W9-DDH-846

The Long Ships

THE

Long Ships

A SAGA OF THE VIKING AGE

BY

FRANS G. BENGTSSON

TRANSLATED FROM THE SWEDISH

BY MICHAEL MEYER

1 9 5 4

ALFRED A. KNOPF   NEW YORK

L. C. catalog card number: 54–8763

THIS IS A BORZOI BOOK,
PUBLISHED BY ALFRED A. KNOPF, INC.

PUBLISHED SEPTEMBER 13, 1954
SECOND PRINTING, SEPTEMBER 1954

Originally published in Sweden in two volumes as RÖDE ORM by P. A. Norstedt & Söners Förlag. An English translation by Barrows Mussey of Volume I was published in the United States in 1942 under the title RED ORM.

Harp Song of the Dane Women

What is a woman that you forsake her,
And the hearth-fire and the home-acre,
To go with the old grey Widow-maker?

She has no house to lay a guest in—
But one chill bed for all to rest in,
That the pale suns and the stray bergs nest in.

She has no strong white arms to fold you,
But the ten-times-fingering weed to hold you—
Out on the rocks where the tide has rolled you.

Yet, when the signs of summer thicken,
And the ice breaks, and the birch-buds quicken,
Yearly you turn from our side, and sicken—

Sicken again for the shouts and the slaughters.
You steal away to the lapping waters,
And look at your ship in her winter-quarters.

You forget our mirth, and talk at the tables,
The kine in the shed and the horse in the stables—
To pitch her sides and go over her cables.

Then you drive out where the storm-clouds swallow,
And the sound of your oar-blades, falling hollow,
Is all we have left through the months to follow.

Ah, what is Woman that you forsake her,
And the hearth-fire and the home-acre,
To go with the old grey Widow-maker?

RUDYARD KIPLING

Translator's Note

THE ACTION of *The Long Ships* covers, approximately, the years 980–1010 of our era. At that time the southern provinces of Sweden belonged to Denmark, so that Orm, though born and bred in Skania, regarded himself as a Dane.[1]

The Vikings harried the countries of northern and western Europe more or less continuously for a period of over two hundred years, from the end of the eighth century until the beginning of the eleventh. Most of the raids on western Europe were carried out by Danes and Norwegians; for the Swedes regarded the Baltic as their domain, and at the end of the ninth century founded in Russia a kingdom that endured for three hundred and fifty years, until the coming of the Mongols. Ireland was, at first, the favorite western hunting-ground of the Vikings; it was not until 838, forty years after the first attack on Ireland, that they began to raid England in large numbers. For the next sixty years, however, they— especially the great Ragnar Hairy-Breeks and his terrible sons— troubled England cruelly, until Alfred withstood them and forced them to come to terms. Then, from 896 until 979, England enjoyed eighty years of almost unbroken respite from their fury. In France the Northmen were so feared that, in 911, Charles the Simple ceded part of his kingdom to them; this came to be known as Normandy, the Northmen's land. Vikings peopled Iceland in 860, and Greenland in 986. In the latter year a Viking ship heading for Greenland went off its course and reached America, which, because of the good grapes they found there, the men named "Wineland the Good." Several other Viking ships sailed to America during the next twenty years.

The Battle of Jörundfjord, or Hjörungavag, so frequently referred to in the following pages, was one of the most famous battles fought in the north during the Viking age. It was fought between the Norwegians and the Jomsvikings. The Jomsvikings (to quote Professor C. Turville-Petre) were "a closed society of Vikings, living according to their own laws and customs. None of them

---

[1] Denmark also claimed suzerainty over Norway, though the Norwegians regarded themselves as independent.

might be younger than eighteen years, and none older than fifty; they must not quarrel amongst themselves, and each must avenge the other as his brother." No woman was allowed within their citadel, Jomsborg, which was sited on the southern shore of the Baltic, probably in the region of where Swinemünde now stands. According to Icelandic sources, Canute's father, King Sven Forkbeard, invited the Jomsvikings to a feast. As the ale flowed, King Sven swore an oath to invade England and kill Ethelred the Unready or else drive him into exile. The Jomsviking chieftain, Sigvalde, swore in his turn to sail to Norway and kill the rebel Jarl Haakon or else drive him into exile. All the other Jomsvikings, including the two Skanian chieftains, Bue Digre and Vagn Akesson, swore to follow him. They sailed to Norway with sixty ships, but Haakon got wind of their approach and, when at last they turned into Jörundfjord, they found him waiting for them with a fleet of no less than one hundred and eighty ships. At first, despite being thus outnumbered, the Jomsvikings looked likely to prevail; but the weather turned against them and, after a bitter struggle, they were routed and slaughtered almost to a man.

This was in 989. In the following spring another vital battle was fought in Sweden, on Fyris Plain before Uppsala, when the dreaded Styrbjörn, the exiled nephew of King Erik of Sweden, sought to win his uncle's kingdom, but was killed by a chance spear in the first moments of the fight. It is to the echoes of these two battles that *The Long Ships* opens.

M. M.

Contents

x] *Contents*

Part Four: THE BULGAR GOLD

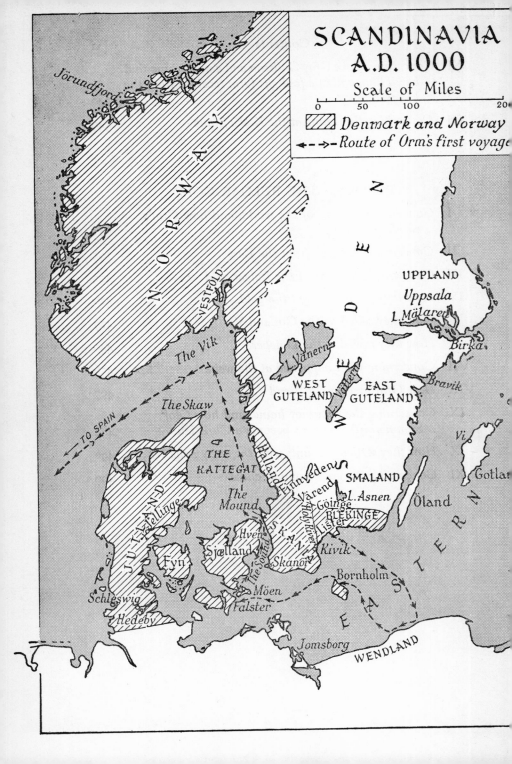

ICELAND

WESTERN EUROPE
A.D. 1000
Scale of Miles

0   100   200   300   400

Denmark and Norway
Moorish Empire
Byzantine   ,,
Route of Orm's first voyage
  ,,   ,,   ,,   second   ,,

← TO GREENLAND & "WINELAND THE GOOD"
(AMERICA)

Jörundfjord

N·O·R·W·A·Y

S W E D E N

Uppsala

Birka

Gotland

Iona

Connaught
Armagh
Limerick Leinster Dublin York
St Finnian's Isle Cashel
Cork Merioneth

Vellinge

Kivik

Schleswig

OBOTRITES WENDLAND

Here they found
the Jew Solomon

R. Maldon
Thames London
Bremen FRISIA SAXONY

Jülich
Maastricht Aachen
Zülpich
Mainz

Goslar

R. Elbe

R. Oder

Normandy Rouen

Brittany Paris

Nantes R. Loire
Tours

Prague

BOHEMIA

R. Rhine R. Danube

BAVARIA

Vienna

H
U
N
G
A
R
Y

Santiago de Compostela

Ramiro's Kingdom Asturia
LEÓN
Navarre
Empty Land Aragon
CASTILE Barcelona
Toulouse

CROATIA

R. Rhone

Lombardy
Cremona

Lisbon
Toledo
S P A I N
Córdoba

Rome

Apulia
Naples

Bari

Cádiz
Njörva Sound
ANDALUSIA
Málaga
Ronda

Granada

Majorca

Tarentum

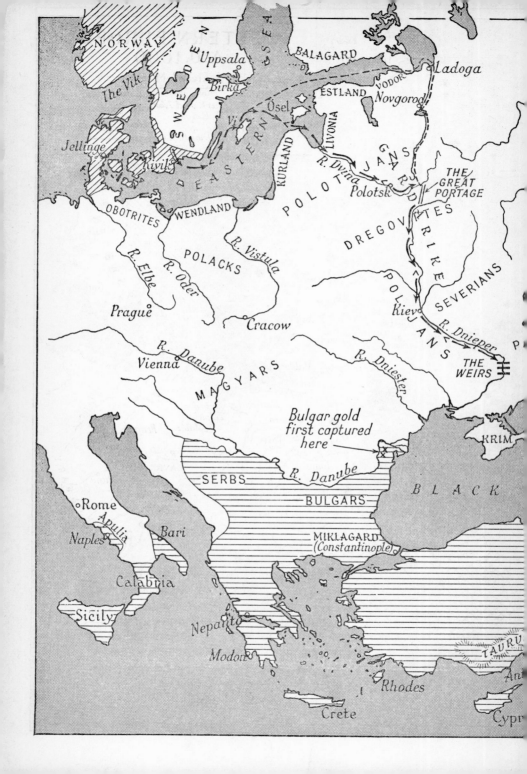

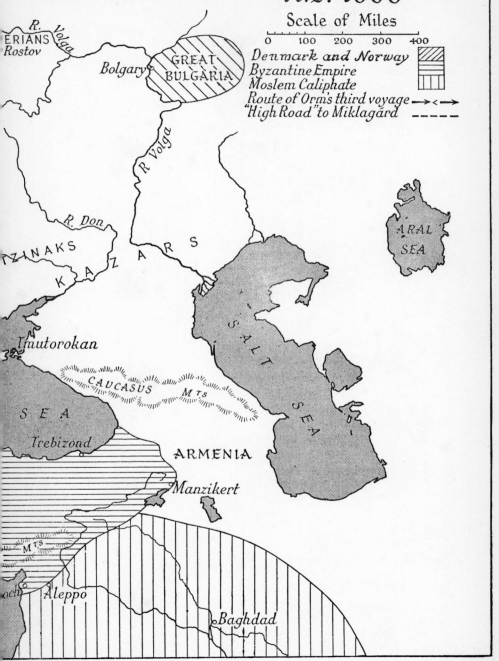

EASTERN EUROPE
A.D. 1000

Scale of Miles

0   100   200   300   400

Denmark and Norway
Byzantine Empire
Moslem Caliphate
Route of Orm's third voyage →—<—→
"High Road" to Miklagård —————

R. Volga

ERIANS
Rostov

Bolgary

GREAT
BULGARIA

R. Volga

R. Don

ARAL
SEA

ZINAKS

K A Z A R S

Tmutorokan

SALT

CAUCASUS

M^{ts}

SEA

Trebizond

ARMENIA

Manzikert

M^{ts}

SEA

och

Aleppo

Baghdad

The Long Ships

PROLOGUE

HOW THE SHAVEN MEN FARED IN SKANIA IN KING HARALD BLUETOOTH'S TIME

MANY restless men rowed north from Skania with Bue and Vagn, and found ill fortune at Jörundfjord; others marched with Styrbjörn to Uppsala and died there with him. When the news reached their homeland that few of them could be expected to return, elegies were declaimed and memorial stones set up; whereupon all sensible men agreed that what had happened was for the best, for they could now hope to have a more peaceful time than before, and less parceling out of land by the ax and sword. There followed a time of plenty, with fine rye harvests and great herring catches, so that most people were well contented; but there were some who thought that the crops were tardy, and they went a-viking in Ireland and England, where fortune smiled on their wars; and many of them stayed there.

About this time the shaven men had begun to arrive in Skania, both from the Saxons' land and from England, to preach the Christian faith. They had many strange tales to relate, and at first people were curious and listened to them eagerly, and women found it pleasant to be baptized by these foreigners and to be presented with a white shift. Before long, however, the foreigners began to run short of shifts, and people wearied of their sermons, finding them tedious and their matter doubtful; besides which, they spoke a rough-sounding dialect that they had learned in Hedeby or in the western islands, which gave their speech a foolish air.

So then there was something of a decline in conversions, and the shaven men, who talked incessantly of peace and were above all very violent in their denunciation of the gods, were one by one seized by devout persons and were hung up on sacred ash trees and shot at with arrows, and offered to the birds of Odin. Others went northwards to the forests of the Göings, where men were less religiously inclined; there they were welcomed warmly, and were tied

up and led to the markets in Smaland, where they were bartered
for oxen and for beaver skins. Some of them, upon finding themselves slaves of the Smalanders, let their hair grow and waxed discontented with their God Jehovah and gave good service to their
masters; but the majority continued to denounce the gods and to
spend their time baptizing women and children instead of breaking stones and grinding corn, and made such a nuisance of themselves that soon it became impossible for the Göings to obtain, as
hitherto, a yoke of three-year-old oxen for a sturdy priest without
giving a measure of salt or cloth into the bargain. So feeling increased against the shaven men in the border country.

One summer the word went round the whole of the Danish
kingdom that King Harald Bluetooth had embraced the new religion. In his youth he had done so tentatively, but had soon regretted his decision and recanted; this time, however, he had
adopted it seriously. For King Harald was by now an old man and
had for some years been tormented by terrible pains in his back,
so that he had almost lost his pleasure in ale and women; but wise
bishops, sent by the Emperor himself, had rubbed him with bear's
grease, blessed and made potent with the names of apostles, and
had wrapped him in sheepskins and given him holy herbal water
to drink instead of ale, and had made the sign of the cross between
his shoulders and exorcised many devils out of him, until at last
his aches and pains had departed; and so the King became a
Christian.

Thereupon the holy men had assured him that still worse tor-
ments would come to plague him if he should ever again offer sacrifice or show himself in any way unzealous in the new religion.
So King Harald (as soon as he had become active again and found
himself capable of fulfilling his obligations toward a young Moroc-
can slave-girl, whom Olof of the Precious Stones, the King of Cork,
had sent him as a good-will present) issued a proclamation that all
his subjects should get themselves christened without delay; and
although such an order sounded strangely from the lips of one who
was himself descended from Odin, still, many obeyed his command, for he had ruled long and prosperously, so that his word
counted for much in the land. He meted out especially severe pun-
ishments to anyone who had been guilty of violence against any
priest; so that the number of priests in Skania now began to mul-

tiply greatly, and churches rose upon the plain, and the old gods fell into disuse, except in times of peril at sea or of cattle plague.

In Göinge, however, the King's proclamation was the occasion of much merriment. The people of the border forests were blessed with a readier sense of fun than the sober dwellers of the plain, and nothing made them laugh so much as a royal proclamation. For in the border country few men's authority extended beyond the limit of their right arm, and from Jellinge to Göinge was a long march even for the mightiest of kings to undertake. In the old days, in the time of Harald Hildetand and Ivar of the Broad Embrace, and even before that, kings had been wont to come to Göinge to hunt the wild ox in the great forests there, but seldom on any other errand. But since those times the wild ox had died out, and the kings' visits had ceased; so that nowadays, if any king was bold enough to murmur a complaint that the people of those parts were turbulent or that they paid insufficient taxes, and threatened to journey thither himself to remedy matters, the answer would be sent to him that there were, unfortunately, no wild oxen to be seen in the district nowadays, but that as soon as any should appear he would at once be informed and a royal welcome would be prepared for him. Accordingly, it had for long been a saying among the border people that no king would be seen in their country until the wild oxen returned.

So in Göinge things remained as they had always been, and Christianity made no headway there. Such priests as did venture into those parts were sold over the border as in the old days; though some of the Göings were of the opinion that it would be better to kill them on the spot and start a good war against the skinflints of Sunnerbo and Allbo, for the Smalanders gave such poor prices for priests nowadays that it was hardly worth a man's trouble to lead them to market.

PART ONE

The Long Voyage

CHAPTER ONE

CONCERNING THANE TOSTE AND HIS HOUSEHOLD

ALONG the coast the people lived together in villages, partly to be sure of food, that they might not depend entirely on the luck of their own catch, and partly for greater security; for ships rounding the Skanian peninsula often sent marauding parties ashore, both in the spring, to replenish cheaply their stock of fresh meat for the westward voyage, and in the winter, if they were returning empty-handed from unsuccessful wars. Horns would be blown during the night when raiders were thought to have landed, so that the neighbors might come to the assistance of those attacked; and the stay-at-homes of a good village would occasionally even capture a ship or two for themselves, from strangers who had not been sufficiently prudent, and so have fine prizes to show the wanderers of the village when the long ships came home for their winter rest.

But men who were wealthy and proud, and who owned their own ships, often found it irksome to have neighbors on their doorstep and preferred to live apart; for, even when they were at sea, they could keep their homes defended by good warriors whom they paid to stay in their houses and guard them. In the region of the Mound, there were many such great lords, and the rich thanes of that district had the reputation of being the proudest in all the Danish kingdom. When they were at home, they readily picked quarrels with one another, though their homesteads lay well spaced apart; but often they were abroad, for they had been used from their childhood to look out over the sea and to regard it as their own private pasture, where any whom they found trespassing would have to answer for it.

In these parts there lived a thane called Toste, a worthy man and a great sailor who, though he was advanced in years, still commanded his ship and set out each summer for foreign shores. He had kinsmen in Limerick in Ireland, among the Vikings who had settled there, and he sailed west each year to trade with them and to help their chieftain, a descendant of Ragnar of the Hairy Breeks, to collect tribute from the Irish and from their monasteries and churches. Of late, however, things had begun to go less well for the Vikings in Ireland, ever since Muirkjartach of the Leathern Coats, the King of Connaught, had marched round the island with his shield-arm toward the sea as a sign of defiance. For the natives now defended themselves better than before and followed their kings more willingly, so that it had become a difficult business to extort tribute from them; and even the monasteries and churches, that had previously been easy to plunder, had now built high stone towers to which the priests betook themselves and from which they could not be driven by fire or by force of arms. In view of all this, many of Toste's followers were now of the opinion that it might be more profitable to go a-viking in England or France, where times were good and more might be won with less effort; but Toste preferred to do as he had been used to do, thinking himself too old to start journeying to countries where he might not feel so well at home.

His wife was called Asa. She came from the border forest and had a ready tongue, besides being somewhat smart of temper, so that Toste was sometimes heard to remark that he could not see much evidence of time having smoothed out the wrinkles in her nature, as it was said to do. But she was a skillful housewife and took good care of the farm when Toste was away. She had borne him five sons and three daughters; but their sons had not met with the best of luck. The eldest of them had come to grief at a wedding, when, merry with ale, he had attempted to prove that he could ride bareback on a bull; and the next one had been washed overboard on his first voyage. But the unluckiest of all had been their fourth son, who was called Are; for one summer, when he was nineteen years old, he had got two of their neighbors' wives with child while their husbands were abroad, which had been the instance of much trouble and sly gibing, and had put Toste to considerable expense when the husbands returned home. This dejected Are's spirits and made him shy; then he killed a man who had chaffed him overlong for his dexterity, and had to flee the country. It was rumored that he had sold himself to Swedish merchants and had sailed with them to the east, so that he might meet no more people who knew of his misfortune, but nothing had been heard of him since. Asa, however, had dreamed of a black horse with blood on its shoulders and knew by this that he was dead.

So after that, Asa and Toste had only two sons left. The elder of these was called Odd. He was a short youth, coarsely built and bowlegged, but strong and horny-handed, and of a reflective temper; he was soon accompanying Toste on his voyages, and showed himself to be a skillful shipman, as well as a hard fighter. At home, though, he was often contrary in his behavior, for he found the long winters tedious, and Asa and he bickered continually. He was sometimes heard to say that he would rather be eating rancid salt meat on board ship than Yuletide joints at home; but Asa remarked that he never seemed to take less than anyone else of the food she set before them. He dozed so much every day that he would often complain that he had slept poorly during the night; it did not even seem to help, he would say, when he took one of the servant-girls into the bed-straw with him. Asa did not like his sleeping with her servants; she said it might give them too high an opinion of themselves and make them impudent toward their mistress; she observed that it would be more satisfactory if Odd acquired a wife. But Odd replied that there was no hurry about that; in any case, the women that suited his taste best were the ones in Ireland, and he could not very well bring any of them home with him, for if he did, Asa and they would soon be going for one another tooth and nail. At this, Asa became angry and asked whether this could be her own son who addressed her thus, and expressed the wish that she might shortly die; to which Odd retorted that she might live or die as she chose, and he would not presume to advise her which state to choose, but would endure with resignation whatever might befall.

Although he was slow of speech, Asa did not always succeed in having the last word, and she used to say that it was in truth a hard thing for her to have lost three good sons and to have been left with the one whom she could most easily have spared.

Odd got on better with his father, however, and as soon as the spring came and the smell of tar began to drift across from the boathouse to the jetty, his humor would improve, and sometimes he would even try, though he had little talent for the craft, to

compose a verse or two—of how the auk's meadow was now ripe
for plowing; or how the horses of the sea would shortly waft him
to the summer land.

But he never won himself any great name as a bard, least of all
among those daughters of neighboring thanes who were of mar-
riageable age; and he was seldom observed to turn his head as he
sailed away.

His brother was the youngest of all Toste's children, and the
jewel of his mother's eye. His name was Orm. He grew quickly,
becoming long and scatter-limbed, and distressing Asa by his lack
of flesh; so that whenever he failed to eat a good deal more than
any of the grown men, she would become convinced that she
would soon lose him, and often said that his poor appetite would
assuredly be his downfall. Orm was, in fact, fond of food, and did
not grudge his mother her anxiety regarding his appetite; but Toste
and Odd were sometimes driven to protest that she reserved all
the titbits for him. In his childhood Orm had once or twice fallen
sick, ever since when Asa had been convinced that his health was
fragile, so that she was continually fussing over him with solicitous
admonitions, making him believe that he was racked with dangerous cramps and in urgent need of sacred onions, witches' incantations, and hot clay platters, when the only real trouble was that he
had overeaten himself on corn porridge and pork.

As he grew up, Asa's worries increased. It was her hope that he
would, in time, become a famous man and a chieftain; and she
expressed to Toste her delight that Orm was shaping into a big,
strong lad, wise in his discourse, in every respect a worthy scion of
his mother's line. She was, though, very fearful of all the perils that
he might encounter on the highway of manhood, and reminded
him often of the disasters that had overtaken his brothers, making
him promise always to beware of bulls, to be careful on board ship,
and never to lie with other men's wives; but, apart from these dangers, there was so much else that might befall him that she hardly
knew where to begin to counsel him. When he reached the age of
sixteen and was ready to sail with the others, Asa forbade him to
go, on the ground that he was still too young and too fragile of
health; and when Toste asked whether she had it in her mind to
bring him up to be a chieftain of the kitchen and a hero of old
women, she exploded into such a rage that Toste himself became

frightened and let her have her way, and was glad to be allowed
to take his own leave, and, indeed, lost little time in doing so.

That autumn Toste and Odd returned late from their voyage,
and had lost so many of their crew that they scarcely had enough
left to man the oars; nevertheless, they were well contented with
the results of their expedition, and had much to relate. In Limerick, they had met with small success, for the Irish kings in
Munster had by now become so powerful that the Vikings who
lived there had their work cut out to hold on to what they had.
Then, however, some friends of Toste (who had anchored his ship
off the coast) had asked whether he might feel inclined to accompany them on a secret visit to a great midsummer fair that was
held each year at Merioneth, in Wales, a district to which the
Vikings had not previously penetrated, but which could be reached
with the assistance of two experienced guides whom Toste's friends
had discovered. Their followers being enthusiastic, Odd had persuaded Toste to fall in with this suggestion; so seven shiploads of
them had landed near Merioneth and, after following a difficult
route inland, had managed to arrive at the fair without giving
wind of their approach. There had been fierce fighting, and a good
many men had been killed, but in the end the Vikings had prevailed and had captured a great quantity of booty, as well as many
prisoners. These they had sold in Cork, making a special voyage
thither for the purpose, for it had long been the custom for slave-
traders to gather in Cork from all the corners of the world to bid
for the captives whom the Vikings brought there; and the King
of those parts, Olof of the Precious Stones, who was a Christian
and very old and wise, would himself purchase any that caught his
fancy, so that he might give their kinsmen the opportunity to ransom them, on which transaction he could be sure of making a
pretty profit. From Cork they had set out for home, in company
with a number of other Viking ships in case of pirates, for they
had little appetite for further fighting, weakly manned as they now
were, besides having much treasure aboard. So they had succeeded
in coming unscathed round the Skaw, where the men of the Vik
and of Vestfold lurked in ambush to surprise richly laden ships returning homewards from the south and west.

After the survivors of the crew had been allotted their share of
the booty, a great quantity remained for Toste; who, when he had

weighed it and locked it into his treasure-chest, announced that an expedition such as this would serve as a fitting conclusion to his wanderings, and that henceforth he would remain at home, the more willingly since he was beginning to grow somewhat stiff of limb; Odd was by now capable of managing the affairs of the expeditions fully as well as he, and would, besides, have Orm to help him. Odd thought that this was a good idea; but Asa was of a very different opinion, observing that, while a fair amount of silver had been won, it could hardly be expected to last for long, considering how many mouths she had to feed each winter; besides which, how could they be sure that Odd would not spend all the prize-money he won in future expeditions on his Irish women, or indeed whether, left to himself, he would ever bother to come home to them at all? As regards the stiffness that Toste complained of in his back, he ought by now to know that this was not the result of his voyages but of the months that he spent idling in front of the fire throughout each winter; and to be falling over his sprawling legs for six months in every year was quite sufficient for her. She could not understand (she continued) what men were coming to nowadays; her own great-uncle, Sven Rat-Nose, a mighty man among the Göings, had fallen like a hero fighting the Smalanders three years after drinking the whole company under the table at his eldest grandson's wedding; whereas now you heard talk of cramps from men in the prime of life who were apparently quite willing to die, unashamedly, on their backs in straw, like cows. However, she concluded, all this could be settled in good time, and meanwhile Toste and Odd and the others who had come home with them were to drown their worries in good ale, of a brew that would please their palates; and Toste was to put these nonsensical ideas out of his head and drink to an equally profitable expedition next year; and then they would all enjoy a comfortable winter together, so long as nobody invented any more of such stupid notions to provoke her, which she trusted they would not.

When she had left them to prepare the ale, Odd remarked that if all her female ancestors had had tongues like her, Sven Rat-Nose had probably fixed on the Smalanders as the lesser evil. Toste demurred, saying that he agreed up to a point, but that she was in many respects a good wife, and ought, perhaps, not to be provoked unnecessarily, and that Odd should do his best to humor her.

That winter, they all noticed that Asa went about her household duties with less than her usual ardor and bustle, and that her tongue ran less freely than it was wont to do. She was more than ever solicitous toward Orm, and would sometimes stand and gaze at him as though contemplating a vision. Orm had by now grown big and could compete in matters of strength with all those of his age, as well as with many older youths. He was red-haired and fair-skinned, broad between the eyes, snub-nosed and widemouthed, with long arms and rather rounded shoulders; he was quick and agile, and surer than most with a spear or with a bow. He was fiery of tongue, and would rush blindly on any man that roused him, so that even Odd, who had previously enjoyed teasing him to a white fury, had now begun to treat him with caution; for Orm's strength made him a dangerous opponent. But in general, except when he was angry, he was quiet and tractable, and always ready to do whatever Asa asked of him, though he occasionally had words with her when her fussing irked him.

Toste now gave him a man's weapons—a sword and a broadax and a good helmet—and Orm made himself a shield; but he found difficulty in obtaining a chain shirt, for nobody in the household was of his size, and there was, at that time, a shortage of good mail-smiths in the land, most of them having migrated to England or to the Jarl at Rouen, where their work was better paid. Toste said that, for the time being, Orm would have to be content with a leather tunic, until such time as he could get himself a good shirt in Ireland; for there dead men's armor was always to be had cheaply in any harbor.

They were talking on this subject at table one day when of a sudden Asa buried her face in her arms and began to weep. They all fell silent and stared at her, for it was not often that tears were seen on her cheeks; and Odd asked her if she had the toothache. Asa dried her face, and turned toward Toste. She said that all this talk of dead men's armor seemed to her to be a bad omen, and that she was already certain that disaster would overtake Orm as soon as he accompanied them to sea, for thrice in her dreams she had seen him lying bleeding on a ship's bench, and they all knew that her dreams could be relied upon to come true. She begged Toste, therefore, to listen to her earnest prayer and not to expose their son's life to unnecessary peril, but to allow him to remain at home with her for this one summer; for she believed that danger threatened him in the very near future and that if he could only survive this immediate hazard, the risk would subsequently decrease.

Orm asked her whether she could see in her dream in which part of his body he was wounded. Asa replied that, each time she dreamed this dream, the sight of him lying thus had awakened her in a cold terror; but she had seen his hair bloody and his face pale, and the vision had weighed heavily upon her, the more so each time that it returned, though she had not previously wished to speak of it.

Toste sat silent for a while, pondering over what she had said; then he remarked that he knew little about dreams and had never himself paid much attention to them.

"For the ancients used to observe," he said, "that as the Spinstress spinneth, so shall it be. If, though, you, Asa, have dreamed the same dream thrice, then it may be that this is intended to serve as a warning to us; and, in truth, we have already lost our share of sons. Therefore I shall not oppose your will in this matter, and Orm shall remain at home this summer, if it is also his wish. For my own part, I begin to feel that I should not mind sailing once more to the west; so perhaps, after all, your suggestion may turn out to be the best solution for us all."

Odd concurred with Toste, for he had several times noticed that Asa's dreams foretold the future correctly. Orm was not overjoyed at their decision, but he was accustomed to obey Asa's will in important matters; so nothing more was said.

When spring came, and sufficient men had been hired from the hinterland to fill the gaps in their crew, Toste and Odd sailed away as usual, while Orm remained at home. He behaved somewhat sulkily toward his mother and sometimes pretended to be sick in order to frighten her, but as soon as she began to fuss over him and dose him with medicines, he would find himself believing that he was in fact ill, so that he gained but little pleasure from his game. Asa could not bring herself to forget her dream and, despite all the worry he caused her, it comforted her to have him safe with her at home.

Nevertheless, and in spite of his mother, he sailed forth that summer on his first voyage.

CHAPTER TWO

CONCERNING KROK'S EXPEDITION, AND HOW ORM
SET FORTH ON HIS FIRST VOYAGE

N the fortieth year of King Harald Bluetooth's reign, six
summers before the Jomsvikings' expedition to Norway, three
ships, fitted with new sails and boldly manned, set sail from the
Listerland and headed southwards to plunder the country of the
Wends. They were commanded by a chieftain called Krok. He
was a dark-complexioned man, tall and loose-limbed and very
strong; and he had a great name in his part of the country, for he
possessed a talent for evolving audacious plans, and enjoyed de-
riding men whose enterprises had gone astray and telling them
what he would have done if he had been in their shoes. He had
never in fact achieved anything of note, for he preferred to talk
of the feats he intended to perform in the near future; but at
length he had so fired the young men of the district with his talk
of the booty that brave warriors might win in the course of a properly conducted expedition against the Wends that they had got
together and fitted out ships and had chosen him to be their chieftain. There was, he had told them, much treasure to be found in
Wendland; above all, one could be certain of a fine haul of silver,
amber, and slaves.

Krok and his men reached the Wendish coast and discovered
the mouth of a river, up which they rowed against a strong current
until they came to a wooden fortress, with piles forming a boom
across the river. Here they went ashore in a gray dawn twilight
and attacked the Wends, having first slipped through their out-
lying defenses. But the fortress was strongly manned, and its defenders shot arrows at them cunningly, and Krok's men were tired
with their heavy rowing, so there was a bitter struggle before the
Wends were finally put to flight. In the course of it Krok lost
many good men; and when the booty was examined, it was found
to consist of a few iron kettles and some sheepskin coats. They
rowed back down the river and made an attempt on another vil-

lage farther to the west, but it, too, was well defended, and after
another sharp struggle, in which they sustained further losses, they
won a few sides of smoked pork, a torn chain shirt, and a necklace
of small, worn silver coins.

They buried their dead on the shore and held counsel, and Krok
had some difficulty in explaining to them why the expedition had
not turned out as he had foretold. But he succeeded in calming
their temper with well-chosen words, reminding them that no man
could insure against bad luck or the whims of circumstance, and
that no true Viking allowed himself to become dispirited by a
little adversity. The Wends, he explained, were becoming redoubt-
able adversaries; and he had a good plan to put to them which
would certainly redound to the advantage of them all. This was
that they should make an attempt against Bornholm, for the rich-
ness of that island's inhabitants was well known to them all, and
it would be weakly defended, many of its warriors having recently
gone to England. A shore-thrust here would meet with little opposition and would be sure to yield a rich harvest of gold, brocades,
and fine weapons.

They found this well spoken, and their spirits rose again; so they
set sail and headed for Bornholm, which they reached early one
morning. They rowed along the eastern coast of the island in a
calm sea and a rising haze, searching for a good landing-place,
pulling briskly and keeping well together, for they were in high
good humor; but they kept silence, for they hoped to land unob-
served. Suddenly they heard ahead of them the clank of rowlocks
and the plash of oar-blades dipping evenly, and out of the haze
appeared a single long ship approaching round a headland. It
made toward them, without slackening its stroke, and they all
stared at it, for it was large and splendid to behold, with a red
dragon-head at its prow, and twenty-four pairs of oars; and they
were glad that it was unaccompanied. Krok ordered all his men
who were not engaged at the oars to take up their weapons and
stand ready for boarding; for here there was plainly much to be
won. But the lone ship headed straight toward them, as though
its helmsman had not observed their presence; and a stoutly built
man, standing in the prow, with a broad beard visible beneath
his bossed helmet, cupped his hand to his mouth as they ap-

proached and roared in a harsh voice: "Get out of our way, unless you want to fight!"

Krok laughed, and his men laughed with him; and he shouted back: "Have you ever seen three ships give way to one?"

"Ay, and more than three," roared the fat man impatiently; "for most men give way to Styrbjörn. But be quick about it and make your choice. Get out of our way or fight!"

When Krok heard the fat man's words, he made no reply, but silently turned his ship aside; and his men rested on their oars while the lone ship rowed past them, nor did any of them unsheathe his sword. They saw a tall young man in a blue cloak, with fair down lining his jaw, rise from his resting-place beside the helmsman and stand surveying them with sleepy eyes, grasping a spear in his hand. He yawned broadly, dropped his spear, and laid himself again to rest; and Krok's men realized that this was Björn Olofsson, commonly called Styrbjörn, the banished nephew of King Erik of Uppsala, who seldom sought refuge from storm and never from battle, and whom few men willingly encountered at sea. His ship proceeded on its course, its long oars sweeping evenly, and disappeared southwards into the haze. But Krok and his men found their previous high spirits difficult to recover.

They rowed to the eastern skerries, which were uninhabited, and there they landed and cooked a meal and held long counsel. Many of them thought that they would do best to turn for home, seeing that bad luck had followed them even to Bornholm. For if Styrbjörn was in these waters, the island was sure to be swarming with Jomsvikings, in which case there would be nothing left for any other raiders. Some of them said that there was little use in going to sea with the sort of chieftain who gave way to a single ship.

Krok was at first less eloquent than usual; but he had ale brought ashore for them all, and after they had drunk, he delivered a speech of encouragement. In one sense, he was ready to admit, it might be considered unfortunate that they had encountered Styrbjörn in this manner; but if you looked at it another way, it was extremely fortunate that they had encountered him when they did, for if they had come ashore and met them or other Jomsvikings there, they would have had to pay dearly for it. All Jomsvikings, and none more so than Styrbjörn's men, were half berserk, sometimes being even proof against iron, and able to lay about them with both hands full as well as the best warriors from Lister. That he had been reluctant to order an assault on Styrbjörn's ship might, at first sight, appear odd to idle-thinking men; nevertheless, he regarded his reluctance as fully justified, and considered it fortunate that he had made his decision so promptly. For a homeless and exiled pirate would hardly be likely to have sufficient treasure stored away in any one place to be worth a bloody battle; and he would remind them that they had not come to sea to win empty honor, but to secure hard booty. In view of all this, he had thought it more proper to consider the general good than his own reputation as a warrior, and if they would reflect, he felt sure that they would agree that he had acted in this affair in a manner befitting a chieftain.

As he thus cunningly dispersed the fog of dejection which had settled on his men's spirits, Krok began to feel his own courage rising anew; and he proceeded to exhort them strongly against making for home. For the people of Lister, he said, were inclined to be uncharitable, and the women in particular would ply them with painful queries regarding their exploits and the prizes they had won, and why they had returned so soon. No man proud of his good name would thus willingly lay himself open to the shafts of their mockery; therefore, he suggested, it would be better if they could postpone their return until they had won something worth bringing home. The important thing now, he concluded, was that they should remain together, face their adversities with courage and resolution, and determine on some worthy goal to which to proceed; on which matter, before he spoke any further, he would like to hear the views of his wise comrades.

One of the men then proposed that they should go to the land of the Livonians and the Kures,[1] where there was a rich harvest to be reaped; but this suggestion won little support, for men of greater experience knew that large shiploads of Swedes descended annually on those regions, and it was not to be reckoned that they would proffer a warm welcome to any strangers who arrived on the same errand. Another man had heard that the greatest single hoard of silver in the world was to be found in Gotland, and he thought that they should try their hand there; but others of his compan-

---

[1] Modern Lithuania and Latvia.

ions, who knew better, said that nowadays, since the Gothlanders had become rich, they lived in large villages, which could be successfully attacked only by a powerful army.

A third man then rose to address them, a warrior called Berse, who was a wise speaker and prized by all for his sound judgment. He said that the Eastern Sea was becoming a crowded and unrewarding pasture, for far too many men were plundering its coasts and islands, so that even such peoples as the Wends were learning how to defend themselves. It would be a poor thing to turn meekly for home—on that point he was of the same opinion as Krok—but it was, he thought, worth considering whether they might not sail out to the lands in the west. He had never himself traveled to those parts, but certain men from Skania, whom he had met at a fair during the previous summer, had been in England and Brittany with Toke Gormsson and Sigvalde Jarl and had had much to say in praise of those countries. They wore gold rings and costly garments, and according to their report certain companies of Vikings had anchored their ships in Frankish estuaries for months on end while they plundered the hinterland, and these men had frequently had burgomasters and abbots to wait on them at table and the daughters of counts to make them merry in bed. How strictly his informants had kept to the truth he could not, of course, say, but, as a general rule, you could believe about half of what Skanians told you; and these men had made an impression on him of considerable prosperity, for they had invited him, a stranger from Blekinge, to join them in a grand drinking-bout and had not attempted to steal his belongings while he slept, so that their story could not be altogether false; besides which, it was more or less confirmed by reports he had heard from other quarters. Now, where Skanians had prospered, men of Blekinge ought to fare at least as well; therefore, he concluded, he, for his part, would suggest that they should sail to the lands of the west, if a majority among his comrades were of the same mind.

Many of them applauded his proposal and cried assent; but others doubted whether they were sufficiently provisioned to carry them through until they came to their goal.

Then Krok spoke again. He said that Berse had made exactly the suggestion that he himself had thought of putting forward. Berse had spoken of the daughters of counts and of wealthy abbots, for the return of whose persons they would receive large ransoms; and he would like to add that in Ireland, there were, as was well known, no less than a hundred and sixty kings, some great, some small, but all of whom possessed much gold and many fine women, and whose soldiers fought wearing only linen garments, so that they could not be difficult to overcome. The most difficult part of their voyage would be passing through the Sound, where they might find themselves attacked by the natives of those parts; but three strongly manned ships, which Styrbjörn himself had not dared to challenge, would be likely to command respect even in the Sound; besides which, most of the Vikings of that region would, at this time of the year, already have sailed westwards; and in any case there would be no moon during the next few nights. As regards food, any that they needed they could easily obtain as soon as they had successfully negotiated the Sound.

By this time they had all recovered their former high spirits. They said that the plan was a good one and that Krok was the wisest and cleverest of all chieftains; and they were all proud to discover how little trepidation they felt at the prospect of a voyage to the lands of the west, for no ship from their district had attempted such a journey within living memory.

They set sail and came to Möen and rested there for a day and a night, keeping a good lookout and waiting for a favorable wind. Then they headed up through the Sound in stormy weather and came that evening to its neck without meeting any enemies. Later, during the night, they anchored in the lee of the Mound and decided to go ashore in search of provisions. Three companies landed secretly, each in a different place. Krok's company was lucky, for they came at once on a sheepfold near a large house and managed to kill the shepherd and his dog before they could give the alarm. Then they caught the sheep and cut the throats of as many as they could take with them; but this caused the animals to bleat loudly, so that Krok bade his men make haste with the work.

They returned to the ship by the way they had come, making as much speed as they could, each man bearing a sheep over his shoulder. They heard behind them the clamor of people who had awaked in the house, and soon there arose the harsh yowling of dogs that had been unleashed on their scent. Then they heard from farther off a woman's voice, which, piercing through the

noise of the dogs and men, cried: "Wait! Stay with me!" and
screamed: "Orm!" several times, and then again cried: "Wait!"
very shrilly and despairingly. Krok's men had difficulty in moving
quickly with their loads, for the path was stony and steep, and the
night was cloudy and still almost pitch-dark. Krok himself went
last in the line, carrying his sheep over his shoulder and holding an
ax in his other hand. He was anxious, if possible, to avoid becoming involved in a fight for the sake of a sheep, for it was not worth
while to risk life and limbs for so little; so he drove his men forward with harsh words of rebuke when they stumbled or slackened
speed.

The ship lay hard by some flat rocks, being held away from
them by the oars. They were ready to pull out as soon as Krok returned, for the other landing-parties had already returned empty-
handed; some of them were waiting on the beach in case Krok
should need any assistance. They were only a few paces from the
ship when two great dogs came bounding down the path. One of
them leaped at Krok, but he jumped aside and struck it with his
ax; the other flashed past him with a huge leap at the man just in
front of him, knocked him over by its impetus, and buried its
teeth in his throat. Two of the others hastened forward and killed
the dog, but when they and Krok bent over the man who had
been bitten, they saw that his throat was badly torn and that he
was rapidly bleeding to death.

In the same instant a spear hissed past Krok's head, and two
men came running down the slope and out on the flat rocks; they
had run so fast that they had outstripped all their companions.
The foremost of them, who was bareheaded and bore no shield,
but carried a short sword in his hand, tripped and fell headlong
on the rocks; two spears flew over him and hit his companion, who
crumpled to the ground. But the bareheaded man was at once on
his feet again; baying like a wolf, he hewed at one man who had
leaped forward with his sword raised when he had fallen, and
felled him with a blow on the temples. Then he sprang at Krok,
who stood just behind him; all this happened very quickly. He
aimed savagely at Krok, but Krok was still carrying his sheep, and
he slipped it round to meet the blow, in the same instant striking
his adversary with the reverse edge of his ax on the forehead, so
that he fell to the ground senseless. Krok bent over him and saw

that he was no more than a youth, red-haired and snub-nosed and pale-complexioned. He felt with his fingers the place where the axhead had landed and found that the skull was unfractured.

"I shall take the calf with me as well as the sheep," he said. "He can row in the place of the man he killed."

So they picked him up and carried him on to the ship and threw him beneath an oar-bench; then, when they had all come aboard, except the two men whom they had left dead behind them, they pulled out to sea just as a large crowd of pursuers appeared on the beach. The sky had now begun to lighten, and some spears were thrown at the ship; but they did no damage. The men pulled strongly at their oars, happy in the knowledge that they had fresh meat on board; and they had already gone a good way from land when the figures on the beach were joined by a woman in a long blue shift with her hair streaming behind her, who ran to the edge of the rocks and stretched out her arms toward the ship, crying something. Her cry reached them as a thin sound across the water, but she stood there long after they had ceased to hear her.

In this wise Orm, the son of Toste, who later came to be known as Red Orm or Orm the Far-Traveled, set forth on his first voyage.

CHAPTER THREE

HOW THEY SAILED SOUTHWARDS, AND HOW THEY
FOUND THEMSELVES A GOOD GUIDE

RROK'S men were very hungry when they reached Weather Island, for they had had to row the whole way there. They lay to and went ashore to gather fuel and cook themselves a good dinner; they found there only a few old fishermen, who on account of their poverty were not afraid of plunderers. When they came to cut up the sheep, they praised their fatness and the evident excellence of the spring pasturing on the Mound. They stuck the joints on their spears and held them in the fire, and their mouths watered as the fat began to crackle, for it was a long time since their nostrils had known such a cheering smell. Many of them exchanged stories of the last occasions on which they had been present at so tasty a meal, and they all agreed that their voyage to the lands of the west had begun promisingly. Then they began to eat so that the juice of the meat ran over their beards.

By this time Orm had regained his senses, but he was still sick and dizzy, and when he came ashore with the others, it was all he could do to keep on his legs. He sat down and held his head between his hands and made no reply to the words that were addressed to him. But after a while, when he had vomited and drunk water, he felt better, and when he smelt the odor of the frying meat, he raised his head like a man who has just waked up, and looked at the men around him. The man who was sitting nearest to him grinned in a friendly way and cut off a bit of his meat and offered it to him.

"Take this and eat it," he said. "You never tasted better in your life."

"I know its quality," replied Orm. "I provided it."

He took the meat and held it between his fingers without eating it. He looked thoughtfully round the circle, at each man in turn, and then said: "Where is the man I hit? Is he dead?"

"He is dead," replied his neighbor, "but no one here stands to avenge him, and you are to row in his stead. His oar lies in front of mine, so it will be well that you and I should be friends. My name is Toke; what is yours?"

Orm told him his name and asked him: "The man I killed—was he a good fighter?"

"He was, as you observed, somewhat slow of movement," replied Toke, "and he was not so handy with a sword as I am myself. But that would be asking a lot of a man, for I am one of the finest swordsmen in our company. Still, he was a strong man, and steadfast and of a good name; he was called Ale, and his father sows twelve bushels of rye, and he had been to sea twice already. If you can row as well as he did, you are no mean oarsman."

When Orm heard this, it seemed to cheer his spirits, and he began to eat. But after a few minutes he asked: "Who was it who struck me down?"

Krok was sitting a short way from him and heard his question. He laughed and raised his ax, finished his mouthful, and said:

"This is the maid who kissed you. Had she bitten you, you would not have asked her name."

Orm gazed at Krok with rounded eyes that looked as though they had never blinked, and then said with a sigh: "I had no helmet and was breathless from running; otherwise it might have gone differently."

"You are a conceited puppy, Skanian," said Krok, "and fancy yourself a soldier. But you are yet young and lack a soldier's prudence. For prudent men do not forget their helmets when they run out after sheep; nay, not even when their own wives are stolen from them. But you seem to be a man whom Fortune smiles on, and it may be that you will bring us all into her good favor. We have already seen three manifestations of her love for you. Firstly, you slipped on the rocks as two spears were flying toward you; then Ale, whom you slew, has no kinsman or close comrade among us who is bound to avenge him; and thirdly, I did not kill you, because I wished to have an oarsman to replace him. Therefore I believe you to be a man of great good luck, who can thereby be of use to us; wherefore I now give you the freedom of our company, provided only that you agree to take Ale's oar."

They all thought that Krok had spoken well. Orm munched his meat reflectively; then he said: "I accept the freedom you offer me; nor do I think I need feel ashamed to do so, though you stole my sheep. But I will not row as a slave, for I am of noble blood; and though I am young, yet I hold myself to be a good soldier, for I slew Ale, and he was one. I therefore claim back my sword."

This provoked a long and complicated discussion. Some of them regarded Orm's demand as altogether unreasonable and said that he ought to think himself lucky to have been granted his life; but others remarked that self-esteem was no great fault in a young man, and that the claims of those whom Fortune smiled on should not be lightly ignored. Toke laughed and said he was amazed that so many men, three full ships' companies, could be anxious about whether or not one boy was to be allowed to carry a sword. A man called Calf, who had spoken against granting Orm's request, wanted to fight Toke for saying this, and Toke said that he would be glad to oblige him as soon as he had finished the good kidney that he was just then occupied with; but Krok forbade them to fight over such a matter. The end of it all was that Orm got his sword back, but that his future behavior would determine whether he was to be treated as a slave or as a comrade. But Orm was to pay Krok for his sword, which was a fine weapon, as soon as he won anything on the voyage.

By this time a light breeze had sprung up, and Krok said that it was time for them to avail themselves of it and set sail. So they all went aboard and the ship made its way up through the Kattegat with its sails filled with the wind. Orm stared back across the sea and said that it was lucky for Krok that they had few ships left at home in these parts at this time of year; for if he knew his mother, she would else by now have been on their tails with half the people of the Mound assisting her.

Then he washed the wound in his head and rinsed the clotted blood from his hair; and Krok said that the scar on his forehead would be a fine thing to show womenfolk. Then Toke produced an old leather helmet with iron bands. He said it was not much of a helmet for these times, but that he had found it among the Wends and that he had nothing better that he could spare. It would, he said, not be of much use against an ax, but still it would be better than nothing. Orm tried it on and found that it would fit him when the swelling had gone down. Orm thanked Toke; and they both knew now that they would be friends.

They rounded the Skaw with a good following wind, and there, after ancient custom, they sacrificed to Agir and all his kin, offering sheep's flesh and pork and ale, and were followed for a long while afterwards by shrieking gulls, which they took to be a good omen. They rowed down the Jutland coast, where the country was deserted and the ribs of wrecked ships were often to be seen in the sand; farther south they went ashore on two small islands, where they found water and food but little else. They proceeded down the coast, for the most part with favorable winds helping them, so that the men became good-humored through being relieved of the tiresome labor of constant rowing. Toke said that Orm was perhaps weather-lucky, as well as being ordinarily fortunate; and weather-luck was one of the best kinds of luck that a man could have, so that, if this were in fact so, Orm could indeed hope for a prosperous future. Orm thought that Toke might be right; but Krok was unwilling to agree with them on this point.

"It is I who bring us this good weather," he said, "for we have

had good weather and winds from the very beginning, long before
Orm joined us; indeed, if I had not known my weather-luck to be
reliable, I should not have ventured on this expedition. But Orm's
luck is good, if not of the same quality as my own; and the more
lucky men we have aboard, the better it will be for us all."

Berse the Wise agreed, and said that men without luck had the
hardest burden of all to bear. "For man can triumph over man,
and weapon over weapon; against the gods we can pit sacrifice, and
against witchcraft, contrary magic; but against bad luck no man
has anything to oppose."

Toke said that, for his part, he did not know whether he had
great good luck, except that his luck in fishing had always been
good. He had always done well enough against men whom he had
quarreled with; but that might be the result of his strength and
skill rather than of his luck.

"But what worries me," he said, "is whether on this expedition
we shall have gold-luck and woman-luck; for I have heard great
tales of all the fine things that are to be found here in the west,
and it is beginning to seem a long time since I felt a gold ring or
a woman. Even if we only find silver instead of gold, and no princesses, such as Berse has spoken of, but simple Frankish house-
wives, I shall not complain; for I am not a fussy man."

Krok said that Toke would have to be patient for a little longer,
however strong his desire for either commodity; and Toke agreed
that it certainly seemed likely that he would have to wait for a
while; for it did not look as though either gold or women grew on
trees in these parts.

They sailed along flat coasts, where nothing was to be seen except sand and marshlands and an occasional fishing-hut. Then they
passed promontories on which tall crosses stood, and knew that
they had come to the Christians' land, and to the Frankish coasts.
For the wise men among them knew that these crosses had first
been set up by the great Emperor Charles, the father of all emperors, to keep Nordic seafarers away from his land; but the gods
of the north had proved stronger than his. They put into creeks
to take refuge from threatening squalls and to rest overnight, and
saw waters more salt and green than any they had seen before,
rising and falling with the ebb and the flood tides. There were no
ships to be seen, and no people; only here and there the traces of

some old building. Many villages had flourished in these parts before the first Northmen came, but everything had long since been
plundered and laid waste, so that nowadays men had to travel far
to the south before they could find any prizes worth the taking.

They came down to where the sea narrowed between England
and the mainland; and there was talk among them of turning toward the English coast. For they knew that King Edgar had recently died and that he had been succeeded by sons who were not
yet of age, which had made the land much sought after by the
Vikings. But Krok and Berse and others among the wisest of them
held that the country of the Franks was still the best, if one went
far enough south; for the King of Frankland and the Emperor of
Germany were at war with each other on a point of dispute concerning their frontiers, and the coastal regions of countries at war
always provided good hunting-grounds for Northmen.

So they continued down the Frankish coast; but here they lay
farther out to sea and kept a sharp lookout on every quarter, for
they had now come to that region which certain Northmen had
won from the King of the Franks. Here ancient crosses were con-
stantly to be seen on promontories and at river mouths, but even
more frequent were pikes with bearded heads set on them, to signify that the rulers of that land had no desire to welcome seamen
from their own northern climes upon their coasts. Krok and his
men thought that this showed scant hospitality on the part of the
men who were now enjoying the fruits of the land; but, they said,
it was only what was to be expected of men from Skania and
Sjælland; and they asked Orm whether he had any kinsmen in
these parts. Orm replied that he had none, as far as he knew, since
his kinsmen always sailed to Ireland; but that he would bear in
mind, when he got home, this idea of putting heads on poles, for
they would make fine scarecrows to protect his sheep. They all
laughed at this and thought that he was well able to speak up for
himself.

They hid in ambush at the mouth of a river and took some fishing-boats, but they found little of worth in them and could elicit
no reply from the men in the boats when they asked where the
rich villages were around there. When they had killed a couple of
them and still could get no intelligible answer from the others,
they let them go alive, since they were of miserable appearance

and would be of no use as rowers and would fetch no price as
slaves. More than once they slipped ashore under the cover of
night, but they won little, for the people lived in large and well-
guarded villages, and several times they had to make haste back to
their ships to avoid being surrounded and outnumbered. They
hoped that they would soon come to the end of the region where
the Northmen held sway.

One evening they met four long ships rowing from the south;
they looked to be heavily laden, and Krok let his ships move near
to them so that he might see how strongly they were manned. It
was a calm evening, and they rowed slowly toward each other; the
strangers set a long shield upon their mast-top, with its point
turned upwards, as a sign that they came as friends, and Krok's
men conversed with them at the distance of a spear's throw, while
each chieftain tried to calculate the other's strength. The strangers said that they were from Jutland and that they were on their
way home after a long voyage. They had plundered in Brittany
with seven ships during the previous summer, and had then ventured far to the south; afterwards they had wintered on an island
off the mouth of the Loire and had ventured up the river, but
then a cruel plague had broken out among them, and now they
were making their way home with such ships as they had strength
to man. When asked what they had won, they replied that a wise
seaman never counts his wealth until he has brought it safely
home; but this they could tell him (since at this meeting they
reckoned themselves strong enough to hold what they had won),
that they had no complaint to make about the amount of their
catch. There was always the possibility of a bad season, compared
with the way things had been in the old days, and that held true
however far southwards one might travel; but anyone who happened on a part of Brittany that had hitherto escaped plunder
would be able to find good reward for his pains.

Krok asked whether they had any wine or good ale that they
would be willing to exchange for pork or dried fish; meanwhile he
tried to come nearer their ships, for he was sorely tempted to hazard an attack on them and by this means get a fine return for his
whole voyage at one swoop. But the Jutish captain at once brought
his ship round to bar their path, with his prow facing them, and
replied that he preferred to keep his wine and ale for his own use.

"But by all means come nearer," he said to Krok, "if there is anything else you care to sample."

Krok weighed a spear in his hand and seemed uncertain which course to take; but at that moment a commotion broke out on one of the Jutish ships. Two men could be seen struggling with each other by the gunwale; then they fell into the water, still locked in each other's arms. Both of them sank, and one was seen no more; but the other rose to the surface at a distance from the ship, only to dive again when a spear was thrown at him by one of the men he had left. There was much shouting on the Jutish ship, but when Krok's men asked them what was the matter, they received no reply. Dusk was now beginning to descend, and after a brief exchange of words the strangers began to row forward again before Krok could decide whether or not to join battle. Then Toke, who sat at his larboard oar just behind Orm on Krok's own ship, cried to Krok:

"Come and look at this! My fishing-luck gets better all the time!"

One hand was gripping Toke's oar, and one Orm's, and a face lay in the water between the hands, staring up at the ship. It was big-eyed and very pale, black-haired and black-bearded.

"This is a bold fellow and a good swimmer," said one of the men. "He has dived under our ship to get away from the Jutes."

"And a wise man, too," said another, "for he sees that we are better men than they."

A third said: "He is black like a troll, and yellow like a corpse, and does not look the sort of man who brings good luck with him. It is dangerous to take such a man aboard."

They discussed the advantages and disadvantages of doing so, and some of them shouted questions at the man in the water; but he lay there without moving, clinging tightly to the oars and blinking his eyes and swaying with the sea. At last Krok ordered him to be brought aboard; he could always be killed later, he explained to those who opposed the idea, if the course of things showed that it would be best to do so.

So Toke and Orm drew in their oars and hauled the man aboard; he was yellow-skinned and strongly built, and naked to his waist, with only a few rags to cover him. He tottered on his feet and could hardly stand, but he clenched his fist and shook it at the

Jutish ships as they merged into the distance, spitting after them and grinding his teeth. Then he cried something and fell headlong as the ship rolled, but was quickly on his feet again, and beat his breast and stretched his arms toward the sky and cried in a different voice, but in words that none of them could understand. When Orm was old, and told of all the things that had befallen him, he used to say that he had never heard so terrible a grinding of teeth, or so pitiful and ringing a voice, as when this stranger cried out to the sky.

They all wondered at him and questioned him profusely as to who he was and what had happened to him. He understood some of what they said and was able to reply brokenly in the Nordic tongue, and they thought he said that he was a Jute and that he disliked rowing on Saturdays and that it was for this reason that he hated the men he had now escaped from; but this made no sense to them, and some of them were of the opinion that he was crazy. They gave him food and drink, and he ate greedily of beans and fish; but when they offered him salt pork, he rejected it with disgust. Krok said that he would do to man an oar, and that when the voyage was over they could sell him for a good sum; meanwhile Berse, out of his wisdom, could try to make something of what the stranger said and discover whether he had any useful information to give them about the lands from which he had come.

So during the next few days Berse sat and talked a good deal with the stranger, and they conversed as well as they could. Berse was a calm and patient man, a great eater and a skillful bard, who had gone to sea to get away from a shrewish wife; he was wise and full of cunning, and bit by bit he succeeded in piecing together most of what the stranger had to say. This he told to Krok and the others.

"He is not crazy," said Berse, "though he seems so; nor is he a Jute, though we thought him to be one. He says that he is a Jew. They are a people from the East who killed the man whom the Christians regard as their God. This killing took place long ago, but the Christians still cherish a great hatred against the Jews because of it, and like to kill them, and will not accept any ransom for them or show them any clemency. For this reason most of the Jews live in the lands ruled by the Caliph of Córdoba, since in his kingdom the man they killed is not regarded as a god."

Berse added that he had heard some talk of this before, and many others said that they, too, had heard rumors relating to it. Orm said that he had heard that the dead man had been nailed to a tree, as the sons of Ragnar Hairy-Breeks had done in the old days with the chief priest of England. But how they could continue to regard him as a god after the Jews had killed him, none of them could understand; for obviously no true God could be killed by men. Then Berse went on to tell them more of what he had managed to grasp of the Jew's story:

"He has been a slave of the Jutes for a year, and there he underwent much suffering, because he would not row on Saturdays; for the God of the Jews gets very angry with a Jew who does anything on that day. But the Jutes could not understand this, though he often tried to explain it to them, and they beat him and starved him when he refused to row. It was while he was in their hands that he learned the little he knows of our tongue; but when he speaks of them, he curses them in his own language, because he does not know sufficient words to do so in ours. He says that he wept much when he was among them and cried to his God for help; then, when he saw our ship approaching, he knew that his cry had been heard. When he jumped overboard, he dragged with him a man who had often beaten him. He asked his God to be a shield to him and not to let the other man escape; that, he says, is why no spear hit him, and how he found the strength to dive under our ship; and so powerful is the name of his God that he will not name him to me, however much I try to persuade him to do so. That is what he says of the Jutes and his escape from them; and he has more to tell us about something else, which he thinks we shall find useful. But much of what he says about this I cannot clearly understand."

They were all curious to know what else the Jew had to say which might be useful to them, and at last Berse managed to discover the gist of it.

"He says," Berse told them, "that he is a wealthy man in his own country, which lies within the Caliph of Córdoba's kingdom. His name is Solomon, and he is a silversmith, besides apparently being a great poet. He was captured by a Christian chieftain who came from the north and plundered the region where he lives. This chieftain made him send for a large sum of money to ransom himself, and then sold him to a slave-trader, for the Christians do not like to keep their word to Jews, because they killed their God. The slave-trader sold him at sea to merchants, from whom he was captured by the Jutes; and it was his bad fortune to be set at once to pull an oar on a Saturday. Now he hates these Jutes with a bitter hatred; but even that is mild compared with the hatred he feels toward the Christian chieftain who betrayed him. This chieftain is very rich and lives only a day's march from the sea; and he says that he will gladly show us how to get there, so that we may plunder the chieftain of all he possesses and burn down his house and take out his eyes and loose him naked among the stones and trees. He says that there is wealth for us all there."

They all agreed that this was the best news they had heard for many a day; and Solomon, who had been sitting beside Berse while he was recounting all this and had been following him as well as he could, leaped to his feet with a great cry and a joyful counte-nance and cast himself full length on the deck before Krok and put a tuft of his beard into his mouth and chewed it; then he seized one of Krok's feet and placed it upon his neck, all the while babbling like a drunken man in words that no one could under-stand. When he had calmed himself a little, he began to search among the words of their language that he knew; he said that he wished to serve Krok and his men faithfully until they had won these riches and he had gained his revenge; but he asked for a definite promise that he himself should be allowed to pluck out the eyes of the Christian chieftain. Both Krok and Berse agreed that this was a reasonable request.

On each of the three ships the men now began hotly to discuss all this, and it put them in the best of spirits. They said that the stranger might not bring much luck to himself, to judge by what had happened to him, but that he might bring all the more to them; and Toke thought that he had never hooked a better fish. They treated the Jew as a friend, and collected a few clothes for him to wear, and gave him ale to drink, though they had not much left. The country to which he wished to guide them was called León, and they knew roughly where it lay: on their right hand between the land of the Franks and that of the Cordoban Caliph; perhaps five days' good sailing southwards from the Breton cape, which they could now see. They sacrificed again to the sea people, were rewarded with a good wind, and sailed on into the open sea.

CHAPTER FOUR

HOW KROK'S MEN CAME TO RAMIRO'S KINGDOM,
AND HOW THEY PAID A REWARDING VISIT

WHEN Orm was old and spoke of the adventures that had
befallen him, he used to say that he had had little to complain
of during the time that he was in Krok's service, though he had
joined his company so unwillingly. The blow he had received on
his skull troubled him only for a few days; and he got on well
with the men, so that before long they ceased to regard him as
their prisoner. They remembered gratefully the good sheep that
they had obtained from him, and he had other qualities that made
him a good shipmate. He knew as many ballads as Berse, and had
learned from his mother to speak them with the intonation of the
bards; besides which, he could tell lie-stories so cunningly that you
had to believe in them, though he admitted that in this particular
craft he was Toke's inferior. So they prized him as a good comrade, and a clever one, well able to while away the dreary hours
agreeably for them during the long days when they had a good
wind in their sail and were resting from their oars.

Some of the sailors were disgruntled because Krok had left Brittany without having first tried to get new supplies of fresh meat;
for the food they had aboard was now beginning to smell old. The
pork was rancid, the stockfish mildewed, the meal stale, the bread
maggoty, and the water sour; but Krok and those of his followers
who had sailed on expeditions of this sort before asserted that this
was as good fare as any sailor could wish for. Orm ate his rations
with a good appetite, though while he did so, he used often to
tell the others of the delicacies to which he was accustomed at
home. Berse remarked that it seemed to him to be a wise dis-
pensation of the gods that a man when at sea could eat and enjoy
food that at home he would not offer to his slaves or his dogs, but
only to pigs; for, were it not so arranged, long sea voyages would
be exceedingly nauseating.

Toke said that the thing that troubled him most was the fact that the ale was now finished. He was, he assured them, not a fussy man, and he reckoned that he could stomach most things when necessity demanded it, not excluding his sealskin shoes, but only if he had good ale to wash them down. It would be a fearful prospect, he said, to envisage a life without ale, either on sea or ashore; and he questioned the Jew much concerning the quality of the ale in the country to which they were journeying, without, however, being able to extract any very clear information from him on the subject. He told the others stories of great feasts and drinking-bouts that he had been present at, and mourned that on those occasions he had not drunk even more than he had.

Their second night at sea a strong wind arose, driving high breakers, and they were glad that the sky remained clear, for they were steering by the stars. Krok began to wonder whether it would be wise to come out into the limitless sea; but the wisest sailors among them said that, however far you might sail to the south, you would always have land on your left, save only in the Njörva Sound,[1] where the waters led in to Rome, which stood at the center of the world. Men who sailed from Norway to Iceland, said Berse, had a more difficult task, for they had no land in whose lee to shelter, but only the open sea, stretching away for ever on either bow.

The Jew knew all about the stars and declared himself skillful at navigation; but in the event, he proved to be of little use to them, for his stars had different names from the ones they were used to, besides which he was seasick. Orm suffered likewise, and he and Solomon hung over the gunwale together in great misery, thinking that they would die. The Jew wailed most piteously in his own language in the intervals of his vomiting; Orm told him to shut up, but he answered that he was crying to his God, who was in the storm wind. Then Orm grabbed him by the scruff of his neck and told him that, though he himself was in poor shape, he yet had enough strength to throw him over the side if he uttered one cry more, for there was sufficient wind about already without his bringing his God any nearer to them.

This quieted Solomon; and toward morning the wind lessened and the sea grew calm, and they both began to feel better. Solomon was very green in the face, but he grinned at Orm in a

---

[1] The Strait of Gibraltar.

friendly way and seemed not to bear him any ill will for his conduct of the night before, and pointed his finger across the sea at the sunrise. He sought among the words he knew and said that those were the red wings of the morning far out in the sea, and that his God was there. Orm replied that his God appeared to him to be the sort of divinity who was best kept at a respectable distance.

Later that morning they discerned mountains far ahead of them. They pulled in to the shore, but had difficulty in finding a sheltered bay in which to anchor; and the Jew said that this part of the coast was strange to him. They went ashore and came at once into conflict with the inhabitants of the place, who were numerous; but these soon fled, and Krok's men ransacked their huts, returning with some goats and other food, as well as one or two prisoners. Fires were lit, and they all rejoiced at having reached land without mishap, and were glad to have the taste of roast meat once more on their tongues. Toke searched high and low for ale, but succeeded in discovering only a few skins of wine, which was so harsh and sour that, he said, he could feel his belly shriveling as he swallowed it; so much so that he could not drink it all himself, but gave away what was left and sat alone for the rest of the evening singing sadly to himself, with tears in his beard. Berse warned them not to disturb him, for he was a dangerous man when he had drunk himself to weeping-point.

Solomon questioned the prisoners, and told the Vikings that they were now in the country of the Count of Castile, and that the place to which he wished to lead them lay far to the west. Krok said that they would have to wait for another wind to carry them in that direction, and that in the meantime they could do no more than rest and eat; though, he added, the situation might become awkward if strong hostile forces should attack them here while the wind was blowing landwards, or if enemy ships should block their exit from the bay. But Solomon explained, as best he could, that there was little danger of this, for the Count of Castile had hardly any ships at sea, and it would take him some time to gather a sufficient force to cause them trouble. In former years, he told them, this Count of Castile had been a powerful ruler, but nowadays he was forced to bow the knee to the Moorish Caliph in Córdoba, and even had to pay him tribute; for, saving only the Emperor Otto of Germany and the Emperor Basil of Constantinople, there was now no monarch in the world as powerful as the Caliph of Córdoba. At this the men laughed loudly, saying that the Jew was doubtless saying what he supposed to be the truth, but that he obviously knew little about the subject. Had he, they asked, never heard of King Harald of Denmark, and did he not know that there was no king in the world as mighty as he?

Orm was still groggy after his seasickness and had little appetite for food, which made him afraid that he might be sickening for something serious, for he worried continually about his health. He soon curled up in front of one of the fires and fell into a deep sleep; but during the night, when the whole camp was still, Toke came and woke him. With tears streaming down his cheeks, he protested that Orm was the only friend he had, and said that he would like, if he might, to sing him a song that he had just remembered; it was about two bear cubs, he explained, and he had learned it as a child at his mother's knee, and it was the most beautiful song he had ever heard. So saying, he sat down on the ground beside Orm, dried his tears, and began to sing. Now, it was a peculiarity with Orm that he found it difficult to be sociable when he had just been waked out of a sound sleep; however, he voiced no protest, but merely turned over on his other side and tried to go back to sleep.

Toke could not remember much of his song, and this made him miserable again. He complained that he had been sitting alone all the evening, and that nobody had come to keep him company. What had hurt him most, he said, was the fact that Orm had not once given him so much as a friendly glance to cheer him up; for he had always hitherto regarded Orm as his best friend, from the first moment that he had set eyes upon him; now, though, he realized that he was, after all, only a good-for-nothing blackguard like all Skanians; and when a puppy like him forgot his manners, a good sound hiding was the only remedy.

So saying, he got to his feet to look round for a stick; but Orm, who was by this time fully awake, sat up. When Toke saw him do this, he tried to aim a kick at him; but as he raised his foot, Orm snatched a brand out of the fire and threw it in Toke's face. Toke ducked in the middle of aiming his kick and fell on his back, but he was on his feet again in an instant, white in the face and

blind with rage. Orm, too, had leaped to his feet, so that they now
stood facing each other. It was bright moonlight, but Orm's eyes
were flickering a dangerous red as he threw himself furiously upon
Toke, who tried to draw his sword; Orm had laid his aside and
had not had time to lay his hand on it. Now, Toke was a huge and
powerful man, broad in the loins, and with tremendous hands,
while Orm had not yet grown to his full strength, though he was
already strong enough to deal with most men. He secured a lock
on Toke's neck with one arm and pinned Toke's right wrist with
his other hand, to stop his drawing his sword; but Toke took a good
grip on Orm's clothing, lifted him from his feet with a sudden jerk,
and threw him over his head like a starfish. Orm, however, managed to hold his lock, though it felt as though his spine would snap
at any moment, and, twisting round, got one of his knees into the
small of Toke's back. Then he threw himself backwards, dragging
Toke down on top of him, and, exerting all his strength, succeeded
in turning him over, so that he had Toke under him with his face
in the dust. By this time several of the others had been roused,
and Berse ran toward them with a rope, muttering that what else
could you expect if you allowed Toke to sozzle himself like that.
They bound him fast, hand and foot, though he struggled wildly
to stop them. He quieted down after a short while, however, and
before long he was shouting to Orm that he had now remembered
the rest of the song. He began to sing it, but Berse threw water
over him, whereupon he fell asleep.

On awakening the next morning, Toke swore fearfully at finding himself tied up, being unable to remember anything of what
had happened. When they told him, he was full of remorse for
the way he had behaved, and explained that it was his great misfortune that drink sometimes made him difficult. Ale, he said, translated him completely, and now, regrettably, it seemed that wine
was going to have the same effect. He inquired anxiously whether
Orm now regarded him as his enemy, in view of his conduct of
the previous night. Orm replied that he did not, adding that he
would be delighted to continue the fight amiably any time that
Toke felt so disposed; but he begged that Toke would promise him
one thing: namely, that he would abstain from song, for the rasp
of a nightjar, or the croaking of an old crow on an outhouse roof,
was far more melodious than his nocturnal serenading. Toke

laughed, and promised that he would try to improve his talents in that respect; for he was a kindly man except when ale or wine distorted his nature.

All the men thought that Orm had come out of the affair remarkably well, especially considering his youth; for few of those who came within the range of Toke's arm once he had reached the weeping stage escaped unscathed. So Orm rose in the estimation of his fellows, as well as in his own. After this incident they began to call him Red Orm, not only because of his red hair but also because he had proved himself a man of mettle, and one not to be provoked without sound cause.

After some days a good wind sprang up, and they put out to sea. They kept well away from the land, to avoid dangerous currents, and headed westwards along the coast of Ramiro's kingdom until they had rounded the cape. Then they rowed southwards along a steep and broken coast, proceeding through a small archipelago, which reminded the men of their own group of islands off Blekinge. At length they reached the mouth of a certain river, for which the Jew had been keeping a lookout. They entered the river on the flood tide and rowed up it until they were halted by weirs; there they went ashore and held counsel. Solomon described the journey that lay ahead of them, saying that bold men might march in less than a day to the fortress of the man upon whom he wished to be revenged, one of King Ramiro's margraves, a man called Ordono, the most villainous and scoundrelly bandit (he said) in all the shores of Christendom.

Krok and Berse questioned him closely concerning the fortress, asking him details of its strength and situation, and how large an army the margrave kept to defend it. Solomon replied that it lay in such a craggy and deserted tract of country that the Caliph's army, which consisted largely of cavalry, never came near it. This made it an excellent hide-out for a bandit, and there was great wealth contained within its walls. It was built of oak trunks and was protected by an earthen dike, surmounted by a stockade; and its defenders might be reckoned to number, at the outside, two hundred men. Solomon thought that they probably did not keep careful watch, because its situation was so remote; and, indeed, the majority of the margrave's men were often absent marauding in the south.

Krok said the number of the defenders worried him less than
the dike and the stockade, which would make a surprise assault
difficult. Some of the men thought it would be a simple matter to
set fire to the stockade, but Berse reminded them that the whole
fortress might then catch, in which case they would gain little profit
from whatever wealth it might contain. In the end they decided
that they would trust to their luck and determine what plan to follow when they reached the place. It was agreed that forty men
should remain on board the ships, while the rest were to set out
when evening fell, for it would then be cooler. Then they drew lots
to determine which of them should stay with the ships, for they
were all keen to be on the spot when the looting began.

They saw to their weapons, and slept during the heat of the day
in a grove of oak trees. Then they fortified themselves with food
and drink and, as evening fell, the company set out, numbering in
all one hundred and thirty-six men. Krok marched at their head,
with the Jew and Berse, and the rest followed, some wearing chain
shirts and others leathern jackets. Most of them were armed with
sword and spear, though a few carried axes; and each man had a
shield and helmet. Orm marched beside Toke, who said it was a
good thing to have this opportunity to loosen one's joints before
the fighting began, after so many sedentary weeks on the oar-bench.

They marched through a barren wilderness, in which no signs
of human life could be seen; for these border regions between the
Christian and the Andalusian kingdoms had for long been deserted.
They kept to the northern bank of the river, fording a number of
small streams; meanwhile the darkness thickened, and after some
hours they rested and waited for the moon to rise. Then they turned
northwards along a valley, making swift progress over flat terrain,
and Solomon proved himself a good guide, for before the skies
grew gray, they reached the approaches to the fortress. There they
hid in the scrub and rested again for a while, peering forward into
the gloom to discern what they could by the pale light of the
moon. The sight of the stockade somewhat daunted them, for it
consisted of rough tree trunks more than twice the height of a
man; and the huge gate, which was fortified on top, looked exceedingly formidable.

Krok observed that it would be no easy task to set fire to this,
adding that he would, in any event, prefer to storm the place with-

out using fire if it was at all possible; but that there might be no other way, in which case they would have to pile brushwood against the stockade and set light to it, and hope that the whole building would not catch. He asked Berse if he had any better suggestion to put forward, but Berse shook his head and sighed and said that he could not think of any alternative, though he, too, disliked resorting to the use of fire. Nor had Solomon anything better to propose; he muttered that he would have to rest content with seeing the infidel burn, though he had hoped to obtain a more satisfying mode of revenge.

At this point in the discussion Toke crawled forward to Krok and Berse and asked what the delay was for, as he was beginning to grow thirsty and the sooner they stormed the fortress, the sooner he would be able to get something to drink. Krok told him that the problem they were debating was how to force an entry. To this, Toke replied that if they would give him five spears, he could, he thought, show them that he was capable of more things than merely rowing and drinking ale. The others asked what plan he had in mind, but he would only answer that, if all went well, he would procure their entry into the fortress, though the owners of the spears would have to be prepared to re-shaft them when they got them back. Berse, who knew Toke of old, advised that he should be given his head; so the spears were brought, and Toke cut off their shafts just where the iron joined the wood, so that he had a short stump left below each blade. He then announced that he was ready to begin; and he and Krok began to steal quietly toward the rampart, taking cover behind rocks and bushes, with a handful of picked men following them. They heard a few cocks crow from within the fortress, but apart from this the night was completely quiet.

They crept up to the rampart a short way along from the gate; then Toke climbed up to the foot of the stockade and drove one of his spears in between two of the piles, a good ell's length from the ground, twisting it with all his strength to make it fast. Higher up in the next chink along, he drove a second blade; then, when he had noiselessly made sure that both of them would take the strain, he stepped carefully up on the shortened shafts and fixed a third spearhead higher up in the next chink. But, placed as he was, he found himself unable to make this blade fast without creating a noise. Krok, who had by now realized what Toke had in mind, signed to him to come down, whispering that they would have to do a bit of hammering now, even at the risk of disturbing certain sleepers from their slumber. Then, carrying the two remaining spearheads in his hand, he took Toke's place on the steps that he had already made fast, and drove the third blade home with a couple of blows from the flat of his ax, immediately afterwards doing likewise with the fourth and fifth spearheads, fastening them higher up and farther along. As soon as he had driven the last blade home, he climbed up them and so reached the top of the stockade.

As he did so, they heard cries and alarums from within the fortress and a great baying of horns; but others of the Vikings followed Krok swiftly up Toke's ladder as fast as they could clamber, and joined him at the top. Along the inside of the stockade there ran a wooden bridge, for bowmen to stand on. Krok and his followers jumped down on to this, encountering some men, armed with bows and spears and still drowsy with sleep, who ran out to intercept them, and cut them down. By this time they were being assailed with arrows from the ground, and two of them were hit, but Krok and the others ran along the bridge to the gate, and there dropped down to the ground, in the hope of being able to open it from within and thus admit the rest of their comrades. Hard fighting ensued, however, for many of the defenders of the fortress had already run to defend the gate, and reinforcements were coming to their aid with every minute that passed. One of the twenty men who had followed Krok up the ladder was hanging from the stockade with an arrow in his eye, and three others had been hit in their passage along the bridge; but all those who had managed to reach the ground safely packed themselves together in a tight phalanx and, raising their battle-cry, fought their way with spear and sword to the gate. Here it was very dark, and they found themselves hard pressed indeed, with enemies behind as well as in front of them.

Then they heard their battle-cry answered from without, for the men waiting on the hillside had run forward to the rampart as soon as they had seen that the attempt to scale the stockade had succeeded, and many of them were hacking at the gate with their axes, while others clambered up Toke's ladder and dropped down

inside the fortress to assist their companions who were fighting
within the gate. There the strife was fierce and chaotic, friends
and foes hardly knowing which was which. Krok felled several
men with his ax, but was himself then struck on the side of the
neck with a club wielded by a huge man with a black, plaited
beard, who appeared to be the defenders' chieftain. Krok's helmet
partially parried the force of the blow, but he staggered and fell
on his knees. At length Toke and Orm succeeded in fighting their
way through a tangle of men and shields, so tightly packed that it
was impossible to use a spear, with the ground so greasy with blood
that their feet several times all but went from under them, and
managed to draw the bolts of the gate. Their comrades poured in
to join them, and such of the defenders in the gateway as did not
flee were overwhelmed and slaughtered.

Then a terrible panic descended on the Christians, and they fled
with death snarling at their heels. Solomon, who had been among
the first to break in through the gate, charged ahead of the Vikings like a fanatic, stumbling over the bodies of the slain. Seizing
a sword that lay on the ground and whirling it above his head, he
shrieked to his companions through the uproar, bidding them all
make haste to the citadel. Krok, who was still dazed from the blow
that had felled him and was unable to regain his feet, cried to
them from where he lay in the gateway to follow the Jew. Many
of the Vikings ran into the houses that lined the inside of the
rampart to slake their thirst or to look for women; but the majority
of them pursued the fleeing defenders to the great citadel that
stood in the center of the fortress. The gate of the citadel was
crowded with Christians trying to get in, but before it could be
closed, their pursuers swarmed in among them, so that fighting
broke out again within the citadel; for the Christians saw that they
had no option but to defend themselves. The big man with the
plaited beard fought bravely, felling two men who attacked him,
but at length he was forced into a corner and sustained blows that
brought him to his knees, sorely wounded. On seeing him fall, Solomon rushed forward and threw himself upon him, seizing him by
the beard and spitting on him and slobbering like a drunken man;
but the bearded man stared at him as though uncomprehendingly,
rolled over on his side, closed his eyes, and so died.

Seeing this, Solomon broke into loud lamentations at having

been cheated of his full revenge, in that he had not been allowed to kill the man himself. Such Christians as remained alive defended themselves no longer when they saw that their leader had fallen, but surrendered to the mercy of their conquerors. Some of them were spared, so that they might be sold as slaves. Having helped themselves handsomely to meat and drink, which included ale as well as wine, the Vikings ransacked the fortress for booty, and disputes broke out concerning the women whom they discovered crouching in various corners, for they had been without women for many weeks. All the booty they found was heaped into an enormous pile—money, jewels, weapons, garments, brocades, coats of mail, household goods, bridles, silver plate, and much besides—and when it had all been counted, the value of it was found to exceed their wildest expectations. Solomon explained to them that it represented the fruits of years of plundering at the expense of the Andalusians. Krok, who was now able to stand on his feet again, and had a rag soaked with wine bandaged round his head, rejoiced at the sight of it and was only afraid lest it might prove difficult to find space for so much on board their ships. Berse assured him, however, that they would be able to find room for it all.

"For no man," he said, "complains of the weight of the cargo when it is his own booty that is putting strain on his oar."

They spent the rest of the day indulging their appetites, in high good humor; then they slept and, when night came, started on their return march toward the ships. All the prisoners were heavily laden with booty, and the men themselves had much to carry. Some Andalusian prisoners had been found in the dungeons of the citadel; they wept with joy at being freed, but looked wretchedly feeble and were incapable of carrying anything. So they were granted their liberty, and accompanied the Vikings on their way back to the ships, whence they were to proceed southwards with Solomon to their own country. Some donkeys had been captured, and Krok mounted one of them and rode at the head of the column, with his feet reaching to the ground. The other donkeys were led behind him, laden with food and ale; but their loads were speedily lightened, for the men stopped frequently to rest and refresh themselves.

Berse tried to hurry them on, that they might reach the ships as soon as possible. He was afraid lest they might be pursued, for some of the defenders of the fortress had managed to escape and could have ridden far enough to have procured help; but the men paid little attention to his exhortations, for they were in high spirits, and most of them were befuddled with drink. Orm had taken a bale of silk, a bronze mirror, and a large glass bowl, which was proving awkward to carry. Toke had a big wooden box balanced on his shoulder, finely embossed and full of various objects; with his other hand he was leading a girl who had taken his fancy and whom he wanted to hold on to for as long as possible. He was in excellent spirits and expressed to Orm the hope that the girl might turn out to be the margrave's daughter; but then he grew melancholy, beginning to doubt whether there would be room for her on board the ship. He was unsteady on his feet, on account of the quantity he had drunk, but the girl seemed already to be solicitously disposed toward him and supported him when he stumbled. She was well proportioned and very young, and Orm said that he had seldom seen a finer girl, and that it would be a good thing to have woman-luck as good as Toke's. But Toke replied that, despite their friendship, he could not share her with Orm, for she appealed to him very particularly and he wished to keep her for himself, if the gods should permit this to be.

At last they reached the ships, and the men who had remained on board were greatly jubilant at the sight of such rich booty, for it had been agreed that this was to be divided among them all. Solomon received many expressions of thanks from them all, and various costly presents; then he departed, together with the prisoners whom they had freed, since he was anxious to get clear of the Christians' country as soon as he could. Toke, who had not yet stopped drinking, began to weep when he heard that Solomon had left them, saying that now he had nobody to help him to converse with his girl. He drew his sword and wanted to run after him; but Orm and the others succeeded in quieting him without having to resort to violence, and in the end he nestled contentedly down beside his girl, having first bound her fast to him so that she should not steal away or be stolen while he slept.

The next morning they began to share out the booty, which proved to be no simple task. Everybody wanted to have as big a share as the next man; but it was decided that Krok and Berse and the helmsmen and one or two others should have three times as

much as the rest. Even then, though the business of sharing everything out fairly was allotted to the wisest among them, it was difficult to satisfy everyone. Berse said that, as it was largely due to
Toke that the fortress had been taken, he, too, ought to have a
triple share; and they all agreed that this should be so. But Toke
replied that he would be content with his single share if he might
be allowed to bring his girl on board and keep her there without
anyone objecting.

"For I should dearly like to bring her home with me," he said,
"even though I cannot be completely sure that she is the margrave's daughter. I am already getting on excellently with her, and
when she is able to speak our language and we can understand
each other's conversation, it will be better still."

Berse remarked that this might not turn out to be such an advantage as Toke supposed, and Krok added that the ships were going to be so heavily laden with all the booty they had won that,
even allowing for the fact that they had lost eleven men in the
fight, he doubted whether there would be room for the girl on
board; as things were, they would probably have to leave some of
the less valuable booty behind.

At this, Toke rose to his feet, lifted the girl on to his shoulder,
and commanded them all to have a good look at her and to note
how beautiful she was and what a fine figure she had.

"I do not doubt," he said, "that she is well able to excite the
lust of any man. Now, if there be any man here who covets her,
I shall be happy to fight him for her, here and now, either with
sword or with ax, whichever weapon he cares to choose. Let the
winner keep the girl; and the man who dies will, by his absence,
lighten the ship more than she will burden it; and in this way I
can fairly take her with me."

The girl held tightly with one hand to the beard on Toke's
cheek, and went red and wriggled her legs and put her other
hand over her eyes; but then she took it away again, seeming to
enjoy being looked at. They all thought that Toke's proposition
had been cunningly devised. But none of them elected to fight
with him, despite the beauty of the girl, for they all liked him and,
besides, feared him for his strength and his skill at arms.

When all the booty had been shared out and stored aboard, it
was decided that Toke should be permitted to bring his girl aboard

Krok's ship, though it was heavily laden; for they agreed that he
had deserved such a reward for his part in the storming of the fortress. They then held counsel regarding the question of the homeward voyage, and agreed that they should return along the
Asturian and Frankish coasts if the weather was bad, but that if
it was good, they should try to make for Ireland, thence to proceed
homewards round the Scottish islands; for, with such booty as they
had, it would be taking an unnecessary risk to sail through fre-
quented waters, where they might encounter other ships.

They ate and drank as much as they could hold, having now
an abundance of food and drink, more indeed than they could
take with them; and all the men were merry and excited, telling
one another what they would buy with their new-found wealth
when they reached home. Krok was by this time himself again;
but the captain of one of the other ships had fallen in the fortress,
and Berse took command of his vessel. Toke and Orm sat down
to their old oars in Krok's ship, finding it easy work with the current to help them; and Toke kept a close eye on his girl, who
spent most of the time sitting by him, and was careful to see
that nobody came near her without good cause.

CHAPTER FIVE

HOW KROK'S LUCK CHANGED TWICE, AND HOW
ORM BECAME LEFT–HANDED

THEY rowed down to the mouth of the river on the ebb
tide and offered up a skin of wine and a pot of flesh for the homeward voyage. Then they set sail, shipped their oars, and moved
out under a gentle wind into the long sweep of the bay. The
heavily laden ships lay deep in the water and made slow progress;
and Krok remarked that they would have to row until their arms
ached before they saw their home shores again. Orm afterwards,
in his old age, used to say that these were the unluckiest words he
had ever heard spoken, for, from that moment, Krok's luck, which
had hitherto been so good, suddenly broke, just as though a

god had heard him speak and had decided there and then to make him a true prophet.

Seven ships appeared round the southern point of the bay, heading northwards. On sighting Krok's ships, however, they turned into the bay and approached them at a great pace, their oars moving nimbly through the water. They were ships such as Krok's men had never before set eyes on, being long and low and very light in the water, and were filled with armed men, wearing black beards and strange coverings on their helmets. The men who were rowing them, two at each oar, were naked, and their skins a polished black-brown. They headed toward the Vikings amid hoarse cries and the sharp tumult of small drums.

Krok's three ships at once came abreast of each other, keeping close to the land on their side of the bay, in order to avoid being encircled. Krok was unwilling to give the order to lower sail; for, he said, should the wind rise, it would be to their advantage. Toke made haste to hide his girl among the bales of booty, piling them around and even on top of her, so as to protect her from spears and arrows. Orm helped him; then they took their places at the gunwale with the others. By this time Orm was well armed, for he had provided himself with a mail shirt and a shield and a good helmet from the fortress. A man standing near them wondered whether these strangers might perhaps be Christians, bent on revenge; but Orm thought it more likely that they were the Caliph's men, since no cross was visible on their shields or standards. Toke said that he was glad that he had quenched his thirst before the fighting began, for it looked as though it might be hot.

"And such of us as survive the day," he said, "will have a story worth telling our children; for these men have a savage air about them, and they far outnumber us."

By this time the foreigners had approached to within a short distance, and they now assailed the Vikings with showers of arrows. They rowed cunningly, slipping round the Viking ships and attacking them from all sides. The ship that Berse was commanding lay next to the shore, so that they could not surround her; but Krok's own ship lay at the extreme right of the three, farthest from the land, and was at once engaged in hard fighting. Two of the strangers' ships drew alongside her on the seaward side, the one lying beyond the other. They grappled the three vessels together with chains and iron hooks; then the men from the outer ship, yelling wildly, jumped across to the inner one, whence they all swarmed on to the Viking ship. They poured aboard her in overwhelming numbers, fighting very fiercely and skillfully, so that Krok's ship, by now very low in the water, lagged sadly behind her two companions. Then a third enemy ship managed to slip round her bows and grapple her on the shoreward side. So the situation now was that Berse's ship and the third Viking vessel had managed to get clear of the bay, though they had four enemy ships harrying them and were hard pressed to hold them off, while Krok's ship was engaging three opponents singlehanded. At this stage of the battle the wind rose, so that both Berse's ships were driven still farther from the shore, with fierce fighting raging aboard them and broad ribbons of blood trailing behind them in the water.

But the men in Krok's ship had no time to worry about how their companion vessels were faring, for they had their hands more than full with their own adversaries. So many foemen had climbed aboard over one of the gunwales that the ship had heeled over and was in danger of sinking; and though many of the raiders were hewn down and fell into the water or back into their own ship, a high proportion of them remained aboard, while others were swarming to their assistance from both sides. Krok fought bravely, and such of the foreigners as challenged him soon ceased their whooping; but before long he recognized that the enemy's superiority in numbers was too great. Then he threw aside his shield, sprang on to the gunwale and, swinging his ax with both hands, severed two of the chains that bound his ship to the enemy; but a man whom he had felled clutched hold of one of his legs, and in the same instant he received a spear through the shoulders and toppled headlong into the enemy ship, where many of his foes fell upon him, so that he was taken prisoner and bound fast.

After this, many of Krok's men were slain, though they defended themselves to the limit of their strength, and at last the whole ship was overrun, apart from a few men who were hemmed forward, including Toke and Orm. Toke had an arrow in his thigh, but was still on his feet, while Orm had received a blow on his forehead and could scarcely see for the blood that was running down into his eyes. Both of them were very weary. Toke's sword broke on the boss of a shield, but as he stepped backwards his foot struck against a firkin of wine that had been captured in the fortress and had been stored in the bows. Throwing aside the stump of his sword, he seized the firkin with both hands and raised it above his head.

"This shall not be wasted," he muttered, and hurled it against the nearest of his foes, crushing two of them and tripping up several others who fell over their bodies.

Then he cried to Orm and the others that there was nothing more to be done in the ship and, with those words, jumped head-first into the sea, in the hope of swimming ashore. Orm and as many of the others as could disengage the enemy followed suit. Arrows and spears pursued them, and two of them were hit. Orm dived, came up, and swam as hard as he could; but, as he was often to observe in his old age, few things are more difficult than swimming in a mail shirt when a man is tired and his shirt is tight. Before long neither Toke nor Orm had the strength left to swim farther, and they were on the point of sinking when one of the enemy's ships overtook them, and they were dragged on board and bound fast, without being able to offer any resistance.

So the Vikings were defeated, and their victors rowed ashore to examine what they had won and to bury their dead. They cleared the decks of the ship they had captured, throwing the corpses overboard, and began to rummage through its cargo, while the prisoners were led ashore and sat down on the beach, well guarded, with their arms bound. There were nine of them, all wounded. They waited for death, staring silently out to sea; but there was no sign of Berse's ships or of their pursuers.

Toke sighed and began to mumble to himself. Then he said:

> "Once, thirsty, I
> Wasted good ale.
> Soon shall I taste
> Valhalla's mead."

Orm lay on his back, gazing up at the sky. He said:

> "At home in the house
> That saw me grow
> Would I were seated now
> Eating sour milk and bread."

But none of them was sicker at heart than Krok; for, ever since the beginning of their expedition, he had regarded himself as a lucky man and as a hero, and now he had seen his luck crumble within the hour. He watched them throwing his dead followers overboard from what had been his ship, and said:

"The plowers of the sea
Earned for their toil
Misfortune and a foul
And early death."

Toke observed that this was a remarkable coincidence, that three poets should be found in so small a company.

"Even if you cannot fully match my skill at composing verses," he said, "yet be of good cheer. Remember that it is granted to the poets to drink from the largest horn at the banquet of the gods."

At this moment they heard a piercing shriek from the ship, followed by a great hubbub, signifying that the foreigners had discovered Toke's girl in her hiding-place. They brought her ashore, and an argument seemed to be developing over who should have her, for several men began quarreling in high-pitched voices, their black beards going up and down. Toke said: "Now the crows are disputing for possession of the hen, while the hawk sits nursing his broken wing."

The girl was led forward to the chieftain of the foreigners, a fat man with a grizzled beard and gold rings in his ears, clad in a red cloak and holding in his hand a silver hammer with a long white shaft. He studied her, stroking his beard; then he addressed her, and they could see that the two of them understood each other's language. The girl had plenty to say, pointing several times in the direction of the prisoners; but to two of his questions, when he also pointed toward them, she made a negative gesture with her hands and shook her head. The chieftain nodded and then gave her an order, which she seemed reluctant to obey, for she raised her arms toward the sky and cried out; but when he spoke to her again, in a severe voice, she became submissive and took her clothes off and stood naked before him. All the men standing around them sighed and tugged their beards and murmured with enraptured voices, for from the crown of her head to the soles of her feet she was exceedingly beautiful. The chieftain ordered her to turn round and examined her closely, fingering her hair, which was long and brown, and feeling her skin. Then he stood up and laid a signet ring, which he wore on one of his forefingers, against her belly and breasts and lips; after which, addressing some remark to his men, he took off his red cloak and wrapped it about her. On hearing his words, all his followers placed their hands against their foreheads and bowed, murmuring obsequiously. Then the girl dressed again, retaining, however, the red cloak, and food and drink were given to her, and everybody treated her with reverence.

The prisoners watched all this in silence; and when it reached the stage where the girl was given the cloak and was offered food and drink, Orm remarked that she seemed to have the best luck of all Krok's company. Toke agreed, and said that it was a hard thing for him to see her in all her beauty only now for the first time, when she was already another man's; for he had had little time with her, and they had always had to hurry; and now, he said, he could weep to think that he would never have the opportunity to split the skull of the potbellied graybeard who had soiled her body with his greasy fingers.

"But I cling to the hope," he added, "that the old gentleman will get little joy out of her; for, from the first moment that I saw her, I found her intelligent and of excellent taste, even though we could not understand each other's conversation; so that I think it cannot be long before she will stick a knife into the guts of that old billy-goat."

All this while, Krok had been sitting in deep silence, weighed down by his fate, with his face turned toward the sea, unable to take any interest in what was happening on shore. But now, all of a sudden, he uttered a cry, and as he did so, the foreigners began to gabble excitedly among themselves, for four ships had appeared far out in the bay, rowing toward the land. They were the ships that had fought Berse, and were rowing slowly; and soon they could see that one of them was lying very deep in the water, badly damaged, with the center of one of its gunwales smashed in, and many of its oars broken.

At this spectacle, the prisoners, though dispirited at their own plight, faint from their wounds and much troubled by thirst, broke into shouts of delighted laughter. For they realized at once that Berse had succeeded in ramming this ship, once the wind had risen out in the open sea, and that the enemy had had to break off the fight when they found themselves with only three sound ships left, and had rowed back with the damaged one. Some of them now began to hope that Berse might return and rescue them.

But Krok said: "He has lost many men, for he had enemies aboard and his hands full when last I saw him. And he must have guessed that few of us can be left alive, since he has not seen our ship come out of the bay; so he is more likely to try to reach home safely with what he has, either in both his ships or, if he has too few men left to man both, in one of them. Should he reach Blekinge safely, even if only with one ship, the story of Krok's expedition will be told in the Listerland and will be well remembered in the years to come. Now, however, these men will surely kill us, for their anger will be greater now that two of our ships have escaped their clutches."

In this, though, Krok was proved a false prophet. They were given food and drink, and a man came to look at their wounds; and then they realized that they were to become slaves. Some of them regarded this as preferable to death, while others were doubtful whether it might not prove a worse fate. The foreign chieftain had his galley slaves brought ashore and let them speak with the Vikings. They seemed to hail from many different lands and addressed them in various strange mumblings, but none of them spoke any language that the prisoners could understand. The foreigners remained in this place for a few days, putting their damaged ship in order.

Many of the oarsmen in this ship had been killed when Berse had rammed it, and the captured Vikings were set to replace them. They were well used to rowing, and at first they did not find the work too arduous for them, especially as, in this ship, there were two men to each oar. But they had to row almost naked, of which they were much ashamed, and each man had one leg chained. Their skin was almost white compared with that of the other slaves, and their backs were sorely flayed by the sun, so that they came to regard each sunrise as another turn of the rack. After a time, however, they became tanned like their fellows, and ceased to count the days, and were conscious of nothing but rowing and sleeping, feeling hunger and thirst, drinking and eating and row-ing again, until at last they reached the stage where, when harder rowing than usual had made them weary, they would fall asleep at their oars and continue rowing, without falling out of time or needing to be aroused by the overseer's whip. This showed them to have become true galley slaves.

They rowed in heat and in fierce rain, and sometimes in a pleas-ant cool, though it was never cold. They were the Caliph's slaves, but they had little knowledge of whither they were rowing or what purpose their labor might be serving. They rowed beside steep coasts and rich lowlands, and toiled painfully up broad and swiftly flowing rivers, on the banks of which they saw brown and black men and occasionally, but always at a distance, veiled women. They passed through the Njörva Sound and journeyed to the lim-its of the Caliph's dominions, seeing many rich islands and fine cities, the names of which they did not know. They anchored in great harbors, where they were shut up in slave-houses until the time came for them to put out to sea again; and they rowed hard in pursuit of foreign ships till their hearts seemed to be about to burst, and lay panting on the deck while battles that they had no strength to watch raged on the grapplings above them.

They felt neither grief nor hope and cried to no gods, for they had work enough to do minding their oars and keeping a watch-ful eye open for the man with the whip who supervised their row-ing. They hated him with a fierce intensity when he flicked them with his whip, and even more when they were rowing their hearts out and he strode among them with big lumps of bread soaked in wine, which he stuffed into their mouths, for then they knew that they would have to row without rest for as long as their strength sustained them. They could not understand what he said, but they soon learned to know from the tone of his voice how many lashes he was preparing to administer as a reward for negligence; and their only comfort was to hope that he would have a hard end, with his windpipe slit or his back flayed until his bones could be seen through the blood.

In his old age Orm used to say that this period in his life was lengthy to endure, but brief to tell of, for one day resembled an-other so that, in a sense, it was as though time was standing still for them. But there were signs to remind him that time was, in fact, passing; and one of these was his beard. When he first became a slave, he was the only one among them so young as to be beardless; but before long his beard began to grow, becoming redder even than his hair, and in time it grew so long that it swept the handle of his oar as he bowed himself over his stroke. Longer than that it could not grow, for the sweep of his oar curtailed its length; and of all the methods of trimming one's beard, he would say, that was the last that he would choose.

The second sign was the increase in his strength. He was already strong when they first chained him to his place, and used to rowing in Krok's ship, but a slave has to work harder than a free man, and the long bouts of rowing tried him sorely and sometimes, in the first few weeks, made him sick and dizzy. He saw men burst their hearts, spewing bloody froth over their beards, and topple backwards over the benches with their bodies shaking violently, and die and be thrown overboard; but he knew that he had only two choices to make: either to row while his fellows rowed, even if it meant rowing himself to death, or to receive the kiss of the overseer's whip upon his back. He said that he always chose the former, though it was little to go for, because once, during the first few days of his slavery, he had felt the whip, and he knew that if he felt it again, a white madness would descend upon him, and then his death would be certain.

So he rowed to the limit of his strength, even when his eyes blurred and his arms and his back ached like fire. After some weeks, however, he found that he was ceasing to be aware of his tiredness. His strength waxed, and soon he had to be careful not to pull too hard for fear of snapping his oar, which now felt like a stick in his hands; for a broken oar meant a sharp lesson from the whip. Throughout his long term as one of the Caliph's galley slaves, he rowed a larboard oar, which involved sitting with the oar on his right and taking the strain of the stroke on his left hand. Always afterwards, as long as he lived, he wielded his sword and suchlike weapons with his left hand, though he still used his right arm for casting spears. The strength he gained through this labor, which was greater than that of other men, remained with him, and he still had much of it left when he was old.

But there was a third sign, apart from the growth of his beard and of his strength, to remind him that time was passing as he labored at his oar; for he found himself gradually beginning to understand something of the foreign tongues that were being spoken around him, at first only a word here and there, but in time much more. Some of the slaves were from distant lands in the south and east and spoke tongues like the yapping of dogs, which none but themselves could understand; others were prisoners from the Christian lands in the north and spoke the languages of those regions. Many, however, were Andalusians, who had been put to the oar because they had been pirates or rebels, or because they had angered the Caliph with seditious teaching concerning their God and prophet; and these, like their masters, spoke Arabic. The overseer with the whip expressed himself in this tongue, and as it was always a wise thing for every slave to try to understand what this man wanted from them, he proved a good language-master to Orm, without causing himself any exertion in the process.

It was a cumbrous language to understand, and even more so to speak, for it consisted of guttural sounds that came from the depths of the throat and resembled nothing so much as the grunting of oxen or the croaking of frogs. Orm and his comrades never ceased to wonder that these foreigners should have chosen to give themselves the trouble of having to produce such complicated noises instead of talking in the simple and natural manner of the north. However, he showed himself to be quicker than any of the others in picking it up, partly, perhaps, because he was younger than they, but partly also because he had always shown an aptitude for pronouncing difficult and unfamiliar words that he had found in the old ballads, even when he had not been able to understand their meaning.

So it came to pass that Orm was the first of them who was able to understand what was being said to them, and the only one who could speak a word or two in reply. The consequence was that he became his companions' spokesman and interpreter, and that all orders were addressed to him. He was, besides, able to discover many things for the others by asking questions, as well as he could, of such of the other slaves as spoke Arabic and were able to tell him what he wanted to know. Thus, though he was the youngest of the Northmen, and a slave as they were, he came to regard himself as their chieftain, for neither Krok nor Toke was able to learn a word of the strange language; and Orm always afterwards used to say that, after good luck, strength, and skill at arms, nothing was so useful to a man who found himself among foreigners as the ability to learn a language.

The ship was manned by fifty soldiers, and the galley slaves numbered seventy-two; for there were eighteen pairs of oars. From bench to bench they would often murmur of the possibility of working themselves free from their chains, overpowering the soldiers, and so winning their freedom; but the chains were strong and were carefully watched, and guards were always posted when the ship was lying at anchor. Even when they engaged an enemy ship, some of the soldiers were always detailed to keep an eye on the slaves, with orders to kill any who showed signs of restlessness. When they were led ashore in any of the Caliph's great military harbors, they were shut up in a slave-house until the ship was ready to depart again, being kept all the time under strict surveillance, and were never allowed to be together in large numbers; so that there seemed to be no future for them but to row for as long as life remained in their bodies, or until some enemy ship might chance to conquer their own and set them at liberty. But the Caliph's ships were many, and always outnumbered their enemies, so that this eventuality was scarcely to be reckoned with. Such of them as showed themselves refractory, or relieved their hatred with curses, were flogged to death or thrown overboard alive; though occasionally, when the culprit was a strong oarsman, he was merely castrated and set again to his oar, which, though the slaves were never permitted a woman, they held to be the worst punishment of all.

When, in his old age, Orm used to tell of his years as a galley slave, he still remembered all the positions that his fellow Vikings occupied in the ship, as well as those of most of the other slaves; and as he told his story, he would take his listeners from oar to oar, describing what sort of man sat at each, and which among them died, and how others came to take their places, and which of them received the most whippings. He said that it was not difficult for him to remember these things, for in his dreams he often returned to the slave-ship and saw the wealed backs straining before his eyes and heard the men groaning with the terrible labor of their rowing, and, always, the feet of the overseer approaching behind him. His bed needed all the good craftsmanship that had gone into its making to keep it from splitting asunder as he would grip one of its beams to heave at the oar of his sleep; and he often said that there was no happiness in the world to compare with that of awakening from such a dream and finding it to be only a dream.

Three oars in front of Orm, also on the larboard side, sat Krok; and he was now a much changed man. Orm and the others knew that being a galley slave fell harder on him than on the rest of them, because he was a man accustomed to command, and one who had always believed himself to be lucky. He was very silent, seldom replying when his neighbors addressed him; and though, with his great strength, he found no difficulty in doing the work required of him, he rowed always as though half asleep and deep in reflection on other matters. His stroke would gradually become slower, and his oar would fall out of time, and he would be savagely lashed by the overseer; but none of them ever heard him utter any cry as he received his punishment, or even mumble a curse. He would pull hard on his oar and take up the stroke again; but his gaze would follow the overseer's back thoughtfully as the latter moved forward, as a man watches a troublesome wasp that he cannot lay his hands on.

Krok shared his oar with a man called Gunne, who complained loudly of the many whippings he received on Krok's account; but Krok paid little heed to his lamentations. At length, on one occasion when the overseer had flogged them both cruelly and Gunne's complaints were louder and his resentment greater than usual, Krok turned his eyes toward him, as though noticing his presence for the first time, and said: "Be patient, Gunne. You will not have to endure my company for much longer. I am a chieftain and was not born to serve other men; but I have one task yet to accomplish, if only my luck will stretch sufficiently to allow me to do what I have to do."

He said no more, and what task it was that he had to perform, Gunne could not wring from him.

Just in front of Orm there sat two men named Halle and Ögmund. They spoke often of the good days that they had spent in the past, of the food and the ale and the fine girls at home in the north, and conjured up various fitting deaths for the overseer; but they could never think of a way to bring any of them about. Orm

himself was seated with a dark-brown foreigner who, for some mis-
demeanor, had had his tongue cut out. He was a good oarsman
and seldom needed the whip, but Orm would have preferred to be
next to one of his own countrymen, or at any rate somebody able
to talk. The worst of it, as far as Orm was concerned, was that the
tongueless man, though unable to talk, was able all the more to
cough, and his cough was more frightful than any that Orm had
ever heard; when he coughed, he became gray in the face and
gulped like a landed fish, and altogether wore such a wretched
and woebegone appearance that it seemed impossible that he could
live much longer. This made Orm anxious concerning his own
health. He did not prize the life of a galley slave very highly, but
he was unwilling to be carried off by a cough; the tongueless man's
performance made him certain in his mind of that. The more he
reflected on the possibility of his dying like this, the more it dejected his spirits, and he wished that Toke had been seated nearer
to him.

Toke was placed several oars behind Orm, so that they seldom
had a chance to speak to each other—only, indeed, while they were
being led ashore or back to the ship; for in the slave-house they
were tethered together in groups of four in tiny cells, according to
their places in the ship. Toke had by now regained something of
his former humor and could still manage to find something to
laugh at, though he was usually at loggerheads with the man who
shared his oar, whose name was Tume and who, in Toke's view,
did less than his share of the rowing and ate more than his share
of the rations. Toke composed abusive lampoons, some about
Tume and some about the overseer, and sang them as chanteys
while he rowed, so that Orm and the others could hear them.

Most of the time, however, he occupied his thoughts with trying
to plan some method of escape. The first time that Orm and he
had a chance to speak to each other, he whispered that he had a
good plan almost worked out. All he needed was a small bit of
iron. With this he could prize open one of the links in his ankle-
chain one dark night when the ship was in port and everybody
except the watchmen would be asleep. Having done this, he would
pass the iron on to the other Vikings, each of whom would quietly
break his chain. When they had all freed themselves, they would
throttle the watchmen in the dark, without making a noise, and

steal their weapons; then, once ashore, they would be able to fend for themselves.

Orm said that this would be a fine idea if only it were practicable; and he would be glad to lend a hand in throttling the guards if they got that far, which he rather doubted. Where, though, could they find a suitable piece of iron, and how could naked men, who were always under close observation, manage to smuggle it aboard without being detected? Toke sighed, and admitted that these were difficulties that would require careful consideration; but he could not think of any better plan and said they would merely have to bide their time until an opportunity should present itself.

He succeeded in having a surreptitious word with Krok, too, and told him of his plan; but Krok listened to him abstractedly and showed little interest or enthusiasm.

Not long afterwards the ship was put into dry dock in one of the Caliph's shipyards to be scraped and pitched. Many of the slaves were detailed to assist with the work, chained in pairs; and the Northmen, who knew the ways of ships, were among these. Armed guards kept watch over them; and the overseer walked his rounds with his whip, to speed the work, two guards, armed with swords and bows, following him everywhere he went to protect him. Close to the ship there stood a large caldron full of simmering pitch, next to which was a barrel containing drinking-water for the slaves.

Krok and Gunne were drinking from this barrel when one of the slaves approached supporting his oar-companion, who had lost his foothold while engaged on the work and had so injured his foot that he was unable to stand on it. He was lowered to the ground and had begun to drink when the overseer came up to see what was afoot. The injured man was lying on his side, groaning; whereupon the overseer, thinking that the man was shamming, gave him a cut with his whip to bring him to his feet. The man, however, remained where he was, with everybody's eyes fixed upon him.

Krok was standing a few paces behind them, on the far side of the barrel. He shifted toward them, dragging Gunne with him; and suddenly it seemed as though all his previous apathy had dropped away from him. When he was close enough and saw that there was sufficient slack in the chain, he sprang forward, seized the overseer by the belt and the neck, and lifted him above his head. The overseer cried out in terror, and the nearest of the guards turned and ran his sword through Krok's body. Krok seemed not to feel the blow. Taking two sideward paces, he flung the overseer head downwards into the boiling pitch as the other guard's sword bit into his head. Krok tottered, but he kept his eyes fixed on what could be seen of the overseer. Then he gave a laugh and said: "Now my luck has turned again," and fell to the ground and died.

All the slaves raised a great shout of joy to see the overseer meet such an end; but the gladness of the Vikings was mingled with grief, and in the months that followed they often recalled Krok's deed and the last words that he had uttered. They all agreed that he had died in a manner befitting a chieftain; and they expressed the hope that the overseer had lived long enough in the caldron to get a good feel of the pitch. Toke wrought a strophe in Krok's honor, which ran thus:

> Worse than the whiplash burned
> The whipper, when his head
> Was drowned deep in the hot wash-
> Tub of the sea-mare's bows.
> Krok, who by cruel fate
> Had slaved at a foreign oar,
> Won his revenge and freedom:
> His luck had turned again.

When they rowed out to sea again, they had a new overseer to supervise their labors; but he seemed to have taken note of the fate of his predecessor, for he was somewhat sparing in the use of his whip.

CHAPTER SIX

CONCERNING THE JEW SOLOMON AND THE LADY
SUBAIDA, AND HOW ORM GOT HIS SWORD
BLUE–TONGUE

THE TONGUELESS man who rowed beside Orm grew
worse and worse until at last he could row no more; so when the
ship anchored in one of the Caliph's military harbors in the south,
called Málaga, he was led ashore, and they waited for another man
to be brought to replace him. Orm, who had had to do nearly all
the work on his oar during the last few weeks, was curious to know
whether he would now have a more congenial workmate. The next
morning the new man appeared. He was dragged to the ship by
four soldiers, who had their work cut out to get him up the gang-
way, and nobody needed to peer closely at him to know that he
still had his tongue. He was a young man, handsome, beardless,
and finely limbed, and he shrieked curses more frightful than anything that had been heard in the ship before.

He was carried to his place and held fast there while the chain
was fixed round his ankle. At this, tears streamed down his cheeks,
though they seemed to be the effect of anger rather than of sorrow. The ship's captain and the overseer came to have a look at
him, whereupon he immediately began to abuse them with curses
and imprecations, calling them many names that Orm had never
heard before, so that all the slaves expected to see him receive a
fearful flogging. The captain and the overseer, however, merely
stroked their beards and looked thoughtful, while they studied a
letter that the soldiers had brought with them. They nodded their
heads at this sentence and shook them at that one and whispered
discreetly among themselves, while all the time the newcomer
howled abuse at them, calling them sons of whores, pork-eaters,
and copulators of female asses. At last the overseer threatened
him with the whip and told him to keep his mouth shut. Then,
when the captain and the overseer had moved away, the new-

comer began to weep in earnest, so that his whole body shook
with it.

Orm did not know what to make of all this, but thought he
would get little help from this fellow, unless they used the whip
on him. Still, he felt it would be something to have a companion
who could at any rate talk, after his experience with the tongueless man. At first, however, the newcomer disdained to hold any
converse with him and rejected Orm's friendly approaches. As Orm
had feared, he turned out to be no oarsman and could not adapt
himself to his new mode of life at all, finding especial cause for
complaint in the food that was supplied to them, which seemed
to Orm to be very good, though insufficient. But Orm was forbear-
ing with him, and did the rowing for both of them, and muttered
words of encouragement to him, in so far as he was able to in
Arabic. Several times he asked the man who he was and why he
had been sentenced to this ship, but received in response merely
haughty glances and shoulder-shrugs. At length the man condescended to address him and announced that he was a man of
breeding and not accustomed to being cross-examined by slaves
who could not even talk properly.

At this, Orm said: "For those words you have just uttered, I
could take you by the neck so that you felt it; but it is better that
there should be peace between us, and that you and I should be
friends. In this ship we are all slaves, you no less than the rest of
us; nor are you the only man aboard who is of good lineage. I am
so myself; my name is Orm, and I am a chieftain's son. It is true
that I speak your language poorly, but you speak mine worse, for
you do not know a word of it. It therefore appears to me that
there is nothing to choose between us; indeed, if either of us has
the advantage, I do not think it is you."

"Your intonation is deplorable," replied the newcomer. "However, you seem to be a man of some intelligence. It is possible that
among your own people you are reckoned to be well-born; but in
this respect you can hardly compare with me, for on my mother's
side I am directly descended from the Prophet, peace be to his im-
mortal soul! Know, too, that the tongue I speak is Allah's own, all
other tongues having been invented by evil spirits to hinder the
spread of the true learning. So you see that there can be no com-
parison between us. Khalid is my name, the son of Yezid; my fa-

ther was a high officer of the Caliph, and I own great possessions and do no work, apart from supervising my gardens, entertaining my friends, and composing music and poetry. It is true, I admit, that I now temporarily find myself otherwise occupied, but this shall not be for long, may worms eat out the eyes of him who set me here! I have written songs that are sung throughout Málaga, and there are few poets living as skillful as I."

Orm commented that there must be many poets in the Caliph's kingdom, as he had met one already. Khalid replied that there were a lot in the sense that many men attempted to write verses, but that very few of them could be considered true poets.

After this conversation they got on better together, though Khalid continued to be a poor oarsman and was sometimes hardly able to pull at all, because his hands were skinned by the oar. A little later he told Orm how he had come to be sent to the ship. He had to repeat himself several times, and use paraphrases to explain what he meant, for he was difficult to follow; but in the end Orm grasped the gist of what he had to say.

Khalid told him that his present plight arose from the fact of the most beautiful maiden in all Málaga being the daughter of the governor of the city, a man of low birth and evil disposition. The beauty of his daughter, however, was such that not even a poet could conceive of anything lovelier, and on one occasion Khalid had been lucky enough to see her unveiled at a harvest feast. From that moment, he had loved her above all other women, and had written songs in her honor that had melted in his mouth as he sang them. At length, by dint of taking up residence on the roof of a house near where she lived, he had succeeded in catching another glimpse of her when she was sitting alone on her roof. He had shouted ecstatic greetings to her and, by stretching out his arms appealingly toward her, had prevailed on her to lift her veil once more. This was a sign that she reciprocated his love; and the surpassing magnificence of her beauty had almost caused him to faint.

Thus assured that the lady was favorably disposed toward him, he had given rich gifts to her maid-in-waiting and so had managed to convey messages to her. Then the governor had gone to Córdoba to present his annual accounts to the Caliph, and the lady had sent Khalid a red flower; whereupon he had disguised himself as an old crone and, with the connivance of the maid-in-waiting, had gained admission to the lady's presence, where he had enjoyed lively sport with her. One day, however, not long afterwards, her brother had drawn upon him in the city and in the ensuing fight had, by reason of Khalid's skill at arms, been wounded. On the governor's return, Khalid had been arrested and brought before him.

At this point in his story Khalid went black with fury, spat viciously, and shrieked horrible curses upon the governor. Then he proceeded: "Legally, he had no case against me. Granted I had lain with his daughter, but in return for that I had immortalized her in exquisite songs, and even he seemed to realize that a man of my birth could hardly be expected to propose marriage to the daughter of a common Berber. I had wounded his son, but only after he had attacked me; indeed, but for the temperateness of my nature, he would not have escaped with his life. For all this the governor, if he had been a true lover of justice, should have been grateful to me. Instead, he took counsel in his wickedness, which is surpassing even in Málaga, and this is the result. Hearken well, O unbeliever, and be amazed."

Orm listened to all this with interest, though many of the words were unfamiliar to him, and the men on the nearest benches listened too, for Khalid told his story in a loud voice.

"He had one of my poems read aloud, and asked whether I had written it. I replied that everyone in Málaga knew the poem and knew that I was the author of it, for it is a pæan in praise of the city, the best that was ever written. In the poem occur these lines:

> This I know well: that had the Prophet e'er
> Tasted the harvest that the grapevines bear,
> He would not blindly have forbidden us
> (In his strict book) to taste the sweet grape's juice.
> His whiskers berry-drenched, his beaker flowing,
> With praise of wine he had enhanced his teaching."

Having recited these lines, Khalid burst into tears and explained that it was for their sake that he had been condemned to serve in the galleys. For the Caliph, who was the protector of the true faith and the earthly representative of the Prophet, had ordained that any who blasphemed against the Prophet or criticized his teaching should be severely punished, and the governor had hit upon this method of securing his revenge, under the pretext of demanding justice.

"But I solace myself by reflecting that this state of affairs cannot last for long," said Khalid, "for my family is more powerful than his, and has, besides, the Caliph's ear, so that I shall shortly be liberated. That is why nobody in this ship dares to bring the whip to me, for they know that no man can with impunity lay his hand on one who is descended from the Prophet."

Orm asked when this Prophet had lived, and Khalid replied that he had died more than three hundred and fifty years ago. Orm remarked that he must indeed have been a mighty man if he could still, after so long an interval, protect his kinsmen and decide what his people might or might not drink. No man had ever wielded such power in Skania, not even King Ivar of the Broad Embrace, who was the mightiest man that had lived in the north. "No man in my country," he said, "lays down the law about what another man may drink, be he king or commoner."

Orm's knowledge of Arabic increased by leaps and bounds now that he had Khalid as his companion, for the latter talked incessantly and had many interesting things to tell of. After some days he inquired where Orm's country was and how he had come to be in the ship. Then Orm told him the story of Krok's expedition, and how he had joined it, and of all that had ensued. When he had recounted his adventures, as well as he could, he concluded: "As you see, much of what happened was the result of our meeting with the Jew Solomon. I think it possible that he was a man of luck, for he was freed from his slavery, and as long as he remained with us our fortunes prospered. He said that he was an important man in a town called Toledo, where he was a silversmith, as well as being the leading poet."

Khalid said that he had certainly heard of him, for his skill as a silversmith was renowned; nor was he a bad poet, as poets went in Toledo.

"Not so long ago," he said, "I heard one of his poems sung by a wandering minstrel from the north, in which he described how he had fallen into the hands of an Asturian margrave, who used him ill, and how he had escaped and had led fierce pirates against the fortress, storming it and killing the margrave and sticking his

head on a pole for the crows to peck at, after which he had returned home to his own country with the margrave's gold. It was
a competent work, in a simple style, though lacking the delicacy
of expression that we of Málaga aim at."

"He does not belittle his achievements," said Orm. "If he is prepared to go to so much trouble to revenge himself on an enemy,
he ought to be willing to do something to help the friends who
rendered him such service. It was we who liberated him from his
slavery, stormed the fortress, and executed his revenge; and if
he is in reality an important man in his country, he is perhaps in
a position to render us who sit here a service comparable to that
which we performed for him. Nor do I see how else we shall ever
regain our freedom, if he does not help us."

Khalid said that Solomon was famous for his wealth, and that
the Caliph regarded him highly, though he did not follow the true
religion. Orm now began to hope, but he said nothing to his countrymen of what Khalid had told him. The outcome of their conversation was that Khalid undertook to send a message, together
with Orm's greetings, to Solomon in Toledo, as soon as he was
released himself.

But the days passed and still no order arrived for Khalid's liberation. The delay made him more unruly than ever, and he in-
veighed furiously again the indifference shown by his kinsmen. He
began to compose a long poem on the pernicious influence of
wine, hoping that he might be able to get this copied out when
they were in port and forwarded to the Caliph, so that his real
feelings on the subject might become known. But when it came
to the point where he had to sing the praises of water and lemon-
juice and to acclaim their superiority to wine, his verses began to
halt somewhat. However, although he continued to shriek imprecations at the ship's crew whenever his dark fits settled on him,
he was still never touched with the whip, and Orm took this to be
a hopeful sign that he would not remain with them for much
longer.

One morning, when they were in one of the eastern harbors, the
ship having returned with many others from a hard chase after
African pirates, four men walked aboard, and when Khalid saw
them, he became faint with joy and paid no heed to Orm's questions regarding their identity. One of the men was an official with

a big turban and a cloak reaching to his feet. He handed a letter to the captain of the ship, who touched it with his forehead and read it reverently. Another member of the four seemed to be some kinsman of Khalid's, for, as soon as the latter had been released from his ankle-chain, they threw themselves into each other's arms, weeping and exchanging kisses and chattering like madmen. The other two men were servants, bearing clothes and baskets. They dressed Khalid in a fine robe and offered him food. Orm shouted to him to remember his promise, but Khalid was already rebuking his kinsman for having forgotten to bring a barber with him, and did not hear. Then Khalid went ashore with his suite, the captain and crew bidding him obsequious farewells, which he acknowledged with condescension, as though barely aware of their presence, and disappeared arm in arm with his kinsman.

Orm was sorry to see him depart, for Khalid had been an entertaining companion, and he feared that in his new-found freedom he would be above remembering to fulfill his promise. Another man was chained beside Orm in Khalid's place, a shopkeeper who had been found guilty of using false weights. He tired quickly and was little use at the oar, and had to be whipped frequently, at which he moaned and mumbled little pieties to himself. Orm gained small pleasure from his company, and this was the period of his life in the galley that he found most tedious. He set all his hopes on Khalid and Solomon, but as more and more time passed, these began to fade.

At last, however, in Cádiz, their lucky day arrived. An officer came on board with a troop of men, and all the Northmen were released from their ankle-chains, were given clothes and shoes, and were removed to another ship, which proceeded up the great river to Córdoba. They were made to lend a hand rowing against the stream, but were not fettered or whipped and were frequently relieved; moreover, they were allowed to sit together, and so could talk without hindrance for the first time for many a day. They had been galley slaves for two years and the greater part of a third; and Toke, who sang and laughed almost the whole time, said that he did not know what would become of them now, but that one thing he did know, that it was high time that he drank the thirst out of himself. Orm said that it would be better if he could wait until he had someone's permission to do so, for it would be a bad thing if they had any violence now, which they would be liable to have, if Orm's memory served him rightly, once Toke began quenching his thirst. Toke agreed that he would do better to wait, though he added that the waiting would be difficult. They all wondered what was going to happen to them, and Orm now repeated to them the details of his conversation with Khalid concerning the Jew. Then they were loud in the Jew's praise, and in Orm's also; and, though Orm was the youngest of them, they all now acknowledged him to be their chieftain.

Orm asked the officer what was going to be done with them, and whether he knew of a Jew called Solomon, but all the officer could tell him was that he had been commanded to conduct them to Córdoba; and he had never heard of Solomon.

They arrived at the Caliph's city and saw it spreading out on both banks of the river, with many houses huddled together and white palaces and palm courts and towers. They marveled greatly as its size and splendor, which surpassed anything they could have imagined, and its wealth seemed to them sufficient to provide rich booty for all the seamen from the whole of the Danish kingdom.

They were led through the city, gazing in wonder on the throngs of people, though they complained that there were too few women among them, and that not much could be seen of those who were abroad, because they were all cloaked and veiled.

"A woman would have her work cut out not to appear beautiful in my eyes," said Toke, "if only I had a chance to talk to one of them; for it is now three years since we fell among those foreigners, and in all that time we have not been allowed to smell a single woman."

"If they set us free," said Ögmund, "we ought to be able to do well for women in this country; for their men are of miserable appearance compared with us."

"Every man in this land is allowed to have four wives," said Orm, "if he has embraced the Prophet and his teaching. But, once having done so, he can never drink wine again."

"It is a difficult choice to make," said Toke, "for their ale is too thin for my palate. But it may be that we have not yet sampled their best brew. And four women is just about what I need."

They came to a large house, where there were many soldiers, and there they slept the night. The next morning a stranger appeared and led them to another house not far distant, where they were well bathed and barbered, and where cool drinks were offered to them in beautiful tiny cups. Then they were given softer garments, which chafed them less; for their clothes felt rough against their skin, since they had for so long been naked. They looked at each other, laughing at the change that had been wrought in their appearance; then, marveling greatly at all this, they were conducted into a dining-room, where a man came forward, greeting them and bidding them welcome. They recognized him at once as Solomon, though he now wore a very different appearance from when they had last seen him, for he had all the bearing and accouterments of a rich and mighty prince.

He greeted them hospitably, bidding them eat and drink and regard his house as their own; but he had forgotten most of what he had formerly known of the Nordic tongue, so that only Orm was able to converse with him. Solomon said that he had done all that he could on their behalf as soon as he had heard of their plight, because they had once performed a very great service for him, which he was glad to be able to repay. Orm thanked him as eloquently as he could; but, he told Solomon, what they were most eager to know was whether they were now free men or whether they were still slaves.

Solomon replied that they were still the Caliph's slaves, and must remain so; in that matter he could not help them; but they were now to serve in the Caliph's private bodyguard, which was recruited from the pick of the prisoners that the Caliph captured in battle and of the slaves that he purchased from abroad. The Caliphs of Córdoba, he went on, had always possessed such a bodyguard, regarding it as safer than being surrounded by armed subjects of their own, since the latter might more easily be bribed by their kinsmen or their friends to lay violent hands on the Caliph's person when discontent pricked the land.

But before they joined the bodyguard, Solomon told them, they would first be his guests for a while, in order that they might in some measure recover themselves after their labors; so they stayed at his house for five days, and were treated as heroes are treated at the table of Odin. They partook of many delicate dishes, and drink was brought to them whenever they cared to call for it; mu-

sicians played for them, and they made themselves tipsy with wine
every evening; no Prophet having forbidden Solomon to taste of
that drink. Orm and his fellows, however, kept a watchful eye on
Toke the whole time, lest he should drink too much and so weep
and become dangerous. Their host offered each of them a young
slave-girl to keep them company in bed, and this delighted them
most of all. They agreed unanimously that the Jew was a fine man
and a chieftain, every bit as good as if he had been of Nordic
blood; and Toke said that he had seldom made a more fortunate
catch than when he had drawn this noble Semite out of the sea.
They slept late in the mornings, in feather beds softer than anything they had previously known; and at table they quarreled merrily about which among them had the prettiest slave-girl, and none
of them would allow that his was not the choicest of them all.

On the third evening of their stay there, Solomon bade Orm
and Toke accompany him into the city, saying that there was
someone else whom they had to thank for their liberation, and
who had perhaps done more for them than he had. They went
with him along many streets, and Orm asked whether Khalid, the
great poet of Málaga, had perhaps come to Córdoba, and whether
it was he whom they were on their way to visit; but Solomon replied that they were going to meet a nobler personage than Khalid.

"And only a foreigner," he added feelingly, "could look upon
this Khalid as a great poet, though he noises it abroad that he is
one. Sometimes I try to calculate how many truly great poets there
can be said to be nowadays in the Caliph's dominions; and I do
not think that that honor can rightly be allowed to more than
five of us, among which number Khalid could not possibly find
inclusion, though he has a certain facility for playing with rhymes.
None the less, you do right, Orm, to regard him as your friend,
for without his help I should never have discovered what became
of you and your men; so if you should meet him and he should
refer to himself as a poet, you need not correct him."

Orm remarked that he knew enough about men not to argue
with poets concerning their respective merits; but Toke broke into
their conversation with the complaint that he wanted to know
why he had been pressed into this evening ramble when it was
impossible for him to understand a word of what was being said
and when he had been enjoying himself so much in Solomon's

house. Solomon merely replied that it was necessary that he should accompany them, it having so been ordered.

They arrived at a walled garden with a narrow gate, which was opened to admit them. They entered, walking among beautiful trees and many strange plants and flowers, and came to a place where a great fountain was playing and clear water ran through rich grasses in small coiling streams. From the opposite direction to that from which they had come, a litter was being carried toward them by four slaves, followed by two slave-girls and two black men carrying drawn swords.

Solomon halted, and Orm and Toke did likewise. The litter was lowered to the ground, and the slave-girls ran forward and stood reverently one on either side of it. Then a veiled lady stepped forth. Solomon bowed low at her thrice, with his hands pressed against his forehead, so that Orm and Toke realized that she must be of royal blood; they remained upright, however, for it seemed to them a wrong thing that any man should abase himself before a woman.

The lady inclined her head graciously in Solomon's direction. Then she turned toward Orm and Toke and murmured something beneath her veil; and her eyes were friendly. Solomon bowed to her again and said: "Warriors from the north, thank Her Highness Subaida, for it is by her power that you stand liberated."

Orm said to the lady: "If you have helped to free us, we owe you a great debt of thanks. But who you are, and why you have showed us such favor, we do not know."

"Yet we have met," she answered, "and perchance you will remember my face."

So saying, she lifted her veil, at which the Jew abased himself again. Toke tugged at his beard and muttered to Orm: "It is my girl from the fortress, and she is more beautiful now than ever. Her luck must indeed have been good, for since we last saw her, she has become a queen. I should like to know whether she is pleased to see me again."

The lady glanced toward Toke and said: "Why do you address your friend and not me?"

Orm replied to her that Toke could not understand Arabic, but that he said that he remembered her and thought her even more beautiful now than when he had last seen her. "And we both rejoice," he added, "to see that luck and power have come your way, for you appear to us to be deserving of the one and worthy of the other."

She looked at Orm and smiled, and said: "But you, O red man, have learned the language of this country, as I have done. Which is the better man, you or your friend who was once my master? "

"We both reckon ourselves to be good men," replied Orm. "But I am young and am less experienced than he; and he performed mighty feats when we took the fortress that was your home. Therefore I hold him to be the better man of us as yet, though he cannot tell you so himself in the language of this land. But better than either of us was Krok, our chieftain; but he is dead."

She said that she remembered Krok, and that good chieftains seldom lived to be old. Orm told her how he had died, and she nodded, and said: "Fate has woven our destinies together in a curious way. You took my father's house and slew him and most of his people, for which I should rightly make you atone with your lives. But my father was a cruel man, especially toward my mother, and I hated and feared him like a hairy devil. I was glad when he was killed, and was not sorry to find myself among foreigners, nor to be made love to by your friend, though it was a pity that we were never able to talk to each other. I did not much care for the smell of his beard, but he had merry eyes and a kind laugh, and these I liked; and he used me gently, even when he was drunk and impatient with lust. He left no bruises on my body, and gave me only a light burden to bear on the march to the ship. I would have been willing to accompany him to your country. Tell him this."

All that she had said Orm repeated to Toke, who listened with a contented expression. When Orm had finished, Toke said: "You see how lucky I am with women! But she is the best I ever saw, and you may tell her that I said so. Do you suppose that she intends to make me an important man in this country of hers?"

Orm replied that she had said nothing about that; then, after repeating Toke's compliment to her, he begged her to tell them what had happened to her since they had parted on the seashore.

"The ship's captain brought me hither to Córdoba," she said. "Nor did he lay his hand on me, though he had forced me to stand naked before him, for he knew that I would make a fine gift

for him to present to his master, the Grand Vizier. Now, therefore, I belong to the Grand Vizier of the Caliph, who is called
Almansur and is the most powerful man in the whole of the Caliph's dominions. He, after first instructing me in the teaching of
the Prophet, raised me from a slave-girl to be his chief wife, since
he found that my beauty exceeded that of all his other women.
Praised be Allah for it! So you have brought me luck, for if you
had not come to destroy my father's fortress, I should still be living in daily dread of my father and should have had some bad
man forced on me as a husband. for all my beauty. When, therefore, Solomon, who makes my finest jewelry, informed me that
you were still alive, I resolved to give you such assistance as lay
within my power."

"We have three persons to thank for freeing us from the galley
benches," said Orm: "yourself, Solomon, and a man from Málaga
called Khalid. Now, though, we know that it was your word that
counted for most; therefore we give our chief thanks to you. It was
lucky for us that we met such people as you and these two poets,
for otherwise we should still be straining on our benches, with
naught but death to hope for. We shall be proud to enter your
lord's service, and to aid him against his enemies. But we are surprised that you succeeded in persuading him to release us, for all
the power you wield; for we seamen from the north are regarded
here as great enemies, and have been so ever since the days of the
sons of Ragnar Hairy-Breeks."

Subaida replied: "You did my lord Almansur a great service
when you took my father's fortress, for he would not else have
known that I existed. Besides this, it is well known among the
people of this country that the men of the north keep their word
and are brave warriors. Both the Caliph Abd-er-Rahman the Great,
and his father, the Emir Abdullah, had many Northmen in their
bodyguards, for in those days your countrymen harried our Spanish coasts sorely; but of late few Northmen have been seen in these
parts, so that there are now none of them in the royal bodyguard.
If you serve my lord Almansur faithfully and well, you will be
richly rewarded, and the captain of the guard will give you and
your men full armor and fine weapons. But first I have a gift for
each of you."

She beckoned to one of the slaves who stood beside the litter, and he brought forward two swords, with splendidly ornamented scabbards and belts embossed with heavy silver buckles. One of these she gave to Toke, and the other to Orm. They accepted them joyfully, for they had felt naked with no swords at their waists during the years that had passed. They drew them forth from their scabbards, examining the blades closely, and weighing them in their hands. Solomon looked at the swords and said: "These were forged in Toledo, where the best smiths in the world, both in silver and in steel, work. They still make swords straight there, as was the fashion in the time of the Gothic kings, before the servants of the Prophet came to this land. No smith alive forges a finer sword than these."

Toke laughed aloud for joy and began to mutter to himself. At length he said:

> "Long have the warrior's hands
> Known the oar's timber.
> See how they laugh to hold
> Once more the war-man's blade."

Orm was anxious not to be outdone as a poet, so he reflected for a few minutes and then, holding his sword before his face, said:

> "The sword the fair one gave me
> I raise with my left hand,
> Like Tyr among the immortals.
> The serpent has won back his sting."

Subaida laughed and said: "Giving a man a sword is like giving a woman a looking-glass; they have eyes left for nothing else. But it is good to see gifts so gratefully received. May they bring you luck."

Then their meeting ended, for Subaida said that the time had come for her to bid them farewell, though it might chance that some time they would meet again. So she stepped into her litter and was borne away.

As they returned with Solomon to his house, the three of them were loud in their praise of Subaida and of the costly presents she had given them. Solomon explained that he had known her for more than a year and had often sold her jewelry. He had realized from the first that she was the same girl that Toke had won in the cruel margrave's fortress, though her beauty had greatly increased since then.

Toke said: "She is fair and kind, and does not forget those who take her fancy. It is a hard thing for me to see her again, knowing that she is the wife of a great lord. Still, I am glad she does not belong to that potbellied old goat with the silver hammer who captured us. I should not have liked that. But, all in all, I cannot complain, for the girl Solomon has found for me suits me very well."

Orm questioned the Jew concerning Subaida's lord, Almansur, asking how he could be the mightiest man in the land. Surely the Caliph must be more powerful than he? Solomon, however, explained how the matter lay. The previous Caliph, Hakam the Learned, the son of Abd-er-Rahman the Great, had been a great ruler despite the fact that he had spent most of his time reading books and conversing with learned men. On his death he had left no heir save an infant son, named Hisham, who was the present Caliph. Now Hakam had ordained that his most trusted counselor, together with his favorite wife, who was the child's mother, should rule until Hisham came of age. Unfortunately, these two had so enjoyed the exercise of their power that they had imprisoned the young Caliph in a castle, on the pretext that he was of too holy a nature to be bothered with earthly matters. This counselor, in his capacity as regent of the realm, had won many victories against the Christians in the north, as a result of which he had received the title of Almansur, meaning "the Conqueror." The Queen, the young Caliph's mother, had for a long time past loved Almansur above all other earthly things, but he had become weary of her, for she was older than he and inclined, besides, to be captious about the division of power; so now she had been imprisoned, like her son, and Almansur ruled alone in the land as the Caliph's regent. Many of his subjects hated him for what he had done to the Caliph and the Queen Mother, but many loved him for the victories he had gained against the Christians; and he was a good master to his bodyguard, for he relied on them as a shield against all who treasured envy and hatred toward him. Orm and his men might, therefore, expect to prosper in Almansur's palace while there was peace, in addition to all the fighting that they could wish for, since each spring Almansur set forth with a mighty army, either against the King of Asturia and the Count of Castile, or against the King of Navarre and the Count of Aragon, far away in the north near the border country of the Franks. All these monarchs lived in perpetual dread of him and were glad to pay him tribute in order to make him postpone his visits.

"But they do not find it easy to buy him off," continued Solomon, "the reason for this being that he is a very unhappy man. He is powerful and victorious, and has succeeded in every enterprise to which he has laid his hand; but, in spite of all this, everyone knows that he is plagued by an incessant fear. For he has turned his hand against the Caliph, who is the shadow of the Prophet, and has stolen his power from him; on account of which, he lives in daily dread of the wrath of Allah and has no peace in his soul. Each year he seeks to propitiate Allah by waging new wars against the Christians, and that is why he never accepts tribute from all the Christian princes at once, but only allows each of them to buy him off for a few months at a time, so that he can always have some of them available for him to put zealously to the sword. Of all the warriors that have ever been born in this land, he is the mightiest; and he has sworn a great oath that he will die in the field, with his face turned toward the false worshippers who believe that the son of Joseph was God. He takes little interest in verses or music, so that these are lean times for poets compared with the favors we enjoyed under Hakam the Wise; but in his leisure hours he finds some pleasure in gold and silver work and in precious stones, so I cannot complain. I bought this house in Córdoba that I might the better serve his pleasure; and long may he flourish and long may fortune smile upon him, for to a silversmith he is indeed a good master."

All this and more Solomon recounted to Orm, and Orm repeated it to Toke and the others; and they agreed that this Almansur must be a notable prince. But his fear of Allah they could not understand, for it was unknown among the Northmen for anyone to be afraid of the gods.

Before the time came for them to leave the Jew's house, he gave them sage counsel on many matters; above all, he warned Toke never to let it become known that he had formerly been Subaida's master.

"For princes enjoy the sight of their women's former lovers no more than we do," he said, "and it was bold of her to allow you to see her again, even though there were witnesses present to swear, if necessary, that nothing untoward occurred. In this, as in all other respects, Almansur is a sharp-eyed master, so that Toke will do well to keep a tight rein on his tongue."

Toke replied that there was no fear of his doing otherwise; and that his most immediate concern was to think of a good name for his sword. For such a sword as his had surely come from the hand of as great a smith as he who had forged Sigurd's sword Gram, or Mimming, which had belonged to Didrik, or Skofnung, which Rolf the Jade had wielded. Therefore it must have a name, as theirs had had. But he could not hit upon any name that pleased him, though he tried assiduously to think of one. Orm, however, called his sword Blue-Tongue.

They left Solomon with many expressions of thanks, and were conducted to Almansur's palace, where they were received by an officer of the royal household and were given armor and a full complement of weapons, and commenced their service in Almansur's bodyguard. And the seven men from the north elected Orm to be their chieftain.

CHAPTER SEVEN

HOW ORM SERVED ALMANSUR, AND HOW HE SAILED WITH ST. JAMES'S BELL

ORM entered the Imperial bodyguard at Córdoba in the year commonly reckoned as the eighth of the reign of the Caliph Hisham; that is, three years before Bue Digre and Vagn Akesson sailed with the Jomsvikings against the Norwegians. He remained in Almansur's service for four years.

The men of the Imperial bodyguard were greatly respected in Córdoba, and were more finely attired than the ordinary citizens. Their mail shirts were light and thin, but more resilient and of finer workmanship than any that Orm and his men had ever previously seen. Their helmets shone like silver, and on occasion they wore scarlet cloaks over their amor; and their shields were engraved round the edge with an arc of lettering, cunningly worked. This same legend was sewn upon Almansur's great banners, which were always borne at the head of his army when he marched to war, and the meaning of it was: "Allah alone is victorious."

The first occasion on which Orm and his men entered Almansur's presence, to be shown to him by the commander of the guard, they were surprised at his appearance, for they had imagined him to be of the proportions of a hero. He was in fact an unprepossessing man, pinched and half-bald, with a yellow-green face and heavy eyebrows. He was seated on a broad bed among a heap of cushions, and tugged meditatively at his beard as he addressed rapid commands to two secretaries seated on the floor before him, who took down everything he said. On a table beside his bed there stood a copper box and, next to the box, a bowl of fruit and a large wicker cage, in which several tiny monkeys were playing and leaping round on a wheel. While the secretaries were writing down what he had just said, he took fruit from the bowl and put it between the bars of the cage and watched the monkeys fighting for the gift and stretching out their dwarfish hands for more; but instead of smiling at their antics, he stared at them with sad eyes and pushed more fruit between the bars and began again to dictate to his secretaries.

After a while he gave the secretaries permission to rest and bade the commander of the guard approach with his men. He turned his face from the cage and gazed at Orm and the other Vikings. His eyes were black and as though grief-stricken, but it seemed as if something burned and glittered deep down in their depths, so that the men found it difficult to meet his gaze for more than a few seconds. He studied them critically, one by one, and nodded his head.

"These men have the bearing of warriors," he said to the commander. "Do they understand our language?"

The commander indicated Orm and said that he understood Arabic, but that the rest knew little or none, and that they regarded him as their chieftain.

Almansur said to Orm: "What is your name?"

Orm told him his name and added that in his language it meant Serpent.

Almansur then asked him: "Who is your King?"

"Harald, the son of Gorm," replied Orm, "and he is the lord of all the Danish kingdom."

"I do not know of him," said Almansur.

"Be glad of it, lord," replied Orm, "for whithersoever his ships sail, kings pale at the sound of his name."

Almansur gazed at Orm for a few moments; then he said: "You are quick-tongued, and deserve the name you bear. Is your King a friend of the Franks?"

Orm smiled, and answered: "He was their friend when his own country was disturbed by insurrection. But when Fortune smiles upon him, he burns their cities, both in Frankland and in Saxony. And he is a King whom Fortune dotes on."

"Perchance he is a good King," said Almansur. "Who is your god?"

"That is a more difficult question to answer, lord," replied Orm. "My gods are the gods of my people, and we think them strong, as we ourselves are. There are many of them, but some of them are old, and few men trouble to worship these, apart from poets. The strongest of them is called Thor. He is red, as I am, and is held to be the friend of all mortal men. But the wisest of them is Odin, who is the god of soldiers, and they say that it is thanks to him that we Northmen are the best warriors in the world. Whether any of our gods have done anything for me, though, I do not know; certain it is that I have not done much for them. And they seem to me to have little sway in this land."

"Now listen carefully, infidel," said Almansur, "to what I am about to say. There is no God save Allah. Say not that there are many, nor that there are three; it shall be well for you on the Judgment Day if you do not say these things. There is but one Allah, the Eternal, the Sublime; and Mohammed is His Prophet. This is the truth, and this you shall believe. When I wage war against the Christians, I wage it for Allah and the Prophet, and ill betide any man of my army who does not honor them. From henceforth, therefore, you and your men shall worship none but the true God."

Orm replied: "We men of the north do not worship our gods except in time of necessity, for we think it foolish to weary them with babbling. In this land we have worshipped no god since the time when we sacrificed to the sea-god to bless our homeward voyage with luck; and that proved to be of little use to us, for not long afterwards your ships appeared and we whom you see here became your captives. Perchance it may be that our gods wield but little power in this land; therefore, lord, I for my part shall willingly obey your command and worship your God while I am your servant. If it be your pleasure, I shall ask my comrades what is their feeling in this matter."

Almansur nodded his assent, and Orm said to his men: "He says that we must worship his God. He has only one God, who is called Allah, and who dislikes all other gods. My own belief is that his God is powerful in this country, and that our gods are weak so far away from our homeland and theirs. We shall receive better treatment if we follow the custom of the people in this matter, and I think it would be foolish of us to go against Almansur's wishes."

The men agreed that they had little choice, and that it would be madness to anger so mighty a lord as Almansur; at length, therefore, Orm turned to Almansur and informed him that they were all willing to worship Allah and to promise to invoke no other god.

Almansur then summoned two priests into his presence, together with a magistrate, before whom Orm and his men were made to repeat the holy creed of the servants of Mohammed, as pronounced to Orm by Almansur: namely, that there is no God save Allah, and that Mohammed is His Prophet. All the men save Orm found difficulty in enunciating the words, though they were carefully spelled out to them.

When this ceremony was completed, Almansur appeared to be well pleased, and told the priests that he felt that he had thereby done a good service to Allah, with which they agreed. Then, putting his hand into the copper box that stood on his table, he took from it a handful of gold coins and gave fifteen pieces to each of the men, but thirty to Orm. They thanked him, and were conducted by the commander back to their own quarters.

Toke said: "Now we have bidden farewell to our gods. This may be a right thing to do in a foreign land, where other gods reign; but if I ever reach home again, I shall bother more about them than about this Allah. Still, I dare say he is the best god in these parts, and he has already provided us with gold. If he can manage to provide a few women too, he will rise even higher in my estimation."

A short while afterwards Almansur declared war against the Christians and set out northwards with his Imperial bodyguard and a mighty army. He plundered for three months in Navarre and Aragon, during which time Orm and his men won both gold and women, so that they declared themselves well satisfied to serve such a master. Each subsequent spring and autumn they found themselves in the field under Almansur's banners, resting in Córdoba during the worst of the summer heat and during those months of the year which the people of the south call winter. They did their best to accustom themselves to the habits of the country, and found little cause for complaint in their employment, for Almansur often rewarded them with rich gifts, to secure their loyalty, and everything that they won by storm or plunder they were permitted to keep for themselves, apart from one fifth, which they had to yield to him.

Sometimes, however, they found it somewhat irksome to be followers of Allah and servants of the Prophet. Whenever on their expeditions they found wine or pork in the Christians' houses, they were forbidden to enjoy either commodity, though they longed for both. This decree, which appeared to them more extraordinary than any they had previously heard of, they seldom dared to disobey, for Almansur punished any disobedience very strictly. In addition to this, they found themselves having to pray to Allah and abase themselves before the Prophet far too often for their taste; for every morning and evening when Almansur was in the field, the whole of his army would fall to its knees, facing the direction in which the City of the Prophet was said to lie, and every man had to bow several times, pressing his forehead against the earth. This seemed to them a debasing and ridiculous thing for a man to have to do, but they agreed that there was nothing for it but to conform to this custom as best they could and do as the rest of the army did.

They excelled in battle and won a great name for themselves in the bodyguard. They held themselves to be the best men in it, and when the time came for the dividing up of booty, no man challenged their right to whatever they chose. There were eight of them, all told: Orm and Toke, Halle and Ögmund, Tume, who had rowed with Toke, Gunne, who had rowed with Krok, Rapp, who was one-eyed, and Ulf, who was the oldest of them. Once, long before, he had had one of the corners of his mouth split at a Christmas feast, ever since when he had been known as Grinulf, because his mouth sat awry and was broader than other men's. Their luck was so good that only one of them lost his life during all the four years that they were in Almansur's service.

They traveled far and wide, for the more Almansur's beard became flecked with gray, the more vehemently he harried the Christians, spending less and less time peacefully at home in his palace at Córdoba. They were with him when he marched far northwards to Pamplona, in the Kingdom of Navarre, where twice they attempted vainly to storm the city; but the third time, they took it and gave it to the sword. Here Tume, who had shared Toke's oar in the galley, was killed by a stone from a catapult. They sailed in Almansur's own ship to Majorca, when the governor of that island had shown himself refractory, and stood guard while his head was struck off, together with those of thirty of his kinsmen. They fought in dust and heat a grim conflict at Henares, where the Count of Castile's men pressed them hard but were at length encircled and annihilated. There, on the evening following the battle, the dead Christians were piled together and built into a great mound of corpses, from the summit of which one of Almansur's priests called the servants of the Prophet to prayer. Then they marched on a huge expedition to the Kingdom of León, where they harried King Sancho the Fat so sorely that in the end his own men found him dispensable (for he was so fat that he could no longer sit on a horse) and deposed him and came with tribute to Almansur.

Throughout all these campaigns Orm and his men never ceased to marvel at Almansur's sagacity and power and at the great luck that always attended his enterprises; but most of all they marveled at the extent of his fear of Allah, and the variety of measures that he was forever devising to placate his God. All the dirt that gathered on his shoes and clothing when he was in the field was carefully scraped off each evening by his servants and placed in a silken bag; and at the conclusion of every campaign this bagful of dirt was brought back to Córdoba. He had ordained that all this dirt that he had collected in his wars against the Christians

was to be buried with him when he died, because the Prophet
had said: "Blessed are those who have trodden dusty ways to
fight against the unbelievers."

Despite all this dirt, however, Almansur's dread of Allah no
whit decreased, and finally he decided to undertake a mightier
enterprise than any that he had yet attempted: namely, to destroy
the holy city of the Christians in Asturia, in which the apostle
James, the great miracle-worker, lay buried. In the autumn of the
twelfth year of the reign of the Caliph Hisham, which was the
fourth year that Orm and his men spent in Almansur's service, he
assembled an army larger than any that had ever before been
seen in Spain, and marched northwestwards, proceeding through
the Empty Land, which was the old dividing barrier between the
Andalusians and the Asturian Christians.

They reached the Christian settlements on the far side of the
Empty Land, which no Andalusian had penetrated in mortal
memory, and each day saw them engaged in hard fighting, for the
Christians defended themselves cunningly among the mountains
and ravines. Then one evening, when the army had pitched camp
and Almansur was resting in his great tent after evening prayer,
the Christians launched a surprise attack. At first they threatened
to overwhelm the Mohammedans, for a troop of them broke into
the camp and created a panic, the air becoming wild with war-cries
and shrieks for help. Hearing these, Almansur hastened forth from
his tent, wearing his helmet and carrying his sword, but without
his armor, to see what was afoot. Now, that evening Orm and two
of his men, Halle and Rapp the One-Eyed, were standing guard
at the entrance to the tent. As Almansur emerged, several of the
enemy's horsemen appeared, galloping toward the tent at full
speed. When they saw Almansur, they recognized him by his green
helmet-veil (for he was the only man in the army who wore that
color) and, yelling triumphantly, cast their spears at him. It was
a dark night, and Almansur was old and could not have evaded
them; but Orm, who was standing nearest to him, flung himself
suddenly at his back, bowling him over on to his face and taking
two of the spears on his shield and a third in his shoulder. A fourth
grazed Almansur's side as he lay on the ground, and drew blood.
Halle and Rapp rushed forward to meet the enemy, casting their
spears at them and bringing one man from his horse; then others

swarmed to their assistance from all directions, and the Christians were killed or put to flight.

Orm pulled the spear out of his shoulder and assisted Almansur to his feet, wondering dubiously how his master would feel about being knocked face downwards on to the ground. Almansur, however, was hugely pleased with his wound. It was the first that he had ever received, and he reckoned it as a piece of great good luck that he had been allowed to spill his blood for Allah's sake, without sustaining any serious injury in the process. He ordered three of his cavalry commanders to be summoned before him, and rebuked them publicly before his assembled officers for not having kept better watch over the camp. They prostrated themselves at his feet and confessed their negligence; whereupon Almansur, as was his wont when he was in a good humor, allowed them time to say their prayers and bind up their beards before being led to execution.

To Halle and Rapp he gave a fistful of gold each. Then, while all the officers of the army were still drawn up before him, he bade Orm step forward. Almansur stared at him and said: "Red-bearded man, you have laid your hand upon your master, which it is forbidden for any soldier to do. What answer have you to make to this charge?"

Orm replied: "The air was alive with spears, and there was naught else to be done. But it is my belief, lord, that your honor is so great that what has happened cannot harm it. Besides which, you fell with your face toward your enemies, so that no man can say that you shrank from them."

Almansur sat fingering his beard silently. Then he nodded and said: "It is a good answer. And you saved my life; and I have work yet to accomplish."

He ordered a neck-chain to be brought from his coffers; it was of gold, and heavy. He said: "I see that a spear found your shoulder. Perchance it may prove painful. Here is balm for the pain."

So saying, he hung the chain around Orm's neck, which was an exceedingly rare honor for him to grant. After this incident Orm and his men stood even higher in Almansur's favor than before. Toke examined the chain and expressed his delight that Orm had won so rich a gift.

"Without doubt," he said, "this Almansur is the best master that a man could wish to serve. All the same, I think it was lucky for you, and for the rest of us, that you did not push him on to his back."

Next day the army continued its march; and at length they came to the holy city of the Christians, where the apostle James lay buried, with a great church built over his grave. Here there was heavy fighting, for the Christians, believing that the apostle would come to their aid, fought to the limit of their endurance; but in the end Almansur overcame them, and the city was taken and burned. Hither Christians from all parts of their country had brought their most valuable treasures for safe keeping, for the city had never before been threatened by any enemy; consequently an enormous quantity of booty was captured, together with many prisoners. It was Almansur's especial wish to raze the great church that stood over the apostle's grave, but this was of stone and would not burn. Instead, therefore, he set his prisoners, aided by men from his own army, to pull it down. Now, in the tower of this church there hung twelve bells, each one bearing the name of an apostle. They had a most melodious note, and were greatly prized by the Christians, in particular the largest of them all, which was called James.

Almansur commanded that these bells should be taken back to Córdoba by the Christian captives, there to be placed in the great mosque with their mouths facing upwards, so that they might be filled with sweet-scented oil and burn perpetually as great lamps to the glory of Allah and the Prophet. They were enormously heavy, and great litters were built to hold them; sixty prisoners were set to carry each bell in one of these litters, working in shifts. But the James bell was so heavy that no litter could be built to take it, and they knew it would not be possible to convey it by ox-cart across the mountain passes. Almansur, however, was very unwilling to leave it behind, for he regarded it as the finest item of spoil that he had ever won.

Accordingly, he had a platform built for the bell to be placed upon, in order that this platform might be dragged on rollers to a nearby river, whence it and the bell could be removed to Córdoba by ship. When the platform was ready and the rollers had been placed beneath it, iron bars were passed through the hasps of the bell, and a number of men tried to lift it on to the platform;

but the southerners lacked either the strength or the enthusiasm for the work; and when longer bars were tried, so that more men might help with the lifting, the bars broke and the bell remained on the ground.

Orm and his men, who had come to watch the work, began to laugh; then Toke said: "Six grown men ought to be able to lift that without much trouble," and Orm said: "Four should be able to manage it."

Then he and Toke and Ögmund and Rapp the One-Eyed walked up to the bell, ran a short bar through the hasps, and lifted the bell up and on to the platform.

Almansur, who had been riding past on his horse, stopped to watch them do this. He called Orm to him, and said: "Allah has blessed you and your men with great strength, praised be His name! It would seem that you are the men to see that this bell is safely conveyed to the ship, and to guard it on its passage to Córdoba; for I know no other men capable of handling it."

Orm bowed, and replied that this task did not appear to him to be difficult.

Then Almansur had a body of good slaves chosen from among the prisoners, and ordered them to draw the bell down to the river at a point where it began to be navigable, after which they were to serve as oarsmen on a ship awaiting them there, which had been captured from the Asturians. Two officials from Almansur's staff were sent with them, to be in charge during the voyage.

Ropes were tied to the platform, and Orm and his men set off with the bell and its slaves, some of the prisoners drawing it, and others placing rollers before it. It was a tedious journey, for the path they had to follow led, for the most part, downhill, so that sometimes the bell slid forwards under its own momentum, and in the early stages some of the slaves who were changing the rollers were crushed. Orm, however, made them fasten a drag-rope to the rear of the platform, so that they might be able to control it where the going was steep. Thereafter, they made better progress, and so eventually came down to the river, where the ship lay at anchor.

It was a merchant ship, smallish, but strongly built, with a good deck, ten pairs of oars, a mast, and a sail. Orm and his men lifted the bell aboard and made it fast with ropes and chocks; then they put the slaves in their places at the oars and moved off down the river. This river ran westwards, north of that river up which Krok's ships had rowed on their way to the margrave's fortress; and the Northmen were happy to find themselves once again in charge of a ship.

The Vikings took it in turns to keep an eye on the rowers, whom they found mulish and very clumsy at their work. They were disappointed to find that there were no ankle-chains in the ship, for this meant that someone had to keep watch throughout the night; and in spite of this, a couple of the prisoners, who had felt the whip, managed to escape. Orm's men agreed that they had never seen such miserable rowing before, and that if it went on like this, they would never reach Córdoba.

When they came to the mouth of the river, they found there many of Almansur's great warships, which had been unable, on account of their size, to sail up the river, though most of the soldiers from them had marched inland to join in the general plundering. Orm's men were glad to see these ships, and he immediately sent both the officials to borrow as many ankle-chains as possible from the various captains, until he had obtained all that he needed. Then the slaves were fettered to their places. Orm also took this opportunity of laying in stores for the voyage, for it was a long way to Córdoba. Having done this, they lay at anchor by the warships in a sheltered bay, to wait for good sailing weather.

In the evening Orm went ashore, together with Toke and Gunne, leaving the rest of his men to guard the ship. They walked down the shore in the direction of some small warehouses, in which traders had established themselves for the purpose of bargaining for the loot that had been won, and to sell necessaries to the ships. They had all but reached the first warehouse when six men from one of the ships entered it, and Gunne suddenly halted in his tracks.

"We have business to transact with those men," he said. "Did you notice the first two?"

Neither Orm nor Toke had observed their faces.

Gunne said: "They were the men who killed Krok."

Orm paled, and a tremor ran through his body.

"If that is so," he said, "they have lived long enough."

They drew their swords. Orm and Toke still carried those which the Lady Subaida had given to them, and Toke had not yet succeeded in finding any name for his sword as good as Blue-Tongue.

"Our duty to Krok comes before our duty to Almansur," said Orm. "All of us have vengeance to reap here. But mine comes first, because I am his successor as chieftain. You two run behind the warehouse, to stop their escaping that way."

The warehouse had a door in each of its shorter walls. Orm entered through the nearest and found the six men inside, talking to the trader. The latter, when he saw Orm enter with his sword drawn, slunk away behind some sacks, but the six men from the ship drew their weapons and shrieked questions at him. It was dark and confined in the warehouse, but Orm at once picked out one of the men who had killed Krok.

"Have you said your evening prayer?" he cried, and hewed at the man's neck so that his head flew from his shoulders.

Two of the others immediately attacked Orm, so that he had his work cut out to defend himself. Meanwhile the other three ran to the back door; but Toke and Gunne were there before them. Toke felled one of them on the spot, crying out Krok's name, and aimed a savage blow at the next man; but there was little room to maneuver, because the warehouse was small and crowded with goods, to say nothing of the men who were fighting in it. One man jumped up on a bench and tried to aim a blow at Orm, but his sword caught in a rafter, and Orm flung his shield into the man's face. The spike on his shield entered the other's eye, and he fell on his face and lay still. After that the fight did not last much longer. The second of the two men who had killed Krok was felled by Gunne; of the others, Orm had killed two and Toke three; but the trader, who had burrowed himself almost out of sight in his corner, they allowed to escape unharmed, because he had nothing to do with this affair.

When they came out of the warehouse with their swords all bloody, they saw men approaching to discover what the noise had been about; but on seeing the Vikings' aspect, they turned and ran. Toke held his sword erect before his face; thick blood ran down its blade and fell from the hilt in large drops.

"Now I name thee, O sister of Blue-Tongue!" he said. "Hereafter shalt thou be known as Red-Jowl."

Orm stared after the men from the ships as they ran away into the distance.

"We, too, must make haste," he said, "for now we are outlaws in this land. But it is a small price to pay for vengeance."

They hastened to the ship and told the others what had happened. Then, at once, though it had by now grown dark, they weighed anchor and put out to sea. They rejoiced in the knowledge that Krok had been avenged, though at the same time they realized that they had no time to lose in getting clear of this country and its waters. They did their best to whip up a good pace from the slaves, and Orm himself took over the steering-oar, while Almansur's two secretaries, who were unaware of what had happened, hurled questions at him but received scant reply. At last the ship came safely out of the bay into the open sea; and a wind sprang up from the south, so that they were able to raise a sail. They steered northwards and away from the land, until the day broke; and there was no sign of any ship pursuing them.

They saw a group of islands off their larboard bow, and Orm put in to one of them. Here he sent both the secretaries ashore, bidding them convey his greetings to Almansur.

"It would be churlish of us to quit the service of such a master," he said, "without wishing him farewell. Tell him, therefore, on behalf of us all, that it has been our fate to have killed six of his men in revenge for Krok, who was our chieftain; though six men's lives are a small return for his death. We are taking this ship with us, and the slaves that man it, for we think that he will scarcely notice its loss. Also, we are taking the bell, because it makes the ship ride stable, and we have dangerous seas ahead of us. We all think that he has been a good master to us, and if we had not had to kill these men, we should gladly have remained longer in his service; but as things have turned out, this is the only course left open to us if we are to escape with our lives."

The secretaries undertook to deliver this message, word for word as Orm had spoken it. Then he added: "It would be well, too, if, when you return to Córdoba, you could bear our greetings to a wealthy Jew called Solomon, who is a poet and a silversmith. And thank him from us for having befriended us so generously; for we shall never see him again."

"And tell the Lady Subaida," said Toke, "that two men from the north, whom she knows, send her their thanks and greetings. Tell her, too, that the swords she gave us have served us well, and that their edges are yet undented, despite all the work that they have done. But, for your own sakes, do not deliver this message when Almansur is within hearing."

The secretaries had their writing-materials with them and noted all this down; then they were left on the island with enough food to sustain them until such time as some ship should find them or they should manage to make their way to the mainland.

When the slaves working the oars saw that the ship was putting out toward the open sea, they made a noisy clamor and complaint, and it was evident that they wished to be left on the island with the secretaries. Orm's men had to go round with switches and rope-ends to silence them and make them row; for the wind had dropped, and they were anxious to lose no time in getting clear of these dangerous waters.

"It is lucky we have them fast in foot-irons," said Gunne, "or we should have had the lot of them overboard by now, for all our swords. It is a pity we did not borrow a proper scourge when we took the fetters. The teeth of these switches and rope-ends are too blunt for mules like these."

"You are right," said Toke, "strangely enough; for we little thought, in the days when we sat on the galley benches, that we should ever come to mourn the absence of an overseer's whip."

"Well, they say that no back is so tender as one's own," replied Gunne. "But I fear these backs will have to itch somewhat more sharply if we are ever to escape from here."

Toke agreed, and they went round the benches again, flogging the slaves smartly to make the ship move faster. But they still made labored progress, for the slaves could not keep the stroke. Orm noticed this and said: "Rope-ends alone will never teach men to row if they are not used to oars. Let us see if we cannot persuade the bell to lend us her aid."

As he spoke, he took an ax and struck the bell with its blunt edge as the slaves dipped their oars. The bell gave out a great peal, and the slaves pulled in response. In this way they soon began to keep better time. Orm made his men take turns in sounding the stroke. They found that if they struck with a wooden club padded with leather, the bell pealed more melodiously; and this discovery pleased them mightily.

After a while, however, a wind sprang up and they had no further need to row. The wind gradually increased, blowing more and more gustily, until it approached gale strength; and things now began to look dangerous. Grinulf remarked that this was only what was to be expected if men put out to sea without first propitiating the people of the water. But others spoke against him, recalling the sacrifice they had offered on a previous occasion and how shortly afterwards they had encountered the ships of Almansur. Gunne ventured the opinion that they might perhaps sacrifice to Allah, for safety's sake, and a few of the men supported this suggestion; but Toke said that, in his view, Allah had little pull in what went on at sea.

Then Orm said: "I do not believe that any man can be certain just how powerful this or that god is, or how much he can do to help us. And I think we should be foolish to neglect one god for the sake of not offending some other. But one thing we know, that there is one god who has served us well on this enterprise; I mean, St. James; for it is his bell that keeps our ship from turning turtle and, apart from this, it has helped the rowers to keep time. So let us not forget him."

They agreed that this was well spoken, and sacrificed meat and drink to Agir, Allah, and St. James, which put them in better heart.

By this time they had little idea where they were, save only that they were a good way from Asturia. They knew, however, that, if they held their course northwards, in the direction in which the storm was driving them, and avoided diverging too far to the west, they would be sure to strike land eventually, either in Ireland or in England, or perhaps in Brittany. So they screwed up their courage and rode out the storm. Once or twice they managed to discern familiar stars, and they trusted that they would find their way.

Their chief worry concerned the slaves, who, though they now had no work to do at the oars, became poorly with fear and seasickness and the wet and cold, so that all of them were green and their teeth chattered; and a couple of them died. They had little warm clothing on the ship, and each day it blew colder, for the autumn was by now far advanced. Orm and his men pitied the wretchedness of the slaves and tended them as well as they could; and to such of them as had stomach to eat they gave the best food, for they knew that these slaves would be valuable booty if they could bring them safely to land.

At last the storm died down, and for a whole day they enjoyed fine weather and a good wind and held their course to the northeast; and the slaves perked up, encouraged by the sun. But that evening the wind dropped completely, and a fog descended on them and began to thicken. It was cold and damp, so that they all trembled with the cold, the slaves most of all; no breath of wind came, and the ship lay still and tossing in a heavy swell.

Orm said: "This is a pretty pass we have come to. If we stay here and wait for the wind, the slaves will die of cold; but if we make them row, they will die just as surely, in the wretched state they are in now. Though we have precious little to row by while we can see neither sun nor stars."

"I think we should make them row," said Rapp, "to warm them up a little. We can steer with the swell, for that gale was blowing from the south; and we have nothing else to guide us while this fog holds."

They thought Rapp's advice good, and the slaves were made to take up their oars, which they did amid much grousing; and, indeed, they had little strength for the task. The men took turns again at beating time on the bell, and it seemed to their ears to sound more sweetly than before, with a long peal following each stroke, so that she was of good comfort to them in the fog. At intervals they allowed the slaves to rest awhile and sleep; but, apart from this, they rowed the whole night through, steering with the swell, while the fog hugged them closely and incessantly.

When morning came, Ögmund was at the helm, with Rapp sounding the bell, while the others slept. Suddenly the two men listened, and stared at each other, and then listened anew. A faint peal had sounded from far away. Much astonished, they roused the others, and all strained their ears. The note was repeated several times, and it seemed to them to come from forward.

"It sounds as though we are not the only sailors who are rowing to a bell," said Toke.

"Let us proceed softly," said Grinulf, "for this may be Ran and her daughters, who seduce men at sea with music and enchantments."

"It sounds to me more like dwarfs at an anvil," said Halle, "and it would be no fun to make their acquaintance. Perhaps we are near some island where trolls hold sway."

The peal still rang out faintly from the distance. All of them were now in a cold sweat, and they waited to hear what Orm should say. The slaves, too, listened, and began to chatter eagerly among themselves; but the tongues they spoke were unknown to Orm and his men.

"What this may be, no man can tell," said Orm, "but let us not be frightened at so small a thing. Let us row on as we have done up to now, and keep our eyes skinned. For my part, I have never heard of witchery practiced by morning light."

They agreed with this, and the rowing continued; meanwhile the distant note began to grow clearer. Light puffs of wind stirred their hair, and the fog thinned; then, suddenly, they all cried out that they spied land. It was a rocky coast and appeared to be either an island or a promontory. They could not doubt that the sound had come from this spot, though it had now ceased. They saw green grass, and some goats grazing: also two or three huts, beside which men stood staring out to sea.

"These do not look to me like trolls," said Orm, "or the daughters of Ran either. Let us go ashore and find out where we have come to."

They did so; and the men of the island showed no fear at seeing armed men come ashore, but came cheerfully toward them and greeted them. They were six in number, all old men, with white beards and long brown cloaks; and no one could understand what they said.

"To what land have we come?" asked Orm. "And whose men are you?"

One of the old men understood his words and cried to the others: "Lochlannach! Lochlannach!" [1] Then he answered Orm in the latter's tongue: "You have come to Ireland, and we are the servants of St. Finnian."

When Orm and his men heard this, they were overcome with joy, for they thought they must be nearly home. They could now

[1] "Men of the lakes."

see that they had landed on a small island, and beyond it they could discern the Irish coast. On this small island there lived only the old men and their goats.

The old men conversed among themselves eagerly and in amazement; then the one who understood Norse said to Orm: "You speak the tongue of the Northmen, and I understand that tongue, for in my young days I associated much with the Northmen before I came to this island. But certain it is that I have never seen men from Lochlann dressed as you and your men are dressed. Where do you come from? Are you white or black Lochlannachs? [2] And how is it that you come sailing to the sound of a bell? Today is St. Brandan's day, and we rang our bell to pay homage to his memory; then we heard your bell reply from the sea, and we supposed that it might be St. Brandan himself answering us, for he was a great sailor. But in Jesus Christ's name, are you all baptized men, that you come sailing with this holy sound?"

"The old man can gab," said Toke. "There is a mouthful for you to answer there, Orm."

Orm replied to the old man: "We are black Lochlannachs, men of King Harald's land, though whether King Harald still lives I do not know, for we have been a long while from home. But our cloaks and garments are Spanish, for we have come from Andalusia, where we served a great lord named Almansur. And our bell is called James, and comes from the church in Asturia where the apostle James lies buried, and it is the biggest of all the bells there; but how and why it has accompanied us on our journey is too long a story to be told now. We have heard of this Christ you speak of, but where we come from he is held in no great honor, and we are not baptized. But as you are Christians, you may be glad to hear that we have Christian men at our oars. They are our slaves, and come from the same place as the bell; but they have been badly knocked about on our journey and are worth but little now. It would be a good thing if they could come ashore here and rest for a while before we continue on our journey homewards. You need fear nothing from us, for you seem to be good men, and we use no violence toward those who do not try to oppose us. We could make use of a few of your goats, but you will suffer no other loss, for we do not intend to stay long here."

[2] I.e., Norwegians or Danes.

When it was explained to the old men what he had said, they wagged their heads and whispered among themselves; and their spokesman said that they often welcomed seafaring men on their island, and that no man did them harm.

"For we ourselves do harm to no man," he said, "and we have no possessions apart from these goats and our boats and huts; the whole isle else is St. Finnian's Isle, and he is powerful in the sight of God and holds his hand over us. This year he has blessed our goats generously, so that you shall not lack for sustenance. Welcome therefore to the little we can offer you; and for us old men, who sit here year after year in loneliness, it will be a joy to listen to the story of your travels."

So the slaves were brought ashore and the ship was beached; and Orm and his men rested on St. Finnian's Isle, living in peaceful harmony with the monks. They fished with them, making fine catches, and fed the slaves so that they looked less wretched; and Orm and the others had to recount all their adventures for the monks to hear, for, though they had difficulty in following his words, the old men were eager for news of distant lands. But most of all they marveled at the bell, which was larger than any they had heard of in Ireland. They acclaimed it as a mighty miracle that St. James and St. Finnian had spoken to each other with their bells from afar; and sometimes at their holy services they smote the bell of St. James instead of their own and rejoiced aloud as its great clang echoed out across the sea.

CHAPTER EIGHT

CONCERNING ORM'S SOJOURN AMONG THE MONKS OF ST. FINNIAN, AND HOW A GREAT MIRACLE OCCURRED AT JELLINGE

WHILE they were resting with the monks of St. Finnian, Orm and his men deliberated deeply what course they should take once the slaves had recovered sufficiently for them to be able to proceed on their voyage. They were all eager to get back home,

Orm no less than the others; nor was there much danger of encountering pirates at this time of year, when few ships were at sea.
But the going was likely to be hard in the winter weather, which
in turn might well result in the slaves dying on their hands; it
would therefore, they thought, perhaps be wisest to sell them as
soon as possible. For that, they could sail either down to Limerick,
where Orm's father was well known, or up to Cork, where Olof
of the Precious Stones had for long been the biggest dealer in
slaves in these parts. They asked the monks which they thought
would be the best plan for them to follow.

When the monks understood what their guests wanted to know,
they chattered eagerly to one another and were apparently much
amused; then their spokesman said: "It is plain that you come
from distant parts and know little about the way things are in Ireland now. It will not be easy for you to trade in Limerick, or in
Cork either; for Brian Boru is powerful in Ireland now, and
though you hail from a far country, you have probably heard of
him."

Orm said that he had often heard his father speak of a King
Brian, who waged war against the Vikings in Limerick.

"He does not wage war against them any longer," said the monk.
"At first he was the chieftain of the Dalcassians; then the Vikings
in Limerick waged war against him. After that, he became King of
Thomond, and then he waged war against them. In time he became King of the whole of Munster, and then he stormed Limerick and killed most of the Vikings there; those that were not
killed fled. So now he is the greatest warrior and hero in Ireland,
King of Munster, and Lord of Leinster; and such foreigners as remain in our coastal cities pay tribute to him. At present he is waging war against Malachy, who is King of all our kings in Ireland,
to win his wife and his power from him. Olof of the Precious
Stones pays him tribute and has to send him soldiers to help him
with his war against King Malachy; and even Sigtrygg Silk-Beard
of Dublin, who is the most powerful of all the foreign chieftains
in Ireland, has paid him tribute on two occasions."

"These are grave tidings," said Orm; "and this King Brian appears indeed to be a mighty chieftain, though it may be that we
have seen a mightier. But even if all that you say is true, I do not
see why this should prevent us from selling our slaves to him."

"King Brian does not buy slaves," said the monk, "for he takes all that he requires from his neighbors and from the men of Lochlann. Besides which, it is known that there are three things that he covets more than anything else in the world, and three things that he abominates—and these last will be to your disadvantage. The things that he covets are these: supreme power, which he has already; the greatest quantity of gold, which he also has; and the most beautiful woman, whom all the world knows to be Gormlaith, the sister of Maelmore, King of Leinster. Her he has yet to win. She was formerly married to King Olof Kvaran of Dublin, who got rid of her because of the sharpness of her tongue; now she is wed to Malachy, the King of our kings, who so disports himself in her boudoirs that he is hardly fit to take the field any more. When Brian has defeated Malachy he will win Gormlaith, for he never fails to get what he wants. But the three things that he most abominates are heathens, men from Lochlann, and poets who praise other kings. His hatred is as violent as his greed, and nothing can assuage either of them; so, since you are heathens and Lochlannachs to boot, we would not advise you to approach him too nearly, for we do not want to see you killed."

The men listened attentively to all this and agreed that it would be unrewarding to trade with King Brian. Orm said: "It seems to me that the James bell was a good guide to us when it led us to your isle and not to King Brian's kingdom."

"St. Finnian's bell helped you, too," said the monk; "and now that you have seen what the saints can do, even for heathens, would it not be a wise thing for you to start believing in God and become Christians?"

Orm said that he had not given the matter much consideration and that he did not think there was any urgency about deciding.

"It may be more urgent than you know," said the monk, "for there are now only eleven years left till the end of the world, when Christ will appear in the sky and judge all mortal men. Before this happens, all heathens will do well to be baptized; and it would be foolish of you to be among the last to do so. Unbelievers are now going over to God in greater numbers than ever before, so that in a short while there will be few of them left in their darkness; and certain it is that the coming of Christ is presently imminent, for the wickedest heathen of all, King Harald of Denmark, has just been baptized. Now, therefore, is the time for you to do as he has done and abandon your false gods and embrace the true faith."

All the men stared at him in amazement, and one or two of them burst out laughing and slapped their knees.

"You will soon be telling us," said Toke, "that he has become a monk like yourself, and shaved off his hair."

Orm said: "We have traveled far and wide in the world, while you rest here with your brothers on this lonely island; nevertheless, you have greater tidings for us than we have to tell you. But this is no small thing that you ask us to believe, when you tell us that King Harald has turned Christian; and I think the most likely explanation is that some seafarer has put this idea into your heads, knowing that you are simple and credulous and thinking to make sport of you."

But the monk insisted that he had spoken the truth and had not merely repeated some sailor's yarn. For they had heard this great news from the mouth of their own Bishop, when he had visited them two years before; and on each of the next seven Sundays they had offered thanks to God, on behalf of all Christians whose homes had been visited by the Vikings, for the great victory He had gained.

This persuaded the men that the monk had told them the truth, though they found it none the less difficult to believe such remarkable tidings.

"He is himself descended from Odin," they said, staring at one another in amazement; "how, then, can he bind himself to any other god?"

"All his life he has had great good luck," they said; "and this was granted to him by the Æsir; his fleets have sailed against the Christians and have returned home laden with their wealth. What can he want with the Christians' God?"

They shook their heads and sat dumbfounded.

"He is old now," said Grinulf, "and it may be that he has become a child again, as King Ane of Uppsala did in former times. For kings drink stronger ale than other men, and have many women; and that can tire a man over the years, so that his understanding darkens and he no longer knows what he is doing. But men who are kings do as they please, even when wisdom has passed from them. Perhaps that is how King Harald has become ensnared into these Christian beliefs."

. The men nodded assent, and recounted stories of people in their homeland who had grown peculiar in their old age and had caused their families great trouble by their crooked fancies; and they all agreed that it was no good thing for a man to live until his teeth fell out and his understanding began to languish. The monks pointed out that worse things than that would befall them, for when the Day of Judgment arrived, in eleven years' time, they would be dragged suddenly out of the earth. But the men replied that they would worry about that when the time came, and that they were not going to bother to go over to Christ for the fear of that.

Orm had much to occupy his mind, for he had to decide what course they would do best to take, seeing that they did not dare to go inland to the markets. At length he said to his men: "It is a fine thing to be a chieftain when there is booty to be divided up and ale to be handed around, but less desirable when there are plans to be made; and I have not been able to think out anything very good. Certain it is that we must sail now, for the slaves are as fit as they ever will be as the result of their rest here and the good food they have had; and the longer we delay, the more difficult our journey will be, because of the weather. The best plan seems to me to be to sail to King Harald, for in his court there are many rich men who will be likely to give us a good price for our slaves; and if he has in fact turned Christian, we have a fine gift to offer him, which should bring us at once into his favor. For my part, I would rather enter his service than sit at home as the youngest son in my father's house, if indeed the old man and Odd, my brother, are still alive, which I do not know; and those of you who yearn to return to your homes will have an easy journey from his court to Blekinge, once we have completed the sale and shared out the money. But the main problem will be to see that the slaves do not die when we come up into the cold of the northern waters."

Then he told the monks that he was prepared to drive a bargain with them. If they gave him all the goatskins they had, together with such clothes as they could spare, he would let them keep the two feeblest of his slaves; for if he took them with him on the voyage, they would die, while if they stayed ashore and regained their health, they would be useful to the monks. In addition to this, he was willing to give them some Andalusian silver coins. The monks laughed, and said that this was a better bargain than most Irishmen managed to drive with Lochlannachs, but that they would most of all like to have the James bell. Orm, however, replied that he could not spare this, and the bargain was concluded on the basis of his original proposal, so that the slaves were provided with something in the way of winter clothing.

They smoked fish and goat's meat to provision themselves for the voyage, taking besides a quantity of the turnips that the monks grew. The monks helped them with everything, behaving in the most friendly way toward them, and did not complain about their herd of goats being reduced to such small proportions by their guests; the only things that worried them were that the holy bell was going to remain in heathen hands, and that Orm and his men would not realize what was best for them and become Christians. When the time came to say farewell, they made one last effort to convince their departing friends of the truth about Christ and St. Finnian and the Day of Judgment, and all the things that would befall them if they neglected to be converted to the true faith. Orm replied that he had little time just then to attend to such matters, but added that he would be a poor chieftain if he went away without giving them some token of gratitude for all the hospitality they had shown toward him and his men. Then, putting his hand into his belt, he drew out three gold pieces and gave them to the monks.

When Toke saw this, he laughed to see such openhandedness; but then he said that he was as rich a man as Orm, and that he intended in due course to marry into one of the best houses in Lister and become a great man in his district. So he, too, gave the monks three gold pieces, while they stood amazed to see such munificence. The other men did not become greatly enthusiastic over the example of their leaders, but for the sake of their good names they, too, gave something; all except Grinulf. The others chaffed him for his thrift, but he grinned with his crooked mouth and scratched the beard on his cheek and was content with the way he had acted.

"I am no chieftain," he said, "besides which I am beginning to grow old; no girl is going to marry me and bring me a fine house to live in, and no gammer neither. So I am only being prudent in being thrifty."

When the slaves had been led aboard again and chained to their places, Orm sailed away from St. Finnian's Isle and headed eastwards along the Irish coast. They had a strong wind to help them and made good progress. All of them were troubled by the autumn cold, despite the fact that they had swathed themselves in goatskins; for Orm and his men had by now been such a long time in the south that they felt the cold in their bones more than they had been wont to. Nevertheless, they were all in good heart at being so near to their homeland, and their only anxiety was lest they should be intercepted by other of their countrymen who might be in these waters; so they kept a sharp lookout, for the monks had said that Vikings from Denmark were to be seen in greater numbers than ever around the English coasts now that most of Ireland had been closed to them by the might of King Brian, so that England was now regarded as being the best hunting-ground. In order, therefore, to avoid encountering other Viking ships, Orm kept the ship well out from the land as they steered up through the English Channel. They had good luck, for they met no ships; so they emerged into the open sea and felt the spray of the waves growing colder and sailed on until they sighted the coast of Jutland. Then they all laughed for joy, for it gladdened their hearts to see Danish soil once more; and they pointed out to one another the various landmarks that they had sighted when they had sailed southwards with Krok long before.

They rounded the Skaw and steered southwards, coming into the lee of the land; and now the slaves had to row again, as well as they could, while the bell of James sang the stroke. Here Orm spoke with some men in fishing-boats who crossed their course, and discovered from them how far they were from Jellinge, where King Harald Bluetooth held his court. Then they polished their weapons and saw to their clothing, so that they might appear before the King in a manner befitting men of worth.

Early one morning they rowed up to Jellinge and made their ship fast to a pier. From where they lay they could see the royal castle, surrounded by a stockade. There were some huts down by the pier, and people came out of them and stared curiously at Orm and his men, for they had the mien and appearance of foreigners. Then the men lifted the bell ashore, using the same platform and rollers that they had employed in Asturia; and while they did so, a crowd of astonished spectators gathered from the huts to gaze upon so great a wonder and to learn where these foreigners had come from. Orm and his men found it very strange to hear their own language being spoken by others again, after having lived among foreigners for so many years. They released the slaves from their chains and harnessed them to the bell, to pull it up to the King.

Suddenly they heard cries and sounds of confusion from the direction of the castle and saw a fat man in a long cowl come running toward them down the hill. He was shaven, and wore a silver cross at his breast and terror in his face. He arrived breathlessly at the huts and, flinging his arms wide apart, cried: "Leeches! Leeches! Is there no merciful soul here who can give us leeches? I must have blood-leeches immediately, fresh and strong."

They could tell he was a foreigner, but he spoke the Danish tongue deftly, though he was gasping for breath.

"Our leeches up in the castle have fallen sick and lost their appetite," he continued, panting, "and leeches are the only thing to relieve him when he has the toothache. In the name of the Father, the Son, and the Holy Ghost, is there nobody here who has any leeches?"

No one in the huts had leeches, however, and the fat priest groaned and began to look desperate. He had by this time arrived down at the pier where Orm's ship was lying at anchor, and there, suddenly, he caught sight of the bell and the men surrounding it. His eyes emerged slowly from their sockets, and he ran forward to examine it more closely.

"What is this?" he cried. "A bell, a holy bell? Am I dreaming? Is this a real bell, or is it a fabrication of the Devil? How has it come here, to this land of darkness and evil spirits? Never in my life have I seen such a magnificent bell, not even in the Emperor's own cathedral at Worms."

"It is called James, after an apostle," said Orm; "and we have brought it here from the apostle's church in Asturia. We heard that King Harald had turned Christian, and thought such a gift would please him."

"A miracle, a miracle!" cried the priest, bursting into tears of relief and stretching his arms heavenwards. "God's angels have turned to us in our hour of need, when our leeches sickened. This is better medicine than leeches. But hurry, hurry! Delay is dangerous, for he has the ache badly."

The slaves dragged the bell slowly up toward the castle, while the priest exhorted the men incessantly to use all the strength they had to pull it faster. He kept up a continual chatter, as though he had taken leave of his senses, mopping his eyes and turning his face skywards and crying out fragments of sacred jargon. Orm and the others gathered that the King had toothache, but could not make out what good their bell was expected to do. But the priest babbled about how lucky something was and called them messengers of God and said that everything would now be all right.

"He has not many teeth left in his mouth, praised be Almighty God!" he said, "but those that he has cause us as much trouble as all the other machinations contrived by the Devil in the whole of this barbarous land. For, despite his age, they often cause him pain, all except the two blue ones; and when they begin to ache he is dangerous to approach, and blasphemes immoderately. There was a time this summer, when one of his molars was hurting him, when he almost sent Brother Willibald to join the martyrs; for he hit him on the head with the big crucifix, which should properly only be used for the soothing of pain. Brother Willibald is himself again now, praise the Lord, but he was sick and dizzy for many weeks. We resigned our lives to the mercy of God, Brother Willibald and I, when we came with Bishop Poppo to this land of darkness with our gospel and our skill in healing; still, it seems a waste to be threatened with martyrdom for the sake of a couple of old teeth. Nor are we permitted to draw any of them out. This he has forbidden us to do, on pain of death, for he says that he is not prepared to become like some old King of the Swedes who ended up drinking milk from a horn. You see the difficulties and dangers we endure from this King in our zeal to spread the faith—Brother Willibald, who is the wisest doctor in the whole diocese of Bremen, and I myself, who am both doctor and precentor, and am called Brother Matthias."

He paused for breath, mopping the sweat from his face, and panted at the slaves to move faster. Then he continued: "The

chief difficulty we doctors have to put up with in this country is
that we have no relics to help us, not even so much as a single one
of St. Lazarus' teeth, which are irresistible healers of the toothache
and are to be found everywhere else in Christendom. For we mis-
sionaries to the heathen are not permitted to carry relics with us,
lest they should fall into heathen hands and so become sullied.
We have to rely on our prayers and the Cross and earthly means
of healing, and sometimes these are not enough. So none of us can
heal by spiritual medicine here among the Danes until we have
relics to assist us; and the time for that has not yet arrived. For
though three Bishops and innumerable minor priests have been
killed by the people here, and some of the bodies of these martyrs
have been recovered and given Christian burial, so that we know
where to find them, yet the Holy Church has ordained that no
bones of Bishops or martyrs may be dug up and used for medicine
until they have been dead thirty-six years. Until that time comes,
this will be a difficult country for doctors to work in."

He shook his head and mumbled sadly to himself, but then appeared to perk up again.

"However," he went on, "now that God has seen fit to allow this
great miracle to take place, things will become easier for Brother
Willibald and me. True it is that I have never seen any reference
in the Holy Scriptures to any special efficacy of St. James as a
healer of the toothache; but in his own bell, fresh from his blessed
tomb, there must surely reside much power against evil of all
kinds, even including bad teeth. Therefore, chieftain, it cannot but
be that you are God's messenger to myself and Brother Willibald,
and to all of the Christian faith in this land."

Orm said: "O wise sir, how can you cure toothache with a bell?
My men and I have been in distant lands and have seen many
marvelous things, but this would be the most miraculous of all."

"There are two cures for the toothache that we who are skilled
in the craft of healing know of," replied Brother Matthias, "and
both of them are good. Personally—and I am sure Brother Willibald will feel as I do in the matter—I am of the opinion that the
ancient prescription laid down by St. Gregory is the most effective.
You will soon have an opportunity to witness it in operation."

By this time they had reached the rampart with its surmounting
stockade, and the great outer door was opened for them by an old

porter, while another man blew on a horn to signify that visitors had arrived. Brother Matthias placed himself at the head of the procession and began exultantly to chant a holy song: "*Vexilla regis prodeunt*." Behind him marched Orm and Toke, followed by the slaves drawing the bell, with the other men urging them along.

Within the stockade lay many houses, all belonging to members of the King's household. For King Harald lived in greater pomp, and with a more extravagant show of power, than his father had done. He had had King Gorm's huge dining-hall enlarged and had added to its splendor, and had had longhouses built for his servants and followers. The completion of his cookhouse and brewery had been celebrated by poets; and men who knew said that they were even bigger than those of the King in Uppsala. Brother Matthias led the way to the King's own sleep-house; for, now that he was old, King Harald spent most of his time there with his women and his treasure-chests.

The sleep-house was a lofty and very spacious building, though nowadays it was less crowded than it had been of old. For since Bishop Poppo had repeatedly warned King Harald that he must take good care in every respect to lead a Christian life, the King had dispensed with the services of most of his women, retaining only a few of the younger ones. Such of the older women as had borne him children now lived elsewhere within the walls. On this particular morning, however, there was a great bustle of activity in and about the house, with many people of both sexes running around in anxious confusion. Some of them stopped to stare at the approaching procession, asking themselves what all this could mean; but Brother Matthias, breaking off his song, cantered like a drunken man through the crowd and into the King's chambers, with Orm and Toke following him.

"Brother Willibald, Brother Willibald!" he cried. "There is yet balm to be found in Gilead! Royal King, rejoice and praise God, for a miracle has been performed for you, and your pain shall soon be driven away. I am as Saul, the son of Kish; for I went out to seek blood-leeches and found instead a holy thing."

While Orm's men were, with great difficulty, contriving to bring the bell into the King's bedchamber, Brother Matthias began to recount all that had taken place.

Orm and his men saluted King Harald with great respect, gaz-

ing curiously upon him; for his name had been in their ears for as
long as they could remember, and they thought it strange to see
him, after all these years, in such a sick and sorry state.

His bed stood against the short wall of the room, facing the
door. It was stoutly timbered and lofty, and was full of bolsters
and skin rugs; and it was of such a size that three or four people
might lie in it without crowding each other. King Harald sat on
its edge, surrounded by cushions, wrapped in a long robe of otter's
fur and wearing on his head a yellow knitted woolen cap. On the
floor at his feet squatted two young women, with a pan of hot
coals between them, and each of them held one of his feet on her
knees and chafed it to keep it warm.

The most ignorant of men, seeing him there, would instinctively
have guessed that King Harald was a great king, though the circumstances of royalty were absent and an expression of unkingly
misery was upon his face. His big round eyes goggled with melancholy anticipation of imminent agony as his gaze wandered around
the faces in his chamber and finally alighted on the bell as it entered the door. He seemed unable to register much interest in the
sight that greeted his eyes, and panted in little gasps, as though out
of breath; for the pain had temporarily gone, and he was waiting
for it to come back and torment him anew. He was heavily built
and of powerful appearance, broad-chested and huge-paunched,
and his face was large and red, with shiny and unwrinkled skin.
His hair was white, but his beard, which was thick and matted and
lay down over his chest in tapering tongues, was a grayish yellow,
though in the middle there was a narrow ribbon, coming down
from his nether lip, which had retained its full yellowness and
contained no gray at all. His face was wet all round his mouth from
the medicines he had taken for the pain, so that both his blue eye-
teeth, which were famous for their length as well as for their color,
glistened even more brightly than was their wont, like the tusks of
an old boar. His eyes stood goggling from their sockets and were
bloodshot, but an awful majesty lurked within them, and in his
broad forehead and great grizzled eyebrows.

Bishop Poppo was not present, for he had been keeping vigil by
the King's bedside throughout the night, offering up prayers for
him, and had had to listen to frightful threats and blasphemies
when the pain had grown especially violent, so that in the end he

had been compelled to retire and get some rest. But Brother Willibald, who had also been up all night experimenting with various medicines in company with Brother Matthias, had managed to remain awake and was still in cheerful spirits. He was a little, shriveled man, with a big nose and pursed lips and a red scar across his temples. He nodded eagerly as he listened to Brother Matthias's account of what had taken place, and flung his arms above his head when he saw the bell appear in the doorway.

"This is in sooth a miracle!" he cried in piercing and exultant tones. "As the ravens of the sky succored the prophet Elijah with food when he was alone in the wilderness, so have these wanderers come to our aid with help sent from heaven. All our worldly medicines have only succeeded in banishing the pain for a few minutes; for as soon as our lord the King's impatience causes him to open his mouth, the pain returns at once. So it has been throughout the night. Now, however, his cure is certain. First, then, Brother Matthias, wash the bell well with holy water; then turn it on its side and wash its interior, for I do not see on its outer surface any of the dust that we shall need. Then, in good time, I will mix this dust with the other ingredients."

So they turned the bell on its side, and Brother Matthias swabbed its interior with a cloth dipped in holy water, which he then wrung out into a bowl. There was a lot of old dust in the bell, so that the water he wrung out of the cloth was quite black, which greatly delighted Brother Willibald. Then Brother Willibald set to work mixing his medicines, which he kept in a big leather chest, all the while delivering an instructive discourse to such of the company as were curious to know what he was attempting to do.

"The ancient prescription of St. Gregory is the most efficacious in cases such as this," he said. "It is a simple formula, and there are no secrets about its preparation. Juice of sloe, boar's gall, saltpeter, and bull's blood, a pinch of horseradish, and a few drops of juniper-water, all mixed with an equal quantity of holy water in which some sacred relic has been washed. The mixture to be kept in the mouth while three verses from the Psalms are sung; this procedure to be repeated thrice. This is the surest medicine against the toothache that we who practice the craft of healing know; and it never fails, provided that the sacred relic is sufficiently strong.

The Apulian doctors of the old Emperor Otto fancied frog's blood to be more efficacious than bull's blood, but few physicians are of that opinion nowadays; which is a fortunate thing, for frog's blood is not easy to procure in winter."

He took from his chest two small metal bottles, uncorked them, smelled them, shook his head, and sent a servant to the kitchen to fetch fresh galls and fresh bull's blood.

"Only the best will suffice in a case such as this," he said; "and when the relic is as powerful as the one we have here, great care must be taken over the other ingredients."

All this had occupied several minutes, and King Harald now seemed to be less troubled by his pain. He turned his gaze toward Orm and Toke, evidently puzzled at seeing strangers clad in foreign armor; for they still wore the red cloaks and engraved shields of Almansur, and their helmets had nose-pieces and descended low down over their cheeks and necks. He beckoned to them to come nearer.

"Whose men are you?" he said.

"We are your men, King Harald," replied Orm. "But we have come hither from Andalusia, where we served Almansur, the great Lord of Córdoba, until blood came between us and him. Krok of Lister was our chieftain when we first set forth, sailing in three ships. But he was killed, and many others with him. I am Orm, the son of Toste, of the Mound in Skania, chieftain of such as remain; and we have come to you with this bell. We thought it would be a good gift for you, O King, when we heard that you had become a Christian. Of its potency in countering the toothache I know nothing, but at sea it has been a powerful ally to us. It was the largest of all the bells over St. James' grave in Asturia, where many marvelous things were found; we went there with our master, Almansur, who treasured this bell most dearly."

King Harald nodded without speaking; but one of the two young women squatting at his feet turned her head and, staring up at Orm and Toke, said very rapidly in Arabic: "In the name of Allah, the Merciful, the Compassionate! Are you Almansur's men?"

They both gazed at her, amazed at hearing this tongue spoken at King Harald's court. She was fair to look upon, with large brown eyes that stood wide apart in her pale face. Her hair was black and hung from her temples in two long plaits. Toke had never been fluent in Arabic, but it was by now a long time since he had talked with a woman, so that he managed to come out readily with his reply. "You surely come from Andalusia," he said. "I have seen women there like you, though none so fair."

She gave him a quick smile, showing her white teeth, but then turned her eyes sadly downwards.

"O stranger, who speak my language," she said in a soft voice, "you see what reward my beauty has brought me. Here sit I, an Andalusian of Celbitian blood, now a slave-girl among the darkest heathens and shamefully unveiled, rubbing this old Bluetooth's decaying feet. There is nothing in this country but cold and darkness and skin rugs and lice, and food such as the dogs of Seville would vomit up. Only in Allah can I seek refuge from the miserable fate to which my beauty has brought me."

"You look to me to be too good for the work you are doing here," said Toke warmly. "You ought to be able to find yourself a man with something better than his toes to offer you."

Again she smiled like the sun at him, though tears had come into her eyes; but at that moment King Harald roused himself and said angrily: "Who are you that mumble crow-talk with my woman?"

"I am Toke, the son of Gray Gull of Lister," replied Toke, "and my sword and the dexterity of my tongue are all that I possess. But I intended no disrespect to you, O King, in addressing your woman. She asked me about the bell, and I answered her; and she replied that she thought it was a gift that would give you as much pleasure as she has given you, and be no less useful."

King Harald opened his mouth to reply, but as he did so, his face went black and he let out a roar and flung himself backwards among the cushions, so that the two young women working on his feet were thrown head over heels on their backs; for the pain had returned savagely into his bad tooth.

At this there was great confusion in the bedchamber, and those who stood nearest the King's bed took a step backwards lest he should become violent. But Brother Willibald had by now prepared his potion and came boldly forward with cheerful mien and encouraging words.

"Now, now, royal King!" he said admonishingly, and made the sign of the cross twice, first over the King and then over the bowl containing the potion, which he held in one of his hands. With his other hand he took a little horn spoon and chanted in a solemn voice:

"The cruel pain
Within thee burning
Now shall be quenched
In the well of healing.
Soon shalt thou feel
The ache departing."

The King stared at him and his bowl, snorted angrily, shook his head and groaned, and then, in his agony, aimed a blow at him and roared violently: "Away from me, priest! Away with your incantations and broth. Ho, there, Hallbjörn, Arnkel, Grim! Up with your axes and split me this louse of a priest!"

But his men had often heard him talk like this and paid no heed to his fulminations; and Brother Willibald, no whit daunted, addressed him boldly: "Be patient, O King, and sit upright and put this in your mouth; for it is rich with the strength of saints. Only three spoonfuls, O King, and you need not swallow them. Sing, Brother Matthias!"

Brother Matthias, who was standing behind Brother Willibald with the great crucifix in his hand, began to intone a sacred hymn:

"Solve vincla reis
profer lumen cæcis,
mala nostra pelle,
bona cuncta posce!"

This seemed to subdue the King, for he patiently allowed himself to be lifted into a sitting position. Brother Willibald promptly inserted a spoonful of the mixture into his mouth, proceeding as he did so to accompany Brother Matthias in his hymn, while everyone in the bedchamber watched them with great expectancy. The King went purple in the face with the strength of the potion, but kept his mouth closed; then, when three verses had been sung, he obediently spat it out, whereupon Brother Willibald, without desisting from his singing, gave him another spoonful.

All the spectators afterwards agreed that it was only a few sec-

onds after receiving the second spoonful, and before the priests
had had time to complete a verse of the hymn, when the King
suddenly closed his eyes and went rigid. Then he opened them
again, spat out the potion, gave vent to a deep sigh, and roared
for ale. Brother Willibald stopped singing and leaned anxiously
toward him.

"Is it better, Your Majesty? Has the pain ceased?"

"It has," said the King, spitting again. "Your medicine was sour,
but it appears to have been effective."

Brother Willibald threw up his arms for joy.

"Hosanna!" he cried. "A miracle has occurred! St. James of
Spain has answered our prayer! Praise the Lord, O King, for better
times are now beginning! The toothache shall no more cloud your
spirit, nor shall anxiety dwell in the hearts of your servants!"

King Harald nodded his head and stroked the corners of his
beard. He seized with both his hands a large vessel that a page
brought to him, and raised it to his mouth. At first he swallowed
carefully, evidently afraid lest the pain might return, but then
drank confidently until the vessel was empty. He ordered it to be
refilled and offered it to Orm.

"Drink!" he commanded. "And accept our thanks for the succor you have brought us."

Orm took the vessel and drank. It was the finest ale he had ever
tasted, strong and full-bodied, such as only kings could afford to
brew, and he drank it with a will.

Toke watched him and sighed; then he said:

> "In my throat there is a feeling
> Of dry rot most unblest.
> Do physicians know the healing
> For me, that ale is best?"

"If you are a poet, you shall drink," said King Harald. "But
afterwards you will have to compose a poem about your drink."

So they filled the vessel again for Toke, and he put it to his
mouth and drank, leaning his head farther and farther backwards;
and all those present in the King's bedchamber agreed that they
had seen few vessels emptied more smartly. Then he reflected for
a while, wiping the froth from his beard, and at length declaimed,
in a voice stronger than that in which he had made his request:

"Thirsting I rowed for many a year,
And thirsting did good slaughter.
All praise to thee, Gorm's gracious heir!
Thou knowest my favorite water!"

The men in the bedchamber praised Toke's poem, and King Harald said: "There are few poets to be found nowadays, and few of those are able to turn out verses without sitting for hours in cogitation. Many men have come to me with odes and lyrics, and it has vexed me sorely to see them while the winter away in my halls with their noses snuffling up my ale, producing nothing whatever once they had declaimed the poem they had brought with them. I like men to whom verses come easily and who can give me some new delight each day when I dine; in which respect, you, Toke of Lister, are more fluent than any poet I have heard since Einar Skalaglam and Vigfus Viga-Glumsson were my guests. You shall both spend Yule with me, and your men too; and my best ale shall be provided for you, for you have earned it by the gift you brought me."

Then King Harald gave a great yawn, for he was weary after his troublesome night. He wrapped his fur more closely around him, snuggled himself into a more comfortable position in his bed, and lay ready for rest, with the two young women on either side of him. The skin rugs were spread over him, and Brother Matthias and Brother Willibald made the sign of the cross above his head and mumbled a prayer. Then they all left the room, and the groom of the bedchamber strode into the middle of the palace yard with his sword in his hand and cried three times in a loud voice: "The King of Denmark sleeps!" so that no noise should be made which might disturb King Harald's slumber.

CHAPTER NINE

HOW KING HARALD BLUETOOTH CELEBRATED
         YULE

GREAT men from all over the north came to Jellinge to celebrate Yule with King Harald, so that there was less than room
enough for them at the tables and in the bedchambers. But Orm
and his men did not complain of this overcrowding, for they had
received a good price for their slaves and had sold them all before
the festival commenced. When Orm had divided up the proceeds
of the sale, his men felt rich and free indeed, and they began to
yearn for Lister and to know whether Berse's two ships had come
home, or whether they themselves were the only survivors of Krok's
expedition. They offered no objection to staying in Jellinge, however, until the festival was over, for it was regarded as a great
honor, and one that added luster to a man's name for the rest of
his days, to have celebrated Yule with the King of the Danes.

The principal guest was King Harald's son, King Sven Forkbeard,[1] who had arrived from Hedeby with a large following. Like
all King Harald's sons, he was the child of one of his father's concubines; and there was little love lost between him and his father,
so that in general they avoided each other as much as possible.
Every Yule, though, King Sven made the journey to Jellinge, and
everybody knew why. For it often happened at Yule, when the
food was richer and the drink stronger than at any other time in
the year, that old men suddenly died, either in bed or on the
drinking-bench. This had been the case with old King Gorm, who
had lain unconscious for two days after a surfeit of Yuletide pork
and had then died; and King Sven wanted to be near the royal
coffers when his father passed over. For many Yules now he had
made the journey in vain, and each year his impatience increased.
His followers were a rough crew, overbearing and quarrelsome,
and it was difficult to keep the peace between them and the men
of King Harald's household, all the more so now that King Harald

---

[1] The father of King Canute the Great.

had turned Christian and many of his men had followed suit. For King Sven still clung to the old religion and made spiteful mock of his father's conversion, saying that the Danes would have been spared all this folly if the old man had had the sense to know when he had lived long enough.

He did not trumpet his opinions too openly when he was at Jellinge, however, for King Harald was easily roused to anger, and when this happened he was liable to do anything to anybody. They wasted no words on each other once they had made formal salutation, nor, from their seats of honor in the great hall, did they toast each other more than the conventions of politeness absolutely required.

There was a snowstorm on Christmas Eve, but it passed, and the weather grew calm and cold; and on Christmas morning, while the priests were singing Mass and the courtyard of the palace lay shrouded in good steam from the preparations afoot in the kitchens, a great long-ship rowed up from the south and made fast to the pier, its sail tattered and its oars glazed with ice. King Harald was at Mass, but they sent a messenger to inform him. Wondering who these new guests could be, he went up the stairs to look at the ship. It was steeply built, with a red dragon's head poised arrogantly upon a curved neck at the prow, its jaws caked with ice from the cruel seas it had passed through. They saw men climb ashore wearing garments barked with ice, among them a tall chieftain in a blue cloak and another, of equal stature, clothed in red. King Harald scanned them as closely as he could from where he stood, and said: "It looks like a Jomsviking or perhaps a Swedish ship, and it is boldly manned, for its crew approach the King of the Danes with no shield of peace upon their masthead. I know of but three men who would dare to come thus: Skoglar-Toste, Vagn Akesson, and Styrbjörn. Moreover, they have brought their ship alongside without removing their dragon-head, though they know well that the trolls of the mainland do not love dragon-heads; and I know of but two men who do not care what the trolls think, and they are Vagn and Styrbjörn. But I see from the ship's condition that its captain disdained to seek shelter from last night's storm, and there is but one man who would have refused to bow to such a tempest. It is my guess, therefore, that this must be my son-in-law Styrbjörn, whom I have not seen these four years; one of them

wears a blue cloak, moreover, and Styrbjörn has sworn to wear
blue until he has won back his inheritance from King Erik. Who
this other with him may be, the man who is as tall as he, I cannot
surely say; but Strut-Harald's sons are taller than most men, all
three of them, and they are all friends to Styrbjörn. It cannot be
Jarl Sigvalde, the eldest of them, for he takes little pleasure in
Yule celebrations now, because of the ignominy with which he
stained his name when he rowed his ships away from the battle at
Jörundfjord; and his brother Hemming is in England. But the
third of Strut-Harald's sons is Thorkel the Tall, and it may be
that this is he."

Thus King Harald surmised in his wisdom; and when the
strangers reached the palace and it became evident that he was
right, his spirits rose higher than they had been at any time since
King Sven arrived. He bade Styrbjörn and Thorkel welcome,
ordered the bathhouse to be heated for them at once, and offered
mulled ale to them and all their men.

"Even the greatest of warriors," he said, "need something to
warm themselves after such a voyage as you have endured: and
there is truth in the old saying:

> Mulled ale for the frozen man,
> And mulled ale for the weary:
> For mulled ale is the body's friend
> And makes the sick heart merry."

Several of Styrbjörn's men were so exhausted by their voyage
that they were hardly able to stand: but when tankards of mulled
ale were offered them, their hands proved to be steady enough,
for not a drop was spilled.

"As soon as you have bathed and rested," said King Harald,
"the Yule feast shall begin: and I shall go to it with a better
appetite than if I had only my son's face to look at across the
table."

"Is Forkbeard here?" said Styrbjörn, glancing around him. "I
should be glad to have a word with him."

"He still cherishes the hope that some day he will see me die
the ale-death," said King Harald. "That is why he has come. But if
I ever should die at a Yule feast, I think it will be because I am
sick of looking at his misshapen face. You will have your chance

to speak with him in good time. But tell me one thing: is there blood between him and you?"

"No blood as yet," replied Styrbjörn, "but as to the future I cannot say. He has promised me men and ships to help me against my kinsman in Uppsala, but none have yet arrived."

"There must be no fighting in my house during the holy festival," said King Harald. "You must understand that at once, though I know that you will find it tedious to keep the peace. For I am now a follower of Christ, who has been a good ally to me; and Christ will tolerate no strife on Christmas Day, which is His birthday, nor on the holy days that follow."

Styrbjörn replied: "I am a man without a country, and as such cannot afford the luxury of being peaceful; for I would rather be the crow than his carrion. But while I am your guest, I think I shall be able to keep the peace as well as any man, whichsoever gods are presiding over the feast; for you have been a good father-in-law to me, and I have never had cause to quarrel with you. But I have news to bring you: namely, that your daughter Tyra is dead. I wish I could have come with more joyful tidings."

"That is sad news indeed," said King Harald. "How did she die?"

"She took it amiss," said Styrbjörn, "because I found myself a Wendish concubine. She became so wrathful that she began to spit blood; then she languished and, after a time, died. In all other respects she was an excellent wife."

"I have noticed of late," said King Harald, "that young people cling less keenly to life than old people. But we must not allow this grief to weigh down our spirits during the Yule feast; and in any case I have more daughters left than I know what to do with. They are a fine-spirited bunch and will not marry any man who is not of noble birth and high renown; so that you need not remain a widower for long if you should find any girl among them who takes your fancy. You shall see them all—though I fear that, when they hear that you are single again, they may have some difficulty in keeping the Yule peace."

"Something other than marriage is uppermost in my mind just now," said Styrbjörn, "but we can speak of that later."

Many glances were cast at Styrbjörn from doorways and loopholes, as he went with his men to the bathhouse; for he rarely ac-

cepted hospitality, and was held to be the greatest warrior that had
been seen in the north since the days of the sons of Ragnar Hairy-
Breeks. He had a short, fair beard and pale blue eyes, and men who
had not seen him before murmured with surprise at finding him so
slim-built and narrow-waisted. For they all knew that his strength
was such that he cleft shields like loaves of bread and split armed
men from the neck to the crotch with his sword, which was called
Cradle-Song. Wise men said that the ancient luck of the Uppsala
kings was his, and that it was this that gave him his strength and
success in every enterprise he undertook. But it was also known
that the curse of his family and their ancient ill luck had in part
descended on him, and that it was because of this that he was a
chieftain without a country; and that it was for this reason, too,
that he was often afflicted with a great heaviness and melancholy.
When the fit attacked him, he would shut himself away from all
company and sit sighing and mumbling darkly to himself for days
on end, unable to endure the presence of any of his fellow beings,
save for a woman to comb his hair and an old harpist to give him
ale and play him sad music. But so soon as the fit passed from
him, he would be eager to go to sea again, and to battle, and then
he would bring the strongest of his men to weariness and despair
by his recklessness and his bad weather-luck.

So he was feared as no other chieftain in the north was feared,
almost as though something of the power and majesty of the gods
dwelt in him; and there were those who believed that some time
in the future, when he reached the zenith of his might, he would
sail to Miklagard and crown himself emperor there, and voyage
in triumph along the round edge of the earth with his terrible
navies.

But there were others who claimed that they could see it written
in his eyes that he would die young and unlucky.

At length everything was ready in King Harald's great dining-
hall for the Yule feast, and all the men were assembled there in
their numbers, seated on benches. No women were allowed to be
present at so tremendous a drinking-bout, for it was difficult
enough, King Harald thought, to keep the peace when men were
by themselves, and it would be many times harder if they had
women to brag to in their cups. When everyone was in his place,
the groom of the bedchamber announced in a gigantic voice that

the peace of Christ and of King Harald reigned in the hall, and that no edged implements might be used except for the purpose of cutting up food; any cut, thrust, or open wound caused by weapon, ale-tankard, meat-bone, wooden platter, ladle, or clenched fist would be reckoned as plain murder, and would be regarded as sacrilege against Christ and as an unpardonable crime, and the miscreant would have a stone tied round his neck and be drowned in deep water. All weapons apart from eating-knives had been left by order in the vestibules, and only the exalted personages who sat at King Harald's own table were allowed to retain their swords; for it was felt that they would be able to control themselves even when drunk.

The hall was built to hold a good six hundred men without crowding, and in the middle stood King Harald's own table, with the thirty most eminent of the company seated at it. The tables for the other guests stretched down the length of the hall from one end to the other. Styrbjörn sat on King Harald's right hand, and Bishop Poppo on his left; opposite them King Sven had Thorkel the Tall on his right, and a red-faced, bald old jarl from the Small Islands called Sibbe on his left. The others sat according to their rank, King Harald himself having settled each man's place personally. Orm, though he could not be reckoned as one of the great chieftains, had yet been allotted a better place than he could have expected, and Toke likewise, for King Harald was grateful to them for their gift of the great bell, and was an admirer of Toke's poetry. So Orm sat three places from the Bishop, and Toke four; for Orm had told King Harald that he would like, if possible, to sit next to Toke, in case the latter became troublesome through drink. Facing them across the table were men of King Sven's company.

The Bishop read grace, King Harald having commanded him to be brief about it, and then they drank three toasts: to the honor of Christ, to the luck of King Harald, and to the return of the sun. Even those of the company who were not Christians joined in the toast to Christ, for it was the first of the toasts and they were thirsty for their ale; some of them, however, made the sign of the hammer over their tankards and murmured the name of Thor before they drank. When the toast to King Harald's luck was drunk, King Sven got ale in his windpipe and had a coughing fit, causing Styrbjörn to ask whether the brew was too strong for his taste.

Then the Yule pork was brought in, and warriors and chieftains alike fell silent when they saw it appear, and took a deep breath and sighed with joyous anticipation; many loosened their belts, to save doing so later. For though there were those who whispered that King Harald was in his old age less openhanded with gold and silver than he had been of yore, this accusation had never been leveled at him in the matter of meat and drink, and certainly never by anyone who had celebrated Yule in his palace.

Forty-eight acorn hogs, well fattened, were slaughtered for his pleasure every Yule; and it was his custom to say that if this did not see them through the whole feast-tide, it would at any rate be sufficient to provide a tasty entrée for every guest, and that they could then fill up with beef and mutton. The kitchen servants entered in a long line, two by two, each pair bearing a great smoking pot, except for some who carried troughs of blood-sausage. They were accompanied by boys armed with long forked spits, which, once the pots had been set beside the tables, they plunged into the stew, fishing out large hunks of meat, which they gave to the guests in order of precedence, so that each had his fair share; in addition to which, every man received a good ell's length of blood-sausage, or more if he wanted it. There were bread cakes and fried turnips set out on clay plates, and at the foot of each table there stood a butt of ale, so that no man's horn or tankard need ever be empty.

As the pork approached Orm and Toke, they sat quite still, with their faces turned toward the pot, watching the boy closely as he fished for the meat. They sighed blissfully as he lifted out fine pieces of shoulder pork to put on their plates, reminding each other how long it was since they had last eaten such a dinner, and marveling that they had managed to survive so many years in a country where no pork was allowed to be eaten. But when the blood-sausage arrived, tears came into their eyes, and they declared that they had never eaten a meal worthy of the name since the day they had sailed away with Krok.

"This is the best smell of all," said Orm in a small voice.

"There is thyme in it," said Toke huskily.

He plunged his sausage into his mouth, as far as it would go, bit off a length, and slowly closed his jaws; then he swung hastily round, grabbing at the boy's coat as he attempted to move on with the trough, and said: "If it be not contrary to King Harald's orders, give me at once another length of that sausage. I have for some years past now fared indifferently among the Andalusians, where they have no food worthy of the name, and these seven Yules I have longed for blood-sausage and had none."

"My case," said Orm, "is the same."

The boy laughed at their anxiety and assured them that King Harald had enough sausage for everybody. He ladled out on each of their plates a good length of the thickest that he had; then they were contented and began to eat in earnest.

For some time now, nobody spoke, either at the King's table or anywhere else in the hall, except when somebody asked for more ale or mumbled a word between bites in praise of King Harald's Yuletide meat.

On Orm's right sat a young man who cut his meat with a knife that bore an engraved silver hilt. He was fair-skinned and had very long and exquisite hair, carefully combed. He belonged to Thorkel the Tall's company, and evidently came of good family, for he was honorably placed at the King's table although he had as yet no beard; besides which his nobility was apparent from his fine clothing and silver sword-belt. After the first flush of eating was over, he turned to Orm and said: "It is good at a feast to sit next to men who have traveled widely; and I think I heard that you and your neighbor have voyaged farther afield than most of us here."

Orm replied that this was correct, and that Toke and he had spent six years in Spain.

"For various reasons," he added, "our journey took longer than we had anticipated; and many of those who set out with us never returned."

"You must have had many adventures worth the telling," said the other. "I myself, though I have not traveled as far as either of you, have also recently been on a voyage from which few came back."

Orm asked him who he was and what voyage he referred to.

The other replied: "I come from Bornholm, and my name is Sigurd; and my father was Bue Digre, of whom you may have heard, despite your long sojourn abroad. I was with him at Jörund-

Fjord when he was killed, and I was captured there, together with Vagn Akesson and many others besides. Nor should I be sitting here tonight to tell the tale if it had not been for my long hair; for it was my hair that saved my life when orders had been given for all the prisoners to be killed."

By this time a number of their table companions had eaten their fill and were beginning to regain the freedom of their tongues for the purpose of speech. Toke now joined in the conversation, remarking that what the Bornholmer had just said had an unusual ring about it and promised a good story; for his part, he had always regarded long hair as being more of a handicap to a soldier than an advantage. Thorkel the Tall sat picking his teeth in the aristocratic manner that was now beginning to be fashionable among great men who had traveled widely, with his face turned to one side and the palm of his hand raised before his mouth. He overheard their conversation and observed that long hair had proved unlucky to many a soldier in the past, and that sensible men always took good care to bind their hair up carefully beneath their helmets; however, he added, Sigurd Buesson would show by his story how a shrewd man might take advantage of the length of his hair, and he hoped that everyone in the hall would listen to what he had to say.

King Sven, by this time, was in a better humor, the appearance of Styrbjörn having shadowed his spirits for a while. He sat lolling backwards in his chair, gnawing a pig's trotter, the bones from which he spat out on the straw that covered the floor. He noted with satisfaction that King Harald, who was engaged in a discussion with Styrbjörn about women, was eating and drinking more than anyone else. He, too, overheard what was being said farther down the table and joined in the discussion, pointing out that a wise soldier also always remembers his beard, for when a battle was being .fought in windy weather a man's beard could easily get into his eyes just when he was preparing to parry a sword-thrust or to avoid a winging spear; wherefore, he told them, he always made a point of having his hair plaited before marching into battle. But now he would be interested to hear how Sigurd Buesson had taken advantage of his long hair, for men who had fought at Jörundfjord usually had adventures worth relating.

Bishop Poppo had not succeeded in finishing all that had been placed before him, and the ale that he had drunk had given him hiccups; nevertheless, he was capable of utterance and he, too, joined in the discussion, saying that he would be happy to tell them the story of Prince Absalom, whose long hair had proved to be his downfall. This, he said, was a good and instructive story, which stood written in God's own holy book. But King Sven cut him off promptly with the comment that he could keep such stories for women and children, if he could persuade them to listen to him. Words were then exchanged between him and the Bishop on this score; but King Harald said:

"A feast such as this, which lasts for six days, will allow us all time in which to tell our stories; and few things are better than to listen to good stories when a man has eaten his fill and has ale left in his cup. For it helps the time to pass easily between one meal and the next, and makes for less quarreling across the tables. But let me say this in the Bishop's favor, that he has good tales to tell, for I myself have listened to many of them with pleasure, concerning saints and apostles and the old kings that used to reign in the Eastern lands. He has told me many stories about one of them whose name was Solomon, who was greatly beloved by God and who seems to have been very much like myself, though it is true that he had more women. I think that the Bishop should tell his story first, before the food and drink make him sleepy, for our Yule drinking does not have the same good effect on him that it has on us, since he has not had sufficient time to accustom himself to it. After him, let other men tell of their adventures at Jörundfjord, or with Styrbjörn among the Wends, or elsewhere. We have, besides, here among us, men who have been as far abroad as Spain, whence they have sailed to my court bearing with them a holy bell, which has been of great service to me; and I wish to hear them tell their story before this feast is done."

They all agreed that King Harald had spoken wisely, and it was done as he suggested; so that evening, after the torches had been brought in, the Bishop told the story of King David and his son Absalom. He spoke loudly, so that everyone could hear him, and he told his tale cunningly, so that all the company except King Sven enjoyed it. When the Bishop had finished talking, King Harald observed that his story was well worth storing away in one's memory, for one reason and another; and Styrbjörn laughed, and raised his glass to King Sven and said: "Be wise, O Prince, and pay heed to this tale, and cut thy hair short as bishops do."

This remark appealed to King Harald, who smote his thigh and fell into such a fit of laughing that the whole bench on his side of the table shook; and when his men and Styrbjörn's followers saw their masters laughing, they all joined in, even those of them who were unaware of the cause, so that the whole hall rang with merriment. King Sven's men, however, were displeased; and he himself glowered sourly and mumbled something into his cup and gnawed his lip-beard and had a dangerous look about him, as though he might at any moment leap to his feet and break into violence. Styrbjörn leaned forward in his seat and stared at him out of his pale eyes, which never blinked, and smiled. There was considerable unrest in the hall, and it looked as though the Christmas peace might shortly be ended. The Bishop stretched out his hands and cried something that nobody heard, and men fixed their eyes upon one another across the table and groped for the nearest thing that might serve as a weapon. But then King Harald's jesters, two small Irishmen who were famed for their skill in trade, jumped up on the King's table in motley-colored tunics, wearing feathers in their hair, and began to flap their broad sleeves and puff their chests and stamp their feet and stretch their necks; then they crew at each other exactly like cocks, so that no man present could remember ever having heard a cock crow as finely as they did; and within a few seconds they had all forgotten their anger and were lolling in their seats helpless with laughter at their antics. So the first day of the feasting ended.

On the next day, when the eating was over and the torches had been carried in, Sigurd Buesson told them of his adventures at Jörundfjord, and how he had been saved by his long hair. They all knew about this expedition; how the Jomsvikings, with men from Bornholm, had sailed out in a mighty fleet under the command of Strut-Harald's sons, with Bue Digre and Vagn Akesson, to win Norway from Jarl Haakon, and how few had returned from that enterprise; so Sigurd did not waste many words on this part of his story, and made no mention of how Sigvalde had fled with his ships from the battle. For it would have been churlish to have spoken of Sigvalde when Thorkel the Tall was among his audience, though they all knew Thorkel to be a bold fighter and were aware that he had been struck on the head by a large stone during the battle soon after the opposing navies had come to grips, so that he had not been conscious when his brother had rowed away.

Sigurd had been aboard his father's ship, and confined himself to such parts of the battle as he himself had been directly concerned in. He told them of his father's death; how Bue had fought fiercely, but at last, when the Norwegians had boarded his ship in overwhelming numbers, had received a slash on his face from a sword which had taken away his nose and the greater part of his jaw; and how he had then seized up his great treasure-chest and leaped overboard with it in his arms. He told, too, how Bue's kinsman, Aslak Holmskalle, had gone berserk, casting aside his shield and helmet, which was something one seldom saw nowadays, and hewing about him with both hands, impervious to the touch of iron, until an Icelandic bard, a follower of Jarl Haakon's son Erik, had picked up an anvil from the deck and with it had split his skull.

"After that," continued Sigurd, "for such of us as remained alive on my father's ship, there was little left to do; for we were few in numbers and very fatigued, and all our ships had now been overpowered, save only Vagn's own ship, which still fought on. We were hemmed in the forecastle, so weary that before long we could lift neither hand nor foot; and at last there were but nine of us left, all wounded, and there they pinned us with their shields and so took us. We were disarmed and brought ashore; and soon the survivors of Vagn's ship were dragged to join us, Vagn himself being among them. Two men carried him, and he bore both sword- and spear-wounds, and was pale and weary and said nothing. They made us sit on a log on the beach, with our legs tied together with a long rope, though they left our hands free; and there we sat and waited, while men were sent to Jarl Haakon to discover what should be our fate. He commanded that we were instantly to be put to death, and Jarl Erik, his son, and many of his followers came to watch our end; for the Norwegians were curious to see how Jomsvikings would conduct themselves in the face of death. There were thirty of us on the log, nine from Bue's ship, eight from Vagn's, and the rest from other ships. Vagn himself sat on our extreme right; and I shall tell you the names of such of the others as were known to me."

Then he gave them a list of all those whose names he knew, in the order in which they sat on the log; and all the company in the great hall listened in silence, for many of those he named were men whom they had known, and some of his listeners had kinsmen among the dead.

He continued: "Then a man came with a beard-ax and stood in front of Vagn and said: 'Do you know who I am?' Vagn glanced at him, but did not seem to notice him and said nothing, for he was very weary. Then the other man said: 'I am Thorkel Leira. Perhaps you remember the vow you made to kill me and bring my daughter Ingeborg to bed?' Now this was true, for Vagn had vowed thus before setting out, since he had heard that Thorkel's daughter was the most beautiful girl in Norway, besides being one of the richest. 'But now,' continued Thorkel Leira, with a broad grin, 'it looks rather as though I am going to kill you.' Vagn curled his lip and said: 'There are yet Jomsvikings living.' 'They shall not live long,' replied Thorkel, 'and I shall see to it myself, so that there shall be no mistake. You will see all your men die beneath my hand, after which you will shortly follow them.' Then he went to the other end of the log and proceeded to behead the prisoners, one after another as they sat there. He had a good ax and went to work with a will; and he never needed to strike twice. But I think that those who were watching the scene had to admit that Vagn's and Bue's men knew how to conduct themselves in the face of death. Two who were seated not far from me began a discussion as to what it would feel like once one's head was off, and they agreed that it was one of those things that are difficult to foretell. One of them said: 'I have a brooch here in my hand. If my brain is still working after I have lost my head, I shall stick it into the ground.' Thorkel arrived at him; but as soon as the blow fell on his neck, the brooch dropped from his hand. That left only two men between Thorkel and myself."

Sigurd Buesson smiled quietly at his listeners, who sat in silent excitement. He raised his cup and drank a deep draught.

King Harald said: "I see that you still have your head on your shoulders; and anyone can hear by the sound of your swallowing that there is nothing wrong with your neck. But that was a sorry situation you were in on that Norwegian log, and it is no easy thing to guess how you managed to escape to tell the tale, however long your hair. This is a fine story, and do not keep us waiting to know how it ended."

They all raised a shout of agreement, and Sigurd Buesson continued: "As I sat there on the log, I do not think I was more frightened than the others were; but I felt it would be a pity to die without having done something worthy for men to speak of after I had gone. So when Thorkel came to my place, I said to him: 'I am afraid for my hair; I do not want it to be stained with blood.' So saying, I drew it forward over my head; and a man who was walking behind Thorkel—I heard later that he was his brother-in-law—ran forward and wound my hair round his fingers and said to Thorkel: 'Now, strike!' He did so; but in the same instant, I pulled my head back as quickly as I could, so that the ax fell between me and his brother-in-law and cut off both his brother-in-law's hands. One of them remained hanging in my hair."

Everyone in the hall burst into a great roar of laughter. Sigurd himself laughed with them; then he proceeded: "You may well laugh, but your laughter, loud as it is, is as silence compared with the merriment of the Norwegians when they saw Thorkel's brother-in-law writhing on the ground, with Thorkel standing scowling above him. Some of them laughed so much that they fell over. Jarl Erik came forward and looked at me and said: 'Who are you?' I replied: 'My name is Sigurd, and Bue was my father; there are yet Jomsvikings living.' The Jarl said: 'You are truly of Bue's blood. Will you accept your life from me?' 'From such a man as you, Jarl,' I replied, 'I will accept it.' Then they untied me. But Thorkel, ill-pleased at this, roared: 'Shall it be thus? Then it were best I lose no time in dispatching Vagn.' Raising his ax, he rushed toward him as he sat quietly on the end of the log. But one of Vagn's men, named Skarde, a good man from Kivik, was seated four places from Vagn; and it seemed to him wrong that Vagn should lose his head before his proper turn arrived. So he threw himself forward over the foot-rope as Thorkel rushed by him, so that Thorkel fell full length over his body and lay at Vagn's feet. Vagn leaned forward and took up the ax, and there was little weariness to be seen in his face as he buried it in Thorkel's head. 'I have fulfilled half my vow,' he said; 'and still there are Jomsvikings living.' The Norwegians laughed louder than ever; and Jarl Erik said: 'Will you have your life, Vagn?' 'If you grant it to us all,' replied Vagn. 'It shall be so,' said the Jarl. So they freed us all. Twelve of us escaped from the log with our lives."

Sigurd Buesson was loudly acclaimed for his story, and everyone praised the good use he had made of his hair. They all discussed his story across the tables, admiring his good luck and that of Vagn; and Orm said to Sigurd: "There is much that is common knowledge in these parts which Toke and I are ignorant of, because we have been out of the country for so long a time. Where is Vagn now, and what happened to him after he escaped from the log with his life? From all that you say, his luck sounds to me greater than that of any other man I ever heard tell of."

"That is so," replied Sigurd, "nor does it stop halfway. We rose high in Jarl Erik's favor, and after a while he sought out Thorkel Leira's daughter, whom he found to be even more beautiful than he had imagined her; nor did she offer any objection to helping him to fulfill the remainder of his promise; so that now they are married, and are well contented. He is thinking of coming back to Bornholm with her, as soon as he can find the time to do so; but the last heard of him was that he was still in Norway and was complaining that it would be many months before he could return home. For he became master of so many fine houses when he married the girl, and of so many great estates attached to them, that it will be no swift matter to sell them for the prices they deserve to command; and it is not Vagn's custom to sell things cheaply when he does not have to do so."

Toke said: "There is one thing in your story that I cannot help wondering about. I mean, your father's, Bue's treasure-chest, which he took with him when he jumped overboard. Did you fish it up before you left Norway? Or did someone else get there before you? If it is still lying on the sea-bed, I know what I should do were I to go to Norway. I should drag the sea for that treasure-chest, for Bue's silver must have been worth a great fortune."

"They fished long for it," said Sigurd, "not only the Norwegians, but also such of Bue's men as survived. Many men dragged for it with grappling hooks, but they caught nothing; and one man from the Vik who dived down with a rope was never seen again. Then all of us concluded that Bue was such a Viking as would wish to keep his treasure with him on the sea-bed, and that he would have no mercy on any man who tried to take it from him; for he was a strong man, and he loved his wealth. Wise men know that those who dwell in the Great Halls are stronger than when they were alive; and this may also be true of Bue, though he does not dwell in the Great Halls but on the deep sea-bed beside his treasure-chest."

"It is a pity that so much silver should be lost," said Toke. "But, as you say, even the boldest of men would not willingly choose to be at the bottom of the sea with Broad Bue's arms locked about his waist."

So that evening drew to its close.

The next evening King Harald wanted to hear about Styrbjörn's adventures among the Wends and Kures. Styrbjörn said that he was no story-teller; but an Icelander who was of his following took up the tale. His name was Björn Asbrandsson, and he was a famous warrior, besides being a great poet to boot, like all wanderers from Iceland. Although he was somewhat drunk, he managed to improvise some highly skillful verses in King Harald's honor in a meter known as *töglag*. This was the latest and most difficult verse-form that the Icelandic poets had invented, and indeed his poem was so artfully contrived that little could be understood of its content. Everybody, however, listened with an appearance of understanding, for any man who could not understand poetry would be regarded as a poor specimen of a warrior; and King Harald praised the poem and gave the poet a gold ring. Toke plunged his head between his hands on the table and sighed disconsolately; this, he muttered, was real poetry, and he could see that he would never be able to succeed in writing the sort of verses that won gold rings.

The man from Iceland, whom some called Björn Champion-of-the-men-of-Breidifjord,[2] and who had been a follower of Styrbjörn for two summers, then went on to tell them of Styrbjörn's various campaigns and the notable things that had occurred during them. He was a fine talker and continued for several hours without anyone wearying of his story; and everybody knew that what he was telling them was the truth, since Styrbjörn himself was among his listeners. He gave them many examples of Styrbjörn's boldness

[2] A good poet and a strong fighter, who is supposed to have ended his days in America.

and of his great luck, and also spoke of the rich booty that his followers had won. Finally he concluded by reciting an ancient poem about Styrbjörn's ancestors, beginning with the gods and ending with his uncle Erik, who was now reigning in Uppsala. To this poem he had himself added a final strophe, which ran as follows:

> Northwards soon
> To crave his birthright
> Styrbjörn shall row
> With a hundred keels.
> His gallant men
> With victory flaming
> Shall make full merry
> In Erik's halls.

This was greeted with tremendous applause, and many of the diners jumped up on their benches to drink to Styrbjörn's luck. Styrbjörn ordered a costly drinking-cup to be brought to him, and presented it to the poet, saying: "This is not your bardic crown, O Icelander; that shall be set upon your brow when I sit on my throne in Uppsala. There shall be wealth worth winning there for every man of my followers; for my uncle Erik is a thrifty man and has hoarded much that we can put to better use than by allowing it to tarnish in his coffers. When the spring buds open, I shall sail northwards to open those coffers, and any man who wishes to accompany me shall be welcome."

Both among King Harald's followers and among King Sven's there were many whose blood was fired by this challenge, and who roared at once that they would keep him company; for the extent of King Erik's wealth was famous throughout the north, besides which, Uppsala had not been plundered since the time of Ivar of the Broad Embrace. Jarl Sibbe of the Small Islands was drunk and was having difficulty in controlling both his head and his wine-cup, but he joined in the thunder of acclamation, roaring that he would bring five ships to row north with Styrbjörn, for, he said, he was now beginning to grow stiff and sleepy, and it was better for a man to die among warriors than upon straw like a cow. King Harald said that he was, alas, too old to take the field, and that he had to keep his soldiers at home to maintain peace in his kingdom; however, he would not stand in the way of his son, Sven, if the latter wished to ally his men and ships to Styrbjörn's enterprise.

King Sven spat meditatively, took a swig from his cup, fingered his beard, and said that it would be difficult for him to spare either men or ships, since he could not neglect his obligations toward his own people, whom he could not leave a defenseless prey to the Saxons and Obotrites.

"I think it fairer," he added, "that if any assistance be lent, it should be provided by my father; for now that he is old, his men have little to do but wait for the next mealtime and listen to the twittering of priests."

King Harald exploded with fury at this remark, and there was uproar in the hall; he said that it was easy to see that Sven would be glad to see him left defenseless in Jellinge. "But it shall be as I command!" he screamed, and his face was scarlet; "for I am the King of the Danes, and I alone! So, Sven, you shall lend ships and men to Styrbjörn!"

Hearing these words, King Sven sat silent, for he was afraid of his father's wrath; besides which, it was clear that many of his men were eager to follow Styrbjörn to Uppsala.

Then Styrbjörn spoke. "I am delighted," he said, "to see how anxious you both are to help me. I think the best solution would be that you, Harald, should decide how many ships Sven shall send; and that you, my good friend Sven, shall determine the extent to which your father shall aid me."

This suggestion caused great merriment among all the feasters, so that the tension in the hall decreased; and finally it was agreed that Harald and Sven should each send twelve well-manned ships to fight with Styrbjörn, in addition to whatever help he might succeed in persuading the Skanians to lend him; in return for which, Harald and Sven were to have a share of the treasure that lay in King Erik's coffers. So that evening, too, drew to its close.

The next day, since they had finished the Yule pork, cabbage soup and mutton appeared on the tables, which they all agreed to be an excellent change. In the evening a man from Halland told them about a great wedding that he had been present at in Finnveden, among the wild people of Smaland. During the celebrations a dispute had broken out concerning a horse deal, and knives had quickly appeared; whereupon the bride and her attendant maidens had laughed delightedly and applauded and had encouraged the disputants to settle the matter there and then. However, when the bride, who belonged to a well-known local family, saw her uncle's eye gouged out by one of the bride-groom's kinsmen, she had seized a torch from the wall and hit her bridegroom over the head with it, so that his hair caught fire. One of the bridesmaids, with great presence of mind, had forced her petticoat over his head and twisted it tight, thereby saving his life, though he screamed fearfully and his head, when it appeared again, was burned black and raw. Meanwhile the fire had caught the straw on the floor, and eleven drunken or wounded men lying in it had been burned to death; so that this wedding was generally agreed to have been one of the best they had had for years in Finnveden, and one that would be long remembered. The bride and bridegroom were now living together in blissful happiness, though he had not been able to grow new hair to replace that which he had lost in the fire.

When this story was finished, King Harald said that it was good to hear of such merry goings-on among the Smalanders, for they were in general a sour and treacherous people; and, he went on, Bishop Poppo ought to thank God every time he said his prayers that he had been sent to Denmark, where men knew how to behave themselves, when he might have fallen instead among the robber folk of Finnveden or Värend.

"But tomorrow," he concluded, "let us hear about the country of the Andalusians, and the strange adventures that befell Orm the son of Toste and Toke the son of Gray Gull on their voyage; for this, I think, will amuse us all."

So that evening ended.

The next morning Orm and Toke debated which of them should tell the story of their travels.

"You are our chieftain," said Toke, "so you must also be our historian."

"You were on the expedition before I joined it," said Orm. "Besides which, you have a readier gift for words than I. Anyway, it is time you had a chance to talk your fill, for I seem to have noticed during these last evenings that once or twice you have found difficulty in listening in silence to all these stories that we have had to hear."

"It is not the speaking that worries me," said Toke, "for I think I have as ready a tongue as most men. The thing that troubles me is that I cannot tell a story unless I am well supplied with ale, for my throat becomes dry easily, and our story is not one that can be told in a few sentences. I have managed to control myself for four evenings, on each of which I have quitted the King's table soberly and peacefully. None the less, it has not been easy for me, though I have had little occasion for talking. It would be a pity if I were to lapse into one of my melancholy moods and gain the reputation of being an ill-conducted man, and one unworthy to eat at the tables of kings."

"Well," said Orm, "we must hope for the best. Even if you should become tipsy during your narration, I do not think that such fine ale as King Harald provides will be likely to make you violent or quarrelsome."

"It shall be as it shall be," said Toke, and shook his head doubtfully.

So that evening Toke told the story of Krok's expedition and of all that had befallen them on their travels; how Orm had come to join them, how they had discovered the Jew in the sea, and how they had plundered the fortress in Ramiro's kingdom; of the sea battle they fought against the Andalusians, and how they had become galley slaves; and he told them how Krok had died. Then he described how they had been freed from their slavery, and the services that the Jew had performed for them, and how they had received their swords from Subaida.

When he reached this point in his story, both King Harald and Styrbjörn expressed their wish to see these swords; so Orm and Toke passed Blue-Tongue and Red-Jowl up the table. King Harald and Styrbjörn drew them from their scabbards and weighed them in their hands, studying them carefully; and both agreed that they had never in their lives seen finer swords than these. Then the swords were passed round the whole table, for many of the guests were curious to examine such fine weapons, and Orm fidgeted nervously until he had Blue-Tongue back at his waist again, for he felt half naked without her cheek against his thigh.

Almost opposite Orm and Toke there sat two of Sven's followers named Sigtrygg and Dyre, who were brothers. Sigtrygg belonged to King Sven's own ship. He was a huge, coarse-framed man, with a broad and extraordinarily bushy beard, which reached right up to his eyebrows. Dyre was younger, but he, too, was rated one of King Sven's boldest warriors. Orm had noticed that Sigtrygg had, for some time during Toke's account of their adventures, been throwing dark glances in their direction and had once or twice appeared to be about to interrupt with some remark. When the swords reached him in the course of their passage round the table, he examined them closely and nodded to himself and seemed reluctant to pass them back.

King Sven, who liked to hear about distant lands, now exhorted Toke to proceed with his story. Toke, who had been utilizing the interval well, replied that he would be glad to continue as soon as the men opposite him had finished looking at his sword and that of Orm. At this, Sigtrygg and Dyre returned the swords, without saying anything, and Toke took up his tale again.

He told them of Almansur and of his might and wealth, and how they had entered his service as members of his Imperial body-guard and had had to worship the Prophet, bowing toward the east each evening and renouncing many of the good things of life; and he told of the wars in which they had partaken, and of the booty they had won. When he came to the story of their march through the Empty Land toward St. James' burial place and described to them how Orm had saved Almansur's life and how Almansur had given him the great gold chain as a token of grati-tude, King Harald said: "If you still have that chain, Orm, I should be interested to see it; for if it is as surpassing an example of the goldsmith's art as your sword is of the smith's, it must in-deed be a marvel to look upon."

"I have it still, King Harald," replied Orm, "I intend to keep it always; and I have always thought it wise to show it to other men as little as possible, for it is of such beauty as to awaken the covet-ousness of any man who is not a king or the wealthiest of lords. It would be churlish of me to refuse to show it to you, O King, and to King Styrbjörn and King Sven and the jarls; but I beg that it shall not be passed round for the other guests to see."

Then he opened his tunic and drew out the chain, which he

wore around his neck, and handed it to Sigurd Buesson. Sigurd
passed it to Hallbjörn, the groom of the bedchamber, who sat on
his right, and Hallbjörn passed it across Bishop Poppo's place to
King Harald; for the Bishop's place now stood empty, he having
had his fill of the Yuletide drinking and being now confined to
his bed, where Brother Willibald was tending him.

King Harald measured the chain, and held it against the light,
that he might the better examine its beauty. Then he announced
that he had spent his whole life collecting jewels and precious ornaments, but that he could not remember ever having seen a finer
work of art than this. The chain consisted of thick lozenges of
pure gold, each lozenge being long and narrow, a good thumb in
length and the breadth of a thumbnail at its middle point, where
it was widest, and from which it tapered inwards toward its ends;
and each lozenge was joined to its fellow by a small gold ring. The
chain comprised thirty-six such lozenges; every first lozenge had a
precious red stone set in its center, and every second, a green.

When Styrbjörn held it in his hand, he said that this was worthy to have come from Weland's smithy; he added, however, that
there might be articles of equal beauty in his uncle's coffers. When
it reached King Sven, he observed that it was the sort of prize for
which warriors gladly gave their blood, and the daughters of kings
their maidenheads.

Then Thorkel the Tall examined the chain, and after he had
praised it as the others had done, he leaned down the table to
hand it back to Orm. As he did so, Sigtrygg thrust out his hand to
take it; but Orm was quicker, and his hand reached it first.

"Who are you to snatch at it?" he said to Sigtrygg. "I have not
heard that you are a king or a jarl, and I do not want it to be
handled by any but them."

"I wish to fight with you for this ornament," said Sigtrygg.

"I can believe that," replied Orm, "for you are plainly a covet-
ous and unmannerly churl. My advice to you is to keep your fingers to yourself and not to meddle with people who know how to
behave themselves."

"You are afraid to fight with me," thundered Sigtrygg. "But
fight you shall, or else surrender your chain to me; for you have
long stood in debt to me, and I demand this chain in payment."

"You have a weak head for ale, and it makes you talk foolishly," said Orm, "for I never saw you in my life before this feast began, so that I cannot possibly be in your debt. The best thing you can do," he added sharply, "is to sit still and hold your tongue, before I beg King Harald's leave to tweak your nose where you sit. I am a man of peace, and loath to dirty my fingers on such a snout as yours; but even the most patient of men would feel an urge to teach you manners."

Now, Sigtrygg was a renowned warrior, feared by all for his strength and ferocity, and by no means accustomed to being addressed in such a manner as this. He leaped up from his bench bellowing like a bull and pouring out a flood of abuse; but louder still rang King Harald's voice through the hall as he called furiously for silence and demanded to know the cause of this disturbance.

"Your good ale, O King," said Orm, "together with this man's greed for gold, have combined to drive his wits out of him; for he screams that he will have my chain and claims that I stand in his debt, though I have never before set eyes on him."

King Harald said angrily that Sven's men were always making trouble, and he demanded sternly of Sigtrygg what had driven him to take leave of his senses and lose control of himself, when he had heard it plainly proclaimed that both the peace of Christ and the peace of King Harald were to be respected in this hall.

"Royal King," said Sigtrygg, "let me explain how this whole matter stands, and you will see that my claim is just. Seven years ago I suffered a cruel wrong, and now, here at your feast, I have heard that these two men were among the perpetrators of it. That summer we were sailing home from the southern lands in four ships, Bork of Hven, Silverpalle, Fare-Wide Svensson, and myself, when we met three ships sailing southwards. We held converse with them, and from this man Toke's story I now know whose ships they were. Now, on my ship there served a Spanish slave, a dark-haired, yellow-skinned man. While we were speaking with the strangers, this man jumped overboard, dragging with him my brother-in-law Oskel, a good man; and nothing more was seen of either of them. But now we have all heard that this slave was taken up on board their ship, and that he was this man whom they call Solomon; and that he served them well indeed. These two men who sit here, Orm and Toke, were the men who pulled him out of the water; we have heard as much from their own lips. For such a slave I could have got a fine price. This man Orm is now the chieftain of such as survive from Krok's company, and it is no more than justice that he should repay me for the loss I thereby incurred. I therefore demand of you, Orm, that you surrender me this chain in payment for the loss of my slave and my brother-in-law, peacefully and of your own free will; failing which, that you meet me in single combat outside this hall, on trodden earth, with shield and sword, now and without delay. Whether or not you give me the chain, I shall in any case kill you; for you have said that you wish to tweak my nose—and to me, Sigtrygg, the son of Stigand, and kinsman of King Sven, no man has ever addressed impertinences and lived to see the end of the day on which he uttered them."

"Two things only have kept my temper cool as I listened to your words," replied Orm. "The first is that the chain is mine and shall remain so, whoever may or may not have jumped from your ship into the sea seven years ago. And the second is that Blue-Tongue and I shall have a say in the matter of which of us two shall live to see tomorrow's sunrise. But first let us hear King Harald's pleasure regarding this affair."

Everyone in the hall was happy to see that there was a good prospect of an armed combat; for a fight between two such men as Orm and Sigtrygg was sure to be worth the watching. Both King Sven and Styrbjörn expressed their opinion that this would add pleasant variety to the Yuletide drinking; but King Harald sat pondering the matter deeply, stroking his beard and wearing an expression of perplexed uncertainty.

At length he said: "This is a difficult case on which to pronounce judgment. I think it doubtful whether Sigtrygg can fairly claim compensation from Orm for a loss that he sustained through no fault of Orm's. On the other hand, it cannot be denied that no man may reasonably be expected to lose a good slave, to say nothing of a brother-in-law, without expecting to receive some compensation for his loss. In any case, now that insults have been exchanged, they are bound to fight it out as soon as they are out of my sight; and such a chain as Orm wears must surely have been the cause of many combats in the past, and will certainly be the cause of many more in the years to come. In the circumstances, therefore, I see no reason why they should not be permitted to settle it here, in armed combat, where we can all enjoy watching them. Therefore, Hallbjörn, see to it that a combat ring be trodden out and roped off here, outside our hall, where the ground is most even, and see to it also that it be well lit with flares and torches; and tell us as soon as it is ready."

"King Harald," said Orm, and his voice sounded strangely unhappy, "I am not willing to be a party to such a contest."

They all stared at him in amazement, and Sigtrygg and a number of King Sven's followers burst out laughing.

King Harald shook his head sadly and said: "If you are afraid to fight, then there is no alternative but that you surrender your chain to him and hope that it may divert his wrath. To my ears, your voice had a bolder tone in it than this a few minutes ago."

"It is not the fighting that worries me," said Orm, "but the cold. I have always been a man of delicate health, and cold is the thing that I can least endure. Nothing is more dangerous for my health than to go out from a hot room, after heavy drinking, into the cold night air, especially now that I have spent so many years in southern climes and am unaccustomed to the northern winter. I do not see why, to please this Sigtrygg, I should have to endure being racked with coughs for the rest of the winter; for coughs and colds tend to hang about me, and my mother always used to say that they would be the death of me if I did not take good care of myself. Therefore, O King, I humbly propose that the fight take place here, in the hall, before your table, where there is plenty of space, and where you yourself will be able to enjoy the spectacle in comfort."

Many of those present laughed at Orm's anxiety; but Sigtrygg did not join in their mirth, bellowing furiously that he would soon settle any fears Orm might cherish concerning his health. Orm, however, paid no attention to him, but remained quietly seated with his face turned toward King Harald, awaiting his decision.

At last King Harald said: "I am sorry to see that young men are growing soft nowadays. They are not what they used to be. The sons of Ragnar Hairy-Breeks never bothered about such trivial considerations as their health or the weather; nor, indeed, did I myself, in my younger days. Really, I do not know of any young man today who is of the old mettle, apart from Styrbjörn. I con-

fess, however, that, now that I am old, it would be a convenience
for me to be able to watch the fight without having to move from
my present chair. It is lucky that the Bishop is ill in bed, for he
would never permit this to take place; still, I do not see that the
peace that we have come here to celebrate can be said to be broken by anything to which I give my assent; nor do I think that
Christ could have any objection to a contest of skill, provided
it be conducted with due propriety and the correct formalities.
Therefore let Orm and Sigtrygg fight here in the cleared hall before my table, with sword and shield, helmet and chain shirt; and
let no man assist them, except with the putting on of their armor.
If one of them be killed, the matter is decided; but if either of
them be no longer able to stand upright, or throw down his sword,
or seek shelter beneath the tables, his adversary shall not continue
to strike at him, for he shall then be deemed to have lost the fight
and the chain with it. And I and Styrbjörn and Hallbjörn my
groom shall see that the contest is fairly fought."

The men hastened to fetch armor for Orm and Sigtrygg, and
the noise in the hall was very great as the rival merits of the cham-
pions were extolled and challenged. King Harald's men deemed
Orm the better fighter of the two, but King Sven's men were loud
in Sigtrygg's praise and said that he had slain nine men in single
combat without sustaining a single wound serious enough to require bandaging. Among those who talked loudest was Dyre. He
asked Orm whether he was not afraid that the cold of the grave
might make him cough; then he turned to his brother and bade
him be content to have Orm's chain for his share of the compensation and allow him, Dyre, to have Orm's sword.

All this while, since they had first interrupted his story, Toke
had been sitting in heavy silence mumbling to himself and drinking; but when he heard Dyre's words, life seemed to return into
his brain. He plunged his eating-knife into the table in front of
Dyre's place, so that it stood quivering in the wood, and tossed his
sword, still in its sheath, beside the knife; then he leaned forward
across the table, so quickly that Dyre had no time to draw away,
seized him by the ears and the beard on his cheeks, and forced his
face downwards toward the weapons, saying: "Here you see weapons as good as Orm's; but if you wish to have them, you must win
them yourself and not beg them from another."

Dyre was a strong man, and he took hold of Toke's wrists and tried to dislodge his grip, but only succeeded in intensifying the pressure on his ears and beard, so that he groaned and grunted but could not free himself.

"I am holding you here in amicable converse," said Toke, "because I have no wish to disturb the King's peace in this hall. But you shall not go free till you have promised to fight with me, for Red-Jowl likes not to hide her beauty from men's eyes when her sister dances naked."

"Let me go," snarled Dyre, his mouth pressing against the table, "that I may waste no time in closing your mouth."

"That is a promise," said Toke, and as he spoke he released his grip and blew from between his fingers the wisps of beard that he had dragged from their roots.

The whole of Dyre's face, apart from his ears, which were scarlet, was white with fury, and at first he seemed to have lost the power of speech. He rose slowly to his feet and said: "This matter shall be settled without delay; and your suggestion is a good one, for by this means my brother and I shall have a Spanish sword apiece. Let us go out and piss together, nor forget to bring our swords with us."

"That was well spoken," said Toke. "You and I can dispense with the formalities of kings. For your acceptance of my suggestion, I shall remain in your debt as long as you live; how long that may be, we shall shortly know."

Then they descended the length of the King's table, each on his opposite side, and strode shoulder to shoulder down the aisle between the long tables that faced each other across the hall, and out through one of the doors in the short wall at the bottom. King Sven saw them go and smiled, for it pleased him to see his men behave arrogantly, because this increased his fame and the fear in which his name was held.

Meanwhile Orm and Sigtrygg had begun to arm themselves for combat, and the part of the floor where they were to fight had been swept, so that they should not slip on the straw or stumble over the bones that had been thrown there for King Harald's dogs to gnaw. The men who had been eating at the top and bottom of the hall now crowded forward to get a better view, squeezing into spaces on the benches and the long tables on both sides of the cleared square, as well as behind King Harald's table and along the wall on the remaining side. King Harald was in high good humor and could scarcely wait for the fight to begin; and when, on turning his head, he noticed two of his women peeping eagerly in at one of the doors, he issued a command that all his women and daughters should come and watch the sport; for it would be a hard thing, he said, if they should be denied the pleasure of witnessing such a spectacle. He made room for some of them on his own royal bench, by his side and on his knees, and for others in the Bishop's empty seat; the two most beautiful of his daughters, however, managed to find a space on either side of Styrbjörn and found nothing to complain of in the tightness of the crush that pressed them against him; they giggled coyly when he offered them ale, and drank it with a bold air. For those women who could not find room on the royal bench, another bench was placed behind the table in such a position that the King and his companions did not impede their view.

Hallbjörn the groom then commanded a fanfare to be blown, and called for silence. He proclaimed that everyone should keep absolutely still while the fight was in progress, and that no man might shout advice to the contestants, or throw anything into the arena. Both the contestants were now ready, and they entered the arena and stood facing each other. When it was seen that Orm held his sword in his left hand, an excited hubbub of discussion broke out, for a fight between one right-handed and one left-handed man provided difficulties for both of them, since it meant that the blows fell on their sword-arm sides, to which their shield offered less protection.

It was plain that neither of them was the sort of adversary that a man would choose to find himself pitted against; nor did either man appear to cherish any anxiety regarding the outcome of the contest. Orm was half a head taller than Sigtrygg and had the longer reach, but Sigtrygg was more squarely built and looked rather the more powerful man of the two. They held their shields well forward across their breasts and high enough to be able to cover their necks promptly, should the necessity arise; and each kept his eyes fixed on his opponent's sword, so as to be able to anticipate the other's blows. As soon as they came within striking distance of one another, Orm aimed a slash at Sigtrygg's legs, but

Sigtrygg evaded the blow nimbly and replied with a vicious swing that landed with a ringing crash on Orm's helmet. After this opening, both men proceeded more cautiously, parrying each other's blows skillfully with their shields, and King Harald was heard to observe to his women that it was good to see experienced swordsmen such as these at work, instead of the sort who rushed crazily into the fight leaving themselves open; for this meant that the spectacle would last longer.

"It is no easy thing to forecast which of these two is likely to prove the master," he said. "But the red man looks to me to be as safe a swordsman as I have seen for many a month, for all his fear of the cold; and I shall not be surprised if Sven is one kinsman the poorer tonight."

King Sven, who, like both the jarls, was sitting on the edge of the table to get a better view of the fight, smiled contemptuously and retorted that nobody who knew Sigtrygg need have any fears regarding the outcome. "Although my men are not averse to the sport of armed combat," he said, "it is seldom that I lose one of them, except when they fight against one another."

As he spoke, Toke re-entered the hall. He was limping badly and could be heard muttering a verse to himself; and as he climbed over the bench to his place, it could be seen that one of his legs was black with blood from his thigh to his knee.

"How went it with Dyre?" asked Sigurd Buesson.

"It took time," replied Toke; "but he finished pissing at last."

Everybody's eyes were now on the fight, which Sigtrygg seemed eager to bring to a quick conclusion. He was attacking Orm savagely, trying to pierce his defense and concentrating on his legs and face and the fingers of his sword-hand. Orm was defending himself ably, but did not appear to be able to achieve anything very positive himself; and it could be seen that he was having trouble with Sigtrygg's shield. This was larger than his own and was of tough wood, strengthened with leather; only the center boss was of iron, and Orm had to take care that his sword should not become embedded in the edge of the shield, for if that were to happen, it would give Sigtrygg the chance to snap it or wrench it from his grasp by a twist of his arm. Orm's shield was made entirely of iron, with a sharp spike in its center.

Sigtrygg sneeringly asked Orm whether it was warm enough for him. Blood was pouring down Orm's cheek from the first blow on his helmet, and he had besides received a thrust in the leg and a slash across the hand, while Sigtrygg was still unmarked. Orm made no reply, but retreated step by step alongside one of the long tables. Crouching behind his shield, Sigtrygg moved swiftly in to the attack, padding forwards and occasionally leaping to one or the other side, while his blows rained ever the more fiercely, so that it seemed to most of the spectators that the end could not now be far distant.

Then Orm suddenly sprang at his opponent and, taking Sigtrygg's blow on his sword, drove his shield against Sigtrygg's with all his strength, so that the spike on his own shield pierced through the leather and into the wood and remained embedded there. He forced the shields downwards so hard that the handles of both of them snapped, whereupon the two men both took a step backwards, freed their swords, and, leaping high into the air, slashed at each other in the same instant. Sigtrygg's blow struck Orm in the side, piercing his chain shirt and causing a deep wound; but Orm's sword buried itself in Sigtrygg's throat, and a great shout filled the hall as the bearded head flew from its shoulders, bounced on the edge of the table, and fell with a splash into the butt of ale that stood at its foot.

Orm staggered, and supported himself against the table. He wiped his sword across his knee, replaced it in its sheath, and gazed down at the headless body lying at his feet.

"Now you know," he said, "whose chain it is."

CHAPTER TEN

HOW ORM LOST HIS NECKLACE

THE FIGHT for the necklace was busily discussed throughout the palace—in the hall, the kitchens, and the women's chambers. All those who had witnessed it were careful to store away in their memories everything that had been said and done, so as to have a good story to tell other men in the years to come. Orm's feat in pinning his opponent's shield was particularly praised, and on the next evening Styrbjörn's Icelander recited some verses in *ljodahattr* on the danger of losing one's head in ale. It was generally agreed that such sport as this was not to be enjoyed every Yule, even at King Harald's court.

Orm and Toke, however, were confined to bed on account of their wounds and could take little pleasure in anything during the next few days, though Brother Willibald used his most soothing salves upon their injured places. Toke's wound began to fester, making him delirious and violent, so that four men were needed to hold him down while Brother Willibald dressed it; and Orm, who had had two of his ribs broken and had lost a quantity of blood, was feeling very sore and enfeebled, and lacked his usual appetite. This last he took to be an evil symptom, and one that boded ill for his recovery; and he became very downhearted.

King Harald had ordered one of his best bedchambers to be prepared for them, with a walled fireplace to warm it, and hay instead of straw in the mattresses. Many of the King's men, and Styrbjörn's also, came to see them on the day after the combat, to discuss the previous evening's happenings and chuckle over King Sven's discomfiture. They made the room very crowded and noisy, and Brother Willibald had to rebuke them and finally drive them out; so that Orm and Toke were not sure whether it was more dispiriting to have company or to be left to their solitude. Shortly after this they lost the comradeship of their own men, who were all anxious to return home now that the Christmas feasting was over; all, that is, save One-Eyed Rapp, who was an outlaw in the Lister country and so preferred to remain at Jellinge. After a few days, a storm having blown up and dispersed the ice, King Sven put sullenly out to sea with few words of farewell. Styrbjörn, too, took his leave of King Harald, being anxious to lose no time in recruiting men for his spring expedition; and Orm's men obtained permission to sail part of the way with them, paying for their passage by taking their turn at the oars. Styrbjörn would have liked Orm and Toke to join his company. He came in person to visit them in their chamber and said that they had made a good contribution to the Yule festivities and that it would be a pity if they were now to spend a week in bed for the sake of a few scratches.

"Visit me on Bornholm when the cranes begin to stretch their wings," he said. "I have room for men of your mettle on the prow of my own ship."

He left them without waiting for their reply, his head being full of urgent matters; so that this was all the converse they had with Styrbjörn. They lay for a time in silence; then Toke said:

> "Welcome the day when
> From the ship's deck I shall see
> Crane and stork and goose
> Steer their course to the north."

But Orm, after reflecting for a while, replied sadly:

> "Speak not of cranes; ere then
> They will have buried me
> Where mole and curious mouse
> Coldly shall brush my mouth."

When most of the guests had departed and there was less confusion in the kitchens, Brother Willibald ordered meat broth to be prepared for both the wounded Vikings twice a day, to fortify them. Several of the King's women thereupon volunteered to carry it from the kitchens to the bedchamber, being curious to see the men at close quarters. This they were able to do without hindrance, for, now that the feasting was concluded, King Harald had taken to his bed, and both Brother Willibald and Brother Matthias, to say nothing of the Bishop, were fully occupied in praying over him and giving him purges to cleanse his blood and his bowels.

The first woman to put her head into their room was the young Moorish girl with whom they had spoken on the first occasion on which they had entered King Harald's presence with the bell. Toke gave a shout of delight on recognizing her and straightway bade her approach nearer. She sidled shyly in, carrying a can and spoon, seated herself on the edge of his bed, and began to feed him. Another girl entered behind her, seated herself beside Orm, and started to feed him likewise. She was young and tall, well made and pale-skinned, with gray eyes and a large and beautiful mouth; she had, besides, dark hair, with an amber hoop around it. Orm had not seen her before, but she did not appear to be one of the servants.

Orm, however, found difficulty in swallowing the broth, for his wound prevented him from sitting up. After a few mouthfuls he got some of the meat into his windpipe and began to cough violently. This made his wound ache and clouded his humor, causing him to groan with the pain. The corners of the girl's mouth rose in a smile as he glowered sourly at her.

When the fit had passed, he said sullenly: "I have not been put here to be laughed at. Who are you, anyway?"

"My name is Ylva," she replied, "and I did not know until this minute that you were the sort of man who could make anyone laugh. How can you, who slew my brother Sven's best warrior, whimper at a spoonful of hot broth?"

"It is not the broth that troubles me," said Orm. "A wound like mine is liable to be painful sometimes. I should have thought even a woman might have guessed that. But if you are King Sven's sister, it may be that the broth you have brought me is bad; indeed, now I think of it, it has an unpleasant flavor. Have you come to avenge the injury I did to your brother?"

The girl sprang to her feet and flung the can and spoon into the fireplace, so that the broth spattered all over the room. Her eyes blazed fiercely at Orm; then, suddenly, she calmed herself and laughed and sat down again on the edge of the bed.

"You are not afraid to show when you are afraid," she said. "That much, at least, must be said in your favor; though which of us is behaving the more sensibly is a question to which two answers might be given. But I saw you fight Sigtrygg, and it was a good combat; and be sure of this, that I regard no man as my enemy merely because he has injured my brother Sven. It was high time somebody taught this Sigtrygg a lesson. His breath stank loathsomely, and there was talk between him and Sven of his having me to wife. Had this happened, he would not have enjoyed many nights of wedlock, for I am not to be pleasured by any chance berserk whose fancy I may happen to tickle. So at least I owe you some thanks for saving me from that extremity."

"You are an impudent and brazen wench," said Orm, "and, I doubt not, a wildcat to boot; but it is always thus with the daughters of kings. I cannot deny, however, that you seem to be too good for such a man as this Sigtrygg was. But I myself have come out of this contest sorely scathed, and I do not know what the end of it will be for me."

Ylva squeezed the tip of her tongue between her teeth and nodded and looked thoughtful.

"There may be others besides you and Sigtrygg and Sven who
have sustained loss and injury through this contest," she said. "I
have heard about this necklace of yours which Sigtrygg coveted.
They say you got it from a southern king, and that it is the finest
jewel that was ever seen. I desire to see it, and you need not fear
that I shall try to steal it from you, though if Sigtrygg had killed
you it might have become my own."

"It is an unlucky thing to possess an object that all men desire
to finger," said Orm sadly.

"If that is the way you feel," said Ylva, "why did you not let
Sigtrygg have it? You would then have been freed from the cares
it brings you."

"Of one thing I am certain, though I have known you for but
a short while," said Orm: "that whatsoever man weds you, there
will be long intervals between those occasions on which he will
enjoy the last word."

"I hardly think you are ever likely to be in a position to prove
the truth of that remark," said Ylva. "The way you look now, I
would not lie in the same bed with you if you were to offer me five
necklaces. Why have you not got someone to wash your hair and
beard? You look worse than a Smalander. But tell me straightway
whether you will show me the necklace or no."

"That is a fine way to speak to a sick man," said Orm, "to liken
him to a Smalander. I would have you know that I am of noble
blood on both my father's and my mother's side. My mother's
grandmother's half-brother was Sven Rat-Nose of Göinge, and he,
as you may know, was directly descended through his mother from
Ivar of the Broad Embrace. It is only because I am sick that I tolerate your impertinences; otherwise I would already have shooed
you out of the room. I will confess, however, that I should like
to be washed, though I am not really well enough to be touched;
and if you are willing to do me that service, I shall have the chance
to see whether you can be more skillful at some things than you
are at serving soup. Though, it may be that the daughters of kings
are not competent to perform such useful duties."

"You are proposing that I act as your slave-girl," said Ylva,
"which no man has dared to suggest to me before. It is lucky for

you that the blood of Broad-Hug runs in your veins. But I confess it would amuse me to see how you look after you have been washed, so I shall come early tomorrow morning, and you will then see that I can perform such tasks as well as anybody."

"I must be combed, too," said Orm. "Then, when you have done all this to my satisfaction, I may, perhaps, show you the necklace."

Meanwhile things were becoming somewhat noisy in Toke's half of the room. The broth and the sight of a woman had considerably raised his spirits. He had managed to pull himself up into a sitting position, and they were endeavoring to converse in her language. This he was able to do but lamely; but he was all the more nimble in the use of his hands, with which he was trying to draw her closer to him. She defended herself against his advances, striking him on the knuckles with her spoon, but made no great effort to move out of distance and seemed not altogether displeased, while Toke praised her beauty as well as he was able and cursed his game leg that kept him sedentary.

Orm and Ylva turned to watch them as their sport became noisier. Ylva smiled at their antics, but Orm shouted crossly to Toke to behave himself and leave the girl alone.

"What do you suppose King Harald will have to say," he said, "if he hears that you have been fondling one of his women above her knees?"

"Perhaps he will remark, as you did," said Ylva, "that it is an unlucky thing to own something that all men wish to finger. But he will hear nothing about it from my lips, for he has more than enough women for a man of his years; and she, unhappy girl, finds little joy among us here, and weeps often and is hard to comfort, since she understands little of what we say to her. So do not let it worry you that she sports with a man whose compliments she can understand, and who seems, besides, to be a bold fellow."

Orm, however, insisted that Toke must control his inclinations while they were enjoying King Harald's hospitality.

Toke, in the meantime, had become somewhat calmer and was now only holding the girl by one of her plaits. He assured Orm that there was no cause for alarm.

"For nobody can accuse me of anything," he said, "while my leg is in its present state; besides which, you heard with your own ears the little priest say that King Harald expressly ordered everything possible to be done to make us comfortable, because of the snub we served King Sven. Now, as everybody knows, I am a man to whose comfort women are an essential factor; and this woman seems to me to be an admirable specimen of her kind. I cannot think of anything that could be more likely to hasten my recovery; indeed, I am beginning to feel better already. I have told her to come here as often as she can, for my health's sake; and I do not think she is afraid of me, though I have been flirting somewhat boldly with her."

Orm grunted doubtfully; but the end of it was that both the women agreed to come the next morning and wash their heads and beards. Then Brother Willibald arrived in a flurry to dress their wounds, and when he saw the spilt broth, he shrieked with fury and drove the women from the room. Not even Ylva dared to gainsay him, for everyone was afraid of the man who wielded power over their life and health.

When Orm and Toke were left alone, they lay on their beds in silence, having much to occupy their thoughts. At length Toke said: "Our luck has turned good again, now that women have managed to find their way to us. Things are beginning to look more cheerful."

But Orm said: "We shall have bad luck on our hands if you cannot curb your itches; and I should be easier in my mind if I were sure that you could."

Toke replied that he had good hopes of his ability to do this, if he really tried in earnest. "Though I doubt whether she would be anxious to spurn my advances," he said, "if I were fit and able to press them; for an old king cannot be much company for a girl of her spirit, and she has been kept under strict surveillance ever since she first came here. She is called Mirah, and comes from a place called Ronda, and is of good family. She was captured by Vikings who came in the night and bore her away with many others of her village and sold her to the King of Cork. He, in turn, gave her to King Harald as a friendship-gift, because of her great beauty; but she says that she would have appreciated the honor more if he had given her to someone younger with whom she could talk. I have seldom seen such a fine girl, so beautifully formed and smooth-skinned; though the girl who sat on your bed is also fine, if perhaps a trifle skinny and less full of figure than she might be. And she seems to be well disposed toward you. Even in such a place as this, our quality is apparent, for we win the favor of women even from our sickbeds."

But Orm replied that he had no room in his thoughts for woman-love, for he felt more sick and enfeebled than ever and doubted whether he had much time left.

The next morning, as soon as it was light, the women came to them as they had promised, bringing warm lye, water, and hand-cloths, and washed Orm's and Toke's heads and beards meticulously. Ylva had some difficulty in attending to Orm, because he was unable to sit up, but she supported his body with her arm and used him carefully, and emerged from her task with credit, for he got no lye in his eyes or mouth and yet became clean and fine. Then she seated herself on the head of his bed, put his head between her knees, and began to comb him. She asked him if he was uncomfortable, but Orm had to admit that he was not. She found difficulty in passing the comb through his hair, for it was thick and coarse, and very tangled as a result of the washing; but she persevered patiently with the task, so that he thought he had never in his life been better combed. She spoke familiarly to him, as though they had been friends for a long time; and Orm felt well content to have her near him.

"You will have your heads washed again before you get up," she said, "for the Bishop and his men like to baptize people when they are lying sick on their backs, and I am surprised they have not already spoken to you about it. They baptized my father when he was sorely ill and had small hope of recovery. Most people regard a sickbed as the best place to be baptized in during the winter, for if a man is ill the priests merely sprinkle his head, whereas if he is well he has to be completely immersed in the sea, which few men fancy when the water is still sharp with ice. It is unpleasant for the priests, too, for they have to stand in the water up to their knees, and become blue in the face, and their teeth chatter so that they can scarcely speak the blessings. For this reason, they prefer in winter to baptize men who cannot move from their beds. Myself the Bishop baptized on Midsummer Day, which they call the Day of the Baptist, and that was not unpleasant. We squatted round him in our white shifts, I and my sisters, while he read over us, and then lifted his hand and we held our noses and ducked under the water. I remained below the surface longer than any of the others, so that my baptism was held to be the best. Then we were all given garments that had been blessed, and little crosses to wear about our necks. And no harm came to any of us as a result of this."

Orm replied that he knew all about such strange customs, having dwelt in the southland, where nobody was permitted to eat pork, and with the monks of Ireland, who had tried to persuade him to allow himself to be baptized.

"But it will take a long time," he said, "before anyone convinces me that the observances of such customs can do a man good or can seriously gratify any god. I should like to see the bishop or priest who could get me to sit in cold water up to my ears, in summer or winter. Nor have I any desire to have water sprinkled over my head, or to be read over; for it is my belief that a man ought to beware of all such forms of sorcery and trollcraft."

Ylva said that several of King Harald's men had complained of the backache after being baptized and had requested the Bishop to give them money for the pain, but that, apart from this, they were apparently none the worse for their experience; indeed, there were many who had now come to regard baptism as being advantageous to a man's health. The priests had no objection to a man's eating pork, as Orm had doubtless observed during the Yuletide feasting, nor did they lay down any regulations regarding diet, save only that when anyone offered them horse-meat they spat and crossed themselves, and had at first occasionally been heard to mutter that men ought not to eat meat on Fridays; her father, however, had expressed his unwillingness to hear any more talk on that subject. She herself could not say that she had found the new religion in any way inconvenient. There were some, though, who held that the harvest was smaller and the cows' milk thinner nowadays, and that this was because people had begun to neglect the old gods.

She drew her comb slowly through a tuft of Orm's hair which she had just untangled, and held it up against the daylight to examine it closely.

"I do not understand how this can be," she said, "but there does not appear to be a single louse in your hair."

"That is not possible," said Orm. "It must be a bad comb."

She said that it was a good louse-comb, and scraped his head so that his scalp burned, but still she could find no louse.

"If what you say is true, then I am sick indeed," said Orm, "and things are even worse than I had feared. This can only mean that my blood is poisoned."

Ylva ventured the opinion that things might perhaps not be quite so bad as he feared, but Orm was much depressed by her discovery. He lay in silence while she finished her combing, acknowledging her further remarks with dispirited grunts. Meanwhile, however, Toke and Mirah had all the more to say to each other and appeared to be finding each other more and more congenial.

At last Orm's hair and beard were combed ready, and Ylva regarded the results of her work with satisfaction.

"Now you look less like a scarecrow," she said, "and more like a chieftain. Few women would run from the sight of you now, and you can thank me for that."

She picked up his shield, rubbed it with her sleeve in the part where it was least scarred, and held it in front of his face. Orm regarded himself in it and nodded.

"You have combed me well," he admitted, "better than I thought a king's daughter could. It may be that you are somewhat above the run of them. You have earned a glimpse of my necklace."

So saying, he loosened the neck of his shirt, drew forth the chain, and handed it to her. Ylva uttered a little cry as her hands closed on it. She weighed it in her fingers and admired its beauty; and Mirah left Toke and ran to look at it, and she, too, murmured aloud with wonder. Orm said to Ylva: "Hang it round your neck," and she did as he bade her. The necklace was long and hung down over the breast-rings of her undergarment. She hastily set the shield on the wall-seat to see how the necklace looked against her throat.

"It is long enough to go twice round my neck," she said, and was unable to take her eyes or her fingers from it. "How should it be worn?"

"Almansur kept it in a chest," said Orm, "where no one ever set eyes on it. Since it became mine, I have worn it beneath my shirt until it chafed my skin, and never showed it to any man until this Yuletide, when it straightway brought me pain. No one, I think, can say that it has not now found a more suitable resting-place; therefore, Ylva, regard it as your own and wear it as you think most fitting."

She clutched the necklace with both hands, and stared at him with enormous eyes.

"Have you taken leave of your senses?" she cried. "What have I done that you should give me such a princely gift? The noblest queen in the world would lie with a berserk for the sake of a poorer jewel than this."

"You have combed me well," replied Orm, and he smiled at her. "We who are of Broad-Hug's line give good friendship-gifts or none at all."

Mirah, too, wished to try on the necklace, but Toke commanded her to return to him and not to tease her mind with trinkets; and he had already won such power over her that she obeyed him meekly.

Ylva said: "Perhaps I would do best to hide it beneath my clothing, for my sisters and all the women in the palace would claw out my eyes to get it for themselves. But why you have given it to me is beyond my understanding, however much of Broad-Hug's blood may run in your veins."

Orm sighed, and answered: "What shall it profit me when the grass grows over my limbs? I know now that I shall surely die, for you have found that not even a louse will live on my body; though, indeed, I had guessed as much already. Perhaps it might have become yours even if I had not been marked for death; though then I should have required something of you in return for it. You seem to me to be well worthy of such a jewel, and it is my guess that you will prove fully able to defend it if anyone should challenge you to a contest of nails. But, for my part, I would rather live and see it glitter between your breasts."

CHAPTER ELEVEN

CONCERNING THE WRATH OF BROTHER WILLIBALD
AND HOW ORM TRIED HIS HAND AT WOO-
ING

THINGS soon turned out as Ylva had foretold, for a few
days later the Bishop began to hint that the two wounded men
should allow themselves to be baptized; but he had no success
with either of them in this matter. Orm lost his patience almost
at once, and told him sharply that he wished to hear no more
about it, as he had in any case but a short time left to live; and
Toke said that he, for his part, would very soon be fit and well
and so had no need of any spiritual assistance. The Bishop then
set Brother Matthias to strive to win them over by patient methods
and gradual education, and he made several endeavors to teach
them the Creed, ignoring their entreaties to be left in peace. Then
Toke had a good spear, slim-bladed and keen-edged, brought to
him, and the next time Brother Matthias came to instruct them
he found Toke sitting up in bed, supported on one elbow, weighing the spear thoughtfully in his free hand.

"It would be an ill thing to break the peace in King Harald's
palace," said Toke, "but I do not think anyone can condemn an
invalid for doing so in self-defense. It would also be a pity to soil
the floor of so fine a chamber as this with the blood of a fat man,
and your veins look full; I have persuaded myself, however, that
if I can nail you cleanly to a wall with this spear, the blood-gush
will be contained within reasonable limits. To do this will not be
a simple task for a bedridden man to perform, but I shall try my
best to execute it competently; and this I swear I shall do the
moment you open your mouth to plague us with your prattle. For,
as we have told you, we do not wish to hear any more of it."

Brother Matthias turned white and raised his hands before him
in fearful supplication. At first he seemed to be about to speak;
then, however, his limbs began to quake and he beat a smart re-

treat from the chamber, slamming the door behind him. After
this they were not disturbed by him any more. But Brother Willibald, who never showed any sign of fear, came at his usual time
to dress their wounds, and rebuked them severely for the fright
they had given Brother Matthias.

"You are a man of mettle," said Toke, "though there is but
little of you; and I confess that I prefer you to other men of your
kidney, though you are rude and peevish. Perhaps it is because
you do not try to badger us into this Christianity, but content
yourself with ministering to our wounds."

Brother Willibald replied that he had been longer than his
fellow priests in this land of darkness and had managed to free
himself from such vain fancies and ambitions.

"When I first came here," he said, "I was as fanatical as any
other member of the blessed Benedict's order in my zeal to baptize
every heathen soul. But now I am wiser and know what is feasible
and what is merely vanity. It is right that the children of this land
should be baptized, together with such women as have not wal-
lowed too deeply in sin, if indeed any such are to be found; but
the grown men of this country are veritable apostles of Satan and
must, in the name of divine justice, burn in hell-fire, however
assiduously one may baptize them; for no redemption can suffice
to wipe away such vileness as their souls are stained with. Of this
I am sure, for I know them well; therefore I do not waste my time
trying to convert such men as you."

His voice became frenzied, and he glared wrathfully from one
to the other, brandishing his arms and crying: "Blood-wolves,
murderers and malefactors, adulterate vermin, Gadarene swine,
weeds of Satan and minions of Beelzebub, generation of vipers
and basilisks, shall you be cleansed by holy baptism and stand as
white as snow in the regiments of the blessed angels? Nay, I tell
you, it shall not be so. I have lived long in this house and have
witnessed too much; I know your ways. No bishop or holy father
shall ever persuade me that such as you can be saved. How should
men of the north be allowed to enter the gates of heaven? You
would scrabble at the blessed virgins with your lewd fingers, you
would raise your war-whoops against the seraphim and archangels,
you would bawl for ale before the throne of God Himself! No, no,
I know what I speak of. Hell alone will serve for such as you,

whether you be baptized or no. Praised be Almighty God, the One, the Eternal, amen!"

He fumbled angrily among his medicines and bandages and bustled across the room to apply salves to Toke's wound.

"Why do you exert yourself to make us well again," said Orm, "if your hatred for us is so great?"

"I do it because I am a Christian and have learned to repay evil with good," he replied, "which is more than you will ever learn to do. Do I not still bear the scar upon my brow where King Harald struck me with the holy crucifix? Yet do I not still daily minister to his contaminated flesh with all the skill that lies at my command? Besides which, it may ultimately be for the best that such fierce fighting-men as you should be kept alive in this land, for you are like to send many of your fellows to hell before you go there yourselves, as you have already done at this Christmas feast. Let wolf rend wolf, that the Lamb of God may dwell in peace."

When he at length left them, Toke said that it looked as though the blow on the head which the little fellow had received when the King had cracked him with the cross had knocked the wits out of him, for most of what he had shouted at them had no sense in it; with which observation Orm agreed. But both of them admitted that he was marvelously cunning in medicine, and very diligent in the care he showed toward them.

Toke was now beginning to be himself again, and before long he was able to limp round the room and even outside it, while Orm lay alone in his bed, finding time heavy on his hands except when Ylva was there to talk to him. When she was at his side, the thought of his impending death troubled him less, for she was always full of merriment and bright talk, so that he found pleasure in listening to her; but he became sullen again as soon as she said that he was looking better and would soon be up and about. In regard to that matter, he said, he thought he knew best what was most likely to happen. Soon, however, he found himself able to sit up in bed without too much pain; and the next time Ylva combed him, she found a louse in his hair that was large and fresh and full of blood. This made him think deeply, and he said that he did not know what conclusion to come to.

"You must not let the matter of the necklace weigh on your mind," said Ylva. "You gave it to me when you thought you were going to die, and the memory of it troubles you now that you see that you are going to live. But I shall gladly give it back to you, though it far surpasses in beauty anything that has ever before been seen in this land. For I do not wish it to be said that I lured your gold from you when you were sick with wounds; which I have already heard muttered more than once."

"Truly, it would be good to keep such a jewel in one's family," said Orm. "But the best solution for me would be to have both you and the jewel; nor will I accept it back on any other condition. But before I ask your father what his feelings are in regard to this, I should like to know whether you yourself are so inclined. For the first time we spoke together you told me that if you had been forced to marry Sigtrygg, you would have driven a knife into him in his bridal bed, and I should like to be sure that you feel differently toward me."

Ylva laughed merrily and said that he should not be too confident about this. "For I am of a stranger temper than you know," she said, "and difficult to satisfy. And the daughters of kings are more troublesome than other women when they marry and leave home. Have you heard what befell Agne, the King of the Swedes, long ago, when he took to wife a king's daughter from a land east of the sea, who was not willing to be his bedfellow? The first night after the marriage, he lay with her in a tent beneath a tree, and when he was sound asleep she fastened a rope to his neck-ring, which was a good, strong ring, and hanged him from the tree, though he was a great king and she had but one slave-girl to help her. So ponder the matter carefully before you seek my hand."

She leaned forward and stroked his forehead and pinched his ears and looked into his eyes, smiling, so that Orm felt better than he had done for many days.

But then she suddenly became solemn and thoughtful and said it was vain to talk of such things before her father had expressed his opinion on the matter; and she thought it would be no easy thing to win his consent unless Orm was better favored than most men as regards property and cattle and gold.

"He complains incessantly that so many of his daughters are unwed," she said, "but he will never admit that any man is sufficiently rich and noble to be worthy of us. It is not such a fine thing as people imagine to be a king's daughter, for many bold youths wink furtively at us and finger the hem of our skirts when no one is watching, but few of them have the courage to carry their suit to our father; and such as do, come crestfallen from the interview. It is a sore pity that he is so intent on getting us worthy husbands, though it is true that a poor man would be no fit mate for me. But you, Orm, who can bestow such a necklace upon me and have the blood of the Broad Embrace in your veins, must doubtless be one of the richest princes in Skania?"

Orm replied that he hoped to be able to prevail upon King Harald into consenting to his suit, for he knew that the King regarded him highly, both because of the bell he had brought him and for the way in which he had vanquished Sigtrygg.

"But I do not know," he continued, "how much wealth awaits me in Skania, for it is now seven years since I left my home, and I cannot tell how it stands with my family. It may be that fewer of them are alive than when I saw them last, and that my inheritance is therefore greater. But in any case I have much gold from the south besides the necklace I have already given you, so that even if I own no more than what I have with me, nobody can call me a poor man. And I can obtain more in the way in which I won this."

Ylva nodded doubtfully and said that this did not sound too promising, her father being a very exacting man. Toke, who had come in while the discussion was afoot, agreed with her and said that this was an occasion when it was necessary to think carefully before deciding what to do.

"It so happens," he added, "that I am able to tell you the best way to win a wealthy woman of noble blood when her father is unwilling but she herself is agreeable. My mother's father was called Nose-Tönne. He used to trade with the Smalanders, and possessed a small house, twelve cows, and a great store of wisdom. One day he was on a business trip to Värend, and there saw a girl called Gyda, who was the daughter of a wealthy lord. He determined to win her, partly for the honor it would bring him and partly because he coveted her fine body and thick red hair. But her father, who was named Glum, was a proud man, and he said that Tönne was not good enough to be his son-in-law, though the girl herself thought otherwise. Gyda and Tönne, therefore, wasted no time in inveighing against the old man's folly, but hastily formed a plan and arranged to meet in the forest while she was nutting there with her maids. The result of this encounter was that she came to be with child, and Tönne had to fight two duels with her brother, the marks of which they both bore till the day they died. In due course she gave birth to twins; whereupon the old man decided that it was no use kicking against the pricks any longer. So they married and lived together in great bliss and contentment, and had seven more children, so that all the people of the district praised my grandfather's wisdom and good luck, and his reputation waxed enormously and became very great, especially when old Glum died and left them a big inheritance. And if my grandfather had not hit upon such a wise method of obtaining the woman of his choice, I should not be sitting here to give you this good advice; for my mother was one of the twins who were begotten under the nut bushes."

"If a marriage can only be brought about by producing twins," said Ylva, "your advice is easier given than followed. And there is a difference between having a farmer from Värend as your father and being daughter to the King of the Danes. I doubt whether such an experiment would turn out as well for us as it did for your grandparents."

Orm thought there was a good deal to be said both for and against Toke's plan, though it was but cold comfort for a man who was sick and unlusty; however, he said, he would make no decision until he was well enough to walk and could sound King Harald's feelings in the matter.

This took some time; but at length he grew better and his wound healed, and his strength began to return to him. The winter was by now almost past. King Harald also had recovered from the effects of Christmas and was in capital spirits, busily supervising the preparation of his warships; for he was making ready to sail to Skanör to collect his herring tax, as well as to dispatch the ships he had promised Styrbjörn at the feast. Orm went to him and explained what was in his mind. King Harald listened to his request amiably, showing no displeasure, but straightway inquired how wealthy Orm was, that he could regard himself as eligible for such a match. Orm furnished him with details of his parentage and ancestry, and enumerated his father's possessions, not omitting to mention all that he himself was bringing home from his travels abroad.

"In addition to all this," he concluded, "there is much land in Göinge which my mother was due to inherit, though I do not know whether it has yet come into her possession. Nor can I say which of my kinsmen are still alive, or how it is with them. For much may have occurred in Skania during these seven years that I have been away."

"The jewel you gave my daughter was a princely gift," said King Harald, "and you have done me several good services, which I have not forgotten. But to marry a daughter of the King of the Danes is the most ambitious match that a man could hope for, and no man has sought the hand of any of my daughters without offering more than all that you possess. Besides which, you have a brother who stands between you and your father's wealth. Now, if he be alive and have sons, how then shall you support my daughter? I am beginning to grow somewhat advanced in years, though a man might not mark it, and I am anxious to see my daughters well married while I am yet alive to make a good match for them. For I do not think that Sven will bother his head about them when I am gone."

Orm was compelled to admit that he had little to offer in return for the hand of such a woman. "But I may well find when I reach home," he said, "that the whole inheritance is mine. My father was already beginning to show his years when I sailed away, and my brother Odd spent all his summers in Ireland and showed little inclination to stay at home. And I have heard that the Vikings in Ireland have fared poorly during the past few years, since King Brian became powerful there."

King Harald nodded, and said that King Brian had caused the death of many Danes in Ireland and of many seafarers who had ventured into his coastal waters; though, in one sense, this had been something of a blessing, since these men included a good many who had been mischief-makers in their own land.

"But this Brian, this King of Munster," he said, "has had his head turned by the surfeit of his successes, so that he is now demanding tribute not only from my good friend King Olof of Cork, but also from my own kinsman, Sigtrygg Silk-Beard of Dublin. Such self-importance sits ill upon the head of an Irish king, and in good time I shall send a fleet to his island to trip his arrogance. It might be a good thing to bring him here and keep him tethered to the door of my hall, not merely to provide sport for my men when they are drinking, but also to teach him a lesson in Christian humility and to provide a warning for other kings. For I have always been of the opinion that the King of the Danes ought to be regarded with veneration by all other monarchs."

"It is my belief, lord," said Orm, "that you are the mightiest of kings. Even among the Andalusians and the blue men [1] there are warriors who know your name and speak of the great deeds that you have done."

"You have chosen your words well," said King Harald, "though previously you showed insufficient humility in begging for the hand of one of my fairest daughters when you were not even certain how you were placed as regards your inheritance and possessions. I shall not condemn you too severely for this, however, since you are young and unreflective. But I shall not immediately accede to your request, nor shall I refuse it. This is my decision. Come to me again in the autumn, when I have returned from my expedition and you are better informed concerning your wealth and expectations; and if I then find them sufficient, you shall have the girl, because of the friendship I bear you. And if not, there will always be a place for you in my bodyguard. Until then you must contain yourself in patience."

When Orm told Ylva how his interview with King Harald had resulted, she flew into a great fury. Tears swelled into her eyes, and she shrieked that she would pluck the old man's beard from his chin to punish him for his closefistedness and obstinacy, and then lose no time in doing as Toke had advised her. But when she had recovered her composure, she thought it wiser, after all, to abandon this plan.

"I am not afraid of his wrath," she said, "not even when he bellows like a bull and flings his ale-cup at me; for I am too quick for him, so that he has never yet managed to hit me, and his fits soon pass. But it is so with him that if anyone gainsays him once his mind is set on a thing, he remembers his grievance darkly and will never cease to seek revenge for it. Therefore I think it best that we should not oppose him in this matter, lest he turn his

---

[1] Negroes.

wrath against us both and give me away to the first rich man who catches his eye, merely to spite me and show which of us is the stronger. But know this, Orm, that I desire no husband but you, and am ready to wait till the autumn for you, though the interval will be long and tedious. If then he still opposes our match, I will wait no longer, but will follow you whithersoever you lead me."

"When I hear you speak like that," said Orm, "I almost begin to feel myself a man again."

CHAPTER TWELVE

HOW ORM CAME HOME FROM HIS LONG VOYAGE

KING HARALD fitted out twenty ships for his expedition. Twelve of these were for Styrbjörn, while with the remainder he intended to assert his authority at Skanör, where a strong force of men was always needed to collect the herring tax. He chose his crews with great care; and every Dane was eager to serve on the ships that were to sail with Styrbjörn, for they knew that much booty might be gained there.

Many men came down to Jellinge to join the fleet; and when King Harald had made his choice, Orm and Toke sought among the ones who were left to find folk whom they might hire to row them home in the ship they had stolen from Almansur; but oarsmen were asking a high price, and this they were unwilling to pay, for, now that they had come so near home, they were reluctant to part with any more of what they had won. Eventually, to save themselves the expense, they made an agreement with a man from Fyn called Ake to the effect that he should buy the ship from them and, in return, crew it and convey them both to their respective homes, Orm to the Mound and Toke to Lister, as well as being responsible for providing food for the voyage. There was a tremendous amount of haggling about this, and at one stage it appeared likely to end in a fight between Toke and Ake, for Toke wanted to have a sum of money as well as his passage, since, he asserted, the ship was practically new and thoroughly stable and seaworthy, if somewhat on the small side. Ake, however, refused to accept this valuation; the ship, he protested, was foreign and of inferior workmanship, and, indeed, virtually worthless, so that he was already on the bad end of the bargain. In the end they asked Hallbjörn, the groom, to arbitrate their case, and the matter was concluded without a fight, though Orm and Toke made little profit on the transaction.

Neither of them felt inclined to join Styrbjörn, for they both had other things uppermost in their minds; and Orm's strength returned but slowly to him, so that he thought he would be an invalid for the rest of his days. He was sad, too, to think that he would shortly have to part from Ylva, who was now permanently chaperoned by a couple of old women, to make sure that she and Orm should not see too much of each other. But although the old women performed their duties conscientiously, they were frequently driven to complain that the King had allotted them a task too arduous for their aged bones.

When the fleet was at last ready to sail, King Harald bade the Bishop bless all the ships; but he refused to take him with him, because of the bad weather-luck that all priests were known to bring. The Bishop wanted to go to Skania to visit his priests and his churches there and to count the number of conversions that had been made; but King Harald told him he would have to wait until another ship sailed to those parts. For he himself, he roundly swore, would never take any bishop to sea with him, nor even a common priest.

"For I am too old to tempt fortune," he said, "and all sailors know that sea-robbers and water-trolls and all sea-powers hate nothing so much as a shaven man, and set traps to drown him as soon as he leaves the land. My nephew, Gold-Harald, once sailed homewards from Brittany with a large number of newly captured slaves at his oars and straightway encountered storms and blizzards and fearful seas, though it was yet but early in the autumn. When his ship was on the point of sinking, he bethought himself and discovered two shaven men among his rowers. He threw them overboard, and enjoyed excellent weather for the rest of the voyage. He could do this because he was a heathen, but it would ill become me to throw a bishop overboard to calm the weather. So he will have to remain here."

On the morning that the fleet was due to sail, which was also the morning that Orm and Toke had fixed for their departure, King Harald came down to the jetties to board his ship. He wore a white cloak and a silver helmet, and had a great company of men with him; and his standards were borne before him. When he reached the place where Orm's ship lay, he halted, bade his followers wait awhile, and climbed aboard unaccompanied to have a few words with Orm in private.

"I honor you thus publicly," he said, "to show evidence of the friendship I bear you, that no man may suppose any enmity to exist between us because I have not yet granted you my daughter's hand. She is now confined in the women's house, where she is the cause of much disturbance; for she is a high-spirited wench and would otherwise be quite capable of running down to your ship the moment I turned my back, to try to tempt you to take her with you, which would be a bad thing for both of you. I and you must now part for a while, and unfortunately I have, at the moment, no adequate gift with which to repay you for the bell you brought me; but I am sure that things will be different when you return in the autumn."

It was a fine spring morning, with a clear sky and a gentle breeze blowing, and King Harald was in a merry humor. He examined the ship closely, noting its foreign workmanship, for he was well versed in the ways of ships and knew as much about decks and rowlocks as any shipwright, so that he found a number of points worth commenting upon. While he was thus engaged, Toke climbed aboard, staggering beneath the weight of an enormous chest. He seemed taken aback to see King Harald there, but lowered his chest carefully to the deck and came forward to greet him.

"That is a fair-sized package you have with you there," said the King. "What does it contain?"

"Only a few oddments for the old woman, my mother, in case she is still living," replied Toke. "It is a good thing to bring home a gift of some sort when a man has been away for as long as I have."

King Harald nodded approvingly and observed that it was good to find young people who still retained respect and affection for their parents. He himself, he added, had noticed little evidence of either quality in his own family.

"And now," he said, seating himself on the chest that Toke had brought aboard with him, "I am thirsty and should like to quaff a cup of ale before we say farewell."

The chest creaked beneath his weight, and Toke, with an anxious look on his face, took a step toward him; but the chest remained in one piece. Orm drew some ale from a barrel and offered it to the King, who drank to their luck for the voyage. He wiped the froth from his beard and remarked that ale always tasted best at sea; he would therefore be obliged if Orm would refill his cup once more. Orm did so, and King Harald emptied it slowly; then he nodded farewell to them, climbed ashore, and departed toward his own great flagship, to the mast of which his standard had already been fixed, displaying two ravens with outstretched wings sewn in black upon a background of scarlet silk.

Orm glanced curiously at Toke. "Why are you so pale?" he asked.

"I have my worries, like other men," replied Toke. "You yourself have not the most cheerful of countenances."

"I know what I am leaving behind," said Orm, "but the wisest of men could not tell me to what I am returning, or whether things will turn out as I fear they may."

At last all the ships put out to sea and steered their separate courses. King Harald and his fleet headed eastwards through the archipelago, and Orm's ship rowed northwards along the coast to the tip of Sjælland. The wind favored the King's ships, and before long they had begun to disappear into the distance.

Toke stood staring after them until their sails had grown tiny; then he said:

> "Dread the hour
> When Denmark's despot
> Bulbous sat
> On brittle box-lid.
> Faintly yet I
> Fear my freight be
> Broken-boned
> By Bluetooth's burden."

He strode to the chest, opened it, and lifted forth his freight, which consisted of the Moorish girl. She looked pale and wretched, for it had been cramped and suffocating in the chest, and she had

been in it for a good while. When Toke released hold of her, her
knees gave under her and she lay on the deck panting and shaking
and looking half-dead until he helped her to her feet again. She
began to sob, glancing fearfully around her.

"Have no fear," said Toke. "He is far away by now."

She sat pale and wild-eyed on the deck, gazing at the ship and
the men without speaking; and the men at the oars gazed back at
her with eyes as wide as her own, asking one another what this
could mean. But none of them was as pale as Orm, or stared more
fearfully, for he looked as though some huge stroke of ill luck had
just smitten him.

Ake, the ship's master, hummed and hawed and tugged his
beard.

"You made no mention of this when we struck our bargain," he
said, "that a woman should be aboard. The least I ask is that you
should tell me who she is and why she came aboard in a chest."

"That does not concern you," replied Orm blackly. "Take care
of your ship, and we will take care of what concerns us."

"He who refuses to reply may have dangerous things to hide,"
said Ake. "I am a stranger in Jellinge and know little of what goes
on there, but a man does not have to be wise to see that this is a
crooked business and one that may easily bring evil in its wake.
Whom have you stolen her from?"

Orm seated himself on a coil of rope, with his hands clasped
round his knees and his back toward Ake. Without turning his
head, he replied evenly: "I give you two choices. Either hold your
tongue or be thrown into the sea, headforemost. Make your choice,
and be speedy about it, for you yap like a mongrel puppy and disturb my head."

Ake turned away mumbling and spat over the side, and they
could see as he moved again to his steering-oar that he was brooding darkly and in an evil humor. But Orm sat still and silent,
staring as he pondered.

After a while Toke's girl recovered her spirits, and they gave
her something to strengthen her; but this at once made her wretchedly seasick, and she hung groaning over the gunwale, refusing to
be comforted by the soothing words that Toke proffered her. In
the end he let her be, fastening her to the gunwale with a rope,
and came and sat beside Orm.

"Now the worst is past," he said, "though this is certainly a troublesome and nerve-racking way of obtaining a woman. I do not think there are many men who would have dared to do as I have done; however, I suppose my luck is greater than that of most people."

"It is better than mine," said Orm. "I grant you that."

"That is not so certain," said Toke, "for your luck has always been good; and a king's daughter is a greater prize than the woman I have won. You must not grieve that you have not been able to do as I have done, for even I could hardly have succeeded in kidnapping a girl as closely guarded as yours was."

Orm laughed between his teeth. He sat silent for a while and then ordered Rapp to replace Ake at the steering-oar, for the latter's ears looked likely to stretch themselves to tearing-point. Then he said to Toke: "I had supposed that a firm friendship existed between us two, since we have been together for so long; but, as the old ones truthfully used to say, it takes a long time to prove a man. In this mad enterprise in which you have now involved us both, you have behaved as though I did not exist or was not worth bothering about."

Toke replied: "You have one characteristic that ill becomes a chieftain, Orm, and that is the ease with which you take offense. Most men would have praised me for stealing the woman single-handed, without endangering anyone else; but you regard yourself as having been insulted because you were not told about everything beforehand. What kind of friendship is it that breaks on so small a rock as this?"

Orm stared at him, white with fury.

"It is difficult to forbear with such addleheadedness as yours," he said. "What do I care about what methods you use to get your women, or whether or not you keep your plans to yourself? What does concern me is that you have earned us King Harald's enmity and wrath, so that whithersoever we go in the Danish kingdom, we shall find ourselves outlaws. You have got your woman, and have barred me forever from mine. A man does not have to be quick to take offense to find fault with such evidence of friendship."

Toke could not find much to say in reply to this charge and was forced to admit that he had not thought of it in this light before. He tried to mollify Orm by saying that King Harald was old and feeble and could not live much longer; but Orm drew scant comfort from this, and the more he thought about it, the more irrevocably he felt himself to be separated from Ylva, and his anger waxed accordingly.

They put in for the night in a sheltered creek and lit two fires. Orm, Toke, Rapp, and Mirah sat by one of them, and Ake and his crew around the other. None of the Vikings was in a mood for talking, but the other men kept up a greedy murmur of discussion. They spoke, however, in low tones, so that the matter of their talk could not be heard.

After they had eaten, the woman curled up to sleep by the fire, with a cloak covering her body. Orm and Toke sat in silence some way apart from each other. Dusk began to fall, and a cold wind sprang up, turning the sea gray; and a storm-cloud appeared in the west. Orm sighed deeply several times and tugged hard at his beard. Both he and Toke were black with anger.

"It would be best to settle this matter," said Toke.

"You have only to say the word," replied Orm.

Rapp had gone to gather fuel for the fire. Now he returned and overheard their last words. He was a silent man, who seldom minded anyone's business but his own. Now, however, he said: "It would be a good thing if you two could leave your fighting till later, for we have other work to do. There are fourteen men in the crew, and we are but three; and that is already difference enough."

They asked him what he meant by this.

"They are planning to kill us, because of the woman," said Rapp. "I heard them discussing it as I was gathering wood."

Orm laughed.

"This is a fine hare you have started," he said bitterly to Toke.

Toke shook his head sadly and stared with troubled eyes at his woman as she slept beside the fire.

"Things are as they are," he said, "and the main thing now is to decide the best way out of this affair. I think the wisest course for us to follow would be to kill the lot of them where they sit, while they are still planning how to dispose of us. They are many, but they are far from being such men as we."

"It looks as though we shall have rough weather tomorrow," said Rapp, "and in that case we cannot afford to kill many of them, for we shall need them in the ship, unless we want to spend the rest of our lives in this place. But whatever we do, let us do it at once, or we shall have a rough night of it."

"They are foolish folk from Fyn," said Toke, "and once we have killed Ake and one or two of the others, the rest will tumble over themselves to do our bidding. But it is you, Orm, who must decide what we are to do. Perhaps it might be wisest to wait till they are asleep and attack them then."

Orm's melancholy had left him, now that there was work to be done. He got to his feet and stood as though making water, so as to be able to survey the group around the other fire without exciting their attention.

"There are twelve of them there," he said when he had sat down again, "which may mean that they have sent two of their number inland to get help, without our noticing their departure. If that is so, we shall soon have a swarm of foes descending on us; so I think we would do best to settle this business without delay. It is plain that they have little foresight or lust for combat, or they would have tried to overpower Rapp when he was in the woods alone. But now we shall teach them that they must manage things more skillfully when they have men of our mettle to deal with. I will go alone and speak with them; then, while their eyes are upon me, come silently up behind them and hew well and quickly or it will go hard for us. I must go without my shield; there is no help for it."

He picked up a tankard they had used at supper, and walked across to Ake's fire to fill it from the barrel that they had brought ashore and set down there. Two or three of the crew had already laid themselves down to sleep by the fire, but most of them were still seated and awake, and their eyes turned toward Orm as he walked toward them. He filled the tankard, blew off the froth, and took a deep draught.

"There is bad wood in your barrel," he said to Ake; "your ale smacks of it already."

"It was good enough for King Harald," retorted Ake sullenly, "and it should be good enough for you. But I promise you that you will not have to drink much more of it."

The men laughed at his words, but Orm handed him the tankard as though he had noticed nothing untoward.

"Taste for yourself," he said, "and see if I have not spoken the truth."

Ake took the tankard without moving from where he sat. Then, as he set it to his lips, Orm gave the bottom of the tankard a great kick so that Ake's jaw was broken and his chin fell upon his breast.

"Does it not taste of wood?" said Orm, and in the same instant he whipped his sword from its sheath and felled the man beside him as the latter jumped to his feet.

The other men, dumbfounded by the suddenness of all this, barely had time to grab for their weapons before Toke and Rapp fell on them from behind; and after that they had little time to show what mettle they were made of. Four of them were killed in addition to Ake, two fled into the woods, and the remaining five ran to the ship and prepared to defend themselves there. Orm cried to them to throw down their weapons, vowing that if they did so he would spare their lives. But they stood wavering, uncertain whether to believe him.

"We cannot be sure that you will keep your word," they shouted back.

"That I can believe," replied Orm. "You can only hope that I am less treacherous than you have proved to be."

They held a whispered conference and then shouted down that his proposal gave them insufficient assurance and that they would prefer to keep their weapons and be allowed to depart, leaving the ship and everything else to the Vikings.

"Then I give you this assurance instead," cried Orm, "that if you do not instantly do as I say, you will all be killed where you stand. Perhaps this knowledge will comfort you."

So saying, he swung himself up on the ship and walked slowly toward them, without waiting for Toke and Rapp to follow him. His helmet had been knocked off by a stone that one of the men had thrown, his eyes were narrow with fury, and Blue-Tongue glittered wetly in his hand as he strode toward them, measuring them as though they were hounds that required the whip. Then they obeyed his bidding and threw down their weapons, muttering baleful curses upon Ake, for they were incensed that everything had turned out otherwise than as he had foretold.

It was by now quite dark, and a blustering wind had sprung up, but Orm thought it unwise for them to remain any longer in the bay. If they lingered, he said, they would have half an army of loyal Sjællanders descending upon them to recover King Harald's woman and restore her to her rightful master. Therefore, despite the darkness and hard weather and the fact that they were so few, he felt there was nothing for it but to try their luck against the sea; for the consequences of Toke's folly, he feared, would dog their heels for many a day.

Having no time to lose, they made haste to bring aboard the food-chest and ale-butt. The woman wept and grated her teeth at the prospect of such a voyage as the weather promised, but obeyed without complaint. Orm stood guard over the prisoners with drawn sword as they sat at their oars, while Toke and Rapp lifted the ale aboard. Toke was handling the barrel very clumsily and awkwardly, and Orm shouted angrily at them to be quicker about it.

"The wood is slippery, and my fingers cannot get a proper hold," replied Toke mournfully, "for my hand is not as it should be."

Orm had never heard him speak so heavily before. His sword-hand had been split at the joint of the third and fourth fingers, so that two of his fingers pointed one way and two the other.

"The loss of blood does not trouble me," he said, "but this hand will be of little use for rowing tonight, and that is a bad thing, for we shall need to row hard if we are to get out of this bay before daybreak."

He rinsed his hand in the water and turned toward the woman.

"You have helped me much already, my poor Mirah," he said, "though it may be that I have done the greater share. Let me now see whether you can help me in this matter, also."

The woman dried her tears and came to look at his hand. She wailed softly when she saw how grave the wound was, but none the less contrived to dress it skillfully. She said she would have been happier with wine to wash it in and cobwebs to lay upon it, but since these were not available she made do with water and grass and chewed bread. Then she bound it up tightly with bandages that she tore from her clothing.

"The most useless things can be turned to useful purposes," said Orm. "And now we are both left-handed."

It was evident from the way he spoke that his anger against Toke had been allayed.

Then they pulled away from the land with seven men at the oars and Toke minding the steering-oar, and the work of getting the ship out of the bay and round the point into the lee of the coast was the hardest that Orm had known since the days when he had toiled as a galley slave. He kept a spear in readiness at his side to kill the first prisoner who flagged; and when one of them caught a crab in the trough of a wave and was thrown on to his back, he was up on his bench and pulling again at his oar within the instant. The woman sat huddled at Toke's feet, rolling her eyes in fear and wretchedness. Toke steadied her with his foot and bade her take up the baling-bucket and perform some useful service; but although she tried to obey him, her work was of no avail, and the ship was half submerged when they at last rounded the point and were able to set sail and bale.

For the rest of the night they were at the mercy of the storm. Orm himself took over the steering-oar, but all he could do was to keep the ship headed toward the northeast and hope that she would not be driven aground before day broke. None of them thought there was much hope of surviving such a tempest, which was worse than that which they had endured on their voyage to Ireland.

Then Rapp said: "We have five prisoners aboard, unarmed and in our power. It is doubtful whether they will be of any further use to us as rowers, but they may help us to calm the storm if we offer them to the sea people."

Toke said that this seemed to him an excellent and proper suggestion, though he felt that they might begin by throwing one or two overboard, to see if that had any effect. But Orm said that they could not do this with any of the prisoners, because he had promised them their lives.

"If you want to give someone to the sea people," he said to Toke, "I can only suggest that you offer them your woman. Indeed, I think it might turn out to the advantage of us all if we could rid ourselves of someone who has brought us so much ill luck."

But Toke said that he would allow nothing of that sort to happen so long as he had breath in his body and one hand capable of wielding a sword.

So no more was said on that subject. As day dawned, a heavy rain began to fall and stood around them like smoke, and the storm began to lessen. When it became light, they could discern the coast of Halland ahead of them, and at last they succeeded in getting the ship into an inlet with her sail slit and her belly half full of water.

"These boards have carried me here from St. James' tomb," said Orm, "and now I have not far to go. But I shall come home without my necklace, and without the James bell, and little profit have I gained from giving them away."

"You are bringing home a sword and a ship," said Toke, "and I have a sword and a woman. And few of those who rowed forth with Krok have as much as that to show for their voyage."

"We carry with us also a great king's anger," said Orm, "and worse than that can hang around no man's neck."

The hardships of their journey were now past. They set the five prisoners ashore and allowed them to depart in peace; then, after they had rested for a while and had put their ship and sail in order, they got good weather and sailed down the coast before a gentle breeze. Even the woman was now in good spirits and was able to help them with one thing and another, so that Orm found himself able to endure her presence better than before.

As evening fell, they drew in to the flat rocks that lay below Toste's house, against which, when they had last seen the place, Krok's ships had been gently rocking. They walked up the path toward the house, with Orm at their head. A short way from the water's edge the path crossed a frothing stream, by means of a wooden bridge consisting of three planks.

Orm said: "Be careful of the one on the left. It is rotten." Then he gazed at the plank and said: "It was rotten long before I left this place, and every time my father crossed this bridge he said that he would have it mended at once. Yet I see that it is still unmended, and still holds together, though it seems to me that I have long been parted from this place. If this bridge still stands, it may be that the old man, my father, has also survived the years that have passed."

A little farther on they saw a stork's nest in a high tree, with a stork standing upon it. Orm stopped and whistled, and the stork beat its wings and clattered its beak in reply.

"He remembers me," said Orm. "It is the same stork; and it seems to me that it was but yesterday that he and I last spoke together."

Then they passed through a barred gate. Orm said: "Shut the

gate securely; for my mother gets angry if the sheep escape, and when she is out of temper our evening fare suffers."

Dogs began to bark, and men appeared at the door and gaped at the three Vikings as they approached the house. Then a woman pushed her way through the knot of men and came toward them. It was Asa. She was pale, but apart from this looked as brisk and spry as when Orm had last seen her.

"Orm," she said, and her voice trembled. Then she added: "God has heard my prayers at last."

"His ears seem to be deafened with prayers nowadays," said Orm. "But I never thought that you, of all people, would turn Christian."

"I have been alone," said Asa; "but now all is well."

"Have your men sailed forth already?" asked Orm.

"I have no men left," she said. "Odd stayed away the year after you left, and Toste died three years ago, in the year of the great cattle sickness. But I have managed to survive because I turned to the true religion; for then I knew that my prayers would be answered and that you would come back to me."

"We have much to speak of," said Orm, "but it would be good if we could eat first. These are my men; but the woman is foreign and is not mine."

Asa said that Orm was now the master of the house and that all his friends were hers; so they entered, and were entertained like heroes. There were tears in her eyes as she carried to the table those dishes which she knew that Orm loved most dearly. They had many things to tell each other, and the telling of them covered many evenings; but no word was said of how Toke had won his woman, for Orm did not wish to temper his mother's joy so soon after his return home. Asa took to Toke immediately and tended his wounded hand with great care and skill, so that it quickly began to mend; and she was fond and motherly toward Mirah, though they could talk but little together, and praised her beauty and black hair. She was disappointed that Orm and his men were not willing to thank God with her for their lucky return; but she was too overjoyed to take offense at their refusal, and said that Orm and the others would understand these things better when they were older and wiser.

At first Orm found such blitheness and gentleness somewhat

strange in Asa, and it was six days before he heard her make one of her sharp-tongued sallies against the servant-maids and could feel that she was beginning to be herself again.

Orm and Toke were now friends again, though neither of them ever mentioned Ylva. As they described to Asa the adventures that had befallen them since Krok's expedition had first rowed forth, Orm felt his old affection for Toke rekindle, and was eloquent in the latter's praise; but whenever his thoughts turned to Ylva, his humor darkened, and then the sight of Toke and his woman gave him little joy. Mirah grew prettier every day, and laughed and sang the whole time, and she and Toke were so happy together that they had little time to notice other people's troubles. Asa prophesied that they would have fine children, and Mirah, when this was explained to her, smiled and said they were doing all they could to ensure that this would be so. Asa observed that she must now begin to look for a wife for Orm, but Orm replied with a dark countenance that she could take her time about that.

As things now were, it was impracticable for Toke to proceed home by sea, at least as long as King Harald's ships were at Skanör; so he decided to journey to Lister by land, with no company save that of his woman (for Rapp was remaining with Orm), and bought horses to carry them. Early one morning they took their leave, with many expressions of gratitude to Asa for her hospitality; and Orm accompanied them for a short distance to show them the right path for the Lister country.

"Here we must part," said Orm, "and with all my heart I wish you a good journey. But it is not easy to be hopeful about the future, for King Harald will not rest until he has hunted you down, whithersoever you may flee."

"I fear it is our fate to be unlucky with kings," replied Toke, "though we are as meek-minded as other men. Almansur, King Sven, and now King Harald; we have made enemies of them all, and the man who brought our heads to any one of them would be well rewarded. None the less, I intend to hold on to mine."

So they parted. Toke and Mirah rode eastwards and disappeared in the woods; and Orm rode back to the house to tell Asa of the danger that hung over them from King Harald's wrath.

PART TWO

In King Ethelred's Kingdom

CHAPTER ONE

CONCERNING THE BATTLE THAT WAS FOUGHT AT
MALDON, AND WHAT CAME AFTER IT

THAT spring many ships were timbered along the coasts of the northern countries, and keels were pitched which had long lain dry. Bays and sounds vomited forth navies, with kings and their wrath aboard; and when summer came, there was great unrest upon the seas.

Styrbjörn rowed early up through the Eastern Sea, with many ships and men from Jomsborg, Bornholm, and Skania. He put into Lake Mälaren and came at length to the plain before Uppsala, where he and King Erik joined battle. There he fell, in the first moments of the fight, and men say that he died laughing. For when he saw the battle array of the Swedes move forward, drawn up in the ancient manner behind horses' heads borne high upon pikes, with King Erik seated in the midst of his army in an old sacred ox-chariot, he threw his head back in a wild frenzy of laughter. In the same instant a spear came between his beard and the rim of his shield and took him in the throat. When his followers saw this happen, their courage broke, and many of them fled there and then, so that King Erik won a great victory.

Then King Sven Forkbeard rowed down through the Danish islands with ships from Fyn and Jutland to take King Harald as the latter sat counting his herring tax at Skanör; for King Sven had at last lost patience at his father's unwillingness to die. But King Harald fled to Bornholm and gathered his ships there, and sharp encounters were fought between these two until at length King Harald took refuge in his fortress at Jomsborg, sorely wounded. Then much of the Danish kingdom was split with strife, for some men held King Harald's cause to be just and some King Sven's; others preferred to fend for themselves and better their own fortunes while the land lay lawless under its warring kings.

But when the summer stood in its flower, King Erik of Uppsala came sailing southwards, with the greatest army that the Swedes

had embarked in any man's memory, driving before him the rem-
nants of Styrbjörn's fleet, which had been harrying his coasts and
plundering his villages in revenge for their chieftain's death. King
Erik had a mind to punish both King Harald and King Sven for
the aid they had lent to Styrbjörn, and many men thought it an
unrewarding prospect to oppose the man who had conquered Styrbjörn and who was already being called "the Victorious." He pursued King Sven to his islands and beyond to Jutland, leaving his
own jarls to rule the places through which he passed. Soon the
rumor spread that King Harald had died of his wounds at Jomsborg, a landless refugee, deserted by the luck that had hitherto favored all his enterprises; but the other two kings continued to war
against each other. King Erik held the upper hand, but King Sven
resisted him stubbornly. Men reported that the royal castle at Jellinge changed hands every few weeks, King Sven and King Erik
taking it in turns to occupy King Harald's old bedchamber; but it
was generally agreed that King Sven was the more likely to have
arrived first at his father's treasure-chests.

But in Skania there were many chieftains who felt little inclined
to involve themselves in this war of kings, thinking it better to let
them settle their own differences, so that honest men might be left
to occupy themselves with more profitable undertakings. One such
was Thorkel the Tall, who had no desire to serve King Sven and
was still less anxious to find himself a minor thane of King Erik.
So he sent word to other thanes and chieftains that he had a mind
to fare forth that summer to Frisia and England, if he could find
sufficient good men willing to accompany him. Many thought this
a good scheme, for Thorkel was an admired chieftain, and his luck
was held to be excellent, ever since he had succeeded in escaping
with his life from the battle at Jörundfjord. Masterless men of
Styrbjörn's army, who had managed to evade King Erik's clutches,
also came to join him, and before long he was lying at anchor in
the Sound off the island of Hven with twenty-two ships; but he
did not as yet reckon himself sufficiently strong to fare forth.

Among those who had joined his banner was Orm Tostesson,
known as Red Orm, from the Mound in Skania. He had brought
with him a large and well-manned ship. Thorkel remembered him
from the Christmas feast at King Harald's castle and welcomed
him joyfully.

It had so turned out with Orm that he had quickly wearied of sitting at home and arranging the affairs of cattle and farmhands; and he had found it difficult to live peaceably with Asa, though she did her best to make him happy. For she still regarded him as a half-grown boy and fussed continually over him with motherly counsel, as though he lacked the sagacity to manage things for himself. He did his best to explain to her that he had, for some years, been accustomed to deciding the affairs of other men as well as his own, but this information did not appear to impress her; nor did her zealous endeavors to convert him to her new religion and find him a wife improve his humor.

The news of King Harald's death had come as a great relief to them both; for when Asa had first learned the truth about how Toke had got his woman, she had been overcome with terror and had been convinced that there was nothing for it but to sell the house and flee to the estate she had inherited from her father in the forests on the Smaland border, where even King Harald's arm would scarcely be able to reach them. Her fear had been ended by the news of King Harald's death; but Orm could not keep his thoughts from Ylva, and he worried more about her safety than about his own. Often he wondered what had become of her when her father had died; whether King Sven had taken her under his wing, as a prospective wife for one of his berserks, or whether, perhaps, she had fallen into the hands of the Swedes, the thought of which troubled him no less. Since he was on evil terms with King Sven, he could not think of any way in which he might regain her for himself, least of all while war was raging through and around the islands.

He said nothing about Ylva to Asa, for he had no wish to listen to the fruitless advice he knew she would immediately shower upon him. But he profited little thereby, for Asa knew several maidens in the district who would admirably suit his needs, and their mothers, being of the same mind as she, brought them to the house and displayed them newly washed, with their plaits fastened with red silk ribbons. The maidens came willingly and sat high-bosomed, a-clink with ornaments, shooting large-eyed glances at him; but he showed no enthusiasm for any of them, for none of them resembled Ylva or was as witty and ready-tongued as she was, so that in the end Asa grew impatient with him, and thought that even Odd had hardly been more difficult to please.

When, therefore, the news came that Thorkel intended to fare forth a-viking, Orm lost no time in procuring himself a good ship and hiring men from the district to come with him, paying little heed to Asa's tears and entreaties. Everybody knew him to be a widely traveled man who had returned with much gold from his voyage, so that he found little difficulty in assembling a good crew. He told Asa that he did not expect to be away for as long this time as when he had previously set forth, and promised her that, when he returned, he would settle down to a peaceful life and take up farming in earnest. Asa wept, and protested that she could not endure such sorrow and loneliness, but Orm assured her that she would live much longer than he, and would help to birch his children, and his grandchildren to boot. But this only caused her to weep the more bitterly. So they parted, and Orm sailed to join Thorkel.

While Thorkel was still lying off Hven, waiting for a favorable wind, a fleet of twenty-eight ships came rowing up from the south; and from their banners and the cut of their stems it was apparent that they were Swedish. The weather was calm and good for fighting, and both sides made ready for battle; but Thorkel shouted across the water to the strangers, proclaiming his identity, and stating that he wished to speak with their chieftain. The Swedes were under the command of two chieftains, of equal sway. One was called Jostein, a man from Uppland, and the other Gudmund, an East Gute. They said they had come to help King Erik plunder in Denmark, and asked what more he wished to know.

"If our fleets join battle," shouted Thorkel, "there will be little booty for the winners, and many men will be killed on both sides. I tell you this, though I am the more likely to prevail."

"We have five ships more than you," roared the strangers.

"That may be," replied Thorkel. "But mine are all picked men, and we have just eaten our morning meal, while your men are weary from rowing, which makes a man less skillful with his spear and sword. But I have a better suggestion to make, which would redound to the advantage of us all; for I can name a more rewarding place than Denmark to go a-viking in."

"We have come to aid King Erik," shouted the Upplander.

"I do not doubt it," replied Thorkel; "and if I join battle with you, I shall have given good aid to King Sven. But if, instead of fighting each other, we join forces and sail together to lands ripe for plunder, we shall have served our kings just as usefully as if we stay and battle it out here. For in either case none of us will take any further part in this war; and the difference will be that, if we do as I suggest, we shall all still be alive, with much fine booty waiting for us to come and collect it."

"You use words skillfully," said Gudmund. "There is wisdom in what you say, and I think we might profitably continue this discussion at closer quarters."

"I know from report that you are both noble chieftains and honorable men," said Thorkel. "Therefore I am not afraid that you will act treacherously if we meet to debate the matter."

"I know your brother Sigvalde," said Jostein, "but I have often heard it said that you, Thorkel, are of stouter mettle than he."

So they agreed to meet on the island to debate the matter, on the beach at the foot of a cliff, in sight of the ships. Jostein and Gudmund were each to bring three men with them, and Thorkel five, bearing swords but no casting weapons. This was done, and from the ships the men of the opposing fleets marked how, at first, the chieftains kept their distance from each other, with their men standing close behind them. Then Thorkel ordered ale to be offered to the Swedes, together with pork and bread; and soon they were seen to sit down in a circle and talk as friends.

The more Jostein and Gudmund considered Thorkel's proposition, the more excellent it appeared to them to be, and before long Gudmund was anxiously supporting it. Jostein at first held out against it, saying that King Erik had a savage memory for men who betrayed his trust in them; but Thorkel regaled them with details of the splendid plunder that awaited sea-rovers in the islands of the west, and Gudmund reckoned that they could worry about King Erik's memory when the time came. Then they came to an agreement regarding the division of command during the voyage, and how the booty was to be shared out, so that no disputes should arise later; and Gudmund observed that so much meat and talk gave a man a fine thirst, and praised the excellence of Thorkel's ale. Thorkel shook his head and said that it was, in truth, the best that he could offer them for the moment, but that it was nothing compared with the ale in England, where the best hops in the world grew. Then even Jostein had to agree that this sounded like a land worth voyaging to. So they took each other by the hand and swore to be faithful and to keep their word; then, when they had returned to their ships, three sheep were slaughtered over the bows of each chieftain's vessel, as a sacrifice to the sea people for weather-luck and a good voyage. All the crews were well satisfied with the agreement that their chieftains had made; and Thorkel's reputation, which was already great in the eyes of his men, waxed because of the wisdom he had displayed in this matter.

Several more ships came to join Thorkel, from Skania and Halland; and when, at last, a favorable wind arose, the fleet put forth, fifty-five sails strong, and spent the autumn plundering in Frisia, and wintered there.

Orm inquired of Thorkel and others of his comrades whether they knew what had become of King Harald's household. Some said they had heard that Jellinge had been burned, others that Bishop Poppo had calmed the sea with psalms and escaped by ship, though King Sven had done his best to catch him. But none of them knew what had happened to the King's women.

In England things were beginning to be as they had been in the old days, in the time of the sons of Ragnar Hairy-Breeks; for King Ethelred had come to the throne. He had not long come of age and taken the reins of government into his own hands before men began to call him the Irresolute, or the Redeless; and honest seafarers from the north flocked joyfully to his coasts to give him the chance to justify his reputation.

At first they came in small bodies and were easily repelled. Beacons were lit along the coasts to signify their arrival, and stout warriors armed with broad shields rushed to meet them and drive them back into the sea. But King Ethelred yawned at his table and offered up prayers against the Northmen, and lay cheerfully with his chieftains' women. He screamed with rage when they brought word to him in his boudoir that in spite of his prayers the long ships had returned; he listened, fatigued, to much counsel and complained loudly at being thus inconvenienced, and otherwise did nothing. Then the invaders began to arrive more frequently and in stronger companies, till the King's levies became inadequate to deal with them, and the larger bands of them would sometimes drive deep inland and return to their ships bent double under the weight of their booty; and the word spread abroad, and many believed it, that no kingdom could now compare with King Ethelred's in wealth and fatness for valiant seafarers who came in good strength. For it was by now many years since England had been properly plundered, save in her coastal areas.

But as yet no large fleet had sailed there, and no chieftains had learned the art of demanding danegeld in minted silver from King Ethelred's coffers. But in the year of grace 991 both these deficiencies were remedied; and thereafter there was no lack of men willing to be instructed in this art as long as King Ethelred was there to pay good silver to such as came and asked for it.

Soon after the Easter of that year, which was the fifth year after King Ethelred's coming of age, the beacons were lit along the Kentish coasts. Men gazed pale-faced into the morning mists and turned and ran to hide what they could and drive their cattle into the forests and take themselves into hiding with them, and word was sent to King Ethelred and his jarls as fast as horse could ride that the biggest fleet that had been sighted for many years was rowing along his coasts, and that the heathens had already begun to wade ashore.

The levies were assembled, but could achieve nothing against the invaders, who split up into powerful bands and plundered the district, gathering into one place everything that they laid hands on. Then the English fell into a panic lest they should drive inland, and the Archbishop of Canterbury betook himself in person to the King to crave help for his city. However, after the invaders had enjoyed themselves for a short while in the coastal area and had carried off to their ships everything that they found worth taking, they embarked again and sailed away up the coast. Then they landed in the country of the East Saxons and did likewise there.

King Ethelred and his Archbishop, whose name was Sigerik, promptly offered up longer prayers than ever; and when they heard that the heathens, after sacking a few villages, had put out to sea again, they had rich gifts distributed among those priests who had prayed most assiduously, believing themselves to be rid at last of these unwelcome visitors. No sooner had this been done than the Vikings rowed in to a town called Maldon, at the mouth of the river Pant, pitched camp on an island in the middle of the estuary, and prepared to assault the town.

The Jarl of the East Saxons was called Byrhtnoth. He had a great name in his country, and was bigger than other men and very proud and fearless. He assembled a powerful army and marched against them, to see whether blows might prove more effectual than prayers against the invaders. On reaching Maldon, he marched past the town toward the Vikings' camp until only the arm of the river separated the two forces. But now it was difficult for him to attack the Vikings, and equally difficult for them to attack him. The tide came in, filling the river arm to the level of its banks. It was no broader than a spear's-throw, so that the armies were able to hail one another, but it did not appear as though they would be able to come to close grips. So they stood facing each other in merry spring weather.

A herald of Thorkel the Tall's army, a man skilled in speech, stepped forward to the river's edge, raised his shield, and cried across the water: "The seamen of the north, who fear no man, bid me address you thus: give us silver and gold, and we will give you peace. You are richer than we, and it will be better for you to buy peace with tribute than to meet men of our mettle with spear and sword. If you have wealth enough, it will not be necessary for us to kill each other. Then, when you have bought your freedom, and freedom for your families and your houses and all that you possess, we shall be your friends and will return to our ships with your freeing-money and will sail away from this place and will remain faithful to our word."

But Byrhtnoth himself stepped forward and, brandishing his spear, roared back: "Hearken well, sea-rover, to our reply! Here is all the tribute you will get from us: pointed spears and keen-edged swords! It would ill become such a jarl as I, Byrhtnoth, Byrhthelm's son, whose name is without spot, not to defend my country and the land of my King. This matter shall be settled by point and blade, and hard indeed must you hew before you find aught else in this land."

They stood facing each other until the tide turned and began again to run toward the sea.

Then the herald of the Vikings cried across the river: "Now we have stood idle long enough. Come over to us, and we will let you have our soil as battleground; or, if you prefer it, choose a place on your bank and we will come over to you."

Jarl Byrhtnoth was unwilling to wade across the river, for the water was cold and he feared lest it might make his men's limbs stiff and their clothing heavy. At the same time he was eager to join battle before his men should begin to feel tired and hungry. So he cried back: "I will give you ground here, and do not delay but come now to fight us. And God alone knows which of us will hold the field."

And these are the words of Byrhtnoth's bard, who was present at this battle and escaped with his life:

> The sea-men's army feared not the flood.
> Blood-wolves waded west through Panta.
> Clear through the current's crystal water
> Bore they their linden shields to the strand.

Byrhtnoth's men stood awaiting them like a hedge of shields. He had ordered them first to cast their spears, and then to advance with their swords and drive the heathens back into the river. But the Vikings formed into battle-order along the bank as they emerged from the water, each ship's crew keeping together, and straightway raised their battle-cries and charged, with the captain of each ship running at the head of his crew. A swarm of spears flew toward them, bringing many of them to the ground, whence they did not rise; but they continued to advance relentlessly until they found themselves shield to shield with the Englishmen. Then there was fierce hewing and loud alarums; and the Vikings' right and left wings were halted and hard pressed. But Thorkel the Tall and the two captains nearest to him—Orm was one, and the other was Fare-Wide Svensson, a famous chieftain from Sjælland, whom King Harald had proclaimed outlaw throughout the Danish kingdom, and who had fought with Styrbjörn at the battle on Fyris Plain before Uppsala—assaulted Byrhtnoth's own phalanx and broke it. Thorkel cried to his men to fell the tall man in the silver helmet, for then the day would be theirs. Straightway the fighting became fiercest in this part of the field, and there was little elbow-room for men of small stature. Fare-Wide hewed his way forward, slew Byrhtnoth's standard-bearer, and aimed a blow at Byrhtnoth, wounding him; but he fell himself in the same instant, with a spear through his beard. Many of the chieftains on both sides were killed; and Orm slipped on a fallen shield that was greasy with blood, and tumbled headlong over the body of a man he had just slain. As he fell, he received a blow on the back of his neck from a club, but at once those of his men who were closest to him threw their shields over his body to cover him and protect his back.

When he regained his senses and was able, with Rapp's assistance, to get to his feet again, the battle had moved away from that part of the field, and the Vikings had gained the upper hand. Byrhtnoth had fallen, and many of his men had fled, but others had formed themselves into a tight ring and, though surrounded, were still resisting valiantly. Thorkel shouted to them over the noise of the battle that he would spare their lives if they cast down their arms; but the cry came back from their midst: "The fewer we be, the fiercer we shall hew, and the shrewder shall be our aim and our courage crueller."

They fought on until they all lay dead upon the ground, together with many of their foemen, about their chieftain's corpse. The Vikings marveled at the valor of these Englishmen, praising the dead; nevertheless, this battle at Maldon, fought three weeks before Whitsun in the year 991, was a grievous setback for King Ethelred and a disaster for his realm. For now, far and wide about them, the land lay helpless before the fury of the invaders from the north.

The Vikings buried their dead and pledged them and the victory they had won. They handed Byrhtnoth's corpse over to the sorrowful envoys who came to beg for it that they might give it Christian burial; then they sent proclamations to Maldon and other towns in the district commanding that the inhabitants should pay fire-tribute and ransom without delay, lest a heavier penalty be demanded of them. They rejoiced at the thought of so much wealth lying in store for them, counting it already as their own; and their anger mounted as the days passed and no Englishman came with surrender and gold. So they rowed up to Maldon and set fire to the stockade on the riverbank and stormed the town and sacked it fearfully. Then they wept because so much

had been burned that there was little left for booty. They swore
that in the future they would be more sparing in their use of fire,
for it was silver that they yearned for and not destruction, which
swallowed up silver with all else; and they set to work to whip
in horses from the whole district, that they might the more speedily descend on those parts of the land which reckoned themselves
safe from the invaders' wrath. Soon bands of them rode forth
in all directions, and returned to the camp laden with booty; and
there was now such dire panic throughout the land that no chieftain dared to emulate Byrhtnoth and challenge them to battle.
Prisoners whom they took reported that King Ethelred was sitting
pasty-faced behind his walls, mumbling prayers with his priests,
wholly redeless.

In the church at Maldon, which was of stone, some of the English were still holding out. They had fled up into the tower when
the Vikings had stormed the city, priests and women being among
them; and they had drawn the steps up with them as they ascended,
that they might not be pursued into their retreat. The Vikings
suspected that they had taken much treasure with them, and strove
their utmost to persuade them to descend from their tower and
bring their treasure with them. But neither by fire nor by force of
arms could they achieve anything; and the people had plenty of
food and drink with them in the tower, and sang psalms and appeared to be in good heart. When the Vikings approached the
tower to try to induce them by words to act sensibly and come
down and part with their treasure, they cast down stones, curses,
and filth upon their heads, yelling with triumph when any of their
missiles met their mark. All the Vikings agreed that stone churches
and their towers were among the most vexatious obstacles that a
man could find himself confronted with.

Jostein, who was an old, hard man, very greedy for gold, said
that he could think of only one way to break down these people's
obstinacy: namely, that they should bring their prisoners to within
sight of the tower and there kill them, one by one, until the people in the tower could endure it no more and so would be forced
to surrender. A number of the men agreed with him in this, for he
had a great name for wisdom; but Gudmund and Thorkel thought
such a plan unwarriorlike and were unwilling to be parties to it.
It would be better, said Thorkel, to bring them down by guile;

he added that he was well acquainted with the foibles of priests and knew how best to approach them and get them to do what one wanted.

He ordered his men to remove a great cross from above the altar in the church. Then he approached the tower, with two men carrying the cross before him, and, halting at its foot, cried up to the people there that he needed priests to tend the wounded and also, which was more urgent, to instruct him personally in the Christian faith. Of late, he explained, he had begun to feel strongly attracted toward the new religion; and he would act toward them as though he was already a Christian, for he would allow everyone in the tower to leave it unscathed in life and limb.

He had proceeded thus far in his discourse when a stone shot out of the tower and struck his shield-arm near the shoulder, knocking him to the ground and breaking his arm. At this the two men dropped the cross and assisted him to safety, while the people in the tower cheered in triumph. Jostein, who had been watching, curled his lip and observed that guile in war was not such a simple matter as inexperienced young men sometimes appeared to imagine.

All Thorkel's followers were inflamed with fury at seeing their chieftain wounded thus, and flights of arrows were loosed at the loopholes in the tower; but this achieved nothing, and the situation appeared to be insoluble. Orm said that in the southland he had sometimes seen Almansur's men drive Christians from their church towers by smoking them out; and they at once set to work to try to do this. Wood and wet straw were piled together inside the church and around the foot of the tower and were lit; but the tower was high and a breeze dispersed most of the smoke before it could ascend. In the end the Vikings lost patience and decided to leave things until the inhabitants of the tower should begin to feel the pangs of hunger.

Thorkel was dejected by the failure of his stratagem, and feared lest his men should taunt him on the subject. Apart from this, he was irked at the prospect of having to sit idly in Maldon guarding the camp, for it was clear that it would be some time before he would be able to ride out and plunder; and he was anxious that men knowledgeable in medicine should come and examine his injury. Orm came to commiserate with him as he sat before a fire

drinking mulled ale with his broken arm hanging at his side. Many
men thumbed his arm, but none of them knew how to put it in
splints.

Thorkel groaned uncomfortably as they thumbed the fracture,
and said it would be medicine enough for the moment if they
could bind up his arm as well as it would allow, with or without
splints.

"Now the words I spoke at the foot of the tower have come
true," he said. "I need a priest badly, for priests understand such
matters as this."

Orm nodded in agreement and said that priests were cunning
doctors; after the Yule feast at King Harald's he had had a much
worse wound than Thorkel's healed by a priest. Indeed, he added,
he would welcome a priest no less than Thorkel, for the blow he
had received on his skull from a shoed club was causing him incessant headaches, so that he was beginning to wonder whether
something might not have come loose inside his head.

When they were alone, Thorkel said to him: "I hold you to be
the wisest of my ship's captains, and the best warrior, too, now
that Fare-Wide is dead. None the less, it is clear that you easily
lose your courage when your body is afflicted, even when the injury
is but a slight one."

Orm replied: "It is so with me that I am a man who has lost his
luck. Formerly, my luck was good, for I survived unscathed more
dangers than most men face in the whole of their lives, and
emerged from all of them with profit. But since I returned from
the southland, everything has gone wrong for me. I have lost my
gold chain, my sweetheart, and the man whose company pleased
me best; and as for battle, it has come to such a pass that nowadays I can scarcely draw my sword without coming to some harm.
Even when I advised you to smoke these English out of their
church tower, nothing came of it."

Thorkel said that he had seen unluckier men than Orm, but
Orm shook his head sadly. He sent his men off plundering with
Rapp in command, and remained himself in the town with
Thorkel, spending most of the time sitting by himself and con-
templating his woes.

One morning not long afterwards the bells in the church tower
rang long and loud, and the people there sang psalms very zealously,

causing the Vikings to shout up and ask them what all the fuss might be about. The people had no stones left to throw down at them, but they shouted back that it was now Whitsun, and that this day was for them a day of rejoicing.

The Vikings found this reply astonishing, and several of them asked the English what on earth they could have to rejoice about, and how they were placed as regards meat and ale. They replied that in that matter things were as they were; nevertheless, they would continue to rejoice, because Christ was in heaven and would surely help them.

Thorkel's men roasted fat sheep over their fires, and the odor of roasting was wafted up to the tower, where all the people were hungry. The men cried up to them to be sensible and come down and taste their roast, but they paid no attention to this invitation and began shortly to sing afresh.

Thorkel and Orm sat munching together, listening to the singing from the tower.

"Their singing is hoarser than usual," said Thorkel. "They are beginning to get dry in the throat. If their drink is finished, it cannot be long before they will have to come down."

"Their plight is worse than mine, and yet they sing," said Orm; and he contemplated a fine piece of mutton mournfully before putting it in his mouth.

"I think you would make a poor songster in any church tower," said Thorkel.

The same day, around dinnertime, Gudmund returned from a-viking inland. He was a large, merry man, with a face that still bore traces of old wounds he had received when a bear had clawed him; and he now rode into the camp, drunken and voluble, with a costly scarlet cloak flung across his shoulders, two heavy silver belts around his waist, and a broad grin in the center of his yellow beard.

This, he cried, as soon as he spied Thorkel, was a land after his own heart, wealthy beyond imagination; as long as he lived, he would never cease to be grateful to Thorkel for having tempted him to come here. He had plundered nine villages and a market, losing only four men; his horses were tottering beneath the weight of their booty, though only the choicest articles had been selected, and following them were ox-carts loaded with strong ale and other delicacies. It would be necessary in due course, he added, to get hold of several more ships, with plenty of cargo-room, to take home all the booty that they would, in a short time and with little expense of effort, have gathered in this excellent land.

"Besides all this," he concluded, "I found a procession of people on the road—two Bishops and their suites. They said they were envoys from King Ethelred, so I offered them ale and bade them follow me here. The Bishops are old and ride slowly, but they should be here soon; though what they can want with us is not easy to guess. They say they are coming with an offer of peace from their King, but it is we, and not he, who shall decide when there is to be peace. I suspect that they also want to teach us Christianity; but we shall have little time to listen to their teaching with such fine plunder to be had everywhere."

Thorkel roused himself at these tidings and said that priests were what he had most need of just now, for he was anxious to get his arm set properly; and Orm, too, was pleased at the prospect of being able to talk to a priest about his sore head.

"But I shall not be surprised," Thorkel said, "if the errand on which they have come is to ransom our prisoners and those people up in the tower."

A short while afterwards the Bishops rode into the town. They were of venerable aspect, with staffs in their hands and hoods covering their heads. They had with them a great company of outriders and priests, grooms, stewards, and musicians; and they pronounced the peace of God upon all who met their eye. All of Thorkel's men who were in the camp came to gaze at them, but some shrank away when the Bishops raised their hands. The people in the tower broke into loud acclamations at the sight of them and began again to ring their bells.

Thorkel and Gudmund showed them every hospitality; and when they had rested and had given thanks to God for their lucky journey, they explained their mission.

The Bishop who appeared to be the senior of the two, and who was called the Bishop of St. Edmund's Bury, addressed Thorkel and Gudmund and such others of the Vikings as had gathered to hear what he had to say. These, he said, were evil times, and it was a great grief to Christ and His Church that men did not know how to live peacefully with one another in love and tolerance. Fortunately, however, he continued, they now had in England a King who loved peace above all other things, and this despite the magnitude of his power and the legions of warriors that lay awaiting his command. He preferred to win the love of his enemies rather than to destroy them by the sword. King Ethelred regarded the Northmen as zealous young men who lacked counsel and did not know what was best for them; and, after having consulted his own wise counselors, he had decided on this occasion not to march against them and put them to the sword, but rather to point out peacefully to them the error of their ways. He had, accordingly, sent his envoys to find out how the gallant chieftains of the north and their followers could be persuaded to turn their thoughts toward peace and abandon the dangerous paths which they were now treading. It was King Ethelred's desire that they should return to their ships and depart from his coasts to dwell in their own land in peace and contentment; and to facilitate this and win their friendship for all time, he was ready to give them such presents as would fill them all with joy and gratitude. Such royal munificence would, he trusted, so soften the hardness of their young hearts that they would learn to love God's holy law and Christ's gospel. If this should come to pass, good King Ethelred's joy would know no bounds and his love for them would become even greater.

The Bishop was bent with age and toothless, and few of the Vikings could understand what he said; but his words were translated for them by a wise priest of his suite, and all those who stood there listening turned and stared at one another in bewilderment. Gudmund was seated on an ale-butt, drunken and contented, rubbing a little gold cross to polish it, and when they explained to him what the Bishop had said, he began to rock backwards and forwards with delight. He shouted to Thorkel that the latter should lose no time in replying to this excellent discourse.

So Thorkel replied, in a manner befitting a chieftain. He said that what they had just heard was without doubt something worth pondering. King Ethelred had already a great name in the Danish kingdom, but it now appeared that he was an even finer king than they had been led to believe; and this proposal of his, to give them all presents, accorded well with the opinion of his worth that they had hitherto held.

"For," he continued, "as we told Jarl Byrhtnoth, when we spoke with him across the river, you who dwell in this land are rich, and we poor seafarers are only too anxious to be your friends if you will but share your wealth with us. It is good to hear that King Ethelred himself shares our feelings in this matter; and, seeing that he is so rich and powerful and full of wisdom, I do not doubt that he will show himself most liberal toward us. How much he intends to offer us we have not yet been told; but we need a lot to make us merry, for we are a melancholy race. I think it best that his gifts should take the form of gold and minted silver, for this will be easiest to count, and easiest, too, for us to carry home. While everything is being settled, we shall be glad if he will permit us to remain here undisturbed, taking from the district what we need for our upkeep and pleasure. There is, though, someone who has as much say in this matter as Gudmund and myself, and that is Jostein. He is at present away plundering with many of his followers, and until he returns we cannot decide how large King Ethelred's gift is to be. But there is one thing I should like to know at once, and that is whether you have any priest skilled in medicine among your followers; for, as you see, I have this damaged arm which needs plastering."

The younger Bishop replied that they had with them two men who were learned in the craft of healing, and said he would be glad to bid them attend to Thorkel's arm. He requested, however, that in return for this service Thorkel should allow the people who were shut up in the tower to descend and go their ways without hindrance; for it was a heavy thing, he said, to think of them up there tormented by hunger and thirst.

"As far as I am concerned," said Thorkel, "they can come down as soon as they like. We have been trying to persuade them to do so ever since we took this town, but they have resisted our offers most obstinately; in fact, it was they who broke my arm. Half of what they have in the tower they must give to us. This is small repayment for the injury to my arm and all the bother they have caused us. But when they have done that, they may go whithersoever they please."

Soon, therefore, all the people in the tower descended, looking

pale and wasted. Some of them wept and threw themselves at the
Bishop's feet, while others cried piteously for water and food.
Thorkel's men were disappointed to find that there was little of
value in the tower; nevertheless, they gave them food and did
them no harm.

Orm happened to pass a water-trough where a number of those
who had been in the tower were drinking. Among them was a
little bald man in a priest's cowl, with a long nose and a red scar
across his forehead. Orm stared at him in astonishment. Then
he went up and seized him by the shoulder.

"I am glad to see you again," he said, "and I have something to
thank you for since the last time we met. But I little thought to
meet King Harald's physician in England. How did you come
here?"

"I came here from the tower," retorted Brother Willibald wrathfully, "where you heathen berserks have compelled me to spend
the last fortnight."

"I have several things to discuss with you," said Orm. "Come
with me, and I will give you food and drink."

"I have nothing to discuss with you," replied Brother Willibald.
"The less I see of Danes, the better it will be for me. That much,
at least, I have learned by now. I will get my meat and drink elsewhere."

Orm was afraid lest the little priest, in his anger, might dart away
and give him the slip, so he picked him up and carried him away
under one arm, promising him as he did so that no harm should
come to him. Brother Willibald struggled vigorously, demanding
sternly to be put down and informing Orm that leprosy and fearful
battle-wounds were the least retribution that would descend on any
man who laid his hand on a priest; but Orm ignored his protests and
carried him into a house he had chosen as his quarters after they
had stormed the town, which now contained only a few members
of his crew who had been wounded and two old women.

The little priest was obviously famished, but when meat and
drink were placed before him, he sat for some time staring bitterly
at the platter and tankard, making no effort to touch them. Then
he sighed, muttered something to himself, made the sign of the
cross over the food, and began to eat greedily. Orm refilled his
tankard with ale and waited patiently until Brother Willibald had

appeased his hunger. The good ale appeared to have no soothing
effect upon his temper, for the harshness of his retorts did not
diminish; he found it in himself to answer Orm's questions, however, and before long he was talking as ebulliently as ever.

He had escaped from Denmark, he explained, with Bishop
Poppo when the evil and unchristian King Sven had descended
upon Jellinge to destroy God's servants there. The Bishop, sick
and fragile, was now living on the charity of the Abbot of Westminster, grieving over the destruction of all his work in the north.
Brother Willibald, though, felt that there was in fact little to grieve
about when you considered the matter aright; for there could be
no doubt that what had happened was a sign from God that holy
men should cease their efforts to convert the heathens of the north
and should instead leave them to destroy one another by their evil
practices, which were, in truth, past all understanding. For his
own part, Brother Willibald added, he had no intention of ever
again attempting to convert anyone from those parts; and he was
prepared to proclaim the fact upon the Cross and Passion of
Christ in the presence of anyone who wished to hear it, including,
if necessary, the Archbishop of Bremen himself.

His eyes smoldering, he drained his tankard, smacked his lips,
and observed that ale was more nourishing than meat for a starving man. Orm refilled his tankard, and he continued with his story.

When Bishop Poppo had heard that Danish Vikings had landed
on the east coast of England, he had been anxious to try to learn
from them how things now were in the Danish kingdom; whether
any Christians were still alive, whether the rumor that King Harald
had died was true, and many other things besides. But the Bishop
had felt too weak to undertake the journey from Westminster himself, and so had sent Brother Willibald to get the information for
him.

"For the Bishop told me I would run little risk of injury among
the heathens, however inflamed their passions might be. He said
they would welcome me on account of my knowledge of medicine;
in addition to which, there would be men among them who had
known me at King Harald's court. I had my own feelings on the
matter, for he is too good for this world, and knows you less well
than I do. However, it is not seemly to contradict one's Bishop; so
I did as he bade me. I reached this town one evening, very ex-

hausted, and, after celebrating evensong, laid myself down to sleep in the church house. There I was waked by screaming and thick smoke, and men and women came running in half-naked, crying that the foul fiends had descended on us. Fiends there were none, but worse adversaries, and it seemed to me that little was likely to be gained by greeting them with words of salutation from Bishop Poppo. So I fled with the rest up into the church tower, and there I should have perished, and the others with me, had God not elected to liberate us from our plight upon this blessed Whitsun day."

He wagged his head mournfully and regarded Orm with weary eyes.

"All this was fourteen days ago," he said, "and since then I have had little sleep. And my body is weak—nay, not weak, for it is as strong as the spirit that inhabits it; still, there are limits to its strength."

"You can sleep later," said Orm impatiently. "Do you know aught of what has happened to Ylva, King Harald's daughter?"

"This much I know," replied Brother Willibald promptly, "that unless she shortly mends her ways, she will burn in hell-fire for her brazenness of spirit and scandalous conduct. And what hope can one cherish that any daughter of King Harald will ever mend her ways?"

"Do you hate our women, too?" asked Orm. "What harm has she ever done to you?"

"It matters little what she has done to me," said the little priest bitterly, "though she did, in fact, call me a bald old owl merely because I threatened her with the vengeance of the Lord."

"You threatened her, priest?" said Orm, getting to his feet. "Why did you threaten her?"

"Because she swore that she would do as she pleased and marry a heathen, even though all the bishops in the world should strive to stop her."

Orm clutched his beard and stared open-eyed at the little priest. Then he seated himself again.

"I am the heathen she wishes to marry," he said quietly. "Where is she now?"

But he received no answer to his question that evening, for, as he spoke, Brother Willibald drooped slowly down on to the table and fell fast asleep with his head upon his arms. Orm did his best to wake him, but in vain; at length he picked him up, carried him to the settle, laid him there, and threw a skin over him. He noted with surprise that he was beginning to grow fond of this little priest. For a while he sat alone brooding over his ale. Then, as he found that he had no desire for sleep, his impatience began again to swell within him, and he got up, crossed to the settle, and gave Brother Willibald a vigorous shaking.

But Brother Willibald merely turned over in his sleep and muttered in a drowsy and peevish whisper: "Worse than fiends!"

When next morning the little priest at length awoke, he proved to be somewhat milder of temper and seemed fairly contented with his situation; so Orm lost no time in extracting from him details of everything that had happened to Ylva since he had last seen her. She had fled from Jellinge with the Bishop, preferring exile to remaining at home in her brother Sven's care, and had spent the winter with him at Westminster, in great impatience to return home to Denmark as soon as good news should arrive of the situation there. Of late, however, the rumor had reached them that King Harald had died in exile. This had caused Ylva to consider journeying north to the home of her sister Gunhild, who was wedded to the Danish Jarl Palling of Northumberland. The Bishop was unwilling to allow her to undertake such a dangerous journey, preferring that she should remain in the south and marry some chieftain from those parts, whom he would help to find for her. But whenever he had brought this subject up, she had turned white with rage and had broken into fearful invective against anyone who happened to be near her, not excluding the Bishop himself.

This was what the little priest had to tell Orm concerning Ylva. Orm was happy to know that she had escaped King Sven's clutches, but it vexed him not to be able to think of any means of seeing her. He worried, too, about the blow he had received on his neck, and the pain he still suffered as a result of it; but Brother Willibald smiled disparagingly and said that skulls as thick as his would survive worse cracks than that. However, he put blood-leeches behind Orm's ears, with the result that he soon began to feel better. Nevertheless, he could not keep his thoughts from Ylva. It occurred to him to try to talk Thorkel and the other chieftains into undertaking a great plundering expedition against London and Westminster, in the hope that this might enable him to make contact with her; but the chieftains were occupied in tedious conferences with the envoys, settling details regarding the gifts they were to receive from King Ethelred, and the whole army sat idle-fingered, doing nothing but eat and drink and speculate on how much so great a King could fittingly be asked to pay.

Both the old Bishops spoke out manfully on their master's behalf, advancing many arguments to show why the sums suggested by the chieftains should be regarded as excessive. They regretted that the Vikings did not appear to realize that there were more valuable things in the world than gold and silver, and that for a rich man to enter the kingdom of heaven was more difficult than for an ox to pass through the smoke-hole of a roof. The chieftains heard them out patiently and then replied that, should any disadvantages accrue to them from the bargain, they would accept them stoically, but they could not accept a sum less than that which they had originally named. If, they added, what the Bishops had said about the kingdom of heaven and the smoke-hole was true, they would surely be doing King Ethelred a good service by relieving him of some of the burden of his wealth.

Sighing, the Bishops increased their offer, and at last agreement was reached as to the sum that King Ethelred was to pay. Every man in the fleet was to receive six marks of silver, in addition to what he had already taken by plunder. Every helmsman was to have twelve marks, and every ship's captain sixty; and Thorkel, Gudmund, and Jostein were each to receive three hundred marks. The Bishops said that this was a sad day for them, and that they hardly knew what their King would say when he heard the sum they had agreed on. It would, they explained, fall all the more heavily on him because at this very moment other envoys of his were negotiating with a Norwegian chieftain named Olaf Tryggvasson, who, with his fleet, was plundering the south coast. They could not be sure, they said, that even King Ethelred's wealth would suffice to meet both demands.

When they heard this, the chieftains began to worry lest they might have asked for too small a sum, and also lest the Norwegians should get in before them. They held a brief conference among themselves and then announced that they had decided not to increase their demand, but that the Bishops had better lose no time in fetching the silver, for, they said, they would take it ill if the Norwegians were paid before them.

The Bishop of London, who was a friendly and smiling man, assented to this and promised that they would do their best.

"I am surprised, however," he said, "to see such valiant chieftains as yourselves bothering your heads about this Norwegian captain, whose fleet is much smaller than yours. Would it not be a good thing for you to row down to the south coast, where this captain is lying, and destroy him and his men, and so win all his treasure? He has lately come from Brittany, in fine ships, and men say that he took much booty there. If you were to do this, it would still further increase the love that our lord the King bears you; and in that case he would have no difficulty in finding the sum you demand, for he would not then have to appease this Norwegian captain's greed."

Thorkel nodded and looked uncertain, and Gudmund laughed and said that the Bishop's suggestion was certainly worth considering.

"I have never myself met any of these Norwegians," he said, "but everyone knows that an encounter with them always provides fine fighting and good tales for the survivors to tell their children. At home, in Bravik, I have heard it said that few men outside East Guteland are their superiors, and it might be worth finding out whether this reputation of theirs is justified. I have in my ships berserks from Aland who are beginning to complain that this expedition is providing them with splendid booty and excellent ale, but little in the way of good fighting; and they say they are not used to a peaceful life."

Thorkel commented that he had, on one occasion, encountered Norwegians, but that he had no objection to doing so again, once his arm was healed; for in a battle with them much honor and wealth might be won.

Then Jostein burst into a great roar of laughter and took off his hat and flung it on the ground at his feet. He always wore an old red hat with a broad brim when he was not actually fighting, because his helmet chafed his skull.

"Look at me!" he cried. "I am old and bald; and where age is, there is also wisdom, as I am about to show you. This god-man can deceive you, Thorkel, and you, too, Gudmund, with his craft and cunning, but he cannot deceive me, for I am as old and as wise as he is. It will be a fine thing for him and his King if he can persuade us to fight against the Norwegian; for then we shall destroy each other, and King Ethelred will be quit of us all and will not need to squander any of his silver on such as survive the battle. But if you take my advice, you will not let any such thing happen."

Gudmund and Thorkel had to admit that they had not thought of it in this light, and that Jostein was the wisest of them all; and the envoys found that they could not prevail upon them any further. So they made ready to return to King Ethelred, to tell him how everything had turned out and to make arrangements to have the silver collected as soon as possible.

But before they departed, they robed themselves in their finest garments, gathered their followers about them, and walked out in solemn procession to the field where the battle had taken place. There they read prayers over the bodies of the dead, who lay half-covered by the richly growing grass, while crows and ravens circled above them in their multitudes, complaining harshly at being thus rudely disturbed from their lawful feeding.

CHAPTER TWO

CONCERNING SPIRITUAL THINGS

THERE was great rejoicing in the camp when the men learned of the agreement that their chieftains had reached with King Ethelred's envoys. They all praised the chieftains for striking such a fine bargain, and acclaimed King Ethelred as the most considerate king toward poor seafarers from the north that there had ever been. Much drinking and merrymaking followed, fat sheep and young women being in great demand; and the scholars among them sat round the fires where the sheep were being roasted and tried to calculate how much silver there would be to each ship, and how much for the whole fleet. This they found a difficult task, and there were frequent disputes over who had calculated most correctly; but on one point they were all agreed: namely, that none of them had ever before believed that such a quantity of silver could exist anywhere in the world, unless perhaps in the Emperor's palace at Miklagard. Some of them thought it surprising that the helmsmen should receive so large a share, seeing that their work was light and they were never required to sit at an oar; but the helmsmen themselves thought that every right-thinking man would appreciate that they were worth more than any other members of the fleet.

Although the ale was good and strong and the excitement great, still, the arguments seldom took a serious turn; for they all now regarded themselves as rich men and found life good, and so were less ready than usual to grope for their weapons.

But Orm sat brooding darkly with the little priest, thinking that few men in the world could find themselves more unhappily placed than he.

Brother Willibald had found plenty to occupy him, for there were many wounded men who required his attention, and he applied himself to their needs with zeal and cunning. He also examined Thorkel's arm and had a good deal to say about the Bishops' doctor and the way he had treated it; for he was unwilling to allow that anyone but himself possessed any skill or knowledge in the craft of medicine. He said that he would have to leave with the Bishops, but Orm was reluctant to let him go.

"For it is always a good thing to have a doctor around," he said, "and it may be, as you say, that you are the best there is. It is true that I should like to send greetings through you to Ylva, this daughter of King Harald; but if I did this, I should never see you again, because of the hatred you bear us Northmen. So I should never know her reply in any case. I cannot decide what is the best thing for me to do, and this uncertainty is having a serious effect on my appetite and sleep."

"Do you intend to keep me here by force?" asked Brother Willibald indignantly. "I have frequently heard you Northmen boast that your fidelity to your word matches your valor in battle; and all of us who were in the tower were promised that we should be free to go as we pleased. But doubtless that has slipped your memory."

Orm stared blackly ahead of him and replied that he seldom forgot things. "But it is hard for me to let you go," he added, "for you are a good counselor to me, even if you can do nothing for me in this matter. You are a wise man, little priest, so answer me this question: if you were in my place and were faced with the problem that faces me, what would you do?"

Brother Willibald smiled to himself and nodded sympathetically at Orm. Then he shook his head.

"You seem to be very fixed on wooing this young woman," he said, "despite the sharpness of her temper. I am surprised at this, for you godless berserks are usually content with any woman who crosses your path and seldom mope for a particular one. Is it because she is a princess?"

"She can expect no dowry from her father," said Orm, "the way things have turned out for him. And be sure of this, that it is herself and not her wealth that I yearn for. Nor is the fact that she is of noble blood any obstacle to our marriage, for I am myself of aristocratic ancestry."

"Perhaps she has given you a love potion," said Brother Willibald, "and that is why your passion for her is so unrelenting."

"Once she gave me drink," said Orm, "but never since. It was the first occasion on which I saw her, and the drink was meat broth. And I drank but little of that, for she lost her temper and threw the cup and the broth into the fireplace. In any case, it was you yourself who ordered the broth to be prepared for me."

"I was not present while it was being prepared," said Brother Willibald thoughtfully, "nor while she was bringing it from the kitchen to your room; and a young man needs but a few drops of one of these potions, when the woman in question is young and well shaped. But even if it be true that she put witchcraft in the drink, there is nothing I can do about it; for there is no cure for love save love itself. That is the verdict of all the wise doctors who have ever practiced since the earliest times."

"The cure you speak of is the cure I wish to have," said Orm, "and what I am asking is whether you can help me to procure it."

Brother Willibald pointed his finger at him magisterially, and in his most fatherly manner said: "There is only one thing to be done when a man is troubled and cannot work out his own salvation; but you, unfortunate heathen, are in no position to follow my advice. For the only remedy is to pray to God for help, and that you cannot do."

"Does He often help you?" asked Orm.

"He helps me when I ask Him sensible things," replied Brother Willibald with feeling, "and that is more than your gods do for you. He does not listen when I complain to Him about trivial afflictions, which He thinks I am well able to endure on my own; indeed, I have, with my own eyes, seen the holy and blessed Bishop Poppo, when we were fleeing across the sea, cry most desperately to God and St. Peter to relieve him from his seasickness and remain unheard. But when I was in the tower with these other good people, and hunger and thirst and the swords of Antichrist were threatening us, we cried to God in our need, and He heard us and granted our prayers, though there was none among us as blessed in the sight of God as Bishop Poppo. For in God's good time the envoys arrived and rescued us; and though they were, in one sense, envoys from King Ethelred to the heathen chieftains, still, they were also envoys from God sent from heaven to succor us, in answer to the many and earnest prayers that we had offered up to Him."

Orm nodded, and admitted that there might be something in what Brother Willibald said, since he had himself been a witness to all this.

"Now I begin to understand," he said, "why my plan to smoke you out of the tower went astray. Doubtless this God, or whoever you cried to, ordered the wind to arise and blow away the smoke."

Brother Willibald replied that this was exactly what had happened; the finger of God had countered their evil machinations and set them at naught.

Orm sat pondering in silence, tugging his beard uncertainly.

"My mother has become a Christian in her old age," he said at length. "She has learned two prayers, which she repeats often, holding them to be most potent. She says it is these prayers that saved me from death and brought me home to her again, after undergoing so many perils; though it may be that Blue-Tongue and I did our share in overcoming them, and you, too, little priest. Now I am beginning to feel that I, too, might ask this God to

help me, since He seems to be such a helpful god. But I do not
know what He will ask of me in return, nor how I should address
Him."

"You cannot ask God to help you," said Brother Willibald de-
cisively, "until you have become a Christian. And you cannot
become a Christian until you have been baptized. And you cannot be baptized until you have renounced your false gods and
professed yourself a convinced believer in the Father, the Son, and
the Holy Ghost."

"Those are a great many conditions," said Orm. "More than
Allah and His Prophet require of a man."

"Allah and His Prophet?" exclaimed the little priest in surprise.
"What do you know of them?"

"I have traveled more widely in the world than you," replied
Orm. "And when I served Almansur in Andalusia, we had to pray
to Allah and His Prophet twice a day, and sometimes even thrice.
I still remember the prayers, if you would care to hear them."

Brother Willibald threw up his hands in horror. "In the name
of the Father, the Son, and the Holy Ghost!" he cried. "Save us
from the machinations of Satan and the devices of Allah the
abominable! Your state is as parlous as a man's could be, for to
worship Allah is the worst heresy of all. Are you still a follower
of His?"

"I worshipped Him while I was Almansur's servant," said Orm,
"because my master commanded me to do so, and he was a man
whom it was folly to disobey. Since I left him, I have not worshipped any god. Perhaps that is why things have gone less well
for me recently."

"I am surprised that Bishop Poppo did not come to hear of this
while you were at King Harald's court," said Brother Willibald.
"If he had known that you had embraced the black impostor he
would have baptized you straightway, so full of zeal and piety is
he, even if it had needed twelve of King Harald's berserks to hold
you in the water. It is a good and blessed thing to rescue a plain
soul from darkness and blindness; and it may be that even the souls
of Northmen should be regarded as deserving of charity, though I
confess I can hardly bring myself to believe it after all I have suffered at their hands. But all good men are agreed that it is seven
times more glorious to save the soul of one who has been seduced

by Mohammed. For Satan himself has not caused more mischief than that man."

Orm asked who Satan might be, and Brother Willibald told him all about him.

"It would appear, then," said Orm, "that I have involuntarily angered this Satan by ceasing to worship Allah and His Prophet, and that all my misfortunes have resulted from this."

"Exactly," said the little priest, "and it is lucky for you that you have come at last to realize the error of your ways. Your present state is as disastrous as could be imagined, for you have incurred the wrath of Satan without having the protection of God. As long as you worshipped Mohammed, accursed be his name, Satan was your ally and so, to a certain extent, you prospered."

"It is as I feared," said Orm. "Few men are in such a desperate plight as I. It is too much for any man to be on evil terms with both God and Satan."

He sat for a while buried in reflection.

At length he said: "Take me to the envoys. I wish to speak with men who have influence with God."

The Bishops had returned from the battlefield, where they had been blessing the dead, and were intending to start on their homeward journey on the following day. The elder of them was exhausted with walking round from corpse to corpse and had gone to rest, but the Bishop of London had invited Gudmund to join him in his lodgings and was sitting drinking with him in a last effort to persuade him to allow himself to become converted to Christianity.

Ever since they had first arrived at Maldon, the Bishops had striven their utmost to win the Viking chieftains over to their religion. King Ethelred and his Archbishop had commanded them to do so, for if they should succeed in this, the King's honor would be greatly enhanced in the sight of God and his countrymen. They had not succeeded in making much headway with Thorkel, for he had replied that his weapon-luck was good enough already and was, in any case, considerably superior to that of the Christians. Accordingly, he said, there seemed no point in his looking round for new gods. Nor had they prevailed upon Jostein. He had listened mutely to their arguments, sitting with his hands crossed upon the handle of the great battleax that he always carried with him, which he called Widow's-Grief, regarding them from beneath wrinkled brows as they explained to him the mysteries of Christ and of the kingdom of God. Then he gave a great roar of laughter, flung his hat upon the floor, and asked the Bishops if they thought that he was a simpleton.

"These twenty-seven winters," he said, "I have served as priest at the great Uppsala sacrifice; and you do me little honor in filling my ears with such prattle as this, fit only for children and gammers. With this ax which you see here I have hewn off the heads of the harvest sacrifices, and hung their bodies on the sacred trees that front the temple; and there were Christians among them, ay, and priests too, naked on their knees in the snow, wailing. Tell me what profit they gained from worshipping this God you speak of."

The Bishops shuddered and crossed themselves and understood that there was no sense in trying to reason with such a man.

But they cherished greater hopes of Gudmund, for he was amiable and good-humored toward them and seemed interested in what they had to say; and sometimes, when he had drunk well, he had even thanked them warmly for their beautiful talk and solicitous regard for his spiritual well-being. He had not as yet, however, committed himself definitely; so the Bishop of London had now invited him to a grand dinner, with food and drink of a very special nature, in the hope of being able to push him to a positive decision.

Gudmund helped himself greedily to everything that was put before him; and when he had eaten and drunk his fill, the Bishop's musicians played for him, so beautifully that tears began to appear in his beard. Then the Bishop set to work on him, speaking in his most persuasive tones and choosing his words with care. Gudmund listened and nodded and at length admitted that there was much that appealed to him in this Christianity.

"You are a good fellow," he said to the Bishop. "You are open-handed and wise, and you drink like a warrior, and your talk is agreeable to listen to. I should like to accede to your request; but you must know that this is no small favor that you are asking of me. For it will be an ill thing if I return home to find myself the laughing-stock of my house-folk and neighbors for having allowed

myself to be deceived by the prattle of priests. Still, it is my belief
that a man like you must doubtless wield considerable power and
be the possessor of many secrets; and I have here an object I have
recently found which I should like you to read one of your prayers
over."

He drew from his shirt the little gold cross and held it in front
of the Bishop's nose.

"I found this in a rich man's house," he said. "It cost me two
men's lives, and a prettier plaything I never set eyes on. I intend
to give this to my small son when I return home. His name is
Folke, and women call him Filbyter. He is a sturdy little ruffian,
with a particular fondness for silver and gold, and once he has
got his hands on a thing, it is no easy matter to get it away from
him. He will hardly be able to contain himself when he sees this
cross. It would be a fine thing if you could bless it and make it
lucky, for I want him to become rich and powerful, so that he
will be able to sit at home in his house and be honored by men,
and see his crops flourish and his cattle wax fat, and have no need
to rove the sea for his livelihood, faring ill among foreigners and
their arms."

The Bishop smiled and took the cross and mumbled over it. Gudmund, greatly delighted, stuffed it back into his shirt.

"You shall return to your home a wealthy man," said the Bishop,
"thanks to good King Ethelred's openhandedness and meek love
of peace. But you must believe me when I tell you that your luck
would be even greater if you were to come over to Christ."

"A man can never have too much luck," said Gudmund, pulling thoughtfully at his beard. "I have already decided which
neighbor's land I shall purchase when I return home, and what
manner of house I shall build on it. It shall be large, with many
rooms, built of the finest oak. To have it the way I want it to be
is going to cost a lot of silver. But if I have a good hoard of silver
left in my coffers after I have built it, I do not think anyone will
feel much inclined to laugh at me, howsoever I may have conducted myself while abroad. So it shall be as you wish. You may
baptize me, and I will follow Christ faithfully for the rest of my
days, if you increase my share of King Ethelred's silver by a hundred marks."

"That," replied the Bishop mildly, "is not the right attitude of mind for one wishing to be admitted into the brotherhood of Christ. I shall not blame you too heavily, however, since you are doubtless unfamiliar with the text which says: 'Blessed are the poor'; and I fear it would take some time to explain the truth of that to you. But you should bethink yourself that you are already about to receive much silver from King Ethelred, more than any other living man could offer you; and, though he is a great and powerful King, still, even his coffers are not bottomless. It is not within his power to grant this demand of yours, even if he were agreeable to doing so. I think I can promise you a baptismal gift of twenty marks, seeing that you are a chieftain, but that is the maximum that I can offer, and he may regard even that as excessive. But now I beg that you will sample a drink that I have specially ordered to be prepared for us and which is, I think, not known in your country. It consists of hot wine blended with honey and with rare spices from the Eastland called cinnamon and cardamom. Men well versed in the subject of drink assert that no beverage is so pleasing to the palate or so effective at dispersing heavy humors and morbid cogitations."

Gudmund found the drink good and wholesome; nevertheless, the Bishop's offer still appeared to him to be inadequate. He would not, he explained, be prepared to risk his good name at home in East Guteland for as little as that.

"However, for the sake of the friendship I bear toward you," he said, "I will do it for sixty marks. I cannot offer myself more cheaply than that."

"The friendship I bear toward you could not be greater," replied the Bishop, "and such is my desire to lead you into the brotherhood of Christ, so that you may partake of the wealth that Heaven has to offer, that I will even plunge into my own poor coffers to satisfy your demand. But I own, alas, little in the way of worldly goods, and ten marks is the most that I can add to my original offer."

Gudmund shook his head at this and closed his eyes sleepily. At this stage in the bargaining a commotion was suddenly heard outside the door, and Orm burst in with Brother Willibald struggling under one arm and two porters hanging on to his clothing and clamoring that the Bishop was not to be disturbed.

"Holy Bishop!" he said. "I am Orm, Toste's son, from the

Mound in Skania, a captain of Thorkel the Tall. I wish to be baptized and to accompany you to London."

The Bishop stared at him in amazement and some alarm. But when he saw that Orm was neither drunk nor out of his wits, he asked him the meaning of his request; for he was not accustomed to Northmen forcing themselves into his presence on errands of this nature.

"I wish to place myself under the protection of God," said Orm, "for my plight is worse than that of other men. This priest can explain it all to you better than I can."

Brother Willibald then begged the Bishop to forgive him for taking part in this intrusion. He had, he explained, not come voluntarily, but had been compelled to do so by the brute force of this heathen berserk, who had dragged him past vigilant porters, despite his desperate struggles and protests; for he himself had realized that the Bishop was engaged upon important business.

The Bishop replied amiably that he need give no more thought to the matter. He pointed a finger at Gudmund, who, with the assistance of a last cupful of spiced wine, had fallen asleep in his chair.

"I have labored long to persuade him to become a Christian," he said, "and yet I have failed, for his soul is wholly occupied with earthly considerations. But now God has sent me another heathen in his place, and one, moreover, who is not called but comes of his own free will. Welcome, unbeliever! Are you fully prepared to join our brotherhood?"

"I am," replied Orm, "for I have already served the prophet Mohammed and his God, and I gather that nothing can be more dangerous than that."

The Bishop's eyes grew round, and he struck the cross on his breast three times and called for holy water.

"Mohammed and his God?" he inquired of Brother Willibald. "What is the meaning of this?"

Between them Orm and Brother Willibald explained to the Bishop how the matter stood. The Bishop then announced that he had, in his time, seen much of sin and darkness, but that never before had he set eyes upon a man who had actually served Mohammed. When the holy water arrived, he took a small branch, dipped it in the water, and shook it over Orm, intoning prayers the while to drive the evil spirits out of the latter's body. Orm turned pale as the Bishop did this, and he afterwards said that this sprinkling was a hard thing to endure, for it made his whole body shiver as though the hairs on his neck were trying to stand on end. The Bishop continued to sprinkle him vigorously for some time, but at length desisted and said that that would suffice.

"You are not rolling about in fits," he informed Orm, "and I can see no froth on your lips, nor can detect any unpleasant smell emanating from your body. All this signifies that the evil spirit has departed from you. Praise God for it!"

Then he sprinkled a little on Gudmund, who immediately leaped to his feet, roaring at them to reef sail, but then fell back on his bench and began to snore resonantly.

Orm dried the water from his face and asked whether this would have the same effect upon him as baptism.

The Bishop replied that there was a considerable difference between baptism and this rite, and that it was by no means so easy for a man to be permitted to undergo baptism, least of all one who had served Mohammed.

"First you must forswear your false gods," he said, "and avow your belief in the Father, the Son, and the Holy Ghost. In addition to this, you must also be schooled in Christian doctrine."

"I have no gods to forswear," said Orm, "and am ready to bind myself to God and his son and this ghost of theirs. As for schooling in Christian doctrine, I have already had plenty of that, first from the monks in Ireland, and afterwards at King Harald's court, and from my old mother at home, as well as she was able. And now I have heard more about it from this little priest, who is my friend and has taught me a great deal about Satan. So that I think I am as learned on the subject as most men."

The Bishop nodded approvingly and said that this was good to hear, and that it was not often that one met heathens who were willing to listen to so much instruction about holy matters. Then he rubbed his nose and stole a thoughtful glance at Gudmund, who was sound asleep. He turned again to Orm.

"There is one other point," he said slowly and with great solemnity. "You have been dyed more deeply in sin than any man I have ever come across, in that you have served the false prophet, who is the blackest of all the chieftains of Satan. Now if, after partaking in such abominable practices, you wish to place yourself under the wing of the living God, it is meet that you should bring with you a gift for Him and for His Church, to show that your repentance is genuine and that you have truly abandoned your evil ways."

Orm replied that was no more than was reasonable, that he should give something to improve his luck and buy the protection of God. He asked the Bishop what would be regarded as a suitable gift.

"That depends," said the Bishop, "upon a man's blood and wealth, and upon the magnitude of his sins. Once I baptized a Danish chieftain who had come to this land to claim his inheritance. He gave five oxen, an anker of ale and twenty pounds of beeswax to the Church of God. In the ancient Scriptures we read of men of noble birth who gave as much as ten marks of silver, or even twelve, and built a church besides. But they had brought all their household with them to be baptized."

"I do not wish to give less than other men," said Orm, "for you must know that the blood of the Broad Embrace runs in my veins. When I reach home, I will build a church; you shall baptize all my crew, and I will give you fifteen marks of silver. But in return for this I expect you to speak well of me to God."

"You are a true chieftain," cried the Bishop joyfully, "and I will do all that lies in my power to help you."

Both of them were delighted with the bargain they had struck; but the Bishop wondered if Orm could have been serious when he had said that all the members of his crew were to be baptized with him.

"If I am to be a Christian," said Orm, "I cannot have heathens aboard my ship. For what would God think of me if I were to allow that? They shall do as I do, and when I tell my crew that such and such a thing is to be, they do not contradict me. I have some men aboard who have already been baptized once, or even twice, but once more cannot hurt them."

He begged that the Bishops and all their followers would honor him by coming aboard his ship the next morning, so that he might convey them up the river to London and Westminster and they might all be baptized there.

"My ship is large and fine," he said. "It will be somewhat

crowded, with so many guests aboard, but the voyage will not take long, and the weather is fair and calm."

He was very pressing about this, but the Bishop said that he could not make a decision in so important a matter before discussing it with his brother in office and with others of their company, so Orm had to contain himself patiently until the following day. He parted from the Bishop with many expressions of thanks, and walked back to his lodgings with Brother Willibald. The latter had not said much in the Bishop's presence, but as soon as they had left the house, he began to cackle mirthfully.

"What are you so amused at?" asked Orm.

"I was only thinking," replied the little priest, "how much trouble you were putting yourself to for the sake of King Harald's daughter. But I think you are acquitting yourself very well."

"If everything goes as it should," said Orm, "you shall not be left unrewarded. For it seems to me that my luck began to improve from the moment I met you again."

The Bishop, left to himself, sat for a while smiling to himself, and then bade his servants wake Gudmund. This they at length succeeded in doing, though he grumbled at being thus disturbed.

"I have been thinking about that matter we were speaking of," said the Bishop, "and, with God's help, I think I can promise you forty marks if you will allow yourself to be baptized."

On hearing this, Gudmund became wide awake, and after a brief argument they shook hands on forty-five marks, together with a pound of the spices that the Bishop used to flavor his wine.

The next day, at Thorkel's lodgings, the chieftains discussed Orm's proposal to convey the Bishops by ship to Westminster. On hearing of the plan, Gudmund announced that he would like to join the party. Seeing that the envoys had promised them a safe conduct, and that peace had been concluded between themselves and King Ethelred, he would, he said, like to be present when the King weighed out his silver, to ensure that the ceremony was carried out in a right and proper manner.

Thorkel thought this a reasonable request, and said he would have liked to accompany them himself if his arm had been better. But Jostein said that it was quite sufficient that one of the three chieftains should go; otherwise the English might be tempted to attack them, and it would be rash to weaken the strength of the main body in the camp before the silver was safely in their hands.

The weather was so fine that the Bishops could not find it in themselves to refuse to return by ship. Their only concern was lest they should fall foul of pirates; so at last it was decided that Gudmund should take his ship as well as Orm's, and that they should sail up to Westminster together. There they were to see the silver weighed out with the least possible delay; and in the event of their meeting the King himself, they were to thank him for his gift and inform him that they intended to start plundering again, on a more extensive scale than before, if he took too long about handing it over.

Orm summoned his crew together and told them that they were now about to sail up to Westminster with the shield of peace upon their masthead and with King Ethelred's holy envoys aboard.

Several of his men expressed uneasiness at this. They said that it was always dangerous to have a priest on board, as every sailor knew, and that a bishop might prove even worse.

Orm calmed their fears, however, and assured them that everything would be all right; for, he explained, these god-men were so holy that no harm could possibly come to them, however cunningly the sea people might contrive against them. He continued: "When we reach Westminster, I am going to get myself baptized. I have discussed the subject thoroughly with these holy men, and they have convinced me that it is an excellent thing to worship Christ; so I intend to begin doing so as soon as possible. Now, in a ship it is always best that everyone should be of the same mind and should follow the same customs. It is therefore my wish that you shall all be baptized with me. This will be to the advantage of you all. You can be certain of this, for I, who know, tell you that it will be so. If any of you is unwilling to do this, let him speak up at once; but he shall leave my ship and take his belongings with him, and shall not be a follower of mine any more."

Many of the men glanced doubtfully at one another and scratched behind their ears; but Rapp the One-Eyed, who was the ship's helmsman, and who was feared by most of the men, was standing in front of the crew as they listened, and he nodded calmly when he heard Orm say this, having heard him speak thus

on a similar occasion once before. When the others saw Rapp do
this, they offered no objection.

Orm continued: "I know that there are among you men who
have already been baptized at home in Skania, perhaps receiving
a shirt or a tunic for your pains, or a little cross to wear on a
band round your neck. Sometimes it happens that one hears one
of these men say that he cannot see that he has profited much
from being baptized. But these were cheap baptisms, fit only for
women and children. This time we are going to be baptized
differently, by holier men, and are going to get protection from
God and better luck for the rest of our lives. It would not be a
right thing that we should gain such advantages without paying
for them. I myself am giving a large sum for the protection
and luck that I expect to receive; and each of you shall pay a
penny."

There was murmuring at this, and some of the men were heard
to say that this was a new idea, that a man should pay to be
baptized, and that a penny was no small sum.

"I am not forcing anyone to do this," said Orm. "Anyone who
thinks this suggestion unreasonable can save his money by meeting me in combat as soon as the baptizing is finished. If he wins,
nobody is going to make him pay; and if he loses, he will also save
his money."

Most of the men thought that this was well spoken, and several
of them challenged any member of the crew who had a mind to
be closefisted to declare himself. But the ones to whom these
words were addressed grinned weakly, thinking that they would
have to make the best of whatever advantages their money might
bring them.

Gudmund and Orm each took one of the god-men aboard his
ship, the elder Bishop and his suite going with Gudmund, and
the Bishop of London with Orm, who also took with him Brother
Willibald. The Bishops blessed their ships, prayed for a lucky
voyage, and set up their standards; then the ships put out and
at once got a good breeze and fine weather, which made the men
regard the Bishops with increased respect. They entered the river
Thames on the flood tide, spent the night in the estuary, and next
morning, in a clear dawn light, began to row up the river.

People stood at their hut doors among the trees that lined the riverbank, staring at the ships fearfully, and men fishing in the river prepared to flee as the ships hove into sight; they were calmed, however, by the sight of the Bishops' standards. Here and there they saw burned villages lying deserted after one of the Vikings' visits; then, farther up, they came to a place where the river was blocked by four rows of piles, with only a small channel left free in the middle. Three large watch-ships lay there, filled with armed men. The Vikings were forced to stop rowing, for the watch-ships stood in the midst of the channel with all their men prepared for battle, and blocked further progress.

"Are you blind?" roared Gudmund across the water, "or have you lost your wits? Do you not see that we come with a shield of peace on our masthead, and have holy bishops aboard?"

"Do not try to fool us," replied a voice from the watch-ships. "We want no pirates here."

"We have your own King's envoys aboard," roared Gudmund.

"We know you," came the reply. "You are full of cunning and devilry."

"We are coming to be baptized," shouted Orm impatiently.

At this, there was loud laughter on the watch-ships, and a voice shouted back: "Have you grown tired of your lord and master the Devil?"

"Yes!" roared Orm furiously, and at this the laughter on the other ships was redoubled.

Then it looked as though there was going to be fighting, for Orm was enraged by their laughter and bade Rapp heave to and grapple the nearest ship, which was doing most of the laughing. But by this time the Bishops had hastily donned their robes, and now, raising their staffs aloft, they cried to both sides to be still. Orm was unwilling to obey, and Gudmund, too, thought that this was asking too much. Then the Bishops cried across the water to their countrymen, addressing them sternly, so that at last they realized that the holy men were what they appeared to be, and not prisoners or pirates in disguise. So the ships were allowed to pass, and nothing came of the encounter, apart from smart exchanges of insults between the rival crews as the Vikings rowed past.

Orm stood with a spear in his hand, staring at the watch-ships, still white with wrath.

"I should have liked to teach them some manners," he said to Brother Willibald, who was standing beside him, and who had not shown any evidence of fear when the fighting had seemed about to begin.

"He who lives by the sword shall perish by the sword," replied the little priest. "Thus it is written in the holy book, where all wisdom is. How could you have come to King Harald's daughter if you had fought with King Ethelred's ships? But you are a man of violence, and will always remain one. And you will suffer sorely for it."

Orm sighed and threw down his spear.

"When I have won her," he said, "I shall be a man of peace."

But the little priest shook his head sadly.

"Can the leopard change its spots?" he said. "Or the blue man his skin? Thus, too, is it written in the holy book. But thank God and the blessed Bishops that they have helped you now."

Soon they rounded a curve in the river and saw London lying before them on the right bank. It was a sight that struck the Vikings speechless with wonder, for the town was so great that, from the river, they could not see its end, and the priests told them it had been calculated that more than thirty thousand men dwelt there. Many of the Vikings found it difficult to imagine what so many men could find to live on in such a crowded place, with no fields or cattle. But the wise ones among them knew and said that such town-dwellers were an evil and cunning race, who understood well how to earn a livelihood from honest countryfolk without themselves ever setting their hands to a plow or a flail. It was therefore, these wise men argued, a good thing for bold sailors to pay occasional visits to these people and relieve them of what they had stolen from other folk. So they all gazed spellbound at the town as they rowed slowly up against the tide, thinking that here indeed there must be riches worth the taking.

But Orm and Rapp the One-Eyed said that they had seen bigger cities, and that this was only a village compared with Córdoba.

So they rowed on toward the great bridge, which was built of huge tree trunks, and which was so high that the biggest ships could row under it, once they had lowered their masts. Many people rushed out to see them, including armed men, yelling at the tops of their voices about heathens and devils; but they broke into shouts of jubilation when they heard their Bishops cry resonantly to them that all was well and that peace had been concluded with the men from the sea. As the ships approached, people crowded on to the bridge to catch a glimpse of them at close quarters. When the crews caught sight of several fine young women among them, they shouted enthusiastically to them to make haste and come down, promising that they would find good prizes aboard, silver and merriment and bold men, as well as plenty of priests to pardon their sins in the best Christian manner. One or two of the young women giggled coyly and answered that they had a mind to do as the men bade them, but that it was a long way to jump; whereupon they were immediately grabbed by the hair by furious kinsfolk, who promised them the birch on their bare bodies for indulging in such lewd chatter with heathen men.

Brother Willibald shook his head sadly and said that young people were very difficult nowadays, even in Christian communities. And Rapp, too, standing at his steering-oar, shook his head as they passed beneath the bridge, and muttered sullenly that women were always full of useless chatter, wherever you found them.

"They ought to have kept their mouths shut," he said, "and to have jumped at once, as they were told to do."

They were now approaching Westminster and could see tall spires rising up behind the trees. The Bishops clothed themselves once more in all their finery; and the priests attending them began to chant an ancient hymn, which St. Columbanus had been wont to sing when baptizing heathens.

> Lo! Here's a host from darkness won
> —Do not reject them, Lord!—
> Who late in need and peril spun
> Upon the sinful flood.
> To the cross which the wide world o'er hath blazed
> They lift their eyes, and Thy name is praised
> By souls which late with the Devil grazed.
> —Do not reject them, Lord!

Their voices rang sweetly over the water in the clear evening; and as soon as the men at the oars had grasped the rhythm of

the hymn, they began to pull in time to it and voted it a fine
chantey to row by.

As the singing ceased, they brought the ship to starboard and
made her fast to one of the piers beneath the red walls of Westminster.

CHAPTER THREE

CONCERNING MARRIAGE AND BAPTISM, AND KING ETHELRED'S SILVER

ING ETHELRED THE REDELESS sat miserably in
Westminster, surrounded by rede-givers, waiting to hear the outcome of his negotiations with the Northmen. He had gathered all
his warriors together about him, partly to protect his own person in
these dangerous times, and partly to keep an eye on the people of
London, who had begun to murmur somewhat after the defeat at
Maldon. He had his Archbishop with him to help and comfort him,
but the latter could achieve little in that direction; and the King's
uneasiness had so increased since the envoys had departed that he
had given up hunting entirely and had lost his desire for Masses
and women. He spent most of his time swatting flies, at which
occupation he was exceedingly skillful.

When, however, he heard that the envoys had returned, having
concluded peace with the invaders, he emerged from his melancholy; and when they told him that the chieftains and their crews
had come with the Bishops to be baptized, his excitement knew
no bounds. He immediately ordered all the bells in the town to
be rung, and commanded that the foreigners should be entertained
sumptuously; but when he heard that there were two strong ships'
companies of them, he became uneasy again and could not make
up his mind whether such tidings should be regarded as excellent
or calamitous. He scratched his beard earnestly and consulted his
priests, courtiers, and chamberlains on their opinions in the matter. Eventually it was decided that the Vikings should be permitted
to encamp in some fields outside the town, but should not be

allowed to enter it, and that the guards on the walls should be strengthened; also, that it should be proclaimed in all the churches that the heathens were flocking to London in their multitudes in search of baptism and spiritual education, so that all the people, when they heard this, might sing praise and thanksgiving to their God and King for causing such a miracle to occur. The very next morning, he added, so soon as he had had a few hours to rest and relax after the anxiety of the past fortnight, the envoys would be granted audience; and they might bring with them the chieftains who were to be baptized.

The Northmen proceeded to their camping-ground, and the King's officers made haste to furnish them with everything that they might require, treating them like royal guests. Before long the air was filled with the crackling of huge fires and the lowing of cattle beneath the slaughter-knife, and there was much demand for white bread, fat cheese, honey, egg-cakes, fresh pork, and ale such as kings and bishops were wont to drink. Orm's men were rowdier than Gudmund's, and more exacting in their demands, for they reckoned that, as they were about to be baptized, they had a right to the best of everything.

Orm, however, had something other than the stomachs of his men uppermost in his thoughts, being anxious to visit another part of the town with Brother Willibald, whom he refused to let out of his sight. He was wretched with anxiety lest Ylva should have come to harm, and could still hardly believe that he would find her safe and sound, despite all Brother Willibald's assurances. He felt certain that she had already promised herself to another, or that she had run away, or been carried off, or that the King, who was said to be much addicted to women, had noted her beauty and had taken her to be his concubine.   •

They passed through the city gate without hindrance, for the guards dared not oppose the entry of a foreigner accompanied by a priest, and Brother Willibald led the way to the great abbey, where Bishop Poppo was residing as the Abbot's guest. He had just returned from evensong, and looked older and thinner than when Orm had last seen him at King Harald's court, but his face lit up with pleasure when he saw Brother Willibald.

"God be praised that you have returned safely!" he said. "You have been away for a long time, and I had begun to fear lest

misfortune might have overtaken you on your journey. There is
much that I wish to learn from you. But who is this man whom
you have brought with you?"

"We sat at the same table in King Harald's hall," said Orm,
"the time you told the story about the King's son who got hanged
by his hair. But there were many others there besides me, and
much has happened since that evening. I am called Orm Tostesson,
and I have come to this land commanding my own ship under
Thorkel the Tall. And I have come to this place this evening to be
baptized and to fetch my woman."

"He used to be a follower of Mohammed," put in Brother
Willibald eagerly, "but now he wishes to abandon his allegiance
to the Devil. He is the man I made well after the last Christmas
feast at King Harald's the time they fought with swords in the
dining-hall before the drunken kings. It was he and his comrade
who threatened Brother Matthias with spears because he tried
to instruct them in Christian doctrine. But now he wishes to be
baptized."

"In the name of the Father, the Son, and the Holy Ghost!"
exclaimed the Bishop in alarm. "Has this man served Mohammed?"

"He has been purged and sprinkled by the Bishop of London,"
said the little priest soothingly, "who found no evil spirit left in
him."

"I have come to fetch Ylva, King Harald's daughter," said Orm
impatiently. "She has been promised to me, both by herself and
by King Harald."

"Who is now dead," said the little priest, "leaving the heathens
to war among themselves in Denmark."

"Holy Bishop," said Orm, "I should dearly like to see her at
once."

"This matter cannot be settled so simply," said the Bishop,
and bade them seat themselves.

"He has come to London to be baptized, and all his crew with
him, for her sake," said Brother Willibald.

"And he has served Mohammed?" cried the Bishop. "This is
indeed a mighty miracle. God still grants me moments of felicity,
even though He has seen fit to condemn me to end my days in
exile with all my life's work ruined and set at naught."

He bade his servant bring them ale and asked for tidings of recent events in Denmark and of all that had happened at Maldon.

Brother Willibald answered him at considerable length; and Orm, despite his impatience, assisted him with such details as he was able to provide; for the Bishop was a gentle and reverend man, and Orm could not find it in himself to refuse him the information he was so eager to obtain.

When they had told the Bishop everything they knew, he turned to Orm and said: "So now you have come to take from me my baptismal child, Ylva? It is no small ambition to seek the hand of a king's daughter. But I have heard the girl express her feelings in the matter; and she is, God witness, a person who knows her own mind!"

He shook his head and smiled silently to himself.

"She is a charge to make an old man hasten toward his grave," he continued, "and if you can rule her judgment, you are a wiser man than I am, or than good King Harald was. But the Lord our God moves along mysterious paths; and, once you have been baptized, I shall not stand in your way. Indeed, her marriage would lift a heavy burden from my old shoulders."

"We have been parted for long enough, she and I," said Orm. "Do not keep me from her any longer."

The Bishop rubbed his nose uncertainly and remarked that such zeal was understandable in a young man, but that the hour was late, and that it might perhaps be more advisable to postpone the meeting until after the baptism. In the end, however, he allowed himself to be persuaded, summoned one of his deacons, and bade him rouse four men, go with them to the Lady Ermentrude, greet her from the Bishop, and beg her, despite the lateness of the hour, to permit them to bring King Harald's daughter to him.

"I have done my best to keep her safe from the eyes of men," he continued when the deacon had left them, "which was very necessary with a girl of her comeliness in such a place as this is, now that the King and his court and all his soldiers have taken up residence here. She is lodged with the blessed Queen Bertha's nuns, hard by this abbey; and a troublesome guest she has proved to be, despite the fact that all the nuns treat her most affection-

ately. Twice she has tried to escape, because, so she said, the life
wearied her; and on one occasion, not so long ago, she inflamed
the lust of two young men of good family who had caught a
glimpse of her in the nuns' garden and had managed to exchange
words with her over the wall. Such was the passion that she
aroused in them that they climbed into the convent grounds early
one morning, accompanied by their servants and henchmen, and
fought a duel with swords among the nuns' flowerbeds to decide
which of them should have the right of wooing her. They fought
so desperately that in the end they both had to be carried away,
bleeding fearfully from their wounds, while she sat at her window
laughing to see such sport. Conduct of this nature is unseemly
in a convent, for it may infect the pious sisters' souls and do them
great harm. But I confess that her behavior seems to me to be
the result of thoughtlessness rather than of evil intentions."

"Did they both die?" asked Orm.

"No," replied the Bishop. "They recovered, though their wounds
were grave. I myself joined in the prayers for them. I was sick and
weary at the time and felt it a heavy burden to have such a charge
upon my hands. I admonished her severely and begged her to
accept the hand of one or other of the men, seeing that they had
fought so desperately for her sake and were both of noble birth.
I told her that I should die easier in my mind if I could see her
wedded first. But on hearing this she fell into a frenzy and
declared that, since both the young men were still living, their
duel could not have been very seriously fought, and that she would
hear no more of their suits. She said she preferred the sort of man
whose enemies needed no prayers or bandages after fighting. It
was then that I heard her mention your name."

The Bishop smiled benevolently at Orm and bade him not to
neglect his ale.

"I had other troubles to contend with in this affair," he continued, "for the Abbess, the pious Lady Ermentrude, had it in
her mind to birch the girl on her bare skin for having incited
these men to combat. But seeing that my poor godchild was only
a guest in the convent, and a king's daughter to boot, I succeeded
in dissuading her from pursuing this extreme course. It was not
an easy task, for abbesses are, in general, unwilling to listen to
counsel and have little confidence in the wisdom of men, even

when they happen to be bishops. In the end, however, she mitigated her sentence to three days' prayer and fasting, and I think it was probably fortunate that she did so. True it is that the pious Lady Ermentrude is a woman of adamant will and no mean strength of body, being broader in the loins than most of her sex; none the less, God alone can say with certainty which of their two skins would have smarted the more had she attempted to bring the birch to King Harald's daughter. My poor godchild might have prevailed, and so have fallen even further from grace."

"The first time she and I spoke together," said Orm, "it was plain to me that she had never tasted the rod, though I doubted not that she had sometimes deserved it. As I saw more of her, though, the question ceased to trouble me; and I think I shall be able to manage her, even though she may occasionally prove obstinate."

"The wise King Solomon," said the Bishop, "observed that a beautiful woman who lacks discipline is like a sow with a gold ring in her snout. This may well be true, for King Solomon was knowledgeable on the subject of women; and sometimes, when her behavior has troubled me, I have been sadly reminded of his words. On the other hand, and it has often surprised me that this is so, I have never found it easy to feel angry toward her. I like to think that her conduct reflects no more than the frenzy and intemperance of youth; and it may be that, as you say, you will be able to curb her without resorting to chastisement, even when she is your wife."

"There is a further point worth considering," said Brother Willibald. "I have often observed that women tend to become more tractable after they have borne their first three or four children. Indeed, I have heard married men say that if God had not ordered it so, the state of wedlock would not be easy to endure."

Orm and the Bishop expressed their agreement with this observation. Then they heard footsteps approaching the door, and Ylva entered. It was dark in the Bishop's chamber, for no lamps had yet been lighted; but she straightway recognized Orm and ran toward him crying excitedly. The Bishop, however, despite his years, sprang nimbly to his feet and placed himself between them, with his arms stretched wide.

"Not so, not so!" he cried importunately. "In God's name, calm yourself, dear child! Enter not into lewd embraces in the sight of priests and in the sacred precincts of an abbey! Besides which, he is not yet baptized. Have you forgotten that?"

Ylva tried to push the Bishop aside, but he stood his ground manfully, and Brother Willibald ran to his assistance and seized her by the arm. She ceased struggling and smiled happily at Orm over the Bishop's shoulder.

"Orm!" she said. "I saw the ships row up the river and knew that men from Denmark were aboard. Then I saw a red beard next to the helmsman of one of them and began to weep, for it looked like you and yet I knew that it could not be you. And the old woman would not let me come to see."

She rested her head upon the Bishop's shoulder and began to shake with weeping.

Orm moved toward her, and stroked her hair, but he did not well know what to say, for he knew little about women's tears.

"I shall thrash the old woman if you so wish it," he said. "Only promise me that you will not be sad."

The Bishop tried to edge him away and to persuade Ylva to sit down, speaking soothing words to her.

"My poor child," he said, "do not weep. You have been alone in a foreign land among strange people, but God has been good to you. Seat yourself on this bench, and you shall have hot wine with honey in it. Brother Willibald shall go at once to prepare it, and there shall be plenty of honey in it; and bright lights also shall be lit. And you shall taste strange nuts from the southland, called almonds, which my good brother the Abbot has given me. You may eat as many of them as you wish to."

Ylva seated herself, drew her arm across her face, and burst into a loud and merry peal of laughter.

"The old man is as much a fool as you are, Orm," she said, "though he is the best god-man I have yet come across. He thinks I am unhappy and that he can comfort me with nuts. But even in his kingdom of heaven I do not think there can be many people who are as full of joy as I am at this moment."

Wax candles were brought in, fair and gleaming, and Brother Willibald followed with the mulled wine. He poured it out into a beaker of green glass, announcing as he did so that it must be drunk at once for its strength and flavor to be fully appreciated; and none of them dared to say that it should be otherwise.

Orm said:

> "Fair the glow
> Of gleaming candles,
> Roman glass
> And god-men's goodness;
> Fairer yet
> The glow that gleams
> Through the tears
> Of virgin eyes.

"And that," he added, "is the first verse that has come to my lips for many a long day."

"Were I a poet," said Ylva, "I, too, should dearly love to make a verse to enshrine this moment. But, alas, I cannot. This I know well, for, when the old Abbess condemned me to spend three days in prayer and fasting, I spent the whole time trying to compose lampoons about her. But I could not, though my father had on occasion tried to teach me the craft, when he was in one of his forthcoming moods. He could not compose verses himself, but he knew how it should be done. And that was the worse part of my punishment, that I was unable to compose a single verse to indict the crone who set me there. But it is all one now, for I shall not be ruled by old women any more."

"That you shall not," replied Orm.

There was much besides that he wished to learn from her, so she and the Bishop told him all that had happened during their last days in Denmark, and about their flight from King Sven.

"But one thing I have to confess to you," said Ylva. "When Sven was almost upon us, and I did not know whether I should manage to escape his clutches, I hid the necklace. For, above all things, I wanted to prevent that from falling into his hands. And I had no time to get it back before we boarded the ship. I know this news will grieve you, Orm, but I could not think of anything else to do."

"I would rather have you without the necklace than the necklace without you," he replied. "But it is a jewel of royal worth, and I fear you will feel its loss more deeply than I shall. Where did you hide it?"

"That, at least, I can tell you," she said, "for I think there is nobody here who will betray the secret. A short way from the great gate of the palace, there is a small rise, covered with heather and juniper, just to the right of the path below the bridge. On that rise, there are three large stones lying together in the undergrowth. Two of them are large and are buried deep in the ground, so that they are scarcely visible. The third lies balanced on top of them, and is not so heavy but that I managed to shift it. I wrapped the necklace in a cloth, and the cloth in a skin, and put them beneath this stone. It was a hard thing for me to have to leave it there, for it was the only keepsake I had by which to remember you. But I think it must still be lying there safely, more so than if it had accompanied me to this foreign land, for no man ever goes near that place, nor even cattle."

"I know those stones," said Brother Willibald. "I used to go there to gather wild thyme and cat's-foot against the heartburn."

"It may prove to be a lucky chance that you hid it outside the rampart," said Orm, "though I fear it will be a difficult enough task to fetch it from its present hiding-place, so near as it is to the wolf's lair."

Now that Ylva had eased her mind of this burden, her heart was lightened. She flung her arms round the Bishop's neck, squeezed almonds into his mouth, and begged him to bless them and marry them there and then. But this suggestion so horrified the Bishop that he got an almond lodged in his windpipe and waved his hands in dismay.

"I am of the same mind as the woman," said Orm. "God Himself saw to it that we should meet again, and we do not intend to part any more."

"You do not know what you are saying," protested the Bishop. "Such ideas are the Devil's prompting."

"I will not return to the crone," said Ylva, "and I cannot stay here. I shall go with Orm in any case, and it will be better if you wed us first."

"He is not yet baptized!" cried the Bishop in despair. "Dear child, how can I marry you to a heathen? It is a scandalous thing to see a young girl so hot with lust. Have you never been taught the meaning of modesty?"

"No," replied Ylva without hesitation. "My father taught me

many things, but modesty was something of which he knew little. But how can there be any harm in my wishing to get married?"

Orm took from his belt six gold pieces, which remained from the small hoard he had brought home from Andalusia, and laid them on the table before the Bishop.

"I am already paying one Bishop to baptize me," he said, "and I am not so poor but that I can afford to pay another to marry me. If you speak well of me to God, and buy candles for His church out of this money, I do not think He will mind if I get married first and baptized later."

"He has the blood of Broad-Hug in his veins," said Ylva proudly, "and if you have any scruples about marrying an unbaptized man, why do you not baptize him yourself here and now? Bid your servants bring water, and sprinkle him as you used to sprinkle the sick in Denmark. What matter if he gets baptized again later, with the others before the King? Twice cannot be worse than once."

"The sacrament must not be abused," said the Bishop chidingly, "and I do not know if he is yet ready to receive it."

"He is ready," said Brother Willibald. "And he might perhaps receive provisional baptism, though that is a ceremony which is seldom performed nowadays. It is lawful for a Christian woman to marry a man who has been provisionally baptized."

Orm and Ylva looked admiringly at Brother Willibald, and the Bishop clasped his hands together and his face grew less troubled.

"Old age has clouded my powers of memory," he said, "unless it is this good wine that has done it, though its effect is, in general, salutary. In ancient times it was a common practice for men who were not prepared to allow themselves to be baptized, but who yet held Christ in honor, to be provisionally baptized. It is lucky for all of us that we have Brother Willibald here to remind us of these things."

"I have felt friendly toward him for some time," said Orm, "and now he stands even higher in my affection. From the very first moment that I met him after the battle, my luck turned for the better."

The Bishop straightway sent a messenger to summon the Abbot and two of his canons, who came readily to help him perform the rite and to see this foreign chieftain. When the Bishop had robed himself, he dipped his hand in holy water and made the sign of the cross over Orm, touching him on the forehead, the breast, and the hands, the while pronouncing blessings upon him.

"I must be growing used to this," said Orm when the Bishop had finished, "for this frightened me much less than when the other fellow sprinkled me with the branch."

All the churchmen agreed that an unbaptized man could not be married in the abbey chapel, but that the ceremony might take place in the Bishop's chamber. So Orm and Ylva were told to kneel before the Bishop, on two hassocks that were provided for them.

"This is a posture I do not think you are used to," said Ylva.

"I have spent more time than most men upon my knees," replied Orm, "in the days when I used to serve Mohammed. But it is a good thing not to have to beat my brow against the floor!"

When the Bishop came to the part of the service in which he had to exhort them to multiply and to dwell together in peace for the remainder of their days, they nodded their affirmation. But when he commanded Ylva to obey her husband in everything, they looked doubtfully at each other.

"I shall do my best," said Ylva.

"It will be hard for her at first," said Orm, "for she is not accustomed to obedience. But I will remind her of these words of yours if ever they should slip her memory."

When the ceremony had been completed and all the churchmen had wished them good luck and many children, it occurred to the Bishop to worry about where they were to spend their bridal night. For there was no room available in the abbey, nor in the houses adjoining it, and he knew of no place in the city where they might find lodgings.

"I will go with Orm," said Ylva contentedly. "What is good enough for him will be good enough for me."

"You cannot lie with him by the campfires, among all the other men," exclaimed the Bishop in alarm.

But Orm said:

> "The voyager,
> Heir to the sea,
> The good plower

Of the auk-bird's meadow,
Hath a bridal bed
For his royal spouse
Better than straw
Or cushioned couches."

Brother Willibald accompanied them as far as the city gate, to make sure the guards allowed them to pass through the postern. There they parted from him, with many expressions of gratitude, and made their way down to the pier where the ships lay. Rapp had left two men on board, to guard against thieves. These men, left to their own devices, had drunk deeply, so that the sound of their sleeping was audible from a good distance. Orm shook them awake and bade them help him pull the ship into midstream, which, though they were still befuddled, they succeeded at last in doing. Then they dropped anchor, and the ship stood swaying upon the tide.

"I have no further need of you now," he said to the two men.

"How shall we get ashore?" they asked.

"It is not far for a bold man to swim," he replied.

They both complained that they were drunk and that the water was cold.

"I am not in a waiting mood," said Orm; and, with those words, he picked one of them up by the neck and belt and tossed him headfirst into the river, whereupon the other promptly followed him, without further ado. From the darkness echoed back the sounds of their coughing and sneezing as they splashed their way toward the bank.

"I do not think anyone will disturb us now," said Orm.

"This is a bridal bed that I shall not complain of," said Ylva.

It was late that night before they closed their eyes, but when at last they did so, they slept well.

When, next day, the envoys appeared before King Ethelred with Gudmund and Orm, they found the King in an excellent humor. After bidding them a warm welcome, he praised the chieftains for their zeal to be baptized, and asked whether they were enjoying their sojourn at Westminster. Gudmund had occupied the night with a tremendous drinking-bout, the effects of which were still noticeable in his speech, so that he and Orm both felt honestly able to reply that they were.

The Bishops began by relating the outcome of their mission and giving details of the agreement they had reached with the Vikings, while everyone in the hall hung upon their words. The King was seated on a throne beneath a canopy, with his crown upon his head and his scepter in his hand. Orm thought that this was a new sort of monarch to see after Almansur and King Harald. He was a tall man, of dignified appearance, swathed in a velvet cloak, and pale-complexioned, with a sparse brown beard and large eyes.

When the Bishops named the amount of silver that they had promised the Vikings, King Ethelred smote the arm of his throne violently with his scepter, whereupon all the gathering in the hall rose to their feet.

"Look!" he exclaimed to the Archbishop, who was seated by his side on a lower chair. "Four flies at a single blow! And yet this is but poorly shaped for the work."

The Archbishop said he thought there were not many kings in the world who could have performed such a feat, and that it testified both to his dexterity and to the excellence of his luck. The King nodded delightedly; then the envoys proceeded with their narration, and everybody began again to listen to them.

When at last they had concluded, the King thanked them and praised the wisdom and zeal they had displayed. He asked the Archbishop what he thought the general reaction to the settlement would be. The Archbishop replied that the sum that the Bishops had named would, indeed, be a heavy burden for the land to bear, but that it was, beyond doubt, the best solution of a difficult situation; to which the King nodded his agreement.

"It is, moreover, a good thing," continued the Archbishop, "a joy to all Christian folk and highly pleasing to the Lord our God that our pious envoys have succeeded in winning these great war-chieftains and many of their followers over to the army of Christ. Let us not forget to rejoice at this."

"By no means," said King Ethelred.

The Bishop of London murmured to Gudmund that it was now his turn to speak, and Gudmund willingly stepped forward. He thanked the King for the hospitality and generosity he had shown them, and informed him that his fame would hereafter stretch as far as the most distant villages of East Guteland, if not farther still. But, he went on, there was one thing that he was anxious to know: namely, how long it would be before the silver was actually placed in their hands.

The King regarded him closely while he was speaking and, when he had concluded, asked him what the scar on his face might signify.

Gudmund replied that it was a wound he had received from a bear he had once attacked rather thoughtlessly, allowing the bear to break the shaft of the spear that he had driven into its chest and then maul him with its claws before he at last managed to fell it with his ax.

King Ethelred's face clouded with sympathy as he listened to the story of this unfortunate incident.

"We have no bears in this land," he said, "much to our loss. But my brother, King Hugo of Frankland, has lately sent me two bears that know how to dance and thereby give us great pleasure. I should have liked to show them to you, but unfortunately my best trainer marched away with Byrhtnoth and was slain by you in the battle. I miss him greatly, for when other men try to make them dance, they move but sluggishly or not at all."

Gudmund agreed that this was a great misfortune. "But all men have their worries," he said, "and ours is: when are we going to get the silver?"

King Ethelred scratched his beard and glanced at the Archbishop.

"You have asked for a considerable sum," said the Archbishop, "and not even great King Ethelred has that amount in his coffers. We shall have to dispatch messengers throughout the land to collect the balance. This may take two months, or even three."

Gudmund shook his head at this. "You must help me now, Skanian," he said to Orm, "for we cannot wait as long as that; but I have talked myself dry in the mouth."

Orm stepped forward and said that he was young and poorly qualified to speak before so great a monarch and so wise an assembly, but that he would explain the case as well as he was able.

"It is no small matter," he said, "to make chieftains and soldiers wait so long for what has been promised to them. For they are men who quickly change their moods and are little inclined toward meekness, and it sometimes happens that they grow weary of the tedium of waiting when they are still hot with the flush of victory and know that good plunder lies ready for them to gather whithersoever they choose to turn. This Gudmund whom you see here is a mild and merry man as long as he is content with the way things are going, but when he is angry the boldest chieftains of the Eastern Sea quake at his approach, and neither man nor bear can withstand his fury. And he has berserks among his followers who are scarcely less fearful than he."

All the assembly looked at Gudmund, who went red in the face and cleared his throat.

Orm continued: "Thorkel and Jostein are men of similar mettle, and their followers are fully as ferocious as Gudmund's. Therefore I would suggest that half the sum due to us should be paid immediately. This will enable us to wait more patiently until the balance has been collected."

The King nodded his head, glanced at the Archbishop, and nodded again.

"And since," continued Orm, "both God and yourself, King Ethelred, find it a cause for rejoicing that so many of us have come up to Westminster to be baptized, it might perhaps be a wise thing to allow all such converts to receive their share here and now. If this should happen, many of our comrades might be driven to wonder whether it would not be beneficial to their souls, also, that they should become Christians."

Gudmund declared in a loud voice that these words exactly expressed his own feelings on the matter. "If you do as he suggests," he added, "I can promise you that every follower of mine who is encamped outside this town will become a Christian at the same time as I do."

The Archbishop said that this was capital news, and promised that skilled instructors would be sent immediately to prepare the men for conversion. It was then agreed that all the Vikings who had come to London should receive their share of the silver as soon as they had been baptized, and that the army at Maldon should have a third of its silver dispatched without delay, the balance to follow in six weeks.

When the meeting had concluded and they had left the hall,

Gudmund thanked Orm warmly for the help he had given him. "I have never heard wiser words issue from the mouth of so young a man," he said. "There is no doubt that you were born to be a chieftain. It will be very advantageous to me to get my silver now, for I have the feeling that some of those who are going to wait till later may experience some difficulty in obtaining their full amount. I do not intend that you shall go unrewarded for this service; so when I receive my share, five marks of it shall be yours."

"I have observed," replied Orm, "that, despite the measure of your wisdom, you are in some ways an excessively modest man. If you were a common or petty chieftain, with five or six ships and no name to speak of, five marks might be regarded as a proper sum to offer me for the service I have rendered you. But, seeing that your fame stretches far beyond the frontiers of Sweden, it ill befits you to offer me so niggardly a sum, and it would ill befit me to accept it. For if this were to become known, your good name might suffer."

"It is possible that you are right in what you say," said Gudmund doubtfully. "How much would you give if you were in my place?"

"I have known men who would have given fifteen marks in return for such a service," said Orm. "Styrbjörn would have given no less; and Thorkel would give twelve. On the other hand, I know some men who would not give anything. But I have no wish to sway your own judgment in this matter; and, whatever the outcome, we shall remain good friends."

"It is not easy for a man to be sure just how famous he is," said Gudmund, troubled; and he went his way buried in calculation.

The following Sunday they were all baptized in the great church. Most of the priests were anxious that the ceremony should be performed in the river, as had been customary in former times when heathens were baptized in London; but both Gudmund and Orm asserted vigorously that there was to be no immersion as far as they were concerned. The two chieftains walked at the head of the procession, with their heads bared, wearing long white cloaks with a red cross sewn on the front of each; and their men followed, also wearing white cloaks, as many as there were enough for in so large a company. All of them carried their weapons, for Orm and Gudmund had explained that they seldom liked to be parted from their swords, and least of all when they were in a foreign land. The King himself sat in the choir, and the church was thronged with people. Ylva was among the congregation. Orm was unwilling to let her show herself in public, for she now appeared to him more beautiful than ever, and he feared lest someone might steal her away. But she had insisted on coming to the church, because, she said, she was curious to see how reverently Orm would conduct himself when the cold water started running down his neck. She sat next to Brother Willibald, who kept a close eye on her and restrained her when she would have laughed at the white cloaks; and Bishop Poppo was also present and assisted with the rites, though he felt exceedingly feeble. He himself baptized Orm, and the Bishop of London Gudmund; then six priests took over from them and baptized the rest of the Vikings as expeditiously as possible.

When the ceremony was over, Gudmund and Orm were received privately by the King. He gave each of them a gold ring and expressed the hope that God would bless all their future enterprises; also, he said, he trusted that they would, in the near future, come and see his bears, which had now begun to show a marked improvement in their dancing.

The next day the silver was paid out by the King's scribes and treasurers to all the baptized men, which caused great jubilation among them. Orm's men were somewhat less jubilant than the others, because each of them had to pay his chieftain a penny; none of them, however, chose the less expensive alternative of challenging him to combat.

"With the help of these contributions, I shall build a church in Skania," said Orm as he stowed the money safely away in his chest.

Then he put fifteen marks in a purse and went with it to the Bishop of London, who, in return, bestowed a special blessing upon him. Later that afternoon Gudmund came aboard carrying the same purse in his hand, very drunk and in capital spirits. He said that all his share of the money had now been counted and stored away, and that, all in all, it had been an excellent day's work.

"I have been thinking over what you said the other day," he continued, "and I have come to the conclusion that you were right in saying that five marks would be too paltry a sum for a man of my reputation to give you as a reward for the service you rendered me. Take, instead, these fifteen marks. Now that Styrbjörn is dead, I do not think I can be valued at less."

Orm said that such generosity was more than he could have anticipated; however, he said, he would not refuse such a gift, seeing that it came from the hand of so great a man. In return he gave Gudmund his Andalusian shield, the same with which he had fought Sigtrygg in King Harald's hall.

Ylva said she was glad to see that Orm had a good head for collecting silver, for it was not a task at which she would shine, and she thought it likely that they would have a good number of mouths to care for in the years to come.

That evening Orm and Ylva visited Bishop Poppo and bade him farewell; for they were eager to sail for home as soon as possible. Ylva wept, for she found it hard to part from the Bishop, whom she called her second father: and his eyes, too, filled with tears.

"Were I less feeble," he said, "I would come with you, for I think I could, even now, perform some useful work in Skania, old as I am. But these poor bones can endure no further hardships."

"You have a good servant in Willibald," said Orm, "and both Ylva and I delight in his company. Perhaps he could come with us, if you yourself cannot, to fortify us in our beliefs and to persuade others to do as we have done. Though I fear he is not greatly enamored of us Northmen."

The Bishop said that Willibald was the wisest of his priests and a most zealous worker. "I know of nobody more skillful at converting heathens," he said, "though, in his own zealous enthusiasm, he is occasionally prone to be somewhat uncharitable toward the sins and weaknesses of others. I think it best that we should ask him his own feelings in the matter; for I do not wish to send an unwilling priest with you."

Brother Willibald was summoned, and the Bishop informed him what they had in mind. Brother Willibald asked, in vexed tones, when they were intending to sail. Orm replied that he wished to depart on the morrow if the wind remained favorable.

Brother Willibald shook his head gloomily. "It is ungracious of you to give me so little time to prepare myself," he said. "I must take many salves and medicines with me when I depart for the shores of night and violence. But with God's good help, and if I make haste, everything shall be ready; for I am loath to be parted from you young people."

CHAPTER FOUR

HOW BROTHER WILLIBALD TAUGHT KING SVEN A MAXIM FROM THE SCRIPTURES

ORM went to Gudmund and bade him greet Thorkel from him and tell him that he would not be rejoining the army, as he was sailing for home. Gudmund was grieved at this news and tried to persuade him to change his mind, but Orm said that his recent luck had been too good to last much longer.

"I have nothing more to perform in this land," he said, "and if you had such a woman as Ylva with you, would you house her among an army of idle soldiers whose tongues slobber out of their mouths at every woman they see? My sword would never be in its sheath, and it is my wish to live with her in peace. And that is her wish also."

Gudmund admitted that Ylva was a woman fit to tempt any man who caught the briefest glimpse of her to wander from the path of discretion. He himself, he added, would like, if he could, to sail home to Bravik without further delay, for it made him uneasy to have so much silver about him. But this he could not do, for he must return to the rest of his men whom he had left at Maldon and must, besides, tell Thorkel and Jostein what agreement they had come to regarding the distribution of the silver.

"My men here are being plundered by quick-witted women," he said, "who swarm like flies round their silver and steal it from their very belts and breeches, once they have made them sufficiently drunk. Therefore I think it best that I should row down the river with you today, if I can get my crew assembled in time."

They went to King Ethelred and his Archbishop to bid them farewell, and saw the bears dance miraculously on their hind legs. Then they ordered the horns to be blown, and the men took their places at the oars, where many of them performed very clumsily at first as the result of fatigue and drunkenness. They made swift progress down the river, however, and this time the watch-ships did not bar their path, though there was a lively exchange of repartee between the crews. They spent the night at anchor in the estuary. Then Gudmund and Orm parted and went their separate ways.

Ylva was a good sailor; nevertheless, she hoped that the sea voyage would not take too long, for she found it very cramped in the ship. Orm comforted her by assuring her that the weather was usually good at this time of the year and would not be likely to delay them.

"The only detour we shall need to make," he said, "will be to a certain hill near Jellinge; and that should not take us long."

Ylva was not sure whether it would be a wise thing to try to regain the necklace now, since nobody knew what the situation was in Jutland or even who sat upon the throne at Jellinge. But Orm said that he wanted to get this business settled by the time he reached home.

"And, whoever sits at Jellinge," he added, "whether it be King Sven or King Erik, I do not think it likely that we shall find him there at this time of the year, when all kings like to fight. We will steal ashore at night, and if all goes well, nobody need know that we have come."

Brother Willibald enjoyed being at sea, though it disappointed him that nobody fell ill during the voyage. He liked especially to squat beside Rapp when the latter was at the steering-oar and to ply him with questions concerning the southland and the adventures he had had there; and though Rapp was somewhat scant in his replies, these two seemed to be becoming good friends.

They rounded the Jutland cape and headed southwards, encountering no other ships; but then the wind turned against them, so that they had much hard rowing to do, and on one occasion they had to seek the shelter of the coast and wait for the gale to lessen. It was night as they rowed up toward the mouth of the river below Jellinge, but the sky had already begun to grow green with dawn when Orm finally beached the ship, some distance below the castle. He told Brother Willibald, Rapp, and two good men from the crew to follow him; but he bade Ylva to remain on board. She was unwilling to obey, but he said that it was to be so.

"In such matters as this, it is I who shall decide," he said, "whatever may be the case later. Brother Willibald knows the place as well as you do; and, if we should encounter anyone and there should be fighting, which is possible now that it is growing light, it will be better that you should be here. We shall not be gone for long."

They walked up from the beach in the direction of the castle, proceeding across the fields that lay on its southern side. Brother Willibald was just remarking that they had almost reached the place when, suddenly, they heard the tramp of feet and men's voices coming from the bridge away to their left and saw a herd of cattle approaching them, driven by several men.

"It will be safest to kill these fellows," said Rapp, weighing a spear in his hand.

But Brother Willibald grabbed him by the arm and forbade him vehemently to use any violence toward men who had done him no harm. Orm agreed and said that, if they made haste, there should be no need for bloodshed.

So they began to run toward the rise. The cowherds stopped and stared at them in amazement.

"Whose men are you?" they shouted.

"King Harald's," replied Orm.

"The little priest!" shrieked one of the herdsmen. "It is the little priest who used to attend King Harald! These men are enemies! Run and rouse the castle!"

Rapp and the two men with him sprang immediately in pursuit of the herdsmen, but the cattle blocked their path, so that the others got a good lead. Meanwhile Orm ran to the rise with Brother Willibald, who at once showed him the place where the three stones lay. Orm heaved the topmost one aside; and there, beneath it, lay the necklace, just as Ylva had hidden it.

"Now we shall have to show our paces," he said as he thrust it into his shirt.

Shouts and alarums could now be heard from the castle; and when they reached Rapp and his men, they found him cursing himself for having failed to stop the herdsmen from giving the alarm. In his anger he had flung his spear at one of them, who, as a result, was now lying outside the great gate.

"But it served little purpose," he said, "and now I have lost a good spear."

They raced as fast as they could across the fields toward the ship. Very soon, however, they heard loud whoops behind them, and the pounding of hoofs. Rapp was a sharp-sighted man with his one eye, and he and Orm glanced back over their shoulders as they ran.

"Here comes King Sven himself," muttered Orm. "That is no mean honor."

"And in a hurry," said Rapp, "for he has forgotten to plait his beard."

Brother Willibald was not so young as the others; nevertheless, he sprinted along nimbly, with his cassock lifted high above his knees.

"Now is our chance!" cried Orm. "Mark them with your spears!"

As he spoke, he stopped in his tracks, turned, and flung his spear at the foremost of the pursuers, a man on a big horse who was galloping just in front of King Sven. When the man saw the spear winging toward him, he pulled his horse back on its hind legs. The spear buried itself deeply in the animal's chest, causing it to topple forwards and roll over, crushing its rider beneath it. Rapp's men cast their spears at King Sven, but failed to hit him; and now he was almost upon them, and they had no spears left with which to defend themselves.

Brother Willibald bent down, picked up a large stone, and flung it with all his might.

"Love thy neighbor!" he grunted as it left his hand.

The stone struck King Sven full on the mouth with a loud smack. With a howl of agony, he crumpled on the horse's mane and slithered to the ground.

"That is what I call a good priest," said Rapp.

The rest of their pursuers crowded round King Sven where he lay on the ground, so that Orm and his men managed to reach the ship unscathed, though somewhat short of breath. Orm cried to the rowers to begin pulling at once, while he and the others were still wading out from the shore. They were dragged aboard and had come a good way from the shore before the first horseman appeared at the water's edge. The wind had sprung up again in the gray dawn twilight and was favorable to them, so that, using both sail and oars, they managed to come swiftly out into the sea.

Orm gave the necklace to Ylva and told her of all that had happened to them; and even Rapp was less scant of speech than usual as he praised the excellence of the little priest's throw.

"I hope he felt it," said Ylva.

"There was blood on his mouth as he fell," said Rapp. "I saw it clearly."

"Little priest," said Ylva, "I have a mind to kiss you for striking that blow."

Orm laughed. "That is what I have always been most afraid of," he said, "that you would become enamored of priests in your piety."

Brother Willibald protested vehemently that he had no wish to be kissed; nevertheless, he appeared to be not altogether displeased at the praises that were being showered upon him.

"That kiss that King Sven received he will not soon forget," said Orm, "and it is not his habit to leave such things unavenged. When we reach home, if we do so safely, my mother will have to pack with speed, for I think it will be safest for us to depart into the forests, where no king ventures. And there I shall build my church."

And of Orm's subsequent adventures in the forest country far north toward the border, the story also shall be told; of his zeal for Christianity, and Brother Willibald's triumphs of conversion; of the opposition they encountered from the Smalanders, and their feuds with them; and of how the wild oxen returned to the land.

PART THREE

In the Border Country

CHAPTER ONE

HOW ORM BUILT HIS HOUSE AND CHURCH AND HOW THEY NAMED HIS RED–HAIRED DAUGHTERS

THREE years had passed since Orm, after selling in haste his father's house on the Mound in order to flee from the wrath of King Sven, had toiled up to the border country with all his household, his wife and mother, his servants, and his little priest, his horses and cattle and as much silver and valuables as his beasts could carry. The estate that Asa had inherited from her father in the border country was called Gröning; but for some years now it had been a neglected wilderness of sagging roofs and overgrown fields, inhabited only by an ancient and infirm bailiff, his wife, and a gaggle of scrawny geese. Orm found little to be enthusiastic about when he saw the place, and thought it a poor homestead for a man of his quality and for a woman who was King Harald's daughter; and Asa ran to and fro weeping and calling to God in her misery, and inveighing violently against the old couple; for she had not visited the place since the days when she had been a girl and her father had lived there in wealth and prosperity, before he and his two sons had been killed in a feud.

But Ylva was contented; for here, she said, they would be safe from King Sven and his ruffianly following.

"This is a place that will suit me well enough," she said to Orm. "if you can prove yourself as skillful at house-building as you have shown yourself to be at fighting and handling a ship."

Their first winter there they fared meagerly, for there was little food for man or beast, and they found their neighbors hostile. Orm sent men to a thane of the district, Gudmund of Uvaberg, whom men called Gudmund the Thunderer, and who was famed for his wealth and pugnacity, to buy hay and hops; but the men returned to Orm empty-handed, having received short shrift, for a newcomer to the border who was a follower of Christ to boot

did not appear to Gudmund to be worthy of his notice. Then Orm
saddled his horse and set forth with One-Eyed Rapp and three
other good men. They arrived at Uvaberg a little before dawn. He
succeeded without much difficulty in gaining entry to Gudmund's
house, picked him out of his bed, carried him out through his own
front door, and dangled him by one leg over his own well, while
Rapp and the others set their backs against the door that the people in the house might not disturb their parley. After Orm and
Gudmund had argued the matter for a while over the mouth of
the well, a bargain was concluded between them by which Orm
was to receive all the hay and hops he required at a fair price;
whereupon Orm turned him right ways up again and set him on
his feet, pleased at having been able to settle the transaction without being forced to resort to violence.

The Thunderer's wrath, though considerable, was equaled by
the respect in which he now held Orm, and was a good deal less
than his astonishment at finding himself still alive.

"For, you must know," he said, "that I am a dangerous man,
even though you are somewhat larger of frame and may therefore
have to wait awhile before you sample the flavor of my wrath.
Few men would have dared to let me escape alive after serving
me as you have done; indeed, I hardly know if I myself would
have been bold enough to do so, had I been in your trousers. But
perhaps your wisdom is not commensurate with your strength."

"I am wiser than you," said Orm, "for I am a follower of Christ,
and therefore possess His wisdom in addition to my own. It is His
wish that a man shall be gentle unto his neighbor, even though
that neighbor should do him mischief. So if you are sensible, you
will go on your knees and thank Him; for your well looked to me
to be somewhat deep. But if it is your wish that we two should be
enemies, you will find that I can be wise in more ways than one;
for I have encountered more dangerous adversaries than you, and
no man has yet worsted me."

Gudmund said that he would have to endure much mockery for
the indignity that he had been forced to undergo, and that his
good name would suffer in consequence; besides which, his leg had
been painfully stretched by having to support his weight over the
well. As he was speaking, the news was brought to him that one
of his men, who had rushed at Orm with a sword as the latter was

carrying Gudmund out of the house, was now being tended by the women for a broken shoulder that Rapp had given him with the blunt edge of his ax. Gudmund then asked what the attitude of Orm and Christ might be to this piece of information, and whether they thought that such an aggregate of injury and insult was not worth some compensation.

Orm pondered this problem for a while. Then he replied that the man whose shoulder had been broken had only himself to blame for his injury, and that he would give him nothing.

"It was lucky for the foolish fellow," he said, "that Rapp is as devout a believer in Christian principles as I am; otherwise the man would not now require any attention from your women. He should count himself fortunate to have escaped so lightly. But as regards the injury and insult that you claim to have suffered, I think there is some justice in what you say, and I shall give you compensation. If you will accompany me, I will introduce you to a holy doctor who is a member of my household at Gröning. He is the cleverest physician in the world and will speedily cure the pain in your leg; indeed, so holy is he that, after he has treated it, you will find it sounder than its fellow. And it will greatly add to your honor, and to the respect in which your name is held, when it becomes known that you have been attended by a man who was, for a long period, King Harald's personal physician and treated him for the many ailments from which he suffered, and cured them all marvelously."

They argued about this at some length, but in the end Gudmund agreed to ride back with Orm to Gröning. There Father Willibald applied soothing salves to the leg and swathed it in bandages, while Gudmund plied him eagerly with questions about King Harald; but when the priest tried to tell him about Christ and the advantages of baptism, he became very violent and told him that he could keep his mouth shut on that subject. For, he roared, if it became known that he had fallen a victim to such nonsense, it would damage his reputation worse than the news of his suspension over the well, and men would never cease to laugh at him. It was a poor thing, he concluded deafeningly, that anyone should hold so low an opinion of his intelligence as to suppose him capable of being gulled by such foolish prattle.

As he took his leave of Orm, having received payment for his hay and hops, he said: "It is not my wish that there should be a blood-feud between our houses; but if the opportunity should arise for me to repay the insult that you have inflicted upon me, be sure that I shall not neglect it. It may be some time before such an opportunity will present itself, but I am a man whose memory is long."

Orm looked at him, and smiled.

"I know you to be a dangerous man," he said, "for you yourself have told me so. Nevertheless, I do not think this vow of yours will cause me to lie awake at night. But know this, that if you attempt to do me a mischief, I shall baptize you, whether I have to hold you by the legs or by the ears to do so."

Father Willibald was dejected by his failure to convert Gudmund and declared himself convinced that his work in the north was doomed to failure. Ylva, however, comforted him with the assurance that things would be easier once Orm had built his church. Orm said that he in good time would fulfill his promise to do this, but that his more immediate concern was to build himself a house; and this, he avowed, he would start work on immediately. He straightway applied himself earnestly to the task, sending his men into the forest to fell trees, lop them, and drag them back, whereupon he himself chopped them into lengths with his ax. He chose his wood most meticulously, using only thick trunks that had no flaw in them; for he intended, he said, that his house should be of fine appearance and built to endure, and no mere forest shack. Asa's estate comprised the land that lay in a bend of the river, protected by water on three sides; the soil was firm, and not liable to flooding. There was room here for all that he wished to build, and he enjoyed the work so much that, the further it became advanced, the more ambitiously he began to plan. He built his house with a walled fireplace and a slide-board in the roof for the smoke to leave by, the same as he had seen in King Harald's castle; and the roof itself he constructed of peeled ash saplings, surmounted by a layer of birch bark and thick turves. Then he built a brewhouse, a cattleshed and a storehouse, all amply proportioned and finer than any that had previously been seen in these parts; and at last, when all these were completed, he announced that the most important buildings were now ready and that he would shortly be able to begin thinking about his church.

That spring the time arrived for Ylva's confinement. Both Asa and Father Willibald took busy charge of her; they had a deal to do, and fell over each other in their eagerness to ensure that nothing might be left undone. The confinement was a difficult one. Ylva screamed fearfully, vowing that it would be preferable to enter a convent and become a nun than to endure such pain; but Father Willibald laid his crucifix upon her belly and muttered priest-talk over her, and in the end everything went as it should, and she was delivered of twins. They were both girls, which was at first a disappointment to Asa and Ylva; but when they were brought to Orm and laid upon his knees, he found little cause for complaint. Everyone agreed that they bawled and struggled as vigorously as any man-children; and, once Ylva had accepted that they were girls and could never become boys, she regained her cheerfulness, and promised Orm that next time she would give him a son. It soon became evident that both the girls were going to be red-haired, which Orm feared might bode ill for them; for, he said, if they had inherited the color of his hair, they might also develop a facial resemblance to him, and he was reluctant that his daughters should be condemned to such a fate as that. But Asa and Ylva bade him desist from such unlucky prophesying; there was no reason, they said, to suppose that they would look like him, and it was by no means disadvantageous for a girl to be born with red hair.

When the question arose of what names to give them, Orm declared that one of them must be called Oddny, after his maternal grandmother, which greatly delighted Asa.

"But we must name her sister after some member of your family," he told Ylva, "and that you must choose yourself."

"It is difficult to be sure which name will bring her the most luck," said Ylva. "My mother was a war captive, and died when I was seven years old. She was called Ludmilla, and was daughter to a chieftain of the Obotrites; and she was stolen away by force from her own wedding. For all warriors who have visited that country agree that the best time to attack Obotrites or any other Wendish people is when they are celebrating some great wedding, be-

cause then they are drunk and lack their usual skill at arms, and
their watchmen lie sleeping because of the great strength of the
mead they brew for such occasions, so that rich booty can then be
secured without much exertion, in the form both of treasure and
of young women. I have never seen a woman as beautiful as she
was; and my father always used to say that her luck was good,
though she died young, for, for three whole years, she remained
his favorite wife; and it was no small thing for an Obotrite woman,
he used to say, to be permitted into the bed of the King of the
Danes and bear him a daughter. Although it may be that she herself had other feelings concerning this, for after she was dead, I
heard her slave-girls whispering among themselves that shortly
after her arrival in Denmark she had tried to hang herself; which
they thought arose from the fact of her having seen her bride-
groom killed before her eyes when they had taken her and were
carrying her away to the ships. She loved me very tenderly, but
I cannot be sure whether it would be a lucky thing to name the
child after her."

Asa said that such a thing must not be thought of, for there
could be no worse luck than being carried away by foreign warriors, and if they gave the child her grandmother's name the same
fate might befall her.

But Orm said that the problem could not be settled as easily
as that. "For I myself was stolen away by warriors," he said, "but
I do not reckon that to have been an unlucky thing for me; for
if that had not happened, I should not have become the man I
am, and would never have won my sword or my gold chain, nor
Ylva neither. And if Ludmilla had not been stolen away, King
Harald would not have begotten the daughter who now shares my
bed."

They found it difficult to make up their minds about this, for,
though Ylva was anxious that her fair and virtuous mother's name
should be perpetuated, she was unwilling to expose her daughter
to the risk of being stolen by the Smalanders or some such savage
people. But when Father Willibald heard what they were arguing
about, he declared immediately that Ludmilla was an excellent
and lucky name, having been borne by a pious princess who had
lived in the country of Moravia in the time of the old Emperor
Otto. So they decided to call the child Ludmilla; and all the house-

folk prophesied a marvelous future for one so curiously named, for it was a name that none of them had heard before.

As soon as the two infants were strong enough, they were baptized by Father Willibald to the accompaniment of much bawling. They waxed fast, enjoying the best of health, and were soon tumbling around the floor with the huge Irish dogs that Orm had brought with him from Skania, or fighting over the dolls and animals which Rapp and Father Willibald carved out of wood for them. Asa doted upon them both and exhibited far more patience toward them than toward any other member of the household; but Orm and Ylva sometimes had difficulty in deciding which of the two was the more obstinate and troublesome. It was continually impressed upon Ludmilla that she had been named after a saint, but this had no noticeable effect on the manner in which she conducted herself. The two infants got on well together, however, though they occasionally went for one another's hair; and when one of them had her bottom smacked, the other would stand by and howl no whit less resonantly than the punished miscreant.

The next year, early in the summer, Orm completed his church. He had sited it on the water's edge, where the bank curved, so that it would shield the other buildings from the river, and he had made it so spacious that there was room for sixty people to sit in it, though nobody could suggest where so large a congregation was likely to come from. Then he built a good rampart across the base of his peninsula, surmounted by a double stockade with a strong gate in the center of it; for, the more he built, the more he worried for the safety of his house, and he was anxious to be prepared against the danger of attack by robbers, as well as by any ruffians whom King Sven might send their way.

When all this work had been completed, Ylva, to her great joy and that of all the household, gave birth to a son. Asa said that this must be God's reward to them for having built the church, and Orm agreed that this might well be the reason for so excellent a stroke of luck.

The new child was without flaw in limb or body and, from the moment of his arrival, leather-lunged. Everyone agreed that he must, without doubt, be destined to become a chieftain, since he had the blood both of King Harald and of Ivar of the Broad-Embrace in his veins. When they brought him to his father for the first time, Orm took Blue-Tongue down from her hook on the wall, drew her from her sheath, and placed flour and a few grains of salt upon the tip of her blade. Then Asa brought the child's head carefully toward the sword until his tongue and lips touched the offering. Father Willibald watched this procedure frowningly. He made the sign of the cross over the child and said that so un-christian a custom, which involved bringing the child into contact with a weapon of death, was evil and not to be encouraged. But nobody agreed with him, and even Ylva, weak and exhausted as she was, cried cheerfully from her bed that there was no sense in his argument.

"It is the custom for children of noble birth to be initiated thus," she said. "For it brings them the courage of chieftains and a contempt for danger, and weapon-luck, and, besides, skill in the choosing of words. I cannot believe that Christ, from all that you tell us about Him, is the sort of god who would be likely to object to any child receiving such gifts as these."

"It is a rite honored by time," said Orm, "and the ancients had a great store of wisdom, even though they did not know about Christ. I myself was made to lick a sword-tip for my first meal, and I do not intend that my son, who is King Harald's grandson, shall have a worse start in life than I had."

So there the matter remained, though Father Willibald shook his head sadly and muttered something to himself about the way the Devil still ruled these northern lands.

CHAPTER TWO

HOW THEY PLANNED A CHRISTENING FEAST FOR KING HARALD'S GRANDSON

ORM was now in better spirits than ever before, for every enterprise to which he laid his hand flourished. His fields bore a rich harvest, his cattle waxed fat, his barns and storehouses were full, a son had been born to him (and he had good hopes that it might not be his last), and Ylva and his children enjoyed the best of health. He took good care to see that there was no idleness among his men once dawn had broken; Asa kept a sharp eye on the female hands as they toiled in the dairy or sat on their weaving-stools; Rapp showed himself to have a good hand at carpentry and smithery and at setting snares for birds and animals; and each evening Father Willibald invoked the blessing of God upon them all. Orm's only regret was that his home lay so far from the sea; for, he said, it sometimes gave him a feeling of emptiness to have no sound in his ears but the murmur of the forest on all sides, and never to hear the whisper of the summer sea or feel its salt on his lips.

But sometimes he was visited by evil dreams, and then he would become so agitated in his sleep that Ylva would wake him to ask whether the night mare was riding him, or whether there was any trouble on his mind. When he had awakened and had fortified his courage with strong ale, she would hear, perhaps, that in his sleep he had returned to the Moorish galley and had been rowing his heart out as the whip snaked across his shoulders and the groans of his fellows filled his ears and their wealed backs bent painfully before his eyes; and on the morning after such a dream he loved to sit beside Rapp, who never dreamed, in the carpenter's shed, and exchange memories with him of those far-off days.

But worse than these were the two dreams that he dreamed about King Sven. For the Moorish galley was but a memory of the past, but when he dreamed of King Sven and his wrath, he could not be sure that they might not be omens of ill luck to come. When, therefore, he had had such a dream, a great unrest would come over him, and he would describe in great detail to Asa and Father Willibald all that he had seen in his sleep, in order that they might help him to arrive at the dream's meaning. On one occasion he saw King Sven standing, smiling evilly, in the prow of a warlike ship that rowed nearer and nearer toward him while he, with but a few men manning his oars, strove desperately, but vainly, to flee. The second time he was lying in the dark, unable to move a finger, listening to Ylva screaming piteously for help as men carried her away; and then, of a sudden, he saw King Sven walking toward him in the light of flames, carrying Blue-Tongue in his hand; and at this he had awakened.

Asa and Father Willibald agreed that such dreams as these must possess some significance, and Asa wept when Orm told her of his second vision. But when she considered the matter more closely, she became less despondent.

"It may be that you have inherited from me the gift of truthful dreaming," she said, "though it is a gift that I would not willingly bestow on anyone, for I myself have never gained profit from it, and it has brought me nothing but anxiety and sorrow that I would not otherwise have known. One thing, however, comforts me, and that is that I myself have not had any dream which could be interpreted as a warning of evil luck to come. For any stroke of bad luck that injured you would touch me no less nearly, so that if anything was to threaten you and your house, I, too, should receive warning of it in a dream."

"For my part," said Father Willibald, "I believe that King Sven has enough to occupy him elsewhere and has little time to spare trying to search you out in these wild forests. Besides which, do not forget that it is against me, and not you, that his anger is primarily directed, for it was my hand that flung the stone that felled him, as David, the servant of God, smote the heathen Goliath; and I have had no evil dreams. It cannot, though, be denied that the paths of evil are long and crooked, and that it is always a good thing to be prepared for the worst."

Orm agreed with this last observation, and had the stockade on his rampart strengthened and tested, and the great gate reinforced with good crossbeams, that he might sleep the more soundly at night. Before long the memory of these bad dreams had almost passed from his mind, and he began to think less of them than of the great christening feast that he was intending to hold in his son's honor.

He lost no sleep in trying to think of a name for the child, for he was determined that the boy should be called Harald.

"There is always the danger," he said, "that, by giving him a king's name, I may expose him to some grievous fate. But few men have enjoyed such luck as King Harald, or have won a greater name; and of all the chieftains I have met, only one, Almansur of Andalusia, was as wise as he. So I think I should be denying my son great possibilities if I withheld from him the name that his grandfather bore so well."

"There is only one thing about that name that worries me,"

said Ylva. "It might cause him to become inordinately greedy for women as my father was. He could never have enough of them. It may be a good quality in a king to be so inclined, but I do not think it is to be desired in other men."

"He will be strong and well-shaped," said Asa. "That I can tell already. And if he is blessed with a merry humor also, he will need no king's name for women to fall ready victims to the snares he will lay for them. My son Are was such a man, though his talent brought him bad luck. Women could not resist him when he winked at them and took them by their plaits. I have heard them confess as much with their own lips. He had laughing eyes and a humor that was never clouded, and was the best of all my sons after Orm; and I pray that God may never allow you, Ylva, to know such grief as I knew when he came to bad luck because of his skill at love-making and went the way to Miklagard and never came back."

"That is my wish, too," said Ylva. "Though, now that I think about it, I would rather that my son had his way with women than that he should stand tongue-tied in their presence and never dare to chance his luck with them."

"You need have no fear of that," said Orm. "There is little bashfulness in his ancestry."

They now began to make great preparations for their son's christening feast, to which many guests were to be invited; for word of it was to be sent to all good people for miles around. It was Orm's wish that there should be no stint of anything, whether baked, brewed, or slaughtered; for he was anxious that these forest people should have the opportunity to see what happened when a chieftain held open house for three whole days. All the eating and drinking was to take place in the church, because there was more room there than in any of the other buildings; then on the third day, when all the guests were merry and replete, Father Willibald would preach them a sermon, after which, Orm doubted not, many of them would offer themselves for baptism.

At first Father Willibald flatly refused to allow a feast to be held in his church, because of the rowdiness and blasphemy that would certainly accompany such an occasion, especially since he had just completed his altar and had carved a fine cross to stand upon it. In the end, however, the consideration that many souls might thereby be won over to the true religion overcame his scruples and he consented. Two things troubled Ylva: first, she was anxious that the ale should not be brewed too strong, since their guests were, many of them, wild folk, and women as well as men would be sitting at the tables; and secondly, she could not make up her mind whether to wear her gold chain or whether it might not perhaps be wiser to keep this hidden.

"For the last time it appeared at a feast," she said, "swords were bared; and the greed for gold is even greater in these parts than it was at Jellinge."

"My advice is that you shall wear it," said Orm. "For I want men to see that you are superior to other women; and you will gain little joy from it if you keep it always locked in a chest."

The whole household now began to busy itself with preparations for the feast. There was great brewing and baking, and every day Orm fingered the flesh of his slaughter-beasts and had them fattened further.

One day a man came out of the forest from the south with two pack-horses and rode toward the house, where they welcomed him warmly and bade him enter. His name was Ole; he was an old man, and had for many years wandered from house to house throughout the forest country peddling skins and salt, for which reason he was called Salt-Ole and was well known everywhere. No one ever offered him violence, though he always traveled alone, for he was cloven-minded and was held to be different from other men; but he knew all there was to be known about skins and was difficult to deceive, and was always welcomed for his salt in such houses as could afford to indulge in such an extravagant luxury. The great hounds bayed as he approached; but he and his old horses paid no heed to their noise. He remained at the door, however, refusing to cross the threshold, until they had assured him that the priest was not in the house, for of him he was terrified.

"Our priest is no wolf or bear," said Asa reprovingly as, with her own hands, she set food before him. "But in any case he is out today fishing with Rapp, so you will not have to meet him. A wise man like you ought not to be afraid of a priest of God. But you are welcome none the less; sit you here and eat, old man. You are particularly welcome with your salt just now, for our stock is nearly at an end, and we shall need more than a little to see us through this christening feast if Orm is to have everything as he wants it. It is his wish that every guest shall have a three-finger pinch of white salt to dip his food in, not merely for his meat and sausage, but for his porridge also, though most folk would say that this was going too far, even for people of our position, and that butter and honey ought to be good enough flavoring for porridge even at the greatest feast."

The old man sat guzzling sour milk, breaking bread into it, and shaking his head at Asa's talk.

"There is nothing like salt," he said. "A man should eat all the salt he can. It gives health and strength and long life. It drives bad things from the body and makes the blood good and fresh. Everybody likes salt. Watch this, now!"

The twins were standing hand in hand, gazing earnestly at the old man as he ate and talked. He took two pieces of salt from his belt and held them out toward the children, making a cheerful clucking noise with his tongue. They approached him hesitantly, but at length accepted the crystals and began at once to suck them.

"You see!" cried the old man, hugely jubilant. "Nobody can say no to salt."

But when he had finished eating and had drunk a cup of ale and been asked for news, and Ylva was ready to argue a price for his wares, it transpired that he had in fact practically no salt left in his bags; none at all of the white, which was called emperor's salt, and which Orm wanted for his feast, and only a little of the brown.

Asa shook her fist at him. "You should have told us this at the beginning," she said, "and I would have given you a different welcome. But it is as I have always said: old men, trolls, and old bullocks, one gets no reward for stuffing them with food."

Ole, however, was by now full and contented, and said that every disappointment brought consolation in its wake. "For there are other peddlers on their way here," he said. "I passed them yesterday while they were resting at Gökliden; eleven men, fourteen horses, and a boy. They had nails in their sacks, and cloth and salt. They had come up through the Long Stocks, they told me, and were heading for Smaland. I did not know them, though I have sometimes thought that I knew all people; but I am growing old, and new ones get born. But of this I am sure, that they will visit you, for their chieftain inquired about you, Orm."

Orm had been taking his midday nap in his room, but had now come out to join the others and listen to the old man's gossip.

"About me?" said Orm. "Who was he?"

"His name is Östen of Öre, and he comes from the Finnveding country, but has never been in these parts before. He said he had spent many years at sea, but had invested all his gains in the wares he was carrying, so as to be able to return home still richer."

"Why did he ask about me?" said Orm.

"He had heard men speak of you as a rich and famous man, such as peddlers like to visit. He had, besides, silver ornaments in his sacks, he told me, and good arrows and bow-sinews."

"Did he ask about anyone else?" said Orm.

"He wanted to know what other great men there were in the district who would be likely to buy his wares without haggling and complaining about the price. But most of the time he asked about you, because he had heard that you were the richest."

Orm sat for a while in silence, looking thoughtful.

"Eleven men?" he said.

"And a boy," replied the old man, "a small one. Such fine wares as he carries need good men to guard them. The boy was there to help with the horses."

"No doubt," said Orm. "None the less, it is a good thing to be warned in advance when strangers come in such strength."

"I marked no evil in him," said Ole; "but I can tell you this, that he is a bold man, for I told him that you have a priest in your house, and he was not frightened."

At this they all laughed.

"Why are you afraid of the priest?" asked Orm.

But to this question the old man would give no answer; only he shook his head and looked cunningly at them and mumbled beneath his breath that he was not so stupid but that he knew that that sort of folk were worse than trolls. Then he got up and left without tarrying longer.

"Seven weeks from now I shall be holding my feast," Orm said to him as he rode away, "and if you are in these parts then, you will be welcome; for it may be that you have this day done me a good service."

CHAPTER THREE

CONCERNING THE STRANGERS THAT CAME WITH SALT, AND HOW KING SVEN LOST A HEAD

HE NEXT evening the strangers of whom Salt-Ole had warned Orm arrived at Gröning. It had begun to rain, and the men and their horses halted a short way from the gate while one of their number came forward and asked for Orm, adding that they would be glad of shelter for the night. The hounds had given warning of the strangers' approach, and Orm was already standing before the gate with Rapp, the priest, and five men of his household, all well armed except for Father Willibald.

The stranger who had addressed them was a tall, lean man, clad in a broad cloak. He brushed the rain from his eyes and said: "Such rain as this is unwelcome to peddlers, for neither bales nor leathern sacks can long withstand it, and I have on my horses' backs salt and cloth, which will suffer if they become damp. Therefore, though I am a stranger to you, I beg, Orm, that you will give me shelter for my wares and a roof to cover the heads of me and my men. I who address you thus am no mere vagabond, but Östen, the son of Ugge, from Örestad in Finnveden, a descendant of Long Grim; and my mother's brother was Styr the Wise, whom all men know of."

As he spoke, Orm looked at him closely. "You have many men with you," he said.

"I have sometimes thought them too few," replied Östen; "for the wares I carry are valuable, and this is not the safest of districts for peddlers to travel in. But so far all has gone well with me, and I trust it may continue so. It may be that I have in my sacks one thing or another that you or your wife might care to buy from me."

"Have you been baptized?" asked Father Willibald.

"Certainly not!" said Östen indignantly; "nor have any of my companions. We are all honorable men."

"Your tongue led you astray there," said Orm sternly. "All of us are baptized men, and the man who asked you that question is a priest of Christ."

"A stranger cannot be expected to know such things," replied Östen humbly; "though, now that I remember it, a man we met on the way did tell me that there was a priest in your house. But it had slipped my memory, for most of what he had to say concerned you, Orm, and your reputation for hospitality and your fame as a warrior."

The rain began to descend more heavily than ever, and thunder could be heard crackling in the distance. Östen glanced toward his wares, and his face began to wear a worried look. His men stood waiting beside the horses with their backs turned toward the wind and their cloaks drawn over their heads, while the rain stood like smoke about them.

Rapp smiled. "Here is a good opportunity for us to buy salt cheaply," he said.

But Orm said: "Your ancestry may be good, Smalander, and I have no wish to think evil of you, but it is a great deal to ask of a man that he should take eleven armed men into his house for the night. I would not appear inhospitable, but I do not think you can blame me for being hesitant. But I give you two choices: either to depart and seek night shelter elsewhere, or to enter my land and take shelter in my bathhouse for the night with your men and your wares, having first surrendered your weapons to me here before my gate."

"That is a hard condition," said Östen, "for if I accept, I place myself and all my wealth in your hands, and no man willingly takes such a risk. But I think you are too great a chieftain to contrive treachery against me, and I am so placed that I cannot but accept your condition. It shall therefore be as you demand."

So saying, he unhooked his sword from his belt and handed it to Orm. Then he turned and bade his men make haste to bring his wares into the dry. They lost no time in obeying his command, but each man had to surrender his weapons at the gate before he was permitted to enter. The horses were tethered in the grass by the river, there being no danger from wolves at this season.

When all this had been done, Orm invited the stranger to take food and ale with him. After the meal he bargained with Östen for salt and cloth and found him an honorable man to deal with, for he asked no more for his wares than what a man might reasonably be expected to pay. They drank upon the bargain as friends; then Östen said that he and his men were tired after their long day's journey, and they thanked him for the good fare he had given them and retired to rest.

Outside, the storm increased in violence, and after a while a noise of lowing was heard from the cattle, which were kept at night in a shed next to the house. Rapp and the old cowman went out to see if the beasts had become frightened and broken loose. It was by now quite dark, apart from an occasional flash of lightning. Rapp and the cowman went carefully round the cattleshed and found it undamaged.

Then a thin voice asked from the darkness: "Are you Red Orm?"

"I am not he," said Rapp, "but I am the next after him in this house. What do you want with him?"

The lightning flashed, and by its light he saw that the speaker was the little boy whom the peddlers had brought with them.

"I want to ask him how much he will give me for his head," said the boy.

Rapp leaned swiftly down and seized him by the arm.

"What kind of a peddler are you?" he said.

"If I tell him everything I know, perhaps he will give me something for my knowledge," said the boy eagerly. "Östen has sold his head to King Sven and has come here to collect it."

"Come with me," said Rapp.

Together they hurried into the house. Orm had gone to bed with his clothes on, for the storm and the strangers had made him uneasy, and Rapp's news at once set him wide awake. He forbade them to strike a light, but slipped on his chain shirt.

"How did they deceive me?" he said. "I have their weapons here."

"They have swords and axes hidden in their bales," replied the boy. "They say your head is worth a deal of trouble. But I am to have no share of the reward, and they drove me out into the rain to keep a watch on the horses, so I shall not be sorry to see them get the wrong end of the bargain; for I am not of their party any more. They will be here any moment now."

All Orm's men were now awake and armed. Including Orm

himself and Rapp, they numbered nine; but some of them were old and could not be reckoned upon for much help when it came to fighting.

"We had better go to their place at once," said Orm. "With luck, we may be able to smoke them in their sleeping-quarters."

Rapp opened the door a few inches and glanced out.

"The luck is with us," he said. "It is beginning to grow lighter. If they try to run, they will make good targets for our spears."

The storm had passed, and the moon was beginning to glimmer feebly through the clouds.

Ylva watched the men as they slipped out through the door.

"I wish this business was over," she said.

"Do not worry," said Orm, "but warm some ale for our return. One or another of us may find himself in need of it when we have finished this night's work."

They walked silently across the grass toward the bathhouse. A woodshed stood beside it, and they had just reached this when they saw the door of the bathhouse slowly open. Through the gap they could see gray faces and the glint of arms. Orm and several of his men immediately flung their spears at the gap, but none found their mark; then the whoop of battle-cries filled the air, and the doorway became thick with figures as the peddlers swarmed forth. Orm bent down and seized hold of the great chopping-block that stood at the entrance to the woodshed. With his arms almost cracking under the strain, he lifted it from the ground, took a step forward, and flung it with all his might at the open doorway. The foremost of his enemies managed to throw themselves aside in time, but several of those behind were hit and fell to the earth groaning.

"That was a useful thought," said Rapp.

The peddlers were bold men, though things had turned out otherwise than they had expected, and such as still remained on their feet rushed at once into the attack. Fierce and confused fighting followed, for as clouds passed across the moon, it became difficult to discern friend from foe. Orm was attacked by two men, one of whom he quickly felled; but the other, a short, thickset, heavy-limbed man, lowered his head and charged Orm like a goat, bowling him to the ground and at the same time wounding him in the thigh with a long knife. Orm let go his sword and gripped the man's neck with one arm, squeezing it as tightly as he could, while with his other hand he grasped the wrist holding the knife. They rolled around in the rain for a good while, for the peddler was short in the neck, as strong as a bear, and as slippery as a troll; but eventually they rolled up against the wall of the bathhouse, and there Orm got a good purchase and slightly altered his grip. The other man began to make a sound like snoring; then something snapped in his neck and he ceased to struggle. Orm got to his feet again and regained his sword; but he was troubled by the knife-wound he had received, and it pained him to move a step, though he could hear two of his men calling for help in the darkness.

Then, over the clang of weapons and the screams of wounded and dying men, there arose a terrible sound of baying, and Father Willibald, with a spear clutched in his hand, came running round the corner of the house with the great Irish hounds, which he had freed from their kennel. All four of them were raging mad, with froth on their lips, and they sprang savagely at the peddlers, who were convulsed with terror at the sight of them, for hounds of the size of four-month calves were a spectacle to which they were unaccustomed. Such of them as could disengage their adversaries turned and fled toward the river, with the hounds and Orm's men at their heels. Two of them were overtaken and killed, but three managed to make good their escape through the water. Orm hobbled after them as fast as he could, for he feared Östen might be among those who were getting away; but when he came back to the house, he found Rapp seated on a log, leaning on his ax, and regarding a man who lay stretched on the ground before him.

"Here is the master peddler himself," said Rapp as he saw Orm approach, "though whether he is alive or not is more than I know. He was no mean fighter, though I say it myself."

Östen was lying on his back, pale and bloody, his helmet split by a blow from Rapp's ax. Orm seated himself beside Rapp and looked down at his defeated enemy, and the sight so cheered him that he forgot the pain from his wound. Ylva and Asa came running out of the house, with joy and anxiety mingled in their faces. They tried to persuade Orm to come indoors at once that they might dress his wounds; but he remained where he was, staring at Östen and mumbling beneath his breath. At last, he said:

> "Now I know
> A gift full worthy
> To be sent
> To Sven my brother.
> Peddler, he
> Shall have his head;
> But the hair on it
> Shall not be red."

Father Willibald now joined them. He examined Orm's wound and ordered him to go at once into the house, saying that if he could not walk he must allow Rapp and the women to carry him there. Then he bent down over Östen and felt with his fingers the place where Rapp's ax had made its mark.

"He is alive," he said at last, "but how long he will live I cannot tell."

"I shall send his head to King Sven," said Orm.

But Father Willibald answered sternly that such a thing was not to be thought of, and that Östen and the other wounded peddlers who were still alive were to be carried into the house.

"This night's work will keep me busy for some time," he said jubilantly.

Father Willibald was always a man of determination, but never more so than when there was any sick or wounded man to be dealt with; for then no man dared to say that it should be otherwise than as he commanded. So everyone who could lend a hand had to help carry the wounded men into the house and make them comfortable there.

Orm had no sooner been assisted to his room and had his wound dressed than he fainted; for he had lost a great quantity of blood. The next day, however, he felt better than he could have expected. He reflected with satisfaction on the way everything had turned out, and said that the peddlers' boy was to remain in his household for always and was to be treated as one of the family. He learned that he had lost two men killed, and that two others had been badly wounded, as also had one of the hounds; but Father Willibald thought it likely that, with God's help, they would all eventually recover, the hound included. Orm was grieved at losing two of his men, but he comforted himself with the thought that things might easily have turned out worse. Of the peddlers, Östen and two others were still alive, apart from the three who had escaped into the river. In the bathhouse they had discovered two men who had been hit by the chopping-block. One of these was dead, and the other had a broken leg and a crushed foot. Father Willibald had had all the wounded men taken into the church, where he had bedded them in straw. There they were receiving the most careful attention, and every day it became more evident that the little priest was by no means discontented with the labor of looking after them. For of late there had been few calls upon his skill as a physician, so that time had begun to grow somewhat heavy on his hands.

Orm was soon on his feet again, with little to show for the wound he had received; and one day Father Willibald came to the dinner table with a more than usually cheerful look on his face and announced that even Östen, who had been the most gravely wounded of them all, now looked to be on the road to recovery.

Rapp shook his head doubtfully at this piece of news. "If that is so," he said, "my aim is less sure than it used to be."

And Orm, too, thought it little cause for joy.

CHAPTER FOUR

HOW ORM PREACHED TO THE SALT–PEDDLER

THE NEWS of the fight at Gröning soon spread throughout the district, and Gudmund of Uvaberg came riding over with a flock of distant neighbors whom Orm had not seen before to learn the details of it from his own lips. They drank deeply of Orm's ale and rejoiced exultantly as he described the battle to them. This, they vowed, was a fine thing, for it would increase still further the good name of the border country and the respect in which its inhabitants were held by the world outside. They had much, too, to say in praise of the great hounds, and begged that their own bitches might be allowed the favor of contact with them; and when all the salt and cloth was shown to them, together with the rest of the booty that Orm had won, they sighed that such luck had not come their way. They bargained for the salt-peddlers' horses, and a satisfactory agreement was soon reached, for Orm had by now many more horses than he required, and felt that he could not honorably ask too high a price, since he had paid nothing for them himself. Then the more muscular of his guests tried their strength at lifting the chopping-block; and though those who watched them named dead men they had known in their childhood who had been able to perform more difficult feats than this, still, nobody was able to throw it as far as Orm had done. This still further improved Orm's spirits, and he told them not to take their failure too hard.

"I am not sure that even I could throw it so far again," he said, "without the help that great anger gives a man."

They were all curious to see Östen and wondered greatly that Orm had spared his life. A knife in the throat, they declared, was always the best medicine for men of that sort; and they counseled him earnestly not to stock up trouble for himself and others by allowing the man to go free. To do so, they said, would surely bring unpleasantness in its wake; of that he could be certain, for they were accustomed to the ways of Smalanders and knew them to be a people who nursed their wrongs. Many of them wanted to go into the church to look at the man and talk to him; it would be interesting, they said, to hear whether he regarded the border country as good terrain for head-hunting. But Father Willibald bolted the door and remained deaf to their entreaties to be allowed to enter. They might, he said, be granted admission at some later date, if God so willed it, but he would not permit them to taunt a wounded man who was still hardly able to lift his head.

So they had to forgo that pleasure; but before riding away, they agreed over their stirrup-cups that Orm must now be regarded as a chieftain even among the Göings, and that he was a worthy scion of Sven Rat-Nose, even though he had allowed himself to become baptized; and they swore that they would take his part in any feud that might develop as a result of all this.

Orm gave each of them his measure of salt as a parting gift and for the maintenance of neighborly relations. Then they rode away from Gröning at a thunderous gallop and in the best of spirits, swaying in their saddles and screeching like jays.

The boy was greatly alarmed when he heard that Östen looked likely to recover, and thought it a bad thing for him; for, he said, if Östen lived he would surely kill him in revenge as soon as he got the chance. But Orm assured him that no harm would come to him, and said that he was to lose no sleep on that score, whatever might be Östen's feelings in the matter. The boy was called Ulf, and from the first he was much cosseted by Asa and Ylva, who hardly knew how to reward him for the great service he had done them all. Asa set to work sewing him better clothes with her own fingers; and she and Father Willibald agreed that the boy was, without doubt, an instrument of God, sent to save them from the machinations of the Devil. They asked him how he had come to join the peddlers. He replied that he had run away from a cruel uncle with whom he had lived down on the coast and at whose hands he had suffered great unkindness and privation ever since his mother and father had been drowned while fishing; and that the peddlers had engaged him to look after their horses.

"But they gave me little to eat," he continued, "so that I was always hungry except when I could steal food from houses; and I had to stay awake each night to watch the horses, and was beaten if anything happened to them. But the worst was that I was never allowed to ride, however leg-weary I became. In spite of all this, I fared better with them than with my uncle; but I never bore them any love, and am glad to be free of them. For here I have what I never knew before: food enough to eat and a bed to sleep in, so that I will gladly remain with you forever if you do not send me away. I am not even afraid to be baptized, if you think it necessary."

Father Willibald said that it was, without a doubt, highly necessary, and baptized he would be as soon as he had received schooling in the Christian doctrine. Ylva set him to watch Oddny and Ludmilla, who were now able to walk and found no difficulty in escaping from the house and on two occasions had alarmed everybody by being discovered down by the river. The boy discharged this function assiduously, accompanying them wherever they went; this, he said, was better work than watching horses. He could whistle better than anyone they had ever heard, and knew many tunes, and could even imitate various birds; and both the girls loved him from the first. In time he came to be known as Glad Ulf, because of his merry temper.

Östen and his two wounded companions were by this time well enough to be moved; so they were taken from the church to the bathhouse, where an armed man kept constant guard over them. Father Willibald now tried to give them some instruction about Christian doctrine; but before long he came to Orm and said that the soil of their hearts was, in truth, stony and unreceptive to the seed of grace. This, though, he added, was no more than was to be expected.

"I am not a vain man," he continued, "and do not hanker after fame or honor. None the less, I should feel that my life's work had been well rewarded if I could become the first priest to baptize a Smalander. For there is no known instance of such a thing ever having been done before; and if it could be brought to pass, great indeed would be the rejoicing in heaven. But whether I shall be able to prevail upon these men is, I fear, doubtful, for their obstinacy is inordinate; and it would be a good thing if you, Orm, could help me with a word of admonition to this Östen."

Orm thought this a wise and proper suggestion and said he would be glad to lend what help he could. "This I promise you," he added, "that baptized they shall be, all three of them, before they set foot outside my gate."

"But they cannot be baptized until they have listened to my exposition of the doctrine," said Father Willibald, "which they absolutely refuse to do."

"They will listen to mine," said Orm.

They went together to the bathhouse, and there Orm and Östen met for the first time since the night of the battle. Östen was sleeping, but he opened his eyes as Orm entered. His head was swathed in bandages, which Father Willibald changed every day. He raised himself slowly into a sitting position, supporting his head between his hands, and looked unblinkingly at Orm.

"This is a good meeting for me," said Orm, "for my head still remains on its shoulders, rather more securely, indeed, than yours; and I owe you thanks, too, for all the wealth you have so thoughtfully brought to my door. But I think you expected things to turn out otherwise."

"They would have been otherwise," said Östen, "if the boy had not served me treacherously."

Orm laughed. "I never thought," he said, "to hear you complain of treachery. But here is a question I should like you to answer. You have tried to take my head. Tell me, now, who has the best right to yours?"

Östen sat for some moments in silence. Then he said: "The luck has gone against me in this affair. I have nothing more to say."

"Your luck would have been much worse," said Orm, "if it had not been for this pious man, to whom your debt is indeed great. When I learned that King Sven wanted a head, my first thought was to send him yours, but this priest of Christ dissuaded me from carrying out my plan. He has saved your life and healed your wound, but even that has not satisfied his zeal, for he wants also to save your evil Smaland soul. So we have decided that you shall become a Christian, and your men with you. Nor have you any say in the matter, for your head belongs to me and I shall do as I please with it."

Östen glared blackly at them both. "My family is great and powerful," he said, "and no member of it sustains injury or insult without revenge. Know, therefore, that you will pay dearly for what you have already done to me, and dearer still if you force me to submit to any ignominy."

"There is no question of anyone forcing you to do anything," said Orm. "You are free to make your own choice. Will you have your head sprinkled by this holy man, who wishes you nothing but good, or would you rather have it stuffed in a sack and sent to King Sven? I can promise you that it will be packed very carefully, so that it will arrive in good condition, for I want him to know whose it was. It might be best to pack it in salt; I have plenty of that now."

"No man of my family has ever been baptized," said Östen. "Only our slaves are Christians."

"You are evidently unaware," said Orm, "that Christ specifically commanded that all men should be baptized, including Smalanders. Father Willibald can quote you the passage."

"His very words," said Father Willibald. "He said: 'Go ye out into the world and preach my gospel to all men, and baptize them.' He also said, on another occasion: 'He that believeth and is bap-

tized, his soul shall be saved; but he that believeth not shall burn
in hell-fire.' "

"You see?" said Orm. "The choice is yours:

> Thou shalt to hell
> Without thy head,
> Or else with water
> Be baptizèd."

"Your sins are many and great," said Father Willibald, "and
your spiritual condition most foul; but it is so with most men in
this land. If, though, you allow yourself to be baptized, you will
be numbered among the blessed and, by Christ's mercy, stand in
the ranks of the saved when He appears in the sky to judge mankind, which is due to happen very shortly."

"One other thing," said Orm; "from the moment that you are
baptized, God gives you His support: and you have doubtless observed, from the result of your attempt to kill me, that His hand
is strong. I myself have never prospered so well as since I began
to follow Christ. All that you have to do is to renounce your old
gods and say: 'There is no god save God, and Christ is His
Prophet.' "

"Not His Prophet!" said Father Willibald severely. "His Son!"

"His Son," said Orm quickly. "That is what I meant to say. I
knew the text well; I was not thinking, and my tongue slipped,
because of the false beliefs I used to hold in the days when I
served Almansur of Córdoba, in the Andalusians' land. But that
was long ago, and it is now four years since I was baptized by a
holy bishop in England, ever since when Christ has supported me
in all my enterprises. He delivers my enemies into my hand, so
that not only men such as you are powerless to harm me, but
King Sven also. And I have gained many other advantages besides. I was born with excellent luck, but it has increased considerably since I went over to Christ."

"There is no denying," said Östen, "that your luck is better than
mine."

"But it only became as good as it is now," said Orm, "after I
got baptized. For in former days, when I knew no religion save
that of the old gods, I suffered many misfortunes, and sat for two
years as a slave in Almansur's galley, chained to a bench with iron.

It is true that I won this sword you see here, which is the finest weapon that was ever forged, so that Styrbjörn himself, who knew more about swords than any other man, vowed when he weighed it in his hand in King Harald's hall that he had never seen a better; but even that was scant compensation for all that I underwent to secure it. Then I embraced the religion of the Andalusians, at the bidding of my master Almansur, and thereby won a necklace, a jewel of royal worth. But for that necklace's sake I was wounded almost to death in King Harald's hall, despite my good Andalusian chain shirt, and if it had not been for this little priest and his healing skill I should have died from that wound. Then, at last, I became baptized and came under the protection of Christ and straightway won King Harald's daughter, whom I count the most precious jewel that I own. And now you yourself have witnessed how Christ helped me to overcome you and all the men you brought with you to kill me. If you consider the matter well, you will, being a wise man, realize that you will not lose anything by being baptized, but will, instead, gain much profit, even if you do not regard it as important that your head should remain on its shoulders."

This was the longest sermon that anyone heard from Orm in the whole of his life, and Father Willibald told him afterwards that he had acquitted himself by no means poorly, considering his inexperience in the art.

Östen sat and pondered for a long while. Then he said: "If all that you say is true, I must agree that you have not lost by becoming a Christian, but have rather gained; for it is no small feat to have won King Harald's daughter, nor are the wares that you have got from me to be despised. But in Smaland, where I live, there are Christian men who are thralls, and they have little to show for their religion; and I cannot be sure whether I may not have their luck instead of yours. But there is one thing I wish to know. If I do as you bid me, what do you intend to do with me then?"

"Set you free, and let you depart in peace," replied Orm. "And your men with you."

Östen eyed him suspiciously, but at length he nodded.

"If you are ready to swear this before us all," he said, "I shall believe that you mean to keep your word. Though what good it can do you to see me baptized is more than I can understand."

"It is no more than just," said Orm, "that I should do something to please God and His Son, after all that They have done for me."

CHAPTER FIVE

CONCERNING THE GREAT CHRISTENING FEAST, AND HOW THE FIRST SMALANDERS CAME TO BE BAPTIZED

WHEN the bees had swarmed and the first hay had been garnered, Orm held his great christening feast. As he had intended from the first, it lasted for three days, and was, in every way, a feast unlike all other feasts, not least in that no weapon was blooded from beginning to end of it, despite the fact that every evening all the guests were as drunk as a man could wish to be at a great lord's banquet. The only misfortune occurred on the first evening, when, in the first flush of intoxication, two young men went to play with the great hounds in their kennel. One of them came smartly out again, having sustained nothing worse than a few gashes and the transformation of his clothes into ribbons; but the other attempted to withstand their assault, and it was only after much screaming that two women of the household, who were known to the hounds, rushed in and rescued him with his arms and legs lacerated and one ear missing. When the news of this reached the feasters, it occasioned much merriment, and the hounds were praised as a credit to the district; but there were no further attempts to play with them.

Asa and Ylva had difficulty in finding room for all the guests to sleep, for more had come than had been invited, and many had brought their sons and daughters with them; and though many of the older guests fell contentedly asleep each evening on the benches on which they had dined, or on the floor beneath, and remained there throughout the night, thereby saving much trouble, still, in spite of this, there was little room to spare. The young people managed well enough, for the girls were bedded in one barn and the boys in another, in good, soft hay; and though a surprising number of them experienced difficulty in finding their right barn, or in remaining in it once they had found it, still, no complaints were heard on this score. In the morning the girls mumbled blushingly to their mothers of the strayings that had taken place and of the difficulty of distinguishing one bank of hay from another, and were warned to take care that no other man stumbled over their legs on the following night, since to trip up two different men on successive nights was a thing that might damage a girl's reputation; after which there ensued lengthy and amiable discussions between various parents, so that by the time the feast ended seven or eight marriages were as good as arranged. The news of these happenings delighted Orm and Ylva, for it was a sign that their guests, both young and old, were enjoying the feast; and only Father Willibald muttered blackly to himself, without, however, making any representations about the way things were going.

In other connections, though, Father Willibald had a great deal to say at this feast; and already on the first day, when all the guests had been fitted into their places in the church and every man and woman had received his or her cup of welcome-ale, he lit before his altar, on which his cross had been set up, three fine wax candles that he and Asa had molded, and spoke to the gathering about the holy place in which they now found themselves.

"The God who rules in this house," he said, "is the only true god, and surpasses all others in wisdom, strength, and the ability to impart luck. His house, into which you have been permitted to enter, is the house of peace. For He dwelleth in peace, and rejoiceth in it, and giveth of it to such as come to Him for succor. You have come to this house from the regions of darkness and heresy to rest for a brief moment in His presence; and to darkness and heresy you will return when you have left it, to wallow in sin and luxuriate in abomination until the span of your life is ended, when you will take your places among the regiments of the damned. But Christ offers His infinite friendship even to you, although you daily slight His name and teaching; therefore you have been permitted to enter this house. For He wants all men to be happy; that is why, when He himself was a wanderer on this earth, He turned water into good ale, that He might give joy to His friends. But the time is almost come when He will cease to be meek to such as refuse His friendship; and when they feel the whip of His anger, terrible indeed shall be their suffering, worse than that of the chieftain in the song who perished in a pit of snakes. So I think you will all agree that it will be a bad thing to be counted among His enemies. But as yet His offer still holds good, that any man or woman who wishes to do may become His servant and gain His protection merely by being baptized. Those, however, who will not do this must protect themselves as best they can."

The guests listened with interest to Father Willibald's address and murmured to one another that there was wisdom in a good deal of the things he had said, though some of his observations were difficult to be taken seriously. It was noticeable that the old people listened more attentively than the young, for the latter, whether boys or girls, found it difficult to take their eyes from Ylva. She was, indeed, a sight to marvel at, for she was now in the full prime of her beauty, at peace with the world and full of good-will toward everyone. She wore new garments, made from the costliest cloth that had been found in Östen's sacks, embroidered with silk and silver; and around her throat she wore the Andalusian chain. It was clear from the way so many of the guests gazed at her that such a woman and such an ornament were sights the like of which a man did not often see; and Orm was not the less happy for observing that they were properly appreciated.

When the priest had finished his speech, Orm tried to persuade one or two of the wiser among his guests to agree that a sensible man would be neglecting his own interests if he did not become a Christian; but he got no further than that two men expressed the opinion that the matter was, certainly, worth consideration; and even several hours later, when they were well on the way toward being drunk, they refused to commit themselves further.

The next day was a Sunday, and Father Willibald told the guests how God had built the world in six days and had then rested on the seventh, which they agreed to be an excellent story; also, how on this same day, many years later, Christ had risen from the dead, which they found more difficult to believe. Then Harald Ormsson was brought into the church to be baptized. Asa carried him to the tub, and Father Willibald performed the ceremony with the maxi-

mum of pomp and solemnity, chanting Latin prayers so loudly that
they drowned the infant's bawling and caused the congregation to
tremble on their benches. When the ceremony was over, toasts
were drunk to the infant's luck, and to the memory of the three
great heroes, Harald Blue-Tooth, Sven Rat-Nose, and Ivar Broad-
Hug, whose blood ran in his veins.

Then all the guests trooped out of the church to see the Smalanders baptized in the river. Östen and his two men were led from
the bathhouse and were made to wade a short way into the water.
There they stood in a row, bareheaded and scowling, while Father
Willibald stood before them on the washing-barge, with Rapp
beside him holding a couple of spears in case the men should try to
offer resistance. Father Willibald read over them, his voice quivering with excitement and joy, for this was, for him, a great day;
then he bade them bow their heads and dowsed them one by one
with a scoop. Having done this, he blessed each of them in order,
placing his hands upon each man's head; then he leaned perilously
forward from his barge and gave each of them a brotherly kiss upon
the forehead.

They endured all this with no sign of expression in their faces, as
though they were scarcely aware of Father Willibald's presence
or of what he was doing to them, and as though the spectators on
the banks did not exist at all.

When they had waded ashore again, Orm told them that they
were now free to go whithersoever they pleased.

"But before you leave me," he said, "I wish to give you one
further example of Christian behavior. It is commanded that we
who follow Christ shall be generous toward our enemies, even to
such as have sought our life; and I do not intend to show myself
less religious in my observance of this command than anyone else."

He then ordered each of the three men to be given food for their
journey, the same as the guests had enjoyed in the church on the
previous evening. In addition, he presented every one of them with
a horse, from those that they had brought with them in their
caravan.

"Now depart in peace," he said, "and do not forget that you
belong to Christ."

Östen glared at him and, for the first time that day, words passed
his lips.

"I am a man whose memory is long," he said slowly; and he spoke as though he was very weary.

He said no more, but climbed upon his horse, rode out through the gate, and, together with his two companions, disappeared into the forest.

Then everybody returned to the church, and the feast proceeded amid much merriment and noise, so that when Father Willibald tried to tell them more about the Christian religion, he had difficulty in getting a hearing. They would prefer, the guests declared, to hear about the adventures that Orm had had in foreign lands, as well as about his feud with King Sven; so Orm complied with this request. There was little love lost between King Sven and the inhabitants of these parts, for it was a peculiarity of the border-dwellers that they were always generous in their praise of dead kings, but seldom found anything good to say about living ones. When, therefore, Orm told them how Father Willibald had thrown a stone at King Sven and hit him in the mouth, so that blood had appeared and his teeth had been loosened, there was tremendous applause and jubilation, and all the guests made haste to fill their cups that they might drink to the honor of the little priest. Many of them swayed backwards and forwards on their benches with tears streaming from their eyes, and their mouths wide open, while others were unable to swallow their ale for laughing, and snorted it out on the table in front of them; and they all cried joyfully that they had never heard the like of such a feat by so tiny a man.

"The spirit of the Lord was upon me," said Father Willibald humbly. "King Sven is God's enemy, and so my weak hand brought him down."

"We have heard it said," remarked a man of note called Ivar the Smith who was seated near Orm, "that King Sven hates all Christians, and their priests especially, so that he kills all he can lay his hands on. It is not difficult to guess the reason for his hatred, if he received such a blow as this from the hand of one of them. For there are few greater indignities that a king could undergo, and few that would take longer to forget."

"Especially if he lost a tooth or two," said another good farmer farther down the table, whose name was Black Grim of the Fell.

"For every time he bites a crust of bread, or gnaws a knuckle of sheep, he will be reminded of the incident."

"That is true," said a third, by name Uffe Club-Foot. "It was so with me when I lost my foot, the time I fell out with my neighbor, Thorvald of Langaled. Midway through our argument he aimed a blow at my leg, and I jumped too late. Long after the stump had healed and I had learned to walk with a wooden peg, I still felt tired and feeble, not only when I was standing but also when I was sitting down, and even in bed, as my woman can attest, for she was for a long time no better off than if she had been a widow. But when at last my luck changed, so that I saw Thorvald lying before me on his doorstep with my arrow in his throat, I took a great leap over him and all but broke my good leg, so full of vigor I suddenly found myself. And I have kept that vigor ever since."

"It is not because of Father Willibald that my brother kills Christians," said Ylva. "He has always hated them bitterly, especially since my father took their part and allowed himself to be baptized. He could not set eyes even on the blessed Bishop Poppo, who was the mildest of men, without mumbling against him; though more than that he dared not do as long as my father retained his power. But now, if reports are true, he kills bishops and priests of all ranks whenever he can lay his hand on them, and it will be a good thing if he does not live too long."

"The life of evil men is often long," said Father Willibald, "but it is not so long as the arm of God. They shall not escape his vengeance."

Down at the end of one of the tables, where the young people were seated and the merriment was greatest, they were now beginning to make verses; and there on this evening a lampoon was composed which was sung along the border for many years afterwards, at feasts, threshings, and flax-strippings, and which came to be known as the "Ballad of King Sven." It was a young man called Gisle, son to Black Grim, who began it. He was a shapely youth, dark-haired and fair-skinned; and although there was nothing wrong with his head, it was a remarkable thing with him that he was shy of women, though he was often observed to cast by no means hostile glances in the direction of one or another of them. All his family regarded this as a peculiar and disturbing thing,

which even the wisest among them knew no cure for; and hitherto
he had been sitting bashful and silent in his place, devoting himself solely to his food and drink, though it was well known that he
had as ready a tongue as any young man there. Opposite him there
sat a girl called Rannvi, a comely virgin with a snub nose and a
dimple in her chin, such a woman as might easily cause a young
man to cease his chatter; and ever and anon, from the time that he
had taken his seat on the bench on the first day of the feast, he
had cast stealthy glances toward her, but had not dared to address
her and had become stiff with terror whenever it had so happened
that their eyes had met. Once or twice she had gone so far as to
chide him for his word-meanness, but without avail. Now, however, the good ale had given him better courage, and the story of
King Sven's humiliation at the hand of Father Willibald had
made him laugh very loudly; and of a sudden he began to rock
backwards and forwards on his bench, opened his mouth wide,
and roared in a high voice:

> "You challenged a priest,
> And that was the least.
> For he toppled you into
> The mud, King Sven!"

"Here is something new!" cried those who sat nearest to him.
"Gisle has turned poet. He is making a ballad about King Sven.
But this is only half a verse. Let us hear the rest."

Many of the guests now made suggestions how he might finish
his poem, but it was no easy thing to find words of the right length
and ending; and in the end it was Gisle himself who found the
answer and completed his poem so that it might be sung to an
old and well-known melody:

> "You were always greedy for
> More, King Sven!
> You thought yourself greater than
> Thor, King Sven!
> But the priest threw a stone
> And down with a groan
> You fell on your face to the
> Floor, King Sven!"

"He is a poet! He has written a whole poem!" cried those about him; and none cried with so loud a voice as Rannvi.

"Listen to the young people," said the old ones higher up the table. "They have a poet there among them. Black Grim's son has wrought a ballad about King Sven. Who would have thought such a thing possible? Has he inherited the gift from you, Grim? If not from you, then from whom, pray?"

"Let us all hear this poem," said Orm.

So Gisle was called upon to declaim his verse aloud before the whole company. At first his voice trembled somewhat; but when he saw that his audience approved his work, and that Orm himself was nodding and smiling, his fear fell from him; and now he found himself able to meet Rannvi's eyes without averting his own.

"I can write you more poems, and better," he said to her proudly as he seated himself again.

Black Grim, Gisle's father, sat beaming with pride and satisfaction. He said that he had often felt himself to have a talent for verse-making, in his younger days, but that something had always happened which had prevented him from putting his inspirations into words.

"All the same," he said, "it is strange that he should have this gift; for he is folk-shy, especially when there are girls near him, though he would gladly have it otherwise."

"Believe me, Grim," said Ylva, "he will not need to be shy of them any more. Trust my word for that. For, now that he has shown himself to be a poet, as many as can find space to do so will hang themselves round his neck. My father, who was full of wisdom upon all subjects, often used to say that as flies swarm around food of any kind but abandon it as soon as they sniff the odor of the honey-pot, so is it with young women when they sense the presence of a poet."

Orm sat staring into his ale-cup with an anxious expression on his face, deaf to what they were saying. Asa asked him if anything was on his mind, but he only mumbled abstractedly to himself and made no reply to her question.

"If I know him aright, he is composing a verse," said Ylva. "He always wears that troubled look when the verse mood is upon him. It is a peculiar thing with poets that if there are two of them in the same room and one of them composes a verse, the other cannot rest until he has composed another which he thinks is better than his rival's."

Orm sat with his hands on his knees, rocking backwards and forwards on his bench, sighing deeply and mumbling cavernously to himself. At length, though, he found the words he wanted, gave two nods of relief, thumped his fist on the table for silence, and said:

> "I hear you don't think
> Me your friend, King Sven!
> They tell me you drink
> To my end, King Sven!
> Wouldst catch me off my guard?
> God and my sharp-tongued sword
> Caused you to blink,
> Ay, and bend, King Sven!"

This was received with approbation by such of the company as were in a condition to appreciate the poem. Orm took a deep draught of his ale, and it could be seen that he was once again in excellent spirits.

"We have done well this evening," he said, "for we have composed a poem that has given pleasure to us all, and that will undoubtedly displease King Sven. This is a remarkable coincidence, that two poets should be found at a single feast, for they seem to be somewhat thinly sown in these parts; and even if our quality is not fully commensurate, nevertheless you have acquitted yourself honorably, Gisle, and I shall therefore pledge you."

But when Orm peered down toward the end of the church through the smoke of the pitch torches, Gisle was nowhere to be seen; nor could he be discovered among those who were asleep beneath the tables. But since Rannvi's place was also empty, their parents thought it most likely that they had both become drowsy and, as befitted well-brought-up children, had retired to rest without disturbing their elders.

That evening Father Willibald, thanks partly to the good offices of Asa and Ylva, received promises from four of the women present that he might soon baptize their infants, provided that he did so in the same tub in which he had baptized Harald Ormsson and with equal ceremony. But still none of the guests was willing to be sprinkled personally, despite the merry humor they were all in as a result of the good food and drink they had consumed. So Father Willibald had to contain himself as patiently as he might, though he had hoped for more spectacular results.

The next day, which was the concluding day of Orm's feast, the drinking reached its climax. Orm still had plenty of smoked mutton uneaten, and the greater part of a fresh ox, as well as two tubfuls of feast-ale and a small tubful of strong mead, made from lime honey, and he said that it would reflect little credit on him or his guests if any of this was left when the feast ended. All the guests were anxious to ensure that his honor, and theirs, should not thus be sullied. They therefore promised to do their best and, from the first moment after they awoke that morning, set to with a will. It was their intention, they said, that both their host and his priest should find themselves beneath the table before the last cup was drained to its dregs.

Orm now took the priest to one side to ask his opinion on an important matter. He wanted to know, he said, whether God would regard it as lawful to baptize heathens while they were unconscious from drink. "For, if so," he said, "it seems to me that a good work might be performed this evening, the way the day is beginning."

Father Willibald replied that Orm had raised a moot point, and one that had been much debated by holy men who had devoted their whole lives to studying the craft of conversion.

"Some scholars," he said, "hold it to be lawful, in circumstances when the Devil shows himself particularly unwilling to yield. They support their contention by quoting the example of the great Emperor Charles, who, when he desired to baptize some wild Saxons who held fast to their ancient idolatry, had the more obstinate of them stunned with a club as they were dragged forth to baptism, to quell their violence and blasphemous outpourings. It cannot be denied that such treatment must cause the Devil considerable vexation, and I do not see that there is much difference between stunning heathens with a club and befuddling them with ale. On the other hand, the blessed Bishop Piligrim of Salzburg, who lived in the time of the old Emperor Otto, held the opposite view, and expressed it in a pastoral letter of great wisdom. My good master, Bishop Poppo, always used to hold that Bishop Piligrim was right; for, he used to say, while it is true that the Devil must be

discomforted by seeing his followers baptized while they are unconscious, still, such discomfiture can only be temporary, for, once
they have recovered their senses and have learned what has happened to them, they lose all the feelings of reverence and love of
God that the sacrament has imparted to them. They re-admit the
Devil to their hearts, opening them wider than before to let him
in, and rage more furiously than ever against Christ and His
servants; so that no good results from the ceremony having been
performed. For this reason the holy men whom I have named to
you, and many others besides, hold it inadvisable to baptize men
when they are in this condition."

Orm sighed. "It may be as you say," he said, "since you have it
from Bishop Poppo's own lips; for he understands the ways of God
better than any other man. But it is a great pity that he should be
of that mind."

"It is God's will," replied Father Willibald, nodding sadly. "Our
task would be rendered too simple if we could enlist the assistance
of ale in our endeavors to baptize the heathens. More is required
than ale: eloquence, good deeds, and great patience, which last is
the most difficult of all virtues to acquire and, once acquired, to
retain."

"I wish to serve God as well as I can," said Orm. "But how we
are to further His cause among these good neighbors of mine is
more than I know."

So they left the matter at that, and the drinking proceeded merrily and apace. Later in the day, when most of the guests were still
more or less upright on their benches, the married women went in
to Ylva's son to bring him name-gifts and good-luck wishes, after
their ancient custom; while the men, feeling the need for air, went
out on the grass to indulge in games and tests of strength, such as
finger-tug, wrestling, and flat-buttock lifting, amid shouts of encouragement and laughter; and many a good somersault was
turned; while some of the more daring among them tried their
hands at the difficult sport known as knot-lifting,[1] without, luckily,

---

[1] A sort of invitation to break one's neck, played by strong, drunken men
after a feast. One (the weaker) sits on the ground, while the other (the
stronger) kneels on his hands and knees. The latter is the man who risks his
neck. The weaker man sits with his knees drawn up and wide apart, puts his
arms outside his thighs and locks his hands under his knees. The strong man
then puts his head forward between the other man's knees and into his locked

anyone overtasking his strength and breaking a limb or dislocating his neck.

It was while these sports were in progress that the four strange beggars arrived at Gröning.

CHAPTER SIX

CONCERNING FOUR STRANGE BEGGARS, AND HOW THE ERIN MASTERS CAME TO FATHER WIL–LIBALD'S ASSISTANCE

HEY looked as beggars usually look, trudging on foot with sack and staff, as they arrived at the house craving food and drink. Ylva was seated on the bench before the house in earnest conversation with the mothers of Gisle and Rannvi; for both these young people had come to her that morning in a state of extreme bliss to say that they were well content with each other, and to beg her to speak persuasively on their behalf to their respective parents, so that the wedding might be arranged as soon as possible; in which project Ylva had willingly undertaken to help them to the best of her ability. When news was brought her that there were beggars standing at the gate, she bade her servants request Orm to come to her, for he had ordered that no strangers were to be admitted until he had himself first carefully scrutinized them.

So he examined the travelers, who replied freely to his questions; but they did not seem to him to be like ordinary beggars. Their leader was a big man, broad of loin and well fleshed, with a grizzled beard and sharp eyes beneath his hat-brim. As he moved, he trailed one leg behind him, as though it might be somewhat stiff at the knee. He answered Orm's questions in a bold voice, and it was plain from his accent that he was a Swede. He said that they had come from Sjælland and were heading northwards across the

---

hands, and tries to rise to a standing position, while the victim does his worst by pressing his knees and his locked hands round the strong man's neck. It was (says the author, in a letter to the translator) "a frightful game, only played by drunk men."

border; a fisherman had brought them across the Sound, and they
had begged their way up from Landöre.

"But today we have eaten nothing," he concluded, "for here-
abouts the houses lie far apart, and at the last house we visited
we were given nothing to put in our sacks."

"Nevertheless," said Orm, "you carry more flesh than I have seen
on the bones of some beggars."

"There is nourishment in Danish and Skanian pancakes," replied
the other with a sigh. "But I fear their effect may wear somewhat
thin, and I with it, before I come to the Mälar country."

The man who stood beside him was younger, of slender build
and pale of skin. His cheeks and jaw were black with a short, dense
beard. Orm studied him for a few moments. Then he said: "From
your appearance, a man might suppose that you had been shaven
for the priesthood."

The slender man smiled sadly. "My beard was burned from my
face one evening when I was roasting pork in a wind," he said, "and
it has not yet regained its old fullness."

But it was at the other two beggars that Orm gazed most curiously, for of them he could make nothing. They had the appearance of being brothers, for they were both small and lean,
long-eared and large-nosed, and both of them stared at him with
wise brown eyes like those of squirrels. Although small, they
nevertheless looked to be agile and muscular. They stood with their
heads on one side, listening to the baying of the hounds; then, of
a sudden, one of them placed a finger in his mouth and emitted
a strange whistle, soft and vibrant. Immediately the hounds
stopped howling and began to pant, as they did when no strangers
were about.

"Are you trolls," asked Orm, "or merely conjurors?"

"Neither, alas," replied the man who had whistled, "much as
we should like to be either. For we cannot conjure food from anywhere, despite our hunger."

Orm smiled. "I shall not refuse you food," he said, "and I do not
fear your witchcraft while there is yet daylight; but such beggars as
you I have never before set eyes on. No other stranger has succeeded in quieting my hounds; indeed, I sometimes find it difficult
to do so myself."

"We will teach you a way," said the second of the two small

men, "once we have got a good meal in our bellies, and food for
two more in our sacks. We are wandering men who serve no master, and we understand hounds better than most men."

Orm assured them that he would not send them away with
empty sacks, and bade them enter.

"You have chosen a good time to arrive," he said, "for you have
come in the midst of a great feast, so that there will be pancakes
enough for you all, and perhaps something else besides. It is a pity
for my guests that you cannot play as skillfully as you whistle."

The two small men glanced at each other and winked, but said
nothing; and they and their two companions followed Orm into the
house.

Orm cried to Ylva: "Here are wayfarers, both large and small,
come to crave a plate of your feast-food."

Ylva looked up from her conversation and nodded, with her
thoughts elsewhere; then, as she caught sight of the two small men,
her eyes grew large with wonder, and she sprang up from the
bench on which she was sitting.

"The Erin Masters!" she cried. "Felimid and Ferdiad! My
father's jesters! Are you still alive? In God's name, dear friends,
what has forced you to turn beggars? Have you grown too old to
practice your arts?"

The two small men stared at her in equal astonishment; then
they both smiled. They dropped their staffs and beggars' sacks,
took a couple of paces toward Ylva, and then, in the same instant,
they both sprang head over heels. One of them remained thus
standing on his hands, on which he proceeded to jump to and fro,
uttering small joyful cries, while the other tied himself into a ball
and rolled toward her feet. Then they both leaped to their feet
again and, gravely and expressionlessly, saluted her.

"We have not grown too old," said one of them, "as you can see
for yourself, O fairest of all King Harald's daughters. For you must
know that the years fear such masters as us; though it is a good
while since you sat on your father's knee and saw us frolic for the
first time. But we are hungrier now than we were then."

Many of the guests, both men and women, had come running
up in haste to look more closely at these marvelous men who could
jump on their hands; but Ylva said that the newcomers were to
eat and drink in peace, and that they were to be treated with as

much honor as any guest in the church. She conducted them into the house herself and placed before them the best of meat and drink; nor did they need any persuasion before they set to. The twins and Glad Ulf followed them in and sat silently in a corner, in the hope that the two little men might perform further antics; meanwhile Orm explained to his other guests who these two strange beggars were, who had so aroused their wonder.

"They were King Harald's jesters," he said, "though now they have no master; they come from Ireland, and are widely famed. I saw them once when I was drinking Christmas with the King; but then they were prinked out with feathers and motley, so that I did not recognize them now. What they can be doing as wandering beggars I do not know, and it puzzles me sadly; but let us sit down to our ale again, and then, in a short while, we will hear their story."

When all the beggars had eaten their fill, the jesters offered no objection to joining the drinkers, who, after their short rest, had now begun again in earnest. Both their companions, however, sat staring silently at their empty plates. When asked the reason for their melancholy, they replied that they were weary after the hardships of their journey and the good meal that they had just eaten. So Father Willibald led them to his room, that they might rest there undisturbed. Then he took the two jesters aside and sat with them for some time in earnest conversation, which none dared to disturb; for they had been old friends ever since they had first met at King Harald's court, and were overjoyed to renew their acquaintance after so long an interval of time.

When at last all the guests had taken their places in the church, the two jesters were placed one on either side of Father Willibald. Many questions were asked concerning them, and all were anxious to see them display their skill; but the two jesters sat supping their ale in silence, as though unconscious of the excitement they were causing.

Then Orm said: "It would be ungracious of us to demand that you should show us your skill, for you have a right to be weary after your wanderings, and no guest or stranger who receives hospitality in my house is required to pay for it. But I cannot deny that we should like to take advantage of the fact that two such masters as you have arrived in the midst of my son's christening feast. For I know that you are both famous men, and I have always heard that no jesters in the world can match those of Ireland."

"Chieftain," replied one of the Irishmen, "what you heard was the truth; and I can assure you that even in Ireland there are not two men more famous for their skill than I, Felimid O'Flann, and my brother Ferdiad here, who is as good as I am. My ancestors have been royal jesters ever since our great forefather Flann Long-Ear performed, long ago, before King Conchobar MacNessa of Ulster and the heroes of the Red Branch in the hall of Emain Macha; and it has always been a law in our family that, once we have become proficient in our art and have earned the right to call ourselves master jesters, we display our skill only when commanded to do so by a person of royal blood. And this you must know, that we who jest before kings follow not only the most difficult calling in the world but also that which, more than any other calling, benefits mankind. For when a king is out of humor, and his fighting-men feel the itch of boredom, they are a danger to other men; but when good jesters perform for them, they rock with laughter over their ale and go contented to their beds and let their neighbors and subjects sleep in peace. After priests, therefore, we perform a more useful function than any other sort of men; for priests offer happiness in heaven, through the influence they have with God, while we offer happiness on earth, because of the influence we have on the humors of kings. And since there are many kings in Ireland, the jesters of that land are the best in the world, and are of many different kinds; tumblers, clowns, ventriloquists, imitators of animals, men who contort their bodies, others who contort their faces, sword-swallowers, egg-dancers, and men who snort fire through their nostrils. But the true master jester is not he who can perform one or another of these arts, but he who knows them all. And it is held by wise men in Ireland that the best among us today are almost as good as King Conaire's three jesters were in ancient times, of whom it was said that no man who saw them could help laughing, even though he might be sitting with his father's or his mother's corpse on the table before him."

Everyone in the church had by now fallen silent, and all the guests were hanging on the Irishman's words and staring at him and at his brother, who was sitting on the other side of Father Willibald with a contented look on his face, slowly moving his large ears backwards and forwards. All agreed that the like of these men had never before been seen in these parts.

"You speak well," said Gudmund of Uvaberg, "and yet it is not easy to believe that all you say is true; for if you are both such great masters in your own land, why have you come to the north, where kings are few and live far apart?"

Felimid smiled and nodded his head. "You may well ask that," he said, "for Ireland is a land that no man willingly leaves; and I will gladly tell you how we came to do so, even if what I say may sound like boasting. I must tell you all that my brother and I are exiles from our land on account of a feat which, I think, none but we could have performed. When we were young, but already expert in our art, we were jesters to the good King Domnal of Leighlin. He was a man who loved laughter and music, the word of God, and legends of heroes, poetry, women's beauty, and the wisdom of old men; and he showed us great honor, rewarding our skill with silver and cattle and fine pastures in which to keep them. Because of this we loved him dearly and were well content to be his servants; and our only worry was lest in our contentment we should grow too fat, for that is the worst thing that can happen to any man who practices our art. His neighbor was King Colla of Kilkenny, a dangerous man, very proud, and cunning at planning ways to discomfort those who lived too near him. One Whitsun, King Domnal held a great feast, and his priests, his poets, and we, his jesters, were kept busier than usual; for the King was to wed Emer, the daughter of the King of Cashel. She looked as a princess should, clear-eyed, purple-mouthed, and white of skin, high-breasted, slender of waist, and broad of hip, and with hair so long that she could sit on the ends of it; so that even you, Ylva, would hardly have known which was the lovelier, you or she, if you could have seen her. This marriage was a source of great joy, not only to King Domnal, but to all his men, so that it was as merry a feast as a man could wish for. Then, on the second evening of the feast, when we were all drunk, King Colla descended upon us. King Domnal was killed as he hewed naked about him at his chamber door; many of his men fell with him; his Queen was taken from her bridal bed and carried off with the rest of the booty; and my brother and I suffered the same fate, for such was our fame. When King Colla saw Queen Emer, his lips grew moist and he leered like a hound, but us he threw into one of his dungeons until his wedding-day; for he had set his mind on marrying the woman he had stolen. Then he told us that we were to jest at his wedding feast. At first we refused to do this, for we were still heavy with grief at the death of our master; but when he swore that he would have us flogged with sharp-twigged birches unless we obeyed his bidding, we changed our tone and promised to appear before him and exhibit our finest arts. And that we kept that promise I do not think he could well deny."

Felimid smiled thoughtfully to himself as he drank long and slowly from his cup. All the guests drank to him, crying that he was a fine story-teller and that they were eager to hear about this great feat that he had performed. He nodded, and continued:

"There he sat on his royal throne as we entered his presence, and already he was drunk; and never have I seen any man who looked so well at peace with himself and the world. As he saw us enter, he roared in a loud voice to his guests that the two masters from Leighlin would now display their quality as conjurors of mirth and merriment. Nor did she who sat beside him in her bridal jewels wear a sad face; for young women soon accustom themselves to a change of man, and perchance King Colla seemed to her to be an even finer match than our lord, King Domnal, had been. We began with simple jests, though we spoke them well, and with tricks that we were wont to perform on common occasions; and King Colla was in such a capital humor that he began at once to bellow with laughter. The whole hall laughed with him; and when Ferdiad stood on his head and played the flute, while I danced the bear-dance round him, uttering growls, the applause became tremendous, and the King flung himself backwards on his throne with his mouth wide open, splashing mead from his stoup over his lady's robe. He gasped for breath and shrieked that he had never before set eyes on jesters to compare with us. At this, we pricked up our ears and bethought ourselves and exchanged a word in whispers; for if he had never seen jesters like us, it was no less true that we had never before heard anyone laugh like him at the simple antics which were all that we had yet performed for him. So we turned to more difficult feats and meatier jests, and at these the King laughed like a magpie in May when the sun appears through an Irish mist. Then we began to feel merrier ourselves, and displayed our rarest arts and told our most uproarious jests, such as contort the bellies and pain the jaws even of men who are weighed down with grief or plagued with sickness. All the while, King Colla's laughter grew louder and more breathless until it sounded like the ninth wave breaking upon the coast of Donegal when the spring tide is at its height. Then, of a sudden, his face turned black and he fell from his throne to the floor, where he remained lying; for he had burst inwardly with the violence of his laughter. When this happened, Ferdiad and I glanced at each other and nodded, remembering our master Domnal and thinking that we had now repaid, in some measure, the gifts and kindnesses that he had showered upon us. The Queen screamed wildly with terror, and all those in the hall rushed toward him, save we, who headed for the door; but before we reached it, we heard the cry go up that he was dead. We did not wait to hear more, but took to our heels and fled northwards across the heath as speedily as Bishop Asaph fled across the fields at Magh Slecht when the red ghosts were after him. We sought sanctuary with King Sigtrygg of Dublin, supposing we should be safe there; but Queen Emer sent armed men after us, who told King Sigtrygg that we were slaves whom she had inherited from her former husband, King Domnal, and that now, with evil and malicious intent, we had caused the death of her new husband, thereby doing great damage to her and her good name, and that she therefore wished to kill us. But we escaped in a trading ship and fled to King Harald of Denmark, into whose service we entered; and there we prospered. But never, as long as he was alive, did we tell anyone of what we had done to King Colla, for we did not want King Harald to hear of it. For it might have caused him to worry lest he might suffer a similar fate."

When Felimid had finished telling his story, there was a tremendous uproar at the tables; for many of the guests were now beginning to be drunk, and they cried that, though the Irishman had spoken well, it was not talk that they wanted but an exhibition of the antics that had killed King Colla. Orm himself agreed with this viewpoint.

"You have already heard," he said to the jesters, "that our curiosity has been great from the first moment that we learned your identity; and that curiosity is now much greater, as a result of the story you have just told us. Nor need you be alarmed lest any man or woman here should burst with laughter; for if this should happen, nobody will seek to be revenged upon you, and it will provide an excellent climax to my feast and cause it to be long remembered throughout the border country."

"And if it is as you say," said Ylva, "that you can only jest in the presence of one of royal blood, do I not count as such, as much as any small Irish king?"

"Of course you do," said Felimid hastily, "no one has a better right to be called royal than you, Ylva. But there is another obstacle to prevent us from performing here, and if you will bear patiently with me, I shall tell you how the matter lies. Know, then, that my great-great-great-great-great-great-grandfather, Felimid Goatbeard, after whom I was named, was the most famous of all jesters in the days when King Finechta the Feaster was Ireland's over-king, and he was the first of our line to become a Christian. Now, it so happened that on one occasion, when he was traveling, this Goatbeard met in the place where he was lodging for the night St. Adamnan and became inspired with a great respect and reverence for this holy man, finding him greater than any king. So, to show his admiration for him, he jested before him, while the good man sat at his dinner table, performing the most intricate and difficult antics that he knew with such enthusiasm that at length he broke his neck and lay on the floor as if dead. As soon, however, as the holy man realized his plight, he rose from his table, went over to him, touched his neck, and prayed for him, with powerful words, so that life returned to him, though his head sat crooked on his neck for the rest of his days. In gratitude for this miracle, it has ever since been a tradition in our family that we may jest before the Archbishop of Cashel and the Archbishop of Armagh, the Abbot of Iona and the Abbot of Clonmacnoise, as well as before kings; and also that we never display our art in the presence of any man or woman who has not been baptized. For that reason, we cannot perform for you here, gladly as we would otherwise have done so."

Orm stared at the little man in amazement when he heard these words, for, from his memory of the Christmas at King

Harald's court, he knew them to be a lie; and he was on the point
of saying so when he caught a warning glance from Father Willibald, which caused him to shut his mouth and remain silent.

"It may be that God Himself willed it so," said the other Irishman in a small voice, "for, without boasting, I think it may be said
that many of King Harald's best men chose to be baptized chiefly
in order that they might not have to leave the hall when the time
came for us to display our arts before the King."

Ylva opened her mouth and began to speak, but Orm, Father
Willibald, and both the jesters immediately started talking at the
same time, so that, what with their voices, the cries of disappointment, and the gurgles and snores of drunkenness that were arising
from various parts of the hall, it was impossible to hear what she
was saying.

Orm said: "It is my hope that both you masters will remain here
for some short while longer, so that I and my household may be
able to enjoy your jests and antics when these our guests have left
us; for every man and woman in my house is a good Christian."

But at this many of the young people began to shout louder than
ever that they would see the jesters perform their tricks, whatever
sacrifice might be involved.

"Baptize us, if there is no other way," cried one, "and do not
delay, but let the rite be performed at once."

"Yes, yes!" cried the rest. "That is the best solution. Let us all
be baptized at once."

Some of the older people laughed at this, but others looked
thoughtful and glanced doubtfully at one another.

Gisle, Black Grim's son, jumped up on his bench and shouted:
"Let those who are not willing to be a party to this go and make
themselves comfortable in the hay-barn, that they may be out of
the way."

The excitement and shouting became more and more vociferous.
Father Willibald sat with his head bowed upon his chest, mumbling to himself, while the two jesters peacefully sipped their ale.

Black Grim said: "At this moment it seems to me but a small
thing to be baptized, and no cause for alarm; but that may be
because I have drunk deeply of this excellent ale and am warmed
by the feast and by the wise conversation of my friends. It may
be that I shall feel differently when the ale-joy has gone from me

and I begin to think of the way my neighbors will laugh and gibe at me."

"Your neighbors are all here," said Orm, "and who will laugh or gibe at you if everyone does as you do? It is more likely that you will all be laughing at men who are not baptized when you all find how much you have improved your luck by submitting to the ritual."

"It may be that you are right," said Grim, "for no one can deny that your luck has been as good as a man's could be."

Brother Willibald now rose to his feet and read over them in Latin, with his hands spread wide, so that all the guests sat silent and motionless beneath the sound of his words, and several of the women turned pale and began to tremble. Two of the more drunken men got up and bade their women straightway come with them and leave this witchcraft; but when those addressed remained in their seats as though they had not heard their husbands speak, with no eyes or ears for anyone save Father Willibald, both the men sat down again, with the air of men who have done all they can, and returned with glum faces to their drinking.

Everyone felt a great relief when Father Willibald came to the end of his Latin, which sounded like nothing so much as the squealing of pigs. He now began to address them in ordinary language on the subject of Christ, His power and goodness, and His willingness to take all men and women into His protection, not excluding robbers and adulterers. "So you see," he said, "there is no one here unqualified to receive all the good that Christ has to offer you; for He is a chieftain who bids every man and woman welcome to His feast, and has rich gifts for every one of His guests."

The company were greatly pleased with this speech, and many of them burst out laughing; for everyone found it an amusing and proper thing to hear his neighbors described as robbers and adulterers, comfortable in the knowledge that he himself could not be classed among those sorts of people.

"It is my earnest hope," continued Father Willibald, "that you will be willing to follow Him for the rest of your lives, and that you will appreciate what that involves—namely, that you shall mend your ways and follow His commandments and never worship any other god."

"Yes, yes," cried many of them impatiently; "we appreciate

everything. And now make haste, so that we can get on with the important business."

"One thing you must not forget," proceeded Father Willibald, "is that, from this day forward, you must all come to me in this church of God on every Sunday, or at least on every third Sunday, to hear the will of God and be instructed in the teaching of Christ. Will you promise me this?"

"We promise!" they roared eagerly. "And now shut your mouth. Time is running on, and it will soon be evening."

"It would be most beneficial to your souls if you could all come every Sunday; but for those who live a long way off, every third week will suffice."

"Cease gabbing, priest, and baptize us!" roared the more impatient members of the gathering.

"Quiet!" thundered Father Willibald. "These are the ancient and cunning devils of your false beliefs that tempt you to bawl thus and interrupt my speech, hoping thereby to obstruct the will of God and so keep you for their own. But this is no superfluous information that I give you, when I speak to you of Christ and of the decrees of God, but important instruction, to which you must listen attentively and in silence. I shall now pray that all such devilry may instantly depart from you, so that you may be worthy to receive baptism."

He then began again to read in Latin, slowly and in a stern voice, so that before long several of the older women began to wail and weep. None of the men dared utter a word; they all sat staring anxiously at him with large eyes and open mouths. Two of them, however, were seen to nod; their heads dropped nearer and nearer to their ale-cups, and after a short while they slid slowly beneath the table, whence lengthy snores soon began to emerge.

Father Willibald now commanded them all to come forward to the baptism-tub, in which Harald Ormsson had been baptized; and there twenty-three men and nineteen women, young and old, were duly sprinkled. Orm and Rapp pulled the two sleepers out from under the table and tried to shake some life into them; but, finding that all their efforts failed, they carried them up to the tub and held them in position until they, too, had been sprinkled like the rest, after which they were thrown into a quiet corner to continue with their sleeping. The whole company was now in excellent spirits. They wrung the water out of their hair, went joyfully back to their places at the tables, and, when Father Willibald attempted to conclude the ceremony by pronouncing a general blessing, the noise was so great that little of what he said could be heard.

"Nobody here is afraid of a little water," they roared proudly, grinning at one another across the tables.

"Everything is ready now."

"Up, now, jesters, and show us your skill!"

The jesters exchanged small smiles and rose willingly from their 'benches. Immediately a deep silence fell on the hall. They saluted Ylva with great courtliness when they had come into the center of the hall, as though she were their only spectator; then, for a long while, they held the gathering alternately dumb with amazement and helpless with laughter. They turned somersaults both backwards and forwards, without the help of their hands, landing always on their feet; they imitated birds and beasts, played ditties on small pipes while dancing on their hands, and juggled with tankards, knives, and swords. Then out of their sacks they produced two great dolls, clad in motley and with faces carved in the likeness of old women. These they held in their hands, Felimid taking one and Ferdiad the other, and immediately the dolls began to speak, at first amiably, then shaking their heads and hissing angrily, and at the last furiously abusing each other, vituperating tirelessly like squabbling crows. A shiver went through the gathering as the dolls began to talk; the women ground their teeth, and the men went white and reached for their swords; but Ylva and Father Willibald, who knew the Irishmen's tricks of old, calmed them with the assurance that all was the result of the jesters' skill and that there was no witchcraft in it. Orm himself looked uncertain for a few moments, but soon recovered his mirth; and when the jesters brought their dolls closer to each other and made them fight with their arms, while their voices cursed each other yet more shrilly, as though they might at any moment seize each other by the hair, he burst into such a bellow of laughter that Ylva leaned anxiously across to him and bade him remember what had happened to King Colla. Orm wiped the tears from his eyes and looked at her.

"It is not easy to be prudent when one is merry," he said. "But

I do not think God will allow any harm to befall me now, when
I have just done Him so great a service."

It was noticeable, however, that he took Ylva's warning seriously, for he was never able to ignore any observation relating to
his health.

At length the jesters concluded their performance, though the
guests begged them many times to continue; and the evening
ended without anyone suffering the fate of King Colla. Father
Willibald then thanked God for all the happiness that they had
enjoyed, and for all the souls that he had been permitted to lead
to Christ. So Orm's great christening feast came to a close; and
the guests rode home from Gröning in the gray dawn twilight,
talking of all the good ale and victuals that they had consumed
and of the marvelous feats that had been performed for them by
these Irish jesters.

CHAPTER SEVEN

CONCERNING THE KING OF SWEDEN'S SWORD–
BEARER, AND THE MAGISTER FROM
AACHEN AND HIS SINS

WHEN all the guests save the four beggars had departed and
peace had returned to Gröning, Orm and all his household agreed
that the feast had passed off better than any of them could have
dared to hope, and that Harald Ormsson had had a christening
that would without doubt bring much honor to himself and them.
Only Asa wore a thoughtful look. She said that his sharp-toothed
guests had consumed practically their entire stock of provisions,
both wet and dry, so that there was scarcely enough left for their
own needs.

"The bakehouse is empty," she said, "save for one small bin;
and the larder looks as though a pack of wolves had visited it.
I tell you both that, if you have many sons, you will not be able
to hold christening feasts like this for all of them, or it will eat

up all your wealth. I do not wish to complain too loudly over so much waste on this occasion, for it is right that the first-born son should be thus honored; but now we shall all have to be content with small-beer with our meals, until the next hop harvest."

Orm said that he had no wish to hear any grumbling over the fact that a little extra food had been consumed. "But I know you mean well," he said to Asa, "and that your grumbling arises chiefly from habit. And I have heard that small-beer is a drink that a man can be content with."

"You must remember, Asa," said Father Willibald, "that this has been no ordinary feast. For it has advanced the cause of Christ, and has caused heathens to become baptized. Let us, therefore, not complain that so much has disappeared, for God will repay us tenfold."

Asa admitted that there might be something in this argument, for she never liked to oppose Father Willibald, even when she was in her sharper moods.

Father Willibald was especially jubilant because he had achieved so much during the feast, not only having converted all the guests but having also become the first of all Christ's servants to succeed in baptizing men from Smaland.

"Now, indeed, I can truthfully say," he said, "that patience has earned its reward and that I have not accompanied you to this foul land in vain. During these three feast-days forty-five souls have received baptism at my hand. True, alas, it is that none of them can be said to have been impelled by a genuine heartfelt longing for Christ, though I told them so much about Him. Our guests were persuaded by the Irish Masters, and the men from Smaland were baptized against their will. But it is my belief that if a servant of Christ were to sit and wait for the people of this land to come to him out of the longing of their hearts, he would have to wait a long time. And I believe that much good may result from all that has happened during this feast. But the credit for all this is not mine; but belongs to these two Irish Masters; and it was certainly a true miracle of God that they were sent here at the very time when their art was most needed."

"Only God could have thought of it," said Asa.

"But now," said Orm to the four strangers, "it is time for us to hear something more about you curious men who have come to us

in the guise of beggars.We should like to know why you two masters wander thus about our land, and who your two companions
are, and on what errand you are bound."

The large man with the grizzled beard glanced at his companions
and nodded his head slowly. Then he said, in a heavy voice: "My
name is Spjalle and my home is in Uppsala. I have accompanied
King Erik on all his campaigns, and have stood beside him as his
shield-bearer, because of my size and strength. But now I no longer
perform that task; instead, it has been commanded that I shall return to Uppsala in the guise of a beggar, with a sword bound to my
leg."

He ceased speaking, and all the others stared at him in astonishment.

"Why have you a sword bound to your leg?" asked Ylva.

"There is much that I could say in reply to that question," he
replied. "And much else besides; but perchance I have already said
too much, for I know that you, woman, are King Sven's sister. But
my chief news is my worst; which is that King Erik, whom men
called the Victorious, is dead."

They all thought that this was news indeed and were eager to
know more.

"You need have no fear on my account," said Ylva, "though I
am King Sven's sister. For there is no love lost between us, and the
last greeting we received from him was when he sent men here to
seek our lives. Was it he who killed King Erik?"

"No, no!" cried Spjalle indignantly. "Had that been so, I should
not now be here to tell the tale. King Erik died of witchcraft; of
that I am sure, though whether his death was plotted by the gods,
or whether by the foul Gute woman Sigrid, Skoglar-Toste's daughter and King Erik's Queen—may she toss perpetually in the whirl-
pool of hell among sword-blades and serpents' fangs!—I do not
know. The King lay off the Small Islands plundering with a mighty
fleet, intending shortly to sail against King Sven, who was hiding
in North Sjælland; and good luck attended all our enterprises, so
that our hearts were merry. But while we were in harbor at Falster,
our luck changed; for there a madness descended upon the King,
and he made it known to the whole army that he was intending
to become baptized. He said that his luck against King Sven would
become better if he did this, and that it would not then be long

before he put an end to him for good. He had been seduced into this folly by priests who had come to him from the Saxons and who had long been mumbling in his ear. The army liked this news but little, and wise men told him openly that it ill became the King of the Swedes to think of such foolishness, which might serve for Saxons and Danes but would be of no use to him. But he glowered fiercely at them when they counseled him thus, and answered them shortly; and as they knew him to be the wisest of men and one, besides, who always followed his own inclinations, they said no more to him on the matter. But his Queen, the crazy Gute woman, who had sailed south with us, bringing all the ships she had inherited from her father, loathed Christ and His followers with a savage loathing and refused to let King Erik silence her; so that a terrible enmity sprang up between these two, and it was rumored among the soldiers that she had said that there was no more pitiful object in the world than a baptized king, and that King Erik had threatened to have her flogged if she dared to mention the matter again. But it was too late to talk to her of flogging; she ought to have tasted the birch long before, and many times at that. As a result of their strife, the army became divided, so that we Swedes and the Queen's men looked askance at one another and exchanged sharp words, and often drew our swords upon one another. Then the witchcraft gripped him, so that he began to sicken and lay helpless, unable to move his limbs; and early one morning, while most of our men were still asleep, Skoglar-Toste's crazy daughter sailed away with all her ships and deserted us. Many of us thought she had sailed to join King Sven, and the King thought so too when he heard of her departure; but there was nothing we could do, and the King was by now so weak that he was scarcely able to speak. Then a great panic descended upon the army, and all the ships' captains wanted to desert and return to their homes as soon as they might; and there was much wrangling about the King's treasure-chests and how they might best be divided among his followers so as to prevent them from falling into King Sven's hands. But the King called me to his bedside and commanded me to carry his sword back to his son in Uppsala. For this is the ancient sword of the Uppsala kings, which was given them by Fröj and is their dearest possession. 'Take my sword home, Spjalle,' he said, 'and guard it well; for in it resides the

luck of my family.' Then he begged me to give him water to drink,
and from this I knew that he had not long to live. Soon afterwards he, whom people called the Victorious, died miserably in
his bed; and there were scarcely enough of his followers left to
build his pyre. But we performed the task as well as we could,
and killed his thralls and two of his priests and laid them on the
pyre at his feet, that he might not appear before the gods alone
and unaccompanied like a man of low degree. Then, while the pyre
was yet aflame, the people of the islands fell upon us in great
strength. When I saw them coming, I straightway fled, not from
fear, but for the sword's sake, and with these three men escaped
across the water to Skania in a fishing-boat. Now I carry the sword
bound to my leg beneath my clothes, to hide it as best I can. But
what will happen in the world now that he is dead is more than I
can guess, for, of all kings, he was the greatest, though by the foul
witch's contriving he met so mean an end and now lies far away
on Falster's strand with no mound to cover his ashes."

Such was Spjalle's story, and all his listeners stood open-eyed and
silent to hear such tidings.

"These are evil times for kings," said Orm at last. "First
Styrbjörn, who was the strongest; then King Harald, who was the
wisest; and now King Erik, who was the most powerful; and not
long since we heard that the great Empress Theofano had also
died, she who ruled alone over the Saxons and the Lombards.
Only King Sven, my wife's brother, who is more evil than other
kings, does not die, but flourishes and waxes fat. It would be good
to know why God does not destroy him and let better kings live."

"God will smite him in His own good time," said Father Willibald, "as He smote Holofernes, who had his head hewn off by the
woman Judith, or Sennacherib, the Lord of the Assyrians, who
was slain by his sons as he knelt praying before his idols. But it
sometimes happens that evil men cling hard to life; and in these
northern climes the Devil is stronger and more powerful than in
more civilized regions. That this is true has just been dreadfully
testified before us; for this man Spjalle sits here telling us how he
himself slew two of Christ's servants to sacrifice them on a heathen's pyre. Such devilry exists nowhere in the world save in these
climes and among certain of the Wendish tribes. I do not rightly
know what action I should take against the perpetrator of such a

crime. Of what use would it be for me to tell you, Spjalle, that you will burn in hell-fire for this deed; for even if you had not committed it, you would burn there just the same."

Spjalle's gaze wandered thoughtfully around the small group in which he sat.

"In my ignorance, I have said too much," he said, "and have made this priest angry. But we acted only according to our ancient custom, for we always do thus when any Swedish king sets out on his journey to the gods. And you told me, woman, that I was not among enemies here."

"She spoke the truth," said Orm. "You shall suffer no harm here. But you must not be amazed that we, who are all followers of Christ, hold it an evil thing to have killed a priest."

"They are among the blessed martyrs now," said Father Willibald.

"Are they happy there?" asked Spjalle.

"They sit on the right hand of God, and live in bliss such as no mortal man can conceive of," replied Father Willibald.

"Then they are better off than when they were alive," said Spjalle, "for in King Erik's household they were treated as thralls."

Ylva laughed.

"You deserve more praise than blame," she said, "for helping to bring them to this happy state."

Father Willibald glared angrily at her and said that it distressed him to hear her dismiss the matter so lightly. "Such foolish talk was pardonable in you when you were but a thoughtless girl," he said, "but now that you are a wise housewife with three children, and have received much Christian instruction, you should know better."

"I am my father's child," replied Ylva, "and I cannot remember that he gained much spiritual profit from begetting children or from all the instruction he received from you and Bishop Poppo."

Father Willibald nodded sorrowfully and passed his hand gently over the crown of his head, as was his wont when anyone mentioned King Harald's name; for he still bore there the imprint of a crucifix with which the King, in an impatient moment, had struck him a violent blow.

"It cannot be denied that King Harald was a dreadful sinner," he said; "and on the occasion to which you have referred, I all but joined the regiments of the blessed martyrs. In many ways, though, he was not altogether unlike King David—the resemblance is, perhaps, more noticeable if one compares him with King Sven—and I do not think he would have been pleased to hear one of his daughters jest on the subject of priest-murder."

"We are all sinners," said Orm. "Even I am no exception; for I myself have more than once laid violent hands on a priest, during our campaigns in Castile and León, when we stormed the Christians' towns and burned their churches. Their priests fought bravely against us, with spear and sword, and it was my master Almansur's command that we should always kill them first. But that was in the days when I knew no better, so that I think God will not judge me too severely for it."

"My luck is better than I had feared," said Spjalle. "For I see that I have fallen among honorable men."

The pale young man with the short black beard, who was the fourth of these beggars, had till now sat silent and heavy-eyed. Now, however, he sighed and spoke.

"All men are sinners," he said. "Alas, it is too true! But none of you bears as heavy a burden on his soul as I carry. I am Rainald, an unworthy priest of God, canon to the good Bishop Eckard of Schleswig. But I was born at Zülpich in Lotharingia and was formerly magister in the cathedral school at Aachen, and I have come to these northern climes because I am a sinner and a most unlucky man."

"A man would have to look far before finding more rewarding beggars than you," said Orm, "for not one of you but has a tale to tell. If your story is good, Rainald, let us hear it."

"Stories about sin are always good to hear," said Ylva.

"Only if one listens to them in a pious frame of mind, and profits from them," said Father Willibald.

"There is, I fear, much profit to be gleaned from my story," said the magister sadly, "for ever since my twelfth year I have been the unluckiest of men. Perhaps you know that in a cave in the earth between Zülpich and Heimbach there lives a wisewoman called Radla, who has the power of seeing into the future. I was taken to her by my mother, who wished to know if it would be a lucky thing for me to enter the priesthood; for I had a great longing to become a servant of Christ. The wisewoman took my hands

in hers and sat for a long while rocking and moaning with her
eyes closed, so that I thought I would die of terror. At last she
began to speak, and said that I would be a good priest and that
much of what I did would prosper. 'But one piece of bad luck
you must carry with you,' she said. 'You shall commit three sins,
and the second shall be worse than the first, and the third shall
be the worst of all. This is your fate, and you cannot escape it.'
Those were her words, and more than that she would not say. We
wept bitterly, my mother and I, as we walked home from her
cave, for it was our wish that I should be a holy man and free from
sin. We went to our old priest to ask his advice, and he said that
a man who committed only three sins in his life should be regarded as lucky; but I derived little comfort from that. So I entered the priest-school at Aachen, and none of the students was
more zealous or industrious than I, or more assiduous in his avoid-
ance of sin. Both in Latin and in liturgy I was the best in the
school, and by the time I was twenty-one I knew the Gospels and
the Psalms by heart, as well as much of the Epistles to the Thessa-
lonians and Galatians, which were too difficult for the majority
of the students, so that Dean Rumold praised me highly and took
me to be his deacon. Dean Rumold was an old man with a voice
like a bull and large glaring eyes. People trembled when he addressed them, and he loved two things above all else in the world,
after Christ's holy Church: namely, spiced wine and knowledge.
He was expert in sciences so obscure and difficult that few people
even knew the meaning of their names, such as astrology, mantik,[1]
and algorism,[2] and it was said that he was able to converse with
the Empress Theofano in her own Byzantine tongue. For in his
younger days, he had been in the Eastland with the learned Bishop
Liutprand of Cremona and had rare and wonderful stories to tell
of those regions. All his life he had collected books, of which he
now possessed more than seventy; and often in the evenings, when
I brought the hot wine to him in his chamber, he would instruct
me in learned matters, or let me read aloud to him from the
works of two ancient poets who were in his library. One of these
was called Statius; he sang in difficult words about old wars that
had been fought between the Byzantines and a town called Thebes.

[1] Black sorcery.
[2] Counting with Arabic numerals, a science little practiced at this time.

The other was called Ermoldus Nigellus, and he was easier to understand; he told of the blessed Emperor Ludwig, the son of the great Emperor Charles, and of the wars he had fought against the heathens in Spain. When I made errors in reading Statius, the old Dean would curse me and swipe at me with his stick saying that I ought to love him and read him with care, because he was the first poet of Rome who had turned Christian. I was anxious to please the Dean and to escape his stick, so I did my best to obey him; but I could not come to love this poet greatly, much as I tried to do so. There was, besides, a third poet whose works the Dean possessed, bound more finely than the others, and sometimes I saw him sitting mumbling over them. Whenever he did this, his mood would mellow, and he would send me to fetch more wine; but he would never let me read to him from that book. This made me all the more curious to know what it might contain, and one evening, when he was visiting the Bishop, I went into his chamber and searched around for this book, finding it at last in a small chest that stood beneath his wall-seat. The first thing in the book was 'Rules for a Magister,' which is the blessed Benedict's counsel on how to lead a godly life; and after that there came a discourse on chastity by a man from England called Aldhelmus. Following this was a long poem, beautifully and most carefully inscribed. It was called *Ars amandi*, which means the *Art of Love*, and was written by a poet of ancient Rome called Ovid, who most assuredly was not a Christian."

The magister looked sadly at Father Willibald as he reached this point in his narrative, and Father Willibald nodded pensively.

"I have heard tell of this book," he said, "and know it to be highly regarded by foolish monks and learned nuns."

"It is as Beelzebub's own brew," said the magister, "and yet it is sweeter than honey. It was difficult for me to understand it completely, for it was full of words that do not appear in the Gospels or the epistles, nor in Statius either; but my eagerness to discover its meaning matched my fear at what it might contain. Of its content I will say nothing, save that it was full of details concerning caresses, sweet-smelling substances, strange melodies, and every form of sensual pleasure that man and woman can indulge in. At first I feared lest it might not be a great sin to read about such matters, but then I bethought myself (it was the Devil speaking to me) and decided that what was fit matter for a wise Dean could not be sinful reading for me. This lustful Ovid was, in sooth, a great poet, though wholly of the Devil's party, and I was surprised to find that his verses remained in my head without my making any effort to memorize them—far more so than the Epistle to the Galatians, though I had struggled most assiduously to memorize that. I continued reading until I heard the Dean's footsteps outside the house; when he entered, he gave me a sharp drubbing with his stick because I had neglected to meet him with torches and help him home. But I scarcely noticed the pain, for other things were uppermost in my mind; and on two later occasions when he was absent, I stole again into his room, and so read the poem to its end. The result of this was that a great change came over me; for from that time my head was filled with sinful thoughts in most melodious verse. Shortly afterwards, because of my knowledge, I was made magister at the cathedral school, where all went well for me until I received a summons to appear before the Bishop. He told me that the rich merchant Dudo, in the town of Maastricht, a man known for his piety, who had bestowed rich gifts upon the Church, had asked for a godly and learned priest to be sent to him to instruct his son concerning the Christian virtues, and also to teach him to write and reckon; for which post the Bishop had chosen me, because the Dean held me to be the best of the young teachers, and the only one skilled in the difficult art of reckoning. In order that I might also conduct services for the merchant's household, the good Bishop raised me to the rank of presbyter, with the right to hear confession; and I straightway departed for the town of Maastricht, where I found the Devil awaiting me."

He clasped his head between his hands, and groaned aloud.

"That is not much of a story, so far as it goes," said Orm. "But now perhaps it will get better. Let us hear what happened when you met the Devil."

"I did not meet him in his bodily form," said the magister, "but it was enough as it was. The merchant Dudo lived in a large house by the river; he welcomed me warmly, and each morning and evening I led his household in prayer. I applied myself with industry to the task of teaching his son, and sometimes Dudo himself would come and listen to us, for he was, in truth, a godly man, and often bade me not to be sparing with my rod. His wife was named Alchmunda. She had a sister who lived in the house with them, a widow called Apostolica. They were both young, and fair to look on. They conducted themselves most modestly and virtuously; when they walked, they moved slowly, with their eyes directed toward their feet, and at prayer-time no one showed greater zeal than they. But since the lewd poet Ovid yet nested in my soul, I dared not glance too closely at them and avoided speaking with them; so all went well until the time came when the merchant had to go on a long business voyage southwards and into Lombardy. Before he set out, he confessed himself to me and vowed to give rich gifts to the Church to ensure his safe return; he delivered parting admonitions to his household, made me promise that I would pray for his safety every day, and so, at last, departed with his servants and horses. His wife and her sister wept loudly as he left; but once he had gone, their weeping quickly ceased, and they now began to conduct themselves otherwise than as they had done before. At household prayers they behaved as piously as ever; but they often came to hear me instructing my pupil at his lessons, sitting whispering together with their eyes on my face. Sometimes they expressed concern lest the child might be overstraining his mind, and suggested that he should go and play, in order, they whispered to me, that they might ask my advice on matters of serious import. They were amazed, they said, that I was such a solemn and earnest young man, in view of my youth, and Mistress Apostolica asked whether it was true that all young priests were timid of women. She said that she and her sister might both now be regarded as poor widows in mourning, and that they were in grievous need of comfort and exhortation. They told me they were both anxious to confess all their sins before Easter, and Alchmunda asked whether I had the power of granting absolution. I replied that the Bishop had given me that power, because, he had explained, this good household was known for its piety, so that its members would, in any case, have few confessions to make. At this they clapped their hands in joy; and from that moment the Devil began to make me his plaything, so that these two women occupied more and more of my thoughts. For their good names' sake, Dudo had strictly forbidden them ever to walk alone in the town, and had commanded his steward to see that they did not disobey this order; for which reason they often cast glances at me and so, in time, tempted me into the cave of sin. I should, alas, have been steadfast and resisted their entreaties, or else have fled from their presence, as the blessed Joseph did in the house of Potiphar; but Joseph had never read Ovid, so that his situation was less perilous than mine. When I looked at them, my mind was no longer filled with piety and chastity, but rather with lust and sinfulness, so that I trembled when they passed close to me; but I dared do nothing, being as yet youthful and innocent in such matters. But these women, who were as full of sinful thoughts as I, and far less timid, lacked not the courage. One night, when I was lying asleep in my chamber, I was awakened by a woman coming into my bed. I could not speak, being filled with great fear and joy; she whispered that it was beginning to thunder, and that she was much afraid of storms. Then she flung her arms around me and began to kiss me furiously. Suddenly a flash of lightning lit up the room, and I saw that the woman was Apostolica; and although I, too, greatly feared the thunder, I had little time to think of such things now. A short while later, however, after I had enjoyed pleasure with her which far surpassed anything that Ovid had described, I heard the thunderclap just above the roof, and at that I became greatly frightened, for I supposed that God would strike me with His thunderbolt. This, though, did not happen; and on the following night, when Alchmunda came to me as eagerly as her sister had done, there was no thunder at all, and my lust was even greedier than before, so that I surrendered myself to the pleasures of sin with gay courage and a hard heart. These women were of a sweet and gentle temper, never upbraiding me or quarreling with each other, and there was no evil in them, save only their great lust; nor did they ever show fear or remorse at what they had done, apart from their anxiety lest any of the servants should come to suspect what was afoot. But the Devil was strong in them; for what could be more pleasing to him than to cause the downfall of a servant of Christ? When Easter arrived, the whole household came to me in turn to confess their sins. Last of all came Alchmunda and Apostolica. Solemnly they described to me all that had taken place between them and me, and I had no alternative but to pronounce God's absolution upon them. This was, indeed, a terrible thing for me to have to do; for although I was by now steeped in sin, yet it felt as though I had deliberately betrayed God."

"I sincerely hope that your conduct underwent a change for the better," said Father Willibald severely.

"I hoped it would," replied the magister, "but fate willed it otherwise, as the wisewoman told me when she warned me about my three sins. As yet, however, the Devil had not wholly ensnared my soul, for every day I prayed for the merchant as I had promised to do, that he might be preserved from danger and return safely home; indeed, after a time I prayed for him twice and thrice a day, to soothe the remorse and terror with which my heart was filled. But my terror waxed greater every day, until at last, on the night after the festival of Christ's resurrection, I could stand it no longer and fled secretly out of the house and the town and made my way, begging, along the weary roads until I came to my home, where my mother was yet living. She was a godly woman, and when I told her of all that had taken place, she wept bitterly; then, however, she began to comfort me, saying that it was no great wonder that women lost their prudence when they saw me, and that such things happened more often than people generally supposed. The only course for me to follow, she continued, was for me to go back to the good Dean and tell him of all that had happened; and she blessed me as I left her to obey her bidding. Dean Rumold stared at me in amazement when I arrived at his house, and asked why I had returned; then, weeping, I gave him a truthful account of the whole matter, from beginning to end. He simmered furiously when he learned that I had read Ovid without his permission; but when I told him what had taken place between me and the two women, he slapped his knee and broke into a thunderous bellow of laughter. He wanted, he said, to know about this business in detail, and whether I had found the women satisfactory; then he sighed, and said that there was no time in life to be compared with youth, and that no deanery in the whole of the Empire was worth the loss of it. But as I proceeded further with my story, his face began to darken, and when I had concluded, he smote the table with his fist and roared that I had behaved most scandalously, and that this was a matter for the Bishop to decide. So we went to the Bishop and told him everything; and he and the Dean agreed that I had acted most wickedly, having doubly betrayed my trust; firstly, in that I had abandoned the post to which I had been appointed, and secondly, in that I had betrayed the secrecy of the confessional by telling my mother what had occurred between me and the women. That I had committed fornication was, of course, a grievous sin, but not an uncommon one, and not to be compared with these others which I had committed, which could only be wiped out by the most rigorous penance. Since, however, I had acted out of youthful folly rather than with evil intent, they would, they said, punish me as mildly as possible; so they gave me three penances to choose from: either to spend a year as chaplain to the lepers in the great hospital at Jülich, or to make a pilgrimage to the Holy Land and bring thence to the crowning-church oil from the Mount of Olives and water from the river Jordan, or to go as a missionary to convert the Danes. Fortified by their compassion, and fired with the desire to wipe out my sin, I therefore chose the most difficult penance. So they sent me to Bishop Eckard of Hedeby. He received me warmly and soon made me one of his canons, because of my learning; and I remained with him for two years, applying myself assiduously to the cause of piety and teaching in the school that he had founded there, until, again, my fate overtook me; and I committed my second sin."

"You are a strange kind of priest," said Orm, "with your sins and your crazed women. But you still have not told us why you came here."

"Why did you not marry, like a sensible man," said Ylva, "since your lust for women is so strong?"

"Some men hold that a priest should not marry," said the magister. "Your own priest, here, is wifeless; though it may be that he is more godly than I and so better able to resist temptation."

"I have had more important things to bother about than women," said Father Willibald. "And now, God be praised, I have reached the age where such temptations no longer exist. But the blessed apostles have held differing views on this subject. St. Peter himself was married, and even went so far as to take his wife with him on his travels among the heathens. St. Paul, however, was of another mind and remained unmarried throughout his life; which may be the reason why he traveled farther and wrote more. For many years now godly men have inclined to the opinion of St. Paul, and St. Benedict's abbots in France now hold that priests should avoid marriage and, if possible, all forms of carnal indulgence. Though it is my belief that it will be some time before all priests can be persuaded to deny themselves to that extent."

"You speak aright," said the magister. "I remember that the French Abbot Odo and his pupils preached that marriage was an evil thing for a servant of Christ, and I hold their opinion to be correct on the matter. But the Devil's cunning is immeasurable, and many are his devices; so that now you see me here, an outcast and a lost wanderer in the wilderness, because I refused to enter into marriage. This was the second of the sins that the witch-woman prophesied would be my lot. And I dare not imagine what the third will be."

They begged him earnestly to continue with his story, and after Ylva had fortified him with a strong drink, he told them about his second sin.

CHAPTER EIGHT

CONCERNING THE SINFUL MAGISTER'S SECOND SIN AND THE PENANCE TO WHICH HE WAS CONDEMNED FOR IT

T O continue with my story," proceeded the magister in a melancholy voice, "I must tell you that not far from Hedeby there dwells a woman by the name of Thordis. She is of noble birth, and is one of the richest women in those parts, with broad estates and many herds; and she was born and brought up a heathen. Because of her wealth, she has been married three times, though she is still but young; and all her husbands have died violent deaths in wars or feuds. When the third was killed, she fell into a deep melancholy and came of her own accord to Bishop Eckard to tell him that she desired to seek help from God. The

Bishop himself instructed her in the Christian doctrine and subsequently baptized her; after which she attended Mass regularly, riding to church at the head of a large procession of followers with as much noise and clanging of weapons as any war-chieftain. Her pride was great and her temper refractory, and at first she refused to allow her followers to divest themselves of their weapons before entering the church; for if they did so, she said, they would make a poor show as they marched down the aisle. Eventually, however, the Bishop succeeded in persuading her to consent to this; and he bade us treat her always with the utmost patience, because she was in a position to do much good to God's holy Church. Nor can I deny that she came several times to the Bishop with rich gifts. But she was difficult to handle, and especially so toward me. For she had no sooner set eyes on me than she conceived a fierce passion for my body, and on one occasion after Mass she waited alone for me in the porch and asked me to bless her. I did so; whereupon she allowed her eyes to roam over my body and told me that if I would only pay some attention to my hair and beard, as a man should do, I would be fitted for higher duties than that of conducting Mass. 'You are welcome to visit my house whenever you please,' she added, 'and I shall see to it that you do not regret your visit.' Then she seized me by the ears and kissed me shamelessly, though my deacon was standing beside us; and so I was left in great bewilderment and terror. By God's help, I had by now become strong at resisting the temptations of women and was determined to conduct myself unimpeachably; besides which, she was not so beautiful as the two women who had led me astray in Maastricht. I had, therefore, no fears of being seduced by her; but I was alarmed lest she might act crazily, and it was a great misfortune that the good Bishop Eckard happened to be away at this time, at a church conference at Mainz. I persuaded the deacon to say nothing of what he had seen, though he laughed much about it in his ignorance and folly; and that evening I prayed to God to help me against this woman. When I rose from my prayers, I felt wonderfully strengthened, and decided that she must have been sent to show me how well I was now able to resist the temptations of the flesh. But the next time she came to the church, I found myself no less fearful of her than before; and while the choir was still singing, I fled as fast as I could into the sacristy, that I might avoid meeting her. But, disdaining all modesty, she pursued me and caught me before I could leave the church, and inquired why I had not been to visit her, despite her invitation that I should do so. I replied that my time was wholly occupied with important duties. 'Nothing can be more important than this,' she said, 'for you are the man I wish to marry, though you are one of the shaven sort; and I should have thought that you would have had better sense than to let me sit and wait for you to come to me, after the evidence I had given you of my affection.' By this time I was greatly confused and could not at first think of any more courageous reply than that, for various reasons, I could not leave the church while the Bishop was absent. Then, however, my courage rose, and I told her in a determined manner that marriage was not a pleasure in which the servants of Christ could indulge, and that the blessed fathers of the Church would not approve of a woman entering upon marriage for the fourth time. She grew pale as I addressed her, and came menacingly nearer to me while I was yet speaking. 'Are you a gelding?' she said, 'or am I too old to excite you?' She looked very dangerous in her wrath, so I seized a crucifix and held it before her and began to pray that the evil spirit might be driven out of her; but she snatched it from my hand so violently that she fell over backwards and struck her head against the great robe-chest. But she leaped instantly to her feet, crying loudly for help; and I—I know not what I did. Then my destiny, from which there is no escape, was further fulfilled; for in the fight that now ensued, in the church and the porch and in the square outside, between her men, who were trying to help her, and good men from the town, who were trying to help me, men were killed on both sides, including a subdeacon, who had his head cut off by a sword, and Canon Andreas, who came rushing out of the Bishop's palace to stop the fight and received a stone on the skull, from which he died the next day. At last the woman was driven off, together with such of her followers as were still able to run; but my despair was great when I surveyed the scene of the battle and reflected that two priests had been killed because of me. When Bishop Eckard returned and heard the news, he found that I was mostly to blame; for, he said, he had strictly ordered that the woman Thordis was to be handled with the utmost care and patience by us all, and I had disobeyed that instruction. I ought, he said, to have complied with her wishes. I begged him to condemn me to the severest possible punishment, for the thought of my sin pained me grievously, even though I knew that I could not have avoided it. I told him of the wisewoman's prophecy and how I had now committed the second of the three sins of which I was fated to be the author. The Bishop said that he would prefer that I should not be at Hedeby when the time came for me to commit the third; and at last they thought of a fit penance for me to undergo. He bade me make a pilgrimage northwards to the country of the wild Smalanders, to ransom from them God's zealous servant Father Sebastian, who three years ago was sent to preach the gospel to them, ever since when he has languished there in bitter serfdom. Thither am I now bound, and this is the mission on which I have come. Now you know as much as I do about me and my misfortunes."

With this he ended his story. Ylva laughed and gave him more ale.

"It seems that you are unlucky with women, whichever way you treat them," she said, "despite all that you have read in the book which tells everything about the art of love. And I do not think you will be likely to have better success with them in these parts."

But Magister Rainald replied that he was done with all such vanity.

"You must be a very foolish man in more respects than one," said Orm, "and your holy Bishop too, if you think you have any hope of ransoming your priest from the Smalanders, or even of escaping from them with your life, without the aid of silver and gold."

The magister shook his head and smiled sorrowfully.

"I have no gold or silver," he said, "for I do not intend to offer metal to the Smalanders in exchange for Father Sebastian. I wish to offer myself to be their slave in place of him. I am younger than he, and stronger, so that I think they will agree to the exchange. By this means I hope to atone in some measure for causing the deaths of the two priests."

They were all amazed at this reply and at first refused to believe that he could be serious in what he said. But the magister swore that this was so.

"I think I am as good a Christian as most men," said Orm, "but

I would rather commit all manner of sins than offer myself as a thrall."

Father Willibald said that such Christian zeal was not what every man might feel, but that the magister was acting rightly.

"Your thralldom will not last for long," he added, "for there are now no more than five years left before Christ shall return to the earth, according to the best calculations. If, therefore, you avoid women and meet no further misfortunes at their hands, it may be that you will succeed in baptizing many Smalanders before that day arrives, in which case you will be able to appear with a calm conscience before the judgment throne of God."

"What you say is true," replied the magister, "and the same thought has occurred to me. But the worst is that I still have my third sin to commit, and the wisewoman said that this would be the most heinous of all."

None of them could think of any comfort to offer him, but Orm said that he hoped it would be some time before this third sin might be due.

"For I should not like you to commit it while you are a guest in my house," he said. "But be sure of this, priest, and you, too, Spjalle, and both you Irish masters, that you are welcome to stay in my house for as long as you please."

"That is my wish also," said Ylva.

They thanked them both for this invitation, but Spjalle said that he could not accept for more than a few days.

"For I must not loiter on my journey," he explained, "with the luck of the Kings of Sweden bound to my leg."

Both the jesters said that they would go with Spjalle, since they, too, were heading for Uppsala. If they did not find things to their satisfaction there, there were other kings elsewhere who would make them welcome.

"We can go to Norway," they said, "where Olaf Tryggvasson is now King; for he is said to have become a zealous Christian. Or we could voyage to the Eastland, to Prince Valdemar of Gardarike, who has a great name for power and wealth, and is said to be well disposed toward men skillful in the arts."

"That will be a long journey for you to travel," said Orm.

"We have no home," they replied, "and it is our life to wander over the earth; but where kings are, thither will we gladly journey, for all kings welcome us. Beyond Gardarike is the kingdom of Basil, him whom they call the Hammer of the Bulgars, and who is the most powerful of all the monarchs in the world, now that King Harald and King Erik are dead; though it may be that the young Emperor of Germany would be displeased to hear us say so, and King Brian, too, who rules in Ireland now. We have heard it said by far-traveled men that the jesters of the Emperor in Miklagard have a great name and can perform marvelous feats; men speak especially of a performance they gave before the envoys of the old German Emperor, in the days when Nikeforos ruled at Miklagard. They are said to have climbed miraculously upon a pole; and this is a trick new to us, though we reckon that we know more tricks than most men. It might, therefore, be worth our while to journey there to see how skillful they really are, and to show them what the Erin Masters can perform. It would, besides, be a great honor for us to jest before the Emperor Basil, and for him to receive a visit from us. But first we shall go to Uppsala, to the young King there, and we think it best that we should travel there in Spjalle's company. For he is a good man to go a-begging with."

They held to this decision; and after a few days, when he had regained his strength, Spjalle once again bound his royal sword to his leg, and he and the two masters took up their sacks and beggars' staffs. Asa and Ylva gave them fine fare for their journey, so that they said they had small hope of encountering again such hospitality as it had been their fortune to receive here at Gröning.

As they parted, Felimid said to Orm: "If we should meet again, you may be sure that you will always have good friends in us."

"I dearly hope that we may meet again," said Orm. "But if you set forth for Miklagard, I fear my hope is not likely to be fulfilled. For I shall remain here, a man of peace, watching my children grow and my herds fatten, and shall never wander across the seas any more."

"Who knows?" said the small, long-eared men. "Who can tell?"

They wagged their heads, received a blessing from Father Willibald, and departed with Spjalle on their journey.

But Magister Rainald remained with Orm for a while longer, it having been decided that this was the wisest thing for him to do. They all agreed that it would be madness for him to go alone

across the border to look for Father Sebastian, for if he did so, he
would be caught or killed without achieving anything. So it was
decided that he should stay at Gröning until the time arrived for
the border peoples to hold their great annual conference, which
they called Thing, at the Kraka Stone; for the time for this was
shortly due. At the Thing, said Orm, they might be able to come
to some agreement with the Smalanders about the matter on
which his mind was set.

CHAPTER NINE

HOW THE MAGISTER SEARCHED FOR HEIFERS
AND SAT IN A CHERRY TREE

SO Magister Rainald remained with them over the summer.
He helped Father Willibald to minister to the spiritual needs of
the household and to such of the newly baptized Christians as
thought it worth their while to keep their promise to attend divine service. The magister was greatly praised by them all for his
singing at Mass, which was more beautiful than anything that had
been heard in these parts before. At first the newcomers to Christianity showed some reluctance to appear on Sundays, but as the
news of the magister's singing spread, more and more people began to turn up; and tears could be seen standing in the women's
eyes as he sang. Father Willibald was much gratified to receive this
assistance, for he himself had an unmelodious voice.

The magister was poorly qualified, however, to do other forms of
useful work. Orm wanted to give him something to occupy him
during the week, and did his best to discover some task that he
might be able to perform competently; but they could not find
anything at which he was of the slightest use. He knew no trade
and was unable to handle any sort of tool. Orm said: "This is a
bad thing; for soon you will be a thrall in Smaland, and if you
can do nothing but sing, I fear you will have a hard time of it
up there. It would be best for you if you could learn to do some-

thing useful while you are staying here with me, for this will save you many stripes on your back."

Sighing, the magister concurred; and he tried his hand at many simple tasks, but could not succeed with any of them. When they set him to cut grass, his efforts were pathetic to see, for he could not learn to swing the scythe. He was useless at carpentry, though Rapp and even Orm himself spent long hours trying to teach him the craft; and when he tried to chop wood for the bake-oven, he hit himself in the leg, so that when they came to fetch the wood, they found him groaning on the ground in a puddle of blood. When he had recovered from this, they sent him out with a man to watch the fishing-lines in the river; but there he was attacked by an enormous eel, which twined itself round his arm. In his terror he upset the punt, so that all the fish they had caught fell into the water, and it was only with difficulty that he and his companion managed to reach the bank safely. So he gained the name of being a hero in church, and a good man to have in the house of an evening, when everybody would be seated at his or her handicraft and he would tell them stories about saints and emperors; but in all matters else he was regarded as an incomparable duffer, unable to do any of the simple things that every man has to know about. Still, he was not disliked; and least of all by the women, who, from Asa and Ylva to the youngest serving-girls, fussed over him continually and, at the least excuse, spoke out manfully in his defense.

Early in the spring of that year, One-Eyed Rapp had taken himself a wife, a plump farmer's daughter called Torgunn, whom, despite his one-eyedness, he had had no difficulty in winning, on account of the great name he possessed as a widely traveled and weapon-skillful man. Rapp having ordered her to get herself baptized, she had lost no time in doing so, and had never since failed to attend a service; she was well liked by everyone and performed her duties industriously, and Rapp and she were well content with each other, though he was occasionally heard to mumble that she was difficult to silence and slow to bear him a child. Ylva liked her greatly, and these two often sat together exchanging confidences; nor did the flow of words from their mouths ever slacken.

It happened one day that all the people of the household had to go into the woods to look for strayed heifers; and a lengthy search ensued. Toward evening, while Rapp was on his way homewards, having found nothing, he heard a sound from a birch copse; and on approaching nearer he saw Torgunn lying in the grass by the side of a great boulder, with Magister Rainald arched above her. More than that he could not see, because of the height of the grass; and both of them rose hastily to their feet as soon as they heard his footsteps. Rapp stood there without saying anything, but Torgunn immediately hopped toward him on one leg, with her mouth full of words.

"It is indeed lucky that you have come," she said, "for now you can help me home. I twisted my knee, falling over a root, and was lying there crying for help when this good man came to my aid. He lacked the strength to pick me up and carry me; instead, therefore, he has been reading prayers over my knee, so that it has already begun to feel better."

"I have only one eye," replied Rapp, "but with that I see clearly. Was it necessary for him to lie upon you while he prayed?"

"He was not lying upon me," said Torgunn indignantly. "Rapp, Rapp, what is in your mind? He was kneeling beside me, holding my knee, and praying thrice over it."

"Thrice?" said Rapp.

"Do not make yourself more stupid than you are," said Torgunn. "First in the name of the Father, secondly in the name of the Son, and lastly in the name of the Holy Ghost. That makes three."

Rapp looked at the priest. The latter was pale, and there was a tremble in his mouth, but otherwise he looked as usual.

"If you had been out of breath," said Rapp thoughtfully, "you would by now be a dead man."

"I have come to this land in search of martyrdom," replied the magister mildly.

"You will find it, sure enough," said Rapp. "But first let me look at this knee of yours, woman, if you can remember which it is that is hurting you."

Torgunn grumbled plaintively and said that she had never been treated thus before; however, she seated herself obediently on the stone and bared her left knee. They found difficulty in agreeing whether or not there was any swelling to be seen; but when he thumbed it, she screamed aloud.

"And it was worse a few minutes ago," she said. "But I think I might manage to hobble back to the house, with your help."

Rapp stood with a dark face, thinking to himself. Then he said: "Whether any harm has come to your knee I do not know, for your screams mean nothing. But I do not want Orm to be able to say that I killed a guest of his without good cause. Father Willibald knows best about these things, and he will be able to tell me whether the limb is really damaged."

They started homewards and made fair progress, though Torgunn often had to stop and rest because of her great pain. Over the last stretch she was forced to support herself on both of the men, with one arm round the neck of each.

"You are hanging heavily enough on me," said Rapp, "but I still do not know whether I can believe you in this matter."

"Believe what you will," replied Torgunn, "but of this I am sure: that my knee will never be right again. I caught my foot between two roots, as I was jumping down from a fallen trunk; that was how it happened. I shall be lame for the rest of my days as the result of this."

"If that is so," replied Rapp bitterly, "all his praying will have been to no purpose."

They carried Torgunn to bed, and Father Willibald went to examine her. Rapp at once took Orm and Ylva aside and told them what had happened and what he believed to be the truth of the matter. Orm and Ylva agreed that this was a most unfortunate occurrence, and that it would be a sad thing for all of them if there should be discord between Rapp and Torgunn as a result of this.

"It is a good thing that you think before you act," said Orm, "otherwise you might have killed him, which would have been a bad matter if he should turn out to be innocent. For to kill a priest would bring God's punishment down upon us all."

"I have a better opinion than you of Torgunn, Rapp," said Ylva. "It is an easy thing to twist a knee when one is clambering among logs and stones. And you have admitted yourself that you saw nothing take place."

"What I saw was bad enough," said Rapp, "and they were in the darkest part of the forest."

"It is wisest not to judge too hastily in such matters," said Orm. "You remember the judgment delivered by our lord Almansur's magistrate in Córdoba, the time when Toke Gray-Gullsson had managed by cunning to gain entry to the woman's room in the house of the Egyptian sugar-baker, the one that lived in the Street of Penitents, and a wind blew aside the curtain that hung across the window so that four of the sugar-baker's friends, who happened to be walking across the court, saw Toke and the sugar-baker's wife together on her bed."

"I remember the occasion well," said Rapp. "But the husband was a heathen."

"What happened to the woman?" asked Ylva.

"The sugar-baker presented himself before the magistrate with his garments rent and with his four witnesses behind him, and begged that Toke and the woman should be stoned as adulterers. My lord Almansur had himself commanded that the case should be judged strictly according to the law, though Toke was a member of his bodyguard. The magistrate listened carefully to the evidence of the four witnesses concerning what they had seen take place, and three of them swore upon oath that they had distinctly witnessed certain things occurring; but the fourth was old and had weak eyes and so had not been able to see as clearly as the others. Now, the law of Mohammed, which stands written by Allah's own finger in their holy book, states that no person may be convicted of adultery unless four pious witnesses can be found who have clearly and unmistakably seen the offense committed. So the magistrate found Toke and the woman not guilty and sentenced the sugar-baker to the bastinado for bringing false accusation."

"That sounds a good land for a woman to live in," said Ylva, "for much can take place before one is seen in the act by four witnesses. But I think the sugar-baker was unlucky."

"He did not think so for long," said Orm, "for as a result of this incident his name became known to the whole bodyguard, and we would often visit his shop to chaff him and drink his sweet Syrian mead, so that his trade increased greatly, and he praised Allah for the magistrate's wisdom. But Toke said that, though the affair had ended well enough, he would take it as a warning, and he never again ventured to go in to the woman."

Father Willibald now came to them and told them that Torgunn had been telling the truth when she had asserted that she had twisted her knee. "Before long," he said to Rapp, "it will be so swollen that even you will have no doubts upon the matter."

They all supposed that Rapp would feel relief at this news, but he sat for some time buried in his thoughts. At length he said: "If that is so, the magister must have lain there a good while, holding her knee with both his hands, or perhaps with one only. It is difficult for me to believe that he stopped at that, for he has himself told us that he is weak-willed where women are concerned, and that he has learned from Roman books secret methods of pleasing them. It is my belief that he did more than read over her knee; for if he had confined himself to that, the swelling would not have arisen, if there is any virtue in his godliness."

This was the longest speech that any of them had ever heard Rapp deliver, and none of them could persuade him that he was of a wrong opinion in the matter.

Then Ylva said: "At first you were suspicious because you could not see any swelling; now you are suspicious because you have been told that there is one. But this does not surprise me, for you men are always the same once you have an idea fixed in your head. I shall go myself to Torgunn and have the matter out with her; for she and I are close friends, and she will tell me the truth of what really happened. And if anything has taken place which she does not wish to speak of, I will know from her replies what it is that she is trying to hide. For a woman knows at once whether another woman is telling the truth or not; which is, God be praised, more than any man is capable of."

With this she left them; and what she and Torgunn said to each other no man knows, for none heard their talk.

"You can put your mind at rest now, Rapp," said Orm, "for in a short while you will know the truth about this matter. There is no more cunning woman in the wide world than Ylva; of that I can promise you. I marked that the very first time I met her."

Rapp grunted, and they began to discuss two heifers that had escaped and had not been discovered, and where it would be best to search for them on the following day.

Ylva was absent for a long while. When at last she returned, she shook her fist under Rapp's nose.

"I have discovered the truth of this matter," she said, "and it was as I had supposed. You can set your mind at rest, Rapp, for nothing blameworthy took place between these two in the forest. The only one who has behaved badly is you. Torgunn does not know whether to laugh at you for your suspicions, or whether to weep at the memory of the hard words you used to her; and she tells me that she almost regrets not having seduced the priest when she had the chance. 'We could have had much pleasure before Rapp came,' she told me, 'and since I shall in any case have to endure his suspicions and be looked upon as a woman of shame, I might as well have got what enjoyment I could out of the affair.' Those were the words she used; and if you are as wise a man as I hold you to be, Rapp, you will never mention another word about this business; if you do, I cannot answer for her behavior. But if you handle her tenderly, I think she will be willing to let the matter drop; and it would be a good thing if you could get her with child, for then you would not have to worry yourself any more about this poor unfortunate magister."

Rapp scratched his scalp and muttered something to the effect that any state she might be in was not the result of any lack of endeavor on his part. But they could see that he was much relieved by what Ylva had told him, and he thanked her for having put the matter to rights.

"And it is a good thing that I myself possess some small stock of wisdom," he said, "even though I am not as wise as you, Ylva. For if I had been an impatient man, I would have killed the magister and would now be wearing a long nose, and you and Orm would no longer be my friends. But now I will go to Torgunn, to comfort her and make things well again."

When Orm and Ylva had gone to bed, they talked for a time about this business before falling asleep.

"All this has passed off better than I could have expected," said Orm, "thanks to your good offices. For if I had been called upon to decide in this matter, I should have adjudged that they had busied themselves with more things in the forest than with this knee of hers."

Ylva lay for a while in silence. Then she said: "Orm, you would have judged correctly, but you must never let anyone know this. I promised her that I would not repeat what she told me, and that I would talk Rapp into believing that nothing had taken place; and we must leave things as they now are, and nobody must know anything, not even Father Willibald; for if the truth were to come out, it would cause great distress to both Rapp and Torgunn, as well as to this unfortunate woman-crazy magister. But to you I will tell the truth, which is that there was more done between these two than praying over her bad knee. She says that she liked him from the first, because of his beautiful singing voice and the unlucky fate to which he is condemned; besides which, she says that she could never say nay to a holy man. She says she trembled throughout her whole body like a trapped bat when he touched her knee as she lay there on the ground, and that he did not appear embarrassed but straightway guessed what was in her mind. Before long they were both in a state of desire; she says that she could not help this. Later, when they had become calm again, he began to groan and weep and took up his prayers where he had left them off; but he had only had time to say a few sentences before Rapp appeared. That, doubtless, is why the swelling has become worse, for he should, properly, have repeated the prayer thrice for it to be effective. But she will thank God for the rest of her life, she says, for not allowing Rapp to arrive a few minutes earlier than he did. Now if you let Rapp or anyone else know the truth of this, you will make me exceedingly unhappy, and others also."

This story delighted Orm hugely, and he gladly promised never to repeat a word of it, to Rapp or anyone else.

"As long as Rapp never knows that they have cuckolded him," he said, "no harm need result from this incident. But this magister is, indeed, a remarkable man; for in all other manly pursuits he is wholly incompetent, but his handling of women leaves nothing to be desired. It would be a bad thing if he should see any more of Torgunn without other people being present; if that were to happen, this business might end evilly, for Rapp will not allow himself to be gulled a second time. So I must think out some regular task for him to perform, which will keep him away from her, and her from him; for I cannot be sure which of the two would be the more desirous of promoting a second meeting."

"You must not treat him too harshly," said Ylva, "for the poor creature has enough suffering ahead of him at the hands of the Smalanders. I myself will do what I can to keep him and Torgunn apart from each other."

The next morning Orm called the magister to him and told him that he had at last found him a task that he thought he would be able to perform to everyone's satisfaction.

"Hitherto," he said, "you have not shown much skill in any of the labors to which we have set you; but now you will have the chance to do us all a real service. Here you see this cherry tree which is the best of all my trees; and that is not only my opinion, but also that of the crows. You are now to climb to the top of it, and I would advise you to take food and drink with you, for you are not to come down until the crows and magpies have gone off to their night branches. You shall sit there every day; and you shall take your place there early, for these crows awake in the gray twilight before dawn. It is my hope that you will succeed in protecting the berries for us, if you do not eat too many of them yourself."

The magister looked gloomily up at the tree; the fruit there was larger than that usually found on cherry trees and was just beginning to darken toward ripeness. All the birds were especially fond of these cherries, and both Rapp and Father Willibald had tried to keep them away by shooting arrows at them, but had been able to achieve little.

"This is no more than I deserve," said the magister, "but I am afraid to climb so high."

"You will have to accustom yourself to that," said Orm.

"I easily become dizzy."

"If you hold on tightly, the dizziness will not affect you. If you show that you have not the courage to undertake this task, everybody will laugh at you, and the women most of all."

"I have, in truth, deserved all this," said the magister sadly.

After some argument he succeeded, with much difficulty, in climbing part of the way up the tree, while Orm stood on the ground below, exhorting him continually to ascend higher. At length, amid much praying, he managed to reach a fork where three branches met; it swayed beneath his weight, and, seeing this, Orm commanded him to remain there, since his rocking would make him more visible to the birds.

"You are quite safe up there," he shouted up at the magister, "and nearer heaven than we poor creatures who must remain on the ground. There you can eat and drink to your heart's content, and discuss your sins with God."

So there he sat; and the crows, which came flying eagerly from all directions to peck at the good fruit, fled in terror and amazement when they saw that there was a man in the tree; they circled over him, cawing with anger, and the magpies sat in the trees around him mocking him with spiteful laughter.

It was on the sixth day, on an afternoon when the heat was very great, that he fell. He had become drowsy with the heat, and swarming bees had come to the tree and had selected his head as a resting-place. Awaking in terror, he whirled his arms violently to drive them away, lost his balance, and fell shrieking to the ground in a shower of bees, cherries, and broken branches. The twins and their playmate were the first to reach the place of the accident; they stared at him in wonder, and the boy Ulf asked him why he had fallen down. But he only lay there groaning and saying that his last moment was at hand. The children now began joyfully to pluck the good fruit that had fallen with him; but this aroused the bees, who attacked them, so that they fled shrieking. All the house people were gathering reeds down by the river, and it was left to Ylva herself and two of her maids to rush to their help. They bore the magister into the weaving-room and put him to bed. When the maids heard of the misfortune that had befallen him, they became so mirthful that Ylva lost patience with them and boxed their ears, and bade them go at once and fetch Father Willibald, who was down by the river with the others.

Ylva was moved with pity for the magister and did what she could to make him comfortable; she also gave him a strength-drink of her best ale. He had sustained no injury from the bees, but suspected that the fall had broken his shoulder. Ylva wondered whether this might not be God's punishment for his conduct with Torgunn in the forest; and he agreed that this might well be the case.

"But how much do you know of what happened between us in the forest?" he asked.

"Everything," replied Ylva, "for Torgunn has told me with her own lips; but you need not fear that anyone else will come to hear of it, for both she and I know how to keep our tongues quiet when there is need for it. And this comfort, at least, I can give you, that she had plenty to say in your praise, and that she does not regret what took place between you, though it came so near to bringing disaster on you both."

"I regret it," said the magister, "though I fear there is little to be gained by that. For God has so cursed me that I cannot be alone with a young woman without straightway becoming inflamed with desire. Nor have even these days that I have spent in the tree cleansed me of this passion, for my thoughts have dwelt less upon God than upon the sins of the flesh."

Ylva laughed. "The bee-swarm, and your fall from the tree, have helped you now," she said, "for here you are, alone with me, in a place where nobody will be able to disturb us for a good while; and I think I am not less comely than Torgunn. But from this temptation, at least, I think you will be able to emerge without sin, poor foolish man."

"You do not know," replied the magister sadly, "how powerful the curse is," and he stretched his arm toward her.

What then happened between these two, nobody ever knew; and when Father Willibald came to the house to examine the magister's injuries, he found him asleep, purring contentedly, while Ylva sat working industriously on her weaving-chair.

"He is too good a man to have to climb trees," she said to Orm and the house-folk that evening as they were sitting at their meal, full of merriment at the manner in which the magister had ended his sojourn in the tree, "and he shall not be forced to do it any more."

"I know little of his goodness," said Orm, "but if you mean that he is too clumsy to do so, you have my agreement. What he is fitted for is more than I know; but the Smalanders will, no doubt, be able to hit upon something. Most of the cherries are ripe now and can be picked before the birds steal them, so that we shall lose little by this accident. But it is good that the time for the Thing is almost upon us."

"Until that time arrives," said Ylva firmly, "I myself will keep watch over him; for I do not want him to be mocked and fare miserably during the last days that he will spend among Christians."

"Whatever he does, women swarm to his assistance," said Orm. "But you may do as you think best in this matter."

Everybody in the house laughed themselves crooked whenever any mention was made of the magister and his bee-swarm; but Asa said that this was a good omen, for she had often heard wise old people say that when bees settled on a man's head it meant that he would have a long life and many children. Father Willibald said that in his younger days he had heard the same asserted by learned men at the Emperor's court at Goslar; though, he added, he was not sure whether this was altogether applicable when the person in question was a priest.

Father Willibald could not find anything very wrong with the magister's sore shoulder; none the less, the magister preferred to remain in bed for the next few days, and even when he felt well enough to get up, he continued to spend most of his time in his room. Ylva watched over him with care, preparing all his meals herself, and saw to it strictly that none of her servant-girls should be allowed to come near him. Orm chaffed her about this, saying that he wondered whether she, too, might not have gone crazy about the magister; besides which, he said, he could not but grudge all the good food that was taken daily into the weaving-room. But Ylva answered firmly that this was a matter for her to decide; the poor wretch, she said, needed good food to put a little flesh on his bones before he went to live among the heathens, and, as regards the servant-girls, she was merely anxious to preserve him from temptation and spiteful mockery.

So Ylva had her way in this matter; and things continued thus until the time arrived for the dwellers on both sides of the border to ride to the Thing at the Kraka Stone.

CHAPTER TEN

CONCERNING THE WOMEN'S DOINGS AT THE KRAKA STONE, AND HOW BLUE– TONGUE'S EDGE BECAME DENTED

EVERY third summer, at the first full moon after the heather had begun to bloom, the border peoples of Skania and Smaland met, by ancient tradition, at the stone called the Kraka Stone, in order to take vows of peace, or of war, against one another until the time of their next meeting.

To this place came chieftains and chosen men from Finnveden and Värend and from all the districts of Göinge, and a Thing was held, which usually continued for several days. For even when peace prevailed along the border, there were always many problems to be settled; disputes regarding hunting and pasturing rights, murders resulting from these disputes, cattle-thefts, woman-thefts, and the extradition of slaves who had escaped across the border. All such matters were duly weighed and judged, by wise men from all the various tribes, sometimes in a manner satisfactory to everyone, as when, for example, murder could be repaid by murder, or rape by rape, and sometimes by an agreed fine. When, though, a difficult altercation had arisen between stubborn men, so that no agreement could be arrived at, the matter would be decided by single combat between the parties concerned, on the flat grass before the Stone. This was regarded as the best entertainment of all, and any Thing during which at least three corpses had not been carried from the combat ground would be thought a poor and unworthy session. Most often, however, the Thing sustained its reputation as an occasion of much sport and displaying of wisdom, and everyone left it well contented, with fine stories to tell their wives and housefolk on their return home.

Much buying and selling also took place there, of slaves, weapons, and oxen, forged iron, and cloth, skins, wax, and salt, so that sometimes traders came to it from as far afield as Hedeby and Gotland. In former times the King at Uppsala and the King of the Danes had been wont to send trusted men to the Thing, partly to safeguard their rights and partly to keep an eye for outlaws who had escaped their clutches; but the farmers had greeted these envoys by removing their heads, which they had then smoked over juniper fires and sent back to their masters, to signify to the kings that the border peoples preferred to manage their own affairs. But stewards and ships' chieftains from the jarls of Skania and West Guteland still occasionally came there, to enlist the services of any good warrior who had a mind to go a-viking overseas.

Accordingly the Thing at the Kraka Stone had come to be regarded by the border peoples as a great occasion, so that they often reckoned time from Thing to Thing.

Men said that the Stone had been set up in ancient times by Rolf Krake, during a journey that he had made through these parts; and neither kings nor border-dwellers had dared to erase this mark which he had raised to show where the country of the Danes ended and that of the Swedes began. It was a tall and mighty stone, such as only heroes of ancient times could have had the strength to raise; it stood in open ground on a hill, and was shadowed by a hawthorn tree, which was held to be sacred and of equal age with the Stone. On the evening before each Thing, it was the custom of the Virds, the inhabitants of Värend, to sacrifice two goats at the Stone and perform strange rites; their blood was allowed to spread over the ground, and it was held that this blood, together with that which was spilled around the Stone during combats, gave much strength to the tree, so that it continued to flourish, despite its age, and always bloomed most richly in the year following a Thing. But few saw it bloom save the birds that nested in its branches, and eagles and kites and the wandering animals of the earth; for all around the Kraka Stone for many miles the land was desert and uninhabited.

As Orm was making ready to journey to the Thing, many farmers came to Gröning to accompany him thither—Gudmund of Uvaberg, Black Grim, and others. Orm left Rapp behind to guard the house and took with him both the priests and two of his men. All the women wept because the magister was now leaving them to become a slave, but he said that there was nothing else for it, and that it was to be so. Asa and Ylva had sewn new clothes for him, a tunic and shirt and skin breeches; Orm said that it was well that they had done this, for it would make it easier for them to negotiate the exchange if he had good clothes on his back, which his new employer would be able to make use of.

"For you must not suppose," he said, "that he will be able to wear them for long himself."

Torgunn brought the magister a basket of birch bark filled with good food for his journey, which she had herself prepared specially for him. Rapp scowled when he saw it, but she insisted that the magister should have it, saying that she was giving it to him as a thanks-gift for the prayers he had read over her knee; besides which, she said, she hoped to get a good blessing from him in return for it. The magister sat palely on his horse and blessed her and all the others with beautiful words, so that tears appeared in all the women's eyes. Father Willibald, who was also seated high on a horse, then offered up a prayer for a lucky journey and protection against wild beasts, robbers, and all dangers that threaten men who travel. Then the company rode away to the Thing, strong in numbers and well armed.

They reached the Stone a short while before dusk and pitched camp, together with other groups of men, on the ground that the Göings had, by ancient custom, been used to occupy, on the bank of a brook that ran through birch trees and thickets on the southern side of the Stone. Traces could still be seen there of campfires around which they and their predecessors had sat at previous Things. On the other side of the brook the Finnvedings were encamped, and from them there came much noise and shouting. It was said to be a greater hardship for them than for other men to sit without ale around the Kraka Stone, and it was, accordingly, an ancient custom among them to arrive at the Thing already drunk. Both the Göings and the Finnvedings were encamped a short way from the brook, and only came to it to water their horses and fill their pots; for they had always thought it wisest not to crowd unnecessarily close to one another if the peace of the Thing was to be maintained between them.

The Virds were the last to arrive at the meeting-place. Any man looking at them could see at once that they were a race apart, without resemblance to other peoples. They were enormously tall men with silver rings in their ears, and their swords were longer and heavier than those of other men. They had shaven chins, long cheek-beards hanging down on either side of their mouths, and eyes like the eyes of dead men. They were, moreover, short of speech. Their neighbors said that the cause of this aloofness was that they were ruled by their womenfolk and were afraid lest, if they spoke, this might be discovered; but few dared to ask them directly how much truth there was in this report.

They were encamped in a grove east of the Stone, where the brook ran broadest; there they were apart from the other tribes, which was the way they liked it to be. They were the only men who had brought women with them to the Thing. For it was an old belief among the Virds that the best cure for a woman's barrenness was to be found at the Kraka Stone, if a man did as the wise ancients had prescribed; and young married women who had borne no children to husbands of proved virility were accordingly always eager to accompany their menfolk to the Thing. What they had to do would be seen tonight, under the full moon; for the whole of this evening the Virds would be in possession of the Stone, and their concern that no stranger should see what their women did after the moon rose was well known among both the Göings and the Finnvedings. For it had happened on more than one occasion that those who to satisfy their curiosity had approached too near the Stone while the women were there had seen a winging spear or a hewing sword as their last sight on earth, and this before they had had the chance to witness that for which they had come. Nevertheless, inquisitive young men of the Göings, and such of the Finnvedings as had not drunk too deeply, nursed the prospect of a fine evening's entertainment; and as soon as the moon's glimmer could be discerned above the edge of the trees, some of them climbed up into the branches to good vantage points, while others crept forward through the thickets and undergrowth as near to the Stone as they dared.

Father Willibald was much displeased at all this, especially at the fact that young men of Orm's following, who had received baptism at the great feast and had since paid several visits to his church, were as eager as the rest to see as much as they could of witchcraft at the Stone.

"All this is the Devil's work," he said. "I have heard tell that it is the custom of these women to run around the Stone in shameless nakedness. Every man who has received baptism should arm himself with strength from Christ against such abominations as this. You would be better employed in axing a cross for us to raise before our fire, to protect us this night from the powers of evil. I myself am too old for such work; besides which, I cannot see well in this dense wood."

But they replied that all the crosses and all the holy water in the world would not prevent them from seeing the Vird women perform that evening.

Magister Rainald was seated beside Orm in the circle around the food-pot. He sat with his arms round his knees and his head bowed, rocking backwards and forwards; he had been given bread and smoked mutton like the rest, but showed little appetite. It was always so with him when he was contemplating his sins. But when he heard Father Willibald's words, he stood up.

"Give me an ax," he said, "and I will make you a cross."

The men round the fire laughed and expressed doubt whether he was capable of performing this task. But Orm said: "It is right that you should try; and you may find it more profitable than climbing into the trees."

They gave him an ax, and he went away to do the best he could.

Clouds now began to pass over the moon, so that at times it was quite dark; but in the intervals the curious among them were able to see what the Virds were doing up at the Stone. Many men were assembled there. Some of these had just finished cutting a strip of turf, long and broad, and were now raising it from the ground and placing stakes beneath to hold it up. Others were collecting brushwood, which they placed in four piles at equal distances from the Stone. When these preparations had been completed, they took their weapons and walked some distance toward the ground where the Göings and the Finnvedings were encamped. There they remained as sentries, with their backs to the Stone, some of them going down as far as the brook itself.

The noise of bleating was now heard; and from the direction of the Vird camp four old women appeared, leading two goats. With them came a small, bald man with a white beard, very old and bent, holding a long knife in his hand. After him followed a crowd of women, all wearing cloaks.

When they reached the Stone, the old women tied the legs of the goats together and fastened long ropes around their backs. Then all the women helped to heave the goats up over the top of the Stone and make the rope fast, so that the goats were left hanging down, one on either side of the Stone, head downwards. The little old man gesticulated and chattered petulantly until they had got them into the exact position in which he wanted them. When at last he was satisfied, he ordered them to lift him to the top of the Stone, which they succeeded, with difficulty, in doing. They pushed the knife up to him on a stick, and, taking it, he seated himself astride the Stone just above the goats. Then he raised his arms above his head and cried in a loud voice to the young women: "This is the first! Go ye through earth!"

The women tittered, and nudged one another, and looked coyly hesitant. At length, however, they slipped their cloaks from their bodies and stood naked; then they walked in a line toward the raised strip of turf and began to creep under it, one by one. A terrific crash from the direction of the Finnvedings' camp suddenly echoed through the silence of the night; then cries and groans were heard, followed by loud laughter, for an old leaning tree, into the branches of which many of the young men had climbed, had collapsed under their weight and had crushed several of them as it fell. But the women continued to creep under the turf until all of them had passed beneath it, whereupon the old man raised his arms again and cried: "This is the second! Go ye through water!"

At this the women walked down to the brook and waded out into the midst of it. They squatted down on their haunches where the water was deepest, held their hands over their faces, and, amid much shrieking, plunged their heads beneath the water, so that their hair floated on the surface, after which, without delay, they came up again.

Then the old women lit the piles of brushwood around the Stone, and when the young women had returned from the water, the old man cried: "This is the third! Go ye through fire!"

The women now began to run around the Stone and to leap nimbly over the fires. As they did so, the old man slit the throats of the goats, so that their blood ran down the sides of the Stone, while he mumbled words of ritual. Nine times the women had to run around the Stone, and nine times lap blood, that it might give them strength and make their wombs fruitful.

A great cloud passed over the moon, but by the light of the fires the women could still be seen gamboling around the Stone. Then a voice was suddenly heard to begin singing, in words which none of them could understand; and as the moon shone forth again, the magister could be seen walking up toward the Stone. He had crossed the brook and passed the sentries without being spotted, for in the darkness they had turned round to watch the women dancing. He had bound two birch rods together with osiers, so that they formed a cross, and this he held raised before him as he walked swiftly toward the Stone.

The old women began to shriek with all the force of their lungs, partly from rage and partly from fear, and the old man stood up on top of the Stone, brandishing his bloody knife like a madman and screaming in a loud voice. The women ceased their gamboling and stood still, not knowing what to do; but the magister walked through their circle, held the cross up toward the old man, and cried: "Get thee hence, Satan! In Jesus Christ's name, depart, thou unclean spirit!"

The old man's face became convulsed with fear as the magister threatened him with the cross; he shrank away, his foot slipped, and he toppled backwards from the Stone to the ground, where he remained lying with his neck broken.

"He has killed the priest!" shrieked the old women in confusion.

"I, too, am a priest," cried the magister, "and a better priest than he!"

Heavy footsteps were now heard approaching, and a powerful voice demanded to know what all this screaming might be about. A tremor passed through the magister's body, and, gripping his cross in both hands, he placed himself with his back against the Stone. Pressing the cross against his breast, he closed his eyes and began to mutter in a rapid monotone: "I am ready! Christ and all ye holy martyrs, receive me into your blessed kingdom. I am ready! I am ready!"

The sentries remained motionless at their posts, despite the screams of the old women. They had been put there to see that no Göings or drunken Finnvedings came to meddle with or gloat at the women of their tribe, and it would have been unseemly for them to come near to other men's naked wives on open ground, lest by doing so they might provoke strife.

But a man now came from the Virds' camp, tall and powerfully made, who appeared not to be worried at the prospect of coming near naked women. He wore a broad-brimmed hat and a blue skirt of costly cloth and carried a red shield by its strap, while his sword dangled from a broad belt of silver. The women looked bashful as he approached them, and tried to cover their nakedness as well as they could. Some took grass to cleanse the blood from their mouths; but all remained where they were.

The newcomer glanced along the line of them and nodded.

"Have no fear," he said in a friendly voice. "Such things do not bother me, save in the springtime, and then women who take my fancy have no need to prance through fires. One thing I will not deny, now that I see you at close quarters, and that is that several of you are more comely naked than clothed—which is as it should be. But who is this shivering fellow who stands with his eyes closed in the midst of your circle? Does the sight of you displease him?"

"He is a Christ-priest!" cried the old women. "He has killed Styrkar!"

"It is the nature of priests to fight one another," replied the man calmly, "I have always said so." He walked up to the body of the old man and stood with his thumbs in his belt looking down at it. He rolled it over with his foot.

"Dead as a herring," he said. "So here you lie, Styrkar, for all your cunning and trollcraft. I do not think many people will mourn you. You were an evil-minded old snake, as I have told you more than once; though no one can deny that you were a crafty priest and full of learning. Go, now, to the trolls, to whom you belong; for the gods will kick you from their door if you try to gain admittance there. But you, my good women, why do you still stand naked in the night air? Your stomachs will surely suffer for it."

"We have not completed the rite," they replied. "We still have half our laps to run around the Stone. But what shall we do, now that our priest, Styrkar, is dead? Must we depart, having gained nothing? We do not know what to do."

"What has happened has happened," said the man. "But do not grieve at it, for it is my belief that you can find better remedies for your emptiness than frolicking around this Stone. When my cows bear not, I change my bull. That usually does the trick."

"No, no!" wailed the women sorrowfully. "You are wrong, you are wrong! We are not so foolish as you think; this is the only remedy left to us!"

The man laughed, turned round, and clapped his hand across the magister's shoulders.

"I stand here talking foolishly," he said, "though you all know that I am in fact the quickest-witted of men. Your priest Styrkar is dead, but we have here a Christ-priest to replace him. One priest is as good as another; believe me, for I have come across every variety."

He seized the magister by one leg and the scruff of his neck, swung him up, and deposited him on the top of the Stone.

"Use your tongue now," he said, "if you have priest-words in your mouth. Up with your chin and spout the best incantations you know. Whether we shall then kill you or let you live depends on how you acquit yourself. Spell boldly, and spell children into the wombs of these Vird women; if you can make it twins, so much the better."

Standing on the Stone, the magister trembled, and his teeth were heard to chatter. But the man who stood beneath him, sword in hand, wore a dangerous and purposeful look. So the magister held the cross before him and began desperately to gabble prayers; and once he was properly under way, his voice rang out manfully.

The newcomer stood and listened; then he nodded.

"This is a real priest," he said. "I have heard this sort of talk before, and there is much strength in it. Start your antics again, women, before he grows weary and the fires die to ash."

Screwing up their courage anew, the women began again to prance around the Stone; and once the magister had got over the worst of his fright, he acquitted himself nobly, dipping his cross over their heads as they came up to the Stone to lap the blood, and blessing them with his finest blessings. The women trembled as the cross touched them; and when the ceremony was completed they agreed unanimously that this was a good priest, and that they had been more sensible of his sacred power than they had been of Styrkar's.

"Let us not kill this man," they said. "He shall come with us and be our priest in Styrkar's stead."

"If it is your wish," said the man in the hat, "let it be so; and may he bring you better luck than Styrkar did."

But as he said this, a powerful voice was heard to roar from the direction of the brook: "Give this priest to me!"

Orm and his men had seen the old priest fall down from the Stone and a few minutes later the magister standing there in his place, which had filled them with amazement.

"It may be that he had gone crazy," said Father Willibald, "or, on the other hand, it may be that God's spirit has entered into him. That is a cross he holds in his hand."

"It does not take much to drive him to a place where women are," said Orm darkly. "None the less, it would be a shameful thing if we allowed him to be slaughtered like a goat."

They took men with them and walked up from the stream. The moon was clouded over, and as Orm shouted up toward the Stone, not much could be seen. The women turned back nervously toward the camp, and the magister descended from the Stone. But the man in the broad hat strode down toward Orm, accompanied by several of the Vird sentries.

"Who is that who screams in the night?" he said.

"Give me back that priest," said Orm grimly. "He is mine and has not my permission to depart."

"What loud-mouthed fellow might you be?" asked the other.

This was a mode of address to which Orm was not accustomed, and he was seized by a fury such as seldom came over him.

"A man who is not afraid to teach you manners," he cried, "and that straightway."

"Come over here," said the other, "and we shall see which of us is the better teacher."

"Have I peace from your following?" said Orm.

"You have peace from us," said the Virds calmly.

Orm drew his sword and leaped across the brook.

"You come here nimbly," said the other, "but you will be carried back."

Orm charged at his adversary, and their swords met so fiercely that sparks came from them. Then the hatted man said:

> "Dame Red-Jowl,
> Thou hardly forged one,
> Hard the fight
> When sparks fly from thee."

Orm took a fierce slash on his shield, and his voice was changed as he replied:

> "Friend, thy word
> Was timely spoken.
> Know, Red-Jowl
> Hath joined with Blue-Tongue."

They lowered their swords and stood motionless.

"Welcome, Orm Tostesson, chieftain of the sea. What do you among these Göing savages?"

"Welcome, Toke Gray-Gullsson, warrior of Lister! What do you among the Virds?"

Both of them now began to talk eagerly and simultaneously,

laughing with joy; for the friendship between them was very great, and it was several years since they had last seen each other.

"We have much to talk of," said Toke. "And it is fortunate that you are swift at composing verses, the way I taught you to be; for if it had not been so, we two might have hewn at each other for a while longer, and might have suffered thereby. Though I do not think your verse was so good as mine."

"In that you may claim superiority without offense," said Orm. "I have had but little practice at making verses since last we parted."

Toke drew his finger along Red-Jowl's edge.

"There is a dent here, where our swords met," he said. "She was never dented before."

Orm likewise passed his finger along his blade.

"It is the same with mine," he said. "Andalusian-forged iron can only be dented by Andalusian blades."

"It is my hope," said Toke, "that they will not kiss edges again."

"That is my hope also," said Orm.

"It would be good to know whether she who gave them to us is yet living," said Toke. "And how our lord Almansur now fares, and where his great war-banners now wave before him, and whether his luck still holds."

"Who can tell?" said Orm. "That land is far from here, and these things happened long ago; though it is true that my thoughts often turn to him. But come with me now, that we may talk alone; I wish I had ale with which to bid you welcome."

"Have you no ale?" asked Toke in alarm. "How can we talk without ale? Ale is the best friend of friends."

"Nobody has brought ale to the Thing," said Orm. "Ale is the provoker of quarrels—which I think you know as well as the next man."

"Our luck is good tonight," said Toke, "and yours is better than mine. For one man has brought ale to the Thing, and I am he. You must know that I am now a great man among the merchants of Värend, and I deal particularly in skins; and no skin-sale can be arranged without ale. I have brought five pack-horses to the Thing, all laden with ale, and I shall not be taking any of it home again if all goes as it should; for I intend that they shall carry nothing but skins. Therefore come with me."

"It shall be as you wish," said Orm. "Perhaps I shall find my lost priest there, too."

"The women took him with them," said Toke. "They said they liked the sorcery he practiced, so you need not worry your head about him. He looked to me to be a bold fellow, the way he went for Styrkar with his cross. Though what will happen to him for killing the old goat is a matter for the Thing to decide."

"I have another priest with me here," said Orm, "an old friend of yours."

Father Willibald had come across the brook to discover what had happened to the magister. Toke greeted him joyfully.

"I remember you well," he said. "You shall come with us and sample my ale. I owe you a great debt for the way you mended my leg in King Harald's castle, better than any other man could have done. But what are you doing here, so far from the Danish court?"

"I am God's priest to Orm's household," said Father Willibald. "And my mission is to Christianize heathens in this wild outpost of the world, as I have already Christianized him. Your turn likewise shall come, though I remember you as a man deep in godlessness; it is the finger of God that has led you here to meet us."

"That is a point that might be argued," said Toke, "but what is certain is that we three shall now sit down together in friendship. *Bismillahi, er-rahmani, er-rahimi!* as we used to say when we served my lord Almansur."

"What is that you said?" asked Father Willibald. "What language is that? Are you, too, a victim of southern witchcraft?"

"It is the tongue of Spain," said Toke. "I remember it still, for my woman is from that land and still likes to speak her own tongue, especially when she is in an ill humor. It enables me to keep in practice."

"And I can tell you the meaning of what he said," said Orm. "It is: In the name of God, the Merciful, the Compassionate. The Merciful One is Christ, as everybody knows; and the Compassionate One evidently refers to the Holy Ghost, for who could be more Compassionate than He? You can see that Toke is practically a Christian already, though he pretends otherwise."

Father Willibald mumbled doubtfully to himself; but without more argument about the matter they proceeded with Toke to the Vird camp.

CHAPTER ELEVEN

CONCERNING TOKE GRAY–GULLSSON AND A MIS-
FORTUNE THAT BEFELL HIM, AND OF A
FOUL GIFT ORM RECEIVED FROM THE
FINNVEDINGS

THEY sat over Toke's ale late into the night, talking of all
that had happened to them since they had parted. Orm told how
he had gone a-viking in England under Thorkel the Tall, and of
the great battle at Maldon and all the booty they had won there;
how he had chanced to meet Father Willibald and had been
baptized and had found again King Harald's daughter (here the
little priest had a good deal to add to Orm's narrative), and of the
great sum of silver that King Ethelred had elected to pay to buy
himself and his country relief from the Northmen's fury. Then he
spoke of his voyage home, of his visit to Jellinge, and of his encounter with King Sven there; of what had happened at this meeting, and how he had then been forced to flee in haste to his
mother's estate in the border country, in order to escape the vengeance of his brother-in-law.

"But his memory is long, like his arm," said Orm, "so that even
in these distant parts he still pursues me, to avenge the nose-burn
that this good priest gave him when last we met. This very spring
I had to fight in night-darkness outside my own door with a
traveler who was staying in my house as my guest, a man from
Finnveden named Östen of Örestad, who had served at sea with
the Danes. He had come with a strong band of followers to slay
me secretly and send my head to King Sven. But instead he lost
many men, and his horses and goods, and suffered a split skull into
the bargain; which affair will, I doubt not, come up for discussion
during the Thing. For as soon as his head had healed, I let him
depart in peace, and two of his men with him; but first I forced
him to become a Christian, because Father Willibald here, whose

will I seldom oppose, preferred that they should be Christianized rather than killed."

"Even the wisest of men sometimes act foolishly," said Toke, "and a man who lets his enemy live has only himself to blame if he comes to regret it. I know that Christians sometimes do this, to put themselves in good odor with their god; but in these parts the old method is still regarded as the best. Next time you may find difficulty in killing the fellow, for he will certainly seek revenge for all he lost and for the insult you did to him by baptizing him."

"We acted rightly," said Father Willibald. "Let the Devil and his minions do their worst."

"Besides which, Toke," said Orm, "God's hand is stronger than you would like to think. But tell us, now, how things have gone with you since last we met."

Toke began to tell them his story. He said that he had not undertaken any long voyage abroad, nor undergone such adventures as Orm had enjoyed; but that he had none the less had just as many troubles to contend with, if not more.

"For coming home to Lister was like tumbling into a snake-pit," he said. "Scarcely had I reached my father's house and greeted the old people and deposited my woman and my goods inside the door when men came running to me with urgent tidings; and before long I found myself involved in a feud that embroiled the whole district."

This was a feud that had been started by Orm's men, Ögmund, Halle, Gunne, and Grinulf, as soon as they had reached home, having journeyed thither on Styrbjörn's ship from King Harald's castle, while Orm and Toke were still lying there wounded. On their return they discovered that they were not the only ones to have come back alive from Krok's expedition. Seven years before, Berse had arrived home in one ship, with only thirty-two men at his oars but with a rich cargo, consisting of the best of all the booty from the margrave's fortress, which he had managed to bring away in his two ships after the Andalusians had surprised them.

"Berse was a man of much wisdom," said Toke, "even if it is true that he ate himself to death soon after his return; for in the matter of food he was greedier than other men, and his greed

proved his downfall when he found himself a rich man with no
need to bestir himself. He had lost so many men in the fight with
the Andalusians that he only had enough left to man one ship,
and barely that; but he took all the best of the booty from the ship
he had to leave behind, and managed to reach home without any
further misfortunes. His men worked themselves almost to death
at the oars, but did so cheerfully, knowing that the fewer of them
survived, the more each man would receive when the booty came
to be shared out. Before Krok sailed forth from Lister, few of them
had been fat enough to feed a louse, but when they returned,
there was no man in the district whose wealth could compare
with theirs. And there they sat, happy in their satiety, until the
time came when our men returned and discovered how things
were."

"But our men did not lack for silver or gold," said Orm.

"They were not poor," said Toke. "Far from it; for they were all
prudent and sensible men, so that they had brought much back
with them from Spain, besides what they had received as their
share of the price we got for the Andalusian rowers we sold at
Jellinge. And until they reached home, they thought their luck
good and felt well contented with their lot. But when they heard
how Berse's men had fared and saw them sitting fatly on their
broad estates, with plump cattle and well-timbered ships, in such
prosperity that even their slaves came puffing from their porridge
without the appetite to scrape their platters clean, then their
humor changed. Brooding and discontented, they reminded one
another of all the hardships they had been forced to undergo
during the seven years that they had spent in Andalusia, and so
became still more inflamed with wrath against Berse's men, who
had barely set foot in Spain before turning for home with a ship-
load of gold and silver. They sat hunched on their benches, spitting
on the ground as they reflected, and thinking that the ale they
drank lacked its proper flavor.

"Man is always so," said Father Willibald, "be he heathen or
baptized; content with his lot only as long as he meets no neighbor
who possesses more."

"It is good to be rich," said Orm. "Nobody can deny that."

"Gunne was the only one who had anything to smile about,"
continued Toke. "He was a married man when he sailed forth with

Krok; and when Berse returned, all those who did not come with him were presumed dead. So his wife married again and, by the time Gunne reappeared at her door, had already borne her new man a lapful of bawling sons. She had, to Gunne's eyes, aged, and was no longer the sort of woman that a man who had served in Almansur's bodyguard would lust after, so that he now felt free to look for a younger and more beautiful woman on whose arms to set his fine silver bracelets. But even this consolation was soon swallowed up in the fury he felt at being cheated, and in the end the four of them agreed that they could not honorably tolerate so ostentatious a display of wealth by their former comrades. They gathered their kinsmen and went round the district demanding their rightful share of all that Berse had brought home. But they received only rough answers, barred doors, and weapons bared against them. This still further increased their indignation, and they began to think that Berse's men not only owed them many marks of silver but were, besides, dishonorable traitors, who had fled like cravens from the battle, leaving Krok and ourselves to face the reckoning, and were, in short, to blame for our ship being captured."

"There was nothing they could have done to help us," said Orm, "for they had lost more than half their numbers. It was our fate to be chained to slave-oars."

"That may be," said Toke, "but the district was thick with Krok's kinsmen, and their minds soon began to work similarly. They demanded that his share, as chieftain, should be paid to them. Then both sides unhooked their weapons from the walls, and a feud was declared and was waged without quarter. By the time I arrived, both Halle and Grinulf were abed wounded, having been surprised in an ambush; but in spite of this they were in excellent heart and lost no time in acquainting me with the situation. Several of their enemies, they told me, had been found dead in this place or that; two had been burned in their houses by Ögmund and a brother of Krok's; and others, having grown soft with good living, had paid up in order to be allowed to grow old in peace. But others, it appeared, were more obstinate and had demanded that Ögmund, Halle, Gunne, and Grinulf should be declared outlaws; also, that the same sentence should be pronounced against me if I should take their part."

"One thing I can guess," said Orm, "and that is that you did not long remain neutral in this affair."

Toke nodded unhappily and said that he would have liked to settle down peacefully with his woman and avoid quarrels, for they were well content with each other, as, indeed, they had been ever since the day he had stolen her; he had not been able to refuse his friends help, however, for if he had done so, his good name would have suffered. He therefore immediately agreed to take their part; whereupon, a short while later, at the wedding of Gunne and his new woman, he had been the victim of a fearful misfortune, a ludicrous and shameful humiliation that had caused him incalculable misery and had cost several men their lives.

"And you must know, both of you," he said, "that when I tell you what happened, you may both laugh without fear that I shall draw upon you, though I have killed more than one man for twisting his mouth at this affair. What happened was as follows. On the evening of the wedding I went drunk to the privy and fell asleep as I sat there, as often happens to a man at a good feast; and there I was speared in the rear by two men who had crept up secretly behind the wall. I leaped high into the air, with all my sleep and good drunkenness gone from me instantly, thinking that I had been mortally wounded; which was also the belief of the two men, for I heard them laugh with delight as they ran away. But they had fumbled their thrusts, perhaps because the spears were somewhat long in the shaft, so that I escaped with lighter injuries than I at first feared to have sustained. None the less, I had to lie a long while abed, and on my stomach the whole time; and it was still longer before I was able to sit comfortably on a bench. Of all the things that have happened to me in my life, this was the worst—worse than being a galley slave among the Andalusians."

"Then you never discovered the men who had wounded you?" asked Orm.

"I discovered them," replied Toke, "for they could not keep their mouths shut, but had to boast of the deed to their women; so that the story came out and became known through the whole district. They were called Alf and Steinar, insolent fellows of good family, nephews of Ossur the Braggart, who was helmsman in Berse's ship, that fellow who was always boasting that on his mother's side he was descended from King Alf Woman's Darling of Möre. I learned that they were the culprits while I was still in bed from my wounds. Then, as I lay there, I vowed that I would never enjoy ale nor woman before I had killed them both; and, whether you believe it or not, I kept that vow. As soon as I was upon my feet again, I was out after them every day; and at last I came upon them one day, just as they were wading ashore from fishing. I almost wept with joy when I saw them step on to the land; and there, sword in hand, the three of us fought until I killed Steinar. Then the other fellow fled, with me at his heels. It was a beautiful race, well run by us both, through groves and fields among herds at pasture and across the meadows toward his father's house. He was a nimble-footed man, and was running for his life; but I was running for his life too, as well as to purge myself of my shame and of the great longing I had to be free of my vow. A short way from the house I caught him as my heart seemed to be about to burst, and cleft him to the teeth in the sight of his harvesters; and never have I felt so good as when I saw him there, lying on the ground at my feet. I went home with a merry heart and drank ale for the rest of the day and told my woman that our troubles were over. But this, as it turned out, was not so."

"What troubles could you have left, after such a fine revenge?" asked Orm.

"The people of the district, my friends no less than my enemies," said Toke darkly, "could not forget the circumstances in which I had received my wound, and there was no end to the mock they made of me. I had supposed that my revenge would put a stop to all this, seeing that I had killed both of the men singlehanded in fair fight; but this seemed to make little impression on their foolish minds. More than once I and Red-Jowl had to rid men of the habit of hiding their faces behind their hands when I appeared; but even this helped little, and soon I found myself scarcely able to endure the most solemn countenances, because I knew what lay behind their gravity. I composed an excellent poem about my slaying of Alf and Steinar, but soon discovered that there were already three poems in circulation describing the circumstances in which I had been wounded, and that in every house people were laughing themselves crooked every time they heard them. Then I realized that I would never be able to live down the shame of this incident; so I took my woman and everything else that I possessed, and journeyed up through the great forests until I came to Värend, where I have kinsmen. There I bought a house and have dwelt contentedly ever since, being now a richer man than when I arrived first, thanks to the good skin-trade. I have three sons, all of whom promise well, and a daughter, whose suitors will be hewing hard at one another before many years have passed. But never until this evening have I told anyone the reason for my leaving Lister. Only to you, Orm, and to you, little priest, have I told these things, because I know I can trust you both never to repeat them to a living soul. For should you do so, I would once again become a public butt, even though four years have now passed since this catastrophe occurred."

Orm praised Toke for the way in which he had told his story, and assured him that he need have no fears about anyone hearing it from his lips. "I should like," he added, "to hear these poems that were written about you; but no man enjoys repeating lampoons directed against himself."

Father Willibald emptied his cup, and announced that stories of this kind, dealing with feuds and jealousies, with spear-thrusts delivered in this place or that, revenge and lampoons and the like, gave him little pleasure, whatever Orm's attitude toward them might be.

"And you can be sure of this, Toke," he said, "that I shall not run around gossiping to people of such matters, for I have more important things to tell them. If, though, you are a man who is willing to learn from events, you may yet gain some profit from this distressing experience. From the little I saw of you in King Harald's castle, and from what Orm has told me about you, I know you to be a bold and fearless man, sure of yourself, and merry in your disposition. But in spite of all this, you have only to undergo some misfortune that causes foolish people to laugh at you, and you at once become cowardly and downhearted, so that you had to flee from your home district as soon as you found that you could not bully your enemies into silence. We Christians are more fortunate, for we do not care what men think of us, but only what God thinks. I am an old man and have little strength left in my bones; nevertheless, I am stronger than you, for no man can scare me with mockery, because I care not a jot for it. He who has

God behind his back flinches from no man's ridicule; and all their smirks and gossipings trouble him not at all."

"Those are wise words," said Orm, "and worth pondering; for, be sure of this, Toke, that this priest possesses more wisdom in his small head than we in our large ones, and it is always a good thing to mark his words."

"I see that the ale is beginning to work on you both," said Toke, "for you would not address such nonsense to me if you were sober. Is it in your mind, little priest, to try to make me a Christian?"

"It is," retorted Father Willibald purposefully.

"Then you have set yourself a difficult task," said Toke, "and one that will cause you more trouble than all the other religious duties you have ever performed."

"It would be no shame for you to turn Christian," said Orm, "when you consider that I have been one for these five years. I am not less merry than of old, nor has my hand weakened, and I have never had cause to complain about my luck since the day I received baptism."

"All that may be true," said Toke, "but you are not a skin-trader, as I am. No skin-trader can afford to be a Christian in this land; it would arouse distrust in the minds of all my customers. If he changes his gods, the Virds would say, who can rely on him in other matters? No, no. For our friendship's sake, I would do much for you, Orm, and for you too, little priest; but this I will not do. Besides which, it would drive my woman, Mirah, crazy, for she retains this characteristic of her countrymen, that she hates Christians above all things else; and, to my way of thinking, her humor is brittle enough already, without whetting it with ideas such as this. It is therefore useless for you to try to convert me, little priest, though I am your friend and hope to remain so."

Even Father Willibald could find no good answer to this argument; and Orm yawned, and said that the night was growing old and that it was time to seek sleep. They parted from Toke with many expressions of friendship; he and Orm were delighted with their luck at having once again found each other, and vowed to meet often in the future.

Orm and Father Willibald walked back to their camp. There all was peace and stillness, and in the moonshine men lay snoring under ribbons of pale smoke from the dying fires. But one of

Orm's men was sitting awake, and he lifted his head as they approached.

"A message came for you both," he said sleepily. "See, here, this bag; the owls have not ceased to screech since the moment I received it. I was down at the brook, drinking, when a man came from the Finnvedings' camp and asked for you, Orm. I told him that you had gone to the Virds. Then he threw his bag across the water, so that it fell at my feet, and shouted that it was a gift for Orm of Gröning and his long-nosed priest. I asked him what the bag might contain. Cabbage-heads, he replied, and laughed and went away. It is my belief that it contains something worse. Here is the bag; I have not touched the strings."

He dropped the bag at Orm's feet, laid himself down, and fell asleep at once.

Orm stared darkly at the bag and then at the priest. Both shook their heads.

"There is devilry here," said Father Willibald. "It cannot but be so."

Orm untied the strings, and shook out the contents. Two human heads rolled on to the ground, and Father Willibald fell to his knees with a groan.

"They are both shaven!" he cried. "Priests of Christ, murdered by heathens! How can human understanding comprehend the will of God when such things are allowed to gladden Satan?"

He peered more closely at the two heads and flung his arms toward the sky.

"I know them, I know them both!" he cried. "This is Father Sebastian, a most pious and worthy man, whom our crazy magister was to release from his slavery. Now God has released him and has set him high in heaven among the blessed martyrs. And this is Brother Nithard of Reims, who was at one time with Bishop Poppo at King Harald's court. From there he went to Skania, since when nothing has been heard of him; he, too, must have been made a slave. I know him by his ear. He was always ardent in his zeal and passion for the true faith; and once, at the Emperor's court, he had an ear bitten off by one of the Empress Theofano's monks from Constantinople, that city which Northmen call Miklagard, during an argument concerning the nature of the Holy Ghost. He used to say that he had given his ear in the fight against heresy, and that he was ready to give his head in the fight against heathendom. And now his words have been fulfilled."

"If he wished it to be so," said Orm, "we should not weep; though it is my belief that the Finnvedings did not render these god-men headless as an act of favor, however holy they may have been, but that they have done this deed and sent their heads to us as an insult and to cause us grief. This is our reward for having baptized Osten and his two men and allowed them to go in peace instead of killing them when we had them in our power. Perhaps you now regret, as I do, that we acted thus mercifully."

"A good deed remains good and should never be regretted," replied Father Willibald, "whatever consequences it may bring with it. These holy heads I shall bury in my churchyard, for from them much strength will come."

"A stink is coming from them already," said Orm darkly. "But you may be right."

Then, at Father Willibald's bidding, he helped to gather grass and leafy branches, with which they stuffed the bag. Among these, with great care, they placed the two heads, after which they refastened the strings.

CHAPTER TWELVE

CONCERNING THE THING AT THE KRAKA STONE

𝕿HE NEXT morning twelve men were chosen from each of the three border tribes, the Virds, the Göings, and the Finnvedings; and these men went to the places traditionally reserved for them, in a half-circle facing the Stone, with each twelve seated together. The rest of the men grouped themselves behind their chosen representatives to listen to what these wise men had to say. The twelve Virds sat in the center of the half-circle, and their chieftain rose first. His name was Ugge the Inarticulate, son of Oar; he was an old man, and had the reputation of being the wisest person in the whole of Värend. It had always been the case with him that he was never able to speak except with great difficulty, but everyone was agreed that this was a sign of the profundity of his thinking; it was said that he had been marked out as a wise man even in his youth, when he would sometimes sit through a three-day Thing without uttering a word, only now and then slowly shaking his head.

He now advanced to the Stone, turned to face the assembly, and spoke.

"Wise men," he said, "have now gathered here. Very wise men, from Värend and Göinge and Finnveden, after the ancient custom of our fathers. This is good. I greet you all and pronounce that our decisions shall be received peacefully. May you judge wisely, and to the advantage of us all. We have come here to talk about peace. It is the way with men that some think one thing and some another. I am old and rich in experience, and I know what I think. I think that peace is a good thing. Better than strife, better than burning, better than murder. Peace has reigned between us tribes for three whole years now, and no harm has come as a result of this. Nor will any harm come if this peace is allowed to continue. Those who have complaints to make shall be heard, and their complaints judged. Those who wish to kill one another may do so here at the Stone, for such is the law and ancient custom of the Thing. But peace is best."

When he had finished his speech, the Virds looked this way and that, for they were proud of their chieftain and his wisdom. Then the Thing-chieftain of the Göings rose. His name was Sone the Sharp-Sighted, and he was so old that the two men who were seated next to him took hold of his arms to help him get up; but he brushed them angrily away, hobbled nimbly forward to the Stone, and took his stand beside Ugge. He was a tall and scraggy man, desiccated and bent crooked with age, with a long nose and thin wisps of mottled beard; and although the day was fine and the late summer sun shone warmly, he wore a skin coat reaching to his knees, and a thick cap of fox fur. He looked immeasurably wise and had had a great reputation for as long as anyone could remember. His sharp-sightedness was famous; he could find where hidden treasure lay, and could look into the future and foretell the bad luck that lay there. In addition to all this, he had been married seven times and had twenty-three sons and eleven daughters; and it was said that he was doing his best to get round dozens of both, which made him much admired and honored by all the Göings.

He, too, pronounced peace upon the assembly and spoke in fine words of the peaceful intentions of the Göings, which, he said, were proved by the fact that they had undertaken no campaigns against either the Virds or the Finnvedings for four whole years. This, he continued, might be taken by foolish strangers to signify that weakness and sloth had begun to flourish among them; but if anyone thought this, he was wrong, for they were no less ready than their fathers had been to teach manners with point and blade to any man who sought to do them wrong, as could be testified by one or two people who had made the effort. It was also wrong to suppose that this peaceful attitude was the result of the good years they had enjoyed recently, with rich harvests, lush pasture, and freedom from cattle sickness; for a well-fed Göing was as doughty a warrior as when starvation cramped his belly, and of as proud a temper. The true cause of this desire for peace, he explained, was that men of wisdom and experience now prevailed, their counsel being accepted by the tribe.

"So long as such men are to be found and their advice listened to," he concluded, "we shall prosper. But as the years pass, the number of wise men grows less, and I think that, of those men whose judgment can be fully relied upon, no more than two are alive who are likely to survive much longer, Ugge and myself. It is therefore more than ever necessary that you young men who have been chosen to represent your tribes, though you have not yet any streak of gray in your beards, should listen carefully to what we say and thereby glean wisdom, which as yet you lack. For it is a good thing when old men are listened to and young men understand that they themselves have but a small measure of understanding."

A third now joined them at the Stone. He was the chieftain of the Finnvedings, called Olof Summerbird; and he had already won himself a great name, though he was yet young. He was a finely proportioned man, dark-skinned, and with piercing eyes and a proud look. He had been in the Eastland, having served in the courts of both the Prince at Kiev and the Emperor at Miklagard, whence he had returned home with great wealth. The name Summerbird had been given him on his return because of the splendor and bright color that he affected in his dress. He himself was well pleased with this nickname.

All the Finnvedings, both the chosen men and those who sat behind them, shouted with pride and triumph as he strode forward, for he looked in sooth like a chieftain; and when he took his place by the other two in front of the Stone, the difference between himself and them was manifest. He wore a green cloak, sewn with gold thread, and a shining helmet of polished silver.

After pronouncing peace upon the assembly, as the others had done, he said that his belief in the wisdom of old men was perhaps not fully commensurate with their own. Wisdom, he thought, could sometimes be found in younger heads; indeed, there were some who thought that it more often resided there. He would not disagree with the old men when they said that peace was a good thing; but everyone ought to remember that peace was nowadays becoming more and more difficult to keep. The chief cause of this, he said, was the unrest that was being aroused everywhere by the Christians, who were very evil and cunning men.

"And, believe me," he continued, "when I speak of the Christians, I know what I am talking about. You all know that I have spent five years at Miklagard, and have served two Emperors there, Basil and Constantine. There I was able to see how the Christians behave when they are angry, even when they have only one another to vent their spite upon. They clip one another's ears and noses off with sharp tongs, as revenge for the smallest things, and sometimes geld one another. Their young women, even when they are beautiful, they often imprison in closed stone houses and forbid to have intercourse with men; and if any woman disobeys, they wall her up alive in a hole in the stone wall and let her die there. Sometimes it happens that they weary of their Emperor, or that his decrees displease them; and then they take him and his sons and bind them fast and hold glowing irons close to their faces until their eyes sweat and so go blind. All this they do for the glory of Christendom, for they hold it to be less of a crime to maim than to kill; from which you may gather what kind of men they are. If they behave so toward one another, what will they not do to us, who are not Christians as they are, if they should become strong enough to attack us? Everyone should therefore beware of this danger, that it may be met and stifled before it grows greater. Have

we not all witnessed how, in this very place, a Christian priest only
last night forced his way to this Stone and committed murder
here, in the full sight of the Vird women? He had been brought
here by the Göings, perhaps so that he might commit this foul
deed. This is a matter between them and the Virds, which does
not concern us Finnvedings. But it would surely be good if the
Thing could declare that any Christian priest who appears among
the Göings, the Virds, or the Finnvedings shall instantly be killed
and shall not be kept alive as a slave, much less be permitted to
practice his witchcraft undisturbed; for otherwise much mischief
may be caused and strife be provoked."

Thus spoke Olof Summerbird, and many nodded thoughtfully
at his words.

He and the other two chieftains now seated themselves on the
three chieftain-stones, which rested on the grass bank before the
Kraka Stone, and the Thing began. It was an ancient custom that
those quarrels should first be decided which had originated in the
arena itself, so that the first case to be debated was that of the
magister. Ugge demanded compensation for the death of Styrkar,
and wished to know to whom this Christ-priest belonged, and why
he had been brought to the Thing. Orm, who was among the
chosen twelve of the Göings, rose and replied that the priest might
be regarded as belonging to him, though he was in fact no slave,
but a free man.

"And one would have to travel far," he added, "before finding
a more peaceable man. He has no appetite for violence, and the
only things he knows how to do are reading manuscripts and singing and winning the favors of women. And he came here on a mission which he will never, now, as things have turned out, be able
to fulfill."

Orm then told them about the magister and his mission; how
he had been sent from Hedeby to offer himself in exchange for a
priest who had been enslaved by the Finnvedings, but who had
now been killed by them. "Which matter," he said, "will doubtless be discussed later. But as regards the manner in which Styrkar
met his death, those who saw it happen can testify. For my part,
I do not think this priest capable of killing a grown man."

Sone the Sharp-Sighted agreed that those who had witnessed the
affair should be heard. "But whatever the judgment of the Thing

shall be in this matter," he said, "it shall not result in a feud being declared between the Virds and the Göings. You, Ugge, shall judge this case alone. The man is a foreigner, good for little, and a Christian to boot, so that he will not be missed much, whatever your decision. But you cannot demand compensation from us Göings for something that has been done by a man who is a stranger to our tribe."

The witnesses were now heard. Many men had seen Styrkar topple backwards from the Stone with a loud cry; but whether anyone might have struck him from the farther side of the Stone, none could say. Not even Toke Gray-Gullsson, who sat among the Vird twelve and who had been the first to arrive at the scene of the crime, knew for certain; but he declared that the cross which the Christ-priest had been holding in his hands, and which had been his only weapon, was made of such frail twigs that it might have served as a good instrument to kill a louse with, but would have made little impression on such a tough-hided old fox as Styrkar. It was his belief, he concluded, that the old man had slipped and had broken his neck in the fall; but the people who knew best what had happened, he added, were the women, for they had been on the spot and must have seen everything; provided, he said, some means could be found of persuading them to speak the truth.

Ugge sat for a while deep in thought. At last he said that there seemed to be nothing for it but to hear what the women had to say.

"According to our ancient law," he said, "women can be regarded as admissible witnesses; though how such a decision ever came to be arrived at is more than a man can guess. It is not our custom to use women's evidence where we can avoid it; for while to look for truth in a man can be like looking for a cuckoo in a dark wood, to look for the truth in a woman is like looking for the echo of the cuckoo's voice. But in this case the women are the only persons who saw exactly what happened; and the murder of a priest on holy ground is a matter that must be investigated with care. Let them, therefore, be heard."

The women had been waiting to be called, and now appeared, all together, the young ones who had danced round the Stone and the old women who had assisted with the ceremony. They were all wearing their finest apparel and ornaments, bracelets and necklaces and broad finger-rings and colored veils. At first they appeared somewhat bashful as they walked forwards into the space between the judges and the semicircle of chosen men. They had the magister with them, looking woebegone, with his hands tied and around his neck a rope, by which two of the old women led him, as they had led the goats to the Stone on the previous evening. A great shout of laughter arose from the assembly at the sight of him entering thus.

Ugge cocked his head on one side, scratched behind his ear, and looked at them with a worried expression on his face. He bade them tell him how Styrkar had met his death; whether their prisoner had killed him or not. They were to speak the truth and nothing else; and it would be a good thing, he said, if no more than two or three witnesses should speak at the same time.

At first the women were afraid of the sound of their own voices and whispered among themselves, and it was difficult to coax any of them to speak aloud; but before long they were persuaded to overcome their shyness and began to testify vigorously. Their prisoner, they said, had gone up to the Stone and cried in a loud voice and had then hit Styrkar over the head with his cross, causing the latter to cry also; then he had dug his cross into Styrkar's stomach and pushed him off the Stone. On this they were all agreed, though some said that the priest had struck once, and some twice, and they began to quarrel about this.

When the magister heard them testify thus, he became white in the face with terror and astonishment. Raising his bound hands toward heaven, he cried: "No, no!" in a loud voice. But nobody bothered to listen to the rest of what he had to say, and the old women gave a tug on the rope to silence him.

Ugge now said that this evidence was more than sufficient, for even the speech of women could be regarded as credible when so many of them said the same thing. Whether the murderer had struck once or twice did not affect the issue; here, he said, they had before them a clear case of priest-murder committed on holy ground.

"This crime," he proceeded, "has been regarded ever since the most ancient times as one of the foulest that it is possible to perpetrate, and occurs so rarely that many men sit through a whole lifetime of Things without ever having to judge an instance of it. The penalty for it, which is also of ancient prescription, is, I think, known to no one here save us two old men, Sone and I; unless, perhaps, you, Olof, who reckon yourself to be wiser than us, also know it?"

It was evident that Olof Summerbird was displeased at this question; nevertheless, he answered boldly that he had often heard that the penalty for this crime was that the culprit should be hung by his feet from the nethermost branch of a tree, with his head resting on an ant-hill.

Ugge and Sone beamed with delight when they heard him give this answer.

"It was not to be expected that you would know the correct sentence," said Ugge, "so young as you are; for to attain wisdom and knowledge takes longer than you would like to think. The proper punishment is that the murderer shall be handed over to Ygg, which in former times was our fathers' name for Odin; and now Sone will tell us the manner in which the presentation is to be made."

"Twenty good spears shall be found," said Sone, "with no rot in their shafts; and to each spear, just below the end of the iron shoe, a crosspiece shall be fixed. Then the spears shall be driven into the ground to half their length, close together with their points facing upwards. On these the murderer shall be cast, and there he shall remain until his bones drop to the ground."

"Such is the law," said Ugge. "The only detail you omitted to mention is that he shall be cast so as to land on the spears on his back, in order that he may lie with his face toward the sky."

A murmur of satisfaction passed through the whole assembly as they heard this punishment described, which was so ancient and rare that nobody had seen it. The magister had by now become calm and stood there with his eyes closed, mumbling to himself; the women, however, received the news of his sentence much less placidly. They clamored that this was a crazy punishment to condemn him to, and they had not intended, when testifying, that anything like that should happen; and two of them, who were related to Ugge, pushed their way through the crowd toward him, called him an old fool, and asked why he had not told them of this penalty before they had testified. They had, they said, given

the evidence that he had heard because they wished to keep the
Christ-priest, whom they liked and held to be more potent than
Styrkar, fearing that if he was acquitted, he would be set free and
go back to the Göings.

The most vehement protests came from one of the old women,
who was Styrkar's niece. Eventually she succeeded in quieting the
others so that her voice might be heard alone. She was large and
coarse-limbed and shook with fury as she stood there before Ugge.
She said that in Värend no decision was taken about anything until the women had passed judgment, and that old men there were
put out to play in the woods.

"I have nursed Styrkar, troll that he was, for many years," she
shrieked, "gaining my livelihood thereby. How shall I live now
that he is dead? Are you listening to me, you crookbacked imbe-
cile? Another priest, young and beautiful, and, from his appearance, wise and tractable also, has come and killed him, and nobody
can deny that it was high time that somebody did so. And what
do you suggest we should now do! Throw this young man upon the
points of spears! What good will that do to anybody? I tell you
that he shall be handed over to me, to replace the priest I have
lost. He is a fine priest, and when the dance round the Stone was
finished he performed to the satisfaction of us all; in nine months
the whole of Värend will be able to testify to the efficacy of his
magic. The services of such a priest will be sought by many, and all
who come will bring him gifts; and I shall thereby be compensated
for my loss, whether I have him as husband or as slave. What purpose will be served by throwing him upon spears? It would be better if you sat on them yourself, for it is plain that your age and
learning have driven you crazy. He shall be mine, as payment for
the murder he has committed, if there be any justice in the world.
Do you hear that?"

She shook her clenched fist in front of Ugge's face and appeared
to be considering whether to spit in it.

"She is right, she is right! Katla is right!" cried the women.
"Give him to us in Styrkar's place! We need a priest of his mettle!"

Ugge waved his hands and shouted as loudly as he could in an
endeavor to quiet them; and beside him Olof Summerbird was
near to falling backwards from his stone in his delight in the wise
man's discomfiture.

But Sone the Sharp-Sighted now rose from his stone and spoke in a voice that made everyone suddenly quiet.

"Peace has been pronounced upon this assembly," he said, "and it is a quality of wise men to endure women patiently. It would be an ill thing if we should allow the peace to be broken, and particularly ill for you, women; for we could then sentence you to be birched before the assembly, with good switches of birch or hazel, which would be sadly ignominious for you. If that were to happen, all men would snigger at the sight of you for the rest of your days, and I think none of you would wish that to happen. Therefore let there be an end to your screamings and vituperations. But one question I would ask of you before you depart from this place. Was Styrkar struck by the Christ-priest, or was he not?"

The women had now become calm. They replied with one accord that he had not so much as touched Styrkar; he had merely shouted something and raised his cross, at which the old man had fallen backwards and died. This, they declared, was the pure truth; they could, they said, tell the truth as well as anyone, if only they knew what purpose it would serve.

The women, including Katla and her captive, were now ordered to leave while Ugge debated with his chosen twelve over a suitable sentence. Several of them thought that the priest ought to be killed, for there could be no doubt that he had slain Styrkar by trollcraft, and the sooner one got rid of a Christ-priest, the better. But others opposed this argument, saying that any man who had managed to troll the life out of Styrkar was worth keeping alive. For if he had succeeded in doing this, he must also have been able to perform efficaciously upon the women; besides which, there was the old woman's argument to be considered, for, as she had asserted, it was true that no compensation could be claimed from the Göings for the loss of her man. The end of it was that Ugge declared that Katla should keep the Christ-priest as a slave until the fourth Thing following this one, extracting from him as much service as she could during that period. Neither Sone nor anyone else had any fault to find with this judgment.

"I could not have judged the matter better myself," said Orm to Father Willibald when they were discussing the case later. "Now he will have to get along with the old woman as best he can. He was reckoning on becoming a slave of the Smalanders anyway."

"For all his weaknesses," said Father Willibald, "it may be that God's spirit was upon him last night when he went up to denounce the heathen priest and his abominable practices. Perhaps he will do great works now, for the glory of God."

"Perhaps," said Orm, "but the best of it is that we are now rid of him. When a man is campaigning or a-viking, it is only right that he should indulge his lust for women, even if they belong to someone else; but it seems wrong to me that a man of his mettle, a Christ-priest and a good-for-nothing, should cause women to lose all sense of decency as soon as they set eyes on him. It is not right; it is unnatural."

"He will have plenty of opportunities to atone for his sins," said Father Willibald, "when that old crone Katla gets her claws into him. Certain it is that I would rather be in the hungry lions' den with the prophet Daniel, whose story you have heard me recount, than in his clothes now. But it is God's will."

"Let us hope," said Orm, "that it will continue to coincide with our own."

The Thing continued for four days, and many cases were judged. The wisdom of Ugge and Sone was praised by all, save those who received the wrong end of their decisions; and Olof Summerbird, too, showed himself to be a shrewd judge, rich in experience despite his youth, so that even Ugge was forced on more than one occasion to admit that he might, with the passing of the years, attain some wisdom. When difficult cases arose, in which the parties refused to come to any agreement and the representatives of the tribes involved in the dispute could not agree, the third judge was called upon to help them reach a decision, such being the ancient custom; and on two occasions, when the dispute lay between the Virds and the Göings, Olof Summerbird officiated as the impartial judge and acquitted himself with great honor.

Thus far all had gone well; but gradually the common members of the assembly began to show signs of increasing unrest as time went on without any good fight developing. A combat had, indeed, been ordered on the second day, as the result of a dispute between a Finnveding and a Göing concerning a horse-theft, for no witnesses could be found and both parties were equally obstinate and equally cunning at prevarication; but when they fronted each other on the combat place, they proved so unskillful that they straightway ran their swords through each other's belly and fell dead to the ground, like two halves of a broken pitcher, so that nobody gained much pleasure from that contest. The tribesmen made wry faces at one another when this happened, thinking that this was proving a very disappointing Thing.

On the third day, however, they were cheered by the appearance of a complicated and difficult case, which promised excellent results.

Two Virds, both known men of good reputation, named Askman and Glum, came forward and told of an instance of double woman-theft. Both of them had lost their daughters, buxom young women in the prime of their beauty, who had been stolen by two Göing otter-hunters in the wild country east of the Great Ox Ford. The identity of the thieves was known; one of them was called Agne of Sleven, son of Kolbjörn Burnt-in-His-House, and the other Slatte, known as Fox Slatte, nephew to Gudmund of Uvaberg, who was one of the twelve Göing representatives. The theft had taken place a year previously; the two young women, it appeared, were still in the clutches of their captors; and Askman and Glum now demanded treble bride-money for each girl, as well as reasonable compensation for the injury caused to the Widow Gudny, Glum's sister, who had been with the girls when the theft had taken place and had been so affected by the incident that for a good while after it she had been out of her proper mind. This good widow, they explained, they had brought with them to the Thing; she was well known to have an honest tongue, and, since many could testify that she had by now returned to her full senses, she would, they claimed, be the best witness to tell the assembly exactly what had happened.

The Widow Gudny now came forward. She was of powerful and impressive appearance, not yet old enough to frighten men; and she described clearly and earnestly how the incident had taken place. She and the girls had gone into the wild country to gather medicinal herbs and had had to spend the whole day there, because these herbs were rare and difficult to find. They had wandered farther afield than they had intended, and a terrible storm had suddenly broken over them with thunder and hail and pelting rain. Frightened, and drenched to the skin, they had lost their way; and after wandering for some time without coming upon any track or landmark, they had at last arrived at a scraped-out cave in the earth, in which they had taken shelter. Here they began to feel the effect of cold, hunger, and fatigue. There were two men already in the cave, hunters who lived there while trapping otters; and she was relieved to see that they did not look dangerous. The men had given them a friendly welcome, making room for them at their fire and giving them food and hot ale; and there they had remained until the storm ceased, by which time it was night and very dark.

Up to then, she continued, she had only worried about the storm and the ache that she was beginning to feel in her back as the result of being cold in wet clothes. But now she began to fear for the girls, which worried her much more. For the men were now in high spirits and were saying that this was the best thing that could have happened, for it was a long time since they had seen any women; and they were liberal with their ale, which they kept in a keg in their cave, and warmed more of it against the cold, so that the girls began to grow muzzy, being young and inexperienced. She had asked the men, in a pointed manner, to describe to her the way back to their home, and they had told her; but apart from this they had shown no concern for the girls' safety except by sitting close to them and feeling them to see if they were dry. This went so far that after a while Fox Slatte picked up two small bits of wood and told the girls that they were now to draw lots to decide which man each was to sleep next to. At this she had declared vigorously that the girls must straightway go home, finding their way as well as they might in the dark. For her own part, she was compelled to remain in the cave because of the severe pain in her back.

"I spoke thus," she said, "because I thought that the men might give way and let the girls go in peace if I undertook to remain with them. I was ready to make this sacrifice for the girls' sake, since, whatever the men might do to me, it would be less horrible for me than for them. But instead of being accommodating, the men grew angry and addressed me in the most insulting terms and seized hold of me and threw me out of the cave, saying that they would speed me on my way with arrows if I did not instantly depart from the place. I spent the whole night wandering in the forest, in terror of wild beasts and bogies. When I reached home and told what had happened, people went to the cave and found it empty, with no trace of the men or the girls or the otter skins. For a long while after this I was sick and half crazed because of the treatment I had endured at the hands of these foul ruffians."

Here the Widow Gudny ended her testimony, having spoken her last few sentences in a voice dimmed by weeping. Gudmund of Uvaberg now rose and said that he would present the case of the two young men. He was doubly qualified to do this, he said, partly because he was wiser than they, and so better able to choose his words, and partly because he had on more than one occasion heard the whole story of events, not only from Agne of Sleven and his nephew Slatte, but also from the mouths of the young women themselves. He therefore was as well informed about this matter as anyone, if not better; and as regards the testimony of the Widow Gudny, to which they had just been listening, he would say this, that much of it was according to the facts, but most of it contrary to them.

"Slatte and Agne both say," he continued, "that they were sitting in their cave during the storm, which was so severe that they were barely able to keep their fire from blowing out, when they heard groans outside. Slatte crept out and saw three figures moving in the rain with their skirts wrapped round their heads. At first he feared them to be trolls; and the women supposed him to be one when they saw his head suddenly appear from the earth, so that they quaked and screamed with terror. Realizing from this that they must be mortals, he approached and calmed them. They accepted his invitation to join him in his cave and seated themselves round the fire. The girls were very fatigued, and were sniveling with distress; but there were no tears coming from the widow, and she showed little evidence of exhaustion. She kept her eyes fixed upon them incessantly as she sat drying herself before the fire; she wanted her back rubbed, and every part of her body warmed with otter skins; then, after she had drunk of their hot ale like a thirsty mare, she became merry and took off most of her clothes. She did this, she explained to them, so that she might feel the heat more, since heat was what she needed most.

"Now, Slatte and Agne are both young," continued Gudmund, "but not more foolish than the run of men; and they knew well enough what thoughts tend to enter the minds of widows when

their glance falls on a man. When, therefore, she suggested that
the girls should go into a corner of the cave to sleep, but said that
she herself would remain awake to see that no harm came to them,
the men's suspicions were aroused and they exchanged a knowing
glance. Both Agne and Slatte have assured me that they would
gladly have obliged the widow had she come to them unaccompanied, but that it seemed to them an unmanly and dishonorable
thing for the two of them to share a widow when there were two
fair young women also present who might well be as eager for
pleasure as she was; for had they done so, they would have been
laughed at by every right-thinking person to whose ears the story
might have come. So they seated themselves beside the young
women and spoke calmingly to them and helped them to warm
their feet at the fire. By this time the girls were in better spirits,
having swallowed food and drink and become warm; they scarcely
dared, however, to glance at the men and were shy of speech.
This increased the men's respect for them, for it testified to their
modesty and good upbringing; and their liking for them became
so strong that eventually they decided to draw lots for them, so
that there should be no quarreling over who was to have which,
and so that all should be satisfied. But when they suggested this,
the widow, who had been growing more and more restless because
no attention was being paid to her, jumped to her feet shrieking
wildly. She protested that the girls must go home at once or terrible things would happen. They were young, she said, and able
to endure the hardships of the night; but for herself she must beg
hospitality until morning, since she was too fatigued and racked
with backache to undertake the journey. This suggestion astonished the men, who asked her whether it was her intention to kill
the girls; for this, they swore, she would certainly do if she drove
them out into the wild forest to face the darkness and rain and
all the evil things that lurked there. Such cruelty and wickedness
they had never before heard the like of, and they would not allow
it, for they were determined to protect the girls from her mad
caprices. Nor, they told her further, were they so careless of their
own safety that they were prepared to allow such a murderous
character as she to remain in their cave; for if they did so, they
could not be sure what might not happen to them while they
were asleep. So they commanded her to go; she looked, they say,

as strong as an ox, so that there would be little danger for her in
the forest, and if she should encounter a bear or a wolf, the animal would certainly flee at the sight of her. Seizing hold of her,
therefore, they ejected her from the cave, throwing her clothes
after her. The next morning they thought it best to move on; and
the girls, when they heard of this decision, volunteered to accompany them, to help them carry their traps and skins. There are
witnesses present here at the Thing who have heard this from the
girls' own mouths. These young women are now married to Agne
and Slatte and are well contented, and have already borne their
husbands children.

"Now, I do not think," concluded Gudmund, "that this business can properly be called woman-theft. The fact of the matter
is that these men saved these young women's lives, and that not
once but twice; first when they took them into their cave and
offered them warmth and shelter, and secondly when they prevented them from being driven out into the forest as the wicked
widow would have done with them. The men are therefore willing to pay ordinary bride-money for them, but no more."

Thus reasoned Gudmund, and his words were greeted with great
acclamation by the Göings. The Virds, however, appeared to approve them somewhat less, and Askman and Glum would not relax
their demand. Had the two men stolen the widow, they said, they
could have had her cheaply; but virgins could not be considered as
being in the same category as widows; nor would any wise man
place much reliance on the defense that Gudmund had put up
for them. They thought it only right that the Widow Gudny
should receive compensation for the insults and injuries that had
been done to her; they knew her well, and she had never shown
herself to be as man-crazy as Gudmund had made her out to be.
In this matter of her compensation, however, they would accept
whatever sum might be offered, but they were not prepared to
haggle over the young women.

Witnesses were then heard for both sides, both those who had
heard the story from the young women's lips, and those who had
been addressed on the subject by the Widow Gudny on her return from the cave. Ugge and Sone agreed that this was a difficult
case to judge; and the spirits of the assembly rose, for there ap-

peared to be an excellent prospect of a four-handed combat, provided no unlucky chance intervened.

Ugge said that he felt half inclined to allow Sone to judge the case alone, because of his great wisdom and for their ancient friendship's sake; but he could not persuade his chosen twelve to agree to this, and so Olof Summerbird was co-opted as third judge. This honor, he said, was one that gave him little joy, for much silver and several lives depended on the result of the case, so that whoever judged it would bring upon himself the hatred and abuse of many, however just his decision might be. At first he suggested, as a compromise, that the husbands should pay double bride-money instead of the treble portion that was demanded; but neither the Göings nor the Virds would have any of this. Gudmund said that Slatte was already in strained circumstances, it being impossible for those who lived by trapping otters and beavers to amass a fortune, because of the poor prices that were paid for skins nowadays; while Agne of Sleven had lost his whole inheritance through his father's having been burned in his house. The most they could afford would be the ordinary bridal portion, and even that they would hardly be able to pay without assistance. The Vird representatives, on the other hand, thought that Glum and Askman were demanding no more than was reasonable.

"For," they said, "we Virds have, ever since ancient times, held our women in great honor, and our neighbors must not be allowed to suppose that our virgins can be picked up cheap in any forest."

Several thought that the best solution would be for the four parties concerned to fight it out; they thought that Askman and Glum, despite their disadvantage in age, would emerge with honor from the contest.

The matter was debated this way and that for a good while, but both Sone and Ugge were reluctant to declare that it should be decided by combat.

"Nobody can say," said Ugge, "that either of the two stolen women has any guilt to bear in this business; and it would be a bad judgment that condemned them to the certain misfortune of having to lose either a husband or a father."

"If we are to pass unanimous judgment on this case," said Olof Summerbird, "we must first decide whether woman-theft has been committed or not. I know my opinion, but I should prefer that those who are older should speak before me."

Ugge said that in his mind there was no doubt; that which had occurred must be regarded as woman-theft. "It is no excuse to say that the young women went with the men of their own free will," he said. "For they did not do so until the following morning, by which time they had spent the night with them. This we know, for it has been admitted that the men drew lots for them. And every wise man knows that a young woman is always ready to go with a man whose couch she has shared, especially if he is the first with whom she has done this."

Sone hesitated for a considerable while before announcing his decision, but at length he said: "It is the duty of a judge to speak the truth, even if in so doing he speaks against his own people. This is woman-theft, and I do not think anyone can deny it. For when they ejected the widow from the cave, they forcibly separated the young women from their guardian and so stole them from her care."

Many of the Göings complained loudly when they heard Sone speak thus, but none dared to say that he was wrong, because he had such a great name for wisdom.

"Thus far, at least, we are agreed," said Olof Summerbird, "for I, too, judge this to be woman-theft. This being so, we must also agree that greater compensation is required than the ordinary bridal portion that Gudmund offers. But still we are far from reaching any satisfactory conclusion. For how shall we get the parties to accept our decision if the fathers will not accept, nor the husbands pay, double bride-money? It is my opinion that if either party has the right to maintain its demand, it is the Virds."

Up to this moment Orm had been sitting silent in his place, but he now rose and asked what the Virds reckoned to be the value of a bridal portion, either in oxen or in skins, and what would be regarded as the equivalent in silver.

Ugge replied that the men of Värend had, from ancient times, reckoned the bridal portion in skins: thirty-six marten skins for a good farmer's daughter in the prime of youth, fresh and strong and without fault or blemish; in which case, the skins must be good winter skins, with no arrow-holes; alternatively, thirty beaver skins, also of the first quality; in return for which, no dowry was required to accompany the bride save the clothes she wore and the shoes she walked in, together with a new linen shift for the bridal night, a horn comb, three needles with eyes, and a pair of scissors.

"Which," he continued, "amounts to eighteen dozen marten skins, for two treble portions, or, alternatively, fifteen dozen beaver skins, if my reckoning is correct. That is a great quantity, and to calculate its equivalent in silver is a problem that would tax the brain of the most skillful arithmetician."

Several of the representatives who were experienced in calculation endeavored to come to his assistance, among them Toke Gray-Gullsson, who was used to reckoning in skins and silver; and after they had taxed their brains for a good while, they declared unanimously that treble bride-money for two virgins would amount to seven and a quarter marks of silver, no more and no less.

"To reach that even figure," explained Toke, "we have subtracted twopence three farthings for the shifts, which will not be needed in this instance."

When Gudmund of Uvaberg heard this great sum named, he burst into a tremendous bellow of laughter.

"No, no!" he roared. "I could never agree to such a sum. Do you think me mad? Let them fight it out; whatever the result, it will be the cheapest way."

And other voices from the assembly echoed his words: "Let them fight!"

Orm now rose and said that a thought had occurred to him which might perhaps help to deliver them from this quandary; for he was of that party which felt that it would be a pity to allow the matter to be settled by blows.

"Gudmund is right," he said, "when he says that seven and a quarter marks of silver is a great sum, enough to alarm the richest man; and few there are who have ever held so much in their hands, save those who have gone a-viking against the Franks, or have been present when my lord Almansur of Andalusia shared out his booty, or have taken geld from King Ethelred of England, or served the great Emperor at Miklagard. But if we take a third of this sum, we find it to be two and one-third marks, plus one twelfth of a mark; and if we split this third into two parts, we have one and one-seventh marks, plus one twenty-fourth. Now, we have been told that Agne of Sleven and Slatte are prepared to pay ordinary bridal portions. That means that we have two sixths of a total sum accounted for. I have been thinking that it would be no dishonor to these men's kinsmen and neighbors if they were to provide a like sum. I know Gudmund of Uvaberg and would not like to think him less openhanded than other men; and one and one-seventh marks, plus one twenty-fourth of a mark, are not a sum that it would ruin him to pay, even if he had to do so unaided. But I am sure that there are others besides him who are willing to help Slatte, and I do not doubt that it is the same with Agne's kinsmen. If they are prepared to do this, we shall have four sixths of the total sum already promised and only the last third to find. As regards this final portion, I have been thinking that here among our chosen twelve there sit men who would be prepared to give something for good neighbor's sake and for the sake of their own good names. I could wish that I were richer than I am; nevertheless, I am prepared to give my share; and if we can but find three or four others to do likewise, the last third of the sum will be paid and the business settled to the satisfaction of all."

When Orm had concluded and had seated himself again, the representatives of the three tribes glanced at one another, and several of them were heard to murmur approval. Sone the Sharp-Sighted was the first to voice his thoughts.

"It is good to hear that wisdom will not wholly depart from the border country when Ugge and I die," he said. "Orm of Gröning, despite your youth you have spoken words of wisdom. I will not content myself with saying that your suggestion is good; I shall even offer to pay a part of the last third of the sum myself. This may surprise some of you, for you all know how many children I have to support; but there are certain advantages in having a large family. Even if I contribute as much as a quarter of this third, I shall be able to afford it; for I shall collect the sum from my sixteen grown sons, who spend most of their time wandering about the forest. So that if I take two skins from each of them, I shall be able to pay my share and have a few left over for myself; and I am prepared to do this to help Agne of Sleven, because his mother was second cousin to my fourth wife. But let no man sit here with his tongue tied; let all who wish to join with me in this speak freely and so win honor before the whole assembly."

Toke Gray-Gullsson rose at once and said that it was not his custom to be closefisted when other people were being open-handed.

"And I say this," he said, "though I am only a skin-merchant who has, alas, all too often been skinned himself. I possess no great wealth, and am never likely to attain to any; many of you who sit here know that well, for you have got good money from me for skins of little quality. But at least I have enough to join with Orm and Sone in contributing toward this excellent cause; so whatever they give, I shall give the same."

Ugge the Inarticulate now began to stutter and stammer, as he always did when anything excited him. At last, he managed to say that this solution would bring honor to both the Göings and the Virds, and that he himself was prepared to contribute as much as those who had spoken before him.

Two of the Göing representatives, Black Grim and Thorkel Hare-Ear, now cried that the Virds must not be allowed to outdo them in generosity, and that they, too, wished to give a share; and Olof Summerbird said that he saw no reason why other men should have all the honor, and that he therefore proposed to offer twice as much as anyone else.

"And if you take my advice," he added, "you will gather in the contributions at once, for money melts forth most freely when the flame of giving is still warm. Here is my helmet to collect it in; and you, Toke Gray-Gullsson, being a merchant, will be able to weigh each man's contribution, to make sure that it is correct."

Toke sent a slave to fetch his scales, and more and more of the representatives, both Virds and Göings, rose to make their offers; for they saw that they might now win honor cheaply, for the more people contributed, the smaller each man's gift would have to be. But Olof Summerbird reminded them that nobody had yet heard Gudmund of Uvaberg say how much he and the other kinsmen of Slatte and Agne were prepared to give.

Gudmund rose to his feet with an uncertain expression on his face and said that it was a matter that needed much consideration, for a sixth of the whole sum was a great amount for himself and his kinsmen to find between them.

"No man can call me mean," he said, "but I am, alas, only a poor farmer, and Orm of Gröning is mistaken in suggesting to you that I am anything else. There is little silver to be found in my house,

and I think the same is true of Slatte's other kinsmen. Such a burden would be too heavy for us to bear. If, however, we were asked
to find one half of the sixth, I think we might manage to scrape
it together. Here among us sit so many great and famous men,
with their belts distended with silver, that they would hardly notice
it if they gave another half-sixth, in addition to the third that has
already been promised. Do this, and your honor will be increased
yet more; and I shall be saved from destitution."

But at this the judges and representatives and the whole assembly seated at their backs hooted and howled with laughter; for it
was well known to all of them that Gudmund's wealth was only
surpassed by his meanness. When he found that he could win no
support for his suggestion, he at length yielded; and two men,
acting as spokesmen for Agne's kinsmen, promised that their due
share would be paid.

"It would be best," said Sone to Gudmund, "if you, too, could
gather in your share now, since you have, I doubt not, many kinsmen and friends among the assembly here; and I myself will collect
the sum due from Agne's kinsmen."

By this time Toke's silver-scales had arrived and he was attempting to calculate how much each man would have to pay.

"Thirteen men have promised to contribute," he said, "and each
of them is giving the same amount, except Olof Summerbird, who
is giving a double portion. That makes fourteen lots that we have
to calculate. What one fourteenth of one third of seven and a
quarter marks of silver comes to is not easy to say; I do not think
the wisest arithmetician of Gotland would be able to tell us at
once. But a man who is shrewd can find a way out of most difficulties, and if we work it out in skins the problem becomes easier.
That way, each lot will be one fourteenth of six dozen marten
skins, which is one seventh of three dozen; and each lot must be
reckoned to the nearest skin, for one always loses a little in weighing, as I know from experience. By this reckoning, each man should
give the equivalent in silver of six marten skins, a small price to pay
for such an honor. Here are the scales and weights, and anyone
who wants to do so is welcome to test them before I begin the
weighing."

Men who knew about such things now tested the scales carefully;
for merchants' scales were often cunningly adjusted, so that the

test was well worth making. But the weights could only be tested by touch; and, when two men expressed doubts regarding their accuracy, Toke immediately replied that he would gladly fight any man to prove that they were correct.

"It is part of a merchant's trade," he said, "to fight for his weights; and anyone who is afraid to do so must be regarded as unreliable and should not be dealt with."

"There shall be no fighting about weights," said Ugge sternly. "All the silver that is collected in the helmet shall be given at once to Glum and Askman; and what good would it do Toke to weigh falsely, when his own silver is to be weighed with the rest?"

All those who had promised to contribute now took silver from their belts and had it weighed. Some gave small silver rings, others twists of silver thread, and others yet handed over silver that had been chopped up into small squares. Most, however, gave their contribution in the form of silver coins, and these were from many different countries and the farthermost parts of the earth, some of them having been struck in lands so remote that no man knew their name. Orm paid in Andalusian coin, of which he still possessed a quantity, and Olof Summerbird in beautifully engraven Byzantine pieces that bore the head of the great Emperor John Zimisces.

When all the contributions had been collected, Toke poured them into a small cloth bag and weighed them all together; and the scales showed that his calculations had been correct, for they made up a third of the sum required. But there was also a small surplus.

"This is too little to divide up and give back to all of you," said Toke, "for I cannot measure such small amounts on my scales."

"What shall be done with it?" asked Ugge. "It seems unnecessary that Glum and Askman should receive more than they demanded."

"Let us give it to the Widow Gudny," said Orm. "Then she, too, will have some compensation for the distress and disappointment that has been caused to her."

All agreed that this was an excellent solution; and soon Sone and Gudmund came back with their respective sixths, which they had collected from their kinsmen and friends in the assembly. Sone's sixth was weighed and found correct; but Gudmund's was deficient, though he produced a pile of skins and two copper kettles to add to his silver. He bewailed the deficiency loudly, saying that he was prepared to swear upon oath that this was all that he could raise, and begging that some rich man of the chosen twelve should lend him the money that was lacking. But this nobody was willing to do, for everyone knew that lending money to Gudmund was like casting it into the sea.

At length Sone the Sharp-Sighted said: "You are a stubborn man, Gudmund, as we all know well; but all men can be persuaded to change their attitudes by some means or other, and I think you are no exception to this rule. I seem to remember that Orm of Gröning managed to persuade you to do so not long after he had arrived in the border country, when you were unwilling to sell him hops and cattle fodder at a fair price. I fancy that a well entered into the story; but I forget exactly what happened, for I am beginning to grow old. While, therefore, you, Gudmund, think how you may find the rest of your share of the silver, perhaps Orm will tell us the story of how he prevailed upon you. It would be interesting to know the method he used."

This suggestion was enthusiastically received by the assembly, so Orm rose and said that the story of what had happened was short and simple. But before he could go further, Gudmund leaped to his feet and roared that he did not wish it to be repeated.

"We made this matter up a good while ago, Orm and I," he declared, "and it is not a story worth listening to. Wait but a short while, for I have just remembered another man whom I might ask, and I think he will be able to supply what is lacking."

With that, he lumbered hastily away toward his camp. As he disappeared, many shouted that they wished, nevertheless, to hear the story of how Orm had persuaded him. But Orm said that they would have to get somebody else to tell it to them.

"For what Gudmund says is true," he said, "that we made this matter up long ago; and why should I provoke him to no purpose, when he has already gone to fetch his silver to avoid having this story repeated? It was only to make him do this that Sone, in his wisdom, referred to the incident."

Before anyone could say more, Gudmund returned, puffing, from his camp with the missing money. Toke weighed it and found it correct; so two thirds of the bride-money due from Slatte and Agne was handed over by Ugge to Glum and Askman, whereupon these two admitted the men who had stolen their daughters to be good and blameless sons-in-law. The remaining third, which was to be paid by Slatte and Agne themselves, they were to receive at the end of the winter, so that the young men might be able to collect the necessary amount in skins.

But as soon as this matter was settled, Olof Summerbird said that he would now like to hear the story that had been promised them of how Orm had persuaded Gudmund to change his mind. All the representatives cried assent to this, and Ugge himself supported the suggestion.

"Instructive stories," he said, "are always worth hearing, and this is one that is new to me. It may be that Gudmund would prefer that we should not hear it, but you must remember, Gudmund, that you have caused us all a great deal of inconvenience by your attitude toward this case, and that we have paid a third of the money demanded of your kinsmen, though you were wealthy enough to have given it yourself. Seeing that you have been saved so much silver, you can put up with the shame of hearing this story repeated. If, though, you would prefer to tell it yourself, by all means do so; and Orm Tostesson will doubtless be able to refresh your memory if any details should escape you."

Gudmund now flew into a fury and began to roar. This was an old habit with him when he was angry, and because of it he had come to be known as the Thunderer. He sank his head down between his shoulders and shook throughout his whole body and brandished his fists before his face and roared like a werewolf. It was his hope that people might suppose from this that he was about to go berserk, and in his younger days he had often succeeded in frightening men by this means; but nobody was deceived by it any longer, and the more he roared, the louder the assembly laughed. Suddenly he fell silent and glared around him.

"I am a dangerous man," he said, "and no man provokes me without regretting it."

"When a representative breaks the peace of the Thing," said Toke, "by threat or abuse, drunken talk or malicious accusation, he shall be required to pay a fine of—I forget the sum, but doubtless there are men here who can remind me."

"He shall be expelled from the precincts of the Thing by the

judges and representatives," said Sone. "And if he should resist or
attempt to return, he shall pay with his beard. Such is the ancient
law."

"Only twice in my life have I known a representative to be
deprived of his beard," said Ugge reflectively. "And neither of them
was able to endure life for much longer, after suffering such shame."

Many now began to be incensed with Gudmund, not because
he had howled at them, which nobody bothered much about, but
because the honor that they had won by their openhandedness had
cost them so much silver; and they now blamed Gudmund for this.
So they roared furiously at him to depart from the Thing, swear-
ing that otherwise they would take his beard from him. Gudmund
had a very fine beard, long and luxuriant, of which he evidently
took great care; he therefore yielded to their clamor and left the
Thing rather than risk exposing his beard to danger. But as he
departed, he was heard to mumble: "No man provokes me without
living to regret it."

Orm was now commanded to tell the story of his first meeting
with Gudmund and how he had persuaded him to change his mind
by holding him over his own well. This hugely delighted the
assembly; but Orm himself was not greatly pleased at having to
repeat the tale and, when he had finished, said that he would now
have to be prepared for some attempt by Gudmund at revenge.

So this difficult case of woman-theft was successfully concluded.
Many had won honor through it, but it was the general opinion
that Olof Summerbird and Orm of Gröning deserved the most
praise for the way they had spoken.

Ever since the opening of the Thing, Orm had been expecting
to hear some accusation from the Finnvedings about the way he
had treated Östen of Öre, or some reference to the two heads that
had been thrown across the brook on the first evening. But as
nobody mentioned either matter, he decided to find out for himself whether they felt bound as a tribe to avenge the insult inflicted
upon one of their members. Accordingly, on the evening of this
the third day of the Thing, he went alone to the Finnveding camp,
having first requested and obtained safe-conduct to do so, in order
that he might discuss the matter privately with Olof Summerbird.

The latter received him in a manner befitting a chieftain. He
had sheepskins spread out for Orm to sit on, offered him fried

sausage, sour milk, and white bread, and commanded his servant to bring forth his feasting-cup. This was a tall clay cup with handles, narrow-necked, and terminating in a leaden stopper. It was placed carefully on flat ground between them, together with two silver mugs.

"You conduct yourself like a chieftain," said Orm, "here, as at the Thing."

"It is a bad thing to sit talking without ale to drink," said Olof Summerbird; "and when chieftain entertains chieftain, they should have something better to swallow than water from the brook. You are a man who has traveled widely, as I have, and perhaps you have tasted this drink before, though it is seldom offered to guests here in the north."

He took the stopper from the cup and poured a liquid from it into the two mugs. Orm nodded as he saw its color.

"This is wine," he said, "the Roman drink. I have tasted it in Andalusia, where many people drank it secretly, though it was forbidden them by their prophet; and once again, on a later occasion, at the court of King Ethelred in England."

"In Constantinople, which we call Miklagard," said Olof Summerbird, "it is drunk by everyone, morning and evening, especially by the priests, who thin it with water and drink twice as much as anyone else. They hold it to be a sacred drink, but I think that ale is better. I pledge you welcome."

They both drank.

"Its sweetness is soothing to the throat when a man has eaten fat sausage with salt in it," said Orm, "though I agree with you about ale being the better drink. But it is time for me to tell you why I have come to speak with you, though I think you know the reason already. I wish to know whether the two heads that were thrown to me across the brook were sent by your kinsman Östen. They belonged to two Christian priests who had become your slaves. I also wish to know whether this Östen still seeks my life. If he does so, it is without cause, for I spared his life and gave him his freedom when he was in my power, the time he treacherously gained entry to my house to get my head, which he had promised to King Sven. You know that I am a baptized man and a follower of Christ; and I know that you regard Christians as evil men, because of the way you saw them act in Miklagard. But I promise you that I am not that sort of Christian; and here at this Thing I have learned that you, too, are a man who hates evil and villainy. It is because I know this that I have come to you this evening; otherwise I would have been foolish to cross the brook."

"How you could have become a Christian," said Olof Summerbird, "is more than I can understand. Nor can I make much of your little bald priest; for I hear that he helps all members of the Thing who come to him with ailments, and refuses reward for his labor. So I hold you both to be good men, as though you had never been tainted with Christianity. Nevertheless, you must admit, Orm, that you and your priest laid a cruel burden on my kinsman Östen when you forced him to receive baptism. The shame of that has driven him mad; though it may be that the ax-blow he received on his head also had something to do with it. He has become folk-shy and spends most of his time wandering in the forest or lying in his room groaning to himself. He refused to come to the Thing; but he bought these two slave-priests from their owners, paying a big price for them, and straightway hewed off their heads and sent them here by his servant, that he might give them to you and your little priest as a reminder and a greeting. He has, indeed, been well punished for his attempt against your life, for he has been baptized and has lost all the wares you took from him, and his understanding too; but though he is my kinsman, I will not say that he has got more than he deserved, for he was too rich a man, and too nobly born, to be a party to such a bargain as he made with King Sven. I have told him as much myself and have said that I shall not order any feud against you to avenge him; but it is certain that he will gladly kill you if he gets the chance. For he believes that he will become brave and merry again, as he was before, once he has killed you and your little priest."

"I thank you for this information," said Orm. "Now I know how I stand. There is nothing I can do about the two priests whose heads he took, and I shall not seek revenge for their death. But I shall be on my guard, in case his madness drives him to make some further attempt against me."

Olof Summerbird nodded and refilled their mugs with wine.

It was now quite still in the camp, and there was no sound to be heard save the breathing of sleeping men. A light breeze stirred the trees, and the aspen leaves rustled. They pledged each other again, and as Orm drank, he heard a branch crack in the wood behind him. As he leaned forward to replace his mug on the ground, he heard a sudden gasp at his ear, as of a man fighting for his breath. Olof Summerbird sat up alertly and gave a cry, and Orm turned half around, saw a movement in the woods, and crouched closer to the ground.

"It is a lucky thing I am sharp of hearing and moved quickly," he said afterwards, "for the spear flew so close to me that it scarred the back of my neck."

There was a howl from the woods, and a man rushed out at them whirling a sword. It was Östen of Öre, and they could see at once that he was mad, for his eyes stared stiffly out of his head like a ghost's, and there was froth on his lips. Orm had no time to seize his sword or get to his feet. Flinging himself sideways, he managed to grip the madman's leg and throw him across his body at the same time as he received a slash across the hip from his sword. Then he heard a blow and a groan, and as he got to his feet he saw Olof Summerbird standing sword in hand, and Östen lying still on the ground. His kinsman had hewed him in the neck, and he was already dead.

Men came running toward them, awakened by the noise. Olof Summerbird looked with a pale face at the dead man.

"I have killed him," he said, "though he was my kinsman. But I do not intend that any guest of mine shall be attacked, even by a madman. Besides which, his spear broke my feasting-cup; and whoever had done that, I would have killed him."

The cup lay in fragments, and he was much grieved at its loss, for such a one he would not easily find again.

He ordered his men to carry the dead man to the marsh and sink him there, driving pointed stakes through his body; for if this is not done, madmen walk again and are the most fearful of earthbound spirits.

Orm had come out of this adventure with a scar on his neck and a wound in his hip; but the latter was not dangerous, for the sword-blade had struck his knife and eating-spoon, which he wore on his belt. He was accordingly able to walk back to his camp; and as he said farewell to Olof Summerbird, they took each other by the hand.

"You have lost your cup," said Orm, "which is a pity. But you are the richer by a friend, if that is any consolation to you. And I should be happy if I could think that I had won as much."

"You have," replied Olof Summerbird. "And this is no small prize that you and I have won."

From this time the friendship between them was very great.

On the last day of the Thing, it was agreed that peace should reign throughout the border country until the time of the next Thing. So this Thing at the Kraka Stone ended, though many thought that it had been disappointing, and nothing to boast of, because no good combat had been fought during it.

Father Willibald went to the Vird camp to look for the magister and say farewell to him, but the woman Katla had already taken him away. Orm wanted Toke to come back to Gröning with him, but Toke refused, saying that he had to buy his skins. But they promised to entertain each other honorably in the near future and always to keep their friendship firm.

All now rode off toward their respective homes; and Orm felt much relieved that he was rid of both the magister and his enemy, Östen of Öre. When Christmas came, Toke and his Andalusian wife Mirah visited Gröning; and all that Orm and Toke had to tell each other was as nothing compared with what Ylva and Mirah had to say to each other.

At the beginning of spring Rapp's wife, Torgunn, bore her man a boy. Rapp was much pleased at this; but when he reckoned the months backwards, he felt somewhat suspicious, for the date of conception was not far from that time when the magister had read over Torgunn's injured knee. All the house-folk, men and women alike, praised the child and his resemblance to his father; this comforted Rapp, but did not completely allay his fears. The only man whose word he wholly relied upon was Orm; so he went to him and begged him to examine the child and say whom he thought it most resembled. Orm looked at the child closely for a long while; then he said: "There is a great difference between him and you, and nobody can fail to see it. The child has two eyes, and you have only one. But it would be churlish of you to resent this, for you, too, had two eyes when you came into the world. Apart from this disparity, I have never seen a child that more resembled its father."

Rapp was calmed by this assurance and became exceedingly proud of his son. He wanted Father Willibald to christen him

Almansur, but the priest refused to give the child a heathen name, and he had to be content with calling him Orm instead. Orm himself carried the child to the christening.

A fortnight after this child was born, Ylva gave birth to her second son. He was black-haired and dark-skinned, and yelled little, but gazed about with serious eyes; and when the sword's point was offered to him, he licked it even more avidly than Harald Ormsson had done. All agreed that he was born to be a warrior, and in this they prophesied rightly. Ylva thought that he resembled Gold-Harald, King Harald's nephew, in so far as she could remember this great Viking from her childhood days; but Asa would have none of this, insisting that he bore a marked likeness to Sven Rat-Nose, who had been similarly dark of skin. But he could not be christened Sven, and they already had one child called Harald; so in the end Orm gave him the name of Blackhair. He behaved very quietly and solemnly during the christening, and bit Father Willibald in the thumb. He became his parents' favorite child, and in time the greatest warrior on the border; and many years later, after many things had happened, there was in the court of King Canute the Mighty of Denmark and England no chieftain of greater renown than the King's cousin Blackhair Ormsson.

PART FOUR

The Bulgar Gold

CHAPTER ONE

CONCERNING THE END OF THE WORLD, AND HOW
ORM'S CHILDREN GREW UP

AT length that year arrived in which the world was due to
end. By this time Orm was in his thirty-fifth and Ylva in her
twenty-eighth year. All good Christians believed that in this, the
thousandth year after His birth, Christ would appear in the sky
surrounded by hosts of shining angels and judge every man and
woman, both living and dead, to decide who should go to heaven
and who to hell. Orm had heard Father Willibald talk about this
so often that he had become resigned to it. Ylva could never make
up her mind whether she really believed that it would happen or
not; but Asa was happy in the thought that she would be able to
attend this great occasion as a living person, in her best clothes,
and not as a corpse in a winding-sheet.

Two things, however, troubled Orm. One was that Toke still
refused to be converted. The last time he had visited him Orm
had striven earnestly to persuade him that he would be wise to
change his faith, enumerating to him all the advantages that
Christians would shortly enjoy; but Toke had remained obstinate
and had chaffed Orm for his zeal.

"The evenings will be long in heaven if Toke is not there," said
Orm to Ylva more than once. "Many of the great men I have
known will be elsewhere; Krok and Almansur, Styrbjörn and Olof
Summerbird, and many other good warriors besides. Of the people
who have meant most to me, I shall only have yourself, our children, Asa, Father Willibald, Rapp, and the house-folk; and also
Bishop Poppo and your father, King Harald, whom it will be good
to meet again. But I should like to have had Toke there. It is his
woman who holds him back."

"Let them do as they think best," said Ylva. "Things may turn
out otherwise than as you anticipate. For my part, I do not think
God will be in such a hurry to destroy the world, after having put
Himself to so much trouble to create it. Father Willibald says

we shall all sprout wings, and when I picture him thus, or you, or
Rapp, I cannot but laugh. I do not want any wings, but I should
like to be allowed to take my gold chain with me, and Father
Willibald does not think I shall be allowed to. So I am not looking
forward to this event as eagerly as he is, and will believe in it when
I see it happen."

Orm's other concern was whether it would be wise to sow his
crops. He was anxious to know at what season of the year Christ's
advent might be expected, but Father Willibald was unable to
enlighten him on this point. Orm doubted whether it would be
worth the labor, for he might never be able to reap the year's
harvest and would not be likely to need it even if it should ripen
in time. Soon, however, he succeeded in solving this problem to
his satisfaction.

From the very first day of this year every young Christian woman
had sought the delights of bodily pleasure more greedily than ever
before, for they were uncertain whether this pleasure would be
allowed them in heaven and were therefore anxious to enjoy as
much of it as they could while there was yet time, since, whatever
form of love heaven might have to offer them, they doubted
whether it could be as agreeable as the sort practiced on earth.
Such of the servant-girls as were unmarried became wholly intrac-
table, running after every man they saw; and even in the married
women a certain difference was evident, though they clung virtuously to their husbands, thinking it imprudent to do otherwise
when the Judgment Day was so close upon them. The result of
all this was that by the spring most of the women at Gröning were
with child. When Orm discovered that Ylva, Torgunn, and the
rest were in this condition, his spirits perked up again, and he
ordered that the sowing should take place as usual.

"No children can be born in heaven," he said. "Therefore they
must all be born on earth. But this cannot be until the beginning
of next year. Either the god-men have calculated wrongly, or God
has changed His mind. When nine months have gone by without
any woman becoming pregnant, then we shall know that the end
of the world is imminent, and can begin to prepare for it; but
until then we can live our lives as usual."

Nothing that Father Willibald said could persuade him that he
was wrong in this surmise; and as the year wore on and nothing

happened, the priest himself began to have doubts about the matter. It might be, he said, that God had altered His plans, in view of the fact that there were still so many sinful men on earth to whom the gospel had not yet penetrated.

That autumn a band of foreigners came from the east and made their way on foot along the border. They were all soldiers, and all wounded; some of their wounds were still bleeding. There were eleven of them, and they trudged from house to house craving food and night shelter; where this was granted them, they remained for one night, or sometimes two, and then proceeded on their way. They said they were Norwegians and were journeying homewards, but more than this they would not reveal. They conducted themselves peaceably, using no violence toward anyone; and where night shelter was refused them, they continued on their way without complaint, as though unconcerned whether they ate and slept or no.

At length they arrived at Gröning, and Orm came out to speak with them, accompanied by Father Willibald. When they saw the priest, they fell on their knees and besought him earnestly to bless them. He did so willingly, and they seemed overjoyed at having come to a Christian house and especially at having found a priest. They ate and drank ravenously; then, when they had consumed their fill, they sat silent and large-eyed, paying scant heed to the questions that were addressed to them, as though they had other things uppermost in their minds. Father Willibald saw to their wounds, but his blessings were what they were most eager for, and of these it seemed that they could not have enough. When they were told that the morrow was a Sunday, they begged to be allowed to stay and attend Mass and to listen to the sermon. This request Orm granted them willingly, though he was vexed that they would tell him nothing about themselves or whence they had come.

That Sunday was a fine day, and many people came riding to church, mindful of the promise they had made to Father Willibald on the evening of their baptism. The foreigners were given places on the front benches and listened earnestly to all that the priest said. As usual during this year, he took as his theme the end of the world, assuring them that it might be expected to occur very shortly, though it was difficult to say exactly when, and that every Christian must mend his ways in order that he might not be found wanting when the day arrived. As he said this, several of the foreigners were seen to smile contemptuously; others, however, wept, so that the tears could be seen on their cheeks. After Mass they begged to be blessed again, with a great blessing; and Father Willibald did as they asked him.

After he had blessed them, they said: "You are a good man, priest. But you do not know that the event of which you warn us has already happened. The end of the world has come; Christ has taken our King from us to live with Him, and we have been forgotten."

Nobody could understand what they meant, and they were unwilling to say more. At length, however, they explained what had happened to them. They spoke with few words, and in voices such as dead men might have, as though nothing any longer had any meaning for them.

They said that their King, Olaf Tryggvasson of Norway, the best man who had ever lived on earth, save only Christ Himself, had fallen in a great battle against the Danes and Swedes. They themselves had been captured alive by the Swedes; their ship had been boarded by great numbers and they, fatigued, had been pinned between shields or else, because of their wounds, had been unable to resist longer. Others of their comrades, more fortunate, had followed their King to Christ. Then they had been led, together with many others, aboard one of the Swedish ships to be taken to Sweden. There had been forty of them in the ship, all told. One night they lay in an estuary, and someone observed that this river was called the Holy River. This they took to be a sign from God, and as many of them as had the strength to do so broke their fetters and fought with the Swedes in the ship. They killed them all; but most of their comrades were slain also, so that only sixteen of them were left alive. These had then rowed the ship up the river as far as they could. Five, wounded more grievously than the rest, had died at their oars, smiling; and they, the eleven survivors, had taken weapons from the dead Swedes and abandoned the ship, thinking to march overland to the Halland border and so into Norway. For, realizing that they were the most unworthy of King Olaf's men, since they alone had been left behind when all their comrades had been permitted to accompany him, they had not dared to take their own lives, for fear lest he should refuse to know them. They believed that this was the penance demanded of them, that they should return to Norway and bring to their countrymen tidings of the death of their King. Every day they had said all the prayers they knew, though these had been fewer than they could have wished, and had reminded one another of all the King's commandments regarding the conduct of Christian warriors. It was a great joy to them, they said, that they had at last found a priest and been permitted to attend Mass and receive God's blessing; now, however, they must continue on their journey, that they might lose no time in bringing their sad tidings to their countrymen. They believed that when they had done this, a sign would be given them, perhaps by their King himself, that they had at last been deemed worthy to join him, though they were the poorest of his men.

They thanked Orm and the priest for their kindness and went their way; and nothing more was heard of them at Gröning, nor of the end of the world.

The year ended without the smallest sign having appeared in the sky, and there ensued a period of calm in the border country. Relations with the Smalanders continued to be peaceful, and there were no local incidents worth mentioning, apart from the usual murders at feasts and weddings, and a few men burned in their houses as the result of neighborly disputes. At Gröning, life proceeded tranquilly. Father Willibald worked assiduously for Christ, though he was not infrequently heard to complain at the slowness with which his congregation increased, despite all his efforts; what particularly annoyed him was the number of people who came to him and said that they were willing to be baptized in return for a calf or heifer. But even he admitted that things might have been worse, and thought that some of the men and women he had converted were perhaps less obdurately evil than they had been before baptism. Asa did what she could to help him; and although she was by now beginning to grow old, she was as active as ever and had plenty to occupy her in looking after the children and the servants. She and Ylva were good friends and seldom exchanged words, for Asa was mindful that her daughter-in-law was of royal blood; and when they disagreed, Asa always yielded, though it could be seen that it went against her nature to do so.

"For it is certain," said Orm to Ylva, "that the old woman is even more obstinate than you, which is saying not a little. It is good that things have turned out as I hoped they might, and that she has never tried to challenge your authority in the house."

Orm and Ylva still found no cause for complaint in their choice of each other. When they quarreled, neither of them minced words; but such incidents were rare and quickly passed, nor did either of them cherish rancor afterwards. It was a strange peculiarity of Orm's that he never birched his wife; even when a great anger came over him, he restrained his temper, so that nothing more came of it than an overturned table or a broken door. In time he perceived a curious thing: namely, that all their quarrels always ended in the same way; he had to mend the things he had broken, and the matter about which they had quarreled was always settled the way Ylva wanted it, though she never upturned a table or broke a door, but merely threw an occasional dish-clout in his face or smashed a plate on the floor at his feet. Having discovered this, he thought it unrewarding to have any further quarrels with her, and a whole year would sometimes pass without their harmony being threatened by hard words.

They had two more children: a son, whom they called Ivar, after Ivar of the Broad Embrace, and whom Asa hoped would, in time, become a priest, and a daughter, whom they called Sigrun. Toke Gray-Gullsson was invited as the chief guest at the christening, and it was he who chose her name, though only after a long exchange of words with Asa, who wanted the child to be given a Christian name. Toke, however, asserted that no woman's name was more beautiful than Sigrun, or more honored in old songs; and as Orm and Ylva wished to show him all honor, it was allowed to be as he wished it. If all went well, Toke said, she would, in good time, marry one of his sons; for he could not hope to have either of the twins as a daughter-in-law, none of his sons being old enough to be considered as future husbands for them. This, he said to himself sadly as he sat gazing at Oddny and Ludmilla, was, in truth, a great pity.

For the two girls were, by now, beginning to grow up, and nobody could any longer doubt whether they would be pleasing to the eye. They were both red-haired and well-shaped, and men were soon glancing at them; but it was easy to perceive one difference between them. Oddny was of a mild and submissive temper; she was skillful at womanly tasks, obeyed her parents willingly, and seldom caused Ylva or Asa any vexation. On the few occasions when she did so, her sister was chiefly to blame, for, from the first, Oddny had obeyed Ludmilla in everything, while Ludmilla, by contrast, found it irksome to obey and pleasing to command. When she was birched, she yelled more from anger than from pain, and comforted herself with the reflection that before long she would be big enough to give as good as she got. She disliked working at the butter-churns or on the weaving-stools, preferring to shoot with a bow, at which sport she soon became as skillful as her teacher, Glad Ulf. Orm was unable to control her, but her obstinacy and boldness pleased him; and when Ylva complained to him of her perversity and the way she played truant in the forest, shooting with Glad Ulf and Harald Ormsson, he merely replied: "What else can you expect? It is the royal blood in her veins. She has been blessed with a double measure, Oddny's as well as her own. She will be a difficult filly to tame, and let us hope that the main burden of taming her will fall on other shoulders than ours."

In the winter evenings, when everyone was seated round the fire at his or her handicraft, she would sometimes behave peaceably, and even now and then work at her spinning, provided that some good story was being told, by Orm of his adventures in foreign lands, or by Asa of the family in the old days, or by Father Willibald of great happenings in the days of Joshua or King David, or by Ylva of her father, King Harald. She was happiest when Toke visited Gröning, for he was a good story-teller and knew many tales of ancient heroes. Whenever he seemed to flag, it was always she who jumped up to fill his ale-cup and beg him to continue, and it was seldom that he found the heart to refuse her.

For it was always so with Ludmilla Ormsdotter that from her earliest youth men found it difficult to gainsay her. She was pale-complexioned, with skin tightly drawn over her cheekbones, and dark eyebrows; and although her eyes were of the same gray as those of many other girls, it nevertheless seemed to men who studied them closely and returned their gaze that there were none to compare with them anywhere else in the whole border country.

Her first experience with men occurred in the summer after her

fourteenth birthday, when Gudmund of Uvaberg came riding to
Gröning with two men, whom he suggested that Orm should take
into his service.

Gudmund had not been seen at Gröning since Orm had insulted him at the Thing, nor had he ridden to any Thing since
that day. But now he came full of smiles and friendliness and said
that he wished to do Orm a kindness, so that their old quarrel
might be made up.

"I have with me here," he said, "the two best workers that ever
were; and I now offer them to you. They are not serfs, but free
men, and each of them does the work of two, and sometimes more.
This is therefore a fine service I am doing you by offering them to
you, though it is equally true that you will be doing me a good one
by accepting them. For they are both tremendous eaters, and
though I have kept them for four months, I find myself unable to
do so any longer. I am not so rich as you are, and they are eating
me out of house and home. I dare not ration them, for they have
told me that if this is done, they become dangerous; unless they eat
themselves full each noon and evening, a madness comes upon
them. But they work willingly for anyone who will feed them full,
and no man has ever seen workers to match them."

Orm regarded this offer with suspicion and questioned both
Gudmund and the two men carefully before accepting them. The
men did not attempt to conceal their shortcomings, but said honestly how things were with them and how they wished them to
be; and as Orm had good need of strong workers, he at length
accepted them into his service, and Gudmund rode contentedly
away.

The men were called Ullbjörn and Greip. They were young, long-
faced, and flaxen-haired, and a man had only to look at them to
tell that they were strong; but as regards intelligence, they were
less fortunately equipped. From their speech it could be heard
that they came from a distant part of the country; they said they
had been born in a land far beyond West Guteland, called Iron-
Bearing Land, where the men were as strong as the bears, with
whom they would often wrestle for amusement. But a great famine
had afflicted their land, and so they had left it and journeyed
southwards in the hope of reaching a country where they would be
able to find enough to eat. They had worked on many farms and

estates in West Guteland and Smaland. When food began to become scanty, they explained, they killed their employer and went on.

Orm thought that they must have worked for a tame lot of masters if they had allowed themselves to be killed as easily as that, but the men stared earnestly at him and bade him take good note of what they had said.

"For, if we become hungry, we go berserk, and no man can withstand us. But if we get enough food, we conduct ourselves peaceably and do whatever our master bids us. For we are made that way."

"Food you shall have," said Orm, "as much as you want; if you are such good workers as you claim to be, you will be worth all the food you can eat. But be sure of this, that if you enjoy going berserk, you have come to the wrong place here, for I have no patience with berserks."

They gazed at him with thoughtful eyes and asked how long it was until the midday meal.

"We are already beginning to feel hungry," they said.

As fortune had it, the midday meal was just due to be served. The two newcomers set to with a will and ate so greedily that everyone watched them in amazement.

"You have both eaten enough for three men," said Orm. "And now I want to see each of you do two men's work, at the very least."

"That you shall," they replied, "for this was a meal that suited us well."

Orm began by setting them to dig a well and soon had to admit that they had not exaggerated their worth, for they quickly dug a good well, broad and deep and lined from top to bottom with stone. The children stood and watched them work; the men said nothing, but it was noticeable that their eyes often turned toward Ludmilla. She showed no fear of them and asked them how it was with men when they went berserk, but received no reply to this question.

When they had completed this task, Orm told them to build a good boathouse down by the river; and this, too, they did quickly and well. Ylva forbade her daughters to go near them while they were working there, for, she said, one could never be sure what such half-trolls as they might not suddenly do.

When the boathouse was ready, Orm set them to clean the
cowshed. All the cows were at pasture, and only the bull was left
in the shed, he being too evil-tempered to be allowed loose. A
whole winter's droppings lay in the pens, so that Ullbjörn and
Greip had several days' stiff work ahead of them.

The children and all the house-folk felt somewhat afraid of the
two men, because of their strength and strangeness. Ullbjörn and
Greip never had much to say to anyone; only sometimes, when
they were spoken to, they told briefly of feats of strength they had
performed, and how they had strangled men who had not given
them enough to eat, or had broken their backs with their bare
hands.

"Nobody can withstand us when we are angry," they said. "But
here we get enough to eat and are content. So long as things continue thus, nobody has anything to fear from us."

Ludmilla was the only one not afraid of them, and several times
went to watch them work in the cowshed, sometimes accompanied
by her brothers and sisters and sometimes alone. When she was
there, the men kept their eyes fixed on her; and although she was
young, she understood well what they were thinking.

One day when she was there alone with them, Greip said: "You
are the sort of girl I could fancy."

"I, too," said Ullbjörn.

"I should like to play with you in the hay," said Greip, "if you
are not afraid to do so with me."

"I can play better than Greip," said Ullbjörn.

Ludmilla laughed. "Do you both like me?" she said. "That is a
pity. For I am a virgin, and of royal blood, and not to be bedded
by any chance vagabond. But I think I prefer one of you to the
other."

"Is it me?" said Greip, throwing aside his shovel.

"Is it me?" asked Ullbjörn, dropping his broom.

"I like best," said Ludmilla, "whichever of you is the stronger.
It would be interesting to know which that is."

Both the men were now hot with desire. They glared silently at
each other.

"I may perchance," added Ludmilla softly, "allow the stronger
man to sit with me for a short while down by the river."

At this they straightway began to growl fearfully like werewolves and seized hold of each other. They appeared to be of equal strength, and neither could gain an ascendance. The beams and walls shook as they stumbled against them. Ludmilla went to the door to be out of their way.

As she was standing there, Orm came up.

"What is that noise?" he asked her. "What are they doing in there?"

Ludmilla turned to him and smiled. "Fighting," she said.

"Fighting?" said Orm, taking a step toward her. "What about?"

"Me," replied Ludmilla happily. "Perhaps this is what they call going berserk."

Then she scampered fearfully away, for she saw a look on Orm's face that was new to her, and understood that a great anger had come over him.

An old broom was leaning against the wall. Orm wrenched the shaft out of its socket, and this was the only weapon he had as he strode in, slamming the door behind him. Then his voice was audible above the snarling of the men, and for a moment all was silence in the shed. But almost at once the snarling broke out afresh and with redoubled violence. The servant-girls came out into the yard and stood there listening, but nobody felt inclined to open the cowshed door to see what was happening inside. Someone shouted for Rapp and his ax, but he was nowhere to be found. Then one of the doors flew open and the bull rushed forth in terror, with its halter hanging loose about its neck, and fled into the forest. Everyone shrieked aloud at this sight; and now Ludmilla began to be afraid and to cry, for she feared she had started something bigger than she had intended.

At length the uproar ceased and there was silence. Orm walked out, panting for breath, and wiped his arm across his brow. He was limping, his clothes were torn, and part of one of his cheek-beards had been wrenched away. The servant-girls ran up to him with anxious cries and questions. He looked at them and said that they need not lay a place for Ullbjörn or Greip at supper that evening.

"Nor tomorrow, neither," he added. "But how it is with this leg of mine I do not know."

He limped into the house to have his injury examined by Ylva and the priest.

Inside the cowshed all was disorder, and the two berserks were lying across each other in one corner. Greip had the sharp end of the broomstick through his throat, and Ullbjörn's tongue was hanging out of his mouth. They were both dead.

Ludmilla was afraid that she would now be birched, and Ylva thought she had deserved it for having gone in alone to the two berserks. But Orm pleaded for her to be treated leniently, so that she escaped more lightly than she had thought possible; and she described what had happened before the fight in such a manner that they agreed that no blame could be attached to her. Orm was not displeased with the incident, once Father Willibald had examined his leg and declared the injury to be slight; for though he was now certain that Gudmund of Uvaberg had offered him the two men in the hope of gaining his revenge, he was well pleased with his feat of having overpowered two berserks singlehanded and without the help of any proper weapon.

"You did wisely, Ludmilla," he said, "to turn them against each other when they would have molested you, for I am not sure that even I could have defeated them if they had not already tired each other somewhat. My advice, therefore, Ylva, is that she shall not be birched, though it was rash of her to go in to them alone. For she is too young to understand the thoughts that are liable to enter men's heads when they look at her."

Ylva shook her head doubtfully at this, but allowed Orm to have his way.

"This affair has turned out well," he said. "Nobody can deny that these two ruffians have done good work since they arrived here. I now have a well, a boathouse, and more honor to my name, and Gudmund has been well snubbed for his pains. So everything is as it should be. But I will take care to let him know that if he provokes me again, I shall pay him a visit that he will not forget."

"I will come with you," said Blackhair earnestly; he had been sitting listening to their conversation.

"You are too small to wear a sword," said Orm.

"I have the ax Rapp forged for me," he replied. "He says there are not many axes with a sharper edge than mine."

Orm and Ylva laughed, but Father Willibald shook his head frowningly and said it was a bad thing to hear such talk from a Christian child.

"I must tell you again, Blackhair," he said, "what you have already heard me say five, if not ten times, that you should think less about weapons and more about learning the prayer called *Pater Noster*, which I have so often explained to you and begged you to learn. Your brother Harald could recite that prayer by the time he was seven, and you are now twelve and still do not know it."

"Harald can say it for us both," retorted Blackhair boldly. "I am in no hurry to learn priest-talk."

So time passed at Gröning, and little of note occurred; and Orm felt well content to sit there peacefully until his days should end. But a year after he killed the berserks, he received tidings that sent him forth upon the third of his long voyages.

CHAPTER TWO

CONCERNING THE MAN FROM THE EAST

OLOF SUMMERBIRD came riding to Gröning with ten followers and was warmly welcomed. He stayed there three days, for the friendship between him and Orm was great. The purpose of his journey, however, was, he said, to ride down to the east coast to Kivik to buy salt from the Gotland traders who often anchored there. When Orm heard this, he decided to go with him on the same errand.

As things now were, salt was scarcely procurable, however large a price people might be willing to pay for it, thanks to King Sven Forkbeard of Denmark and the luck that attended all his enterprises. For King Sven was now ranging the sea with larger fleets than any man had heard tell of before, laying violent hands on any ship that crossed his path. He had plundered Hedeby and sacked it, and was reported to have laid waste all the country of the Frisians; it was known, moreover, that he had a mind to conquer the whole of England and as much more as he had time for. Trade and merchandise interested him not at all, but only long ships and sworded men; and things had come to such a pass that of late no salt-ships had come from the west, because they no longer dared to brave the northern waters. So no salt was procurable except that which the Gothlanders brought from Wendland, and this was bought up so eagerly by the coastal dwellers that little or none ever found its way inland.

Orm took eight men with him and rode with Olof Summerbird down to Kivik. There they waited for several days in the hope that a ship might soon arrive, while many people gathered there from all parts on the same errand. At last two Gotland ships were sighted. They were heavily laden and dropped anchor a good way outside the harbor. For the hunger for salt had become so great that the Gothlanders now drove their trade cautiously, to avoid being killed by overzealous customers. Their ships were large, high-gunwaled, and well manned, and anyone who wanted to buy from them had to row out in small boats, from which they were only allowed aboard two at a time.

Olof Summerbird and Orm hired a fishing-boat and were pulled out to the ships. They wore red cloaks and polished helmets. Olof grumbled at the smallness of the boat, for he had wanted to be rowed out in greater state. When their turn arrived, they climbed aboard the ship, which bore a chieftain's standard, and as they did so, their rowers, one of Orm's men and one of Olof's, cried out their names in a loud voice, so that the Gothlanders might understand at once that they were now being honored by a visit from chieftains.

"Olof Styrsson the Magnificent, Chieftain of the Finnvedings, whom many call Olof Summerbird," cried one.

"Orm Tostesson the Far-Traveled, Chieftain of the Sea, whom most men call Red Orm," cried the other.

There was murmuring among the Gothlanders when these names were heard, and some of the men came forward to greet them; for there were several in the ship who had known Olof in the Eastland, and others who had sailed with Thorkel the Tall to England and remembered Orm from that campaign.

A man was seated by the gunwale, near to the point where they had come aboard. Suddenly he began to moan excitedly and stretched out one of his arms toward them. He was a large man with a matted beard, which was beginning to grow gray; across his face he wore a broad bandage covering his eyes, and as he stretched his right arm toward Orm and Olof, they could see that the hand had been severed at the wrist.

"Look at the blind man," said the Gothlanders. "There is something he wishes to say."

"He seems to know one of you," said the ship's captain. "Besides what you can see, he has also lost his tongue, so that he cannot speak; nor do we know who he is. He was led aboard by a merchant from the East, while we were at anchor trading with the Kures, at the mouth of the river Dvina. The merchant told us that this man wished to go to Skania. He had silver to pay for his passage, so I accepted him. He understands what is said to him and, after much questioning, I have discovered that his family lives in Skania. But more than that I do not know, not even his name."

"Tongue, eyes, and right hand," said Olof Summerbird thoughtfully. "Surely it is the Byzantines who have treated him thus."

The blind man nodded eagerly.

"I am Olof Styrsson of Finnveden, and have served in the bodyguard of the Emperor Basil at Miklagard. Is it I whom you know?"

The blind man shook his head.

"Then perhaps it is I," said Orm, "though I cannot guess who you may be. I am Orm, the son of Toste, the son of Thorgrim, who lived at Grimstad on the Mound. Do you know me?"

At this the blind man nodded several times excitedly, and sounds came from his throat.

"Were you with us when we sailed to Spain with Krok? Or to England with Thorkel the Tall?"

But to both these questions the stranger shook his head. Orm stood deep in thought.

"Are you yourself from the Mound?" he asked.

The man nodded again and began to tremble.

"It is a long while since I left those parts," said Orm. "But if you know me, it may be that we were neighbors there. Have you been abroad for many years?"

The blind man nodded slowly and heaved a deep sigh. He raised the hand that was left to him, spread the fingers wide, and closed his fist again. He did this five times and then held up four fingers.

"This conversation goes better than one would have supposed possible," said Olof Summerbird. "By this, if I understand him aright, he means that he had been abroad for twenty-nine years."

The blind man nodded.

"Twenty-nine years," said Orm reflectively. "That means that I was thirteen when you left. I ought to remember if anyone left our district for the East around that time."

The blind man had risen to his feet and was standing in front of Orm. His lips were moving, and he gestured with his hand as though beseeching Orm to remember quickly who he was.

Suddenly Orm said, in a changed voice: "Are you my brother Are?"

Into the blind man's face there came a kind of smile. He nodded his head slowly; then he tottered on his feet, sank down on his bench, and sat there trembling in every limb.

Everyone in the ship was amazed at this encounter and thought he had witnessed an incident worth recounting to other men. Orm stood staring thoughtfully at the blind man.

"I should be lying if I said that I recognize you," he said, "for it is a long while since last I saw you, and in the meantime you have changed cruelly. But you shall now ride home with me, and there you will find someone who will straightway recognize you if you are the man you claim to be. For our old mother is still alive, and often speaks of you. Surely it is God Himself who has steered your steps, so that, despite your blindness, you have found your way home to me and her."

Orm and Olof now began to bargain with the Gothlanders for salt. They were both amazed at the great meanness that the Gothlanders showed as soon as they turned to any question of business. Many of the crew owned shares in the ship and her cargo, and they all proved to be birds of a feather, merry and friendly when other matters were being discussed, but as sharp as knives when it came to striking a bargain.

"We force no man to act against his will," they said, "concerning salt or anything else; but anyone who comes to buy our wares must either pay our price or go without. We are richer than other men, and intend to grow richer still; for we Gothlanders are cleverer than the run of mankind. We do not rob or kill like most men, but increase our wealth by honorable trading; and we know better than you what salt is worth just now. All honor to good King Sven, who has enabled us to raise our prices!"

"I should not regard any man who praises King Sven as clever," said Orm bitterly. "I think it would be easier to get justice from pirates and murderers than from such men as you."

"Men often speak thus of us," said the Gothlanders, "but they do us injustice. Look at your unfortunate brother here, whom you found in our ship. He has silver in his belt, and not a little; but none of us has taken any of it, save only what we originally demanded for his passage and food-money. Other men would have taken his belt and flung him into the sea; but we are honorable men, though it is true that many think otherwise. But if he had been carrying gold, he would have been less safe, for no man can withstand the temptation of gold."

"I begin to long to go to sea again," said Orm, "if only for the chance of encountering such a ship as yours."

The Gothlanders laughed. "Many men cherish that longing," they said, "but such as try to requite it go home, if at all, with grievous wounds to nurse. For you must know that we are strong fighters and are not afraid to show our strength when the need arises. Styrbjörn we feared, but no man else. But enough of this talk. Let us know at once whether you wish to buy from us or no; for there are many others waiting their turn."

Olof Summerbird bought his sacks and paid for them with few words; but when Orm reckoned up the amount he would have to pay, he began to grumble loudly. His brother touched him with his hand; opening his fist, he revealed a small heap of silver coins, which he carefully placed in the palm of Orm's right hand.

"You see!" said the Gothlanders. "We spoke the truth. He has plenty of silver. Now you cannot doubt any longer that he is your brother."

Orm glanced uncertainly at the silver. Then he said: "From you, Are, I will accept this money; but you must not suppose that I am either mean or poor, for I have enough wealth for both of us. But it is always humiliating to pay money to merchants, especially when they are such men as these."

"They outnumber us," said Olof, "and we must have salt, whatever the price. But it is certainly true that a man has to be rich to deal with men from Gotland."

They bade the merchants a curt farewell, rowed their salt ashore, and started homewards; and Orm hardly knew whether to rejoice or be sad that he was bringing home a brother so fearfully maimed.

During their journey, when they had pitched camp for the night, Orm and Olof sought, by means of many questions, to learn from Are what had befallen him. Olof Summerbird could not remember having seen him in Miklagard; after much questioning, however, they at length gathered that he had been a chieftain in one of the Emperor's warships. He had not been maimed as a punishment, but while in captivity, after some fight; Olof had been correct, however, in guessing that it had been the Byzantines who had treated him thus. But more than this they could not discover, though they worded their questions skillfully; for all that Are could do in reply was to signify either yes or no, and they could see that it galled him bitterly that they could not find the right questions to ask him and that he could not guide their thoughts. They understood that he had been involved in some strange adventure, in which gold and treachery had played their part, and that he possessed some knowledge that he wished to impart to them; but all their efforts to discover what this might be proved vain.

"There is nothing for it but to be patient," said Orm at length. "It is useless for us to plague you with any more of this guessing, for it will lead us nowhere. When we reach home we will get our priest to help us, and then we may, perhaps, find a way to your secret; though how we shall manage to do so is more than I know."

Olof Summerbird said: "Nothing that he has to tell us can be more amazing that the fact of his having found his way home across so many miles of land and sea in such a state of helplessness. If so strange a thing can happen, let us hope that it may not be impossible for us to hit upon some way to discovering his secret. Certain it is that I shall not go home from Gröning until I know more of what he has to tell us."

Are sighed and wiped the sweat from his brow and sat rigid.

When they came to within sight of Gröning, Orm rode ahead of the others to break the news to Asa, for he feared that otherwise the joy and sorrow of seeing Are again might prove too great a shock for her. At first she was confused by what he told her and began to weep bitterly; then, however, she fell on her knees to the

floor, beat her head against a bench, and thanked God for returning to her the son whom she had so long regarded as lost.

When they led Are to the house, she ran wailing to embrace
him, and for some time would not let him go; then she began
straightway to chide Orm for having doubted that this was his
brother. After she had calmed herself, she said she would make a
better bandage for his eyes; then, when she heard that he was hungry, she became more cheerful and went to prepare with her own
hands those dishes which she remembered he liked best. For several days she moved as though in a dream, thinking of nothing but
Are and what she might do to comfort him. When he showed a
good appetite, she sat watching him happily; when, once, he placed
his hand on hers to signify his thanks, she broke into tears of joy;
and when she tired him with incessant prattling, so that he pressed
his hand and the stump of his wrist against his ears and moaned
aloud, she closed her mouth and sat humbly silent for a full minute before commencing afresh.

All the house-folk were filled with compassion toward Are and
helped him in every way they could think of. The children feared
him at first, but soon came to like him. He loved especially to be
led down to the river in the mornings and sit fishing on the bank,
with someone to help him bait and cast his line. Blackhair was
his favorite fishing companion, and Rapp, too, whenever the latter
had time, perhaps because, of all the household, they most liked
to sit in silence like himself.

Everyone was curious to know more of the bad luck that had
befallen him, for Orm had told them all that he had been able to
learn during the journey from Kivik. Olof Summerbird sent his
men home with his salt, keeping only two of them with him at
Gröning; he told Ylva that he would like, if he might, to stay until
they had succeeded in discovering more of Are's secret, as he had
the feeling that it might contain matter of some importance. Ylva
was happy to let him stay, for she liked him and was always glad
when he visited them; besides which, she observed that his eyes
turned ever more frequently toward Ludmilla, who was by now a
full-grown woman of fifteen, waxing lovelier every day.

"It is lucky for us that you are willing to stay," said Orm, "for
we shall never learn much from Are without your help; you are the

only one of us here who knows Miklagard and the people who live in it."

But, despite all their efforts and those of the priest and the women, they could not elicit much more of Are's story. The only certain new fact they learned was that what had been done to him had been done on the river Dnieper, in the land of the Patzinaks, near the great portage beside the weirs. But more than that they could not discover; and Olof Summerbird found it difficult to imagine what Byzantines could be doing there.

Then Orm thought of a plan that might help them. Are was skilled in the use of runes; so Orm bade Rapp make a board of limewood, white and smooth, in order that Are might write on it in coal with the hand that had been left to him. Are was eager to do this and worked hard at it for a time; but with his left hand he could write only awkwardly and, in his blindness, he blurred his runes into one another, so that nobody could make out what he wished to say. At length he was seized with anger and flung the board and the coal away and would try no more.

In the end, it was Rapp and the priest who thought of a better method, one day while they were sitting and scratching their heads about the matter. Rapp axed a short beam of wood, smoothed and polished it, and carved on its surface the sixteen runes, very large and clear, with a deep groove separating each from the next. They put the beam into Are's hands, bidding him feel it; and when he understood what they intended, it could be seen that his heart was lightened. For now he was able to touch rune after rune to make the words he wished to say, and Father Willibald sat beside him with sheepskin and pen, writing down the words as Are spelled them out. At first the work went slowly and with difficulty, but gradually Are came to learn the position of each rune, and everyone sat full of joy and expectation as intelligible sentences began to appear on the sheepskin. Each evening the priest read out to them what he had written down during the day. They listened greedily, and after three weeks the whole story lay written there. But the first part of it, which told where the treasure lay hidden, he read only to Orm.

CHAPTER THREE

CONCERNING THE STORY OF THE BULGAR GOLD

ℬAM the poorest of men, for my eyes have been taken from me, and my tongue and my right hand, and my son, whom the Emperor's treasurer killed. But I can also call myself the richest, for I know where the Bulgar gold lies hidden. I shall tell you where it lies, that I may not die with the secret still hidden in my breast, and you, priest, shall repeat it to my brother, but to no other man. He shall then decide whether he wishes it to be repeated for other ears.

In the river Dnieper, where the portage climbs beside the great weirs, just below the third weir as a man comes from the south, off the right bank between the skull-mound of the Patzinaks and the small rock in the river on which the three rosebushes grow, under the water in the narrow channel where the rock-flat is broken, hidden beneath large stones where the rock-flat juts out and hides the bed beneath—there lies the Bulgar gold, and I alone know its hiding-place. As much gold as two strong men might carry lies drowned there, in four small chests sealed with the Emperor's seal, together with silver in five sacks of skin, and the sacks are heavy. This treasure first belonged to the Bulgars, who had stolen it from many wealthy men. Then it became the Emperor's, and from him it was stolen by his treasurer, Theofilus Lakenodrako. Then it became mine, and I hid it where it now lies.

I shall tell you how all this came about. When I first came to Miklagard, I entered the Imperial bodyguard, as many Northmen had done before me. Many Swedes serve in it, and Danes too, and men from Norway, and from Iceland also, far out in the western sea. The work is good, and the pay also, though I came too late to partake in the plundering of the palace when the Emperor John Zimisces died, which was a fine plundering, still much talked of among those who took part in it. For it is the ancient custom there that whenever an emperor dies, his bodyguard is permitted to plunder his palace. There is much that I could tell you, priest, but I shall speak only of those things that it is necessary to know, for this fumbling upon a beam wearies me. I served in the bodyguard for a long while, and became a Christian and took a woman to wife. She was called Karbonosina, which means with coal-black eyebrows, and was of good family according to Byzantine reckoning, for her father was brother to the wife of the second wardrobe-master of the three royal Princesses.

You must know that in Miklagard, as well as the Emperor Basil, who is childless, there rules also Constantine, his brother, who is also called Emperor. But Basil is the true Emperor. It is he who rules the land and crushes revolts and goes to war each year against the Bulgars and Arabs, while Constantine, his brother, sits at home in the palace playing with his treasure and his courtiers and the eunuchs who crowd about him. When any of them tells him that he is as good as his brother, or better, he strikes the speaker on the head with his little black staff, which bears a gold eagle on it, but the blow is always light, and the speaker is afterwards rewarded with rich gifts. He is a cruel man when his humor is darkened, and worst when he is drunk.

It is he who is father to the three Princesses. They are held to be greater than all other people in the world, save the Emperors themselves; for they are the only children of Imperial blood. Their names are: Eudokia, who is hunchbacked and disfigured by the pox, and whom they keep hidden; Zoe, who is one of the fairest of women, and who has lusted eagerly after men since she was a young girl; and Theodora, who is weak-brained and pious. They are unmarried, for there is no man in the world worthy to marry them, say the Emperors—which has for years been a source of vexation to Zoe.

We of the bodyguard took it in turns to go to war with the Emperor Basil and to remain in the palace with his brother. There is much that I remember and would tell you, but this telling goes slowly, and I shall now speak to you of my son.

My woman called him Georgios and had him christened thus, I being in the field with the Emperor when he was born. For this I whipped her on my return, and called him Halvdan, a good name. When he grew up, he was known by both names. With her and others he conversed in the Greek tongue, which is the speech that women and priests use there, but with me he spoke our tongue, though the learning of it came more slowly to him. When he was seven years old, my woman ate a surfeit of mussels and died; and I took no other wife, for it is a bad thing to marry a foreign woman. The women of Miklagard are worth little. As soon as they marry, they become thoughtless and lazy, and childbearing ages them and makes them fat and insubordinate. When their husbands try to tame them, they run shrieking to their priests and bishops. They are not like our women, who are understanding and work diligently and whom childbearing makes wiser and more comely. This was the opinion of all of us Northmen who served in the bodyguard. Many of us changed our wives every year and still were not satisfied.

But my son was my joy. He was shapely and swift-footed, quicktongued and merry. He was afraid of nothing, not even of me. He was such that women in the street turned to look at him when he was little, and turned more swiftly as he grew to manhood. This was his misfortune, but there was no help for it. He is dead now, but is seldom out of my thoughts. He and Bulgar gold are all I can think about. It could have become his, if all had gone well.

When my woman died, my son spent much time with her kinsfolk, wardrobe-master Symbatios and his wife. They were old and childless, for the wardrobe-master, as befitted one who worked in the royal women's apartments, was a eunuch. He was married, though, as Byzantine eunuchs often are. He and his wife both loved Halvdan, though they called him Georgios, and when I was away with the Emperor they took care of him. One day I returned from the wars to find the old man weeping for joy. He told me that my son had become the Princesses' playmate, especially Zoe's, and that Zoe and he had already fought and proved equally strong, she being two years older than he. Although they had fought, she had said that she much preferred him as a playmate to the Metropolitan Leo's niece, who fell on her knees and wept when anyone tore her clothes, or chamberlain Nikeforos's son, who was harelipped. The Empress Helena herself, he said, had clapped the boy on the head and called him a little wolf cub and told him he must not pull Her Imperial Highness Zoe's hair when she maltreated him. Gazing up at the Empress, the boy had asked her when he might pull it. At this the Empress had condescended to laugh aloud with her own mouth, which, the old man said, had been the happiest moment in his life.

These are childish things, but to remember them is one of the few joys that remain to me. In time things changed. I pass over many things, which would take too long to tell. But some five years later, when I was commanding a company of the bodyguard, Symbatios again came weeping to my chamber, but not this time for joy. He had that day gone to the innermost clothing chamber, where the coronation garments were kept, and which was seldom visited, to see if there were any rats there. Instead of rats, he had found Halvdan and Zoe playing a new kind of game together, a game the sight of which had terrified him exceedingly, on a bed they had made of coronation garments that they had dragged from their chests. As he stood there speechless, they had grabbed their clothes and disappeared, leaving the coronation robes, which were of purple-dyed silk from the land of the Seres,[1] severely crumpled, so that he knew not what to do. He had pressed them as well as he was able, and had replaced them carefully in their chests. There could, he said, be only one fate for him if this business was discovered—namely, that he would lose his head. It was lucky that the Empress was sick abed, for all the courtiers were in her chamber and had no time to think of anything else, which was the reason the Princess was less carefully guarded than usual and had been able to find this opportunity to seduce my son. There could be no doubt, he said, that the blame was wholly hers; for nobody could suspect a boy still in his thirteenth year of harboring such ideas. But nothing could alter what had happened, and he held this to be the worst stroke of ill luck that had ever befallen him.

I laughed at his story, thinking the boy had behaved like a true son of mine, and tried to comfort the old man by telling him that Halvdan was too young to be able to present Princess Zoe with a little emperor, however hard they might have striven to do so; and that though the coronation robes might be crumpled, they could hardly have sustained any real damage. But the old man continued to weep and moan. He said all our lives were in danger— his, his wife's, my son's, and my own—for the Emperor Constantine

---

[1] China. (The word "China" was not used in those times.)

would immediately order us to be killed if he ever learned of what had happened. Nobody, he added, could suppose that Zoe had been frightened at being discovered thus with Halvdan, for she was by now a full fifteen, and of a temper more akin to that of a burning devil than of a blushing virgin, so that it could not be doubted that she would shortly start afresh with Halvdan, he being the only person she was allowed to associate with who was not a woman or a eunuch. In time the scandal must inevitably be discovered, when Princess Zoe would receive an admonition from a bishop, and Halvdan and the rest of us would be killed.

As he spoke, I began to be afraid. I thought of all the people I had seen maimed and killed for offending the imperial humor during the years I had served in the bodyguard. We sent for my son and remonstrated with him for what he had done, but he said that he regretted nothing. It had not been the first time, he said, and he was no child who required seducing, but knew as much about love as Zoe. I realized that nothing now could keep them apart and that disaster would overtake us all if the affair was allowed to continue. So I shut him up in the wardrobe-master's house and went to call on the chief officer of the bodyguard.

He was called Zacharias Lakenodrako, and bore the title of Chief Sword-bearer, which is an office much honored among the Byzantines. He was an old man, tall and venerable-looking, with red and green jewels on his fingers, a wise and skillful talker, but sly and malignant, like everybody who holds high office in Miklagard. I bowed humbly before him, said that I was unhappy in the bodyguard, and begged that I might spend the remaining years of my service on one of the Emperor's warships. He considered this request and found it difficult to grant. At length he said he thought he might be able to arrange it if I did him a small service in return. It was his wish, he said, that the Archimandrite Sophron, who was the Emperor Constantine's confessor, should receive a sound drubbing, for the latter was his worst enemy and had of late been talking evil of him to the Emperor behind his back. He wanted, he said, no bloodshed, so that I must use no edged or pointed weapons against the Archimandrite, but merely stout sticks, which would make his flesh smart. He said the deed would best be done beyond the palace gardens in the evening when he was riding home from the Emperor on his white mule.

I answered that I had long been a Christian, and that it would be a great sin for me to thrash a holy man. But he admonished me like a father, explaining that I was wrong in my supposition. "For the Archimandrite," he said, "is a heretic, and confuses the two natures of Christ, which was the reason why we first became enemies. So it will be a pious action to thrash him. But he is a dangerous man, and you will be wise to take two men to help you. For before he became a monk he was chieftain of a band of robbers in Anatolia, and is still easily able to kill a man with a blow from his fist. Only strong men, such as serve in the bodyguard, will be able to give him the whipping he deserves. But I am sure your strength and wisdom will see the matter through. Take good sticks and strong men."

Thus spoke sword-bearer Zacharias, deceiving me and leading me into sin. God has since punished me for striking a holy man; for though he may have been evil, he was still holy. But I did not understand this then. I took with me two men on whom I could rely, Ospak and Skule, gave them wine and money, and told them we were going to beat a man who confused the two natures of Christ. It surprised them that three of us should be needed to beat one man, but when that evening we attacked the Archimandrite, their wonder ceased. As we rushed at him, I received a kick from his mule; and with his rosary, which he wore on his wrist and which consisted of heavy leaden beads, he gave Skule such a blow on the temples that he fell to the ground and remained there. But Ospak, a good man from Öland with the strength of a bear, dragged him from his saddle and threw him to the ground. By this time our blood was roused, so that we beat him worse than we would otherwise have done. He bellowed curses and roared for help; but nobody came, for in Miklagard, when anyone hears a cry for help, everyone runs in the opposite direction, lest he be arrested as perpetrator of the crime. At last we heard the sound of hoofs and we knew that the Khazar bowmen of the city watch were approaching; so we left the Archimandrite, who was by now unable to do anything save crawl, and departed. But we had to leave Skule there with him.

On the next day I went back to sword-bearer Zacharias, who was so pleased with the way everything had turned out that he acted honorably toward me. Everything, he said, leering with satisfaction,

had gone better than he could have hoped. Skule had been dead
when the watch had found him, and the Archimandrite was now
in prison charged with street-brawling and murder. There was
good hope that he would not be released before his ears had been
clipped, for the Emperor Constantine feared his brother, and the
Emperor Basil always meted out severe punishment to any monk
convicted of disorderly behavior and, moreover, disliked having
men of his bodyguard murdered. As a reward for the success of
my efforts, my request was to be granted immediately. He had, he
said, already spoken with important friends of his who held high
positions in the navy, and before long I would find myself a ship's
chieftain in one of the red ships, which were regarded as the finest
in the fleet.

Things turned out as he had promised, for even Byzantine
courtiers sometimes keep their word. So I was appointed to a good
ship and departed with my son from the palace and the perils it
contained for us. We rowed westwards to the land of Apulia,
where we fought Mohammed's servants, both those of Sicily and
those who belong to more distant lands. We stayed there a long
time and underwent many adventures, which it would take long
to relate. My son waxed strong and comely. I made him an archer
in my ship. He liked the sea, and we were happy there. But when
we were ashore, he was often foolish with women, as young people
are, and this caused quarrels between us. When we anchored in
the Emperor's harbors, Bari or Tarentum in Apulia, or Modon, or
Nepanto, where the great shipyards are, and where we received
our pay, there were always plenty of women to choose from, for
wherever sailors are with booty and pay, thither women always
flock eagerly. But there were also in these towns officers called
strategi, and silver-booted naval chieftains, and officials called
secretices and *logothetes* who dealt with matters of pay and booty.
They had their wives with them, beautiful women with dovelike
voices and white hands and painted eyes. They were full of witchcraft, and not for seafaring men, as I often told Halvdan.

But he paid small heed to my counsel. It was his fate that
women's eyes always turned toward him, and he thought none but
the best good enough for one who had lain with the Emperor's
daughter. The Byzantine women are fiery, and swift to cuckold
their husbands once their lust is aroused. But their men dislike

being cuckolded, and those in high office order the death of any young man who arouses their suspicions, and often kill their wives, too, that their minds may be set at rest and that they may marry again and be luckier. My advice to Halvdan was always to leave married women alone and to content himself with those whose virtue was their own business. If he had heeded my counsel, that which afterwards happened would never have happened. He would not be dead, and I should not be as I am. Neither should I be sitting here telling you of the Bulgar gold. It would have been better so.

It was not for the woman's sake that he was killed, but for that of the gold. But it was the woman who caused our ways to separate, and the rest followed.

It was then that sword-bearer Zacharias Lakenodrako spat the communion bread into the face of his enemy, the Archimandrite Sophron, who had by this time returned into the Emperor's favor, crying aloud before the assembled court that the Archimandrite had poisoned it. The Archimandrite was whipped for this and exiled to a distant monastery, but Zacharias, too, was dismissed from his office and had his ears clipped for dishonoring Christ. For it was held that, once a man had taken the body of Christ into his mouth, he ought to have the faith to swallow it, even if he knew it to be poisoned. When this news reached me from Miklagard, I laughed aloud, thinking that it would be difficult to decide which of the two men was the more evil, and that the ambitions of both to have the other's ears clipped had now been satisfied.

But Zacharias had a son called Theofilus. He was already thirty years old and was serving at the court. When his father lost his ears and his office, the son went to both Emperors and prostrated himself on the ground at their feet. He said that the sin his father had committed was, indeed, most foul, and the punishment inflicted upon him so mild that he wept for joy whenever he thought of it. In short, he praised the goodness of the two Emperors so enthusiastically that before very long the Emperor Basil appointed him naval treasurer. This meant that, for the future, he was to supervise the division of all booty won anywhere by the Emperor's ships, and was, besides, to be in complete charge of all matters concerning sailors' pay.

We came with the red fleet to Modon, to have our keels scraped and to be paid. Treasurer Theofilus was there, with his wife. I never saw her, but my son quickly did so, and she him. It was in church that their eyes first met, and although he was but a young archer and she a rich woman, it was not long before they met in secret and indulged their lust for each other. Of this I knew nothing until he came to me one day and told me he was weary of the sea and had hopes of a better position in the treasurer's household. The woman had told her husband that Halvdan was son to a man who had once done his father a service by spiting the Archimandrite, so that now Halvdan stood high not only in the woman's favor, but in that of her husband also.

When I heard the reasons for his appointment, I told him he might as well run a sword through his breast there and then as do what he intended to do. I also said that it was cruel of him to leave me alone and kinless for a woman's painted eyes. But he would have his way, and refused to hearken to my counsel. The woman, he said, was like a flame, and without flaw, and he would never be able to live without her. Besides which, he said, he would now grow rich and famous in the treasurer's service and would no longer have to continue as a poor archer. There was no danger, he said, of his being found out and killed, for, he bade me remember, he was half Byzantine and therefore better able than I to understand many things, including women. When he said this, I was gripped with fury and cursed his mother's name; and so we parted.

This was a great grief for me. But I thought that, in time, the woman would tire of him, or he of her, and that then he would come back. "Then," I thought, "when my service is finished, he will return with me home to the north and take a wife there and forget his Byzantine blood."

So time passed, and the Emperor Basil, who is the greatest warlord who has ever ruled in Miklagard, began a new campaign against the Bulgars. These people are bold warriors and terrible bandits, and plague their neighbors fearfully, so that they have excited the wrath of many emperors; and now the Emperor Basil had sworn an oath to destroy their kingdom and every man of them and hang their King in chains above his own city gate. He invaded their land with a mighty army, and his red fleet sailed up into the Black Sea to harry their coasts.

But twelve of the best ships were detailed upon a special mission, and mine was among them. We took soldiers from the army aboard, as many as the ships could hold, and sailed northwards along the coast till we reached the mouth of a river called Danube, which is the greatest of all rivers. The commander of our flotilla was named Bardas; he was in the biggest of our ships, and I heard, as we rowed up the river three abreast, that the naval treasurer was on board with him. At this I rejoiced, hoping to see my son again, if he was still alive. But why the treasurer should be accompanying us, none could say.

We heard the trump of war-horns ahead and, rounding a bend in the river, sighted a great fortress. It stood behind dikes and stockades on a hill not far from the river. All around was marsh and wilderness, with nothing to be seen but reeds and birds. We all marveled that our Emperor had sent us to so desolate a place as this. We put soldiers and archers ashore to storm the fortress. The Bulgars fought valiantly on their ramparts, and it was not until the second day that we gained the upper hand. I was wounded in my shoulder by an arrow and went back to my ship. There they drew out the arrow and dressed the wound; and as night fell, I sat on the deck and saw the fortress burn and the treasurer's men come back with prisoners, who staggered beneath the weight of the booty they were carrying. The ship that had carried Bardas and the treasurer lay at the end of our line, nearest to the fortress; then came two other ships, then mine, and then the rest in a line up the river. A short while after darkness had fallen, we heard shouts and alarums from one of the ships below us, and men cried from other ships to ask what might be afoot. I thought some of the men had probably been trying to steal the booty, and that Bardas was teaching them a lesson. But soon the noise ceased and everything became quiet, save for the baying of wolves who had scented meat. So I sat there, sleepless because of the pain in my arm.

Then a man came swimming toward my ship. I could hear him in the water, but could see nothing. I took a spear and bade him say who he was, for I feared the Bulgars might be upon us, but when I heard him reply, my heart leaped, for the voice was that of my son. When I had pulled him aboard, he sat there panting. I said: "It is good to see your face. I had small hope that we should meet again." He replied in a low voice: "Bardas has been murdered in his ship, and many others with him. The treasurer and his father have fled with the gold—more gold than anyone has ever seen. We must go after them and take it from them. Have you archers aboard?"

I gave him drink to calm him, and answered that I had some fifteen archers left aboard, the rest being ashore, but that I wished to know more about this gold, for this was the first I had heard of it.

Eagerly he replied: "The gold belonged to the Bulgar King, who kept it hidden here. The Emperor learned of this and sent us here with his treasurer, whom he trusted. I saw the gold as they were carrying it aboard, and helped to seal it with the Emperor's seal. But the treasurer hates the Emperor for what he did to his father. The old man is here with him, and they planned this together. All his men were bribed to help him, and when darkness fell they killed Bardas and his officers and the archers of his bodyguard. It was easy, for the others suspected nothing. But I thought to myself: 'This was lately the Emperor's gold, and while it was his it was a crime for any man to touch it. Now it is the treasurer's; but if it should be taken from him, whose will it be then?' I reasoned thus; then, when no one was looking, I slipped overboard into the river and swam here to you. They will not miss me, for they will think I have been killed in the fighting. But now answer me this question: whose shall the gold be if it is taken from them?"

I said: "This must be the reason that the treasurer anchored his ship farthest downstream, so that they might more easily escape in the darkness. If they have already fled, the gold will belong to whoever can take it from them and keep it; for such is the unwritten law of the sea. First they will float silently downstream in silence; then, when they are out of earshot, they will unship their oars. When it begins to grow light, they will set sail, and with this wind they will soon be well out to sea. It would be good to know where they are making for. There is much here that requires thought, and I do not want to do anything before I am sure which is the wisest course to follow."

Halvdan said: "The treasurer told me that we should flee to Tmutorokan, beyond Krim, where we would divide up the treasure, and then proceed to the country of the Khazars, to be safe from the Emperor's wrath; after which, he said, we might go where we pleased. He said this to the others also; so it is certain he does not intend to go there. But a short while before we started on this voyage, I heard him sitting mumbling with his father, just after some message had reached them, and I heard the old man say it was a good thing for them that the great Prince of Kiev had begun again to beget children upon his concubines and no longer honored his High Princess, our Emperor's sister, so that there was small friendship between him and the Emperor. I therefore think that they intend to flee to Kiev with the gold."

I said: "Halvdan, you are a wise boy, and I think you have guessed rightly. If they are heading for Kiev, they are sailing in a direction that suits us well, for they are taking it halfway home for us. If we let them reach Kiev, we shall find good men there willing to help us take it from them, if we find we cannot do so ourselves unaided. There is no need for us to start yet, for we must not let them see us following them over the sea, lest they should grow suspicious and alter their course. But a short while before it is light, when even the best ship's watchmen are asleep, let us leave this place silently. I have grieved much that you left me, Halvdan, but perhaps what happened was for the best, for this affair looks as if it may prove most luck for us both."

Thus spake I, foolishly; for what known god likes to hear men praise their luck before it has come to them?

I asked him about the woman who had seduced him. He replied that the treasurer had wearied of her and imprisoned her in a nunnery, because she had taken to defending herself when he tried to birch her. "And," he said, "when I found that she was lusting after other young men besides me, I, too, wearied of her."

This pleased me, and I promised him far finer women when we should bring the gold home to the north.

As the first gray appeared in the sky, we weighed anchor and swung out into the river, with our oars shipped and our rowers asleep on their benches, and glided downstream without anyone crying to ask whither we were going. When the crew and the archers awoke, I gave them better food than that to which they were accustomed, and stronger drink; then I told them that we were pursuing thieves who had fled with the Emperor's booty. More than that I did not tell them. It was not my intention to act dishonorably and steal one of the Emperor's ships, for I wished but to borrow it until I had achieved my purpose. I thought this not unjust, seeing that he owed me a year's pay.

We came out of the river and sailed across the sea, uncertain whether we had guessed rightly; but when we reached the mouth of the river Dnieper, we saw fishermen there and learned from them that one of the Emperor's red ships had entered the river the day before. My ship was smaller than the treasurer's, but I was not afraid, for I had Lezghian and Khazar archers aboard, good men for a fight, while he had only men of his own household.

Then there was heavy rowing with few intervals for resting, but whenever the rowers began to complain, I gave them a double measure of wine and comforted myself with the thought that the treasurer, with his heavier ship, must be in a worse plight. I saw no horse-herds on the banks, and no Patzinaks, at which we were glad; for when the Patzinaks are on the warpath, or are pasturing their horses on the riverbanks, they regard the river and all that moves on its surface as their own, so that no sailor dares land to cook his food. They are the most arrogant of peoples, and the worst robbers, and the Emperor himself pays them friendship-money every year.

On the fourth day the bodies of three men floated down the river. By the marks on their backs it could be seen that they were oarsmen of the treasurer who had grown tired. This I took as an encouraging sign, and I now began to hope we might overtake him at the weirs. On the next day more bodies floated downstream, but they did not belong to the treasurer's men. Then we found his ship, stranded on a tongue of land and empty. I realized from this that he had encountered a river ship and captured it, that he might proceed more swiftly and take his treasure more easily across the portage when he came to the weirs. For a keeled warship is no easy thing to drag overland.

Toward the evening of the eighth day we heard the splash of the weirs and reached the portage. There was nothing to be seen there save two oarsmen who had been left because they were too weak to row farther. We gave them wine, which revived them, and they told us that the treasurer had put his new ship on rollers that very day. But he had been unable to find either horses or oxen to harness to it, for the riverbanks were deserted, so that he had only his oarsmen to pull it, and they were all exceedingly weary. They could not, therefore, have got far.

Halvdan and I rejoiced when we heard this. We took archers with us and followed the tracks of the ship. Between the second and third weir, we sighted them. Then we turned inland and crept swiftly forward behind the burial mound of the Patzinak chieftains, which stands on a rise there, surmounted by skulls, and waited beside it with arrows in our bows until they had almost reached the spot where we were hiding. I saw the treasurer and his father walking beside the ship in full armor, with swords in their hands. I ordered four archers to mark them, and the others to kill the men who were in charge of the harnessed rowers.

The bows sang, men fell to the ground, and we all drew our swords and charged, whooping our battle-cry. The rowers dropped their ropes and fled, and all was confusion; but the treasurer and his father fell not, because the Devil and their good armor protected them. Zacharias the sword-bearer, who had been grazed by several arrows, fled quicker than anyone else, running like a youth. But I gave most of my attention to the treasurer. I saw him turn in astonishment, his face a sickly white above his black beard, as our arrows and war-whoops reached him. He gathered his men about him, roaring at them in a terrible voice, being pained at the prospect of being parted from so much gold. I wish he had stood his ground there longer.

Halvdan and I and the master of the archers, a Lezghian man named Abchar, were the first to reach them, and we fought with the men who stood protecting the treasurer. I saw him bare his teeth as he recognized Halvdan; but we could not get at him, for his men fought bravely, even though their leader was cowering behind them. Then the archers joined us, and we forced the treasurer's men back toward their ship; but when at last we broke their resistance, we found him fled and several of his men with him.

It was by now almost dusk, and I was uncertain what to do. The master of the archers was a man who always did as he was bidden without asking questions; I bade him take his men and pursue the enemy up the river as swiftly as he could, not pausing until darkness fell. I told him that the Emperor had put a price of a hundred pieces of silver on the treasurer's head, and a like sum on his father's, and that this would be paid in full to whoever brought me their heads. So he hastened away with his men.

So soon as Halvdan and I were left alone, we climbed up into the ship. There, in the cabin, hidden behind sacks and casks, lay the treasure, in four small chests and seven skin sacks, all sealed with the Emperor's seal. But sight of so much wealth caused me less joy than concern as to what we should do next, and how we should succeed in bringing it home without anyone else learning of its existence. Halvdan said: "We must hide this before the archers return." I said: "Where can we find a place large enough to hide so much?" He said: "Perhaps in the river." "You are right," I said; "wait here while I investigate."

I went to the river, and there found the place of which I have spoken, with the river frothing as it coursed over it. Together we carried the treasure there and hid it well, save two sacks of silver which, after much thought, I left in the ship.

Abchar and his men now returned. They carried three heads, but not those I most wished to see. Together we ate and drank food and wine that we found in the ship. Then I said to him: "Here, Abchar, you see these two sacks, sealed with the Emperor's seal. This is the treasure that the treasurer Theofilus and his father stole from the Emperor. Whether it is silver or gold I know not, for none may break the Emperor's seal. Now we are in a sore plight, for all this must speedily be brought intact to the Emperor; but I was commanded by him not to return without the treasurer's head. This, therefore, is what we must do. I and my son will go up the river to search for the treasurer, as far as Kiev; and two of your men, volunteers, shall go with us. But you and the rest of your men shall return to our ship with this treasure and bid the helmsman convey you to Miklagard. We four shall find our own way back, when our task has been accomplished."

Those were my words, and Abchar nodded and felt the weight of the sacks. He spoke to his men, and two Khazars volunteered to come with us. Abchar and the others departed with the silver-sacks, and I was glad that thus far all had gone well. I needed the two archers to help me in my quest for a boat, lest we should encounter robbers, or perhaps the treasurer himself, if he had managed to rally his men. I thought he would probably continue his flight from us, but in that I was wrong.

We were tired, and that night I took the first watch myself. Then I bade one of the Khazars replace me; but he must have slept, in order, perhaps, that our fatal destiny might be fulfilled. For during the night, while we were all asleep in the ship, the treasurer, with his father and four men whom he still had, fell upon us unawares. I was awakened by the clatter of stones as someone stumbled, and sprang to my feet with my sword drawn. Two men leaped at me and as I met them, I saw the treasurer fell one of the Khazars and charge at Halvdan, whirling his sword above his head. Halvdan must have been sleeping deeply, for he had barely managed to draw his sword; I would have given my life and all the gold to have come between them. The men who had engaged me fell dead, but I scarcely noticed them go down, for as I turned upon the treasurer, Halvdan was already lying at his feet. I hewed with both hands; it was my last blow, and my best. It cleft his helmet and chain hood, and split his skull so deeply that I saw his teeth fall out through his throat. But as death bit him, his sword entered my eye. I fell to the ground and knew that I was about to die; but the thought of that did not trouble me, for I thought: "Halvdan is dead, and I have avenged him, and everything is now finished."

This story wearies me, and there is little more to tell. The next I knew was that I was lying bound, and that sword-bearer Zacharias was sitting beside me, laughing, with a laugh that was not that of a man. He told me how I was to be maimed, and croaked much about the gold. I spat in his face and bade him show me his ears. He had one man left, and between them they chopped off my hand and heated oil from the ship to dip the stump in, so that I should not die too quickly. But he promised me a quick death if I would tell him where the gold was. I did not oblige him, fearing no pain, for my soul was dead. I told him the gold was on its way to the Emperor, and he believed me. We spoke no more.

Then I heard a scream, and a man whimpered and began to cough and then fell silent. Then I was lying in a boat that was being pulled across the ground. I was given drink, and knew nothing. Then the boat was floating on the water, and it seemed to me that I was dead. The man who was rowing talked much, and I understood some of what he said. He was the second Khazar. He was singing and whistling, and very merry. He had run away when we had been attacked, and had fled back to my ship, but it had gone. So he had returned and, creeping up close behind the men who were working on me, and killed them both with arrows. Why he troubled to save what remained of me no one can know; he may have been a good man, as Khazars often are. Two poor peasants had come over from the other bank to plunder the dead, and he had given them the treasurer's ship with all that it contained, on condition that they gave him their small boat and helped him carry me up the portage. Thus it happened; I know only what he said.

He laughed all the time and praised his luck, for on the bodies of the treasurer and his father he had found much silver and gold, and the arms and weapons that he had taken from them were of the finest workmanship. On the bodies of the other men, too, he had found money and jewels, and had, besides, taken a fine gold ring from the finger of my son. He was now, he told me, intending to buy horses in Kiev, and a woman or two, after which he would return to his own people, a rich man, in armor. He cared for me as well as he could while telling me all this. I wanted to drag myself over the side of the boat and drown, but was too weak to do so.

He knew that I wanted to go to Kiev, and when we reached the city, he handed me over to some monks. I wanted to reward him with silver, for he had left my belt untouched, but he would accept nothing. He had, he said, enough already, and had, besides, won favor with God for the way he had treated me.

I stayed with the monks and was nursed by them, until at length I grew better and began again to think of the gold. Then men from the north visited the monks and asked me questions. They understood that I wished to go home and learned that I had the means wherewith to pay them. So I ascended the river, one ship passing me on to another, until at last I came aboard the Gothlanders' ship, where I met Orm.

All the time the thought weighed heavily on me that I would never be able to tell anyone about the Bulgar gold and where it lies, even if, by some marvel, I should reach home and rejoin my kinsmen. But now, thanks to your cunning, priest, I have been enabled to tell everything and can die happier.

As to the gold, Orm may do as he thinks best. It is a great

treasure, enough for many men, and none can say what so much gold is worth, or how much blood has been spilled for its sake. It lies there in the place I spoke of and will not be hard to find for anyone who knows where to look for it. There is, besides, a mark near by which shows the place; the bones, by now pecked clean by crows, of the treasurer Theofilus and the sword-bearer Zacharias —may their souls wander without refuge till the end of time—and of my son, Halvdan, on whose soul God have mercy.

CHAPTER FOUR

HOW THEY PLANNED TO GET THE GOLD

AS soon as he learned about the gold, Orm sent a man with a message to Toke.

"Tell him," he said, "that there is question of a voyage after a great treasure in the Eastland, that he is the man whose advice I would most value on the matter, and that it would be good if he could come here quickly."

Toke needed no further persuasion than this, and before Are and the priest had finished telling their story he arrived at Gröning, eager to learn more of what was afoot. After he had been welcomed and had drunk a cup of ale, he said:

> "I heard word
> Of bellied sailcloth,
> Creak of oars,
> And gold in Eastland.
> Then I smelled
> A smell remembered:
> Salt of spray
> And black-pitched boat's keel."

But Orm replied, more soberly:

> "Twoscore years
> And their stored wisdom
> Curb men's lust

For distant faring;
No slight task
By stealth to pilfer
Far-drowned gold
In Gardarike.

"But the treasure is rich beyond imagination," he added, "and I have never needed counsel so urgently as in this affair. Ylva will not advise me; she says it is a matter that I must decide for myself, and it is not every day that she speaks thus. I have therefore asked you here to counsel me what to do. Here you see Olof Summerbird, who has himself been in the Eastland, and who is a man of much wisdom. Three heads are better than two when such an important matter as this has to be decided."

Orm then told Toke of all that had happened to Are and of the Bulgar gold; the only thing he did not tell him was where the gold lay hidden.

"That knowledge," he said, "I shall keep to myself until we reach the place. For gold can cause much bad luck; and if it should become known too soon where the gold lies, the information might come to the wrong ears, and other hands might touch it before mine. If this gold is ever to be lifted, it shall be lifted by my hands and no one else's; for it has been bequeathed to me by Are, who thinks of himself as dead. But to those who help me get it I shall, if our journey proves successful, give good shares of it. I have been restless ever since I heard of this gold, and sometimes have hardly been able to sleep for thinking of it. What troubles me most is that, if I go in search of it, I shall be away from my home here for a long while and shall continually be plagued with anxiety for the safety of my house and family. Besides which such a voyage will necessitate the expenditure of much money on a good ship and crew. And if, in spite of all this, I seek the gold and then find that some thief has got there before me, I shall have wasted a great deal of money."

Toke said unhesitatingly that, for his part, he was ready and willing to make the voyage. "And my advice to you, Orm," he said, "is to go in search of this gold. For if you do not, you will sit here brooding over it until you can neither sleep nor eat, and will never again be merry-hearted. Indeed, I should not be surprised if you brooded yourself out of your senses. It is your fate to go and look for this gold, and you cannot escape it; and I have known men have worse fates than that. True, it will be a long voyage, but you cannot expect to get so large a treasure as this without some trouble. As for me, the skin-trade is bad just now, and my wife pregnant, so that I have nothing to keep me from coming with you."

"Rapp gave me the same advice," said Orm, "but when he did so, he supposed that he would be accompanying me. But when I told him that he would have to remain here to guard the house and my family, he changed his tone and bade me forget the gold and stay at home. Father Willibald advised me as I had known he would, telling me that I am rich enough already, and old enough to be thinking more of heavenly than of earthly riches. But I find it difficult to be at one with him in this matter."

"The priest is wrong," said Toke, "however wise he may be in other matters. For it is so with men that the older they become, the more they hanker after goods and gold. So it was even with King Harald, my woman tells me, and he was the wisest of men, even if he was once fooled by me. I myself grow yearly more resentful of the Gotland merchants at Kalmarna, even when they pay me value for my skins, which is seldom."

"The years affect a man in more respects than one," said Orm, "and I am not sure that I could endure a long voyage as well as I used to."

"I am older than you," said Toke, "and the years do not weigh upon me. Besides which, it is not so long since, if reports be true, you killed two berserks with a broomstick. That may, without exaggeration, be described as a bold feat, and shows that you still retain some remnant of your youthful vigor, even though you yourself would like to believe that it is otherwise. I am told that your daughter Ludmilla was the subject of the quarrel; if that is so, she will be much envied by women and coveted by men. But let us hear what Olof Summerbird has to say about the matter."

"Orm and I have discussed it deeply," said Olof thoughtfully, "and I have been as double-minded as he, unable to decide which will be the wisest course for him to take. I know better than most men how arduous this voyage will be, and how great the dangers we shall encounter; but when a man has a ship filled with good men, much may be achieved. Orm wishes me to join him in this expedition, if he decides to undertake it. There are reasons why I should not; but it is true that my presence would be of use to you, for I know the whole long road to Miklagard, and the great river, and the perils that lie in its water and on its banks. I have at last decided and my answer is this: seek the gold, Orm, and I will come with you if you will give me your daughter Ludmilla to be my wife."

Orm stared at him in astonishment. Toke roared with laughter.

"What did I say?" Toke said. "Here is the first of the flock."

"You have a wife already," said Orm.

"I have two," said Olof, "for such is the custom of chieftains in Finnveden. But if you give me your daughter, I will send them away."

"I could think of worse sons-in-law," said Orm reflectively, "and it might be good to marry her off before more berserks come roaring around her. But this is a serious matter, which requires consideration. Have you talked with my women about it?"

"It would have been dishonorable of me to have spoken with them before I had asked your feelings in the matter," replied Olof. "But I think Ylva will not be unwilling to have me as a son-in-law. She knows, as you do, that I am the richest chieftain in all Finnveden, with sevenscore head of cattle, and heifers besides; and that I come of a very ancient line."

"Of my own line I shall say nothing," said Orm, "though some would regard it as better than most men's, for the blood of Ivar of the Broad Embrace flows in my veins, and it was after him that my youngest son was named. Do not forget that my daughter is granddaughter to King Harald Bluetooth, so that you could not find a bride of nobler blood if you were to search every great house in Smaland. You will have to drive your present wives farther from your straw than to the brewhouse or garden cottage if you wish to wed my daughter; and you will not find her a meek wife if you take other women to your bed once you have married her."

"She is worthy to be accorded such an honor," said Olof, "and, indeed, I have already noticed that it is difficult to keep the peace in the house when a man has more wives than one. But I am happy that you are not opposed to the match, and thank you for it."

"Do not thank me yet," said Orm. "First we must hear what

Ylva has to say about it. It is I who shall decide whether or not
the marriage will take place, but a wise man always allows his
wife to speak when so important a matter as this has to be decided."

So Ylva was sent for. When she heard what the matter was, she
said that it did not altogether surprise her.

"And I think such a suitor should not be denied," she said, "for,
Olof, you are both rich and of noble family, so that a better match
would not easily be found in these parts. Besides, you are a man
of good sense, which has always seemed to me to be a quality worth
having in a husband. It is true that you would have impressed me
more with your wisdom if you had asked for Oddny, who is meek
and submissive and no less well-shaped than her sister; but in matters such as this a man must choose as his inclinations lead him
and cannot choose otherwise. It suits me well that you have chosen
Ludmilla, for she is unruly and difficult to live with; but women
sometimes improve when they have found a man."

"That is true," said Toke. "There is no harm in the girl. Her
temper is no worse than yours was when Orm and I first met you
in your father's castle. But you tamed quickly, and I have never
heard Orm regret his choice."

"You talk nonsense, Toke," said Ylva. "I was never tamed. We
of Gorm's blood do not tame; we are as we are, and shall be so
even when we appear before the judgment throne of God Himself.
But Orm killed Sigtrygg, you must remember, and gave me
Almansur's chain; and then I knew that he belonged to me, for
no other man would have acted thus. But do not speak to me of
taming."

"That chain proved useful," said Orm. "I do not think anyone
can deny that. Perhaps we shall have another such for Ludmilla
when we have returned home with the gold. You must now speak
to the girl yourself, Olof; and then she shall be regarded as your
betrothed. You shall be married to her as soon as we have returned
from our voyage if you can get rid of your wives as easily as you
claim to be able to."

Olof said that such matters presented no difficulty in Finnveden;
one merely paid one's women well, and they went. This would
take no time, and he saw no reason why the marriage should not

take place before they started. But both Orm and Ylva opposed this suggestion, and at length he yielded.

So far all had gone well for Olof Summerbird in this business, even if he had not had matters entirely as he wished them to be. Ludmilla received his suggestion amiably, and they began at once to discuss their plans. It was evident that she was well satisfied with the prospect of becoming his wife, even if she afterwards confided in Oddny and Ylva that she felt that so great a chieftain might have come with his hands full of ornaments. She asked him if he was ill-tempered when he was drunk, and whether he was merrier in the mornings or the evenings; and she wished to know exactly how the two women looked of whose company he was depriving himself for her sake, as well as details concerning his house and cattle, the number of his slaves and serving-maids, and a precise account of all that he had in his coffers. To all these questions he returned satisfactory answers.

But when Father Willibald heard what was afoot, he was by no means pleased. For in their excitement it had not occurred to them that Olof Summerbird was not a Christian, and this fact greatly troubled Father Willibald. A Christian maiden, whom he had baptized with his own hand, could not, he said, be bestowed upon a heathen; and this marriage could only take place if Olof first allowed himself to be baptized. On this point there was now a sharp exchange of opinions among the women, for Asa sided with the priest, while Ylva and Ludmilla opposed him. At length Orm told them to stop arguing and close their mouths; their immediate concern, he said, was to plan the voyage, and they would have time enough to discuss this other matter later. If Olof was prepared to allow himself to be baptized, he said, all would be well; if not, he was to have the girl none the less.

"For she will have plenty of opportunities to convert him," he said, "if she thinks it worth her while to try."

Asa rebuked him sharply for this judgment; but Orm bade her think of Are and remember that his present condition was the work of Christian hands.

Father Willibald sat dejected in his chair. He said that since the thousandth year had passed without Christ appearing in the sky, people had shown less willingness to become converted. "If things continue the way they are going," he added, "the Devil will triumph after all, and you will all become heathens again."

But Orm bade him be cheerful and not think so ill of them all. "I am content with Christ," he said, "and I hope He will remain content with me, even if I marry my daughter to the suitor who pleases me best. Much will have to happen before I abandon Him, for He has always helped me well."

Toke said that this reminded him that he had news from Värend which would interest them all.

"You doubtless remember the priest Rainald," he said, "the fellow who, for Christ's sake, knocked old Styrkar down from the Stone. The old woman to whom he was given as a slave is now dead, and he is a free man and much admired and respected. He is still a priest, but no longer serves Christ. For he wearied of Him while he was the old woman's slave, and now he curses everything that has to do with Him, and follows the old god Frey instead, and is amassing great wealth by his knowledge of witchcraft. All women obey him, whatever he commands them to do, and hold him to be the best priest there has ever been among the Virds. And I have heard it said that he has gathered a band of followers and has set himself up as a chieftain for vagabonds and outlaws."

Father Willibald heard this news with horror. Hereafter, he said, he would no longer offer prayers for this man; he had never before heard of a Christian priest giving himself openly to the Devil.

Ylva thought that he had had good qualities, and that it was a pity that things had gone so ill with him. But Orm laughed.

"Let him and the Devil do as they please together," he said. "We have more important matters to worry about."

He was now no longer doubtful whether or not to voyage after the gold. Between them they decided that if they managed to buy a good ship down at the coast, they would sail at midsummer.

"Our hardest task will be to find a good crew," said Orm. "We must have good sailors, who know the ways of ships, but there are few of them to be found here, inland, and it will be dangerous to hire men who are not known to us, with such a cargo as we hope to be bringing home. It might be wise to take but a few men, for then we shall have less money to pay out; but it might be wiser to take many, for we do not know what dangers await us."

CHAPTER FIVE

HOW THEY SAILED TO THE GOTLAND VI

OLOF SUMMERBIRD rode home to make ready for the voyage and to hire men whom he knew in Halland to serve as crew, while Orm, Toke, and Harald Ormsson rode down to the coast in search of a ship. At the mouth of the river they found one for sale. The man who owned it was growing old and wanted to sell it in order to have a good inheritance to leave his daughters when he died. They examined it carefully and found it in good order. It carried twenty-four pairs of oars; ships of such a size were reckoned to be large, but Orm thought it could without harm have been bigger, and Toke agreed with him.

"For great chieftains will be sailing in it," he said, "and thirty pairs of oars would not be too many for us."

"When we come to the portage, which Olof Summerbird has told us of," said Harald Ormsson, "we may be glad that it is no larger."

"You are luckier even than I had supposed you to be, Orm," said Toke, "for I see that wisdom does not reside in you only, but in your children also."

"It is a bad thing when a man receives instruction from his son," said Orm, "and it shall not happen in my house, so long as I retain my tongue and my good right arm. But in this instance I admit that the boy is right. This will be heavier work than when we dragged St. James' bell."

"We were young men then," said Toke. "Now we are great chieftains and shall not need to touch the rope ourselves. The young men will strain at the harness, while we walk beside them with our thumbs in our belts, marveling at the paucity of their strength. But it may be that a ship such as this will be too big for them to manage."

At length, after much bargaining, Orm bought the ship.

Around the mouth of the river, there lay great houses; and from these he bought malt, hogs, and oxen and arranged with the farmers that they should brew, butcher, and smoke his purchases, that the ship might be well provided with food and drink. He was astonished when he discovered how much all this was to cost him in silver; his astonishment became even greater when he sought to hire a number of young men from the houses for a year's voyage; and he rode dejectedly home with the others, mumbling that this Bulgar gold would surely bring him into poverty and wretchedness.

"One thing I have learned," said Harald Ormsson, "namely, that a man needs to have much silver before he can go in search of gold."

"That is well said," said Toke. "If you continue as you have begun, you will, with experience, become as wise as your mother's father was. The old ones used to say that from Odin's bracelet a new bracelet used to issue every Wednesday, so that he came to have many; but that if he had not had the first, he would never have had any. Never set yourself up as a Viking if you have not plenty of silver; nor as a skin-trader, neither. That is my advice to you. Only poets can win wealth with empty hands; but then they must make better songs than other poets, and competition spoils the pleasures of composition."

On their way home, they rode in to speak with Sone the Sharp-Sighted, for Orm had a request that he wished to make to him.

Sone's house was large, with many rooms, and was everywhere full of his sons and their children. He himself, by this time, was immeasurably old and very frozen, and spent all his time sitting by the fire and mumbling to himself. Orm greeted him respectfully. After a few moments Sone recognized him, nodded amiably, asked him for news, and began to talk about his health. This was less good than it had been, but nothing to grumble about; and one good thing, he said, was that he still had his understanding left to him, in prime condition, so that it was still, as before, better than other men's.

A crowd of his sons had come in to greet the visitors and listen to them. They were powerful men, and of all ages. When they heard their father speak of his understanding, they cried that the old man was talking nonsense; there was, they said, nothing left of his understanding, but only his tongue and chatter. Resenting this, Sone brandished his stick and quieted them.

"They are foolish boys," he said to Orm. "They think that my understanding has been used up by begetting all of them, and that I have none left for myself. But that, as may easily be observed, is not the case; for little of it have they inherited from me. Sometimes it happens that I confuse their names, or forget one altogether, and that angers them, so that they talk ill of me. But the truth is that names are not a thing that it is important to remember."

"I have come here partly to see you," said Orm, "and partly to see your sons. I intend to sail forth shortly on a long voyage, to Gardarike, to claim an inheritance. I have already bought a ship. It may be that I shall need good fighting-men on this voyage. Now I have always heard your sons praised as bold men, and it therefore seemed to me that it would be a good thing if I could have some of them with me in my ship. I shall pay them honorably, and if all goes well, there may be silver to be shared out among such of us as survive the voyage."

Sone became excited at this news. Better tidings he had not heard for many a day, he said, and he would be glad to send a flock of his sons to aid Orm. It was time that they went out into the world and learned wisdom and understanding. Besides which, he said, it would make things less crowded in the house.

"They are too many for me, now that I am old," he said. "Take half of them with you, and it will be to the advantage of us both. Do not take the eldest ones, nor yet the youngest, but a half score of those between. They have never been in a ship, but will serve for fighting."

Some of his sons were immediately willing to go; others pondered the matter and then agreed to come. They had heard tell how Orm had killed his two berserks, and thought him a chieftain after their liking. They conferred with Orm about the voyage late into the evening, and the end of it was that eleven of them agreed to come with him. They promised to be ready by midsummer, when Orm would come to collect them.

Toke thought this a good addition to their strength, for these men looked to him likely to render good service. Orm, too, was pleased, so that when they rode away on the following morning, his dejection had left him.

When they reached home, everyone came running out to meet

them with sad news. Are was dead; his body had lately been fished up out of the river. Blackhair was the only person who had seen what had happened, and he had little to tell. He and Are had been sitting together fishing, and Are had been as usual, save that he had, once and then again, stroked Blackhair across his cheeks and hair. After a short while he had risen suddenly to his feet, made the sign of the cross thrice upon his breast, and had then strode forth into the river with bold steps until, reaching that part where the water was deepest, he had disappeared. He had not been seen again, and Blackhair had been unable to do anything to save him. It had been a long time before Rapp had found his body.

When the news of this had been brought to Asa, she had taken to her bed and prayed that she might die. Orm sat with her and comforted her as well as he could. Any man, he said, who had been treated as Are had been treated might be forgiven for wearying of life; and it was clear that he longed to escape from his wretchedness and seek peace with God, now that he had imparted to his kinsfolk his knowledge of the Bulgar gold.

"From God," he said, "he will by now have received back his sight, his tongue, and his right hand; besides which, I doubt not, he has also found his son again. That is no small sum of things to win, and any wise man would have done the same."

Asa agreed with his reasoning; none the less, she found his death a hard thing to endure, and it was three days before she was able to move about again. They buried Are beside the church, near the place where Father Willibald had interred the two heads that Östen of Öre had hewn from the holy men. Asa chose a place for herself next to Are, for she thought it would not be long before she would go to join him.

Toke now rode home to make preparations for the voyage, and shortly before midsummer he and Olof Summerbird arrived at Gröning with good men accompanying them. Olof had had much to do; he had given his two wives rich compensation and driven them out of his house, though one of them had been unwilling to go and had resisted stubbornly. There was, therefore, now no obstacle to his taking Ludmilla in honorable marriage, and when he appeared at Gröning he expressed his wish that the ceremony might be performed immediately. But Orm held to his decision, finding it

foolish of Olof to think of marrying the girl before the voyage
was completed.

"She is betrothed to you," he said, "and with that you must rest
satisfied. A newly married man is a poor comrade to have on a long
voyage. We have shaken hands upon the bargain, and you must
stand by our original agreement. First let us get the gold; then,
when that is done, you shall have my daughter as reward for your
good help. But it is, I think, nowhere customary to pay first and
receive help afterwards."

Olof Summerbird was a reasonable-minded man in all matters,
and he could not deny that Orm had spoken wisely; he himself had
no argument to advance but the great desire he felt for the girl,
which was such that it was a source of merriment to them all. She
could not come near him but his voice changed and he struggled
hard for breath; he said himself that such a thing had never happened to him before. Ludmilla was as eager as he was that the
marriage should take place as soon as possible, but knew that Orm
was not to be persuaded from his original decision. Olof and she
agreed, however, that there was no reason for them to be downhearted, seeing that they felt the same toward each other.

Before his departure Orm made careful plans to arrange how
everything should be in the house during his absence. Rapp was
to remain at home and be in charge of everything, though up to
the last moment he grumbled in the hope that Orm might change
his mind and allow him to go with the others. Orm saw to it that
he had sufficient men left with him to do the work and protect
the house. Ylva was to see to the house itself and all that went on
inside it, and nothing important was to be done without her
consent. Harald was to remain at home, for Orm was unwilling to
risk his first-born on so dangerous a voyage, and Harald himself
showed no particular desire to go; but Glad Ulf was allowed to
come with them and, at length, Blackhair also, after he had besought Orm and Ylva with many prayers. The obstinacy of his
desire to go drove Ylva more than once to weep tears of grief and
rage. She asked him what he thought a thirteen-year-old boy could
do in a company of full-grown fighting-men; but he said that if
he was not permitted to sail in this ship, he would run away and
join another, and Glad Ulf promised to take better care of Blackhair than of himself. That, thought Blackhair, was not necessary;

however, he promised always to be careful, though he said that he fully intended to do his worst to men who robbed honest people of their eyes, if he should happen to encounter any of them. He now had both a sword and a spear, and regarded himself as a fully-fledged warrior. Orm was pleased at the prospect of having him with him, though he did not allow Ylva to know this.

Father Willibald preached a great sermon about people going down to the sea in ships, and blessed them all with a lengthy blessing. Toke and Olof Summerbird and the heathen men they had brought with them sat and listened to the sermon with the others and agreed that they all felt hugely strengthened after the blessing. Many of them after the service went to the priest and, drawing their swords, asked for a blessing on them also.

When the time came for their departure, the women wept loudly, and among those who were going away there were not a few who felt grief. But most of them were glad at the prospect of adventure and promised to bring fine things home with them when they returned; and Orm felt well contented to be riding at the head of so proud a company.

They came to Sone the Sharp-Sighted to collect his sons, who speedily made themselves ready. The old man was sitting on a bench against the house wall, warming himself in the sun. He ordered his sons, the eleven who were leaving him, to come to him one by one, that he might bid them each farewell. They did so, and he gazed earnestly at them, mumbling their names and addressing each one correctly without exception. When the last of them had saluted him, he sat silent, staring straight before him; then a tremor ran through his limbs, and he laid his head back against the wall and closed his eyes. At this his sons shifted their feet and murmured uneasily: "Now he sees! He sees!" After a while he opened his eyes again and looked around with an absent expression, as though he had just awakened from a long sleep. Then he blinked, moistened his lips, nodded to his sons, and said that they might now start on their voyage.

"What did you see?" they asked.

"Your fate," he answered.

"Shall we come back?" they all cried eagerly.

"Seven shall come back."

"But the four others?"

"They shall remain where they shall remain."

All the eleven crowded round him, begging him to say which of them would not return.

"If four of us are doomed to die out there, it is best that those four should stay at home, so that no harm may come to them."

But the old man smiled sadly.

"Now you talk foolishly," he said, "as you often do. I have seen the web that the Spinners are spinning, and for four of you there is but a short time left. Their thread no man can lengthen. Four of you must die, whether they go or stay; which four will be revealed to you in good time."

He shook his head and sat buried in thought. Then he said: "It is no joy for a man to see the Spinners' fingers, and few are they who see them. But I am granted that vision, though I would gladly not see it. But the faces of the Spinners I have never seen."

Again he sat silent. Then he looked at his sons and nodded.

"Go now," he said. "Seven of you will return. That is enough for you to know."

His sons protested no longer, for it was as though a shyness had come over them in the old man's presence; and so it was also with Orm and all his following. But as they rode away, the sons continued for some time to mutter bitterly against the old man and the strangeness of his ways.

"I should have liked to ask him how I would fare," said Toke, "but I dared not."

"I had the same thought," said Olof Summerbird, "but I, too, lacked the courage."

"It may be that his words were but empty talk," said Orm, "though it is true that the old woman at Gröning, too, sometimes sees what is to be."

"Only a man who does not know him could think his words empty talk," said one of Sone's sons who was riding beside them. "It will happen as he has foretold, for so it has always been. But by telling us this he has made it worse for us than he knows."

"I think he is wiser than most men," said Toke. "But is it not a comfort to you all to know that seven of you will return safe and sound?"

"Seven," replied the other darkly, "but which seven? Now we brothers cannot have a merry moment until four of us are dead."

"So much the merrier will that moment be," said Orm; at which Sone's sons grunted doubtfully.

When they had reached the ship and sent their horses home, Orm straightway set his men to repaint the dragon-head; for if their ship was to enjoy good luck, it was necessary that its dragon-head should gleam as redly as blood. They carried everything aboard, and each man took his place. At first Orm was unwilling to sacrifice a goat for luck on the voyage; but in this everyone opposed him, so that at last he yielded.

"You may be as Christian as you will," said Toke, "but at sea the old customs are still the best; and if you do not comply with them, you may as well jump headfirst into the sea where the water is deepest."

Orm agreed that there might be some truth in this, though he found it hard that the price of a goat should now be added to all that he had had to pay out for this voyage before it had yet begun.

At last all was ready; and as soon as the goat's blood had streamed down the bows, they sailed out in fine weather with a good favorable wind. Ever since his boyhood Toke had known the waters as far east as Gotland, and he had undertaken to pilot the ship until they reached the Gotland Vi. Beyond, few knew how the waters ran; but they reckoned to be able to hire a pilot there to help them, for there were many pilots in Gotland.

Orm and Toke were both happy to be at sea again; it was as though many of the burdens that oppressed them ashore had suddenly fallen from them. When they sighted the coast of Lister in the distance, Toke said that the life of a skin-trader was, in truth, a hard one, but that now he felt once more as light of heart as when he had first sailed forth with Krok.

"I cannot understand why I have kept away from the sea for so long," he said, "for a well-manned ship is the best of all things. It is good to sit contented ashore, and no man need be ashamed to do so; but a voyage to a far land, with booty awaiting a man and this smell in his nostrils, is as good a lot as could be desired, and a sure cure for age and sorrow. It is strange that we Northmen, who know this and are more skillful seamen than other men, sit at home as much as we do, when we have the whole world to plunder."

"Perhaps," said Orm, "some men prefer to grow old ashore rather than to risk encountering that surest of all cures for age that seafarers sometimes meet with."

"I smell many odors," said Blackhair in a distressed voice, "but think none of them good."

"That is because you are unaccustomed to them and know no better," replied Orm. "It may be that the sea-smell here is not so rich as that in the west, for there the sea is greener with salt and so has a richer tang to it. But this smell is nothing to complain of."

To this Blackhair made no reply, for the seasickness had come over him. At first he was much ashamed of this, but his shame became less when he saw that many of the inland-dwellers were also beginning to hang over the ship's side. One and another of them were soon heard to beg in unsteady voices that the ship might be turned back at once, before they all perished.

Orm and Toke, however, stood by the steering-oar and found everything to their liking.

"They will have to grow used to it, poor wretches," said Orm. "I, too, once suffered thus."

"Look at Sone's sons," said Toke. "Now they have something besides their father's prophecy to worry about. It takes time for landlubbers to appreciate the beauty of life at sea. With this wind, though, they can vomit to windward without its blowing back into the face of the next man, and many quarrels between irritable persons will thereby be avoided. But I doubt whether they appreciate this. Understanding does not come naturally to a man at sea, but only by experience."

"It comes in time," said Orm, "however painful the process. If the wind drops, they will have to take to the oars, and I fear those who are not used to rowing will find the sport somewhat strenuous in such a sea as this. Then they will look back regretfully on the time when they were free to vomit in peace and had no need to toil."

"Let us make Olof overseer," said Toke. "The task needs someone who is used to commanding obedience."

"Obeyed he may be," said Orm, "but his popularity will suffer for it. It is a hard office for a man to perform, and hardest when the rowers are free men who are not used to the whip."

"It will occupy his mind," said Toke. "From his face, his thoughts would appear to be elsewhere; which I can well understand."

Olof Summerbird was in a deep melancholy. He had seated himself on the deck beside them; he looked sleepy and said little. After a while he mumbled that he was unsure whether it was the seasickness or the lovesickness that was weighing on him, and asked whether they would be putting in to land for the night. Orm and Toke agreed, however, that this would be unwise if the wind held and the sky remained clear.

"To do so," said Toke, "would merely be pandering to the landlubbers, more than one of whom, I doubt not, would disappear during the night. For they would easily be able to find their way home from here, happy at having escaped further misery. But by the time we reach Gotland, they will have found their sea-legs, and there we shall be safely able to let them ashore."

Olof Summerbird sighed and said nothing.

"We shall save much food, besides, by keeping on our course," said Orm. "For if we went ashore, they would eat a good meal, and then vomit it up again the next day, so that it would be wasted."

In this he was right; for the wind remained favorable to them, and barely half of the men succeeded in doing themselves justice at mealtimes before they sighted Gotland. Blackhair soon collected himself, and Glad Ulf had been used to the sea from boyhood; and they took great pleasure in munching their food and praising its quality, watched by pale men who had no stomach to eat. But as soon as they reached calmer water near Gotland the men began to find their appetite, and Orm thought he had never seen such gluttony as they now displayed.

"But I must not grudge it them," he said, "and now, perhaps, they will begin to be of some use."

In the harbor of the Gotland Vi so many ships lay at anchor that Orm was at first doubtful whether it would be wise to sail in. But they took down the dragon-head, set up a shield of peace in its place, and rowed in without any ship opposing their passage. The town was very great, and full of seamen and rich merchants; and when Orm's men came ashore, they found much to marvel at. There were houses built entirely of stone, and others erected for

the sole purpose of drinking ale in; and the wealth of the town
was such that whores walked the streets with rings of pure gold
in their ears and spat at any man who had not a fistful of silver to
offer for their services. But one thing in this town they marveled
at most of all and refused to believe in till they had actually seen
it. This was a man from the Saxons' land who spent the whole
of every day scraping the beards from the chins of the rich men
of the town. For this he received a copper coin from every man
he scraped, even when he had cut them so that they bled freely.
Orm's men thought this a more astonishing custom than any they
had ever before seen or heard tell of, and one that would be un-
likely to afford a man much pleasure.

Olof Summerbird was now in a more cheerful humor, and he
and Orm went in search of a skillful helmsman. Few men remained
on board, for all wanted to stretch their legs and refresh themselves. Toke, however, stayed behind to guard the ship.

"The ale these Gothlanders brew is so good," he said, "that once,
when I was a young man, I drank somewhat too deeply of it in this
very harbor. As a result, I became miserable and killed a man, and
only with difficulty managed to swim away with my life. These
Gothlanders have a long memory, and it would be an ill thing if
I were to be recognized and taken to task for such an old and trivial
offense when we have important work ahead of us; so I shall remain
on board. But I would advise such of you as go ashore to conduct
yourselves peacefully, for they have little patience with strangers
who cause disturbances."

Some while later Orm and Olof came aboard with the helmsman
they had chosen. He was a small, thickset, grizzled man called
Spof. He had been many times in the East and knew all the
routes, and would not agree to go with them until he had carefully
inspected the whole ship. He said little, but nodded at most of
what he saw. Finally he asked to be allowed to sample the ship's
ale. This was the ale that Orm had had specially brewed in the
estuary before they had embarked, and nobody had yet found
cause to complain of it. Spof tasted it and stood thinking.

"Is this all the ale you have?" he said.

"Is it not good enough?" said Orm.

"It is good enough to drink during the voyage," said Spof, "and
I shall not object to drinking it. Now, these men you have with

you, are they meek and submissive, addicted to hard work and easily contented?"

"Easily contented?" said Orm. "That they are not; indeed, the only time they do not complain is when the seasickness is upon them. Nor did I choose them for the meekness of their nature; and as for hard work, I do not think they like it better than most men."

Spof nodded thoughtfully.

"It is as I feared," he said. "We shall arrive at the great portage in the worst of the summer heat, and you will need better portage-ale than this if all is to go well."

"Portage-ale?" said Orm to Toke.

"We Gothlanders," said Spof, "have sailed the rivers of Garda-rike more often than other men and have penetrated them farthest. We know all their currents and hazards, even beyond the portage of the Meres, beyond which no man has voyaged in large ships save we. And it is thanks to our portage-ale that we have succeeded in making progress there, where all other men have been forced to turn back. This ale needs to be of extraordinary strength and flavor, so that it fortifies the spirit and cheers the heart; and it is to be given to the men only while they are hauling the ship across the portage. At no other time during the voyage must they be allowed to drink it. This device have we Gothlanders invented, and because of it we brew finer ale than any other people, for on the excellence of it our wealth depends."

"Unless I am much mistaken," said Orm, "this ale is not to be bought at a low price."

"It is dearer than other ales," replied Spof, "in proportion as it is superior to them; possibly a fraction more. But it is well worth its price, for without its help no ship can cross the portage into the hinterland of Gardarike."

"How much shall we need?" asked Orm.

"Let me see," said Spof. "Twenty-four oars; sixty-six men; Kiev. That will involve seven small portages, but they will not be diffi-cult. It is the great portage to the Dnieper that presents the prob-lem. I think that five of our largest barrels will suffice."

"Now I understand," said Orm, "why most men prefer to sail westwards."

And when he had paid for the ale and had given Spof half of

his hire-money for the voyage, he began to wish more strongly still that Are's treasure had been buried in some river in west-oversea instead of in Gardarike. As he reckoned out the silver, he mumbled heavily that he would never reach Kiev save as a beggar, armed only with his staff, for he would certainly have pawned his ship and weapons to the Gothlanders long before he sighted its walls.

"Still, you seem to me to be a good man, Spof," he said, "possessing both cunning and wisdom; and it may be that I shall not regret hiring you as my helmsman, though your price is high."

"It is with me as with the portage-ale," replied Spof, unoffended. "I am expensive, but I am worth my price."

They remained at anchor in the Gotland Vi for three days, and Spof ordered the men to carpenter strong cradles to hold the ale-casks firmly in position, until everything was as he wanted it. The ale occupied a deal of room and weighted the ship heavily, but the men did not grumble at the extra labor it would cost them, for they had already sampled it in the town and knew its flavor. By the end of their first day ashore many of them had drunk up all their silver and besought Orm to advance them part of their hire-money for the voyage, but nobody succeeded in persuading him to comply with this request. Some of the men then tried to barter their skin jackets in exchange for ale, and others their helmets, and when the Gothlanders refused to accept them, fights were started, as the result of which law-men from the town came to the ship demanding stern compensation. Orm and Olof Summerbird sat arguing with them for half a day until they had reduced their original demands by half, though even that sum, Orm thought, was more than sufficiently large. Thereafter they let no man ashore without first divesting him of his weapons.

Sone's sons were well supplied with silver of their own and drank deeply in the town, but found it difficult, none the less, to put their father's prophecy wholly out of their minds. On the second day ten of them returned to the ship, carrying the eleventh, who was on the point of expiring. They had warned him, they said, to control his passions, but in spite of this he had crept up upon a young woman whom he had seen chopping cabbages behind a cottage and had managed, by persuasive use of his tongue and hands, to put her on her back. He had no sooner done this, however, than a crone had emerged from the house, picked up the chopper, and deposited it in his head, which they had not been able to prevent.

Toke examined the wound and said that the man had not long to live. He died during the night, and his brothers buried him sadly and drank to a lucky death voyage for him.

"It was his fate to die thus," they said. "When the old man sees, he sees the truth."

But although they mourned their brother and had nought but good to speak of him, it was noticeable that something of their melancholy had been lifted from them. For now, they reminded each other, there was bad luck in store for three of them only, so that a quarter of their troubles were past.

The next morning they put out to sea and steered northwards, with Spof at the helm. Orm said that how they might fare in the future was uncertain, but that he dearly cherished one hope at least: namely, that he would not soon find himself anchored in another harbor as ruinous to seafarers as the Gotland Vi.

CHAPTER SIX

HOW THEY ROWED TO THE DNIEPER

THEY rounded the tip of Gotland, headed eastwards, past the island of Ösel, and entered the mouth of the river Dvina. This river formed the beginning of the low road to Miklagard, which was that most used by Gothlanders. The high road, which the Swedes favored, went along the coast of the Dead Land,[1] up the Vodor River to Ladoga, and thence through Novgorod to the Dnieper.

"Which is the better road no man has yet decided," said Spof. "I myself cannot say, though I have traveled them both. For the labor of rowing against the current always makes the road one has chosen seem the worse, whichever that may be. But it is lucky for us that we are starting late and so will miss the spring tide."

---

[1] Balagard; that is, the southern coast of Finland.

The men were in good heart as they entered the river, though they knew there was hard rowing ahead of them. After Orm had arranged matters so that each man should row for three days and rest for one, they proceeded upstream through the country of the Livonians and that of the Semgalls, occasionally passing small fishing villages sited on the banks, and beyond into a land deserted of men, with nothing to see save the river stretching away behind them and dense forest hugging them endlessly on both sides. The men felt awed by this country; and sometimes, when they had gone ashore for the night and were sitting around their fires, they heard a distant roaring that was like the voice of no animal they knew, and murmured to one another that this might, perhaps, be the Iron Forest, which the ancients spoke of, where Loki's [2] progeny still roamed the earth.

One day they met three ships moving down the river abreast, heavily laden and well manned, though with only six pairs of oars out to each ship. They were Gothlanders, on their way home. The men were lean and burned black by the sun, and they glanced curiously at Orm's ship as it approached them. Some of them recognized Spof and shouted greetings to him; and words were flung across from ship to ship as they glided slowly past. They had come from Great Bulgaria, on the river Volga, and had rowed down the river to the Salt Sea,[3] where they had traded with the Arabs. They were carrying a good cargo home, they said: fabrics, silver bowls, slave-girls, wine, and pepper; and three men in the second ship held up a naked young woman and dangled her over the side by her arms and hair, crying that she was for sale for twelve marks between friends. The woman shrieked and struggled, fearful lest she should fall into the water, and Orm's men drew deep breaths at the sight of her; but when, nobody having made an offer, the men drew her in again, she screamed foul words and thrust her tongue out at them.

The Gotland chieftains asked Orm who he was, whither he was heading, and what cargo he had aboard.

"I am no merchant," replied Orm. "I am going to Kiev to claim an inheritance."

---

[2] Loki was the spirit of evil and mischief in Norse mythology; it was he who contrived the death of Balder.

[3] The Caspian Sea.

"It must be a great inheritance if it is worth the labor of such a voyage," said the Gothlanders skeptically. "But if it is plunder you seek, seek it from others, for we always travel well prepared."

With that the ships passed on and grew small down the river.

"That woman was not contemptible," said Toke thoughtfully. "By her breasts, I adjudge her to be twenty at the most, though it is always difficult to be sure with a woman when she is hanging with her arms above her head. But only Gothlanders could ask twelve marks for a slave-girl, however young. None the less, I expected you, Olof, to make a bid for her."

"I might have done," said Olof Summerbird, "if I were not so placed as I am. But there is only one woman I long for, and I shall not forfeit my right to her maidenhood."

Orm stood scowling darkly after the disappearing ships.

"I am surely fated to fight with Gothlanders before I die," he said, "though I am a peaceful man. Their arrogance is great, and I am beginning to weary of always letting them have the last word."

"Perhaps we could fight them on our way home," said Toke, "if our other enterprise comes to nothing."

But Spof said that if those were his intentions, Orm would have to find another helmsman, for he would not take part in any fight against his own people.

In the afternoon of the same day they had a further encounter. They heard the harsh creak of oars, and around the nearest bend there emerged a ship, rowing swiftly. They had all their oars out, and were rowing with all their strength. At the sight of Orm's ship, they slackened their pace; the ship carried twenty-four pairs of oars, as Orm's did, and was filled with armed men.

Orm shouted immediately to his rowers to continue strongly and steadily, and to the rest of his men to make ready for battle; and Toke, who was standing at the steering-oar, altered course so as to be able to grapple the other ship without being rammed, if there should be fighting.

"What men are you?" came the cry from the strange ship.

"Men from Skania and Smaland," replied Orm. "And you?"

"East Gutes."

The river was broad here, and the current weak. Toke shouted to the larboard rowers to pull, and told the starboard men to rest on their oars, so that the ship swung swiftly round toward the East Gutes until both the ships were gliding side by side down-stream, so close that their oars were all but touching.

"We had you at our mercy then, if we had wished to ram you," said Toke, pleased at the success of his maneuver. "And that even though you had the current with you. We have been in situations like this before."

The East Gute, seeing their willingness to fight, spoke more humbly.

"Have you met Gothlanders on the river?" he asked.

"Three ships this morning," replied Orm.

"Did you speak with them?"

"In friendliness. They were carrying a good cargo, and asked if we knew if there were any East Gutes near."

"Did they speak of East Gutes? Were they afraid?"

"They said they found life tedious without them."

"That is like them," said the East Gute. "Three ships, you said? What freight have you aboard?"

"Arms and men. Is there anything you want from us?"

"If what you say is true," said the other, "you carry the same cargo as we, and there is nothing for us to fight for. I have a sug-gestion to make. Come with me and let us surprise these Goth-landers. They carry booty worth winning, and we will share it like brothers."

"What quarrel have you with them?" asked Spof.

"They have riches aboard and I have none. Is not that cause enough? The luck has been against us since we started for home. We came rich from the Volga, but the Meres were waiting for us at the portage by the weirs and ambushed us. We lost one of our ships and most of our cargo, and have no wish to return home empty-handed. Come now with me, if you are the men you look to be. Gothlanders are always worth attacking. I have heard at home that they are beginning to shoe their horses with silver shoes."

"We have business elsewhere," said Orm, "and urgent business at that. But I doubt not the Gothlanders will be glad to see you. Three against one is the sort of odds they like."

"Do as you wish," said the other sullenly. "It is as I have always heard, that Skanians are swinish bladders of men with no thought save for themselves, and never stretch out a hand to a stranger."

"It is true that we seldom think of East Gutes except when forced to," replied Orm. "But you have wasted our time for long enough. Farewell!"

Orm's ship was gliding slightly behind that of the Gutes, and Toke now swung her round facing upstream. While he was swinging her, the Gute chieftain's anger outgrew his patience, and of a sudden he flung his spear at Orm, crying as he did so: "Perhaps this will help you to remember us!"

Olof Summerbird was standing beside Orm, and he now performed a feat that many had heard tell of, but few had ever had the good fortune to behold. As the spear winged its way toward Orm, Olof took a step forwards, caught it in its flight just below the blade, turned it in his hand, and flung it back with such speed that few of those present realized immediately what had happened. The East Gute was not prepared for so swift a reply, and the spear took him in the shoulder, so that he staggered and sat down on his deck.

"That was a greeting from Finnveden," shouted Olof, and his men roared with approval of his feat and nodded to one another, hugely proud of their chieftain's performance. All the sailors rejoiced with them, though they doubted not that the East Gutes would now attack them. But the Gutes seemed to have lost their stomach for fighting and proceeded downstream without further words.

"Such a throw I have never before seen," said Orm, "and I thank you for it."

"I am as skillful with weapons as most men," said Toke, "but I could never match that feat. And you may be sure of this, Olof Styrsson, that few men have received such a tribute from Toke Gray-Gullsson."

"It is a gift one is born with," said Olof, "though perhaps an unusual one. I could do it even as a boy, finding it easy, though I have never been able to teach it to anyone else."

That evening Olof's feat was much discussed around the campfires on the bank, and they speculated on what would happen when the Gutes caught up with the Gothlanders.

"They cannot attack three good ships with only one," said Toke, "however strong their itch for trouble. I think they will follow the Gothlanders out into the open sea, and hope they may become separated by bad weather. But the Gothlanders will not yield their cargo easily."

"East Gutes are dangerous men," said Orm. "We had some of them among us when I sailed to England with Thorkel the Tall. They are good fighters and regard themselves as the best in the world, which is perhaps the reason why they find it difficult to live peaceably with other men and take few pains over their behavior. They are merry when drunk, but otherwise take little pleasure in jests. But they are worst when they suspect that anyone is laughing at them behind their backs; rather than be mocked, they would run upon a spear-point. Therefore I think it best that we should keep good watch tonight, lest they should regret their continence and decide to return."

But nothing further came of this encounter; and, cheered by this meeting with their countrymen, they rowed on into the limitless land.

They came to a place where the water boiled around great stones. There they hauled their ship on to the bank and emptied her. Then they dragged her up a trodden track past the weir and slid her back into the water. When they had brought the ship's contents up by the same path and had replaced them in the ship, the men asked confidently if it was not now time for them to be given some of the good portage-ale. But Spof said that only novices at the work could suppose that they had yet earned it.

"This was not a portage," he said, "but a lift. The ale will only be served after we have passed the portage."

Several times they came to similar weirs, and to some where the climb was longer and steeper. But Spof always gave the same reply, so that they began to wonder what the appearance of the great portage might be.

Every evening, after they had gone ashore for the night, they fished in the river, always making fine catches. So they did not lack for food, though they had by now eaten most of what they had brought with them. In spite of this, however, they sat dejected around their fires as they cooked their fish, longing for fresh meat and agreeing with one another that too much fish made a man distempered. They began, too, to grow weary of the heavy rowing; but Spof comforted them, saying that things would soon be different.

"For you must know," he said, "that the heavy rowing has not yet begun."

Sone's sons liked the fish less than anyone else and went out each evening to hunt. They took spears and bows and were cunning at discovering the tracks of animals and their watering-places. But although they were tireless and always came back late to the camp, it was a long time before they found anything. At last they sighted an elk, which they managed to corner and kill, and that night they did not return to the camp before dawn. They had lit a fire in the forest and eaten themselves full; and such meat as they brought back with them they were loath to part with.

After this they had better success with their hunting. Glad Ulf and Blackhair joined them on their sorties, and others also; and Orm regretted that he had not brought with him two or three of his great hounds, thinking that he could now be using them to good purpose.

One evening Blackhair came running back to the camp exhausted and breathless, shouting for men and ropes. There was now, he said, meat for all; and at this every man in the camp leaped quickly to his feet. They had driven five large animals into a bog, where they had killed them, and many men were needed to drag them out. All the men rushed joyfully to the spot, and they soon had the good meat on dry land. The animals looked like great bearded oxen, but oxen such as Orm had never before seen. Two of Toke's men, however, said that these were wild oxen, such as were still sometimes to be found near Lake Asnen in Värend, where they were held sacred.

"Tomorrow we shall have a holiday," said Orm, "and hold a feast."

So they had a feast, at which no complaints were heard; and the wild oxen, which were praised by all for the flavor and good texture of their flesh, disappeared with what was left of the ale they had brought with them when they had started.

"It is no matter if we finish it," said Orm, "for it is already beginning to grow sharp."

"When we come to the town of the Polotjans," said Spof, "we shall be able to buy mead. But do not let anyone tempt you to touch the portage-ale."

When they had recovered from this meal and had continued on their course, they had the good fortune to be favored with a strong wind, so that for a whole day they were able to proceed by sail. They were now entering country where traces of man's habitation could be seen on the banks.

"This is the country of the Polotjans," said Spof. "But we shall not see any of them before we reach their town. Those who live in the wild country here never come near the river when word has come to them that ships are approaching, for fear lest they should be taken to serve at the oars and then be sold as slaves in a foreign land."

Spof told them also that these Polotjans had no gods save snakes, who lived with them in their huts; but Orm looked at Spof and said that he had been to sea before and knew how much to believe of that story.

They came to the town of the Polotjans, which was called Polotsk and was of considerable size, with ramparts and stockades. Many men went naked there, though no women did so; for, a short while before, they had all been commanded to pay taxes, and the chieftain of the town had ordered that no man might wear clothes until he had paid what he owed the great Prince. Some of these looked more resentful than the rest; they had, they said, paid their tax, but must still go naked, because they had no clothes left after having pawned them to raise the money. In order to be ready for the cold season, they offered their wives for a good shirt, and their daughters for a pair of shoes, and found Orm's men willing customers.

The chieftain of this town was of Swedish blood, and was called Faste; he received them hospitably and asked anxiously for news of events at home. He was aged, and had served the great Prince of Kiev for many years. He had Polotjan women in his house, and many children, and, when drunk, spoke their tongue in preference to his own. Orm bought from him mead and pork, and many other things also.

When they were ready to proceed, Faste came to bid them farewell and begged Orm to take with him his scribe, who was going to Kiev with a basket of heads. The great Prince, he explained, liked to be reminded that his town chieftains served him zealously, and was always pleased to receive evidence of their zeal in the shape of the heads of the more dangerous criminals. Lately it had become difficult to ensure a safe passage to Kiev, and he was reluctant to neglect so good an opportunity as this of sending his gift. The scribe was a young man, a native of Kiev; besides the heads, he carried a sheepskin on which were written the names of the former owners of the heads, together with an account of their misdeeds.

In view of the hospitality that Faste had shown him, Orm felt unable to deny him this request, though he was unwilling to comply with it. The heads awoke unpleasant memories in him, for he had received a present in that shape once before; he recalled, also, that his own head had been sold to King Sven, though the transaction had never been completed. Accordingly he regarded this basket as likely to bring bad luck with it, and all his men thought the same. It was, besides, noticeable in the summer heat that the heads were beginning to age, and before they had gone far the men began to complain of their stink. The scribe sat by his basket as though smelling nothing; he understood the Northmen's tongue, however, and after a while suggested that the basket should be tied to a rope and allowed to trail in the water. This proposal won general approval; so the basket was tied firmly to a rope's end and heaved overboard. They had, by this time, set sail again and were making good speed; and later that day Blackhair cried that the basket had detached itself and disappeared.

"The best course for you now, scribe," said Toke, "is to jump overboard and fish for your treasure; for if you arrive without it, I fear things may go somewhat ill for you."

The scribe, though vexed at this occurrence, appeared not to be greatly alarmed by it. The sheepskin, he explained, was more important than the heads; as long as he still had the former, he could manage without the latter. There were only nine of them, and he doubted not that he would be able to borrow substitutes from public officials in Kiev with whom he was friendly; for there were always plenty of malefactors in their custody awaiting execution.

"We are taught to be merciful, after the example of God," he

said, "and therefore think it good to help one another when we
are in distress. And one head is as good as another."

"Then you are Christians in this land?" said Orm.

"In Kiev," replied the scribe, "for the great Prince has so commanded us, and we think it best to comply with his wishes."

They reached a place where two rivers joined. Their course lay
along the right-hand fork, which was called Ulla, and it was now
that the hard rowing began. For here the current soon became
stronger and the river narrower, and often they found themselves
unable to make progress and had to haul the ship ashore and drag
her forward along the bank. They had to toil long and strenuously,
so that even the strongest among them felt it, and regretted the
good days they had spent on the Dvina. At last they reached a
place where Spof ordered them to bring the ship ashore, though
they were making good progress and it was yet early in the day;
for this, he said, was the great portage.

The ground here was scattered with various kinds of timber, left
by travelers ascending or descending—broken planks, rollers, and
a type of rough runner. Some of them were still usable, and the
men axed others from fallen trees. They drew the ship up on the
bank and after a great deal of carpentry managed to fasten runners down both sides of the keel. While they were thus occupied,
some men were seen to come out of the forest a little farther up
the river and stand there uncertainly watching them. Spof appeared pleased when he saw them; he waved to them, held up a
tankard, and shouted the two words that he knew of their language: "oxen" and "silver." The men came nearer and were offered drink, which they accepted; and Orm was now able to make
use of Faste's scribe, who was able to interpret between him and
the strangers. They had oxen they were prepared to hire out, but
only ten, though Spof wanted more. These oxen, the men explained, were grazing deep in the forest where robbers and tax-
collectors would be less likely to find them, but they would be
back with them in three days. They asked only a small price for
the use of them, and begged that they might be paid in sailcloth
instead of silver, as their women liked the striped woof; but in the
event of any ox dying, they wanted to be given good compensation.
Orm found their demands reasonable, and thought them the first
honest people he had dealt with on this voyage.

All the men now set busily to work chopping and carpentering, and in a short time they had built a broad wagon, with strong rounds of oak to serve as wheels. Upon this they piled the portage-ale and made it fast, together with most of the other things from the ship.

The strangers then returned with the oxen as they had promised; and when everything was ready, two oxen were harnessed to the wagon and the rest to the ship.

"If we had six more oxen," said Spof, "all would be well; as things are, we shall have to help with the dragging ourselves. But we must be thankful that we have got any help at all, for to drag a ship up the great portage without oxen is the worst task that a man could be faced with."

When the dragging began, some of the men walked ahead to lift fallen trees out of the way and smooth the track. Then came the wagon. They guided the oxen cautiously, lest anything should give way; and when the wheels began to smoke, they greased the axles with pork and pitch. Then came the ship, with many men harnessed to the ropes beside the oxen. Where the track led downhill, or over grassland and moss, the oxen were able to manage without assistance; but where it led uphill, the men had to lend all their strength, and where the going was rough, rollers had to be placed beneath the runners. The ox-drivers spoke to their beasts the whole time, and sometimes sang to them, so that they dragged willingly, but when Orm's men spoke to them, using the words they used to address oxen at home, they received no response, because these oxen could not understand what they were saying. This surprised the men greatly; it showed, they said, that oxen were far wiser beasts than they had hitherto supposed, for here was evidence that they possessed a characteristic in common with men—namely, that they could not understand the speech of foreigners.

The men grew weary with the heat and toil and the business of changing the rollers; but they kept bravely on, for it was a great incentive to them to see the wagon with the portage-ale moving ahead of them, and they did all they could to keep pace with it. As soon as they pitched camp for the night, they all cried loudly for portage-ale; but Spof said that this first day's work had been light, and that Faste's mead was reward enough for it. They drank of this, grumbling, and soon fell asleep; but the next day's work

proved more arduous, as Spof had told them it would. Before the
afternoon was far advanced, many of the men began to flag; but
Orm and Toke cheered them with words of encouragement, sometimes lending a hand themselves with the dragging so that the
men might be stimulated by their example. When evening came
on this day, Spof at last said that the time had come for the
portage-ale to be opened. They breached a cask and gave a good
measure to every man; and although they had all tasted the same
brew in the Gotland Vi, they declared unanimously that they had
not until this moment appreciated its quality to the full, and that
the labor they had undergone had been well worth while. Orm ordered that the ox-drivers, too, should have their share; they accepted this offer willingly, and at once became drunk and sang
noisily, for they were only accustomed to thin mead.

On the third day they soon came to a lake, long and narrow
between asses'-backs, and here their task was lightened. The wagon
and the oxen proceeded by land, but they launched the ship into
the lake, with her runners still on her keel, and, favored by a mild
breeze, sailed down the water, encamping at length on the farther
shore. On a hill not far from their camping-ground lay a village
with rich pastures below it; here they saw fat cattle being driven
in from their grazing, though it was yet a good while before evening. The village, which appeared to be large, was curiously fortified, for, though it was surrounded by a high rampart of earth and
stone, this was broken in places by a stockade of rough logs which
did not look difficult to scale.

The men were in good spirits, for this was the lightest day's
work they had had for a long while, and the sight of the cattle
awakened in them a longing for fresh meat. Neither Orm nor Olof
was prepared to pay out any more silver for food, reckoning this to
be an unnecessary expenditure after all they had already been put to;
but many of the men, unable to control their longing, determined,
none the less, to go and fetch their supper. Faste's scribe said that
the people who lived in these parts were wild men of the Drego-
vite tribe, who had not as yet paid their taxes, so that the men
might act as they chose toward them. Spof said that the previous
time he had been here, seven years before, this village was in the
process of being built; but they had seen no cattle on that occasion, and so had not disturbed the inhabitants. Orm told the men

that they must not kill anyone in the village without due cause, and must not take more cattle than would be enough to meet their needs. They promised, and set out toward the village. Sone's sons were the most anxious to go, for, ever since they had rowed in to the river Ulla, they had had no opportunity to go hunting, because of the incessant work to which they had been subjected.

Shortly afterwards the men who had been coming by land with the wagon arrived at the camp. When the ox-drivers learned from the scribe that men had gone to the village to get cattle, they fell to the ground shaking with laughter. Orm and the others won-' dered what they could find in this news to be amused at, and the scribe tried to get them to explain the cause of their mirth, but in vain. They would only reply that the cause would in a short while become evident, and then began again to shriek with laughter.

Suddenly shouts and screams were heard from the direction of the village, and the whole company of cattle-raiders emerged, running down the hill as fast as their legs would carry them. They whirled their arms above their heads and yelled fearfully, though nothing else was in sight, and two or three of them fell to the ground and remained there, rolling from side to side. The rest ran down to the lake and jumped into the water.

Everyone in the camp stared at them in amazement.

"Have they devils or ghosts after them?" said Orm.

"I think bees," said Toke.

It was evident that he was right, and all the men now began to laugh as loudly as the ox-drivers, who had known about this from the beginning.

The refugees from the bees had to sit in the lake for a good while longer, with only their noses showing above the surface, un- til at length the bees tired of their sport and flew home again. The men returned slowly to the camp, greatly dejected, with swollen faces, and sat with few words in their mouths, thinking they had lost much honor in fleeing thus from bees. The worst of the business, though, was that three men were lying dead on the hill, where they had fallen: two of Olof Summerbird's men and one of Sone's sons. They grieved at this, for the dead had all been good men, and Orm ordered that portage-ale should be drunk again that evening, to honor their memory and to cheer the stung survivors.

The ox-drivers now told them about the Dregovites, the scribe translating what they said.

These Dregovites, they said, were more cunning than other men and had found a means to live peacefully in their villages. They had many swarms of bees which lived in the tree trunks that formed part of their fortifications, and which, as soon as any stranger touched the trunks or tried to climb over them, came out and stung him. It was fortunate for the men, they continued, that they had tried to invade the village during daylight, for if they had made the attempt by night, they would have suffered far worse. The bees could only guard the village by day, since they slept during the night; accordingly, the wise Dregovites had also equipped themselves with bears, which they trapped when young and trained and gave good treatment. If robbers came in the night, the bears were released and mauled the invaders, after which they returned to their masters to receive honey-cakes in reward for their services. Because of this, nobody dared to enter the villages of the Dregovites, not even the important men who collected taxes for the great Prince.

The next day they remained in this place and buried the dead. Some of the men wanted to throw fire into the village as a revenge, but Orm strictly forbade this, because no man had raised his hand against the dead men, who had only themselves to blame for their fate. Those who had been worst stung were in a sorry plight, for they were too ill to move; but the ox-drivers went up to the village and, standing at a distance from it, shouted to the inhabitants. A short while later they returned to the camp bringing with them three old women. These old women looked at the men who had been stung and placed a salve on their swellings, consisting of snake's fat, woman's milk, and honey, blended with the juices of healing herbs, which soon made the sick men feel better. Orm gave the women ale and silver; they drank eagerly, being careful to leave no drop in their cups, and thanked him humbly for the silver. The scribe spoke with them; they gazed curiously at him, curtsied, and returned to their village.

After a while some men appeared from the village, bringing with them three pigs and two young oxen. The scribe went to greet them, but they brushed him aside, walked up to Orm and Olof Summerbird, and began to talk eagerly. The scribe stood listening,

and then, of a sudden, uttered a yell and fled into the forest. Nobody could understand the villagers except the ox-drivers, and
these knew but few words of the Northmen's tongue; but by gestures they managed to explain that the villagers wished to make
Orm a gift of the pigs and oxen if he would hand the scribe over
to them; for they wished to give him to their bears, because they
disliked any man connected with the great Prince. Orm found
himself unable to accede to this request; however, he gave them
ale and bought their beasts with silver, so that they parted on amiable terms. Later that afternoon several more old women came to
the camp with great cheeses, which they gave to the men in exchange for a good draught of ale. The men, who had already begun
to roast the meat, thought that everything was turning out better
than could have been expected. The only pity, they said, was that
old women had come instead of young ones; but these the Dregovites would not allow out of the village.

Toward evening the scribe slunk back into the camp from his
hiding-place, tempted by the odor of the roasting meat. He begged
Orm to lose no time in getting away from these wild people. The
great Prince, he said, would be informed of their behavior.

They proceeded on their way and at length came to a lake
larger than that which they had just left; then, on the seventh day
of their portage, they reached a river that Spof called the Beaver
River and the ox-drivers Berezina. There was great rejoicing among
the men when they saw this river, and here they drank the last
of the portage-ale, for the worst hardships of the voyage were now
past.

"But now," said Orm, "we have no ale to help us on our homeward journey."

"That is true," said Spof, "but we shall only need it on the way
out. For it is with men as with horses; once their heads are turned
homewards, they move willingly and do not need the spur."

The ox-drivers were now paid off, and received more than they
had demanded; for it was so with Orm that he often felt mean
toward merchants, who for the most part seemed to him to be no
better than robbers and often worse, but never toward men who
had served him well. Besides which, he now felt that he was a
good deal nearer to the Bulgar gold. The ox-drivers thanked him
for his generosity and, before departing, took Spof and Toke to

a village, where they spoke to good men who were willing to hire out oxen for the return journey. Orm ordered his men to dig a hiding-place, where they hid the rollers and runners until they should need them again, having worn out three sets of runners during the long land drag. The wagon he took with him, thinking that it might prove useful when they reached the weirs.

They sailed down the river, past fishermen's shacks and beavers' huts and dams, rejoicing that the going was now light. The river ran black and shining between broad-leaved trees, rich with foliage, and the men thought that the fish from this river tasted more wholesome than those they had caught in the Dvina. Only a few men were needed at the oars; the rest sat in peace and contentment, telling one another stories and wondering whether the whole voyage might not be completed without any fighting.

The river broadened more and more, and at last they came out into the Dnieper. Orm and Toke agreed that even the biggest rivers in Andalusia could not be compared with this; and Olof Summerbird said that, of all the rivers in the world, only the Danube was greater. But Spof thought that the Volga was the biggest of them all, and had many stories to tell of the voyages he had made on its waters.

They met four ships laboring upstream, heavy-laden, and spoke with them. They were manned by merchants from Birka, who were on their way home from Krim. They were very tired, and said that trade had been good but the homeward journey bad. They had been engaged in fighting at the weirs and had lost many men; for the Patzinaks had come west, waging war against all men, and were trying to stop all traffic on the river. It would be unwise, they said, for anyone to travel beyond Kiev before the Patzinaks had left the river and returned again to their eastern grazing-grounds.

This news gave Orm much to think about, and when they had parted from the merchants he sat for a long time pondering deeply.

CHAPTER SEVEN

CONCERNING WHAT HAPPENED AT THE WEIRS

THAT evening they went ashore for the night close to a village, where they found both sheep and mead for sale. After they had eaten, Orm sat in counsel with Toke and Olof over the news they had just heard, to decide what course they would be best advised to take now that they were approaching their goal. They went out to the empty ship, to be able to speak without fear of disturbance or of being overheard; and there they sat together in the evening stillness, while dragonflies played over the surface of the water, and the river chuckled slowly around the ship.

Orm thought that he had many difficult problems to decide.

"Such is our present situation," he said, "that we must plan wisely if we are to bring this voyage to a successful conclusion. Nobody knows anything about the treasure except you two and myself, and the two boys, who know how to keep their mouths shut; no one else. All that the men have been told is that we are going to Kiev to collect an inheritance, and I have not revealed our true purpose even to Spof. But we shall soon have to tell them that we are going beyond to the weirs, and that my inheritance lies hidden there. If we tell them this, though, it is certain that the whole of Kiev will also know of it a short while after we have come to the town; for men who drink in a good harbor cannot keep such a secret longer than the time it takes to drink three cups of ale, even if they know they will lose their heads for it. And if the purpose of our journey comes to the ears of the great Prince and his men, it will be a sad piece of ill luck for us, for then there will be many who will wish to share our silver and gold with us, if not to kill us and keep the lot for themselves. In addition to all this, we now have these Patzinaks to think about, who will be lurking in wait for us at the weirs."

Olof and Toke agreed that there was much here for a man to scratch his head about. Toke asked how far it might be from Kiev to the weirs, and whether they would be able to find food on the river once they had passed beyond the city.

"From Kiev to the weirs is, I think, nine days' hard rowing," said Olof, "though Spof will be able to tell you more accurately than I. The time I voyaged there we bought food from the herdsmen on the banks, and also took much from a rich village of the Severians. But things may be different now that it is no longer peaceful on the river."

"It would be foolish of us to come to Kiev without first telling the men that we intend to proceed," said Toke. "For there is much that will tempt them in the city, and it may be that many of them will refuse to go farther, pleading that we misled them."

"A worse danger," said Olof, "is that the great Prince himself will immediately conscript many if not all of us into his service. I have served the great Prince Vladimir and know how things are in Kiev. He has always given good pay, and if he now has trouble on his hands, he will be offering more than before. It is so with him that he can never have enough Northmen in his bodyguard; for he holds us to be the boldest and most loyal of men, as indeed we are, and loves us dearly, having done so ever since the Swedes helped him to his throne when he was a young man. He himself is of Swedish blood. He knows many ways to tempt Northmen to remain in Kiev, even if his gold should fail to seduce them."

Orm nodded and sat pondering, staring down into the water.

"There is much to be said against our visiting the great Prince Vladimir," he said, "though his fame is so great and his wisdom so renowned that it would be a pity to pass through his town without seeing him. It is said that, now that he is old, men worship him as holy, though it has taken him a long time to attain to that condition. He must be nearly as great a king as King Harald was. But that which is most important must come first. We have come on a particular errand, to collect the gold; then, when we have found it, we shall have another errand—namely, to carry it quickly and safely home again. I think we are all agreed that it would be wisest to proceed directly to the weirs."

"That is so," said Toke. "None the less, I think we would do well to take Spof's counsel on the matter. He knows the route better than we do and, perchance, knows these Patzinaks better also."

The others nodded, and Orm summoned Spof to him from the bank. When he had climbed aboard, Orm told him about the gold.

"I said nothing of this to you when I engaged you," he concluded, "because I was not yet sure of you. But now I know you to be a good man, and honest."

"This is to be a longer journey than I had bargained for," said Spof, "and more dangerous. The price I asked for my services you found dear, but I must tell you that if I had known we were going to the weirs, it would have been dearer still."

"You need have no worry on that score," said Orm. "For this voyage to the weirs you may name your own price. And I promise you, and Toke Gray-Gullsson and Olof Styrsson will be your witnesses, that you shall have your share of the treasure, too, if we find it and bring it safely home. And it shall be a full helmsman's share."

"Then I am content to go with you," said Spof. "We Gothlanders are happiest when we know that our services will be well rewarded."

When he had reflected on the matter, Spof said that he, too, thought that they would do best to proceed directly to the weirs.

"There will be no difficulty about procuring food," he said. "It is cheap and easy to find farther down the river; I have known men get five fat pigs for a single broadax, with a sack of oats thrown in. We have rich villages ahead of us now, both on this side of Kiev and beyond, and shall be able to get enough food to last us to the weirs and back again. But it would be best if you could pay for it, as you have done hitherto, if your silver will stretch to it, for it is unwise to take things by force on an outward voyage when one intends to return by the same route."

Orm replied that he still had a little silver to jingle, though most of it had gone by now.

"Our chief problem will be the Patzinaks," continued Spof. "We may find ourselves forced to buy a safe-conduct from them. It is possible, though, that they will not let us through at any price. It would be good if you could tell me off which bank the treasure lies, and between which weirs."

"It lies off the eastern bank," said Orm, "between the second and third weir, reckoning from the south. But the hiding-place itself I shall reveal to no man until we have reached it."

"Then it lies a good way from where we shall have to beach the ship for the portage," said Spof. "It would be best if we could go there by night. It would have been a good thing if we could have brought someone with us who understands the language of the Patzinaks, in case we should find them unwilling to talk peaceably with us. But that cannot be helped now."

"That difficulty we can overcome," said Toke, "by taking Faste's scribe with us. He can do his business at Kiev on the way back. Nobody will complain of his lateness, for nobody will know when he started. If we should speak with the Patzinaks, there is sure to be someone among them who will understand his language, even if he cannot understand theirs."

With that, their conference ended. The next morning, before they continued with their journey, Orm spoke to the men. He told them that they were going beyond Kiev, to a place where his inheritance from his brother lay hidden.

"There may well be fighting there," he added, "and if you prove yourselves bold men, so that I win my inheritance safely, it may be that each of you will receive a share of it, besides the good money that you have already been promised for your hire."

The men had little complaint to make, save Sone's sons, who were heard to mumble among themselves that two of them would surely die there and that they needed ale rather than the sweet drink which was all that this land had to offer them, if they were to fight with their full strength.

They landed several times during their passage down the river, to visit the villages of the Poljans, where wealth abounded. There Orm bought food and drink, so that they were as well furnished as when they had started. Then, late one evening, when a fog lay over the river, they rowed past Kiev, unable to discern much of the city.

Faste's scribe grew uneasy when he found that they did not intend to put him ashore here.

"I have an important message for the great Prince," he said, "as you all know."

"It has been decided that you shall accompany us to the weirs," said Orm. "You are clever at speaking with all kinds of men and may prove useful to us there. You will be put ashore here on our way back."

At this the scribe showed great alarm; however, when he had prevailed upon Orm to swear an oath by the Holy Trinity and St. Cyril that he would neither force him to row nor sell him to the Patzinaks, he calmed himself and said that the great Prince would have to wait.

Soon the villages along the bank began to grow fewer, until at last they ceased altogether and were replaced by unending grass-land, where the Patzinaks held sway. From the ship they could sometimes see herds of sheep and horses at their watering-places, tended by men on horseback wearing tall skin caps and carrying long spears. Spof said that it was a good thing that they saw such herds only on the left bank of the river and never on the right bank. The reason for this, he explained, was that there was a high tide on the river which prevented the Patzinaks from bring-ing their herds across to the right bank; if they attempted to do this, they would lose many animals at the fords. Henceforth, therefore, they always beached the ship on the safe bank, though they did not relax the sharp watch they kept each night.

When they had come to within three day's rowing of the weirs, they became yet more cautious and rowed only by night. By day they kept the ship hidden among tall reeds in creeks in the right bank. On the last day they anchored within hearing distance of the weirs and, when darkness fell, rowed over to the left bank, where the dragging-tracks began.

It had been decided that twenty men should remain in the ship. They had drawn lots to determine which these should be, and Toke found himself among them. They were to row the ship out into the center of the stream and lie there at anchor during the night until they heard voices calling them from the land. Toke was reluctant to sit idle in the ship, but had to obey when the lot went against him. Orm would have liked to leave Blackhair with him, but in that matter he was unable to have his way.

Orm and Olof Summerbird now set off with the rest of their band up the long dragging-track, taking Spof with them as guide. All the men were armed with swords and bows. Spof had come this way several times before. He explained that the place to which they were going lay beyond the seventh weir, reckoning from the north. This would be three hours' brisk marching, so that, allow-ing for the time it would take to find and raise the treasure, they would be hard put to get back before it began to grow light. They had with them the wagon that they had used at the great portage, to put the treasure in, and also the scribe, though he was not greatly pleased at having to accompany them. They began their march in pitch-darkness; but they knew that the moon would soon rise and, despite the added dangers that this would bring, Orm was glad that it was to be so, since otherwise he feared he might be unable to find the spot where the treasure lay.

But when the moon rose, it straightway brought them trouble, for the first object upon which its rays shone was a rider in a pointed hat and a long coat standing motionless on a hill ahead of them. At the sight of him, they at once halted and stood silent. It was still dark in the hollow where they were, but the horseman seemed, they thought, to be peering in their direction, as though their footsteps or the creak of the wagon might have come to his ears.

One of Sone's sons touched Orm with his bow.

"It is a long carry," he muttered, "and moonlight is deceptive to shoot in; but we think we could mark him so that he will stay where he is, if you so wish it."

Orm hesitated for a moment; then he muttered that hostilities were not to be opened from his side.

The horseman on the hill uttered a whistle, like a pewit's call, and another horseman appeared beside him. The first horseman stretched out his arm and said something. They both sat still for a few moments; then they suddenly wheeled their horses, rode off, and disappeared.

"Those must have been Patzinaks," said Orm, "and now things promise less well, for it is certain that they saw us."

"We have already reached the fifth weir," said Olof. "It would be a pity to turn back when we have come so far."

"There is little pleasure to be gained in fighting horsemen," said Orm, "especially when they outnumber those who oppose them on foot."

"Perhaps they will wait till it is light before they attack us," said Spof, "for they like this moonlight no more than we do."

"Let us proceed," said Orm.

They made all the speed they could, and when they had reached and passed the seventh weir, Orm began to look about him.

"Those of you whose eyes are sharpest must help me now," he said. "There should be a rock in the water here with three rose-bushes on it, though there will be no flowers on them at this season."

"There is a rock with bushes on it," said Blackhair, "but whether or not they are rosebushes I cannot tell."

They crept down to the water's edge, and thence managed to discern three more rocks. All of these, however, appeared to be bald. Then Orm found the cleft where the rock-flat was broken and where the water boiled and bubbled, just as Are had described it.

"If we can now find a hill which is called the skull-mound of the Patzinaks," he said, "we shall not be far from that which we have come to seek."

It did not take them long to find this, for almost at once Spof pointed toward a high mound that lay a short way from the bank.

"They have buried a chieftain there," he said, "I remember that I was once told so. And whenever they have been fighting here at the weirs, it is their custom to set the heads of their enemies on poles upon his mound."

"Then let us make haste," said Orm, "lest they put ours there too."

He walked out along the edge of the cleft until he came to the spot that lay directly between the rock with the rosebushes on it and the mound with the skulls.

"This should be the place," he said. "Now we shall know whether we have made this long voyage in vain."

All the men were much excited. With a spear they measured the depth of the water beneath the cleft.

"We shall need tall men to catch these fish," said Orm, "but I can feel a pile of stones here against the base of the rock, and that is as it should be."

Two brothers of Olof's following, named Long Staff and Skule, Hallanders by birth, were the tallest men in the band. They expressed their willingness to go into the water and do their best to see if anything lay there. When they stood on the bottom the water came up to their necks, and Orm bade them plunge their heads under and bring up, one by one, the stones that lay piled against the rock. They came spluttering up with huge stones, continuing thus for a good while; finding the work strenuous, they rested to regain their breath and then continued. Suddenly Skule said that his fingers had touched something that was not stone, but that he could not pull it free.

"Be careful with it," said Orm, "and clear all the stones away first."

"Here is something that is not stone," said Long Staff, heaving an object out of the water. It was a sack and evidently contained something heavy, so that he had to get a good grip on it. Just as he had got it halfway up the rock facing him, the sack burst in the middle, because the skin it was made of had rotted, and a broad stream of silver coins ran out and fell splashing into the water. At this sight, a great cry of fear and anguish arose from the men on the bank. Long Staff tried to stem the flow with his hands and face, and the men threw themselves over one another to get the sack up and save as much as possible, but in spite of their efforts much of its contents fell into the water.

"This is a fine beginning," said Orm bitterly. "Is that the way you handle silver? How much will be left for me if you continue like that? However," he added in a calmer voice, "now at least we know that we have come to the right place, and that nobody has been here before us. But be careful with the rest, Hallander. There should be four sacks more."

All the men jeered angrily at Long Staff, so that he began to sulk and swore he would remain in the water no longer. It was not his fault, he said, that the sack was rotten; if he had had as much silver as that to hide, he would have taken the trouble to store it in stronger sacks. Let others take his place and see whether they could do better.

But both Orm and Olof said that it was not his fault that this had happened. This encouraged him, and he continued with his fishing in a calmer spirit.

"Here is something else," said Skule, pulling up something that he had caught, "and this is heavier than stone."

It was a small copper chest, very green and exceedingly heavy, bound many times with fine red ropes, which were sealed with lead.

"Ah, yes, the chests," said Orm. "I had forgotten them. There should be four small chests like that. They contain trash for women. But all the silver is in the sacks."

With the other sacks they had better luck, managing to get them up on the rock without spilling any of their contents. As each new find appeared, their merriment increased, and they had no thoughts now for the Patzinaks or for the fact that time was passing. They had to search for a good while before finding the last two chests, for they had sunk down into the gravel in the riverbed; but at last they discovered these, too, and stacked all the treasure into the wagon.

By this time the better part of the night was gone, and as soon as they started on their homeward journey their old fear of the Patzinaks once more came over them.

"They will come as soon as it is light," said Spof.

"Orm's luck is better than that of most men," said Olof Summerbird, "nor is mine among the worst. It may be that we shall avoid these Patzinaks altogether. For a long time has now passed since the two horsemen saw us, and since that moment we have not seen a single man. This may mean that the Patzinaks are now waiting for us below the bottom weir, where the portage ends; for they could not know that we were only intending to come halfway before turning back. They will not pursue us until they have realized their mistake, and if all goes well, we shall by that time have reached our ship safely."

But in this he proved a false prophet, though his words almost came true; for a short while after daybreak, when they were but a little way from the ship, they heard a great thunder of hoofs behind them and turned to see the Patzinaks riding after them like Odin's storm.

Orm bade his men halt and position themselves in front of the wagon with their bows drawn. The men were in the best of spirits, and ready to fight for their silver with all the Patzinaks in the Eastland.

"No stranger shall touch this wagon as long as four or five of us are left alive to defend it," they said stolidly.

But the Patzinaks were cunning, and difficult to mark; for instead of riding straight at the Northmen, they whipped their horses up to a full gallop and rode past them at the distance of bowshot, releasing their arrows as they thundered by. Then they reassembled and, after a brief pause, repeated the maneuver in the opposite direction. Most of Orm's men were skilled huntsmen, and expert with a bow, so that they were able to give a good account of themselves, and a great shout of triumph arose from them every time an enemy tumbled from his horse. But sometimes it happened that a Patzinak arrow, too, found its mark, and after a time Orm and Olof agreed that if things continued in this wise, they would not be able to hold out for much longer.

Between two attacks Orm called Blackhair and Glad Ulf to him. They had both been grazed by arrows, but were in good heart, and each proudly declared that he had killed his man. By good fortune, at the place where they had halted, the rocks dropped steeply down to the river, so that they were secured against attack from that direction. Orm now bade the boys creep down the rocks and run along the bank as fast as they could to where the ship was anchored. Then they were to shout across the water to Toke and tell him to come at once to their aid, bringing with him every man on board.

"Whether this adventure will end well depends on you," he said, "for our arrows will not last much longer."

Proud at being entrusted with so important a mission, the boys obeyed and made swiftly down the rocks. Soon the Patzinaks attacked again, and during this assault Olof Summerbird fell with an arrow in his chest. It had penetrated his mail shirt and was embedded in his flesh.

"That was shrewdly aimed," he said. "You will have to fight the rest of this battle without my assistance."

As he spoke, his knees bent suddenly beneath him, but he managed to remain on his feet and, climbing on to the wagon, lay down upon it, resting his head on one of the sacks of silver. Other wounded men were already sprawled there among the sacks and chests of treasure.

The next time the Patzinaks swept past, Orm's men shot their last arrows at them. As they did so, however, they heard from behind them a great cry of joy.

"The old man's prophecy is fulfilled," cried several voices. "Finn Sonesson has fallen! There is an arrow through his throat, and he is already dead! Kolbjörn, his brother, fell but a few moments ago. Four are now gone; the rest of us cannot die before we have returned home!"

And it turned out as they said, for as they ceased crying, the others heard the sound of war-whoops from the direction of the ship, signifying that Toke had landed with his men. The sight of them seemed to slake the Patzinaks' thirst for battle, for as Orm's men ran eagerly to search for spent arrows that might be used again, they heard the thunder of hoofs grow fainter instead of louder and at last die away in the distance.

Orm ordered his men not to kill any of the men who lay wounded on the ground. "Let them remain where they lie," he said, "until their kinsmen come to collect them."

Their own wounded, those who were unable to walk, were lying in the wagon. Seven others lay dead on the ground, and these the men took up and carried with them, that they might give them honorable burial as soon as the opportunity arose. In the meantime, however, they made haste to return to the ship before the Patzinaks should return.

Faste's scribe had disappeared; but when they went to pull the cart forward, they discovered him asleep beneath it. He was roused with a spear-shaft and was much mocked. He said that this fight had been no concern of his, since he was a state official whose business was collecting taxes, and he had not wished to be in anyone's way, besides which, he had been tired after the night's marching. The men admitted that it testified to his calmness of mind that he had been able to sleep throughout the battle.

They soon met Toke and his men, and there was great rejoicing on both sides. Toke had disposed of the enemy without much difficulty; as soon as he had come against them with war-whoops and arrows, they had turned and fled. The men thought it possible that they, too, had used up all their arrows.

When they arrived at the ship, Orm looked around him. "Where are the two boys?" he asked Toke.

"The boys?" replied Toke. "You had them with you."

"I sent them along the bank to call you to our aid," said Orm in a changed voice.

"What can have become of them?" said Toke, scratching his beard. "I heard hoofbeats and war-cries and saw the Patzinaks ride toward us and wheel their horses, and at once rowed ashore to help you. But I have seen nothing of the boys."

One of Toke's men said that, just before the ship had reached the bank, he had seen three Patzinaks emerge on foot from among the rocks, dragging something along; dead men, he had supposed, or possibly prisoners. They had dragged them toward their horses; but, he said, he had not given the matter more thought, because at that moment the ship had touched land and he had started thinking about the forthcoming battle.

Orm stood speechless. He took off his helmet and let it drop to the ground; then he sat down on a stone on the bank and stared into the river. There he sat, motionless, and none of the men dared speak to him.

The men stood muttering among themselves and gazed at him; and even Toke knew not what to say. Spof and Faste's scribe carried the wounded aboard.

At length Orm rose to his feet. He walked up to Toke and unclipped from his belt his sword, Blue-Tongue. All the men opened their mouths in fear as they saw him do this.

"I am going to the Patzinaks," he said. "Wait here with the ship for three days. If Blackhair returns, give the sword to him. If none of us returns, take it home for Harald."

Toke took the sword.

"This is bad," he said.

"Divide the treasure fairly," said Orm, "as it would have been divided had I lived. It has brought little luck to us of Toste's line."

CHAPTER EIGHT

HOW ORM MET AN OLD FRIEND

ORM took Faste's scribe with him and went to search among the fallen Patzinaks. They found one who was wounded but not dead, a young man, who had received an arrow in the side and another in the knee. He appeared to be in good heart, for he was sitting up and gnawing a piece of dried meat, with a long wooden flask in his other hand, while his horse grazed beside him.

This man was able to understand something of what the scribe said, and was pleased when he learned that they had not come to take his head. Orm bade the scribe say that they wished to help him on to his horse and accompany him back to his village. After the scribe had repeated this message several times, the Patzinak nodded and pointed at his knee. The arrow had gone right through it, just behind the kneecap, so that the head was sticking out from the inner side of his leg. He had tried to pull it out, he explained by gestures, but had not been able to do so. Orm cut the leg of his skin breeches and worked the arrow a little, pushing it farther into the knee until the whole of the metal head appeared, so that it might be cut off and the shaft drawn out from the other side. The Patzinak snapped his fingers as Orm did this, and whistled slowly; then, when the operation was completed, he set his flask to his mouth and drained it. The other arrow he had succeeded in extracting himself.

Orm took from his belt a fistful of silver and gave it to the man. His face lit up at the sight of it, and he seized it eagerly.

Near them there stood other horses, waiting patiently by the bodies of their fallen masters. They moved away as Orm and the scribe approached them; but when the Patzinak called them with a special whistle, they came willingly to him and allowed halters to be put round their necks.

They helped the wounded man on to his horse. He crooked his wounded leg up on the saddle and appeared not to be troubled by it. The scribe was unwilling to go with them, but Orm told him curtly to do as he was told.

"If you protest, I shall wring your neck," he said. "It is I, not you, who am to become their prisoner."

The scribe mumbled that this sort of thing was no fit occupation for a state officer whose concern was collecting taxes; he obeyed, however, and no more was said about this.

They rode away into the grassland, which was the Patzinaks' domain. Orm said afterwards that a man might search long for a worse land and not succeed; for there were no trees or water, beasts or men to be seen there, but only grass and the empty air above it, and, occasionally, a kind of large rat that slunk away among the tussocks. Twice the Patzinak reined in his horse, pointed to the ground, and said something to the scribe, who then dismounted from his horse and pulled up the plants that the Patzinak had indicated. These, which were broad-bladed, the Patzinak then wrapped round his wounded knee, and bound them fast with a bowstring. This seemed to soothe the pain of his wound, so that he was able to ride on without becoming exhausted.

When the sun had climbed to half of its midday height, they reached the Patzinak camp. It lay in a hollow on either side of a stream, along the banks of which their tents stood in their hundreds. As they approached, hounds began to bay and children to yell, and the camp suddenly became full of horses and men. The Patzinak rode proudly in with his prisoners; then, when they had helped him from his horse, he showed the silver he had received and pointed at Orm.

Orm told the scribe to say that he wished to speak to their chieftain. At first nobody appeared to understand what he said, but at length a little bandy-legged man appeared who understood him and was able to reply in the scribe's own tongue.

"Tell him this," said Orm to the scribe. "Both my sons, who are very young, were captured by you during the battle at the weirs last night. I am a chieftain and have come to buy them free. I have come unarmed, as a proof of my peaceful intentions and good faith."

The bandy-legged man pulled thoughtfully at his long cheek-beard and exchanged a word or two with the wounded man who had brought them. Their talk sounded to Orm's ears more like the clucking of owls than the speech of men, but they seemed to be able to understand each other without difficulty. Many of those who stood watching grinned broadly at Orm and took out their knives and drew them across their throats. This, said Orm afterwards, was the worst moment of his life, for he took it to mean that they had already cut the throats of their prisoners, though he hoped that it might merely signify that they intended to perform the operation on him. This seemed to him by far the lesser evil, if, by allowing this to happen, he could enable Blackhair to go free.

He said to the scribe: "Ask him whether his two captives are still alive."

The bandy-legged man nodded, and shouted to three men, who stepped forward. These were the men who owned the prisoners.

Orm said: "Tell them that I wish to buy their prisoners for much silver. They are my sons."

The three men began to jabber, but the bandy-legged man said that it would be best that Orm and the scribe should go with him to the chieftains. They came to three tents that were larger than the rest, and followed the little man into the center one.

Three old men, wearing furs and with shaven heads, were seated on a sheepskin on the ground, their legs crossed beneath them, eating a mess from a large clay bowl. When they had entered, the bandy-legged man halted and signed to Orm and the scribe to remain silent. The three old men ate greedily, blowing on their spoons and smacking their lips with relish. When the bowl was empty, they licked their spoons and stuffed them into holes in their furs. Then, at last, they condescended to notice that somebody had come in.

One of them nodded at the bandy-legged man. He bowed to the ground and began to speak, while the chieftains sat listening with dull expressions, giving vent to an occasional belch.

The one who sat in the middle was smaller than the other two and had very large ears. Tilting his head to one side, he stared piercingly at Orm. At length the bandy-legged man stopped talking, and there was a silence. Then the little chieftain croaked a few words, and the bandy-legged man bowed reverently and went out, taking the scribe with him.

When they had gone, the little chieftain said slowly: "You are welcome here, Orm Tostesson, though it is better that we should conceal the fact that we know each other. It is a long time since we last met. Is Ylva, King Harald's daughter, who played as a child upon my knees, still alive?"

Orm drew a deep breath. He had recognized the little man as soon as he had begun to speak. It was Felimid, King Harald's Irish jester.

"She is alive," replied Orm, "and remembers you well. It is her son who is one of your prisoners here. This is certainly a strange meeting, and one that may prove lucky for us both. Are you a chieftain among these Patzinaks?"

Felimid nodded. "When one is old, one must take the best that comes," he said. "But I cannot really complain."

He spoke to his two fellow chieftains, turned round, and shouted toward the back of the tent. A woman entered with a great drinking-cup, which they passed around and which soon became empty. The woman filled it again; then, when it had again been emptied, the other two chieftains rose with difficulty to their feet and tottered out.

"They will sleep now," said Felimid to Orm when they were alone. "It is so with these people that they easily become drunk, and then they at once fall asleep and remain thus for half the day. They are simple souls. Now you and I can sit and talk here undisturbed. You have had a long ride and are, perhaps, hungry?"

"You have guessed rightly," said Orm. "Since I recognized you my anxiety has been lightened, and the three things that I long for most are to see my son again and to eat and drink."

"You shall see him as soon as we have decided the question of his ransom," said Felimid. "This will, I fear, cost you silver; for if I commanded otherwise, the whole tribe would become enraged with me. But first you shall be my guest."

He shouted orders, and six women entered and began to set out food on a mat that they spread on the floor of the tent.

"These are my wives," explained Felimid. "They may seem a lot for an old man, but such is the custom here. And I must have something to keep me amused, now that Ferdiad is dead and I can no longer practice my art."

"This is sad news about your brother," said Orm. "How did he die? And how did you come here?"

"Eat, and I will tell you; I have already eaten enough. We have no ale, alas, but here is a drink that we make from mare's milk. Taste it; you have drunk worse."

It was a clear drink, with a sweet-sour taste, and Orm thought it would be difficult to find kind words to say of it; however, he soon noticed that there was good strength in it.

Felimid made Orm eat all the food that had been brought, and shouted to the women to bring more. Meanwhile he told what had happened to him and his brother since they had trudged away from Gröning.

"We roamed widely," he said, "as we told you we would when last we parted; and finally we came to the great Prince in Kiev. We remained in his palace for two years, delighting all men with our arts and earning great honor; but then we began to notice that we were putting on flesh. At this we were greatly afraid, and determined to leave, though everybody begged us to remain, because we wished, while our skill yet remained to us, to perform before the great Emperor at Miklagard, as had been our intention from the beginning. But we never reached him, for at the weirs we were taken by the Patzinaks. They found us too old to be of any use and wanted to kill us, so as to be able to set up our heads on poles, as is their custom. But we displayed our arts before them, the simplest that we know, until they prostrated themselves on their bellies in a circle around us and worshipped us as gods. Nevertheless, they would not let us go; and as soon as we had learned something of their language, they made us chieftains, because of our wisdom and knowledge of witchcraft. We soon grew accustomed to our new life, for it is easier to be a chieftain than a jester; besides, we had realized for some time that old age was, at last, beginning to stiffen our limbs. The great Archbishop Cormac MacCullenan spoke truly when he said, long ago: 'A wise man, once he is past fifty, does not befuddle his senses with strong drink, nor make violent love in the cool spring night, nor dance on his hands.' "

Felimid took a draught from his cup and nodded sadly.

"He spoke too truly," he said, "and my brother Ferdiad forgot this warning when one of his women produced male twins. Then he drank deeply of this yeasty mare's-milk and danced on his hands before all the people, like the King of the Jews before God; and in the midst of his dance he fell and remained lying, and when we lifted him up he was dead. I mourned him deeply, and mourn him still, though nobody can deny that it was a worthy death for a master jester to die. Ever since then I have remained here with these Patzinaks, in peace and contentment. They are like children, and venerate me deeply, and seldom oppose my will except when they go head-hunting, which is an ancient custom with them which they will not abandon. But now tell me how it has been with you and yours."

Orm told him all that he wished to know. When, however, he

came to speak of the treasure at the weirs, he thought it best to mention only the three sacks of silver; for he did not wish to pay more than need be when it came to fixing the ransom for Black-hair and Ulf. Lastly he described the battle with the Patzinaks. When he had concluded, Felimid said: "It is lucky that your son and foster son were taken alive. This was because of their youth; the men who captured them hoped to make a good profit by sell-ing them to the Arabs or the Byzantines. You must therefore be prepared to pay a large price for them. It is lucky that you have the treasure within easy reach."

"I shall pay whatever price you name," said Orm. "It is no more than right that a large sum should be demanded for King Harald's grandson."

"I have not myself seen the boy," said Felimid, "for I do not bother myself with the thefts and rapes of my subjects, except where absolutely necessary. They are always capturing men and treasure at these weirs. But it is time for us to settle this matter without delay."

They went out of the tent, and Felimid shouted orders to this man and that. The two other chieftains were awakened, and emerged sleepy-eyed; then, when they and Felimid had seated themselves on a grass slope, all the people in the camp came run-ning to the place and grouped themselves around them in a tight circle. Then the two prisoners were led forth by their captors. They were both pale, and Blackhair had blood in his hair; but their faces lit up as they saw Orm, and the first thing that Black-hair said was: "Where is your sword?"

"I came here unarmed, to obtain your release," said Orm. "Be-cause it was my fault that you were captured."

"They came on us from behind among the rocks," said Black-hair sadly, "and we could offer no resistance."

"They clubbed us," said Glad Ulf, "after which we knew nothing until we awoke to find ourselves bound upon horses."

Felimid now spoke to the other chieftains and to the boys' captors, and a long argument followed as to the amount of the ransom Orm should pay.

"It is our custom," explained Felimid to Orm, "that all those who have taken part in the fighting shall have their share of the ransom, while those who have actually captured the prisoners shall have a double share. I have told them that Blackhair is your son, and that you are a chieftain among your people; but I have not told them that he is a great King's grandson, for if they knew this there would be no end to their demands."

At length it was agreed that they should ride to the ship the next day, and that Glad Ulf should be ransomed with as much silver as could be contained in four of the Patzinaks' tall hats. For Blackhair, though, they demanded his weight in silver.

Orm thought this an exorbitant sum to demand, even for so important a person as his son. But when he remembered his feelings of the morning, after he had learned that Blackhair had been captured, he reflected that, on the whole, things had turned out better than he could have expected.

"He is sparely built," said Felimid consolingly. "You would have to dive deeper into those sacks of yours if you yourself had to be weighed. And a son is worth more than any amount of silver. I can see from his looks that he is Ylva's child. It is a great grief to me that I have no son. I had one, but he died young, and now I have only daughters. Ferdiad's sons will have to succeed me as chieftains."

Later that day the Patzinaks went to the camp which the Northmen had pitched by the weirs, to fetch their wounded. Their dead they left lying where they had fallen, for it was not their custom to bury them, save when a great chieftain had died. But they were vexed that the Northmen had taken away their dead, thus depriving the men who had killed them of their heads, and declared that it was only right that Orm should pay them for robbing them of their lawful trophies.

Felimid upbraided them for making this demand, which he found unreasonable. When, however, they persisted, he said to Orm that it would be unwise to press the point too strongly, for their greed for heads was a kind of madness with them, against which no amount of reason would prevail.

Orm disliked acceding to this request, and thought that these Patzinaks looked likely to skin him to the bone; but since he was in their hands, he thought it would be unwise of him to refuse. He reflected miserably that his silver-sacks would become much lightened by the time he had paid the large sum demanded for the boys' ransom and had given each of his men their share. After he had pondered the matter for a while, however, he hit upon a solution of the problem.

"I shall pay them for my men's heads, since you so counsel me," he said, "and will give them a sum the size of which will surprise them. When we were taking the sacks out of the river, we were in a great hurry, for we feared we might be attacked and outnumbered. In our haste we burst one of the sacks, so that most of its contents ran out into the water; and it contained nothing but fair silver coins. We had no time to gather up this money, so that at least a third of it is still lying there on the riverbed; and if your men are not afraid of water, they will be able to fish themselves great wealth there."

He described the place, and how they would easily find it by the stones lying on the rock-flats, where they had put them after dragging them out of the water. Felimid translated his words to the gathering, and before he had finished, all the young men of the tribe were rushing to their horses so as to be the first to arrive at the place and dive for these unusual fish.

When these questions had been decided, Felimid suggested that they should dine and make merry together, for old times' sake. He spoke much of King Harald and of his brother Ferdiad, and recalled the time he had visited Orm at Gröning and helped Father Willibald to convert the heathens after dinner in the church.

"But now that the Erin Masters have ceased to jest," he said, "there are no good jesters left in the world. For we had no brothers, but were the last of the line of O'Flann, who had jested before kings ever since the days of King Conchobar MacNessa. In my loneliness here I have tried to teach some of the young Patzinaks something of my art, but have failed. The boys can do nothing at all, and when I turned in despair to the girls and tried to teach them to dance like a master jester, I found them too stupid to be able to follow my instructions, though I took pains with them and showed them how everything should be done. They were not quite so hopeless as the boys of this tribe, however, and one of them got as far as being able to dance reasonably well on her hands, and pipe the while. But that was the most she could attain to; and neither her piping nor the movements of her legs were all that could be desired."

He spat meditatively and shook his head.

"Although she was but a novice in the art, and will never be more," he said, "she became so vain of her supposed skill that she performed incessantly, until at last I grew tired of her and packed her off as a gift to Gzak. This Gzak you have doubtless heard of, for he is one of the three mightiest men in the whole world. He is the overlord of all the Patzinaks, and mostly grazes his flocks around Krim. Being a simple soul, who knows little about the arts, he was delighted with the girl. Then he sent her to the Emperor at Miklagard, as a thanks-gift for all the friendship-money that the Emperor had sent him. In Miklagard there must indeed be a dearth of dancers and jesters, for she danced before the Emperor himself and his court and won great praise and fame until, after a year, her vanity became such that she died for it. But my troubles are not at an end, for last winter Gzak sent messengers to me bidding me send him two new dancers of equal skill, to replace her at Miklagard; and my whole time is spent in training them. Their stupidity and clumsiness nauseate me, though I chose them carefully, and they are nothing for you to see, who have watched me and my brother display our art. If you would care to look at them, though, I have no objection to their appearing; they may amuse your sons."

Orm said that he would like to see them, and Felimid shouted orders. When the members of the tribe heard what he said, they began to clap and cheer.

"The whole tribe is proud of them," said Felimid dolefully, "and their mothers wash them in sweet milk every morning, to make their skins clear. But they will never learn to dance properly, whatever pains I may expend upon them."

Mats were spread out on the ground in front of the chieftains, and men brought flaming torches. Then the dancers appeared and were greeted with a great sigh of anticipation from all the tribesmen. They were well-shaped and appeared to be about thirteen or fourteen years old. They wore red hats over their dark hair, and strings of green glass beads round their breasts, and were dressed in broad breeches of yellow silk from the land of the Seres, tied at the ankles.

"It is a long time since I last saw dancing-girls," said Orm. "Not since I served my lord Almansur. But I do not think I ever saw any of a more engaging appearance than these."

"It is not by their appearance, but by their dancing, that they are to be judged," said Felimid. "But I designed their costumes myself and think them not displeasing."

The dancers had with them two boys of the same age as themselves, who squatted on their haunches and began to blow on pipes. As the music started, the girls began to hop around in the torchlight to the time of the pipes, strutting and giving sudden leaps and bouncing backwards and twirling round on one leg, so that everybody except Felimid sat entranced. When the girls stopped, great applause broke out, and they looked gratified when they observed that the strangers, too, appeared pleased with their performance. Then they glanced timidly at Felimid. He nodded toward them, as though satisfied, and turned to Orm.

"I cannot tell them what I really feel," he explained, "for it would make them miserable, and the whole tribe with them. And they are doing their best this evening, with strangers present. But the pipers pain me more than the girls, although they are Khazar slaves who have been given much leisure for practice, and the Khazars are said to be skillful pipers. But that is evidently a false reputation."

The girls began to dance anew, but after a while Felimid shouted angrily at them, so that they ceased.

"I am glad my brother Ferdiad was spared this," he said to Orm. "He had a more tender ear than I."

He said something to the pipers, and one of them came over and handed him his pipe.

As Felimid set his lips to it, it seemed as though witchcraft entered into its reeds. It was as though he piped of joy and luck, jests and laughter, the beauty of women and the gleam of swords, the shimmer of morning upon a lake, and the wind blowing over spring grasses. Blackhair and Ulf sat rocking backwards and forwards, as though they had difficulty in remaining seated; the two chieftains sitting on either side of Felimid nodded piously and fell asleep; the Patzinaks stamped their feet and clapped their hands rhythmically, some laughing, others crying; and the dancing-girls spun and hovered as though they had been translated into thistledown by the notes of Felimid's pipe.

At last he took the pipe from his lips and twitched his huge ears contentedly.

"I have played worse," he said.

"It is my belief," said Orm, "that there is still no master in the world who can compare with you, and it is not surprising that these men worshipped you from the moment you came among them. But it is beyond any man's power to understand how you can conjure such music as that from this simple pipe."

"It comes from the goodness that is in the wood of the pipe, when the pipe is truly made," said Felimid, "and that goodness is revealed when the pipe is blown by someone who has a similar goodness in his soul, as well as patience to seek out the secrets that lie hidden within the pipe. But there must be no wood in his soul."

Faste's scribe ran forward and, falling on his knees before Felimid, besought him to lend him the pipe. There were tears running down his cheeks.

"What do you want it for?" asked Felimid. "Can you play a pipe?"

"No," said the scribe. "I am a state official, employed in the department of taxes. But I shall learn. I wish to remain with you and play a pipe."

Felimid handed him the pipe. He set it to his mouth and began to blow. He managed to produce a tiny squeak, but no more, and the Patzinaks contorted their bodies with laughter at his futile endeavors. But he continued to blow, his face pale and his eyes staring, while Felimid gazed earnestly at him.

"Do you see anything?" asked Felimid.

The scribe handed him back the pipe. Shaking with sobs, he replied: "I see only that which you lately blew upon."

Felimid nodded. "You may stay," he said. "I will teach you. When I have finished training these girls, I shall make you good enough to play before the Emperor himself. You may keep the pipe."

So the evening ended; and next morning Felimid rode with his guests to the ship, with a great host of Patzinaks accompanying them. But before they took their leave of him, Felimid gave them all parting gifts. To Orm, Blackhair, and Ulf he gave each a knife, with gold engraving on the hilts and cunningly worked silver sheaths; and for Ylva he gave them a bale of Serean silk. They thanked him for his gifts, and thought it a bad thing that they had no fine present to give him in return as a token of friendship.

"I take pleasure in few things," said Felimid, "and gold and silver are not among them. So it matters little that you have nothing to give me, for I do not need gifts to be sure of your friendship. There is, though, now that I think of it, one thing that I should like to have, if you should ever find an opportunity to send it to me. Are your great hounds still alive?"

Orm said that they were, and in good health, and that there had been fourteen of them when he had left home. Then Felimid said: "Soon, Blackhair, you will be a full-fledged warrior, and it cannot be long before you will set forth on a long voyage of your own, now that you have started so young. It may be that you will journey to Kiev, or perhaps to Miklagard. If this should happen, bring two or three of the great hounds with you, as a present for me. That would be a friendship-gift that I would cherish indeed, and I cannot think of one that would give me greater pleasure; for they come from Erin, which is my home also."

Blackhair promised that he would do this if he came again to the Eastland; then they broke camp and turned their faces once again to the north. Faste's scribe nodded abstractedly at them as they rode away, his mind being otherwise occupied; for he was sitting with the Khazar slaves, practicing busily on his pipe. Both Blackhair and Ulf would have liked to stay longer with the Patzinaks, to watch the dancers and partake in other pleasures with them; but Orm was impatient to get back to his ship and his men, for he felt half naked, he said, and a mean man, without Blue-Tongue at his waist.

When they reached the river, the Patzinaks halted a short way from the bank, so that there should be no trouble between them and Orm's men; but neither the men who had captured Blackhair and Ulf nor the rest of the band would release their prisoners before the ransom had been paid in full. Orm went alone toward the ship, and when the men aboard saw him they raised joyous cries and put out a boat. Toke handed him his sword and asked eagerly how he had fared. Orm told him how he had met Felimid and how they had settled the whole matter between them, including the amount of the ransom they were to pay for Blackhair and Ulf.

Toke laughed with joy.

"Our luck, too, has been nothing to complain of," he said, "and you need waste no silver to free the boys. We have nine Patzinaks aboard, bound hand and foot, and they will be more than sufficient ransom for our two."

He added that Spof and Long Staff and many of the others had been unable to rest for thinking of all the silver that had been spilled into the water.

"They begged and badgered me," he said, "until at last I yielded. Spof went with twenty men along the right bank, where there was no danger of their being attacked. Midway between the two weirs they crossed the river, at a place where the water was so shallow that they scarcely needed to swim, and crept stealthily through the dusk to the place where the treasure lay. Then they heard merry shouts and saw horses grazing, and came upon these Patzinaks as they were fishing up the silver. We captured the lot of them without difficulty, for they were unarmed and we seized them before they could climb out of the water. With them we captured all the silver that they had fished out. We were just debating whether to free one of them and send him back to his people to obtain the release of you and the boys."

Orm said that this was, indeed, good news, though he doubted whether the Patzinaks would think so. He stood for a while pondering.

"I shall not demand ransom for these prisoners," he said, "and no man in the ship shall lose by this, but only I myself. But they shall not be released until the boys are freed."

"You are a great chieftain," said Toke, "and must act like one. But in this you are being generous to men who do not deserve such treatment. For it was they who attacked us in the first place, and not we them."

"You do not know Felimid," said Orm. "He is worth much generosity. This matter shall be settled the way I wish it."

So he and Toke fetched a sack of silver and carried it between them to the waiting Patzinaks. When they saw what the sack contained, the Patzinaks ran around measuring each other's hats, to find the biggest, but Felimid grew vexed at this and took off his own hat and ordered that the silver should be measured out in that; nor did they dare to say that it should be otherwise.

Then men were sent to search among the pieces of timber that lay on the ground at the beginning of the dragging-tracks, and returned shortly with a plank. This was placed across a stone and axed so that it weighed evenly on either side. Then Blackhair sat on one end of it. The Patzinaks lay saddlebags across the other end, and into these Toke poured silver from the sack until Blackhair's end was lifted from the ground. All the Patzinaks, said Felimid, agreed that this business of the weighing had been carried out in a chieftainlike manner, for they realized that if Blackhair had taken his clothes off before sitting on the plank, Orm would thereby have saved silver, and nobody could have complained that he was acting dishonorably.

When the weighing was completed, Toke went back to the ship with the silver that remained, and Orm said to Felimid: "I have enjoyed a deal of luck since I started on this voyage, and not the least of it was that I met you. When we rode from your camp, you gave us friendship-gifts, and now I have one to offer you in return. You see these men?"

Toke had freed his prisoners, and Felimid and his men stared at them in amazement.

"They are the men who rode out to fish for silver," said Orm. "My men went on a similar errand, and captured them at the fishing-place. But I give them back to you free of ransom, though I doubt not that many men would think me foolish to do so. But I have no wish to haggle with you, Felimid."

"You are worth all your luck," said Felimid, "and that is a great deal."

"I shall bring the great hounds with me, none the less," said Blackhair, "the next time I pass this way. And that may not be long hence, for now that I have been weighed in silver I consider myself a full man."

"Be sure you have dancing-girls washed in milk ready to greet us," said Glad Ulf, "at least as pretty as the ones we saw today."

Felimid scratched behind his ear. "That is all you think me capable of," he said, "to provide dancing-girls for you on your return. I shall choose the ugliest I can find, and have them steeped in horse-droppings, lest you foolish children should take it into

your heads to steal them from old Felimid, after all the pains
he has taken to train them."

They said farewell to the master jester and his Patzinaks and
returned to the ship. Then they weighed anchor and started on
their homeward voyage. The wounded among them seemed to be
on the way to recovery, and even Olof Summerbird, who was the
worst hurt, was in good heart. The men pulled at their oars with
a will, though they knew they had a long row ahead of them
against the current. Sone's seven sons were the merriest of all,
though they had the bodies of their two dead brothers aboard,
intending to bury them at their first camp, with the men who had
been killed by the bees. Toke thought that this had, indeed, been
a strange voyage, for they had come a long way and won a great
treasure, and yet Red-Jowl had not left her sheath. He thought,
though, they might find themselves somewhat busier on the way
home, with so much gold aboard. Ulf and Blackhair sat happily on
the deck, telling the other men of all that had happened to them
while they had been prisoners of the Patzinaks. Orm alone wore
a thoughtful face.

"Do you regret having let those prisoners go without ransom?"
asked Toke.

"No," replied Orm. "What troubles me is that my luck has
been too good, so that I begin to fear that all may not be as it
should be at home. It would be good to know how things are
there."

CHAPTER NINE

CONCERNING THEIR JOURNEY HOME, AND HOW
OLOF SUMMERBIRD VOWED TO BECOME A
CHRISTIAN

THEY buried their dead, in ground where their bodies would
not be disturbed, and journeyed up the great river without adventure, getting good help from wind and sail. Olof Summerbird
remained sorely sick; he had no appetite for food, and his wound

healed slowly, so that there was talk among them of putting in at Kiev in order that men skilled in medicine might examine him. But he himself would not hear of this, being as anxious as Orm and the others to reach home swiftly. The men rowed past the city without complaint, for they all now regarded themselves as rich men and had no desire to hazard their silver among foreigners.

When they reached the Beaver River, and the rowing became hard, Blackhair took his turn with the others, saying that he was henceforth to be treated as a grown man. The work was heavy for him, but, though his hands were skinned, he did not desist until the time came for him to be relieved. For this he won praise even from Spof, who seldom said an approving word about anyone.

At the portage they found plenty of oxen, in the village where they had bespoken them, so that this time they had less difficulty in dragging the ship overland. When they reached the Dregovites' village, where the bees and bears were, they rested for three days at their old camping-ground and sent messengers to the village to beg the wise old women to come and look at Olof's wound, which had been made worse by the bumping of the ship during the drag. They came willingly, examined the wound, opened it, and dripped into it a juice made of crushed ants and wormwood, which made him scream aloud with the pain. This, the crones said, was a good sign; the worse he shrieked, the better the medicine. They smeared it with a salve of beaver's fat, and gave him a bitter drink, which greatly strengthened him.

Then they returned to their village and came back with a great quantity of fresh hay and two plump young women. The crones undressed Olof, washed him in birch sap, and bedded him in the hay with a bearskin under him and one of the two young women on either side of him to keep him warm; then they gave him more of the bitter drink and covered the three of them with oxhides. He fell asleep almost immediately, and slept thus for two nights and a day in great warmth; and as soon as he awoke, the young women cried that his health was returning to him. The crones were richly paid for this; and the young women, too, were well rewarded, though they steadfastly refused to perform the same service for any of the other men.

Olof Summerbird recovered swiftly after this. By the time they reached the city of the Polotjans, his wound was healed, and he was able to eat and drink as well as the best of them. Here the chieftains visited Faste again and told him what had happened to his scribe, but the news did not appear to trouble him greatly.

In this town the men felt as though at home. They remained there for three days, drinking and love-making, to the profit and delight of all the people there. Then, as the leaves were beginning to fall, they rowed down at their leisure to the mouth of the Dvina, reaching the sea just as the first frost-nights came.

One morning, off Ösel, they were attacked by Estonian pirates in four small ships full of howling men. Spof saw them as they emerged out of the mist, and straightway bade the men at the oars pull as hard as they could; then, as the pirates drew abreast, two off either bow, and prepared to grapple, he swung the helm smartly round and rammed one of them so that those aboard her had to pull smartly for the shore, sinking swiftly. One of the others succeeded in grappling Orm's ship, but no sooner had they done this than Sone's seven sons swarmed over into the pirate ship, shieldless and whooping triumphantly, and hewed about them so furiously with sword and ax that they cleared the ship of its occupants well-nigh unaided. When the other pirates saw this happen, they realized that they had encountered berserks, and rowed hastily away.

Sone's sons were much praised for this feat, but several of them climbed back over the gunwale in an ill humor, cursing the old man their father. One of them had lost two fingers, another's cheek had been split by a spear, a third had had his nose pulped, and scarcely one of them had come through unscathed. Those of them who had been wounded most severely said that the old man was to blame for this, having lured them by his prophecy into attempting too much; for they had assumed that they would suffer no hurt. But the others spoke against them, saying that the old man had promised no more than that seven of them should return home alive; he had said nothing about wounds and scratches. It looked as though there was going to be fighting between the brothers, but Orm and Toke calmed them with wise words, and they proceeded on their journey without more incident.

They had good weather all the way from Ösel to the river mouth

and made the whole journey under sail. Meanwhile Orm measured out silver to every man aboard, both their hire-money and
their share of the treasure. No one was discontented, for he gave
each man more than he had expected to receive.

One morning at dawn, as Toke stood at the steering-oar and the
rest of the men were sleeping, Orm seated himself beside him, and
it was plain from his face that he was heavy-hearted.

"Most men would be merry in your clothes," said Toke. "Everything has gone well, you have won a great treasure, and we shall
soon be home."

"My mind is troubled," said Orm, "though I cannot say why.
Perhaps it is the gold that makes me uneasy."

"How can the gold make you uneasy?" said Toke. "You are
now as rich as a king, and kings do not hang their heads because
their wealth is great."

"There is too much of it," said Orm gloomily. "You and Olof
shall both have your good shares, but even so, too much will remain for me. I have deceived the men, telling them that the
chests contain trash for women, and my lie will bring me bad
luck."

"You meet bad luck before it comes," said Toke. "None of us
yet knows what the chests contain; it may be only silver. It was
wise of you to say that they contained women's trash, and I
should have done the same in your clothes; for even the best of
men become crazed when they know that gold is near."

"Before God," said Orm, "I now make this vow. I shall open
one of these chests, and if it contains gold, I shall divide it among
the men. We shall then have three chests left, one of which shall
be yours, one Olof's, and the third mine. Now that I have said
that, I feel better."

"You shall do as you please," said Toke. "As for me, I shall no
longer need to be a skin-trader."

Orm fetched one of the small chests, set it down on the deck
between them, and cut away the red ropes that were sealed with
the Emperor's seal. The chest was strongly locked, but Orm drove
his knife and Toke's under the lid and leaned upon them with all
his weight until the lock broke. Then he lifted the lid, and the
two of them stared silently into the chest.

"Not Fafnir [1]
In time of yore
Guarded e'er
A brood more bonny,"

said Toke reverently; and Orm remained silent, though usually, when Toke wrought a verse, it was his habit to reply with one as good or better.

The sun had by now risen, and its rays struck into the chest. It was filled with gold, which the river water had not tarnished. Most of it was coins, of many different sorts and sizes, filling the chest to its rim; but among them many precious ornaments lay bedded—rings great and small, chains, necklaces, clasps, bracelets, and suchlike, marvelously worked—"like lovely pieces of pork," thought Toke, "in a soup of good pease."

"This trash will please our women well enough when we bring it home," he said. "Indeed, I fear the sight of it may make them mad."

"It will be no easy task to share this out," said Orm.

The men had by now begun to wake up. Orm told them that one of the chests of women's trash was to be shared out among them, and that its contents were better than he had expected them to be.

The division of the gold lasted the whole day. Each man received eighty-six coins, of varying sizes; the same amount was held back for each man who had been killed, to be given to his heirs, and Spof got a helmsman's quadruple share. Sharing out the ornaments fairly proved a more difficult task, and sometimes they had no alternative but to chop rings and bracelets into pieces, to make sure that nobody received less than the next man; though often the men bargained with one another, giving coins in order that they might have the whole of some trinket that had particularly taken their fancy. One or two arguments began, but Orm said that they would have to wait till they reached land before fighting them out. Several of the men had never seen gold coins before; and when Spof told them how much silver went to a piece of gold, they sat gazing foolishly at the deck, with their heads in their hands, unable to calculate how rich they were, though they racked their brains to do so.

When everything had at last been shared out and the chest was empty, many of the men set to work with needle and twine to

[1] The dragon who guarded the Nibelungs' gold.

enlarge the pockets of their belts. Others rubbed and polished their gold, to make it brighter; and there was great cheerfulness among them as they talked of their luck and the fine homecoming they would have, and the deep drinking that would then take place.

They reached the river mouth and rowed upstream until they came to the land of a farmer whom Orm knew. There they dragged the ship on to the bank, amid the crunch of fresh night-ice, shedded her, and went about hiring horses. Some of the men departed for their homes, but the majority remained.

Spof was uncertain what to do. It might be best for him, he told Orm, to stay with this farmer, who was said to be a good man, until the spring, when he would be able to find a ship to take him home to Gotland.

"But it will be a sleepless winter for me," he added, shaking his head gloomily. "For what farmer is so good that he will not instantly kill me in my sleep as soon as he discovers what I have in my belt? Besides which, all men have a tendency to kill Gothlanders without asking them questions, because of the wealth they think we all possess."

"You shall come with me," said Orm, "and be my guest for the winter. It is no more than you have deserved. Then you can return to this place when spring comes and find a ship home."

Spof thanked him for this offer and said that he would gladly accept it.

They rode their horses away; and it was difficult to guess whether Orm or Olof Summerbird was the more anxious to see Gröning again.

They came to a place where the road forked, and one of the paths led to Sone's house. But the seven brothers stood sourly scratching their heads. Orm asked them what might be troubling them.

"We are lucky now," they replied, "more so than other men. For we are rich and know that we cannot die before we reach home. But as soon as we see the old man again, the spell is broken, and we can die as easily as anyone else. Before we left home, we had no fear of death; but things are different now, when we have so much gold to live for."

"Then you shall come with me," said Orm, "and join with me in my homecoming feast. You are good men, and it may be that

I can find sleeping-room for you all until the spring. Then you can ride forth on a new adventure if you feel so inclined, and thus live as long as you want to."

Sone's sons accepted this offer gladly and promised each other that it would be a long while before they revisited their father. Their best plan, they thought, would be to make another voyage to Gardarike.

"If that is your intention, come as my men," said Blackhair. "It will not be long before Ulf and I return there."

"You are young to use the words of a chieftain," said Orm. "You must wait awhile yet."

As they drew near to Gröning, Orm's impatience increased, and he and Olof rode ahead of the others. The first sight that met their eyes was that of men repairing the great gate. Then they saw that the church had been burned. At this, so great a fear came over Orm that he scarcely dared to ride up to the house. Then the men working on the gate saw him and uttered a glad cry, and Ylva came running from the house. It was good for him to see that she, at least, was safe.

"It is good that you have come home at last," she said. "But it would have been better if you had returned five days earlier."

"Has bad luck come upon the house?" asked Orm.

"Bandits attacked us during the night," she said, "four days ago. Harald is wounded and Rapp dead, and three others besides. They took Ludmilla, and the necklace, and much else, and three of my women. Father Willibald was clubbed on the head and is lying half-dead. I managed to escape with the little ones and Oddny and Asa. We spent all the next day hiding in the forest. They were Smalanders; that I know. They took the cattle too, but the hounds went after them and came back with fourteen head. Asa thinks that things might have been unluckier, and I think so too, now that you have come safe home."

"They are unlucky enough," said Orm. "Rapp dead, Ludmilla stolen, and the priest wounded almost to death."

"And the necklace," said Ylva.

"Do not grieve for that," said Orm. "You shall have all the trinkets you need. It is lucky that I have so many men still with me, for this business shall not go unavenged."

"You speak the truth, Orm," said Olof Summerbird. "It shall not go unavenged. Does anyone know where the robbers came from?"

"Nobody knows anything," said Ylva. "Harald was wounded in the beginning of the fight and dragged himself to the bathhouse and remained lying there. Only Father Willibald may have something to tell us, if he ever recovers sufficiently to be able to do so. The strangest thing is that they set fire to the church only; he was down there when they hit him. They stole all they could lay their hands on, and we could tell from their voices that they were Smalanders. There were very many of them. They took their dead with them; five were killed by Rapp and his men as they fought at the gate. That is all I know."

Orm's men had by now reached the house, and Ylva laughed with joy to see Blackhair safe. The first thing Orm did was to send men on horseback to rich neighbors to beg them to lend him food, for there was little left in the storehouse, and nothing at all in the brewhouse, as the result of the bandits' depredations.

Then he turned his attention to the wounded. Harald had received a spear in his chest and an ax-wound in his shoulder, but was in good heart. He assured them that he would soon be strong again, and said that what he most wanted was to hear Glad Ulf and Blackhair tell him of the adventures that had befallen them.

Asa sat with the priest, nursing him like a son. His head was swathed in bandages, and he was still half senseless. When he saw Orm, his eyes lightened, and he said in a weak voice: "Welcome home!" but then drowsed back into unconsciousness. Asa said that he often mumbled to himself as he lay there, but that nobody could understand what he was saying.

The sight of Orm greatly revived her spirits, and she straightway began to reproach him for not having returned in time to avert this calamity. But when she heard that he had Are's treasure with him, her temper softened, and she thought that this had been a trivial attack compared with some she could remember from her young days. That Ludmilla had been stolen, she said, was only what she had always said would happen, because of the unlucky name they had given her. Father Willibald, she was sure, would recover, though he had been near to death, for sometimes now he understood what she said to him, which was a good sign. What worried her most was the empty storehouse and all the cattle that had been stolen.

Toke, Spof, and Blackhair took men and followed the tracks of the bandits to see whither they led; Sone's sons assured them that they would not be difficult to follow, since there had been no rain since the attack. While they were gone, Orm questioned the survivors of Rapp's men closely, in the hope of discovering more about the identity of the bandits; but they could add little to what he had already learned from Ylva.

The day before the attack, they told him, had been the holiday that the priest called All Saints' Day; he had preached a great sermon to them all, and in the evening they had drunk to the honor of the saints. Then they had all slept soundly until the gray dawn, when the bandits had fallen on them. The hounds had begun to bay, and almost at once the bandits had attacked the gate with rams made of tree trunks and had broken it open.

Rapp and Harald had been the first to engage them, though the rest of the men had quickly joined them; they had done what they could, so that most of the women had succeeded in escaping with the children out of the back of the house and then down the river and into the forest. But they had been heavily outnumbered and had not been able to hold the gate long. The priest, who had begun of late to grow harder of hearing, had not awakened immediately, despite the hubbub, and when he at last came out, Rapp had been killed and the bandits were everywhere. He had seen them set fire to the church, and at the sight of this had cried in a loud voice and run down toward it, so that the hounds had not been slipped in time to achieve anything.

This, they said, was all they knew; for, on seeing Rapp fall, and others with him, they had realized they were hopelessly outnumbered, and had given up the battle and taken to their heels. Later, when the bandits had gone, the hounds had been released; the bandits had not dared to approach them. The hounds had followed their traces and, after being away for a whole day, had returned with some of the cattle.

Orm listened blackly to all this, thinking that things had been poorly handled; but there seemed little point in upbraiding them now for what could not be mended, and he did not reproach them for saving their own lives after they had seen Rapp killed and Harald wounded.

He hardly knew whether to grieve more over Ludmilla's fate or

Rapp's; but the more he thought about the business, the greater his anger waxed, and he determined to lose no time in settling accounts with this rabble of bandits. He thought it likeliest that they were men from Värend, though there was peace between them and the Göings and he could not remember that he had enemies there.

The next day Father Willibald was conscious again, though still very weak, and had important news to tell them.

By the time he came out of the house, he said, the bandits had already stormed the gate, and the first sight that met his eyes was flames leaping from a pile of straw that the bandits had heaped against the church and ignited. Rushing toward the flames, he had cried to them to leave God's church in peace.

"Then," he continued, "a man with a black beard strode toward me. He laughed, and cried in a loud voice: 'God's church shall burn, for I have renounced God. This is my third sin. Now I can sin no more.' Those were his words; then he laughed again, and I recognized him. It was Rainald, the priest who lived here long ago, and gave himself up to the Smalanders at the Thing. He it was, and none other; we had already heard, you remember, that he had turned himself over to the Devil. I cursed him and ran to the blazing straw to pull it clear; but then a man struck me, and I knew no more."

All those listening cried aloud with amazement at this news. Father Willibald closed his eyes and nodded.

"It is the truth," he said. "One who was God's servant has burned my church."

Asa and Ylva began to weep loudly, for it seemed to them a terrible thing that this priest should have given himself so utterly to the Devil's service.

Olof Summerbird ground his teeth and drew his sword slowly from its sheath. Reversing it, he rested it hilt-downwards on the floor and crossed his hands upon its point.

"This I swear," he said. "I shall not sit at table, nor sleep in a bed, nor take pleasure in anything, until my sword stands in the body of this man called Rainald, who was a priest of God, and who has stolen Ludmilla Ormsdotter. And if Christ helps me, so that I find her again, I shall follow Him for the rest of my days."

CHAPTER TEN

HOW THEY SETTLED ACCOUNTS WITH THE CRAZY
MAGISTER ·

AS soon as the news spread of the attack on Gröning and of Orm's return, neighbors came flocking to the house with men and horses, anxious to help him secure a good vengeance. Such opportunities, they complained, occurred all too seldom nowadays, and they greatly looked forward to what might come of it. Those who were Christians said that they were entitled to a share in the vengeance because of what had been done to their priest and church. Orm bade them all welcome and said that he was only waiting for the return of Toke and the others before setting forth.

On the third day, toward evening, Toke returned. They had followed the tracks of the bandits far to the north and east; and their best news was that they had with them Torgunn, Rapp's widow, whom they had found starving and half-dead in the wild country. She had escaped from the bandits and had run and walked as far as her legs would take her. Toke's men had taken turns carrying her back, and three of them had already proposed marriage to her, which had revived her spirits; but none of them, they said sadly, had seemed to her to be as good a man as Rapp.

She had important information to give them. Father Willibald was right; the man whom they called the magister was the chieftain of the band. He had recognized her and had spoken with her while they were returning to the bandits' village. He told her that he had renounced God and could now do whatsoever he wished. He had burned the church in order to drive God out of the district; for, now that that was destroyed, there was no church standing within many miles.

His band, Torgunn continued, consisted of outlaws, criminals, and all kinds of ne'er-do-wells, some from as far distant as West Guteland and Njudung, who had sought shelter with him and now lived by plundering. They were strong in numbers and feared no man, and the magister wielded great power over them.

Of Ludmilla she could tell them little, save that she had been in good heart and had threatened the magister and the rest of them with speedy retribution. While the bandits were taking them back to their village, the great hounds had overtaken them. Several of the bandits had been bitten, one to death, and the hounds had driven off a number of the cattle, which had greatly angered their captors. She and Ludmilla had tried to run away during the confusion, but had been recaptured.

At length they had arrived at the bandits' village, which lay near the northern tip of a great lake, which they had had on their right hand during the final stages of the journey. The bandits called their village Priestby. There Torgunn had been allotted to a man called Saxulf, a large, coarse churl of evil disposition. He had tied her up and thrown her on to a pile of skins in his cottage. In the evening he had come to her drunk. He had untied her arms and legs, but had brought neither meat nor drink for her. She had realized that she was now a widow; nevertheless, it had irked her to be forced to lie with a man who conducted himself so coarsely. Accordingly, a short while after he fell asleep, she had slipped out from under the skins and, looking round for a weapon, had happened upon a rolling-pin. Strengthened by God, and also by her hatred of the man and her desire to avenge Rapp, she had hit Saxulf over the head with this pin. He had not uttered a sound, but had merely twitched his limbs. Then she had crept out into the night and escaped from the village without being observed. She had made what speed she could for a day and more, following the tracks along which they had come, terrified lest they might be after her, with nothing to eat save a few cranberries she picked from hedges; then, overcome by exhaustion, she had lain down, unable to move farther, expecting death from starvation and fatigue, or possibly from the jaws of wild beasts, until Blackhair and his men found her and gave her food. She had had to ride home on the men's shoulders; now, however, she was already beginning to recover from this dreadful experience.

Such was Torgunn's story, and it told them what they most wished to know: where the bandits' hide-out lay. Men who had been along their track, and who knew the country, said that the great lake she spoke of was that called Asnen; and two of Olof Summerbird's men claimed to know those deserted parts and a way by which the place might be reached. They undertook to lead Orm and his companions there. The best plan, they said, would be to turn off after the first day's march and proceed westwards, coming upon the bandits from that direction. Orm and the others thought this a wise suggestion, for by this means they would trap them with the lake at their backs.

Orm counted his men and found they numbered one hundred and twelve. The next day, he declared, they would set forth. Fearing for the safety of his Bulgar gold, he took Toke, Olof, and Blackhair with him late that evening, when all the rest of the men were asleep, and hid the chests in a safe hiding-place in the forest, far from all paths and tracks, a spot to which no man ever came. His great hoard of silver he did not think worth hiding; for he had lost his fear of silver, he said, and was content to let it lie in Ylva's coffers, though the house would only be guarded by the few men who were to be left behind.

The next morning, before dawn, all the men were up and ready. There was some delay, however, before they could start out, for Orm was intending to take the great hounds with him, and they had first to acquaint themselves with all the strangers in the party, so that there might be no misunderstandings and the wrong men bitten. The hounds took but a few moments to accustom themselves to most of the men, merely sniffing them two or three times; but others they were more suspicious of and snarled fearfully at, appearing unwilling to accept them as people who ought not to be killed immediately. This caused much hilarity, for the men whom the hounds distrusted grew surly, claiming that they smelled as good as the next man, and words were exchanged on this subject.

At length, however, everything was ready, and the band set out, the hounds being led by men whom they knew well.

They followed the track by which the bandits had gone, continuing thus the whole day, until they came near the place where Torgunn had been found. There they encamped for the night. Next morning they turned off to the left, with Olof's two knowledgeable men leading them. They proceeded for three days across hard country through marshland and dense forest, broken by steep hills, without seeing a house or meeting a man. The hounds knew what they were hunting and ignored all scent of game; it was a great virtue with them that when they were hunting men, they uttered no sound until the moment when they were slipped from their leashes.

On the afternoon of the fourth day after their departure from Gröning they reached a place where two paths crossed. Here they halted, and the two guides said that the lake was now just ahead of them and that the bandits' village lay between it and them. It had been a hard march, but both Orm and Olof Summerbird agreed that they should attack at once; for they were beginning to run short of food, and both of them were impatient to proceed with the business. Some of the young men in the band then climbed up into a tree on a hill to spy out the lie of the village, and Orm divided the men into three bands. Toke was to lead one, Olof the second, and Orm himself the third. He kept the hounds with him, so that they should not be slipped too soon. Toke was to attack from the north, and Olof Summerbird from the south. Blackhair went with Toke, accompanied also by Sone's sons, who were already beginning to reckon themselves as Blackhair's men. Orm commanded them that they should set fire to no house, and maltreat no woman, since some of them might have been stolen from good husbands. When Toke sounded his horn, both bands were to attack with all speed, though without war-whoops.

Toke and Olof moved quietly off with their men, while Orm and his band crept stealthily forward through the undergrowth until they reached the skirts of the forest a short way from the village. Here the men seated themselves on the ground and began to gnaw at the little food they had left, while they waited for the sound of Toke's horn.

Orm took Spof with him and crept forward into a clump of elderbushes. There they lay, scanning the village. It looked to be large, and many of the houses in it were new. People could be seen working in the spaces between them, both men and women. Spof calculated that a village of that size might be reckoned to contain a hundred and fifty men. Between them and the village, in a dip in the ground, there stood a small pool, which evidently served the village as a well. An old woman, carrying a yoke with two buckets, came down to it, drew water, and trudged back again.

Then two men appeared and watered four horses. After the horses had drunk, they became restless and began to prance, and Orm thought that they must have sensed the presence of the hounds. But the hounds stood stock-still behind Orm, sniffing and trembling and making no sound.

The men at the well got their horses under control and led them back to the village. A short while elapsed, and then three women walked down to the pool carrying a bucket in either hand. There were two men with them who appeared to be their guards. Orm caught his breath, for the tallest of the women was Ludmilla. He mumbled this into Spof's ear, and Spof muttered back that they were within bowshot. Still Toke's horn did not sound, and Orm was unwilling to disclose the presence of his men prematurely; however, he signaled to two men crouching near him who had been with him in the battle at the weirs and who were reckoned to be sure marksmen. They said that they thought they could mark the men at the well, rose to their feet, each keeping himself concealed behind his tree, and set arrows to their bowstrings. But Orm bade them wait awhile yet.

The women had by now filled their buckets, and turned to go back to the village. As they did so, Orm pursed his lips and uttered a cry like a buzzard's call, repeating it once. It was a call that he could skillfully ape, and all his children were acquainted with it. Ludmilla stiffened as she heard it. She took a few slow steps after her companions; then she stumbled, so that all the water in her buckets was spilled. She said something to the men and turned back to the well to refill her buckets. She did this as slowly as she might; then, when they were full, she sat down on the ground and clasped her foot. The two men said something to her in stern voices and went up to her to force her to her feet; but as they reached out their hands to her, she threw herself on her back and began to scream.

Still no sound was heard from Toke's side; but when the hounds heard Ludmilla scream, they began to bay, and Orm knew that their presence was now revealed.

Orm muttered a word to his two archers, and their bows sang as one. Their aim was true, and their arrows found their marks; but the men they struck were wearing thick leather jackets and remained on their feet. They pulled the arrows from their flesh and shouted for help. Then Ludmilla leaped to her feet, struck one of them on the head with a bucket, and ran with all her might toward the forest. The two men made after her and began rapidly to overtake her; meanwhile men appeared from the houses to learn the cause of all this confusion.

"Slip the hounds," said Orm, and sprang out of the bushes. As he did so, Toke's horn wound, followed by violent whooping.

But both the horn and the whoops of the men were quickly drowned as the great hounds, slipped at last from their leashes, began to bay fearfully. As the two men chasing Ludmilla saw them, they halted in terror. One turned tail and fled screaming, until the swiftest of the hounds caught him and, leaping upon his neck, felled him to the ground; but the other, keeping his head, ran into the pool and, turning there, drew his sword and stood his ground. Three of the hounds leaped simultaneously at him; he met one of them with his sword, but the other two knocked him off his feet, so that he disappeared beneath the water; and only the hounds came up again.

Ludmilla danced for joy when she recognized Orm. She began at once to ask about Olof and the gold, and he told her. She herself, she said, had been treated as befitted a chieftain's daughter and had not been forced to lie with any man save the crazy priest, who had treated her not unkindly, so that she might have suffered worse.

Orm sent after Spof, and bade him and two others of the older men take Ludmilla a short way into the forest and remain there with her until the fighting in the village had ceased. The other women came timidly up to them; they were, they said, the priest's women. When the hounds had appeared, they had flung themselves face downwards on the ground and remained motionless, so that the hounds had not touched them.

By the time that Orm and his men reached the village, the fighting was already fierce. Olof's men were engaging a group of bandits in a street between two houses, and his voice was heard to cry above the uproar that the man with the black beard was for his sword alone. Orm attacked the bandits from the rear, losing several men to arrows shot from the houses; but although the bandits defended themselves valiantly, they were at length encircled and overcome. Then Orm led his men into the houses to fight with

the men who were still holding out there. He saw two of his
hounds lying dead with spears through their bodies, but each of
them had his man under him, and the others could still be heard
baying fearfully toward the lake.

Orm met Olof Summerbird; his face was bloody and his shield
heavily scarred.

"Ludmilla is safe!" cried Orm. "I have her in good keeping."

"I thank Thee, Christ!" cried Olof. "But where is the black-
beard? He is mine!"

Toke's men had met the fiercest opposition, for many of the
bandits had rushed to meet them at the first sound of whooping.
Orm and Olof gathered their men and led them to Toke's assistance, attacking their enemies in the rear. Here the fighting became
very violent, and many men fell on both sides, for the bandits
fought like berserks. Orm pursued one, who had managed to
break out, around the corner of a house, but as he passed a doorway, a man clad in a chain shirt and a bald man armed with an
ax leaped out and attacked him. Orm hewed at the chain-shirted
man so that he rolled on the ground, and in the same instant
leaped nimbly aside to evade the other's ax, but as he did so, his
foot slipped on a heap of dung and he fell on his neck. As he fell,
he saw the bald man raise his ax again, and, he said afterwards,
his thoughts went back to the battle at Maldon long before and
the shields that had covered him there, and he felt little joy at the
thought that his next night's camp would be on heavenly ground.
But the bald man opened his eyes and mouth wide and let go his
ax and sank on his hands and knees and knelt there, staring; and
as Orm got to his feet again, he heard his name shouted from a
house ahead of him and saw Sone's sons sitting astride the roof,
waving their bows in pride at their good marksmanship.

Orm felt strangely weary after this experience and stood where
he was for a moment looking about him. The village presented a
scene of wild confusion. Women were shrieking, men were chasing one another throughout the houses, cattle and hogs ran terrified through the streets, and most of the bandits who were still
alive had taken to their heels and were fleeing toward the lake.
Toke and Blackhair appeared out of a doorway. Toke's sword was
dripping redly, and he cried to Orm that he had not enjoyed better sport than this since his youthful days. But he had no time to

say more and rushed furiously after the fleeing men, shouting to his men to follow him. Blackhair, however, remained with Orm, calling his men down from the housetop.

Then a great howl was heard, and a black-bearded man came running toward them with an ax in his hand and Olof Summerbird at his heels. As the man caught sight of Orm, he changed his course, leaped over a low wall, and ran on. But Blackhair, turning, ran after him and struck him over the head so that he fell.

"He is mine! He is mine!" cried Olof breathlessly.

The man was twisting on the ground. Olof went up to him, gripped his sword with both hands, and drove it through the chain shirt and the man's body beneath so that it stood fast in the ground.

"God! God!" screamed the nailed man, in a voice filled with pain and terror, and said no more.

"I have kept my vow," said Olof.

"Is that the man?" said Orm. "It is difficult to recognize him beneath that beard."

"It is an ill thing to wear stolen goods in a battle, so that they can be seen," said Olof, bending over the dead body. "Look at this!"

Above the neck of the man's chain shirt shone the glint of gold. Olof reached his hand inside and pulled something out. It was Almansur's chain.

"It is he," said Orm. "And, now that I think of it, there is another proof. Who in this place but he could have called to God? I wonder what he can have wanted of Him?"

CHAPTER ELEVEN

CONCERNING THE GREAT HOUNDS' CHASE

SOME of the crazy magister's men escaped in boats; but not many, for they were hunted by men and dogs along the shore. Their wounded were killed, since they were all miscreants. Twenty-three of Orm's men had been killed and many wounded;

and all agreed that this had been a good fight, and one that would be much talked about in the years to come.

In the village they found a great qauntity of ale, and many hogs were slaughtered; then the men buried their dead together and raised a mound over them and drank to their death voyage. As they had expected, they found a number of stolen women in the village. Each of these was given a cow and allowed to go whither she pleased, with as much booty as she could carry. Among these were Ylva's two servant-girls, who were both young and were greatly delighted at being thus liberated. They had been forced, they said, to endure great indignities and had been kept indoors, closely guarded, ever since Torgunn had run away. They now wished to be wedded to reliable men.

The hounds were much praised for their part in the battle; only two of them had been killed. When all the cattle had been rounded up as booty, Orm said that the work of driving them back to Gröning could safely be left to the hounds, since they were used to this. Horses were found for all the wounded; then, as soon as these had recovered sufficiently to be able to sit on horseback, Orm rode forth from the bandits' village and headed homewards by the shortest route, which led southwards along the shore of the lake.

Ludmilla rode with the rest, and Olof kept his horse close to hers. He had begged Orm and Toke not to mention the two women who had kept him warm at the Dregovites' village, lest she should take the matter amiss. They had both laughed at this and had replied that he must be sick in the head with wounds or love if he supposed that they would do any such thing. But Olof had shaken his head doubtfully, saying that he was a good deal older than she and so could not be too careful.

They rode slowly, for the sake of the wounded. Ahead of them the hounds drove their herd at leisure; no disputes broke out between them and their charges, though when any cow tried to change her direction or escape from the rest, they were quick to show her her mistake.

They camped early that evening and saw to the wounded; then next morning they proceeded alongside the lake toward the place that old folk called Tyr's Meadows. In former times men had lived there, and the meadows had been the scene of great battles, from

which they had won their name. Men said that so much blood
had been spilled on Tyr's Meadows that the grass flourished more
richly there than elsewhere. But neither man nor house was to
be seen there now.

As they approached these meadows, the hounds grew restless, so
that the men wondered whether they had scented bear, or the
smell of the old blood. Leaving their herd, they roamed into the
woods and ranged this way and that, until, of a sudden, two or
three of them began to bay. Others joined them, and soon the
whole pack of them was snarling savagely and driving deeper into
the woods, as though they had once more been slipped for battle.
Orm could not understand what the cause of this might be, for
none of the bandits had fled in this direction; and he and all the
men ran up to the top of a heathered hill beside the track to see
what was afoot.

Away on their right hand, beyond the woods, there lay open
grassland. Across it the hounds were running, driving before them
a great herd of cattle, but cattle such as few of the men had seen
before.

Suddenly one of Toke's men cried: "The wild ox! They are
driving the wild ox!"

The hounds seemed to have taken it into their heads that these
beasts belonged to their herd and were to be driven home with the
rest. They spared no efforts to see that none escaped, and from the
hill the men could see how they fought with the more obstinate
animals to drive them along with the others. The wild oxen re-
sented this treatment, and their bellowing could be heard even
above the baying of the hounds; but at last all but a few ceased
their resistance, and the herd disappeared southwards into the
wooded hills, with the hounds still gamboling behind and about
them.

Realizing there was nothing they could do to stop them, the men
proceeded on their way, driving the tame cattle themselves. Toke's
men, who knew the ways of wild oxen, said that sometimes, in
the beginning of winter, they came down from West Guteland to
pasture in Tyr's Meadows. While they grazed on the war-god's
land, they were held by old folk to be under his protection and so
were never disturbed there. In former times, as was well known,
they had been far more numerous in these parts, but nowadays

they were only to be seen in Tyr's Meadows, and that but seldom.

They found traces of the wild oxen's flight in the country east of the Kraka Stone; but in the dense forests farther south, it was clear that the hounds had found their task beyond them, for the tracks of the herd showed it to have diminished in strength mile by mile. They had, nevertheless, succeeded in keeping some of them together; and when Orm reached home, he learned that the hounds had arrived there driving two bulls, five cows, and a number of calves. The men had done their best to halt them, but had been unable to do so; and when the hounds saw the beasts proceeding into the country beyond their home, they appeared to have felt that they had done enough for honor and went to their food-troughs, very weary and sore-footed.

After this, wild oxen were seen in various parts of the forest country, and no event for many a year past had aroused so much amazement as their reappearance. Now that, with their own eyes, they had seen wild oxen in their district, anything, men said, could happen; and they all reminded one another of the old saying that no king would ever be seen among them until the wild oxen returned to the land. Wise ancients shook their heads and warned their neighbors to prepare for the worst and to keep their bows and spears ready to hand. Some baptized persons thought that Christ would come to Göinge in a great wagon drawn by wild oxen; but few men agreed with them in this surmise. Most took it to mean that King Sven would march against them; and when certain tidings came that he had died in England, black in the face with anger at the stubbornness of the people there, there was such rejoicing in Göinge that all the ale was drunk up, and men sat hoarse and thirsty at their tables with nothing save milk to fill their cups with.

But such as lived long enough saw the old saying fulfilled, when Canute Svensson the Mighty, King of Denmark and England, sailed to the estuary with the greatest fleet that any man had ever seen or heard tell of, and fought with the Kings of Sweden and Norway on the waters of the Holy River.

And this is the end of the story of Orm Tostesson and his luck. He fared forth no more on voyages or campaigns; but his affairs prospered and he aged contentedly. The only thing he found to complain of was an ache in his back which sometimes troubled him, and which even Father Willibald was not always able to dispel.

Olof Summerbird wedded Ludmilla. They lived happily together, though it was rumored that he had not fully as great a say in the management of his house as he had been wont to have. Spof besought Torgunn many times to marry him. At first she refused, finding him short of limb and gray of beard; but when at last he threw caution aside and revealed to her what his belt contained, she found herself no longer able to resist his prayers. They sailed to Gotland, in the ship that lay in the shed by the estuary; and with them, in the same ship, sailed Blackhair, Glad Ulf, and Sone's seven sons, upon a longer voyage. They took two of the hounds with them, to fulfil the promise they had made to Felimid, and stayed away for seven years.

When they returned, Glad Ulf wedded Oddny, who had steadfastly refused to look at any other man. But Blackhair sailed to England, and in the battle on the Holy River he fought in King Canute's own ship.

Toke Gray-Gullsson gained much pleasure from his chest of gold, and hung so many ornaments upon his wife and daughters that their clatter and jingle gave good warning of their approach whenever they went out in their best attire. He sold his house in Värend and built himself a larger one near Gröning. There he and Orm found much satisfaction in each other's company, as did Ylva in Mirah's, though neither Toke nor his woman ever allowed themselves to be baptized. In good time Orm's youngest daughter was wedded to the eldest of Toke's sons, their fathers having decided long ago that they were well suited to each other.

Both Orm and Toke lived to a ripe age without wearying of life; and never, until the day they died, did they tire of telling of the years when they had rowed the Caliph's ship and served my lord Almansur.

A NOTE ON THE TYPE

This book is set in Electra, a Linotype face designed by W. A. Dwiggins. This face cannot be classified as either modern or old-style. It is not based on any historical model, nor does it echo any particular period or style. It avoids the extreme contrast between thick and thin elements that marks most modern faces, and attempts to give a feeling of fluidity, power, and speed.

The typography and binding were designed by W. A. Dwiggins.

The book was composed, printed, and bound by The Plimpton Press, Norwood, Massachusetts.

WAD

Frans G. Bengtsson

FRANS G. BENGTSSON, SWEDISH AUTHOR, 60

Special to The New York Times.

STOCKHOLM, Sweden, Dec. 19 —One of Sweden's most prominent writers, Frans G. Bengtsson, author of "The Long Ships" died here this morning at the age of 60 of complication of a hip bone fracture that had confined him for more than a year.

A master of anecdote and extremely versatile, Mr. Bengtsson knew success almost from the start of his writing career in the mid-Thirties, when he produced a work on King Charles XII of Sweden and won immediate recognition as a fine writer.

He developed into one of the best Swedish essayists. His style was terse and to the point. In Sweden, his books automatically became best-sellers. Two were translated into English: "A Walk to an Ant Hill," published in Lnodon, 1950, and "The Long Ships," which had instant success when published in England in February of this year, and in the United States, where it was brought out this autumn.

"The Long Ships," a story of a Viking chieftain, was written in two parts, the first in 1941 and the second in 1945. After this work, which was a great success on the Scandinavian book market, Mr. Bengtsson was heard from only at long intervals.

His last book, "The Pleasure Garden I Remember," appeared last year.

Mr. Bengtsson, son of an administrator of one of the feudal estates in southern Sweden, studied at the Academy of Lund, where he obtained a Master of Arts degree in philosophy. His painstaking research into ancient and medieval history furnished abundant material for the books he was to turn out later

DATE DUE

GAYLORD			PRINTED IN U.S.A.